teachers appeared. I am also in a similar community. The parallels are amazing. Reading this book helped motivate me to change. The story is a very enjoyable reading experience. I always looked forward to reading the next page. This book helped teach me how I should live more successfully. The authors showcase their understanding of human nature with skill and insight. Through their copious life experiences, they were able to lay out a wonderful practical society that can help us in our everyday lives."
Pancho Copeland
Intrepid Traveler, Carpenter, and Lover of Books

"Blessings to the authors of City of Hope for creating a deeply inspiring story. It clearly shows how a family can become a model of love with the help of a unified community. May the wisdom in the City of Hope become a manual to help people heal by understanding their behavioral patterns, which stem from their past and how they were raised by parents who themselves perpetuate the same errors in parenting, unknowingly passed on through generations."
Ruth Baumrucker
KXCR Community Radio Volunteer Coordinator

The City of Hope

"The greatness of a community is most accurately measured by the compassionate actions of its members."
Coretta Scott King

The City of Hope

Nicholette Pavlevsky
N·I·N Sharyn Bebeau

IngramSpark

We dedicate this book to all Visionaries
alive today
who are working to guide the world
into a better future.

Table of Contents

CHAPTER 1

Running Away

James's fingers dug into the steering wheel. The car was going nowhere. His thoughts wandered over the last few days and years. Periodically he went into rants at God over a life of disappointments and self-loathing. He felt like a failure, again, torn between anger and sorrow. Yesterday, he lost his job to a mindless robot at the Ford plant after four years of working there. This was the eighth job he had lost during the twenty-two years he had been married. Now, he was too embarrassed to go home, so here he was, sitting on the side of a small road with nothing but empty desert around him.

The morning dawned cool and clear. The dirt road beside him was marked with tire tracks from a passing car or truck. The sun was rising in front of the windshield, blinding him as he woke up. Blinking, his eyes adjusted to the light. He saw vibrant pink and orange rocks around him and colorful hills in the distance, but he did not see the beauty in them. To him, it was all just barren land with ugly shrubs and cactuses. In a proverbial sense, he felt lost in the middle of nowhere, wondering how he got there.

Yesterday, after he received his severance package, he was driving home in a state of dread. The auto-drive was not on, so the car sailed past his exit, and he kept on driving. He ended up on I-15 heading northeast, leaving his wife and two kids in San Bernardino. He kept driving onward into the darkness.

The urge to run as far away as possible kept him driving on past towns and cities that offered warm comfortable hotels. Besides, he could not afford one. When he started nodding off and nearly ran off the highway, he pulled off onto a small road and spent a miserable night in the cold car.

When the morning sun woke him up, near I-40, just past Flagstaff, Arizona, he reached to start the car and a thought stopped him. 'Where should I go!?' The words just hung there in his mind, filled with a numb fear of the unknown.

James, an average man, in stature and in life, had no outstanding features and easily blended into a crowd. His receding hairline, dusty brown hair, and graying temples made him look older than forty-seven. He had been letting himself go for years. Stress and depression were his excuses for sporting a round beer belly and an extra sixty pounds.

His marriage was falling apart from a lack of communication, plus anger and stress from pressures at work and family financial demands. He never even told his wife that he had to empty the kid's college fund to cover their debts and the mortgage.

His kids showed no interest in him anymore. Like many teens, they were self-absorbed, lost in their VR Video Games, Facetime, Avatar Sims Games, and of course, their 4F Social Media Score (based on fame, friends, family, forum popularity and gaming credits). They lived in a cyberworld far away and seemed unreachable to him.

Four years ago, his wife told him that she planned to file for divorce as soon as the kids go off to college. That plunged him into a full-blown depression where he has floundered ever since.

To make matters worse, he still owed a lot of money and that would make it even harder to start over.

James was feeling rather bitter about The American Dream. All the dreams he had as a child had turned to dust, leaving him in despair. His old pretentiousness and the last of his pride had fallen away. Now he was angry at the world for being so unfriendly, and angry at himself for all the missed opportunities. He was just as afraid of living as he was of dying alone. He was desperate for a way out but felt trapped. He sensed that there was an answer but had no idea where to even begin looking for it.

The morning was not bringing more clarity. He pounded on the steering wheel and shouted obscenities. It did not make him feel any better. He started the car. Then he shut it off. Repeatedly he started it and stopped. Mumbling under his breath, he kept changing his mind.

"What am I going to do next!?" He grumbled aloud, feeling as empty as the desert around him.

Hours had passed since he woke up. The cool morning air was long gone, and the sun was warming the car to a stifling level. He argued with himself. He could turn the car around and go home or he could just keep going. At home he could tell his wife that he simply had a lapse in good judgment, or he could cast his fate to the winds and keep on going. He fantasized about finding a new place to live where he could start over. He liked that idea, until he began to question and doubt whether a new place would be any better. The little voices in his head threw darts of doubt at every idea that came to him.

Finally, in a fit of frustration, he got out of the car, slammed the door as hard as he could, and stomped off into the desert. He kicked at dirt, sand, and rocks, took a swing at tumbleweeds and shrubs, screamed obscenities. Somewhere in all that, he lost his balance and fell into a cactus. He cursed the vicious plant as he pulled needles out of his blue jeans and tender skin.

James told himself that he had simply been the unlucky victim of a shrinking job market. First there was downsizing due to the green initiative, which Obama started in the early teens. Then small solar businesses boomed and went bust. And then came the COVID 19 economic depression. After that, the market for hybrid cars collapsed when electric cars completely took over. Then he lost three more jobs due to this automation trend that our latest deadhead President was allowing the corporations to introduce, which was devastating the workforce of America again.

An old memory popped up. He was a young child sitting in the dirt hugging his bruised knee after a failed attempt to ride a bike. His father was looming over him yelling at him to get back up. He tried not to cry but the tears came anyway. He knew men don't cry, at least that is what his father told him. Then, like now, the pain in his heart was much worse than that old bruise and these awful cactus needles in his leg.

To distract himself from the pain, he screamed at God again. "What do you want from me? Why are you punishing me? What am I supposed to do?"

The wind blew softly, and dust settled around him. He did not expect an answer, he was just grabbing for something to help him stop crying, from losing his mind completely in a desert of doom.

He tried to gather himself as he pulled out another cactus needle. It pierced his pants and was stuck in his leg. He hoped the pain would bring him back to reality. He noticed that some of the needles had bits of tattered paper stuck to them. One had the word, *Nothing*, on it and another had, *I am not*, and a third had, *Listen to Me*. He looked at the cactus that had broken his fall. It had the faded remnants of a child's book stuck to it. The big letters on the side facing the sun had faded, but the underside was still readable.

He mused that these words were the answers to his questions, but then, quickly dismissed the thought as nonsense and threw the bits of paper away. He pulled out the rest of the cactus thorns, brushed himself off, and stood up. His white button-down shirt and tan jacket had streaks of dirt. He pulled himself together and took a deep breath. Putting his emotions aside, he went back to his car. He told himself he was a man, so he would find his direction on his own. He just needed time to plan. He succeeded in boosting himself up with false bravado.

James got back into his sixteen-year-old Ford Future Hybrid and drove back to the highway going in the same direction. Once again, he did not turn on his guidance system. According to the radio display, it was midday. It was going to be a while before he could find a town with a decent hotel and good food. He did not want to eat at some greasy spoon diner. The critical voice in his head taunted him, saying, "Your plans never come out right, so why should they now?"

"I need a sign." He said aloud. It amused him to think that God might have answered him through those pieces of paper. He was not sure whether God existed or not; but if he did, he was an ass for letting the world go to hell. If he didn't exist, then that would explain a lot. Anyway, at times like this, God was a convenient person to yell at.

After driving for a while, with only his hunger to keep him company, he came to a dip in the road, followed by a hill. On the other side was a billboard with a bright purple border and tall white lettering. It read, "Lost? Need a new direction? Need new friends?"

James found it irritating. He figured the signs were a Christian thing. He could see a set of them up ahead. 'Great' he thought, 'I ask for a sign and I get Christian rhetoric about God for the next who knows how many miles.'

He drove on feeling disgusted with the world and with himself. The next sign posed the questions, "Need a good home for you and your family? Need a dependable career that you will love?"

'Oh no!' he thought, 'It's one of those alternative communities that have been popping up everywhere.' He wondered, 'Which one is this?'

He once saw a 20/20 program on Christian and non-denominational alternative communities. According to the report, they were based on New Spirituality, a sort of non-religious, New Age way of thinking about God and our relationship to Him or Her. He remembered that people said, they believed in a non-judgmental God, unlike the Christian one he hated.

These communities were based on trust, sharing, and healing one another. Some were against the use of the Net, and some did not even use money within their communities. Many believed that love could overcome fear and they were working together to evolve more peaceful ways of thinking. He figured these kinds of places would not last long, because they had no laws, in the traditional sense.

Another sign soon followed, "Come and join us. Take a vacation at our Navaho Hopi Nations, Wise World Park." It had pictures of kids shooting bows with Native American instructors, a circle of Native American and tourist women making baskets, people horseback riding, and a family making camp in a teepee. The purple border on the edge of the billboards showed that they were all talking about the same place.

The next one said, "Hotels, dining, and entertainment for the whole family! Come for the fun. Stay for a better life! The City of Hope, a Trinitus city." The pictures showed a large dining room, a movie theater, a fun center, miniature golf games, and an energy efficient hotel. He only noticed it was a place to eat, sleep, and think, so he made up his mind to stop there.

He had only been driving for an hour or so, but his back was sore from sleeping in the cramped car and his leg was still stinging from the cactus needles. He was dusty, needed a bath, and had not eaten since lunch at work yesterday. He figured, if he was going to spend money he did not have, he might as well rent a nice place.

More signs with purple borders zipped by showing camping, casinos, and a museum called, Societies of Man. James took little notice of them now that he had a goal. He figured that God, if he existed, had sent him here, but he was unwilling to think there was anything more to it than that.

He saw palm trees in the distance when he reached the exit for the City of Hope and the Hopi Indian Reservation. James tried to remember if the 20/20 show talked about this community, but his mind felt blurry. It was too long ago. He took the exit which crossed back over the highway. From this vantage point, he saw miles of farmhouses with hundreds of high tunnels and a small town. To the northwest, was the Native American Indian Reservation, sporting a grand casino; and to the east, on a large plateau, was a small city with tall buildings. Between the freeway and the towns stood a large solar array on the right, and a wind farm on the left.

After about a mile, he came to a stone and slate sign announcing that he was entering the Hopi Indian Reservation. Two miles further, the road split off in a 'Y'. The longer road on the left had a sign that read, Oak Springs. The shorter road led to a gatehouse. It was called, Another Way. He chose the shorter road and soon came to a large multi-level parking lot with a Native American adobe style roof, covered with solar panels. Beyond the garage was a 'V' shaped hotel with a round tower between two wings.

James rolled down his window at the gatehouse. The small building looked as if it was carved out of color banded sandstone but, it was colored stucco. Decorative Native American carvings, painted in bright colors, were alternately inset and projecting out from the walls. The carport overhead reminded him of the windblown sandstone arches in Arches National Park. Engraved above were the words, "Find Love and you will find joy."

He could not drive directly to the hotel, the city, or to the park gate without first going into the multi-acre garage. On the road that led to the hotel and city, he saw a purple solar tram-bus with the words, 'City of Hope' written on its side. Another bus said, 'Wise World Park.' There was a gate to the main road that led to the hotel and city, but it was closed.

A young man came out of the gatehouse to greet James in his car. He was wearing a light blue shirt and pants, creased to look like a uniform. His bright blue eyes were happy to see James. In a warm friendly voice he asked, "Good day sir. We see you. Will you be visiting the Wise World Park, or coming to live with us?"

Questions?! Decisions? James was still unable to think clearly. Just deciding to get food and sleep was all he could manage right now; so, he mumbled, "I don't know."

"That's okay. This is a good place to find yourself again." The young man said with enthusiasm, as though "I don't know," was a perfectly acceptable answer. He handed James a card with the URL address for two articles on the Trinitus website; one presented information for Visitors and the other, Emergence, was for those who were interested in staying long term.

"This information will tell you everything you need to know, no matter what you decide. Now, do you have any of the items on this list with you?" He pointed to a sign near the door of the gatehouse.

James looked up inquisitively at the bubbly gatekeeper. He was smiling brightly, as he held his hand up to the sign which read:

We are creating a healthy world,
one that does not exploit our sacred resources
and is safe for all.
To create a better experience for you
and to protect our way of life,
we cannot allow the following items:

Weapons   Ammunition   Drugs,
E-Cigarettes   Chewing tobacco   Snuff
World Net Connecters
*We have our own Network.

Gas or Oil run Machinery
Hybrid   Hydro cars   Cycles
*Electric, Solar, and Human Powered
versions are available.

Personal Hygiene Items, Cleaners, and Solvents
containing Perfumes   Detergents
Gas and Oil Products
Parts and Extracts of Endangered Plants and Animals
Non-Recyclable Plastics   Palm Oils
Deforestation Crop Products   Sugar

Thank you for helping us
keep our shared air, water, and earth
clean and plentiful.'

"I just want to sleep in a hotel. Is all this necessary?" James was annoyed that they might search him, not that he had anything to hide. He just wanted to get to bed.

"Do I have to park out here?" he said, pointing a thumb at the garage.

"Yes, we have free electric cars if you need to borrow one," and he smiled.

"How much is this going to cost me?" He was now concerned that the man at the gate was trying to rip him off.

"We have several hotels. Some are quite reasonably priced. We also have more elegant ones in the park. If you're thinking of staying, the Emergence Hotel is free." The gate man overlooked James's tone and stayed chipper.

"What if I change my mind?" asked James with an eyebrow raised.

"That is fine sir. However, if there is a chance that you might stay, then the Emergence Hotel is the best choice. It has free courses and

Emergence lectures which you can attend during meals." The man seemed genuinely excited for him.

James was skeptical now. What kind of brainwashing or sales pitch was he going to have to endure to get a free night's stay?

"During meals?" he asked, concerned that they thought he was a fool.

"Oh yes, to make more time in your day. If you prefer, you can eat after or before a lecture. You could eat in your room or go out to any of our many restaurants. It is just for your convenience." His bubbly nature was unshaken by James's doubts. "You see, we will not try to force you into anything. We believe in freedom and choice here in the City of Hope. The Website articles will explain all of this to you."

James parked in the garage, on the north side of the third floor. He was surprised that it was so full. He did not pack for a trip, so he just grabbed his ComPad and his rechargeable razor. He had not replaced his old broken Smartwatch, so he did not have to leave it at the desk with his ComPad.

The waiting tram driver noted the disheveled and dust covered man boarding with nothing in hand but a razor and a ComPad. He knew he had a Runner. He offered James a tour of the city, promising it would only take thirty-five minutes and added a big toothy smile.

James replied, "Just take me to the hotel."

The driver watched as his passenger just sat and stared at his hands. This was a slow time of the day and James was his only rider, so he decided not to give his usual pitch on the intercom and left James to his thoughts.

James sat looking at his razor resting on top of his ComPad and wondered if this is what he has become, a down-trodden man with only a razor. He did not look up or around. He did not even realize that he had not specified which hotel he wanted.

When the driver said, "This is it." He just got off the tram and walked into the lobby without looking up, until the beautiful marble floor caught his eye. It was a mosaic of the desert with tall almost human shaped cactus made of local marble. The serene landscape of the scene was laced with veins of beautiful pure marble. The whole floor was one peaceful design.

On the left side of the large reception room, he spotted a sweeping purple Sun Stone hotel desk. Above it was a sign that read, "Welcome to the Emergence Hotel and to your new life!"

James scoffed as he wandered over to the desk and took out his wallet. He reached for the temporary ID that he was using until he got a new Smartwatch with a Virtual Wallet.

A woman greeted him, cute in a country girl way, simple but attractive with a bright smile. She said in a friendly voice, "We see you. My name is Nicole. We only need your name for your accommodation. We do not require ID here."

"Um, oh, ok, James Dole. I guess I need a single twin or full bed. Um, a tub if you have it." His mind was out of focus. He was exhausted and barely hanging on to any sense of reality. The beauty of this place seemed so otherworldly. He was too tired to really take in all the colorful art and sculptures or the handmade brass lighting fixtures and knobs.

The polished purple crystals embedded in the Sun Stone glittered in the afternoon light, as it streamed down from several skylights in the half-domed roof above. He gave the woman his old ComPad and she set up a new sleek one for him. In the place allotted for a password, she typed, Tim.

As she handed it to James, she explained. "Tim will be your guide. In this ComPad, you will find a folder labeled, "Welcome to Hope City." It will give you an overview and introduction to our structure, beliefs, and programs. I am sure you will find them very helpful."

She smiled at him and said, "Tim will be your Personal Guide during your Emergence. He will show you to your room and help you with whatever you need." Then she turned to Tim, as he came through from a door behind her, and said, "This is Mr. Dole, please take him to S18."

In a small, tired voice he said, "Um, I need to eat too."

Tim came from behind the counter wearing a matching purple suit. Like hers, it had black lapels and a white shirt. Offering his hand to shake, smiling brightly, he said, "We see you. Would you like to eat in your room or in the dining hall?"

His other hand gestured to the right where a well-appointed family style dining room was visible between two pillars through an arched doorway. There was a lecture going on and robot servers were bringing plates of desserts to thirty or more people in there. Rows of long natural edge wood tables stood on either side of a wide path and another two along both walls.

James was surprised and impressed by the level of service and rich décor. He wondered if he was in the right hotel after all. He neglected to shake the man's hand and looked back at the front door as if it could tell him where he was.

"Um, is this the free hotel?"

"Yes sir, did you want a different one, perhaps a hotel in the park?" The young man smiled at his confused charge, and his heart went out to him. "Are you planning to stay with us in the City of Hope?"

"I don't know what I'm doing here, I'm just tired, hungry, and I need time to think." James was annoyed with himself; he assumed that he looked like an idiot.

"That's okay Mr. Dole. I can help you figure things out if you want. Why don't we take you into your room and order food? You can rest until you feel better. How does that sound?" he said in a chipper and caring voice.

He felt like a helpless child, which made him even more annoyed with himself. He just wanted to get out of people's sight. "Yes well, show me the way then."

Even the elevator was unusual. It had letters instead of numbers for the floors. Tim pressed 'S' and they went up nineteen stories. The back of the elevator was curved glass revealing the whole valley and the Wise World Park sprawling across it. It looked like the Wild West in the eighteenth and early nineteenth centuries. Teepees, wigwams, and pueblo adobe structures were grouped near a dry creek. Horses were running free in a pasture. A western style town was to the east, on the other side of the creek.

On the elevator, no one spoke. Tim sensed that this man needed a quiet space. When the doors opened, Tim smiled and waited for James to exit.

"Your room is to the left of the elevator, at the end of the hall. I can show you the menu in your room if you like and turn down your bed for you. Would you like me to have your clothes cleaned? I can also bring you fresh ones," Tim said as they walked to his room.

"Um, I'm not used to all this. I don't understand what's going on here." James was feeling off balance. He was not familiar with this level of service. "Are you working for a tip? Cause I don't think I have any E-Money on my ComPad now, and anyway I left it at the desk."

"Oh no sir," he said politely with a slight laugh. "We are a non-monetary city. We just believe in serving our fellow man. I have all I need, and I love to help my charges have all that they need, as well."

Feeling a bit like Alice in Wonderland, James had to ask, despite his fatigue, "Then how do you make a living?"

The kind man smiled and with the soft voice of a sage, answered, "We don't make a living sir, we create our lives."

"You'll learn more later when you're up to it. We don't live to work. We enhance our lives by serving others. It pleases us. I have chosen to do this work. You'll see. It is different here than in the outer world. This is all explained on the ComPad under 'Welcome to The City of Hope.'

They reached their destination. A pocket door with a number 18 on it automatically slid open before James and Tim. The door was not locked and there was no key card entry device.

"How did the door open?" James asked in surprise. In his financial bracket and F4 rating, he could not afford a Smart House in San Bernardino.

Expecting the question, Tim smiled kindly and answered, "It is a built-in Smart System. It responds to face recognition." He pointed to a small window beside the door.

"You will find that everything here in Hope is state of the art. The menu, the list of services, and the schedule of events are all on your ComScreen. The room and everything in it respond to voice commands. Here is an instruction booklet, you may need it." Tim tapped a soft covered purple manual sitting on the desk, then turned to the ComScreen and said, "ComScreen on. Meal menu."

The ComScreen on the wall turned on. It was a full-service Comp. The menu listed: lunch, dinner, and in-room menus.

"In room," Tim commanded. "There you go, just say what you want or tap on the screen. Do you want me to run a bath for you, sir?" he asked as he turned down the bed.

"Uh, no I'll do that later." James's attention was on ordering food. Then, remembering his manners, he turned to this helpful man and said, "Thank you."

"Sure thing Mr. Dole. Call me later or tomorrow morning, whenever you're ready for a tour of the facilities and an introduction to the program. I am here every day between 7am and 7pm. Feel free to call me if you need something.

"I'll leave you alone now. Have a good afternoon and evening sir." He gave a slight bow and left the room. The door slid closed behind him.

James was still feeling unsettled by this place. He ordered a black bean burger (because real meat was not on the menu) and French Fries, which was his favorite comfort food. Dinner soon arrived, carried in by a friendly middle-aged man who set a table for James.

He finally took in the room around him. Everything was in an old Western craftsman style, using all natural materials. It even had hand-hewn wooden furniture. The polished brass sconces on the wall held frosted glass bordered with curling brass leaves. There were similar ones in the lobby. Around the walls was a soft pastel scene, a foggy landscape of an unknown place. The painted ceiling had a pale sky with wind-streaked clouds. The room had a glass door leading onto a porch where he found planter boxes on the rails dripping with vines that created a cascade of greenery.

After James ate, he soaked in a luxurious voice operated jet-tub. Set into a solid glass tile wall beside the tub, there was a large *ComScreen*. James felt indulgent as he enjoyed the free high life of this place. "*ComScreen*, show me peaceful images," he said. The screen came awake, displaying a series of relaxing sunsets. Normally this would not be his thing. As stressed as he was, it felt comforting.

He still could not quite think straight. He toyed with the idea of calling his wife to let her know that he was okay but then decided to wait. It was not like she wanted him around anyway. Most likely, she would just yell at him. Maybe, he would never call.

'Judy is always angry at me,' thought James, feeling sorry for himself. 'I work so hard, and she doesn't appreciate me, like last week when she got so angry for no reason. I'm the one that always drives Sammy to his soccer game after work. Why can't she take time off from her job occasionally and take the kid, so I can have a beer with the guys. She acts like her job is more important than mine,' he grumbled. 'She's only an advertising agent. All she does is talk on her *Smartwatch* all day.

'I always take the kid to his games, but then my boss asked me to take on this extra job for an hour after work every day. I can't say no to My Boss! Heaven knows we need the money.

'This extra job will show him what a good worker I am. He always acts like I'm a screw-up, but it is not me, it's the team I work with. Those guys mess up and it makes me look bad. I was scared he was going to fire me. Then the company laid people off. Some jerk screwed up and I lost my job.

'When I didn't show up to take Sammy to practice, he got all bent out of shape. He is so spoiled. Kids don't know what they want. He doesn't know how hard it is to earn a buck. He ran to Judy, and she went ballistic. It wasn't a big deal.

'He's usually a benchwarmer anyway. It's that damn coach's fault, for not letting my kid play a lot. Judy did not help by giving the coach a hard time. I think the coach had him sitting out because she yelled so much. Sammy's been playing more now that Judy's been banned from the games. She always thinks that she knows better than everyone. That's what she does to me too, always demanding and belittling.

'I wasn't much of a soccer player either. I warned the kid to stay away from sports. He was never good at it. Of course, Judy took his side.'

'I feel like I am losing control of my life. I am such a failure. When I come home after a hard day at work, I should have the right to watch ball games on the ComScreen and drink a few beers. She has no right to complain about that. Anyway, I just do it to avoid arguing with her about the bills and the college fund for the kids."

James added a capful of bath salt and lay back in the warm water. His stiff back and sore leg began to feel better. The heavy weight he felt he was carrying melted a little.

The bathroom held all the toiletries he needed. He reached for the shampoo and cream rinse in recyclable plant-based plastic bottles. They felt smoother than regular plastics.

On the sink was an old-time ceramic cup for shaving. Next to it was shaving soap, a lathering brush, toothbrush, and hairbrush, all made of wood and natural bristles. In a ceramic twist-top dish he found nail clippers and dental floss. The mirrored cabinet held body powder, loofa, skin lotion, and toothpaste. The toiletries either had no scent or a hint of fragrance from the essential oils in them. On the paper labels was a brief list of ingredients and a brand name. None of which were familiar to him.

Feeling fresh and clean, he fell into bed, slept for 12 hours, and woke up at 2:22 am.

CHAPTER 2

Synchronicity

When he woke, he did not know where he was at first, but it slowly came to him. He fumbled with the light on the nightstand and then remembered it worked on voice command. The digital clock in the corner of the ComScreen said it was still too early for anything to be going on, but he did not want to just lay in bed thinking, not yet anyway. The truth is, he just was not ready to think. So, he shook his dusty clothes, dressed, and went out for a walk. On a hook, outside his door he found fresh clothes, but he decided to just leave his old ones on.

By the time he got to the lobby after getting a whiff of his clothes in the closed elevator, he changed his mind. He decided to use his ComPad on-line credit in a store if he could. He did not want to feel like a charity case, so he walked over to the lobby desk.

An older plump gray-haired man behind the desk said, "Good Morning, sir. We see you. How may I help you?"

"That's about the fourth time I've heard that phrase 'We see you'. What does it mean? I know it's a greeting, but it is odd."

"Yes, the 'we' refers to our Higher Self and our rational self. It means all of who we are is greeting all of who you are. We recognize that we are all Souls and personality, which makes us equally fallible and equally loving."

"Oh, I see," he said, wrinkling his brow and not sure he did. "Well, I was hoping to buy some clothes and get the ones I'm wearing cleaned. Can I have my ComPad to pay for it?"

"Sorry to disappoint you, but we don't buy or sell here at Hope. Your E-Money is of no use here unless you are just visiting. We will gladly have your clothes cleaned for you. As for getting new clothes, we have a Trade Store down the hall." The night manager directed him to the other side of the dining hall and down the corridor to the Trade Store.

As he crossed the half-domed lobby, he noticed three pillars standing together in a triangle in the center of the dome with writing on them. The one closest to him said, love over fear is the choice; another said, "Gratitude over wanting is a perspective" and the last one said, "Acceptance over control is an attitude." On their shared triangular base he read, "The Three Pillars of Trinitarian Thought." He did not understand them.

At the Trade Store, he found the doors open, but there was no clerk. A sign said, "Clerk hours are from 8 am to 6 pm, help yourself."

Inside were neat wooden racks, shelves, and bins of clothes with paper tags hanging on or wrapped around them. This non-monetary business made James feel like he was stealing or borrowing.

The tags stated that the clothes were made of fine quality organic cotton, hemp, silk, fleece, or wool. There were no synthetic fabrics or plastic wrappings, and the hangers were made of bamboo. The brand names on the sewn-in tags were unfamiliar to him. He picked out a few items that were likely to fit and took them to the dressing room.

He chose a white dress shirt, tan corduroy slacks, fresh underwear, and socks. There was a 'Donation and Returns' laundry bin next to a shoeshine bench. He contemplated tossing his clothes into it but decided to keep them and made a mental note to return for a shoeshine when it opens at 8:00, according to the sign on the seat. Then he took his own clothes to the desk to have them cleaned.

He walked over to the dining hall. It was open twenty-four hours. As he came in, he noticed there was only one other person in the room. The woman, sitting at a table on the left side of the room, appeared to be crying. In front of her was a real hardback book and she was writing in a paper journal. This surprised him. Even poor people have Book Pads. A box of tissues was also there. Many wads of used ones were stuffed in an empty drinking glass. James paused. She looked up and smiled at him with watery eyes.

He wondered, should he ask her if she is alright? But then she looked up at him. Her smile let him know she was fine. Maybe she had just read or wrote something sad in her books. After smiling back, he continued to the rear of the room, near the stage, where food was arranged on a table.

He poured a cup of coffee, but it did not taste very good, so he left it on the table. As he was serving himself sweet rolls and orange juice, he turned to find the woman standing beside him.

"Good morning. You couldn't sleep either huh?" He found her a little too thin for his taste, but nice looking. Her voice was smooth, but he thought it seemed a little deep for her stature. She had long blond hair, but her brown roots were showing. In her pink blouse and white capri pants, she reminded him of cotton candy. He watched her pour a cup of herbal tea.

James nodded having already stuffed a big bit of pastry in his mouth. Not really knowing if he should wait for her, or walk off, he paused and tried to swallow.

"The final seminar last night really threw me, you know. I realized that I have been wasting my life working at a job I hated, and for what? To pay the bills?" She poured some tea, shook her head, and said with a look of disbelief, "Why do we do that?"

She continued talking without noticing that he did not answer, as she put sweet monk fruit in her tea. She just needed to talk to someone, anyone who would listen.

"Um, well I don't know, I just got here last night, I didn't go to...."

"Oh, I'm sorry. Look at me, just assuming things again." She laughed and walked beside him as he started looking for a table.

"Would you like to sit with me?" she offered and asked, "Where are you from?"

He thought, 'Talking to someone is better than thinking alone, but I am not so sure about listening to this exuberant lady. Oh well, I'll go along with it,' and answered, "California, *San Bernardino.*"

"Oh, it must be nice there. I'm from Minnesota where it's cold. I hated it there, but I hate my husband more." She walked back to her table, and he followed her, not wanting to be rude.

"Is that a good book you're reading?" James was not really interested in the book, but he did not know what else to say. He just wanted to avoid what usually comes next, questions about spouses, work, and family.

"Oh yes, the *Conversations with God* books are great. Have you read them?" She was perky. "They are amazing. These books and the Founder's books are what brought me here. The Founder of the *Trinitus Principles* was an avid reader of Neale Donald Walsch. He is famous for channeling God." As she sat down and looked at him, she realized that she was talking outside his experience. "Have you been through the Introduction yet?"

"Um, no, I haven't done anything yet. I haven't even read the introductory articles on the website yet."

He felt a little embarrassed. Maybe he had nothing in common with her to talk about that did not involve his past, but he sat down next to her with his pastries and orange juice anyway.

"Maybe I should ask my counselor why I assume people always know what I'm talking about. There must be a reason I do that." She was just thinking aloud as she jotted a note in her journal. "So, how did you find yourself here?"

He shifted uncomfortably and looked down at the table. She, still writing with her antique ballpoint pen, had missed his reaction completely.

"Well, I just stopped to get some rest from the road." As soon as he said it, he knew the next question would bring him to the subject he did not want to talk about. Desperate to redirect her, he asked. "So, tell me what you think of this place."

Missing the redirect, she said, "You may have come for more rest than you realize. There are no coincidences you know." She looked up after finishing the short entry in her journal and pointed at him with a finger and pen, smiling like she had a secret. "There is a reason you came here. It was your destiny!"

"I do not believe in destiny, or God, or anything like that!" He dismissed the thought with a wave of his hand and a mouth full of pastry. He was glad that he had avoided the question of where he came from, and where he was going.

"Come now, how did you get here? Did you see the signs? Did a friend recommend it? Something brought you here, not somewhere else, but here to this hotel and not any of the others, this one, so how did it happen for you?" She was not going to let him slide on this, she strongly believed in synchronicity.

James began to feel a little trapped, but this woman did not deserve his wrath. A picture of the bit of paper from the cactus suddenly jumped into his head. He thought that since she had left her husband, maybe she would not judge him for leaving his wife and kids.

He looked at her, took a deep breath, swallowed another bit of pastry, and took a risk, "I lost my job, left my wife and kids, and just ended up here."

"Oh, I'm sorry to hear that!" Without skipping a beat, she added, "Did you see the signs and just came in, or did you hear about it?" She did not want to get into his private life, but she was trying to make a point about synchronicity. "Did anything odd happen just before you found this place?"

"Well, I did have a run in with a cactus." He was glad she was not judging him.

"A cactus? What happened?" She leaned in towards him, smiling at the opportunity to hear another neat story about synchronicity.

"I was having a bit of a yelling match with God and asked him what he wants from me, why he is busting my balls, and then I fell on a cactus." He began the story with an 'it-was-no-big-deal' kind of attitude.

She laughed a little and said, "Oh my," then motioned him to go on.

"Well, there was this needle stuck in my leg, well really many of them, and three of them had little pieces of a storybook stuck to them. One said, "Nothing," another said, "I am not," and the third said, "Listen to me." It kind of looked like they were answers to my rantings." He shrugged like it was not important and glanced at her to see if she thought the God part was ridiculous.

Her mouth dropped open, she was smiling at the same time, and her eyes grew wide. "God was talking to you, you know that, right?"

"Well, I don't know," he dismissed it.

"Are you kidding? Many people never get to hear something or see something that obvious!" Her hands were open, palms up, fingers wide. Her pen was still in one hand laced between her long fingers. "Don't you realize how lucky you are?"

"I guess not, it was just an old children's book that got thrown out on the highway." He was not willing to think that God would talk to him.

Her voice took on a playful sarcastic tone as she looked at him from under her eyebrows. "Oh yeah right, you just happen to have a talk with God, in the exact place that somebody threw out something with those exact words on it. Don't you find that a bit unlikely?"

"It's just a coincidence...," he started to defend himself, then thought better of it, and stuffed another bite of pastry in his mouth.

She pointed at him with the pen and nodded to show him she knew what she was talking about. "There is no such thing as just a coincidence, it was synchronicity. God's plans are perfect. We just don't see them that way. She gives us exactly what we ask for, we just have a bad habit of asking from fear."

James could not relate to what she was saying, so he became defensive. The grumbler in his mind said, there is no proof of God or synchronicity and besides, why would God talk to me, why now?

To her, he fumed, "Well, he picked a hell of a time to talk to me. Where was he when I needed him before? Maybe then I could have avoided all this shit." His tone was angrier than he meant it to be.

She spoke more seriously and more gently now that she saw that he was angry, "God talks to all of us all the time. The question is not, why or to whom he talks, but when is someone open to hearing Her for the first time. That usually happens when you run out of your own answers."

Wanting to regain control, he snickered, "Well, ain't that a hell of a thing!" He shifted back in his chair and tossed up his hands, avoiding her eyes.

Her serious tone shifted back to being bubbly again as she asked, "You said you don't believe in God, I'm curious, why?"

"There is no proof," he said with a sigh, turning back to his food again. He glanced at the door, wishing he had the balls to just get up and leave. A short bald man with graying temples walked in holding a large rolling flat case with a bundle of wires in his other hand. He smiled and gave a nod of hello as he walked past.

With only a passing glance at the newcomer, she said in near exasperation, "No proof? You need only look at all the coincidences from the beginning of time to know that randomness is not even mathematically possible!" She used her fingers to make air quotes around the word, coincidences.

Given the mood he was in, he did not want to get into a debate, he sighed again and impatiently quipped, "Well, I just don't know. It's not like God ever popped up to help me or anything." He stuffed another bit of food in his mouth and gulped some orange juice. He just wanted to eat and get out of this conversation.

Getting serious again, she slowly said; "look at me…" she paused; I'm just like you, I didn't hear Her either until a few months ago, but now I cannot deny that She is here, right now, talking to you through me. She is in this book I'm reading and, in that man setting up the ComScreen for the lecture. She is in this place and in all the people in it. She is in you, whether you want to believe it or not."

Still trying to avoid her eyes, he chomped on the last of his sweet roll and shrugged with a well maybe look on his face. Mentally, he gathered his testicles and chugged down more juice.

She could see that once again she pushed too hard and moved too fast. She cursed herself in her mind. Chewing on her bottom lip, she said, "Well, you don't have to believe in a god to live here or to do the work they ask of you here."

He swallowed hard. "Work? What work? What have I gotten myself into?" He was suddenly worried. 'What kind of work are they going to make me do to earn my keep?"

"Not regular work," she clarified, "working on your personal process. You know, reflecting upon yourself and your emotions." She wanted to help him calm down, so she added, "You really need to check out the articles on the website. They will explain everything to you." She reached out to him as if to say, sorry, but he pulled back, drinking down the last of his juice.

"Well, I've got to get going. I've got a lot of miles to cover," he said, as he stood up to leave. He was only half lying to her and to himself. He had no idea if he was leaving or not.

Perplexed and now concerned that she may have scared him off, she stood up too. "I'm sorry if I spoke out of turn. You just got here. Where are you going next?" She looked at him sadly.

This last question hit him harder than he expected. "I don't know." He shook his head and walked a few steps away.

She caught up to him and reached out to touch his sleeve. "Please don't leave because of my stupidity. Give this place a chance to help you. If nothing else, take a few days to decompress here."

He simply nodded and walked away. His mind was whirling as he went back to his room for solitude, his walk forgotten. Where am I going? What am I doing here? What do I do now? Where can I go? Did God lead me here? Am I willing to believe in God just to give me a sense of hope? Or is it all hopeless anyway? Are these people just desperate fundamentalists?

Back in his room, he just stood there not knowing what to do. Should he take his razor and leave, or should he sit down and read the *Welcome* shtick in the ComPad? He stood for a long time, then plopped down on the bed.

He was tired, despite a long night's sleep, he was tired of running. He suddenly realized he had been running his whole life. He went to college to escape his father's disappointment. Then he got married to escape his loneliness. Then he threw himself into his work to escape his distant children and empty marriage. Now he was running from himself. Where can he run to? How can he escape himself?

He hit rock bottom and cried for a long time. He felt lost, emotionally drained, believed he was a failure, and saw no way out of his pain. He was sure no one could love him the way he was, and he would die alone. His four-year depression had come to a head, and he did not know what to do next.

Hours later, he was still trying to pull himself together when the ComScreen rang. The prompt said, "Call from Tim." It displayed the time, 7:30 am, and a choice of buttons, *Answer with FaceTime*, *No FaceTime*, and *Refuse Call*. The tune chimed several times before James walked over and commanded it to answer without the camera.

"We see you. I hope I haven't woken you." Tim said cheerfully. "I thought I'd offer to get you up to speed and give you a tour, if you like."

James sighed audibly. "I don't know what I want to do to tell you the truth. I'm feeling out of sorts right now." He leaned heavily on the cabinet, as he talked to Tim.

"I see." Tim took a gentle and serious tone. "Well, if you like, we can just take a walk, or we can talk in your room. I'm trained in Crisis Communication, so maybe I can help you find some answers."

"I don't know, I can't handle a lot of rhetoric right now. No offence, I'm just not in the mood for a sales pitch." He covered his face with his free hand.

"No sales pitch, I promise," Tim reassured him. "That is not my intention. I would just like to help you through your day. It sounds like you are having a tough one already and could use a friendly ear right now."

James thought about what the lady at breakfast had said about God and giving this place a shot, but he was already reeling from that talk. "Is this place religious or something like that?"

"No, no. We are spiritually based, but not religious at all. There is no push from us about your spiritual choices. You do not have to believe in any specific Higher Power to do your Personal Process." Tim reassured him again, and encouragingly asked, "Have you read the articles on the website yet?"

"No, not yet. Someone sidelined me at breakfast, and I have not gotten to them." He sighed again.

"I am sorry that you got that impression from whomever you talked to," Tim said softly. "Please let me clarify this for you and help you through your confusion," he said as gently and as professionally as he could. After waiting for a response and not getting one, Tim added, "Let me suggest a walk in the flower garden on the south side of the hotel. I will wait for you there. If you just want to walk, we can walk silently, and if you feel like talking, I can listen. We can take it slowly, okay? In any case, I think it is best for you to get out of the room and be with someone," he gently urged.

James needed an aimless walk right now, but he had his doubts that Tim would keep from talking about this place. Surely that is his job, isn't it?

"I don't have to listen to a pitch, do I?"

"No pitch, I promise, "repeated Tim with a gentle smile. "I'll just be a willing ear, if you feel like talking." He said in a matter-of-fact tone.

"Ok, I'll go for a walk with you," James puffed himself up and consented, "but one word of your pitch and I'll be out of here!" He waved his hand flat across the air in front of him. He was clearly in no mood for preaching.

James got directions to the flower garden from the lady at the front desk. He stepped out into the soft morning light. The sun had just risen, and the late summer air was still cool at this early hour. For the first time since he arrived, he looked around at his surroundings.

He noted that no one was wearing TeleCom glasses here.

Everyone wore them where he came from. It is so convenient to have your Smart Phone right on your face. The screen is embedded in the lens, and it responds to simple eye movements.

The garden was a marvelous maze of raised flowerbeds made of man-made colored sandstone like the gatehouse. In them were yellow and orange lantana, lovely yellow desert marigolds; blanket flowers, with daisy-like petals in warm colors of yellow, orange, and red, and beautiful fragrant lavender. These were the flowers he recognized as indigenous to the desert and needed little water. There were also several kinds of succulents in bloom. These desert flowers swayed in the gentle morning light.

Just beyond them to the left was a raised gazebo made of graceful sandstone arches. Surrounding the flower garden and a lawn of tiny green succulents was a long, curved enclosure made to look like a canyon wall. Outside the wall was a cluster of houses with domed roofs. Just beyond them to the north was a tall plateau with a small city nestled on top. He wondered why anyone would choose to live here, on this barren land. Then he remembered, the Native American people did not have a choice.

In the flower garden, the walkways were paved with real sandstone tiles of random shapes, echoing the colors of the desert, in tans, shades of yellow to red, tinged in purple hues. Framing the entrance to the garden, and wherever the paths crossed, there were large black slate stones with words carved into them. The one at the entrance said, *Breathe.*

James spotted a big bubbling fountain in a clearing with Tim sitting on a bench beside it, waiting for him.

James started to walk towards Tim, but the garden paths formed a labyrinth, so there was no direct route to the center. He impatiently went around the path of circles four times before he got close enough to call out to Tim without disrupting other early morning walkers.

"Does this path ever get there?" he grumbled.

Tim called back in a relaxed tone, "We all get to the center, eventually, if we do not give up. The question is, did we enjoy the journey, and did we learn something along the way? Take your time, I'm in no hurry."

Others in the maze heard him and smiled at his wise words. Three people reached out to share the moment with James. They tried to make eye contact, but he looked away, embarrassed.

James cursed under his breath as another walker approached from a side path, leading to another fountain. He was a heavyset man about his own age. "Read the black stones," he said, as he strolled past and pointed down at James's feet.

James did not care to read them. He was only interested in finding the quickest way to the center where Tim sat. Now he glanced down and read, "Something that starts out bad, can lead to a good opportunity."

He started to feel that there was a conspiracy against him and that he was the victim of some kind of joke.

Part of him wanted to scream and yell obscenities at Tim, but he decided on caution and restraint. 'To hell with it!' He thought and gave a feeble wordless yell. It did not make him feel better, just made him more embarrassed. He could feel the need boiling up in him to really yell but suppressed it.

His focus returned to the path, and he decided not to read any more black stones. When he finally reached the fountain, he was ready to rest. He sat down hard on the bench next to Tim and let out an exasperated sigh.

"Is it your job to torture me?"

"No, on the contrary, I'm here to help." In a soft relaxed tone, Tim asked, "Do you want to tell me about your troubles and what brought you here, or would you prefer to sit quietly?" He offered nonchalantly. He trained as a shaman to guide softly, so he approached this angry man by gently offering and was careful not to push.

"What is the end game here anyway? Are you going to sell me a bill of hope and wellbeing if I just change my lifestyle to fit into your little community?"

James was not angry with Tim; he just wanted to know the bottom line. At this point, he could leave if he wanted, not that he knew where else he would go. In any event, he was determined to avoid getting involved in a cult, if that is what this was.

"There is no end game. I just want to help you if you are open to it. You can stay, you can go, you can learn what you are willing to learn or not learn anything. It is not my goal to make you stay. It is entirely up to you." Tim was leaning into James with a helpful concerned look yet spoke in a flat matter-of-fact tone.

James threw up his hands and leaned back against the bench. "So, what do you people want from me?" His voice was louder than required to talk over the gentle sounds of the fountain.

"We require nothing from you. The only question is, how can we help you?" Tim seemed sweet and empathetic.

James tried to calm down, so he took a deep breath. 'Okay,' he thought. 'I'll play along, but just long enough to get to the truth.'

"I lost my job, my wife doesn't want to be with me anymore, and my kids, well let's just say we don't connect."

"May I say something?" asked Tim.

James nodded, okay.

"James, you can get a new job and you can find a new relationship. Kids? Well, they're difficult, but they are doing what they need to do. Just making changes will not help you feel better about yourself or about your life."

'Here comes the pitch!' He thought and steeled himself. "Yeah okay, so what are you going to sell me to make me all better?" James asked sarcastically.

"Not a thing! We are not selling anything. Our program and our help are free. All I want is for you to drop your guard enough to let me talk to you on an intimate level. That's all. You are also free to go about your new life, or your old life, the same way you always have." Tim paused, and added, "Has it been working for you?"

Even though there was no sarcasm in Tim's voice, it cut into James as if it did. James was far from relinquishing control or granting trust.

"No one talks on an intimate level, especially men."

"That doesn't work well in this messed up world, does it? Don't you think it is time for a change that might work better?" Tim's voice was slightly coaxing. "Try being open with me and I promise not to judge you. I won't be as hard on you as you are being on yourself right now. Life is hard enough and made harder by the fact that you were taught not to honestly share your feelings."

"So, the plan is to get in my head and brainwash me into a cult?" James only half believed that. The other half thought Tim was being honest with him. The world had trained James for far too long for him to give into Tim's soft gentle tone very easily.

"No plan. No brainwashing. I will just tell you the truth of my experiences, and you can tell me yours as you see it. I will try to help you see things more clearly, but I will not try to convince you of anything."

"I'm sorry, but I'm having real trouble believing that there is no ulterior motive here." James gave a wave towards the hotel.

"I understand," reassured Tim, "but there isn't. We don't make money off anyone that comes here. We don't lose anything if you leave. We have no power over you, and we don't need you to believe in us to do what we love to do. We want to teach those who seek it, how to live in a community based on *Unconditional Love*."

"I just came to sleep."

Tim was gentle and looked at his charge with honest curiosity and asked, "That's fine. Now, you're here sitting with me trying to figure us out. Why bother?"

James sighed and really looked at his guide for the first time. He guessed Tim was of mid-age, late 30's, early 40's. His brown hair had reddish highlights, and his bright hazel eyes were full of kindness. He saw no animosity, no challenge, no judgment, just concern for James's well-being.

"I'm still here because I don't know where to go or what to do."

Ever so gently, Tim replied, "I can't tell you the answers. That is not my intention, but I can offer this. You are welcome to stay as long as you need while you figure it out, whether you go through the Emergence Program or not."

"No charge? No hooks? No anything?" James was still skeptical.

"None," Tim said flatly.

Despite himself, James felt relieved.

"Do you want to talk about how you came to be here?" Tim was careful. He did not want to push this man too hard. His careful wording left an option open to say, no if he wanted.

More relaxed, but still in a skeptical mood, James replied sarcastically. "Well, a lady told me that it was God and synchronicity."

"But you don't believe in that sort of thing, do you? Is that what set you off this morning?" Tim responded to James's tone.

"Yeah, I guess," admitted James as he started to pace.

"I'm sorry," Tim said softly, "She probably didn't mean to upset you." He was genuine as usual. He stood up to see if James wanted to walk now.

They walked slowly from the fountain area into the garden maze.

"No," James admitted. "She was apologetic about it and said I should give this place a chance."

Like the black slate stones evenly placed around the fountain, there was one at the opening to the maze that read; *Relax, life is not in your control.*

James paused and remembered that he had decided not to read any more stones. He felt that the maze was there just to provoke him.

"Now, what is this supposed to mean?" He pointed to the stone and looked accusingly at Tim.

Tim smiled, and explained, "It means that whether you believe in God or not, you cannot control your life. Control is the opposite of trusting, relaxing, and letting events unfold. It requires that you hold the reins tightly on everything and everyone. Doing that made your life unmanageable in the first place."

"Oh, is that so! I'm supposed to just go willy-nilly into life with no plan or account for my actions?" James stood there waving his hands about.

"It doesn't mean that," Tim patiently replied. "It just means that when you try to force your plan into being, you are not allowing life and others to be as they are. You are not letting life teach you. You're trying to force life to bend to your will. You're in a state of tension, force, and unwillingness. If you let life teach you and guide you, you can relax in the process. If you're listening to your heart, instead of your head, then you can relax and let life unfold naturally. It works much better than you think." His guide's tone was honest and not pushy.

James did not really understand what Tim was saying, but he was satisfied that the black stone was not trying to push a God on him. He walked quietly and kept his head up, to avoid reading another stone.

As they made their way through the maze, they were quiet for a while before Tim asked; "Are you going to give it a chance?"

"What?" James was surprised. "Oh, you mean the program? I don't know. I guess, it's not like I have anything else to do right now but get my head straight."

"I think we can help you do that. We can talk anytime you need to. Just call me." He waited for a moment before asking, "Would you like a tour?"

James thought it through. I don't want to go back to my little room and just sit there wondering what to do. Anyway, it feels good to be out in the morning air.

To Tim he replied, "Well, I guess, I don't know what else to do. I'm a little hungry, but I think right now there is a seminar in the dining room, and I'm not ready for that." He said the word, seminar, like it was a horrible thing.

Tim smiled at his charge's comment. No matter how many times he had done this, it always amazed him how much people resist the love and care given to them here. They find it so hard to believe that what we offer is real and that our love is unconditional, he mused. And how sad it is that the world outside our gates is so unloving and uncaring.' He personally felt great satisfaction in caring for and loving people, especially when they never really experienced it before.

"We can go to the tourist part of town. There are many choices of cuisine there and I can show you the sights and entertainments we offer. Does that sound good?"

"Yeah, okay," James welcomed the distraction.

When they came to the end of the maze, they walked through the lobby and entered a waiting tram. Tim and James sat across from the driver in two front seats, and the solar electric bus silently took off.

Tim and the driver exchanged the greeting that the people of this community used, "We see you."

The driver asked how they were doing and Tim answered with a friendly smile. The tram went around the hotel and followed along the curved wall framing the hotel gardens. James took note that the driver, a different one to yesterday, was also a new arrival in the community. He told them that he liked this job because it gave him time to think and process with his passengers. The tram went through the residential area, stopping now and then to take on more passengers.

Tim finished talking with the driver and turned back to James. He pulled a band out of his pocket and said, "Here put this on your wrist, the one without a watch. It will help people to know your status."

"Status?" James took the band confused.

Explaining further, Tim said, "Well, we are going to the lower town, which is a mix of people, residents, guests, visitors, and staff. The bands help people to know if you are knowledgeable about the program and familiar with personal processing, or not.

"It helps to know this, so there are no misunderstandings. Your band is black, which indicates that you are a guest and thus have not done any personal process yet. This way, if you have an outburst of negative emotions, we will understand that you may need special care and attention."

"Special care?" James looked at his Guide like the man just slapped him.

"Yes, you're not used to the open and disarming ways we tend to communicate. If someone gets too personal with you, you may feel a bit alarmed or confronted. It helps us to know that we may need to move slowly with you. You might take something personally when it was not meant to be, like the lady you encountered this morning."

James sat back looking at the band. It was a soft flexible tube with a black liquid inside and magnetic ends that fastened around the wrist. The liquid seemed to glow softly, like a black light. It had a small bead like solar cell on it.

"Well, it's hard not to take this personally." James was only half kidding as he waved the band.

"That is understandable, but it will make your stay more pleasant."

James put the band on and remembered that the lady he talked to had worn one. He noticed the driver wore a red one, and Tim's was a light purple. He figured that the rainbow colors of the bands had something to do with the status of the wearer and their ability to *process*, whatever that was.

The homes they passed looked like a giant cluster of mushrooms. Then they passed stores that looked like tree houses. Beyond that there were various apartment buildings and hotels. They looked like short fat palm trees or tall evergreen trees. These buildings were up on pillars, like exposed roots.

Further on, they came to the entertainment options. Buildings shaped like clamshells on pillars came into view, all in reddish brown, light tans, and off-white colors.

James noticed that all these buildings were round and curved with southwestern style adobe or stucco. They were all open underneath. Everything was off the ground on pillars made to look like stems or tree roots, for a low-impact footprint. He also noticed that similar businesses and living environments were grouped together. On the right side of the road was a line of buildings with a dry riverbed behind them. On the left side, were houses and businesses right up to the base of a large plateau. The road ahead followed the riverbed up to the top of the plateau, where the main part of the city was situated.

The driver's voice came through the speaker system. He was pointing out the places they passed, but James was only half listening. He was looking at all the unique structures here, while he continued to think about the wristband and the status it conferred. He wondered if wearing the colored bands created prejudices between the different colored groups, and whether this process thing could prevent it.

This led him to think about the 4F scoring system which he hates. The rest of the world is using it, and it is segregating people, forcing them to focus on fame and popularity. It scores you on your posts and friends, your family ties, and your job. The 4F combines likes, retweets, and friend count scores. Then the score is converted into bitcoin and that defines your personal value. If you commit a crime or even a slight to someone, you lose points.

He shook his head thinking, 'Leaving my wife will undoubtedly knock my points down into the negatives.'

James turned his attention back to the driver who was describing the landscape for the passengers, then a thought hit him. He turned to Tim and asked, "So, the wristband colors you wear, do they create prejudices and social classes?"

Tim answered, "I suppose it could; but we haven't had any problems yet. The way we look at life and each other prevents that problem. The community considered it for a long time before they decided to use bands. That was before my time. They concluded that it was worth the risk because it helps peace officers do their jobs and it smooths out interactions between visitors and residents. Our Founding Principles and our personal processing circumvent any prejudices." Tim explained, ever bright, open, and wanting to help his companion understand.

"What color do peace officers wear?" James asked out of curiosity.

"We all wear purple. Purple indicates that we have had therapeutic and crisis training. Anyone dressed like me is a peace officer and can intervene in a crisis." Tim said with a smile.

In surprise, James said, "Oh, so you're a cop, not just a therapist."

"More like a therapist that acts as a peace officer when needed."

James thought about the way things were in his hometown. Cops were more like soldiers patrolling a war zone. Gangs and police were always at war in the bad neighborhoods. Those areas have segregation walls in between different neighborhoods. Whole parts of town looked like walled prisons.

Tim pushed the button for the next stop, interrupting James's thoughts.

They stepped off the tram in the middle of the restaurant district. As the passengers left, they all said, "Thank you" and "Goodbye" to the driver. James assumed they were all friends. He would soon learn that this was how everyone treated each other here.

"What kind of food do you feel like eating?" Tim gestured around them with both hands.

"Well, brunch, I guess. Even though it is still early, I don't feel like traditional eggs and bacon right now. Maybe something lighter?" James was interested in their unusual architecture.

He had once worked for a company that installed solar panels on new buildings. They were passive solar like these structures, but he found it interesting that these arrays were mounted on artistic organic shapes, rather than, on the contemporary flat roofs of San Bernardino.

He saw very few straight lines or corners on anything. All the painted concrete pillars were made to look like tree trunks with branches that held tree house buildings. Since they were above ground, it left open plazas underneath. It looked as if the manmade sandstone, plants, and glass just grew together like a jungle. Every building here had a rooftop garden, and an outdoor Lanais covered with plants and vegetables.

The solar panels, shades over open decks, rain collectors, and even transmitting towers were all disguised as flowers, trees, and leaves. All the buildings seemed to be powered by their own solar or wind array. Walkways between buildings looked like wood and rope bridges, though they were constructed from a lightweight concrete.

Tim saw the look on James's face. "Beautiful, isn't it?" He waited for his charge to take a good look around.

The main street was in the center of a circle of buildings. They walked into a large round outdoor eating area with tables and chairs placed between live palm trees in raised flower beds with benches around them. These cobblestone works of art and function were of different earth tones arranged in a swirling galactic pattern.

James was stunned. Much of the architecture he was used to outside in the cities was in a modernistic contemporary space-age style. It started in Dubai in the late 1900s and early 2000s, flat curves, sharp angles, shiny metal, black glass, and sterile looking.

"Do you like our architecture?" Tim asked.

"Wow! It is fascinating," James realized his mouth was open. He cleared his throat and looked at his guide. "So, where to?"

"I think Oliver's is a good spot. It has sandwiches and salads that are light and different. Would you like to try it?"

"Sure, why not." James was feeling a little better already.

Oliver's was on the west side of the plaza and now mostly in the sun. The restaurant decor had umbrella tables and chairs that looked like an assortment of vegetables, bread, and cheese slices. Out in front of Oliver's, the two men chose a table that looked like a slice of red onion with stools that looked like stuffed olives. Its lettuce leaf umbrella on a curved metal stem pole, leaned to one side.

A server came to the table to greet them and said, "We see you. Thank you for your patronage." He pointed to the ComPad picture menus on the table and went through a list of their specialties made from seasonal foods and imports from Trinitus, alternative cities and other communities in the local area. The waiter spoke and dressed like a maître d' at a 5-star restaurant. The selections were more about the ingredients than they were about any specific dish. Many selections were described as organic, hydroponic, free-range, and true soil.

James looked a little overwhelmed by the range of choices and the new names for the dishes, so Tim offered to do the ordering.

Gratefully, he agreed just to speed things up. He also wanted to avoid asking too many questions. He had no idea which one was a salad or a sandwich. Finally, the waiter asked them what drinks they wanted.

James asked for a regular coffee with cream. The waiter apologized. "In Hope, we don't serve caffeinated coffee, and all our teas are herbal. We avoid crops that destroy endangered ecosystems. I can bring you a herbal coffee, if you like. We have several blends to choose from," he suggested and smiled politely.

"No, I think I had one this morning and I did not like it. It didn't taste like coffee. I'll just have water."

Tim asked for water too. The waiter gave a brief bow and went up a flight of stairs to the kitchen in the tree house. It looked like a quaint little cottage sitting among strong leafy branches.

James looked around at the buildings again. He made small talk about the work he had done in the solar industry and complemented the organic designs they were using. Tim told James that if he chose to stay, he could find work here in this field. James did not have an opportunity to investigate further before the waiter returned.

He was carrying a large round bamboo tray and placed it on a Lazy Susan in the middle of the table. This was a build your own salad or sandwich affair. He also brought a rack of condiments in natural plant-based containers and a small loaf of fresh bread on a wooden cutting board, which he set beside it. There was a selection of cured and cooked meat slices, though none were lamb or beef. A section of lettuce and other live salad greens were growing in a large bowl of water, which he placed beside an assortment of cheeses, uncut tomatoes, marinated veggies, and pickles. The dishes, silverware, and cloth napkins were all made from bamboo. Nothing was made of plastic.

James quickly built a sandwich, while Tim took the time to cut or tear his ingredients into a salad, then added vinegar and oil for dressing. Tim seemed to be very intent on his food. He was creating it slowly and deliberately as if meditating. He also ate silently, so James was quiet while he ate his sandwich.

James looked around at the people there. He noticed that many of them were wearing yellow, green, blue, or purple bands. Their clothing seemed to be a mixture of an Arabian desert style with American Indian designs. They wore a light robe or tunic in bright colors and in some cases, with Indian motifs. He could easily pick out the visitors and guests because they were dressed in the kind of clothes he found familiar. Tim and the staff wore purple suits.

Some of the tables in the circle were taller. They were made for standing rather than sitting. At the one that looked like a cucumber slice, was a woman with long white hair wearing a light purple tunic, covered with a warm brown robe. She was drinking tea, seated in a high folding chair, which she must have brought with her. Her wristband was white. Occasionally a passerby would bow slightly or speak to her before they walked on. She would nod in acknowledgement and then returned to her old well-worn hardback book.

After James finished his sandwich, he waited for Tim to finish. Then he gestured his head toward the woman and asked, "Who is that? What does a 'white' wristband mean?"

Tim smiled and took his time swallowing the last bite of food. "That is the Founder's Proxy. She represents our late Founder who developed the Trinitus Principle by which we live. She became a White Band through her deeper understanding of our teachings and her spiritual connection with our Founder."

"So, you do have a religious leader?" James had an edge to his tone.

"She was voted in by the Council Members. It is more like winning the Peace Prize than anything else. She holds no power over the Council, but they do go to her for advice on difficult matters. She is more like our Elder than our leader." Tim explained, patiently as always.

Tim pushed his plate aside and ate a piece of bread. Meanwhile, James continued to quietly watch the Founder's Proxy. A woman asked her something and waited for an answer with her head bowed, as if in prayer, while the Elder seemed to meditate on the matter.

Tim finished eating and gently asked his charge, "It seems to me that you have doubts about religion and take issue with God, is that right?"

"Hmm, well, yes. I don't know if believing in a god has ever helped anyone get through life better." James was still watching the Elder who was now speaking to her querant with her eyes closed.

"I agree. It is not about believing in a god that does something. It's about having a relationship with your *Higher Power*, plus understanding life and how it works, that makes the difference." Tim's voice stayed soft and even.

James looked Tim squarely in the eyes and in a sharp tone challenged, "Oh really? How can you have a relationship with something you can't see or hear?"

"Again, I agree with you. However, the goal is to be able to see and hear Him or Her when you need to. The woman over there asked the Proxy a question. Now the Elder is talking to God, her version of God. She is channeling her Higher God Self to answer the woman's question. This Higher Power, some call, God, is in all of us. Can you believe that?"

"No, I don't! How can I trust that this *Higher Power* is in all of us, when most of us are so screwed up!" This conversation was getting him agitated, but he did not want to get too adamant in public or take his feelings out on Tim, who was just doing his job. Though his tone remained frustrated, he kept the volume down.

Tim, ever soft and patient, asked, "What if I told you that God's love is in all of us, but the reason you don't see this love in most people, is because they are not connected to it, even when they do believe in Him? They don't know how to put their beliefs aside to hear Her voice inside them."

James sighed impatiently, "I don't want to get into this right now. Can't you just tell me what this place is all about, without getting into the God thing?"

"Yes, I can. As I've said before, you do not have to believe in a god to live here, or to receive help with your difficulties. I am sorry if I have offended you. What would you like to know?" Tim was sincerely apologetic and wanted to be helpful.

"Well, what is the main point of this place, what are you trying to do?" James demanded to know.

"The purpose of our communities is to be an example of what life could be if we all worked diligently on our own traumas and emotional problems. By interacting with unconditional love, instead of fear, we make better decisions for ourselves and our future. We give of ourselves as an open resource to our community." Tim's answer was concise. He spoke in a gentle tone and waited patiently for his charge to ask questions.

"So, all of you work on your traumas?!" James said with scorn. "I'm not traumatized," James added in denial, wanting to exclude himself.

Tim patiently explained, "It depends on how you define trauma. We define it in a way that covers everything from the smallest neglects from your parents to the many common distresses that are part of normal life outside in the cities."

"Oh, I see. So, if my father and wife disapproved of everything I did and I couldn't hold down a job, or cover the bills, would you consider me traumatized? Gee, that means just about everyone is, right? It is a tough world out there. Everyone must fight to survive!" James's tone was both sarcastic and defeated.

"Here in our Trinitus cities, we ask, 'what if it did not have to be this way? What if life was not a struggle? What if we could go through life with guidance and have help in dealing with our emotions. What would our lives be like without the low self-esteem we develop from the harsh way people treat each other?" Tim posed the questions with sincere wondering and James could see that he really wanted to find the answers.

James said with a shrug, "I don't know. I thought life always has to be a struggle. It has always been that way, hasn't it? I don't think people change much. Maybe we just can't change."

Tim leaned in and spoke in a direct and flat tone, "Maybe out in the world, people don't try to change. Maybe they let their children grow up, never knowing how to talk about their feelings and they don't teach them how to manage them better. Maybe parents can't teach something they don't know themselves. Maybe they feel helpless and think they cannot do anything about the world because they have been led to believe it is what it is, and you can't change it."

James leaned forward and stared at Tim across the slice of onion. In a sharp scornful tone, with his chin jutting forward and his lips pursed, he spit out, "So, you think you can change people? How?"

Ignoring James's aggression, Tim sat back relaxed and gently smiled. "We have programs that help people process their emotions, and face their fears to regain their self-esteem, so they can learn to trust in life again, while we provide a stress-free environment."

"A process? Well, how do I know it'll work for me? And more

specifically, how's it going to solve my problems with my wife, kids, and losing my job?"

In a soft even tone, as always, Tim responded. "It is more about you letting it work for you. The process provides guidelines by teaching certain ideas, new points of view, and through talking openly about how you feel and why. The tricky part is that some people are not used to being vulnerable. You will have to learn to trust us. I get the sense that trust is hard for you." Tim carefully ventured.

"Hmm, you think so." answered James sarcastically.

They sat quietly for a bit while James tossed these ideas around in his head. Tim sat patiently waiting and let him work it through.

James thought back to a conversation his Aunt Gracie had once had with him. She was in the habit of talking openly and honestly about her day and about her ailments to anyone who politely asked, "How is your day?" or "How are you?

He was concerned that someone was going to take advantage of her, so he warned her to stop. Her response was, "It is good to be honest. When I talk to strangers about my problems, sometimes they come up with good answers and they share them without judgments."

He thought about her words when he rode on public transportation, but he never dared do it, not that anyone asked how he was doing and really meant it. He also remembered his wife saying that she had no idea how he feels about things and called him passive aggressive. She wanted him to go to couples' therapy at the time, but he refused. He did not want to spend the money.

James weighed his options and could see no downside to trying out this process thing. After all, he told himself. I have nothing more to lose now. This stranger is not judging me. I have been trying to figure out all these things and I haven't gotten very far. I asked the questions, but I didn't get any answers on my own. If Tim and this community can help me move in the right direction, then what the heck. Maybe I can put this program to the test, besides it'll give me more time to think in a free hotel.

"You're right. I don't trust anyone. I guess I feel like everyone is going to judge me and think I'm stupid or something. The world is so messed up. I can't be the only one that doesn't get how life works. I know I'm not the only one struggling. I don't have anyone to give me the answers. No one seems to know what they're doing out there! So, tell me, how is it so different here?" James was curious and maybe he felt a little drop of hope.

In a gentle sage-like tone, Tim explained, "We talk to each other and learn from each other's experiences. Then we apply what we learn to ourselves and teach others. We remind ourselves that we are all going through similar things and see each other as equals on their own paths. We treat our intimate conversations with respect, and we don't cover difficult feelings with platitudes. We let ourselves feel and are honest about it. We try to be authentic and nonjudgmental. We use therapeutic processes to help each other along."

"That's a tall order for most people, don't you think?" James scoffed.

"Sure, at first, but it comes with practice. None of this is an overnight cure. It takes courage to change the ideas you hold about yourself and a willingness to be open to new viewpoints about the world.

"Here in our community, you will have the time you need, whenever you need it. You will have people you can talk to, and you will have less stress pressuring you along the way. We provide a rest from the struggle to survive that you have been facing in the world. It is hard to let go into the process when you are with people who don't value self-reflection, or when you are all wrapped up worrying about money and you don't feel safe."

"Sure, that makes sense. Do you really practice this stuff? Are you trained to guide people through it?"

"Yes, I am," Tim assured him, and waited to see if James would continue the conversation, or commit to doing it later, but James sat silently watching the Elder. She was writing something on a piece of paper. The other woman had left.

When she finished, the Elder looked right at him, smiling. She waved the paper in his direction and gestured for him to come and get it.

Tim noticed and offered to get it for him. James just nodded, not knowing what to do. Tim thanked her, bowed slightly as he received the paper, and returned with it in hand. Without looking at it, he gave it to James.

"What is this about?" James asked with a wrinkled brow.

"I don't know. Read it. It is for you and not necessarily for me to know." Tim sat back down on the olive stool.

James opened the folded paper and in blue ink it read, "We see you. God *is* talking to you." Across the top and below, it said in quotes, "Nothing," "I am not", and "Listen to me." Shocked, James dropped the note on the table like it was on fire. These were the words from the cactus needles!

"What the hell! How could she know about this!?"

Having seen this kind of thing before, Tim just answered calmly. "Words come through her. They show love to those who need it."

James stared at the note, then looked back at Tim, "I saw these words printed on bits of paper on the side of the road, miles from here!" He looked toward the Elder who had turned back to her book. "How could she know about this? I only mentioned it to a lady at breakfast. Could they have talked?" James looked at his guide for answers.

"From what I know about her abilities, I doubt that she talked to anyone, other than her own inner guidance." Tim glanced at the paper tossed on the table and said, "Can you share the story with me?"

James shook his head in disbelief, but then the words started pouring out. He talked about losing his job, leaving his wife, his rant at God in the desert, and lastly about the tattered book on the cactus. He ended by telling Tim that the lady in the dining room said it was God talking to him.

With gentle urging Tim asked, "What do you think about the possibility that God was talking to you through the Elder?"

"I don't know about that. It's hard to explain right now."

After waiting for his charge to absorb what had just happened, and after seeing how agitated he was getting, Tim asked, "Would you like me to show you around, or would you prefer to go back to the hotel, or we could go to a Conversation House?"

"What is a Conversation House?" James wasn't really interested; he was just being polite. He was still reeling in confusion.

"It's partly a tea parlor and coffeehouse, and partly a book trade library. It's a good place to get into conversations about feelings and thoughts. People also read poetry there."

"No, I think I need to go back to my room now and read the Welcome Statement in the ComPad before I experience anything more." James suddenly felt very tired.

"Sure, that's understandable. Let me know whenever you feel overwhelmed or need to take a break. This can all be too much sometimes. Never be afraid to call a stop to it. Okay? Deal?"

"Yeah, sure," James's mind was still reeling from the note. He stuffed it in his pants pocket as they got up to leave. It felt funny not having to wait for a check or pay. Tim explained that whenever they were together, James did not need E-Money to pay for things. The center was busier now. There were more trams coming and going, more people walking or riding small solar Segway scooters. The Elder was packing up her chair and book to leave.

James was quiet on the tram back to the hotel and Tim let him be. As they got off and entered the hotel, Tim asked, "Do you want me to come up and answer any questions about the community?"

"No, I need some time alone right now." James was still preoccupied with this idea that God had chosen now, of all times, to talk to him. "Um, thanks for the walk and for not giving me a sales pitch." He paused for a moment. "Did you mean it when you said, I don't have to believe in God to do this processing thing?"

"Yes, I mean it. It is clear to me that God has other plans for you. It helps to have the support of a *Higher Power*. It can be hard to trust yourself when you are faced with challenges in your life, especially when you have no reason to forgive yourself or others for the traumas you have suffered. Choosing a healthier way of thinking sometimes needs *evidence* as to why it works better. God and His unconditional love can be that evidence." Tim urged gently.

"I just don't understand." James sighed and shrugged hopelessly.

Tim tried to reassure him that it was no big deal, "Don't worry about it for now. You are a long way from getting down to the bottom of your feelings where that question lies. We'll take it slowly. God is just letting you know that He is there, when you're ready for Him."

They returned to the hotel and Tim left him in front of the elevator. James, half waved and stepped inside. He stared at the brass panel of letters. Below A and Lobby there were two other buttons, Pool/Gym and Book Club; and above T was Conference Room and Rooftop Garden Deck. He hadn't noticed them before. He pressed S and went to his room.

On a hook outside his door, he found the clothes that were left for him that morning and the work clothes that had been cleaned. He grabbed them and hung them all in his closet. Then he lay down on the freshly made bed and stared at the ceiling. He did not have it in him to read the *Welcome* material yet.

He thought about synchronicity and the cactus plant. He pulled out the note, went out onto his porch, and sat down in a rocking chair next to a small bubbling fountain.

He looked at the note and thought to himself, 'Okay God, so you want to talk to me. Is it true that you want nothing from me, except for me to listen to you, and you're not punishing me? I have to say it feels like you are!' He did not expect an answer, but he heard the words, "That's right," in his head.

James assumed he was telling himself what he wanted to hear, and this was not the voice of God.

"Why couldn't it be?" answered the voice in his head.

"Because it can't be, you don't exist!" James said out loud.

"Neither do you, really. Not the way you think of anyway."

"Huh? What?" James couldn't figure out if it was his own voice or not. Why would he say that to himself? If there was God, what did He mean by that? Was he really having a conversation, or was he losing his mind? He shook his head like he was trying to shake water off.

"Nope, this is not possible!" he blurted out.

"Okay," was the last thing he heard. Now he was left in silence wondering what had just happened. He could not cope with this just yet. He put his thoughts elsewhere.

He thought about this community and questioned whether to stay or to go. 'If I leave, where would I go? I'm broke and my 4F score is probably tanked. I have no family left, other than my wife and kids. No place I'm particularly interested in going to. I really should do something to pay off our debts. I can't leave my wife in this financial bind, even if she is mostly to blame for it.

'How can I make things right for her and the kids?' He questioned himself. 'I'd at least have to do that, no matter what I do. If this place does not deal with money, I'd have to work outside of it, but I could live here and give all my money to her and the bank anyway.'

'Hey, that sounds like a plan! Great,' he thought, his spirits lifting. 'Maybe I have something to focus on now.'

With new conviction he stood up and leaned over the rail to look around. The garden maze was just below him. Now he could see that it formed a Yin and Yang shape. The two fountains were the dots. In the open area between the maze and the hotel, a group of people were gathering to do some exercise. They put down mats, pillows, and what looked like foam bats.

He watched out of curiosity and thought about calling Tim to see what work arrangements were available to him. There were about twenty people fanned out, side by side, in four rows, with four guides and a teacher standing in front. James went in and called Tim on the ComScreen. He saw the time, 9:05 am.

"Sorry to bother you again so soon, but I was wondering what jobs I might be able to get here, if any, that pay money?"

"No problem. Yes, you can do just about anything you like. We understand the need for money outside our community. Anyone going through the program can earn money for their work, until they no longer need it. What kind of work did you have in mind? What are your skills and most importantly what do you love to do?"

This surprised James. "Uh, well I have a degree in architectural design, and I would love to design buildings like the ones we saw today. Those were so organic, I loved them. I get a job doing what I want, just like that?" he said in disbelief.

"Yes, you can. We have a work and education system that focuses on the needs of the workers and the community, not on industry and profits. If you feel a need to brush up with courses in your field, they are available, otherwise you can go straight to work," replied Tim.

"When can I start?"

"As soon as you like. Have you read the *Welcome Folder* yet? It is all in there," Tim urged gently.

"You can look for work outside in the city, but as you know, that's not that easy, especially in this area. You can stay here regardless. The program is more than a self-help strategy and a set of ideals; it helps you to integrate with our unique way of life. The people who live here and the way things work is a little different. They can take some getting used to. Like I said, it's not about brainwashing, it's about helping you cope with the culture shock you might feel," Tim added in a soft persuasive voice.

"I see, well, I guess I've got some reading to do. I'll get back to you, if I have questions." James reached the website and looked at the two folders. "Do I have to read both, or can I skip one?"

"They are basically the same, but the *Visitor* one is more for people who are here for a vacation or for a few days of retreat. It focuses on our culture and attractions. The other one is for longer stays and describes our Personal Process Program, employment, and educational options."

"Okay, well, that's what I thought, so I'll read the *Emergence* one. Can I place a call to outside the community on this thing?" James waved towards the ComScreen.

"Yes. Just say or select, outside line, after you say, phone."

"Ok great, I'll probably call you in the morning, if I don't have questions between now and then." James said goodbye and touched the end call button on the ComScreen.

CHAPTER 3

The Plan

James set to work, glad to have a direction and purpose. He sat down at the desk. Other than the brief *Welcome Statement*, he found a folder entitled, *Emergence*. It contained seven files: *Adjusting to Our Culture,*" which contained the *Principles of Trinitus*; *Work Opportunities*; *Educational Options*; *Personal Process*; *Environment and Art*; *Most Frequently asked Questions*; and *The New Spirituality*. He was impressed with their comprehensiveness, clarity, and lack of sales pitch. What he read reminded him of a college syllabus or a workplace orientation.

He read *Work Opportunities* first. It described how the needs of the community are addressed through Educational and Work Co-Ops. These Co-Ops operate upon the principles of Horizontal Leadership and Conscious Decision Making. Employee-Owned Co-Ops function without stocks or money.

Everyone in the Co-Op votes on what they will make or change. We work in tandem with other Co-Ops, Trinitus Cities, and local communities. We trade goods and supplies as well.

Our companies are different than those in the outer world, in several ways. We do not work for a company's bottom line, but rather, we create new ideas for our community, ideas that broaden our shared core beliefs and are beneficial to the majority of people. Rather than create a market for our goods and services, we fulfill existing needs in the most ecologically and socially sound way. For example, store clerks have an equal say in what patrons want.

New products, concepts, and services are screened and voted upon by the *Co-Op Council*. Then they are passed on to other councils who seek to integrate it with existing forms.

James was impressed with everything he read until he reached the part about no stocks and no money. Then he laughed to himself at their impractical approach and thought they could never pull this off.

Next, he opened the *Education* file. It described how after Basic School, the equivalent of elementary school, students attended a 6-year high school, which included the curriculum of a 2-year college.

Then they attend a Trade School, which is also run as a Co-Op. He read about how they teach Quested Knowledge, a combination of technical information and on-the-job training. He was intrigued by a statement that read, "Students are guided by their educators and aptitude tests to discover their interests. Then an individual program is designed with the student's participation, which is tailored to their skills and interests.

Some Co-Ops are purely educational. They produce new ideas with innovative intellectual properties. These are our Think Tanks and Intellectual Colleges.

'Wow!' He thought. 'Individual programs tailored to individual interests and the student has full say. That's amazing!' He leaned back and began to daydream about his skills and interests. With a wide smile, he imagined working at something that was fun and satisfying, rather than all the miserable jobs he had had over the years.'

The *Environment and Art* file described how the Cities of Trinitus focus on creating peaceful, integrated, social environments for people. It stressed how important it is to create harmony between nature, people, and an object's function. It stated that there is no advertising anywhere in the cities or on the products because they feel that advertising is manipulative. They want things to be based on their true value not on brand names. The Co-Op's name or the shop's name is the only information presented on small signs. Total transparency of ingredients and manufacturing practices are required.

Trinitus *Cities* focus on creating an integrated environment of ecology, art, social engagement, and natural forms with efficient function. Most of all, it emphasized the importance of fostering serenity, rather than focusing on sales and profit.

James breezed through the two files entitled, *Adjusting to our Culture* and *Frequently Asked Questions*. He decided to read *Personal Process* and *The New Spirituality* files last. Most of the questions in the FAQ were already answered in the other files anyway.

The questions he found most interesting were, 'What happens when someone commits a crime?' and 'Are there any laws?'

The article emphasized that they have only one law, their 'Golden Rule, "Treat everyone, everything, and every situation with Unconditional Love."'

Small crimes are handled by Peace Officers right on the spot. They deal with everyone involved using compassionate counseling. Larger crimes, those that result in bodily harm, or sexual assault, are handled by a judicial court. In some cases, it can lead to incarceration. Once convicted, the prisoner is given the choice of having their case transferred to authorities outside the city or they can stay within the community's jurisdiction.

Those who choose to stay are incarcerated in a humane environment and given a therapeutic program specifically designed for them. They are kept there until they have proven that they are ready to rejoin the community.

Trinitus focuses on mentally healing people, rather than punishing them in a harsh and negative environment. The correction community is a walled off area with mandatory daily therapy.

James wondered, how do they handle divorces? Probably with counseling too. But I bet both parties need to agree to do it, and in my experience, that will never happen.'

TRINITUS

A COOPERATIVE HUMANITARIAN FOUNDATION

MISSION STATEMENT

We at Trinitus are a grassroots movement and a nonaffiliated community of organizations, businesses, and individual volunteer members working together for the common good. We are united in heart and are committed to providing the entire community with a more evolved understanding of human consciousness, of social interaction, of nature, of a natural way of life, and of God as each sees Him/Her/It, as well as dedicated to enhancing everyone's spiritual and personal evolution.

We are accomplishing our goals by participating in Personal Process, by cooperating with each other, by acknowledging our common desire for a better way of life, and through the practice of unconditional love. We combine our knowledge and efforts with other organizations to find new alternatives, to research new methodologies, and seek truth and justice for everyone in our community.

We teach and promote unconditional love, forgiveness, acceptance, and personal processing to foster a higher awareness of how to live together with social emotional maturity. We produce new attitudes, products, positive lifestyles, and working environments that promote growth, a love for life, and a willingness to do more for ourselves and each other.

We take individual responsible action to enhance the overall good of our whole community, a healthier attitude towards the Earth, and towards all the lifeforms it supports. We accentuate the great achievements of humanity and rectify the negative effects of the past. As we face the continuing problems of today, we introduce noninvasive, alternative strategies that balance progress and protection for our environment. We bestow upon all individuals the freedom to express their own ideas and live by their own life choices, so long as they do no harm to people, animals, the environment, or any other living forms.

We recognize that life is a process. We can only strive for better ways of living and can never truly claim that we have the ultimate truth and are without fault. We strive to always learn from each other. We share with each other our revelations, resources, love, care, and help our community evolve towards our greatest potential.

James sat back and let out a long sigh. These ideas seemed exciting and impossible. He wanted to believe in them, but they were so different from anything he had ever experienced, his mind rebelled against it.

He thought these were lovey-dovey ideas that could never be a reality, but then for just a flash, he imagined how it could be. Before he could dismiss this as fantasy, he remembered that he had already seen bits of it in the community. Then the moment passed, and his skeptical mind was back in control.

He was glad to see that there was no indication of this being a cult, at least not yet, but he planned to proceed carefully.

He paced around his room for a minute to get back to a more familiar reality. Then with a sigh, he mustered his courage and read on.

THE TRINITUS PRINCIPLES

LOVING

1

We open our hearts, feelings, and hopes as we accept ourselves and others. By communicating openly with each other and through grace and love, we heal our fears. We believe that fear of loss, feelings of separateness, and a belief in unworthiness cannot exist where unconditional love, a sense of oneness, a feeling of belonging, and self-awareness are present.

2

We see all humanity as one family and respect our children as our future. Thus, we teach each other with unconditional love. We have no limitations when we work together for the future of our children and our children's children.

3

We strive to lead with our hearts and express the highest versions of ourselves. We inspire and support others with unconditional love and encourage everyone to follow their own loving instincts. Thus, we lead by example.

GROWING

4

We apply all our ideals and principles to our communities, knowing they reflect who we are and what we are becoming. We love and care for future generations by protecting our environment and by creating sustainable social structures. Everyone in our community is free and equal.

5

We respect and protect all cultures, including our indigenous population. We protect their lands and their sovereignty. We have much to learn from the First Nation and from the past.

6

We are dedicated to protecting and stewarding our natural wild lands and waterways. We approach all our ecological resources with respect and keep them as natural as possible.

TEACHING

7

We address the needs of the whole person through teaching social emotional integration, unconditional love, good parenting skills, and cooperative working skills. We support each person as they follow their passions. We support all practices that help humanity evolve into a greater loving whole.

8

We develop practices that work in harmony with nature and the science of the universe. We work with the natural world, not against it. We broaden our understanding of the interplay between humanity and nature. We vow to never be controllers or a destructive element to nature.

9

Through honest self-assessment, we seek to discover each person's unique skills and provide them with opportunities to contribute to a healthier future. We support each member of our community in using their innate skills in alignment with our principles and we respect individual uniqueness.

SHARING

10

We promote respect for everyone's intrinsic self-worth, separate from the ownership of things and ideas. We value love for all people above power, influence, or privilege. We promote equality in all forms.

11

We strive to maintain cooperation between all the communities of Trinitus and between us and all our neighbors. We share openly with love and with all our resources be they physical, technical, or intellectual. We are modeling a more harmonious way of living for all humanity. We are exploring innovative ways to move forward and meet the challenges of the limitless frontiers ahead.

12

We, the people of Earth, are all stewards of our only planet. As such, we have the inalienable right and responsibility for self-preservation, sustainability, and healthy expressions for a life-sustaining culture.

Now James understood that the belief system of Trinitus is based on sharing everything. He found it hard to imagine how they were able to share all their goods, services, even their emotions. He had doubts that he could ever openly share his deepest feelings and felt a little nervous about this Personal Process thing they kept talking about.

Did everyone undergo therapy, even the Peace Officers? He reminded himself that Tim said earlier that he, and all Peace Officers, were trained to do therapy with anyone breaking the law of love. Apparently, the 'Law of Love' was their only hard and fast law, the rest were just minor regulations.

The next file made it clear that instead of laws, they had a *Constitution of Courtesies*, a modified version of Richard Bach's book, *Curious Lives*.

THE CONSTITUTION OF COURTESIES

Everyone in the community is asked to live by the Constitution of Courtesies. However, this is an individual choice. The courtesy you show to those you love is a model for how you treat everyone in our extended community. Showing these courtesies to yourself and others creates a lifestyle conducive to justice. It lifts you above strife and destruction, now and forever.

Everyone is asked to take the following vows:

"The same gentleness and respect I pledge to show myself; I vow to show to everyone. Whatever good things come into my life; I will willingly share them with others. I will respect and be kind to myself, to my peers, to my elders, and to all children. I will also cherish the land, air, and water. I do this out of respect and care for future generations.

"I claim freedom for myself. Likewise, I will safeguard the freedom of others. I will safeguard everyone's right to think and believe in accord with the dictates of their own conscience, as long as doing so does no harm. I willingly make the choice to live each day from my highest sense of Right Action.

"I vow not to foster, comply with, or consent to any action, words, thoughts, or choices that cause evil, fear, or malice. I agree to never comply with evil through inaction. I pledge to come from love in all I do.

"I vow to remember that I can only change my own feelings, beliefs, perspectives, and attitudes; I cannot change those of others. I pledge to work with my feelings and my beliefs as part of living consciously and caringly. I pledge to choose the path of Right Action and cultivate my own happiness. I vow to live as an example for others.

"I vow to make the most important goal in my life that of loving, sharing, and caring for myself and others. I pledge to live my truth as I see it. I vow to work on becoming the grandest version of myself in accord with the highest vision I have of who I am."

For inspiration, the article ended with two great quotes:
There are only two paths in life, fear and love.
I will venture on the hardest one, love.
Fear is the only true evil and opposes life."
Nicholette Pavlevsky

"Grant me the serenity to accept the things I cannot change,
the courage to change the things I can,
and the wisdom to know the difference."
Dr. Reinhold Niebuhr

James opened the *Personal Process* file and flipped through it. It was long. For a moment, he felt the weight of it. A shudder of fear rippled through him, but he told himself, he could do this. If all the people here can do it, so can he.

He sat back and read that it had three sections, *Therapeutic Principles and Insights, Eleven Affirmations for Personal Process,* and *Helpful Definitions.*

The program was described as Holistic, meaning that it would address the needs of all parts of the individual; physical, emotional, mental, and spiritual. It went on to describe the process of self-reflection, which would teach him to acknowledge, accept, and integrate all the naturally diverse parts of himself. He stopped reading when he got to the part where it said, your beliefs play a big part in how you see the world around you, and how you see yourself.

His mind drifted off on the question, what do I really believe? He realized that he could quickly recognize what other people believed about him, and what he was taught to believe, but all that aside, he felt confused. Every time he thought he had identified something he truly believed and questioned himself about it, his conviction fell apart. He was shocked to realize how little he knew about his true inner self.

In the introduction to *Therapeutic Principles and Insights* he read about the intrinsic worth of each individual and how people are born whole, but then they are fed negative beliefs, which tear down their self-esteem, and make them doubt themselves.

One paragraph stressed how common parenting techniques are based on reward and punishment. A common cultural belief throughout the ages has been, "Spare the rod and spoil the child."

Punishment instills fear in a youngster. *Fear of punishment* is then used to control the child and the adult they become.

Another common technique used to control people is *shaming*. With shame comes guilt and blame. The fear and pain inflicted by these harsh emotions become a lifelong tool used to force a person to obey external demands.

Shame, blame, and fear are not part of a child's innate nature. These feelings are instilled in them, indoctrinated into them, to control them. To avoid these awful feelings, people do what is expected of them, rather than what they themselves believe to be right. Rather than trust themselves, they give their power away. They become trained to believe that something is wrong with them, when in truth, the problem is that they have been trained to obey others and to not trust their own wisdom and knowing Inner Self.

Many negative beliefs are passed from generation to generation. Parents pass on what they themselves experienced as a child; plus what they see others around them doing. The problem is everywhere because everyone has been indoctrinated into a fear-based belief system. Self-doubt, the product of fear, makes them conform. That is why so many people feel alienated and estranged from their own true Inner Nature.

The result of common negative beliefs is that most people in our society doubt themselves, even hate themselves, and spend most of their lives trying to cover up or compensate for these awful feelings, which the world around them has implanted in them.

Here in the City of Hope, we train people to know themselves. With the knowledge gained through *self-reflection*, as well as many other easy and effective practices. The people in our community have discovered the beauty within them and are thus able to see it in others. Together we are developing healthy ways to express personal power.

Next, James opened *The Eleven Affirmations* file. As he perused the list, it struck him as being very similar to the Alcoholics Anonymous 12 Step Program. He had gone to some AA meetings when he was in college because it was a time when he was drinking heavily. Those meetings helped him become aware of his anger and how he was plagued with feelings of worthlessness. He stopped going to meetings after he got married. It struck him that if he had continued; he might not be in the predicament he was in now.

For a long time, he did not drink. But the pressures of the last few years seemed more manageable with a few drinks in him. He was able to keep to the limit of three beers. Now he began to question whether using drinking to cope with his issues was really the best thing to do. From what he was reading, they were saying that it is important to face events rather than anesthetize away the pain.

James reached for the *New Spirituality* file, but his finger slipped and somehow it hit the power button. Instead of opening the file, it shut off the ComPad. He felt hesitant to turn it on again. He both did and did not want to know what the file said. He shrugged off the feeling and put the ComPad away. He felt safer once it was out of sight. He was not ready to read that article.

He looked at the time on the ComScreen and realized he had been reading for over an hour. He jotted down a few notes and questions to share with Tim. Then he went downstairs to get something to drink.

James arrived at the dining room just before lunch hoping to avoid the lecture. People were just beginning to file in. There were already more than a dozen people in the room. He decided to give the herbal tea a try. He was usually a coffee person, but since they only had that coffee-wannabe, he decided to try the iced herbal tea. It was peppermint and surprisingly refreshing. He strolled over to the buffet table. Feeling brave, he filled his plate with several fresh, though unfamiliar foods that smelled delicious. He looked around for a seat and chose an unoccupied table against the wall. He ate quickly so he could leave before the room filled with people and the discussion began. Not that he would admit it, but he enjoyed all the novel tastes.

Before he could make his getaway, the lady he had met earlier walked over to him.

"Hi," she bubbled, "I'm glad to see you're still here. Did you decide to give it a go?" She smiled warmly.

"Hmm, well yeah, at least until I get on my feet, I guess," and shrugged as if to say it's nothing. "I just need to catch up on some bills. I can't argue with free rent and food!" He sipped his tea.

"May I sit with you? I don't think we properly introduced ourselves this morning. I'm Cathy, Cathy Burns, but I'm thinking of going back to my maiden name, Cartwright."

She was holding her copy of *'Conversations with God'* tight to her chest like it was her Bible and she also carried a pink satin covered journal.

He motioned for her to sit, though he was reluctant to have company. "I'm James. I see you still have the book you were reading earlier. What do you like best about it?" He was not interested in the book; he just wanted to control the direction of the conversation to avoid talking about his life.

"Oh, it's fantastic! It is all about this guy who loses everything and then ends up talking to God. At first, it is more like the guy is ranting at God about all the things he doesn't like about his life. I am about halfway through, and it is great the way these talks are changing the guy's attitudes, beliefs, and perspectives. I can already see where it is going. It is a series. Before this one, I read *What God Said*. That was a real eye-opener.

James almost choked on a sip of tea. "What!? How did he know it was real? I mean, like, how did he know it was God talking?"

"The voice he heard in his head, told him things he did not know. It was like he opened his mind and something calm and wise came out. The man was writing notes on something else when suddenly he started writing a clearly delineated path of action for a problem he had been wrestling with for a long time. It was amazing," she shared excitedly.

"I read the Founder's book, and she called this experience, channeling. Do you know what that is?" Her blue eyes blazed with excitement.

"I'm not exactly sure, but I did hear that word earlier today in the same context." James was taken back by the many coincidences that had happened to him in the last few hours. "What do you mean, 'heard in her head'?"

"I think it's like prayer, or meditation. It's a conversation you have with God or with your Higher God Self...."

"Really? interrupted James. "How do you know it's not just your own thoughts talking to you?"

"There is something in the quality of the voice that feels important. It feels knowledgeable and calm. It tells you things you don't know, or it speaks in a way you never would. It also leaves you with a feeling of wellbeing, like something has been resolved, and sometimes it leaves you feeling expansive like anything is possible," She shared these revelations with a matter-of-fact attitude, as she sipped tea from her glass.

James thought for a moment, unconsciously spinning his glass of tea. Cathy realized that he was asking for a reason to believe. "Did God talk to you James?"

"I don't know." He mumbled. Snapping back from his thoughts, he sat up from his slouched over position. "I don't think so." He tried to dismiss it with a bored expression and turned back to his tea.

"You did, didn't you?" Cathy was not going to let him dodge her. She persisted, "It's ok if you don't believe it at first, what did She say?"

James knew she was trying to corner him again. He avoided the question by nonchalantly taking another approach, "Why do you call *God* a *She*?"

"She, He, It, Shmit, it doesn't matter to a sexless energy force, that's just how I relate to God. You will have your own style." There was no way Cathy was going to let him off the hook.

"So, did He talk to you or not?" She tapped on her book.

Certain that she was never going to let this go, he mumbled again, "I don't know," threw up his hands, looked her in the eyes and said strongly, "I really don't know!"

"What did He say?" She pressed harder. "Maybe I can help you to know."

She was relentless and he was curious about something the voice had said so he ventured, "Okay, God, the voice, or whomever, said that I don't really exist! Why would He say such a thing?"

"See, that proves you were talking to God, because you would never have said that, right?" She smiled knowingly.

"Well, no, and it makes no sense," he admitted uncomfortably.

"Were those the exact words he used?" She probed.

He thought for a moment and then remembered. "I said to God, 'You don't exist' and then I heard these words in my head, 'Neither do you, really. Not the way you think of anyway.'"

"Ahh," she said nodding with a cat-that-ate-the-mouse smile on her face.

"That gives it a slightly different connotation. If you think that you are primarily a mind, separate from nature, and separate from other forms of life, a lone individual surviving in a dog-eat-dog world, if that is what you think you are, God is telling you that this image of yourself is an illusion."

He did not realize he was nodding his head. She had him pegged; that is exactly how he saw himself.

"You didn't read the New Spirituality article, did you?" She was hoping he did because there was so much that she wanted to tell him but did not know how basic to make the explanation.

"You know how the blades of a windmill look far apart from each other at the tips, but at the center hub they are all connected? People are like that. They look very separate in the everyday world, but when you look deeper, you find that they are all connected, not only to each other, but also to a powerful Divine Force.

"This special connection explains why you can meet a stranger and feel like you know them. When you talk to each other, it feels like you share something special in common. This commonality is called the Collective Soul. It's a combination of your Soul and everyone else's all together. The spokes in my analogy represent your spirit and the place where the blades meet the hub is your Soul. This is why they say, 'We are all One'."

"You are primarily a Soul who took on a body to be born, and you shed the body when you die. After death, your Soul continues its journey. It may choose to take on another body, or not. If the Soul does not reincarnate, it continues through other realms.

"While the Soul is immortal, the ego is temporal. It only exists for one lifetime. Therefore, when you identify with your ego, you think this life is all you have. When you are connected to your Soul, given that it is immortal, there is no end to the knowledge that can come through. Accessing this knowledge is called channeling.

"When God spoke to you, He did it using whatever instrument was available. For the man who was writing, God used his pen; for you, He used a torn children's book, later, he used your inner voice. No matter how the message is conveyed, the wisdom comes from God, your Soul, through your spirit, from your Higher Self. Just as the Eskimos have fifty words to describe snow, we have lots of words for the Inner God.

James reflected on the conversation he had with God and how it did have an 'other-than-self' feeling to it. This only made him angrier. "Why did He wait until now to talk to me, when my life has fallen apart!"

"Maybe you were not listening before now. It takes an element of surrender to be willing to listen. Otherwise, you just discount the message as a novel coincidence. When your need for help is strong, you are more willing to surrender your beliefs," she ventured.

She leaned in, her elbows on the table like she was telling him a secret, "I did not hear Her until I ended up in the hospital with a broken jaw from my husband."

"I'm sorry to hear that. A man should never take out his anger on his wife." His mind jumped to a time when he was so frustrated with everything that he wanted to hit someone, especially Judy. This brief thought ended with the words, *'For not rescuing me.'* That startled him. Those words sounded different than the others.

Desperate to move away from that subject, he demanded, "Why does God wait until we are at rock bottom!?"

"I made excuses for my situation, I rationalized it, I told myself it would get better. I was willing to adapt to awful circumstances, rather than face the power within me, rather than listen to this voice warning me. Looking back, it was there, but I discounted this inner advice until I was desperate, so desperate, I was willing to let go of what I believed and was open to hearing the truth. I was so lost. I had no idea what to do.

"That's when God said to me: 'Have you had enough self-punishment?'

"I was pissed at Her for accusing me of doing this to myself. Now that I understand, I can see She was right. I chose to stay. I insisted on believing that it would get better." She took a deep breath and sat up straight and tall.

"I'm glad you're out of that situation now," James commiserated.

"The point is, my God Self was finally able to break through my denial and my need for control. Or rather, I could no longer control my life and deny what was happening." She inhaled and blew it out, straightened her arms in front of her, with hands clasped together.

James huffed and chuckled. "I guess you are saying, 'God tries to get our attention by provoking us.'"

"Sure, She can be a smart ass if She needs to be to get our attention." Cathy laughed nervously, but that is to overcome our resistance. When we are willing to listen, we hear more easily.

"I still have a hard time believing any of this is true," James sighed.

"A nurse gave me the Founder's book and I just started reading it. The Founder also had a tough time believing it, at first. She thought she was crazy for a while. When she challenged God to prove Himself to her, He did. Wait, he will prove Himself to you in time, you will see." She waved her hand like it was a sure thing.

"Hmmm. If he exists, then why doesn't He talk to us all the time; right from birth, so we can avoid hardships altogether!" James crossed his arms, feeling smug that he had won a point.

"Actually, He does. Most little children hear the inner voice of God. By the time they are five, especially when they enter school, they become so filled with socially acceptable beliefs that the voice seems to fade away. These beliefs make it hard for them to listen. In truth, it is their trust in their Inner Selves that fades.

"God has given us free-will. The journey of life is to discover our Life Mission and fulfill it. The challenges we meet hone our skills. Sometimes we need a small homeopathic dosage of a poison to learn to understand and cope with it. The poisons we encounter teach us what specific area of life we came here to heal.

"This is a Gods-Eye-View. Your everyday life is controlled by the society in which you live, and ours out there is based on *Power Over*, rather than *Power With*. When a society is based on *Power Over*, then the people are fed beliefs that make them subservient to maintain control over them. When a society is based on *Power With*, then they promote beliefs that create a more humanitarian way of living. This is the difference between the world you came from and the community we are creating here."

These words were pouring through her. It was not like she was thinking of what to say, but rather, like she had her finger in a light socket and the electricity was moving through her carrying the words with it. James found her fascinating and scary to watch.

"Life is harder when we don't listen to Her. Our *Souls* come into flesh willingly. Throughout life, it tries to guide us but only if we are willing to be guided.

"The world out there is a total mess, and the ego is the scapegoat being blamed. Problems arise because the ego is the servant of the beliefs that it has been fed.

"The world out there runs on Control-Based Beliefs. The ego is specifically fed beliefs that make it feel helpless. These controlling beliefs make you feel that you are to blame, or someone is to blame, whenever life is hard.

"People are trained to be hard on themselves. They are fed beliefs like shame and blame, ideas that generate fear, rules that girdle your choices, laws that hurt rather than support a harmonious community. There are so many unhealthy beliefs in the world. Even the simple ones we all take for granted can make life harder and restrict the ease we experience.

"Some Limiting Beliefs are it is natural to live as a single-family unit, even though more hands make life easier; you must struggle to make a living; everyone out there is either a threat or in competition for the things you want and need. A belief in pride stands in the way of asking for help when you need it, even when it is being offered. Beliefs in nationalism and duty can send a promising young man off to kill men women and children on the other side of the world.

James wanted to jump in and protest, but he just stared in amazement instead.

"Society and most religions generate beliefs that maintain their control, while undermining your belief in yourself. When people started becoming more conscious and began moving towards *Power With*, those in control felt threatened and tightened the reins. There are lots of ways they did it; by inflating prices, so people had to work harder; by eliminating freedoms, like when Roe v. Wade was overturned in June 2022; and politically, like when Israel and Saudi Arabia were on the eve of signing a peace treaty, and Hamas stopped them by starting a war with Israel. Here in the City of Hope, we are trying to change all that."

She smiled at the wide-eyed amazement in his eyes.

"Have I lost you yet?" she asked, worried that as usual she jumped the gun and said too much too soon.

He nodded no, but inside, there was a lot of screaming going on. Her words were attacking everything he ever believed!!!

"Wait a minute!" he protested. "People around us, our schools, our stories, the news media, they don't teach us these things. The Churches certainly do not say, 'God is in you, and God talks straight to you! I think they lock people up for that!" James threw up his hands in protest.

"They certainly don't tell you," she agreed. "That is why we are creating communities like this one, where we can help each other listen better.

"The whole world is at a pivotal time right now. People are

beginning to wake up and see what is really happening.

"The secret is out! This is an exciting time to be alive!" She was animated now; her hands out, palms up in front of her.

James was still angry, and he wasn't sure why. A need to scream was boiling up inside him. He did not want to take it out on Cathy, and he did not want to make a scene in front of all the people in the dining room.

"Well, I'll think about it. But now I've got something to do, I have to go. Thanks for your perspective." He gathered his glass and stood up to leave.

Cathy was worried, "Did I upset you? I know I can come across too pushy. I am sorry."

"No, no, you're fine," he reassured her. "I just need to do something with my guide and get my shoes shined." He smiled at her, put away his glass, and said in a shaky voice, "See you later, maybe." He mused that he was leaving before the lecture began but felt like he had already attended one.

"Yes, I hope so, have a good day." Cathy smiled back.

James went to the front desk. As he waited his turn, he watched several newcomers check in and noted that each person was assigned their own personal guide, even when they arrived in a group or as a couple. When his turn came, he asked Nicole, the young lady behind the counter who originally greeted him, if he could get a Smartwatch.

"Sure, no problem, Mr. Dole," Nicole said with a friendly smile.

"Please, can you also call Tim and ask him to meet me at the *TradeStore*?" James flipped a thumb towards down the hall.

"Sure thing, Sir. He'll be with you shortly." She assured him as she tapped on her pad.

James was having his shoes shined when Tim arrived with a Smartwatch. He was delighted to see that it was the very newest model with a folding screen, the kind that molded itself to his wrist with slap straps, Eye Recognition Software, and a Virtual Wallet.

"It has a hundred credits in it, so you can go into town alone and pay for things when I am not with you." Tim explained as he set up the Smartwatch and put his own number in Contacts.

"Tim, what kind of work can I do in the community?" James brought up the subject.

"It's your choice." Seeing James's eyes light up, reminded Tim of why he loves his work so much. "You can work on construction. Our community is slowly but steadily growing, so new buildings are always going up. Or you can work on design, as long as what you create is aligned with our theme of natural and organic. We do not have bosses to answer to, but we do have councils that approve of designs and oversee budgets for all the projects."

"I want to design structures," James answered excitedly. He wanted to work for the money, but now he was realizing it was going to be more than that. "I have a degree in architecture, which I have never been able to use because the competition in that field is vicious and positions are scarce. Now I need money, a lot of it. I am deeply in debt and I need to dig myself out of a hole."

"Okay. You can report to the Building Council. I will take you there and introduce you to the members. You can work as much or as little as you want. You can take on long hours and earn more, or you can put in shorter hours whenever your emotional process demands your attention.

"In other words, we approach working as an organic process that follows your own rhythm. No pressure. It is amazing how much more effective people are here where they can live without pressure."

"Tim, it looks like you work a lot of hours."

"It varies. I enjoy being with newcomers and supporting them. It is very satisfying, so it does not feel like work. You'll see. When you are doing what you love, it feels almost strange to get paid for it. Sometimes I feel like I should pay them for the privilege of the experience, and I do not get paid anymore. I used to, but now, I have everything I need, so whatever would have been my salary is reinvested in the community which I benefit from.

"Before you can begin working here in our community, you need to attend three intro lectures and two Emotional Management classes. This usually takes two days, but if you're in a hurry, you can cram them into one very full day.

"You could start right now, or first thing tomorrow at breakfast and do the classes in between the mealtime intro lectures," Tim offered.

"That all sounds good to me," said James. He thanked the man for shining his shoes and they left the Trade Store.

"You seem to be feeling better than yesterday when you first arrived. In fact, you seem better than you were just this morning," probed Tim.

"Yes, well, I have a plan to focus on and this place is giving me a way to do things I could not do out in the real world. I still can't believe I can work at what I love and pay off my bills."

"I'm glad we can help. Are you ready to get started? We can go to an intro lunch right now, if you like."

"Not quite yet, I just ate. Could I bend your ear about this God thing, first? I understand that the Founder of these cities channeled God. It was mentioned in the *Emergence* files, plus you and Cathy, the lady I told you about, talked about channeling. What is your take on it?"

When they reached the lobby, Tim motioned James towards a set of chairs, "We can sit here or go to the Book Club downstairs.

There are books there that might help you with your questions."

"I'm not much of a reader, but I'll consider it later. Right here is fine," James said, sinking into a plush comfortable armchair.

Once they settled in, Tim began, "What do you want to know? What sparked your sudden interest?"

"Um, as you know, there was this cactus and then the note from the Proxy lady," he paused and took a deep breath, feeling amazed that he was going to say this out loud. "Well, uh, when I went to my room after our brunch, I had... well, I don't really know what happened but, I think I heard a voice in my head that was not my own.

"Then I met Cathy again, just a while ago, and she was adamant that I was hearing God, channeling God, or my God Self." James's face was a deep rose color, and his voice was uncharacteristically low, but he got all the words out. He trusted Tim, thinking, 'if anyone can explain this stuff, he can.'

"I mean, I'm no guru or Proxy, but I heard something!"

In a kind, gentle voice, Tim reassured him, "I believe you did. Anyone can hear God, if they listen with an open mind. You must have already overcome your resistance. As for channeling, it is a general term for communicating with a Higher Spirit."

"Is that the same thing as mediumship?" James tossed out a word he had once heard related to this kind of woo-woo stuff.

"Not exactly, mediumship is the act of connecting with the Souls of the dead. This is a little different. channeling is opening to a dimension inside yourself. It is more like Gnosis, tapping into knowledge that lies in a deeper dimension within you."

"What? Now I am really confused! Are the words coming from God or from me?" James did not realize his voice was getting louder with each word.

"You will have to stretch to understand," Tim spoke very softly hoping to calm this angry fellow down. He expected this reaction. "The answer is both."

"Riddles, riddles, riddles," James spit the words out. "In any case, I have to tell you, I'm kind of pissed He waited so long!" James said honestly.

With great patience, Tim tried to explain this difficult concept. "If you are going to understand any of this, you cannot look for black and white, hard and fast answers. Life has more colors than that. There is a way to look at life that sees everything as shades of color blending into each other, so nothing is all good or all bad; nothing is absolutely right or absolutely wrong. In fact, God is omnipresent so the Divine Presence can be in heaven, in you, in that statue over there, and in everyone walking through this room at this very moment."

"Okay, let me get this straight." James was getting scared that this really was a cult and all his fine plans for getting out of debt were going to vanish in a split second.

"Nothing is totally wrong, so, that means I can go kill somebody and it would be okay? There is no morality in that! You are preaching chaos and lawlessness! I don't want to be a part of that!" James was quite a bright shade of red by now.

In a calm teaching voice with no defensiveness, Tim responded, "What I am advocating is completely different than that. We can answer to a higher order of morality without tightly defined laws. We can teach people to evaluate situations and take *Right Action*."

As for killing people, if you kill your neighbor, it is a crime, and they send you to prison. If you kill a designated enemy, they pin a metal on you. The system you presently have is not moral. It just serves those in power, and they use it to control you.

If someone is about to abuse your child and the only way to stop him is to kill him, doing so under such extreme circumstances could be *Right Action*. However, anything short of such a dire situation, as saving the life of a child, there is no justification for killing anyone. Making war on innocent people in the name of national pride and duty is morally wrong. Therefore, the circumstances define morality not static rules or laws.

"From a *Gods-Eye-View*, everything is relative. If you see a man fall down drunk in the street, the compassionate *Right Action* might be to help him up. However, if people have always picked him up, then being one more helper does not serve him. Maybe being forced to pick himself up might be his first step towards lasting sobriety. Life is relative.

"If you do not have laws to control people, how do you avoid total chaos?" James demanded to know.

"By training people to trust themselves, trust their intuition, trust their innate sense of balance and to love themselves. If they truly love themselves, they will naturally love those around them.

"People living in Hope are trained to respect the innate dignity and worth of each person. We value the lives of people, animals and all living things. We see all lifeforms as an interweaving of mutual support. With these values at the core of our decision making, we help each other, we help each other grow, and we do not compete.

"Instead, we set up a way of life where everyone can access what they need. If everyone is going to help you get what you want and need, you have no reason to steal, to lie, or to cheat, so you do not need laws forbidding those behaviors. Instead of punishing people after they commit a crime, we create a lifestyle that supports them. We help them satisfy their needs, so they have no reason to commit a crime. We believe in prevention rather than punishment.

"Where does God come in, in all of this? Why didn't he save me?" James was getting impatient. He understood the words, but the concepts made no sense to him.

Tim closed his eyes for a second to gain clarity before beginning. He trusted that whatever needed to be said would come through him.

"God paves the path with tiles of love. Those who walk it barefoot feel supported, calm, and are usually in the right place at the right time. Good things come to them. They love themselves and they believe wherever they are is their home, and whoever they are with is their family, so they feel safe.

"At every crossroads, they see guidance in the symbols, coincidences, and intuitive insights around them, so they feel equipped to make the healthiest choice available. This is living from your Essential Self, your God Self.

"Out in the very unreal 'real world', negative beliefs separate you from the path and from everyone else. You don't feel loved or supported. Life is a struggle, but it does not have to be that way. It is only a struggle because you and everyone around you was trained to believe it is. A society that chooses to structure everyday life based on separation and fear, will increase separation and fear.

As Dr. Charles Bebeau, one of my teachers used to say, "What you believe, you create."

"The Founder understood that if she joined with people who also believed they have the power to create a new and better way of life, then it would come to pass and it has.

James sighed loudly. "Yeah, well, I don't know too many people who think like this, except maybe my mom. She was quite Christian. To humor her, I went to her Church once when I was a teenager, and her preacher said stuff like: "You do not hear God because your ego isn't wounded enough to be ready to receive love. He said you should suffer to find love. It is not because God wants you to suffer, but because your Soul chooses to suffer, and your ego gets in the way. Your ego is all about fear, pain and trying to avoid death. The Soul is all about learning what is 'not' love."

"God wants you to have joy and love in your life. He denies you nothing, including pain if you want it, but you, like all humans, are new to this game. You are still evolving. You are slowly moving from being an animal driven by fight or flight instincts to being self-aware, but still, you live in fear and ego. You are evolving and one day you will choose to love consciously and be joyful but it's relatively new.

"God is just waiting until you grow up because you, are part of a species that is just not well developed yet. You suffer because you do not know any better. You are just learning that you are more than an animal with brains; you are a spirit with a body and a mind. My mother believed everything he said, do you?

"Okay," said Tim enjoying the challenge of this exchange, "so if I have it right, your points are:

"Love requires suffering.
Your Soul chooses to suffer.
The ego is all about fear, pain, and avoiding death.
The Soul's primary focus is on what is not love.
You have pain because you chose it.
Humanity is unevolved and new to life.
Someday you will learn how to love.
God is waiting for you to grow up."

Tim took a deep breath and dived in. "Here in Hope, we share *unconditional love* with everyone, and we try to create a lifestyle for every person in our community that is healthy and comfortable, so we experience a minimum of suffering. We do not believe love requires suffering.

"No one here believes that the Soul chooses to suffer. In fact, the Soul offers comfort when the ego is being battered by the beliefs, rules, and laws of the unhealthy society in which people are forced to live.

"The ego is flexible. It takes the shape of the beliefs it is fed. When the culture is based on *Power Over*, it instills negative beliefs that result in feelings of fear and pain.

"People are more afraid of fully living than they are of dying.

"The Soul is primarily focused on fulfilling its Mission. Love is the willingness to merge with another. The natural state of human consciousness is to merge, but beliefs are the marionette strings that tug at the heart. They can keep you from merging, not only with other people, but also with nature, animals, and even yourself.

"No one chooses pain, unless they have been twisted through punishment to equate love with pain. If that is the way they were indoctrinated in childhood, they will grow up setting up situations and attract to them people to play out painful scenarios, because their Soul is trying to resolve old issues and release old scars.

"Humanity is evolving and always has been. Each generation tries to make life better for their little group. It is only now that the Age of Unity has dawned that humanity is beginning to see itself as part of a global community, rather than part of a little group." Tim expressed his understanding of the principles as clearly as he could, now it was up to James to stretch his mind and understand.

James was boiling. Not knowing what to believe, he said much too loudly, "Really? You're saying God is not to blame, my ego and my Soul are not to blame, then who is?! I just want to scream at God for not coming to me sooner, for not giving me the answers to life before I lost everything!"

Tim smiled lovingly, "I am sorry. I wish life could have been easier for you. I can see how difficult it was. It must also be hard for little chicks to peck their way out of their own shells. They must feel odd suddenly being out in the breeze after always being safe inside.

"I know it does not make you feel any better to know that your Soul needed to walk its own path through the debris of your culture, your family, and all the beliefs you were given. Know this, it has all been to awaken you in ways your parents, and their parents before them, were not able to. No one is to blame, not God, not you, no one. It was all part of your path. If indeed your old life cannot be salvaged, then it means you have outgrown it, like the little chick who has found himself in a new and different world.

"Life has its own timing. Sometimes it takes a long time for you to be willing to let go of your compliance to a toxic way of life, partly because you did not know any better, and partly because you were trained to put your head down, try harder, and find someone to blame for your hardships. Sometimes difficult experiences come from a benevolent God. He is trying to pry your fingers loose from the beliefs that have been indoctrinated into you. He is trying to force you past your beliefs, so you can be free."

James stared at his teacher with fire in his eyes. Tim smiled back with sincere compassion. They stayed that way for what seemed like a long time. Then the deep color subsided from James's face. His shoulders slumped and his voice was a little shaky when he spoke.

"Well, even if all that is true, it makes no sense. Anyway, what am I going to do with all this anger? I feel like I've been robbed of so many years! I feel, like, like I need some redemption for my suffering. It's just not fair! My Soul may think it's guiding me towards some kind of Mission, but I'll tell you, I feel like I've been put through hell!"

The color of his face was growing darker again. James realized his volume was equally harsh and suddenly felt embarrassed. He looked around at the twenty or so people in the lobby expecting to see disapproving stares, but people met his gaze and smiled at him. Some of them had a 'I know how you feel' look of compassion in their eyes.

"As part of your training here, you can attend workshops in Anger Management and Primal Scream Therapy. You will have coursework and exercises as part of your Process Work. Check the schedule, I think there is a Primal Scream Session every morning at 9:00 am and another at 2:00 pm. Until then, practice talking to God, or yell at Him if you need too. He won't mind. He understands and so do we."

"When you can forgive yourself for conforming to the only reality you knew, for believing what you were indoctrinated to believe, and for trying to survive within a toxic environment, when you can forgive yourself, you will find that God has forgiven you as well. When you feel love for yourself, you will feel love from God and from many people around you. Many, not all, some people will fear you for daring to do what they are too afraid to do. Not all chicks are willing to break through the shell."

James and Tim sat quietly for a moment. Once he felt calmer, James continued in a different tone, "Well, thank you for answering my questions. I am sorry I did not understand a lot of it."

"That is okay. You lessened the not knowing," Tim quipped.

"I'm not sure what to do with myself now. I can go outside or to my room and have a chat with my new buddy, God. Or maybe I can work up my courage and call my wife. I have no idea what to say to her, but I owe her a call. I guess I've needed a break from everything, including her. I need to wrap my head around all this, James said, sweeping his arms wide, as if to embrace the whole community.

"This sure was a lot to take in on my first full day here. Thank you for your patience and for the Smartwatch." James got up.

Tim also stood up and said, "No problem. This is a lot to take in. God brought you here, so he must think you can handle it. Give yourself some credit; many people just keep on driving passed our gates."

"Maybe I will just walk around the community. It might calm me. I've wanted to take another look at your architecture," said James, rubbing his hand through his thinning hair.

"Do you want company? I can walk in silence beside you and be there if you have questions," Tim gently offered.

"Don't you have something else to do? Surely, I'm not the only one you are helping."

"You are my only charge, James. I only take one at a time, so I can be available for you, even in the middle of the night if you are in a crisis."

"What do you do when you're not with me?" James raised an eyebrow.

"I write, teach, meditate, work in the garden; as a Peace Officer, I counsel disputes; and sometimes I assist elders. Basically, I follow the course of my day. By that I mean, I am open to help wherever I am needed. At the beginning of last week, I worked at the front desk and at the end of the week, I helped shear some of our Delaine Merino sheep. Mostly, I follow the dictates of my Higher Self and am guided to wherever I can be the most useful. If you need me, no matter what the hour, I will be there for you. While I am your personal guide, you are my priority." Tim smiled.

James thought about it and decided he needed to walk alone.

"Thank you for offering, but I need time to let this all simmer in me," James gave a little half smile.

He climbed the hill to the residential area; his eyes absorbed every building he passed. James let his mind wander over the events of this morning. Between what Tim and Cathy had told him, he was really confused. When he was listening to them, their ideas and concepts made sense, but when he tried to see how they would fit into his life, it made his head spin. He imagined explaining this stuff to Judy and almost laughed aloud.

As he walked by the houses, he marveled at how each one was small, compact, and unique. It surprised him to see so many people outdoors. At home, the streets were usually crowded with vehicles, but the sidewalks were almost always empty. In fact, new neighborhoods rarely have sidewalks these days. They usually had only small hiking paths.

Where he lived, it was rare to see anyone outdoors. But here, he saw people tending gardens, one man was painting a watercolor of the nearby plateau, several children were running around chasing each other, a few boys were playing a ballgame, a couple of girls were building a haphazard playhouse, neighbors were chatting, one woman was carefully arranging a rock garden, and two white-haired men were playing pickleball. He passed four plant covered gazebos where people were working on ComScreens. There was such a sense of vitality in this bustling community.

As he strolled past their homes, friendly people greeted him with the phrase, "We see you," and many waved.

At first, he felt like he was naked, and these people could see right through him. What were they seeing? But after so many smiles and waves, he stopped feeling like an invader who did not belong in this neighborhood. He began to relax and accept that *'we see you,'* was just their way of saying, 'hello.'

James passed two women tending a hanging vegetable garden. One was a young Chinese woman with long black hair and the other looked Irish, with flaming red curls. The redhead asked; "We see you. Are you looking for an open house?"

He was not sure what she meant, so he mustered his courage and answered her, "What do you mean by, 'open house'. I'm new here."

She glanced down at his black wristband. "Oh, I see. You are not even in the program yet. I thought you were looking for a house, I was going to give you a tour of one in a nearby cluster."

"Well, actually, I would love a tour, I'm an architect and I'm interested in seeing how these structures are built." James jumped at the opportunity.

"Okay, I will just put the hose away and take you there." She pushed a button on the nozzle. The water immediately stopped, the hose automatically retreated, wound itself around a wheel, and withdrew inside a cover.

James noticed that she was wearing a green wristband and the light desert clothing that was popular here.

She waved goodbye to her friend and joined him on the pathway. "An architect, that must be interesting work. I wasn't artistic at all before I came here. Now I do Pour Painting. It is easy and fun. My real thing is math. I live over there," she pointed to a very colorful group of mushrooms, "in a School Cluster and I teach in the school. The Open House I am about to show you is not part of any Career Designated Cluster."

"That was my friend Ming Ying, she lives here. I came over to help her with her garden. I live in the next Cluster. "I'm Fiorella. I come from Italy."

James introduced himself as they walked along past three brown mushroom shaped homes. Then they passed a very colorful large honeycomb structure composed of small hexagon units. Fiorella pointed to it and said, "This is our school. We draw children from nine Clusters.

"Each Cluster has a central yard. The school has an exceptionally large one because it is our playground. It has excellent equipment, colorful playhouses, and several little forts.

"The next Cluster has a community vegetable garden. We all tend the garden, and all share the produce," she explained. "Over there in that Cluster is our soccer field and the one beyond it has a baseball diamond."

"What is that big one over there?" he asked, pointing to a large mushroom standing high above the ground on eleven strong cement stems?"

"That's our Community Center," she answered.

The houses they passed had vegetable gardens out front rather than grassy lawns. When he asked why, she explained, "Water is too precious for water guzzling grass. We grow mostly drought tolerant or desert plants, and food.

They came to a Cluster of hexagon houses about 40 feet apart. Like the others, it had no fences and a wide cultivated area in the center.

Fiorella pointed out that every house had its own Wind Spinners and Solar Coverings for power, Solar Tubes for heating water, plus Skylights and Sun Tunnels for lighting.

He was surprised to see no power or telephone lines anywhere.

Smiling brightly, Fiorella stopped in front of a house and said, "This is it."

He was delighted with the structure. He had never seen anything like it. Like the other houses in this Cluster, it stood on nine thick pillars which created a six-foot-high open area underneath. It looked like a cool place to hang out in the heat of the day.

James followed her up the front steps to a wide porch with long narrow planter boxes built into the railing. The outer walls of the house were hempcrete made to look like stucco adobe.

The two beautifully beveled glass doors before him were unlocked. There was a small camera near the door like the one by his hotel room. The doors opened into a small mudroom and then into a large central room capped with a dome. When the doors closed, they made a little pop sound indicating they were almost perfectly airtight, and he noticed the two large windows beside the doors were triple paned glass.

In the central atrium, she opened her arms wide and asked, "What do you think?"

This large central room had a dome ceiling with a round skylight at the top and exposed wooden beams forming arches curving down from the center.

"I see this house has a lot of glass; tall doors and windows, and the skylight, doesn't that let in a lot of heat?" He was confused.

"Does it feel hot in here?" She asked.

"No, quite the contrary. It is very comfortable," he marveled.

"All glass is covered with Transparent High Heat UV Blocking and Protection Film. It lets in all the light and none of the heat."

"The house also has excellent insulation and is 98% airtight."

"Fiberglass?"

"No," she smiled amused. "We use Merino wool. Sheep's wool is a renewable resource. We shear our sheep once a year. It is a very efficient insulation material. It keeps the house warm in winter and cool in summer. Wool insulation can last a lifetime, and, unlike old-fashioned fiberglass, wool is 100% biodegradable.

"The hardwood floors have in-floor heating. There are lightweight panel room dividers, so the family can customize the space," she explained as they walked to the back of the atrium where the dining room and kitchen were located.

The kitchen had lots of hidden cabinets and a walk-in pantry. The walls had panels made of resin that looked like wood. One beautiful panel hid an energy efficient solar refrigerator and behind another was a solar composter and a garbage Compact Recycler.

When he wrinkled his brow, she explained, "It makes small bricks that we use in construction here."

Along a wall was a long, polished stone counter upon which sat several individual electric appliances. Among them were a microwave, a griddle, and a solar wok.

"Individual appliances are much more energy efficient than big clumsy stoves," she said proudly.

'Back home,' he thought, Judy still uses an old-fashioned electric stove. Boy, would she be thrilled if she lived here. It is so airy and light.

Two tall glass doors in the kitchen opened onto a covered deck with a beautiful view of the plateau. The deck was cool and comfortable. It had vines of grapes crawling over a pergola, green peas cascading down from railings, and an assortment of trees and bushes framing the communal yard. He recognized figs, jujube, dragon fruit, macadamia nuts, persimmons, loquat, pineapple guava, prickly pear, and pomegranate bushes and trees providing shade and food. She pointed out that they were all drought resistant plants.

To finish the tour, they returned to the central atrium. Off to the left were two large master bedrooms with skylights and Sun Tunnels in their domes.

"Little round reflective tubes are inserted in the ceiling," she pointed out. "They look like lights, but they are tubes made of reflective metal to bring in a lot of light during the daytime. At night, heat and motion guided LED lights automatically come on and off when someone enters or leaves the room," she sounded like a tour guide. It was his turn to smile amused. She had obviously forgotten that he was an architect and knew all about this stuff.

On one side of the open living space were two large bedrooms each with a bathroom and on the other were four smaller rooms. Altogether the space formed an octagon.

"Why do you have so many rooms? Do you have a lot of children?"

She laughed, "No, all family houses have grandparent suites included, for extended family living. We believe elders are important in raising healthy children. If you don't have grandparents, you can use the rooms for other purposes."

"Wow, this is nice." James admired the exposed ceiling beams and the tall church-like windows in each room. "There is so much natural light in here."

"Do you have a family, James? I could reserve this for you," she offered helpfully.

"No, that's alright. I need to talk to them before I can commit to anything," he said hurriedly, suddenly feeling awkward. "I just wanted to see how the house was built. Thank you for showing me around."

James was suddenly a little red in the face.

"I didn't mean to hit a sore spot, I'm sorry," she said with sincerity, responding to the shift in his tone.

"No, it's okay. I just haven't told them what I'm doing yet. I need to do that first before I commit to anything."

He thought, 'Sandra and Sammy would love this place.' Suddenly he felt a pang of yearning. He missed his kids but shook off the feeling.

"Oh, by the way, what are the requirements if I want to live in this house?"

He headed down the stairs and Fiorella followed. "Anyway, I am not ready to do that yet. I'm at the hotel for now. I have some things to do first."

James reached out his hand to shake goodbye and said," "Thank you, for taking the time to show me this house."

She gave him a sincere smile and said, "Anytime. It was nice meeting you. I hope you choose to stay."

"Well, I know I want to work here for a while. As for the long term, I'll have to see about that later."

"If you want to see more homes another time, I will be glad to show you. I'm the Neighborhood Guide." She waved and turned to leave.

"What is that?

"A Neighborhood Guide is a community representative. Here in Hope, we have a council for each area containing nine home Clusters and an assortment of community buildings like the school and the Community Center. Our council brings issues to the attention of all our neighborhood members. We are a Co-Op, so everyone votes every two years to elect a new Neighborhood Guide, and this term it is me."

"Do all neighborhoods have this governing structure?"

"Yes, we have a horizontal platform of self-governance. Everyone has an opportunity to voice their opinions and is free to participate in their own way. As the Neighborhood Guide, I represent nine Clusters and have a seat on all the larger governing bodies."

"Oh, that sounds interesting." James was curious. "I was wondering, do you have much crime here? Back home we have armed guards everywhere and a Neighborhood Watch, but these measures are just like bandaids on a hemorrhage in a city of crime."

"No, there's little if any crime; that's one of the reasons I came to Hope. It is much safer here! We have no shootings, and no guards are needed here. It is nice to finally relax about things like that."

"That sounds unbelievable!" James was truly surprised. In his world, there were armed guards everywhere, campuses were fenced in, and on average, there was at least one attempted mass shooting a year.

"I came to the States because I was offered a great paying job. At first, I lived in the city. My health was soon in shambles from all the stress. Then I came here, and it literally saved my life. I quickly lost 60 lbs., my hair stopped falling out, and I never had another panic attack again!"

James was still not sure if this place was legit or not. "What do you think of Hope? I mean, is it what it says it is? Does it really have a new way of thinking and a healthier way of living, or is there some hidden agenda?"

She smiled, "In this community people practice being authentic with each other. They walk their talk. Being new, you probably find this hard to believe. If we have any agenda, it's to spread love to every town and city around the globe. The world would be better off if it followed our lead.

"We circumvent most of the problems of the outer world. Our kids don't need a gang to feel they belong. Here we help each other and work together for the benefit of everyone, so the festering grievances that lead to violent crimes just can't take root here.

"Our children are given respect, appreciation, and support. From the youngest age they have opportunities to be heard, acknowledged; practice problem solving and decision making. They are given a variety of avenues for meeting their needs and for voicing issues arise.

"In school, we begin with bonding exercises, so the class is a peaceful cooperative place. Lesson plans are based on group projects where the students are trained to help each other. We also have openings on all the Boards for youngsters to participate in the governing process. Children here do not feel helpless and powerless as many do in the outside world. Here they even have a say on all our councils."

James thanked her again and headed back to his hotel. He wanted to call his family, hoping they would take him back. At least now, he had something to offer. First, he wanted to talk it over with Tim.

On the walk back, James's plan expanded. If he could convince his family to move here, he could sell their house and pay off part of their debt. Maybe he could help his wife break her habit of spending money they do not have and take away her need to shop. Each new exciting idea made James walk faster. After a brisk walk back to the hotel, he arrived a bit out of breath.

He used his Smartwatch to call Tim and paced around the room while he waited the two minutes for Tim to arrive.

"We see you. How may I help you, James?" Tim smiled but there was a raised eyebrow in concern at seeing James still catching his breath. "Are you alright?"

"Yes, can we go somewhere to talk? I need your advice and some information about moving my family here. Also, do I need to do anything special to get housing?"

"It's just the same requirements as work. You and your family need to attend the initial courses. Is this what you want my advice for?"

"Yes, can we go somewhere to talk?"

"Sure, let's go to your room, it has the best privacy." It was apparent to Tim that James was anxious about this subject.

"Yeah, I guess that will do." He started for the elevator.

Tim stopped by the front desk, picked up a brochure from Nicole, handed it to James, and said, "This booklet should cover most of your questions about housing."

James began reading it while they waited for the elevator and on the way up to his floor.

The leaflet detailed how to go about finding housing. He read, "Housing is on a first come first serve basis. You sign up at the Housing Bureau. They will recommend a house based on your real needs in terms of size and type. You can choose a professional Cluster like the School Cluster," he thought of Fiorella "or a special interest Cluster like the Musicians Cluster. As with everything in the City of Hope, no money is required.

"Okay, this sounds straightforward, but it is hard to believe. Is it really saying whether I work or not, housing is free once I start the program?"

"That's right, James. At Hope, we do not require people to work. Most people choose to work because it means they get to do something they love. As a community, we believe in our people. We trust each other to do what is right without adding the pressure to perform."

"Boy. That would make life so much easier, especially with my wife!"

When they reached James's room, they sat around the table.

"Well Tim, I don't know! I often think this place is hard to believe, I can't imagine how my wife will take it." James lowered his brows in concern. "I don't know how to begin explaining all this to her, even if she gives me a chance to say a word. She can be a bit challenging even when she is not mad, and she is going to be mad at me."

"I understand," Tim sympathized. "Just stand solid, breathe deeply, use a minimum of words, and be honest. I mean honestly presented with gentle care and concern. Give her time to adjust to each detail you present.

"Well, to tell you the truth, I'm willing to take the chance that this place is not a cult. I want to go for happiness once in my life.

"If this means she leaves me, like she has threatened before, I am willing to cope with that. We have been unhappy for a long time now.

"There are a couple of big obstacles I can foresee. First, I don't think she is willing to live without money and fancy clothes. Secondly, there's her job. How can I ask her to leave it? She is happy there."

In a small childlike voice, James hesitantly suggested, "I was thinking you could do a much better job of explaining it all to her. She might listen to you. Then we would have a better chance of her agreeing to come here."

"I would be willing to talk to her," Tim consented and then changed the subject.

"How do you think she feels about you being gone these last couple of days?"

"I'm not sure. She has been threatening to leave me for a while now. I don't know how much is just blowing off steam and how much is real. I think she is just staying with me for the extra money. It doesn't feel like she loves me anymore. At least, that is the way she acts lately."

"Her real reasons probably run deeper than that, but I'm not her counselor, I'm yours.

"How do you feel about her wanting to leave you?"

"I have been trying to please her from the beginning and it gets harder all the time. I think I want a divorce as much as she does. But at the same time, I know that it will be hard on my children. She said she's waiting until they go off to college, but that is still a year away. What she does not know is that there is no money left to send them to school. Once she finds that out, she might leave a lot sooner, if she really means it.

"What do you want, James? She is not the only one deciding here." Tim prodded carefully.

"Hmmm, well, I always ran from my problems. I don't know what I want. I just don't want to get yelled at for losing another job. She is not very understanding about my situation. She thinks I'm a fuck up. It really wasn't my fault. The company was downsizing, so I was released. It was nothing I did, but she'll say it was my fault for not making myself indispensable!"

"I understand," said Tim sympathetically, "but you still have not answered my question. What do you want? Do you want a divorce? Why are you leaving it all for her to decide? Don't you have a say in this?"

James was startled by the idea that he could have an equal say in this major decision. He thought about it for a few minutes. He looked at his guide who encouraged him with a look of raised eyebrows.

"You're right! I am leaving it up to her. I am letting her decide my future! I want to do what is right. I don't want to leave them in the financial jam they are in now. I think I want to stay here whether they come or not."

"If your wife agrees to come, do you want to stay married to her?" Tim tried again.

"I don't know. I'd be surprised if she willingly chose to come here. I don't think she will."

"That is not what I asked you," Tim persisted.

James blew out the breath he was holding, rubbed his head and said in a small voice, "No, I don't think so. I have had it. I can't stand the way she treats me. Even if she were willing to do Personal Process, which I don't think she would, I would still have a hard time dealing with her.

"If I could talk them into living here, it would be to lessen my bills and give the kids a better life, better education; not to make our dead marriage work. That is the truth. I think divorce is inevitable for us, now or later."

"Okay. If I understand you right, you want to offer your kids and your wife a new home. If she agrees, you will all live together here in the community, otherwise, you want a house for you and your kids, assuming you can arrange joint custody, right?" Tim clarified.

Yeah, I guess." James sighed.

"Do you think there is any chance that she will give up her job and come here to live with you?"

"No. Thinking that is just setting myself up for failure and disappointment again."

"It is important for you to clarify what you want and see that it is separate from what your wife wants. It will help you know what you are trying to achieve here."

"You're right. I've been kowtowing to her needs long enough. I need to take care of me; but I also want to pay off our debts."

"How did you get so far in debt?" Tim gently asked.

"Hmmm. Well, I've always made less than her. She does advertising, which is work she probably can't do here. She has always made more than me, but then she also spends more. She is the one that bought all that stuff we cannot afford, and I can't afford a financial battle with her in court either."

"We have free lawyers here if it comes to that, but you may want to get your financial accounts in order first." Tim suggested.

"I'm glad we talked it over. I was just focusing on how hard it would be to explain this place to her, now I see that I'm also having trouble admitting what I need to myself. Thank you for helping me see that. So, now what?"

"You might want to assess your financial debts first and then have an honest discussion with your wife about your needs and directions. Get clear with yourself whether you really want a divorce or want to look for other options," Tim suggested.

"You're right. I need to see where I stand with her, and I need to think about what I really want first. I love my kids, but lately they don't seem to care much about me. I don't know if fighting for custody is even worth it."

Tim sat quietly, letting James make his own decisions.

"All I know for sure is that I need a break from the world right now." James stood up and waved his arms up and wide. "Living here seems to be the best way to take one. This God thing is new and strange to me, but I need people around me who understand it. So, I'm staying here, that's for sure."

He took a deep breath and slowly let it out. "Well, I guess I have to call Judy now that I know what I want."

Tim stood up, "Then I should go and give you some privacy."

"Thanks," James sighed.

"Call me whenever you need me," Tim smiled and left.

James stared at his Smartwatch wishing it could handle the call for him. It was Saturday, so she would probably be at home. As soon as he said, "Hello", she started yelling. She dived in with how stupid he was for not coming home and demanded to know why. Her volume went up several notches when he said he lost his job. She accused him of running off to some weird place just to get out of his responsibilities. He tried to reassure her that he had every intention of paying the bank what he owed them, but she cut him off midsentence and accused him of lying or pipe dreaming. He got angry and accused her of spending too much on unnecessary things. That made her even more irate! She spit out the threat of divorcing him. Before he could say another word, she hung up without even asking where he was.

Even though James expected it to go just the way it did, he was fuming. He picked up a chair. It took all his willpower to resist throwing it through a glass door. Then he stomped out onto the porch and screamed at the top of his lungs.

He was fuming! 'She never shuts up long enough to let me explain anything! She just automatically assumes everything is my fault!'

James stewed for a while and then said out loud, "That's just fine. I expected that reaction from her! She has faults too, but she never admits them! Everything is always my fault. I am so done with this! The kids will be fine, and I'll pay the alimony."

He threw himself on the bed and started thinking about his finances. 'Our joint checking account and savings account are both nearly empty. I owe quite a bit on my car, but I won't need it here so I can sell it, and that debt will be gone. I need to pay off my credit cards, but I'll tell her, her cards are her problem!' These ideas felt comforting.

'Alimony will cover the kids and their school, but what about the college fund?' His ability to think clearly vanished as he got into an argument with himself over who was responsible for draining that account. 'Sure, I am the one who withdrew the money, but it was only because we had to pay for HER overspending. Maybe some little bit of it is mine and the kids, but most of it is HER obsessive splurging!'

These thoughts were just frustrating, so he decided to think about something else for a while. His mind wandered back to his talk with God earlier in his room.

'Look at me, I talked with God!' He laughed at himself.

'Have I fallen into madness or what? I can't believe God really spoke to me, but it did seem real at the time. Maybe I belong here with all these nuts; but Tim seems like a solid person. He is smart. Whether they are all crazy or not, living here will give me a chance to get my life back on track, get a handle on my anger, and not have to pay a dime to live here. Meanwhile, I can get back into my real career in architecture. What have I got to lose?'

He sat up and asked the ComScreen to show him the events calendar. He looked it over and took note of the schedule of classes and introductory seminars. He needed to attend them before he could get the work and housing he wanted. He decided to start right away.

A seminar on *Living within a Non-Monetary System* was going to be held at dinner tonight.

But that was four hours away. He needed to do something right now while his determination was strong. He perused the calendar again and found an *Eleven Affirmations for Life* meeting starting at 2:00, in just a few minutes, so he left his safe room and headed for the Affirmation Room across from the Trade Store.

The room had soft lighting and pictures of serene landscapes. There was a podium pushed to the side against a wall, and a circle of chairs in the center. The Eleven Affirmations for Life appeared as a hologram in the center of the circle. James took a seat and began to read them. They were obviously patterned after the twelve steps of Alcoholics Anonymous (AA). Then he clicked his ComPad, and a welcome packet appeared. He had just begun to read it when the meeting began with everyone reciting the affirmations:

ELEVEN AFFIRMATIONS FOR LIFE

1. I have realized that my life is a choice between fear and love and only love can restore my peace of mind. I can only change myself, not others.

2. I can restore myself to calm only by recognizing my conscious loving self, which is greater than my rational ego. I need only to accept love and release my fears, anger, apathy, and disillusionment.

3. I accept that I am the co-creator of my destiny with my conscious loving Self as I understand it. I accept love and self-responsibility as my new way of life.

4. I will make a constant fearless search of my personal issues with acceptance and honesty. I ask my conscious loving Self to help me overcome my shortcomings. I will admit my shortcomings firstly to myself and to others.

5. I will embrace other people as my equals. I will endeavor to accept others as they are. I will not judge or try to control another's program. I can only be responsible for myself.

6. I will endeavor to treat myself and others with love and acceptance. I realize that this program is about progress, not perfection.

7. I believe that real control is to be found in my ability to change and redefine myself through personal processing. I am finding that true self-esteem comes from working with these affirmations and changing my perspectives.

8. I believe that expectations are a form of control, assuming that someone or something should do or be a certain way, is to set myself up for disappointment. Life is as it's supposed to be, and people are on their own path. People are there for me to reflect on and learn from.

9. I will keep in constant contact with my conscious loving Self, as I understand it. I will continue to act with unconditional love as best I can. I will continue to search out my fears and through personal process release them.

10. I will endeavor to share my experiences with others through my example, keeping in mind that others have their own paths and that my path may not fit their needs. I will listen, be patient, compassionate and only give advice when others are receptive to it.

11. I must keep myself humble and always strive to learn and improve, because the day I say, 'I know it all' is the day I stop growing. I must continue to search for Higher Understanding and reach deeper levels within myself by listening to others and to my conscious loving Self.

A short man with curly black hair and sparkling eyes, a bulbous nose, and plump pink cheeks stood up, introduced himself as Godfrey and read a blessing. Then each of the twenty-two people sitting in a circle briefly shared some part of their current process. When each one introduced themselves, they stated their name and what step they were working on.

While he listened, James took note of the array of colored wristbands, mostly red, orange, and yellow.

When James's turn came, he was surprised to hear how calm he sounded when that was not how he was feeling, and said he was working on step two. He is building a new relationship with God.

After the Affirmations meeting, he still had time for a short lecture before dinner, so he headed down to the Book Club and was just in time for the Anger Management meeting.

All four walls of the Book Club were covered with bookshelves separated by fluted columns. There was an abundance of books in several languages. In the center were inviting sofas, chairs, and bean bags, accompanied by lamps. Three large chandeliers shed yellow light on the rest of the room. It was a very comfortable place to read. The ceiling was painted in a Michelangelo style, depicting present-day scenes from Trinitus City.

The seats here were also arranged in a circle with open space around them. Twelve men and women were mulling around the coffee and tea table located beside a sliding ladder against the wall. James poured a cup of tea and sat down. While the others settled in, he looked at their wristbands. Like his, most of them were black with a few reds.

Once again, there was a hologram projected into the center, this time showing the guidelines of the group. A woman with purple and green dreadlocks and intense eyes, in her late forties was dressed in a flowing robe like many people around the community. She had a Purple Band and was obviously the leader of the group.

"Welcome to the Anger Management group. My name is Katja. I am from Russia, and I will be your guide. Please feel free to ask me any questions. We have a few important guidelines. Remember, respect for everyone is primary here. It is important that everything you say to each other in this room is non-judgmental. If you wish to ask a question or say a few words after someone shares, please ask the speaker for permission first. There will be no cross talking. No one is allowed to talk about anyone else's sharing outside this group. You can talk about your experience only. To be a member of this group, you must maintain absolute confidentiality."

Just like in the Affirmation group, the meeting began with a blessing. A young man with red hair and a military style haircut, who introduced himself as Pancho, stood up and gave a short blessing of forgiveness. After that each person was given five minutes to share.

The first speaker, Akisha, a lovely young African woman with a fountain of long black braids, talked about her anger towards an unfair system. A few others echoed the same theme. The next speaker, Sergio, a gray-haired Italian man talked about his wife in a very loud tone. The theme of his complaint was also a common one. A few, mostly younger members, expressed anger at their parents. It surprised James when a few mature women and one older man also blamed their parents for their problems. One shy, slender, Frenchman spoke about his anger at himself. His sharing struck a deep chord in James.

A hefty African American man stood and took a deep breath before he spoke. Nevertheless, his words came out with a fury. "My name is Jordan and I'm angry with God, I know I shouldn't be, but I am. Seems to me that if humanity needed to be in touch with their emotions and process them all this time, it should have been in the Bible. Right? It seems so simple to me now. Once we get our heads and hearts working together, suddenly everything's hunky-dory.

"But I was taught that we screwed up in the Garden of Eden, so the Devil's been running things ever since. Why does life have to be this way? With the Bible as the only manual on how to be a good human, it can get confusing. There is a lot of begetting and conquering in that book, and then we are told not to do that stuff. Why doesn't the Bible tell us how to live together, rather than divide everything apart?" He threw up his hands in protest.

Katja thanked Jordan and said, "That is an intriguing idea, "The Devil is running this world." After our sharing circle, we can open that one up for discussion. Agreed?" Everyone nodded.

When it was James's turn to speak, he looked around the circle and a huge lump lodged itself in his throat. He gave a lame smile and croaked out the word "Pass." It was going to take him some time before he felt safe enough to talk about his anger to anyone, let alone a group.

As promised, after the sharing circle, Katja asked, "Briefly tell us, do you believe the Devil is running this world?"

A variety of perspectives were tossed around, most of which James had never considered before. He was going to need time to ponder these ideas.

Sergio spoke with great conviction saying, "The Devil is just a perverted idea introduced by a controlling Church to get people to pay for salvation. They tell you there is hell and then make you follow their rules to keep you from going to this place they made up to begin with."

Akisha said, "Maybe the Devil is made up, but so many people have believed in it for so long, that the thoughtform now has a life of its own. It is real enough now to make people do a lot of terrible things."

Godfrey put in his opinion, "I don't believe in the Devil or evil. I think people are infinitely gullible. The culture programs people to believe all this ugly stuff, so people filter their emotions through these ugly beliefs. If we raise children in a safe environment and treat them fairly, they will act in a loving and caring way towards the people around them."

Katja turned to James and asked, "What do you think James?" He felt singled out and froze like a deer in a headlight. A minute ago, he had lots of opinions, but now his mind went blank, so he shrugged his shoulders and grunted.

Katja said, "That's okay James, take your time. We look forward to the day when you are ready to share your thoughts and feelings with us."

Someone else jumped in to share their opinion, but James did not notice who it was or what they said. He was busy pondering why he was so comfortable in the Affirmation group and so blocked in this group. Then again, he did not see himself as an angry person. The only reason he came here is because it was available in this time slot, and because Judy was always telling him he is an angry man.

When the session ended, James headed for the door. Godfrey fell into step beside him and said, "Hi Man, nice to meet you."

James said, "Thanks, it is good to be here."

"It was a pretty tame session today," Godfrey said, shaking his head. "That's probably because everyone is recovering after yesterday. The fur was really flying the other day. Jordan and Akisha got into it something fierce. We had to do deep breathing for almost a half hour to ground that much fury. I just wanted to slug Jordan. He was being so bullheaded. Today, he was a sweet puppy dog."

"Why did we spend so much time today talking about the Devil, I thought we were supposed to talk about God?" asked James.

"In this Anger group, a lot of people believe the Devil made me do it, so they don't have to be accountable for their outbursts. In Affirmation, they talk about God, here you are more likely to hear about the Devil or feel the handiwork of his claws.

"God gets the credit for all the good stuff and the Devil gets blamed for the bad." Godfrey was shaking his head at the world's stupidity. "It is all bullshit! People are all a mixed bag. I think, once we learn to trust ourselves, we blame others less. At least that is what I am working on. What about you?"

"I'm new here. I have only been in Hope for a couple of days and today is my first day of meetings."

Godfrey smiled, "Man, you are in for a wild ride. Keep a journal. Whenever I read mine, it blows my mind how much I change every day. I have been here two months, and I am nothing like I used to be.

"I told you how I wanted to slug Jordan, well, a few months ago I would have done it without a second thought, but now, I just watch the fury rise in me and I have several tools to cool the fire down. See you tomorrow?"

James nodded and they walked their separate ways.

James returned to his room to shower before the dinner lecture. Then he dressed in the clothes that were left for him the night before, a blue button-down shirt and grey slacks. "I will need to get clothes and shoes at some point." He said aloud to no one. "I guess I have to do some shopping if I'm going to stay here after all."

When James entered the dining hall, he found it quite full. He looked around for a seat and found one towards the back. On each table was a ComPad. James looked at it confused, a young Asian man sitting beside him noticed his Black Band and said, just touch the screen and the menu will appear. Order whatever you want, and AI robots will deliver your order.

James was impressed with the wide array of foods being offered. There were several offerings for every kind of diet. He ordered poached salmon with caramelized onions and a lemon sauce, scalloped potatoes, and roasted asparagus with mushrooms.

A dusty blond man in his fifties entered the stage. He was dressed in a long tan robe, tied with a red cummerbund sash around his rather ample belly. "We see you. Dear community of friends, my name is Randal Kauffman.

"We are here to look at why we don't use money in Trinitus Cities even though it is the system used everywhere else."

"What is money? It is a means of exchanging energy. People work for food and for other necessities. Everything is made by workers, and then the workers buy the things made. Money was introduced because it is a more exact exchange than trade, which was the previous method. In a large, complicated society, it is difficult for trades to always be a fair and even exchange."

Holograms with a Power Point of pictures, diagrams and commentaries suddenly appeared between the tables as soon as the speaker began to talk.

"Even though money itself is not evil, our present economic system is oppressive and divisionary. It creates rich and poor, promotes inequality, and condenses all the power in the hands of a few. In a Capitalistic monetary system where everyone is in competition with everyone else, some will gain while others lose. This creates inequalities. Those with the resources enslave those without them and assume privileges that deprive others of necessities. When the few have too much, the many have too little. Social injustice is a consequence of our Capitalistic money system."

Randal spoke in a soft but firm tone. He had obviously given this lecture many times and was very confident in what he was saying.

"While being rich is wonderful and everyone deserves to have abundance, hoarding is different. Taking ownership of collective resources is immoral and leads to a corrupt social system. When some people have far more than they need, and many have far less, many fathers and mothers are forced to work more than one job just to stay afloat. This dynamic is hard on everyone. It can put a wedge between the parents and the children.

"While a large portion of the population is scrambling to survive and get ahead, those with great power and great wealth approach the acquisition of more and more resources as a competitive game. Political leaders compete to prove who is the mightiest of them all.

"With money comes power and influence. Those who possess great wealth make the rules and rule the world."

"As a byproduct of Capitalism, people are forced to endure many traumas caused by money problems and the inequity of resources. The lack of money has been a major contributor to the perpetuation of crimes, gangs, war, poverty, disease, suicide, and homelessness. We need to cure people, but even more than that, we need to remove the primary causes of their problems. Poverty and hardships lie at the root of many emotional and mental problems. A healthier way of living requires removing the cause of poverty, racism, drug abuse, alcoholism, child abuse, and the destruction of our environment."

A parade of AI servers rolled into the room. Ever so silently they deposited plates in front of each person and rolled right out again. Since most eyes were glued on Randal or the holograms, it felt like the food simply magically appeared.

"Great wealth corrupts leaders. It has led to the implementation of unfair laws and undermined integrity. Collective resources have been siphoned off, exploited to line the pockets of individuals, rather than going into humanitarian endeavors. If the resources were used for the betterment of all, it would go into healthcare, protecting people and our planetary environment, bettering the quality of life on this planet, and the advancement of sciences and arts.

"The desire for money and power, along with an obsession for maintaining control, has led to most of the inequalities in the world. The desire to maintain power, has led to owning or financially supporting the media; thus, controlling what news and information people receive."

Each time Randal made another point, pictures and words appeared on the hologram beside James. A series of headlines proclaimed one thing, while a sentence under it pointed out the distortion, the misleading phrasing, and the scripted lies.

"Owning the media is a power that is often abused. It leads to information that is distorted, slanted against certain racial and ethnic groups to perpetuate prejudice. While people are busy hating some neighbors, fearing others, and scrambling to make ends meet, they are too distracted to see through all the lies and pretense, under too much pressure to realize they are being manipulated and controlled; too preoccupied with their own problems to see that collective resources are being confiscated by a few powerful people. These people contribute heavily to political campaigns, which put our leaders in their pockets.

"The media also convinces people that there is not enough to go around. Thus, people compete for the crumbs left over after the super wealthy divide up the pie. They take what should belong to everyone. They use fear and control to make people believe this is just the way life is and there is nothing you can do about it. They even go so far as to convince people that their supposed superiority is part of the natural order of things, when that is the farthest from the truth.

"Good leaders seek to enhance the well-being of their citizens. Rich leaders use the citizens to feed their own greed. A dark byproduct of this corrupt financial system is the Black Market where animals and people are abused and dark atrocities fester.

"For your mental wellbeing, turn off the news, turn on the internet, and watch programs that report on alternative communities and socially beneficial organizations. These programs will keep you informed about all the wonderful ways men and women are working together and carving out new pathways towards a healthier happier world."

Randal cleared his throat and leaned forward as though he was about to convey something very special, something for their ears only. He took a deep breath and looked over the gathering for a few seconds to build suspense. All eyes were on him.

"Our Founder gathered several great thinkers who had studied the negative effects of the monetary system. They discussed methods for creating a more equitable community and decided that we must begin by eliminating money. Without it, people have no way to commandeer all the resources, no way to control the people who work for them, no way to maintain power over others.

"Our Founder dreamed of creating a better society, one where all the members thrive, not just a select few. She experimented with different ways to remove the stress that constricts people in their daily lives. She recognized that constant stress undermines health and corrodes one's sense of wellbeing. Above all, she wanted to remove the divisionary effects of competition to foster an atmosphere of cooperation.

"She was certain that the first step towards creating a better way of life was to eliminate money and develop other ways of organizing and distributing collective resources.

"Once the element of money was removed, people eased into everyday life with more relaxation and comfort. Members of the community attained higher levels of openness towards each other. Many said their happiness level had improved greatly and the fear of not surviving had all but ceased."

James was surprised and delighted with the quality of the food. He smiled to himself, thinking he was going to like living here, and chuckled that it was free. He savored each bite while he listened to Randal's speech go from the obvious to the impossible.

"Within a small community like ours, everyone can contribute as they are able, for the benefit of all. With the elimination of money came the elimination of greed and no more fear of lack. The next step was to begin healing the scars of the old unjust system. To meet this need, she introduced an emotional support system, that would help people to see life from a different perspective. That's why we require Personal Process.

"Once we eliminated money, the division between rich and poor disappeared. We were able to undermine the whole hierarchical system, which is the cause of most people's physical, mental, emotional, and spiritual problems. Without money, inequalities disappeared. Hatred, the need to blame others for one's own problems, and living in fear, all disappeared. Instead, we were able to create a peaceful way of life that supports the wellbeing of all our members.

"Our communities are dedicated to being an example for the future, a future where people are free to explore their own creativity for the wellbeing of their Souls, while contributing to the wellbeing of all their neighbors. Without a hierarchical society, we are free to flower, each in our own way, for the enhancement of the whole community."

As he came to the end of tonight's lecture, Randal looked over his audience and gauged their level of understanding. He saw that many were enthusiastically nodding their heads. His heart was deeply invested in this material.

"We are the vanguard of a new world, walking into the future with our eyes wide open. Our Founder studied history and took note of the mistakes societies made in the past, so we are not condemned to repeat those mistakes.

"Every one of you is a path blazer, a living example to the world. Together we are demonstrating how to create a healthier, more cooperative, independent, and creative society. As we live our daily lives, we sow the seeds for a world based on love, sharing, and equality, where people are fulfilled and happy.

"We are establishing a solid foundation. Our lives model a sustainable and comfortable lifestyle. In the future people will live better, treat each other with more love and respect, and work together to meet collective needs. They will thrive because of the way we live today.

"The non-monetary system we created is based on an open exchange of services and resources. With this key, our communities are thriving. Our community is now independently prosperous. All the Trinitus Cities share their technologies and resources. We put the welfare and safety of all our citizens first and foremost. Within a safe protected environment, we work to heal each other and thus provide a solid foundation for future generations to carve out lasting peace and universal prosperity."

"Enjoy your dinner. After dessert and beverages, I invite you to join us for a half hour Dialogue Circle. You are welcome to share stories from your experience, ask questions, or offer your ideas."

James loved his dinner and marveled at his good luck. He certainly never imagined he would find his way to paradise when he drove into the desert. Many people had attended similar lectures before, so after dinner, the room emptied out quickly and only a dozen or so newcomers remained.

They pulled the chairs into a small circle. In this intimate group, James felt less nervous and was willing to speak.

He asked Randal, "Since work is voluntary, some people will work, and others won't. That sounds unfair. Why should I work, if I can just lay in the sunshine and play all the time? Meanwhile other people are slaving away."

Randal laughed, "No one in our community is slaving away, and fairness is not a criterion here. No one measures what they do or do not have against anyone else. We each have what we need and want. In the outer world, people work to survive and justify their existence. In our community, we work at what we love for the pleasure it brings. We are nourished by the acknowledgement we receive, by the strong feeling of belonging it brings, and by our growing sense of self-worth. Our contribution to the community is valued by everyone. It makes us feel good about who we are and what we have done. Work is a point of pride. We are motivated by the wonderful feelings our contribution creates in us; how it enhances our lives."

A young East Indian woman with a red dot between her eyes wearing a lovely royal blue chiffon sari dotted with silver stars, spoke next. "Hello everyone, my name is Sattva. I am wondering, since everything here is state of the art. Does that not mean it comes from the outer world and is expensive? I can understand that here you exchange goods and services within the community, but where does the money come from when you interface with merchants out in the world?

Randal expected the question. In every group at least one person asks it. "Trinitus Cities are donation based, and we have some large contributors, people who strongly believe in what we are creating here. We also have several income streams. We offer classes, seminars, and events, which paid guests attend. The hotels and the resort bring in a good income, and we sell our surplus naturally grown food and our fine crafts to outside markets."

"Who owns everything? Does the Founder own all this?" asked a middle-aged man with bushy eyebrows, a bald head, and a thick mustache.

"All our businesses function as Co-Ops, all products and land are shared not owned by the people in the communities. As for the land, the Trinitus Organization owns it and holds it in trust for the whole community. All major decisions affecting the land are made by community vote and everyone is welcome to participate."

A man, wearing a skullcap and a long white robe, asked, "What if we are of another religion. Must we convert to be accepted?"

"No. Trinitus Cities is not a religious organization and does not favor one religion over another. We protect and support all religions with one stipulation. They cannot preach harm to another group or individual."

"Is there a name for this non-monetary open resource lifestyle?"

"Yes, a Holocracy, from the word Holism."

"It sounds like Communism to me," said Akisha. James recognized her from the Affirmations group.

"Randal responded by quoting Marx's Alienated Labor; 'In the Capitalist society, 'His work is not voluntary but imposed, forced labor. It is not the satisfaction of a need, but only a means for satisfying other's needs. – it is not your own work but work for someone else.'

"This can lead to debasing feelings and co-dependence. At Trinitus, we do work that feels fulfilling. At the end of the day, there is a feeling of satisfaction that fills the heart in ways shopping, acquiring, and owning things never can."

"As for true Communism, it only existed on the planet in the 1930s. Though the name lived on, the system quickly morphed into Totalitarianism and an Oligarchy." True Communism is a political and economic system that seeks to create a classless society in which the major means of production is owned and controlled by the public. There is no government or private property or currency, and the wealth is divided among citizens equally or according to individual needs. We are taking Marx's ideals and applying them to a new era while instituting many safeguards to ensure it does not morph into anything else."

James walked out with Akisha. She turned to him and said, "I am so glad I found this place. I only wish I had found it a lot sooner. My life would have been a lot easier!"

James nodded emphatically and said, "Me too."

He returned to his room, plopped down in a plush armchair, let out a deep sigh and said, "Okay God, let's have a talk."

CHAPTER 4

Introduction

James woke up at 6:00 feeling refreshed. It had been a long time since he had slept this deeply. Tim wasn't due until seven, so he stayed in bed and luxuriated in a feeling of wellbeing. His mind went over all the interesting things he experienced yesterday. It was quite a full day. When his thoughts reached last night, he laughed, marveling that he had had the nerve to ask God, to talk with him. He asked almighty God to talk to humble little him. Then the most amazing thing happened; God spoke!

James remembered every detail like a movie replaying itself right in front of him. He was sitting in his room staring at the ceiling when he got up his nerve and growled at God, "Why haven't people done anything before about all the misery in the world!"

No answer came.

'I knew this wouldn't work,' he grumbled to himself and maybe to God, if He was listening.

After sitting quietly for a few minutes, he took a deep breath, let it out slowly and relaxed. He wondered why he never questioned the way life is. 'I was too busy trying to keep my life together to think of anything else.' He thought.

"And you were too scared!" He heard.

'Were those words my own thoughts?' he wondered, then decided, 'Probably not. I would never admit to being scared.'

"God why would I be scared?" he asked.

The answer did not come right away but a few deep breaths later he heard, "You are afraid of change. It kept you in the same old tape loop unable to see life from another perspective."

'So, fear keeps the hamster wheel spinning?' James pondered.

"That and you are trained to obey without questioning."

"You got that right. I would have gotten a fist in the face if I ever talked back to my father and questioned his orders."

After only one deep breath he heard, "It is just a small step from obeying your father without question to obeying the laws of your country without objection."

"Yeah, that's true. I would never have thought of changing the law. Laws are just fixed permanent things. No one can change them, except maybe lawyers."

"Somehow the idea would have to be planted in your mind, the idea of looking at the box your life has put you in and motivate you to get out of the box."

"Yeah, like losing my job and driving off into the desert."

"That was brave," said God. "You usually choose the path of least resistance and followed the norm."

"Yeah, well I didn't want to stand out and be ridiculed or ostracized."

"Those thoughts are what have kept you in the box all these years," God explained.

"Well, I am out of the box now!" This thought came with a thrill soaring through his body, followed by a solid sense of rightness.

It was time to get up. James jumped out of bed, showered, and put on his clean work clothes. As he made his way to the lobby, he thought, 'I bet once word of this place gets out, everyone will want to live here.'

Echoing in his ears were the words, "You would lose that bet."

Startled, James began to worry that God was going to start talking to him all the time now that he had started the dialogue.

"Relax. I only answer your thoughts when your heart is open to hearing what I have to say," God reassured him.

He calmed down and asked, "Why wouldn't everyone want such a wonderful way of life?"

"Some are afraid to be happy and afraid to be free. It feels ungirdled and they are afraid of the unknown. They would rather choose an awful known to a possibly pleasurable unknown."

"Yeah, I'm not so sure Judy would be open to coming here. It might be hard for her to trust this strange new way of living and she is addicted to buying more and more stuff."

"She is trying to fill a hole in her Soul. She keeps shopping, not because she craves the things, but rather because she craves the feeling it gives her. For a few minutes she feels good about herself and feels like she is in control of her life," God informed him.

Not knowing what to make of that statement, James changed the subject. "I have some doubts that this system could work on a global scale."

"It can, if it is organized as interconnected circles." He saw an image in his mind. If he believed in visions, which he didn't, not yet, he would have realized he was having one. He saw small communities all interconnected by common values and mutual interests.

By the time the elevator door opened, a very different version of James stepped out. He may not have achieved enlightenment, but he wasn't his usual close-minded self anymore either.

James met up with Tim and they headed for the dining room. On the way to the morning lecture, Jams asked his Guide if he could recommend a book on channeling. Tim nodded yes and said, "After breakfast, we can go to the Book Club room, and I will give you one that the Founder wrote."

"I might also want one on dealing with anger," James admitted.

"Okay. I know a couple of good ones. There's *Anger Management Workbook* by Aaron Karmin. You might also like *Healing the Angry Brain* by Ronald Potter-Efron. You can find them in the Book Club or on the ComScreen in audio and eBook form."

In the dining room, they found a couple of seats near the stage and ordered breakfast on the ComScreen. James ordered Eggs Florentine and felt very indulgent. Tim ordered granola with fresh fruit and oat milk.

A very tall Scandinavian woman with long cream-colored hair down to her waist took the stage and introduced herself as Annika.

"Today, I will be giving you an overview and introduction to the structure of Trinitus Cities." Our unique design has several elements to it. We address the needs of the whole individual, which means we care about meeting their spiritual, mental, emotional, and physical needs. We want everyone to thrive. It is the key to our success as a cooperative community.

"Spiritually, we do not ask anyone to change their religion, we only ask that you know what you believe and develop a strong relationship with your own Spiritual Source. To that end we offer classes on intuition and channeling. To address your mental needs, we have a well-stocked library and classes on a variety of subjects. These classes are free to our members and at an equitable fee to guests. We also offer counseling to those who request it with the same financial arrangement. Emotional needs are often the most neglected out in the world, so it has become a major focus here. Everyone is required to participate in Personal Process for a specified number of hours in accordance with the color of your wristband. Our community is very different than the outer world because it is based on very different principles.

"All our businesses are structured to have horizontal management as a Co-Op. All members of the Co-Op have a vote. Certain key positions have veto power, which sends the issue back for further discussion, so new information can be provided. We approach the land with great respect and emphasize renewable and sustainable agriculture. Regenerating the soil is given top priority. We take recycling, repurposing, renewing, and redeveloping objects, very seriously. If you attended last night's lecture, you are familiar with our resource economies. Our products and their production are all environmentally safe and employ recycled materials as much as possible.

"The Trinitus Organization oversees outreach. It has established a network of mutually cooperative communities that work together in fair and equitable ways for our mutual benefit. These are alternative communities, Co-Ops, green businesses, as well as third world villages and towns. We send educational teams worldwide to struggling communities that are economically challenged. We help them stabilize their economy and teach them how to set up a Co-Op system so they can become independent and self-sufficient. When they become stable, we establish trade with them. Our grassroots approach is gaining influence and having a quiet but increasing influence on the world.

"We offer therapeutic programs that address the needs of the whole person. We have set up several clinics in countries all over the world that address spiritual, mental, emotional and physical issues. These clinics are also a revenue source. The client is charged on a sliding scale according to what they can comfortably pay. At first, we offered our services for free, but found that out in the world, people value a service by its price. Free became equated with not worth much. We had to charge our clients to gain their respect for the work being done.

"We run private prisons throughout the United States, where we provide therapy and Personal Process to the inmates. After they are released, we vocationally retrain the parolees and provide them with satisfying jobs. We also assign them a Guide, not a Probation Officer, but rather a support person they can talk to, so they have continuous assistance and encouragement in their reentry process. Going back into the world, especially once you have seen the world from a new perspective, can be quite challenging.

"We also work with the court system to provide reconciliation programs in the hopes of preventing people from going to jail in the first place.

"Our Outreach Programs work with gangs in many cities across the country, especially those in poverty-stricken areas. We provide safe living environments and counseling for families that need help; mostly those dealing with physical and/or substance abuse. These programs were funded by contributions, grants, and endowments. We charge only what they can comfortably afford, and it may only be $1.00 but at least the individual feels good about contributing something.

"Economically, these outreach programs pay their own way and bring in a little income. Most of Trinitus's income comes from the Co-Ops, green businesses, the food, arts, and the crafts we sell, the Living History parks, our resorts, and our Wildlife Refuges. The remainder of our income comes from our trade with other communities that Trinitus has influenced and helped.

"Thank you for joining me today. After breakfast, we will have a Dialogue Circle where you can ask questions and share your ideas. We are always open to suggestions on how we can refine our process. Those of you with Red Bands may want to sit in to get a better idea where you might like to contribute your energy."

"Tim, that was amazing! I did not realize Trinitus was so extensive and had such an influence around the world. I've never even heard of it before. How can that be?" James was finding more things to like about this place all the time.

"There are a great many organizations, thousands upon thousands of people around the world, working cooperatively to better people's lives and rehabilitate the environment. You just never hear about all the good work they do every day because the news does not report on them. Let's go up to the roof deck, it offers the most expansive view of the land around here. It will give us a good perspective on the way the land and the houses work together."

They walked out onto the garden deck and a cool breeze whipped through James's light shirt, reminding him that he wanted to get more clothes. Tim volunteered to go with him.

They caught a tram into town. The shops were all on stilts like a network of treehouses. The walkways connecting them looked like a series of rope bridges but were made of strong hempcrete and steel. This skyline level could be reached by moving stairs and elevators. On the ground level were booths and stalls where individuals sold an assortment of things they had crafted. These hand-made products were beautiful, unique, and fun to explore.

Like most areas in the community, the structures were arranged in a circle with Open Space in the center. They passed one that had a playground with an assortment of brightly colored objects to climb and play on. Around this fun zone were comfortable benches. Since it was a safe enclosed area, children could be left alone there to play while parents attended to their tasks. There were always a few adults taking in the sun with half an eye on the children.

"I just want to buy a few things, a change of clothes, a few warm things, jacket, a robe, some pajamas. I am not a shopaholic like my wife. That woman can go through money like water through a sieve."

Tim listened patiently. He noticed that James took every opportunity to criticize his wife, especially about her spending, but saw no need to mention it for now.

James was not keen on the robe and tunic look but tried one on for the fun of it. Tim pointed out that all the clothes were made from natural organic fibers, created here in the community. "People dress in lose clothes because they enjoy the feeling of freedom. We enjoy living simply."

James chose the kind of clothes he was used to wearing, slacks and solid-colored shirts. He also got a warm jacket for the coming winter, well-made running shoes, and a warm cushy bath robe. Not paying for them was beginning to feel more natural. A stray thought crossed his mind. 'If I get used to this and ever go back to the real world, I might walk out of a store without paying and get arrested.'

They were in and out in record time. Tim suggested they go to the juice bar. On the way he asked James, "Did you call your wife?"

James nodded yes.

"How did it go?"

James huffed and rolled his eyes so hard his head went around with them. "Oh yeah, a freaking delight that was! She wouldn't let me get a word in edgewise, just ran off at the lip and hung up. It was just as I expected. She blamed me for getting laid off, said I was a coward for leaving, and that I'd lost my mind joining this cult. She went ballistic when I told her she spends too much, and it is her fault we are in debt. She told me to expect divorce papers and hung up, without even asking for my address." He took a sip of juice and had a coughing fit. Emotions were blocking his throat.

"What are you going to do next?"

"Well, I guess I'll write her an email. At least, then she can't interrupt to curse me out. If she wants to know where I am, to serve me papers, she will have to react in a civil way to my email, if she is capable of that! I doubt that we can have a real conversation on the Smartwatch."

"If your wife is open to it, we do offer Marriage Counseling with a therapist or arbitration with a lawyer." Tim suggested.

"There is too much water under the bridge for counseling. She'd never be willing to do that. She is just perpetually nasty these days."

"Why?"

"Too many reasons to go into right now."

"Do you want to enter into counseling with her?"

"She'd never do it."

"I asked about you, not her. Are you trying to avoid conflict by not considering counseling?" Tim questioned.

James looked at him startled and then cast his eyes downward. "Yep, probably," he let out a big sigh. "Who wouldn't want to avoid it? No matter what I say or do, she is going to use it as a platform for screaming at me and accusing me. With her, everything is my fault."

"Think of it as a challenge that you can overcome, as a puzzle you know you can solve. Look at your feelings and anticipate hers. Be willing to go behind the yelling, to the underlying hurt. Think about the part you might have played in that hurt. Be aware of your own feelings and try to understand hers. Can you feel some bit of compassion for this woman you loved enough to marry, if you can understand some of her pain; when you talk to her, you will be less emotionally triggered. You can consciously choose how you want to respond rather than respond automatically to every hook she puts out."

James's wrinkled brow showed he did not know what Tim meant by a 'hook.'

"Arguments are like fishing. You put bait on a hook. The bait is some statement guaranteed to get a rise out of the other person. When they jump in to defend or attack, then you have them hooked. The only way to avoid the same old circle is to try something different. Do not get hooked and avoid tossing out barbs. Think of a new way to respond." Tim advised.

"I don't think I can muster that much emotional control around her. I'm new to this stuff. All I know how to do is shut down and not say anything. If I concede to her demands and give up, the screaming stops." James's shoulder deflated in defeat and he sighed.

"If you always give in, then what could you do that is different?' Tim prompted.

James shrugged and looked away.

Tim stood quietly and waited. James was getting uncomfortable with the prolonged silence and ventured a guess, "Maybe I can write a letter and acknowledge some of the things she said that were true, exaggerated for sure, but partly true. I can tell her that I am open to getting a divorce now. We don't have to wait for the kids to go to college. That's still a few years off. Why spend the next few years torturing each other, when we can get it over with now." Once the words were out, James felt a lot better, like a heavy weight was lifted from his overburdened shoulders.

Tim nodded. James gave a weak smile and continued, "The email has to be worded just right. If it is too angry, she will retaliate. If it is too soft, she will try to tear my guts out. Can you help me word it?"

"Sure," Tim gave him a compassionate look and smiled. "We can also direct her to our website, so she can read about our community. That way, she can make an informed decision about us without you there."

James nodded, "Sounds good."

He was ready to change the subject. "So, Tim, I was thinking of taking a Personal Process class today. Could I do one before lunch? I want to get all the prerequisites in as soon as possible, so I can start my new job."

Tim looked at his Smartwatch and said, "We had better head back then."

They rode the tram back to the hotel. James put his purchases in his room and met Tim in the Conference Hall for 'Introduction to Personal Process'.

This large round chamber was airy and bright. Sky lights from the garden roof lit up the room. The walls were a circle of windows that let in even more sunlight. Above the windows were louvered vents for more air flow which helped because the room was comfortably warm from the sun.

Greek style pillars stood like sentries between the windows, giving the room the feeling of an Ancient Temple of Knowledge. Comfortable chairs were set up in an arc, like an amphitheater, with twenty-two seats across and twelve rows deep, all facing a large stage. About half the seats were full. As far as James could see, there were an equal number of Black Bands and Guides like Tim. The two of them sat down in the first row, right in the center of the arc.

Alberto walked to the center of the stage where four people were already seated on chairs behind him.

"We see you. I am Alberto Fornelli," said this tall slender man with black curly hair and an old-fashioned handlebar mustache. "Today, it is my pleasure to share a very exciting innovation with you. Our community is proud of the Personal Process Program. Our members are implementing what they are learning, and it is contributing greatly to the stability, sustainability, and wellbeing of our dynamically peaceful community.

"We have made this program a daily practice, which sets us apart as innovative pioneers. I will be your MC. Welcome to an 'Introduction to Personal Processing.'" He paused for the last few people to settle in and double checked his ComScreen. When the room was quiet, he began.

"We are here to answer the question, what is Personal Process? It is simply self-reflection, looking at your mind and trying to understand how it works. It is looking at your life and seeing why you made the decisions that you did and continue to do. It is knowing yourself, so you can learn to trust yourself. Once you have mastered self-trust, you will be able to trust others. Once you understand yourself, you can begin to understand others. Self-understanding and self-trust are the keys to living peacefully within yourself and with others. That is why it is so important here in our community.

"When you are aware of why you do things, you can make informed conscious decisions. When a part of you is denied, hidden, rejected, a source of guilt and shame, or a cause for blame, it is pushed down into your depths where it gathers more power and becomes the marionette strings that make you act in detrimental ways. We call these compulsions and obsessions. They have great power and influence over you and cause the key dramas in your life.

As Alberto continued his explanation, a huge holographic image appeared at the back of the stage behind him. In the hologram, people were working their way through challenging interactions in everyday situations. Then a dialogue appeared showing possible interpretations and reactions. A debate ensued between the rational and unconscious minds. Their different reactions were listed in brightly differing colors so it was easy to track the difference between healthy creative responses, compared with negative, or self-centered, or low self-esteem responses.

"Undigested beliefs that you carry around in the depths of your mind cause or attract the terrible things that happen in your life. Your beliefs hold tremendous attracting power, drawing people and events into your life. Here in Trinitus, we believe that helping you work your way through the traumas, the scar tissue of your dramas, is the path to peace.

"In your quest for self-discovery, we can help you put all the events of your life into meaningful sequences and see the sense in it all. We can even help you see that your traumas played an important part in awakening you to the healing needed in this wounded world. We will also help you recognize and reclaim the power you left behind in those traumatic events.

"When you were a child, you were fed a barrage of beliefs, which formed the framework through which you interpret reality. Some of those beliefs were purposely implanted in your mind to make you behave in a certain way, make you doubt yourself in several ways, and siphon off your power, to control you and make you obedient. The work you will do here will disentangle you from the toxic beliefs this culture has implanted in your mind. We will help you sort through your beliefs so you can discard the ones that no longer serve you.

As he spoke, holograms appeared throughout his lecture adding visual depth to everything being said.

"No matter how much you have suffered from growing up in this unfair world, one truth remains. The consciousness you call, 'Me,' is more than what the world tells you, you are. The I, the Conscious Psyche, that sees out through your eyes, the Pure Consciousness that you are, is what we call, your Soul. Your Soul looks out at the world and sees its own reflection. This is where processing begins.

"There is an old parable about a group of blind men who come upon an elephant. They each lay their hands on the beast and get into an argument. Each is certain they alone know the nature of this new creature. Is it the man holding the snake-like tail, or the hands wrapped around the thick tree trunk leg? Is it the wee man dangling from the gigantic wing flapping ear? They argued endlessly, certain that each knew the truth.

James almost jumped when a full-size group of blind men and an elephant appeared as a holograph beside Alberto.

"Here in Trinitus, we know that an elephant has all these parts and more. We know that human consciousness is capable of so much more than the world out there allows. We know from experience that you can wrap your mind around a great vision, an inspiring ideal, answer an awakening bell, or take a practical approach to look deeper; deeper into your mind and body, deep enough to see the patterns, the repetitious patterns weaving through your life.

"On your path, you experienced people and events that were part of your Destiny. They may have wounded, healed, transformed, released, or rebirthed you. They happened for a reason; to lead you to discover your own truth so you can release the old beliefs that diminish you. Each test and challenge you faced was your teacher, guiding you to know yourself. These events happened to test and transform you.

"The human psyche is powerful, and it hosts forceful energies. When powerful energies surge through you, they attract equally intense forces. Then whatever happens becomes the gist of your life story. Here is where your successes and your wounds occur.

"Doing Personal Process requires you to be an explorer and an honest evaluator. It means looking inside you to find valuable truths. To do this work, you need to be a brave warrior ready to cut away the chains of the past, so you can discover who you truly are, and what you have come into this life to accomplish.

"Here in Trinitus, we offer tools from a wide array of disciplines to help you on this journey. You also have a Guide who has volunteered to walk this path beside you. Guides have been training for a while and have advanced along their own journey of self-discovery.

"Diving into the depths can be scary. When you are navigating through the darkness of your fears, it is comforting to have someone beside you, someone holding a light of understanding. Your Guide is your lamp holder, trained to help you navigate through difficult memories as you revisit old battles. They support you when you face the old wounds and reclaim the power you left behind.

"Your Personal Process leads you to look into the mirror of your Soul and clearly see who you are. First, you may need to clear away obstacles - your old fears and remove the old detrimental beliefs that have caused you to retreat from life. You will be guided to face the old traumas still lodged in your body, those overwhelming events that you could not digest when they happened, so those energies are still there, blocked, frozen in time, still denied, still pulling the strings of your behavior, still crying out to be healed.

"When you face the past and reclaim the power you left behind, you also find an important key. It is hidden in your traumas. When an experience is intense, it is important. It is where you find the key that unlocks the Life Mission you came into this world to fulfill.

"Your traumas, your war wounds, came from the battles you fought, many of which were caused by the beliefs you carry. These beliefs, which you may think are absolute truth, were implanted in you by a hierarchical, greed-ridden, unjust society. No one here is a victim, but rather a battle worn warrior.

Holograms flashed disturbing pictures of the way the world is organized and showed the damage it causes.

"When you know who you are on a profound level, you are better able to activate your greatest potential. With this goal in mind, we can help you look at all your wounding experiences and see them as Ariadne's thread, leading you out of the labyrinth; or as Hansel and Gretel's breadcrumbs, leading you home.

"When you look at your traumas as signposts, you can see that they point the way to your Life Mission. This is what you came into life to heal. Unfortunately, people sometimes need a homeopath dosage of the poison to awaken them to what needs healing. These are your traumas. These are the issues you are driven to understand and resolve. This is your apprenticeship in healing.

"From your first awareness as a baby, and on through your life, your experiences and especially your traumas, implant beliefs. Beliefs are crucial in framing your reality. They create the baseline themes of your life.

"Your traumas form sequences. The events may have occurred years apart, but they hold a thread of similarity which binds them together. You can travel along those threads of association to find hints about your Life Mission. Embedded in your traumas, issues, grievances, and wounds, are the keys to your empowerment. Facing your issues and your traumas sets you free from their repressive influence.

"The process of following intense memories and talking about them was first formally recognized by Sigmund Freud. He called it Talk Therapy. It works for 30% of the clients, primarily those who feel they need to say things they were never allowed to say and acknowledge the truths they never realized before.

"The reason Talk Therapy only works for 30% of the clients is because humans are complex creatures. Understanding human consciousness requires a broader perspective than just engaging the rational mind. We do not all need the same thing, nor do we all function the same way. In fact, some of us are more physical, mental, emotional, or spiritual.

"We acknowledge all four aspects of human nature and offer different ways to do Personal Process to match their differing needs. Many people are a mixture, so we offer a mixture of therapeutic modalities for you to choose from.

"Talk Therapy appeals to people who are mentally dominant. These people read lots of books because they want to collect maps. They need these maps to navigate the pathways into deeper awareness. They are motivated by a yearning to be informed, understand, and know the truth.

"The people who live primarily on an earth plane, need physical challenges to reach the inner realms. They need to be in their bodies and get past their self-sufficiency, before they are willing to open and go deeper.

The Hologram now showed inspirational images. James felt excited and inspired when a huge mountaintop appeared beside him and he felt like he was standing on top of the world.

"To address their needs, we have a well-equipped gym, regularly scheduled hikes, rock climbing walls of varying levels of challenge, and competitive sports.

"Every practice and game begin and ends with a Sharing Circle. They activate their prowess and then, as a group, tackle the wounds they share. Three guides are always present. One is the Keeper of the Heart to help them stay in their hearts. Another is a psychotherapist who helps them delve deeper, and the third is a coach who helps them clarify their goals and develop strategies for reaching them.

"For those working on an emotional level, we offer several forms of therapy: Primal Scream, Cathartic Expression, Reichian Energy and Breathwork, Hallucinogenic Therapy, Music Therapy, Sound Healing, Pujas, and others.

"For those who are most comfortable working on a Spiritual level, we offer support. Everyone has a Soul. Through the events of your life, your Soul acquires wounds. We do not compare battle wounds or put band aids on them. We are not interested in making you a better adjusted robotron who does what you are told.

"We are here to help you use your traumas to ferret out your core wounds, uncover your core beliefs, and see how these beliefs, (which were indoctrinated into you when you were very young) control you. We help you free yourself from the marionette strings that make you say and do things that are not in your best interest.

"Everyone has incarnated with a Life Mission. What is yours? Discovering the answer to this question is the Spiritual Path you are on. We will use rituals to mark your progress along your chosen path. If your religion supports your development, we respect the part it plays in your life. If your religion is thwarting you, we will help you explore other options. You need a higher force to connect with; otherwise, you will be a feather on the wind, tossed about and slammed by Destiny's whims.

"This has been an overview of the principles and framework we promote.

"Behind me are four chairs representing four approaches to therapy, one for each of the four aspects of human nature. I would like to invite four of our top therapists to represent four legendary path blazers who helped humanity advance. These four brilliant and insightful disciplines are powerful tools for understanding and living life.

"We will take a five-minute break for you to move and stretch."

James was grateful for this opportunity to move around. He was glad that he was able to fit all these meetings in, so he could advance quickly, but sitting through so many lectures was challenging.

When they were ready to begin again, Alberto stepped forward and said, "Let me introduce our guest speakers.

"Representing a physical earthy style of therapy, we offer the work of Virginia Satir. I would like to turn the stage over to Gilda who is trained in Transformational Systemic Therapy, Satir's style of family therapy.

"Thank you, Alberto, that was a very informative overview." Turning back to the audience, she said, "In Virginia's words, "Feelings of worth can flourish only in an atmosphere where individual differences are appreciated, mistakes are tolerated, communication is open, and rules are flexible - the kind of atmosphere that is found in a nurturing family."

Gilda came down from the stage and walked through the rows as she explained, "The process I offer, works to improve the connections between family members. We address the problems underneath common behaviors to see how family members impact each other."

As she marched through the rows, she stopped at one big buff man and said to him, "Sir, please go up on the stage."

"I like to use people to demonstrate the principles I teach.

"You, Miss, please join him.

"Right now, I am picking these people to build a family unit.

"You, with all the piercings and tattoos, please go to the stage.

"Today we will look at different styles of family structure.

"You, in the next row, please go up." She pointed to the stage.

"We also put on plays where everyone has a part. You are both the audience and the actor. One person is the director and everyone else takes the part of one of the Director's ancestors to demonstrate how issues are passed down through a lineage.

Gilda returned to the stage and told the man to stand on a chair overlooking the family. She put boxing gloves on the woman standing beneath him. The daughter with all the piercings and tattoos was asked to wear a lion mask with sharp teeth and growl. The son, who turned out to be a rather short man in his forties with the air of a teenager, was asked to sit down on the floor with his back to the others.

"In an actual Process Group, this is where we would begin. During our session, you can talk about how you feel when you play your part. You can also sculpt others to demonstrate your issues. We understand that people resonate with other people's issues, so undoubtedly someone else in the group will have similar issues even if it is packaged in different circumstances. The core pain and suffering are the same. Thus, when you act out someone else's drama, you can resonate with the experience."

Gilda gave a brief half bow and sat down.

Alberto returned to center stage and announced, "Addressing emotional needs, is the work of Carl Rogers presented today by Raj."

Raj remained seated, leaned forward and spoke to the audience like they were his brother sitting beside him in front of a fire.

"I feel your pain. It makes me admire your courage. I look at all your yearning faces and my heart goes out to you. I wish you could have had an easier life. I wish your path could have been paved with love. I am so sorry it was not. I am here for you, not as your Guide. I don't think I could guide anyone who is holding the map. I am here to hold up a mirror or hand you the tools you need. If you work with me, we can breathe together, we can cry together, we can lament, savor, remember, and forgive together.

"Our group will meet in the hot tub down in the gym and in the sauna. Sometimes we will meet at night in a candlelit room. We will walk this path together and hold each other up, if need be. We will be looking for the naked truth, threads of truth that you can consciously use to weave your own unique garment which will serve you in the world.

"Thank you for letting me be part of this great pioneering endeavor to transform human consciousness one person at a time." He smiled with great sincerity and looked around the room making eye contact with many people in the audience.

Alberto's voice rang through the mic announcing, "Our next speaker is Shareen. She will share with you how she uses the mind to shine the light of awareness back upon itself and introduce you to a process called *the Chain of Questions*.

Shareen took center stage and said, "*The Chain of Questions* was developed by Nicholette Pavlevsky. This technique was born out of her own healing process. The work starts with a client describing a problem they are having. The therapist begins asking a series of questions to uncover the primary emotion underlying the problem. The quest takes the client deeper and deeper as he recalls other experiences that also had this same emotion attached to it. These questions lead the mind into the beliefs underlying the events. By following the emotion through several experiences, and following the accompanying beliefs, it leads the mind to uncover the core belief that is generating these problems."

Alberto smiled and said into his Micro Mic, "Thank you Shareen. Next, to introduce you to the Spiritual Realm, the greatest deep-sea diver into the unconscious realm was Carl Jung. Marlena will acquaint you with his brilliant work."

"Jung was truly a Renaissance Man," said Marlena in a strong stage voice as she strode to the center of the stage. "He combined a vast array of different disciplines to understand human consciousness. Through psychology, astrology, mythology, art, mysticism, and many other unorthodox methods, he explored the Soul and delved into the deep psyche. His pioneering work uncovered truths about the core of our being never before known. In the depths of human consciousness, he found radiantly divine immortal forces, which he called *Archetypes*. Following his lead, you can experience your own inner divinity.

"Jung did not see people as flawed creatures stumbling through life entangled in random chaos. He saw meaningful, purposeful, orderly, unfolding forces moving the individual towards their Destiny.

"Charles Bebeau modernized Jung's work to create Archetypal Psychotherapy. He incorporated a wide variety of therapeutic techniques to help his clients see the amazing synchronicities happening in their lives. He interpreted the symbols in these synchronicities, to show that the same meaningful patterns were present in their inner and outer lives. Interpreting the patterns revealed that their psyche was always moving towards a healing purpose, a Soul Mission.

"All the strange, wonderful, terrible experiences of your life have made you the exact right kind of person to fulfill your Soul Mission. Therefore, our groups work to uncover the meaning, purpose, and order in the events of your life, so you can discover your Soul Mission." Marlena smiled and went back to her seat.

Alberto returned to center stage to end the lecture. "Thank you to all our therapists for sharing an overview of some of the different therapeutic processes we offer. Here in Trinitus, you can choose your own pathway. We recognize that many of you are diverse in nature, so you can choose one school of thought or mix and match. In doing your Personal Process, you are free to choose any lens that enhances your awareness. We acknowledge that you are the captain of this journey. First, your Guide, then your Counselor, will be your First Mate, your Confidant, the person who holds the other end of your tether when you go out on a limb.

"Here in our community, everyone is working on being self-aware and is required to do some form of Personal Process every day while you live in Trinitus.

"You can choose from one of the disciplines presented here today or from another. We offer many. You can stay with one or change periodically, as long as you are continuing to learn, grow, and transform into a happy healthy version of yourself. How you choose to do it is up to you. You are in charge of yourself.

"We see you. Thank you for attending *Introduction to Personal Process*. There will be no Discussion Group or Sharing Circle today. We have tables set up around the room where you will find a schedule for the Process Groups that are being held this week. I recommend that each time you choose a group, you stay with it for a week, at least, before choosing to experience another one. After that, the choice is up to you. Thank you for joining us. I wish you a peaceful day."

James walked around the room twice before he came to a decision. "Oh, Tim, how can I choose. I want to do them all."

"Close your eyes and with your mind's eye look at each therapist who presented. Which one gave you that feeling of 'aha!'"

James tried it and immediately felt that the *Chain of Questions* was the most doable. The others felt weighty in some way. This one seemed more straightforward, and he thought it would be easier.

"I think I'll sign up for the *Chain of Questions*. It seems to be the quickest method. I need the answers right away. The others may go deeper, but I don't think I am ready for them yet."

After James signed up, he walked out with Tim.

"We still have a few minutes before lunch," said Tim. "Would you like to take a walk in the garden?" He always preferred being outdoors.

"I don't know. I need to think about all that stuff they talked about. Maybe I should go to my room.

"How about strolling in the garden? The labyrinth is for thinking. As you walk, you relax your mind and listen. If you hold a question in your heart as you slowly walk, and feel your feet upon the ground, by the time you reach the end, you often find you have the answer that was always within you." Tim smiled patiently.

"Isn't it just easier if you tell me the answer? You have been doing this longer than me. What good is a Guide, if he doesn't tell you the answers?"

"A Guide that helps you find your own answers. Remember the parable about giving a man a fish? If you give a man a fish, he will eat for a day. Teach a man to fish and he will eat for the rest of his life."

"I don't want any fish!" James quipped.

Tim gave him a wrinkled brow look.

"Just kidding, but I am floundering here," James cajoled.

"Very funny; walk the labyrinth and we can talk afterwards."

"You're not going to make me walk that thing again, are you?" James said in lighthearted protest.

Tim laughed. "It is not out to get you, you know. It is just a meditation."

"I like to go straight at things, not go in circles. I would rather spend some time in my room." James chided.

"Well, I can see that. Call me when you are ready."

"Thanks," James called over his shoulder as he dashed to the elevator, glad to escape.

Back in his room, safe at last, James needed some time to think.

The free room and board were very attractive; he liked Tim and was thrilled at the idea that he could practice architectural design again. It all sounded like a dream come true; but...and it was a big but, he was really scared at this idea of having people prowling around in his head.

Finally, after wearing a hole in the carpet, he decided to call Tim and tell him he was going to skip lunch.

"Tim did not protest. James was relieved.

'What to do now?' he asked himself. He ordered lunch delivered to his room and decided to write that letter to his wife that he had been avoiding. After a staring contest with the ComPad, he put his new clothes in the closet. Back at the ComPad he wrote, 'Dear Judy.' He imagined her reading the letter and decided to take a shower, then lunch arrived and he ate heartily.

With the room neat, his body clean and refueled, he ran out of ways to procrastinate, so he sat himself down and willed the ComPad to write itself. He knew it could design an appropriate letter for him but that felt like cheating. After a brief debate with himself (he was torn between using the auto-write and the need to tell his own truth) he wrote the first few words.

It was not easy for him to be frank with her even in a letter. He told her that he was staying here and why. Then he explained what the city was all about as best he could without getting into too much detail. He also repeated his intention to pay the bank everything he owed and give her child support.

He thought about her credit cards, got angry, marched around the room, threatened to smash one of the lamps, cooled down, and stared at the ComPad again. Then courageously wrote the nine bravest words he could think of, 'I am not going to pay your credit accounts.'

He poured himself another cup of herbal coffee from the insulated pitcher that came with his lunch and paced around a few more times.

He settled down again and felt a little calmer as he wrote, "If the kids want to visit me, I need to know. I need to choose between a house for them and a simple apartment for me alone." His hand just seemed to write the rest of the letter while his brain numbed out. It felt like his whole life was fading out. He pictured the house, the car, the neighborhood, the office, all that seemed very far away and long ago, though only a couple of days had passed. It was as though the man who lived that life no longer existed. He also wasn't a member of this community yet. He was just a phantom standing in between.

He heard his father's voice in his head saying, "Men don't cry." That thought was enough to stem this threat of emotion that was threatening to rise in him. He squared his shoulders, finished the letter and wrote, "I am sorry it has come to this. It was inevitable."

He told himself the letter was finished, but it didn't feel finished. He downed the rest of the coffee and stared angrily at the ComPad as though it was its fault that he could not catch the half thought that flashed through his mind. It came through a couple of times, but each time he forgot what it was before he could write it.

He stared at what he had written so far, and then remembered, it was the word, *Divorce*. Slowly, almost mechanically he wrote, "I want a divorce right now. We do not have to wait until the kids go to college. We do not have to stay together torturing each other each day. I want to set you free and I want to be free. This is what you always said you wanted, so now you can have it. You have wasted away all our money. I had to borrow from the kid's college fund to pay your debts. So now there is nothing left. You have milked us dry."

He read it over, and much to his surprise, tears escaped his guard and rolled down his cheek. 'Why am I crying?' he thought, 'It's all her fault. She got us in this financial mess to begin with. It was inevitable.'

He suddenly remembered the $3,000 he invested in his friend's scheme, the one that went belly up. He brushed the thought aside. This was just a pittance of what they owed. Another thought slipped into his mind; there was that huge hospital bill last summer when Sammy broke his arm. He brushed that aside too and reaffirmed that this mess was ALL her fault for overspending on stuff they don't even need. It was her foolishness that put them over the top and made it so hard to catch up.

The letter was done, finished, all there in print. He took a deep breath and was about to hit SEND, when he began to doubt himself, so he decided to show it to Tim first.

Writing this letter made it feel more final. His tidal wave of emotion subsided. He did not throw the ComPad against the wall, though the thought crossed his mind. The lamp still sat on the table unmolested. He felt proud of himself. Maybe all this brain stuff was working.

He splashed some cold water on his face, to clear his mind and called Tim.

"Sorry I missed lunch. I needed to digest all that stuff from this morning. And I wrote that letter to my wife. Could you look at it before I send it?"

"Can you meet me in the garden?" Tim tried to draw him out again.

"No, please come to my room," James whined.

Tim arrived and took a seat. "We see you. Did you finish your letter?"

"Yes, but I value your opinion. Could you read it over and tell me if I said everything I should?"

Tim looked at his charge. The poor man looked like he had come through a battle. His hair was sticking up from all the times he ran his hands through it. His face looked drained and pale.

"What did you decide to do? Mediation or do you still want to file for a divorce?"

James said in little more than a whisper, "Divorce."

"Are you sure?" He raised that eyebrow again.

James nodded like a bobbing head loose on a spring.

"Alright, you can see our lawyer tomorrow at 3:00. But feel free to cancel at any time if you reconsider."

"Why would I reconsider? Do you think I am making a mistake? Oh, this is all happening so fast!" James was troubled.

"Is it too fast?" Tim was concerned.

"I am just scared of making a mistake. The idea makes me sad. I know I must do this."

Tim took the ComPad and read it. "You gave a nice description of Hope. It says everything you told me you want to say, but the ending could use a little softening. Don't you think it sounds a bit harsh, critical, and blaming. It is full of *hooks* and insults."

Reluctantly James reworked the end a couple of times until Tim said it was ready.

Tim said, "I think it sounds good now. What do you think? Are you ready to send it?"

James gave a deep sigh. He wanted to say, "I liked it better before we made the changes. I am so not ready. But he knew he was, so he mumbled, "Yeah, I guess so," and sighed loudly again.

"How are you feeling now?" Tim asked with a quizzical brow. "You sound like you're having an issue with this."

James nodded. "Well, it's just that I feel like a failure, like I should have been able to work things out with her, like this is just one more thing I blotched up. I know I need to put an end to our empty marriage. Judy is just too stubborn to change, and I'm too tired to work through this right now. She is going to divorce me anyway, so that's that. I'm staying here and that's that too. It is unavoidable no matter what."

"I understand that it hurts, but you can work with it. Here in Hope, you do not have to avoid feeling the sadness. No one will judge you for feeling your emotions. It is okay to let go and be sad for a while. It is a lot healthier than giving yourself a hard time or trying to avoid your feelings.

"Well, this just sucks!" James tossed his hands in the air. "The real failure here is that I got in this relationship in the first place. I didn't know who she really was back then. Why did this happen to me? Why did I stay in such an abusive relationship?"

Tim assumed James was just feeling sorry for himself and chose not to respond. He waited for his charge to work the feeling through. When he felt the energy shift in James, he said, "Whenever you are ready, hit SEND and it will go to the external ComScreen. Nicole will forward it to Judy.

"Drum roll," quipped James as he dramatically pushed the button. Suddenly he felt a light sense of relief, and a heavy sense of finality, all at the same time.

"What would you like to do now?

"I signed up for a Process Group tomorrow after breakfast. I don't want to go to any more lectures or groups for today. I am saturated."

"I suggest you go out of this room and find something to do in town. You have done enough learning and accomplishing for one day," with that he left.

Once Tim was gone, James went out on the porch until he felt too restless. He turned on the ComScreen but there was nothing he wanted to watch. He plopped down onto bed and lay there a while lost in thought. His mind reviewed his two long days in Hope. Things were moving fast! He liked Tim, felt he was sincerely caring, and his ideas made sense. A couple of times it felt like Tim had lifted a veil and showed him how things should work. He was happy here, but he could not relax. Part of him was waiting for the other shoe to drop. This place felt so unbelievably good that he assumed that something was inevitably going to go wrong. He was not used to things going right.

James went down to the Book Club and thumbed through, *Anger's Hidden Secret* and *A New God, A New World,* but tossed them aside. He didn't feel like reading.

Then he remembered Tim saying that he needed something that was just fun, so he hopped on the tram and went to town. When he passed a bowling alley, he remembered how much he had liked bowling as a kid. He hadn't done it in decades, so he hopped off the tram and went inside. He played a couple of games by himself and had a fried chicken dinner.

When he returned, he was exhausted, so he fell right into bed. He felt good. It was refreshing to do something that required no thinking, no processing, and no talking. Since he was only wearing a Black Band, and was out without his Guide, he had to use E-Money from his Smartwatch. At least, that felt normal.

The next morning there was no lecture in the dining room, which was a relief. James ate a hearty breakfast and then headed to the Book Club for Personal Process, feeling like a kid entering his first day in preschool, all excited, scared, and nervous.

He sat down next to Akisha, from the Affirmation class, and a minute later Godfrey joined them. They were all grateful to be among familiar faces.

The room was humming as people took their seats. When the sound subsided, the facilitator stood up and said, "We see you. I am Shareen. Welcome to your first Personal Process session.

"In here, you will be given an opportunity to think about how and why you may feel a certain way. You will have opportunities to go beyond thinking about your problems to work on solving them.

"Sometimes the solutions people come up with are not beneficial in the long run. A person who suffers from negative ideas about themselves may come up with strategies for living that are based on avoiding pain, rather than on healing and removing the cause. One common strategy that doesn't work well is that of not letting relationships get too close, to keep from getting hurt. There is a lot of pain hidden behind that belief. This group can help resolve some of these issues.

"We do not always make the best choices. Sometimes deeper

needs arise from the unconscious and compel us to do things and we don't even know why. When we respond with anger, spite, jealousy, and fear, it is because deep, denied issues are being awakened, and they have gathered a list of grievances while they were hiding.

"After a long time, your beliefs take on a life of their own. They can control your thoughts and behavior to avoid being hurt the way you were before. Healing comes when you face the core trauma and reclaim the power you left back there.

"When you pay attention to a feeling in your body, it can take you back in time. You can ride an emotion, like a magic carpet, back to the time when this issue was first seeded. You become aware that you have felt this way many times. It is like many stops on a train taking you to the terminal, the first intense traumatic seeding of that belief.

"Today I am going to introduce you to the Nicholette Method, also known as the *Chain of Questions*. This process focuses on removing detrimental beliefs and bottled-up emotions from your unconscious. It will help you face beliefs from the past that are still hidden deep inside you and still causing anger and prejudice in the present and control your behavior.

"These beliefs may have made your life unmanageable. When you release negative beliefs, it allows you to have steady, balanced emotional interactions. Thus, people get along more peacefully. Here in the City of Hope, self-reflection has improved social interactions in families, business, and even in politics. Our Founder understood that self-reflection is crucial for creating a better society and a better way of life.

"Emotions may seem automatic, sometimes they are, especially when someone suddenly ignites you. If someone cuts you off on the freeway, it might be a knee jerk reaction to call them a vile name. If your partner cheats on you, it might plunge you into depression, anger, or a nasty divorce.

"Even when your first response is automatic, what comes next is choice. Your emotions are all based on the beliefs you hold. Many beliefs come from the society in which you live. It is the way you have been trained to react.

"We all hold beliefs in our unconscious that were ingrained into us when we were very young. Children grow up thinking they are inferior when their parents project their own self-hatred onto the child and say or do damaging things to them.

"Feeling inferior or unworthy becomes a Hot Button. Any situation that reminds them of this feeling will cause an explosion. If someone criticizes an idea they have, it can cause a volatile reaction because it touches that button.

"This is a compound emotion because the explosion occurs in the present, but the cause is rooted in the past. Any current situation that brings up memories associated with that button, will cause a charged response. That is why you need to defuse the underlying issue.

"Anytime you overreact, it indicates that a Hot Button is being activated. Your work is to follow the memories back to find the Core Button and the beliefs it holds."

Shareem invited four people to step forward and participate in a skit to demonstrate this principle. The roles are a child, his dad, the child as an adult, and a board member.

An older bald man was asked to play the dad. Shareem gave a younger man a ballcap to wear as the child. The script begins with the dad talking to the child about his little league game. The father scolds the kid for missing a pitch that he thought the boy should have hit.

"You are a horrible player. You embarrassed me" he shouts and shakes the boy by the shoulders. The child hangs his head and pouts.

In the next scene, another man plays the same child who is now an adult. He is a pharmaceutical executive presenting a new idea to his Board. One Board Member criticized his idea and said it is unworkable. The adult gets furious. He feels rejected and demeaned, just like his father used to do to him. He fumes and tries to coerce the Board Member into accepting his idea; then threatens to quit!

Shareen turned to the group and asked, "Who has an idea on how to resolve this situation?"

James thought the situation looked normal. Men get angry, that is just the way they are. He would have gotten angry in that situation. What was there to resolve?

Alisha raised her hand and stood up.

Shareen nodded to her and she said, "If it was me, I would first try to soothe the man. I would say, 'You misunderstood me, I'm not rejecting you. This idea may not be ready. Maybe I can help you rework it,' so he feels supported."

Godfrey stood up next and said, "I would remind him that I like him and say, 'that's why I went out for drinks with you last week. I still like you, but this idea just does not seem workable, and like Shareen, I would offer to help revise it."

"Thank you, but those are all good ideas for handling the situation in the present, and keep him from quitting, but will they keep him from exploding next time? Is there anything you can do to address that?"

Montgomery, a short thin man with neatly trimmed blue hair and huge holes in his ears stood up and said, "I am new to this process thing, but based on what you said today, and what people have said in other lectures, I guess I could say, "Your idea is not who you are. You are okay, but the idea is not. Why are you getting so angry? What is it about us not liking your idea that makes you feel we do not like you?

"Perhaps an idea you presented when you were young made you feel rejected, and that experience felt like this one in some way. Remember you can still be a great person, even if your idea is not.

"Would you like to tell me about the thing that happened when you were young, the one that made you feel so bad? I am your friend. I want to help you. You can tell me anything and I will not judge you.'

Then I would smile and patiently wait for him to say something."

Shareen said, "Thank you Montgomery. Well done. Your comment is an example of how people in the Trinitus City generally respond to an unwarranted outburst like this one.

"When Montgomery said, 'I am your friend. I want to help you. You can tell me anything and I will not judge you.' Montgomery was establishing rapport and letting the man know that he is a safe person to process with. This offers the man an opportunity to face the real problem on the spot. When people can be there for each other in this way, it creates a high level of trust between them. This is why our culture is different and disarming. We advocate processing on the spot with anyone who is ready to do so. This caring for each other makes us very different than the outer world."

"Out there, an overly intense reaction is generally met with a clash of egos, an argument ensues where both parties want to prove they are right and the other is wrong. Those kinds of arguments do not resolve anything. They just provide vessels for projected, rejected feelings and in the end both parties get hurt.

"When emotional situations polarize, as they do in that world, people become afraid to tell their truth. They don't talk about their feelings, but rather stuff them deep inside, which adds more situations and people to a grievance list they keep in their heads. The irony is that people do not talk about their feelings because they are afraid it will cause conflict; yet stuffing emotions guarantees future conflict because the pressure of denied emotions builds up inside. Acknowledging your true feelings is the only way to stop the experience from happening again."

"Every feeling you have is connected to a belief you have about yourself or about your world. When you look at your beliefs, look for a common thread running through your experiences. Uncover the negative self-deprecating and unloving beliefs that you have held for a long time. They are the ones attacking your self-worth and giving you issues."

"You can start by looking at any situation where you felt charged. Remember, the stronger the charge, the more important the underlying issue. Be honest with yourself.

"Put aside the details of who said or did what. Look for the true motive, need, or belief underneath. Try to remember prior events that felt like this one. They may hold the key to understanding why this kind of situation triggers you so much.

"This is probably a new practice for you. If you have never done this before, be patient. If you ever accuse yourself of anything negative, notice it. Babies don't think badly of themselves, that is a learned behavior. Someone put these hurtful ideas in the baby's head. Go back to a Beginner's Mind. Become an unbiased observer and acknowledge what you see. Look at your motives. What are you trying to prove, express, or heal?

"This is a challenging process, one that becomes easier over time.

Most people have been trained to ignore their feelings, so they are out of touch with themselves. They may have trouble remembering how these feelings started. Children are often trained to hide who they are and deny what they believe.

"When a child spills his milk, the parent doesn't always say, 'It is bad that the milk spilled.' They say, 'You are a bad boy for spilling the milk.' Thus, the action and your self-worth get mixed up together. An attack on your behavior becomes an attack on you.

"This may feel tedious at first because of your resistance, but it gets easier over time. Once you know your core beliefs and are familiar with what kinds of situations trigger you, fewer and fewer situations cause you to overreact because you have very few unresolved feelings to arise.

"Before we move on to the experiential part of the program, I want to cover one more dimension of working with beliefs. Not all of them are yours. There are many negative beliefs that almost everyone has. They define how life is. These ideas can be hard to uproot because they are everywhere. People accept them as universal truths, but they aren't. They were implanted into the minds of children to make them see themselves as good little worker bees.

"Beliefs like, I must work hard to be worthy, I have to earn respect, criminals don't deserve rights, and some races are superior to others, are cultural ideas that do not foster a loving supportive society. Our social norms need to grow like people do.

"Now to begin your Personal Process pick a partner, someone you would like to get to know better."

Once everyone was partnered up, Shareen said, "Now remember a recent aggravating experience." She paused for a minute to let them find the memory. "Decide which one of you will be the Teller who shares their story and who will be the Listener, who questions the storyteller. Now tell your partner about your recent experience."

She paused for a few minutes as a soft hum spread around the room. When the hum was beginning to subside, she told the Listeners to ask a *Chain of Questions*, like What did you feel? What were you thinking? What got you so upset? What meaning did you interpret from what they said? Keep going, be creative, see where it takes you."

Shareen relaxed and listened to the excited hum that filled the room. When the tone softened just a bit, she said, "Now tune into your body and notice what you are feeling. Recall another time when you had this feeling. Tell your partner about these experiences."

Shareen gave them plenty of time. She used the level of murmuring to gauge when they were ready to move on to the next step.

"Pay attention to your emotions and let them take you back into an earlier time. Ask yourself what is similar in all these experiences. Tune into the primary emotion you are feeling. Open yourself to uncover the fear connected with this feeling. Tune into the fear and look for the belief that goes with it. This takes rigorous honesty. Even if it feels painful, stay with it. These negative beliefs have been poisoning your life."

Michela, an older woman with green hair mixed with purple and blue streaks and silver threads tied up in braids around her head, chose James to be her partner.

They introduced themselves and Michela listened patiently while James told her about the phone call he had with his wife and how furious he got over it.

"Why did you get so angry when she blamed you for losing your job. You knew it wasn't true."

"Because I wasn't to blame!"

"Of course not, but why did you feel angry? What was under the anger?"

That really stumped him. "Anger is just anger."

"What do you think she meant by accusing you of not making yourself indispensable?

"She was telling me I am ineffectual and stupid."

"Did she say you were ineffectual and stupid or were those the words you heard in your head?"

That took him back for a second. "I know that is what she meant."

"That is your belief. Do you think you are stupid?

"I'm not stupid and it is insulting to have her assume I am."

Shareen instructed, "Remember to take the story details into the emotions underneath as soon as it feels appropriate."

"When have people assumed you are stupid?" Michela asked, trying to follow his version of what happened.

"They do it at work all the time and my wife Judy says something almost every day."

"How does that make you feel?

"It is infuriating."

"What kinds of situations make you feel like people think you are stupid?

"My boss repeats everything he says to me twice, like he thinks I did not get it the first time."

Michela had an insight into James and wanted to share it but wasn't sure how he would take it. Bravely she ventured, "He may repeat himself because he is not sure that he said it well enough the first time. It may not be a reflection on you, but rather on him, did you ever think of that?"

"No. I assumed he was doing it because he thinks I am stupid."

"Is there any reason you might be afraid that you are stupid and that scares you, so you cover it with anger?

James felt the room too warm, and he was getting bored with this ridiculous game. He wanted it to be over so he could leave.

Michela waited patiently for a few minutes and then repeated her question. "Is there any chance you might think you are stupid?"

"My father sure did. He never missed an opportunity to tell me I was. Nothing I ever did was ever good enough for him. I hated math, but I studied my head off and got a B. Given that my last grade was a D, I was quite proud of my accomplishment. Do you think my father appreciated all the work I put into getting that B? No. He just rattled on about how I was too dumb to get good grades. I was so mad, I wished he was little, and I was big, so I could punch him. He died before I got big enough to show him.

"Do you still hear him in your head telling you, you are stupid?"

"Yes, I guess I do. I feel stupid sometimes. Like around Judy. I often don't know what she wants from me. I'm not just worried that she thinks I am stupid. Sometimes I feel stupid."

James realized he had said too much and felt embarrassed. He was angry that she tricked him into confessing his secret.

Michela sensed his discomfort and noticed his color turning darker, so she quickly said, "Wow! That was great work. I hope I can do as well, when it is my turn. You are a natural at this."

Her kind words made the anger drain away. She sat quietly for a moment to let it all sink in.

James suddenly realized that he thought everyone saw him as stupid. At work, at home, when he was a kid at school, everyone. In a flash, he saw how he always felt hurt by what he thought, they thought. He realized it could have all been in his mind and he was hurting himself, the way his father always hurt him. Suddenly a flood of tears welled up. Before he could pull himself together, big round tears were rolling down his cheeks. Michela just patiently waited for him to move through it.

"I used to see a therapist," shared Michela, "and she told me that crying is a good thing. She said lots of her big burly clients cry. She called it a 'catharsis' and said it is part of the release process, when an energy becomes unblocked. Those tears of yours were hard earned. I hope I do as well when it is my turn."

Shareen observed that several attendees were crying, so to reassure them she said, "Crying is a catharsis. It is part of the process. It comes when you access the anger and move through to the hurt underneath. When the negative feeling is ready to be released, it pours out of you. Well done. Many of you have reached a catharsis. Now that you have faced the truth, now that you have faced a negative belief that had its fangs in you, causing you problems and pain, you have set yourself free from its influence. The next time it tries to raise its ugly head, you can say to yourself, I am not anymore, and I probably never was."

"When you change how you see yourself in the past, you will find that you see yourself differently in the present."

After a few minutes Shareen said, "Allow your experience to come to closure for now. You can revisit this process whenever you want. On your own, you can play both parts, the Teller and the Listener.

She waited a few minutes and asked each couple to change places. Now the previous Listeners had a chance to tell their story and the process began again.

CHAPTER 5

Trauma

James slept deeply and woke up early. He thought he was still in his old bed until he opened his eyes and found himself in this new life. The anticipation of new discoveries pulled him out of bed. He quickly showered, dressed, and was off to discover what this day would hold. In the dining room, he went to the buffet table at the rear, where he found a wonderful array of foods, all healthy and delicious. He took a taste of an unidentified egg dish and then filled his plate with it. It still surprised him that healthy food could taste so good. This delicious, scrambled egg dish had an assortment of interesting flavors, some meaty and other vegetables. He had to admit he liked it better than his usual bacon and eggs.

James scanned the room looking for someone he recognized. Of the twenty or so people sitting in clusters around the room, he recognized one, Cathy Cartwright. He strolled over to her. She was writing in her journal and did not notice him until he was standing next to her.

"Good morning, Cathy, how are you today?" he asked with a bright smile.

Looking up from her writing, she smiled. "Oh, it's James, right? It's good to see you. How is it going?"

"Pretty good. I've decided to stay. I really like this place." He smiled brightly, took a bite of eggs and wanted to moan. They were so creamy and rich.

"Me too. I'm staying. I will graduate today. I'm getting my Red Band. In fact, later this morning, I am going to look at apartments with my Guide."

"Does that mean you finished all your intro stuff?"

"Sure does. I attended all the required lectures, three process groups, got a good report from my Guide, and today I am going to take my vows. Please come and watch."

"How long have you been here?"

"Well, let me think. It feels like years, but in fact, I was here for a week as a visitor, I came to attend a special workshop that my therapist recommended. I fell in love with the place and stayed. I had a Black Band for a week. I guess I've been here a little over two weeks.

"I am glad you're staying too. I attended a few lectures and a process group. I sure hope it gets easier. It feels like my brain is being scrubbed."

She laughed at the image, reached for the pink salt and sprinkled it on the omelet sitting forgotten beside her journal.

"What are you doing today?" She asked just to make

conversation.

"The usual, lectures and group, but there is one other thing." Would saying it out loud jinx it or make it more real, anyway he was reluctant to admit it. He reminded himself that it is inevitable, and bravely confessed to Cathy, "I'm seeing a lawyer this afternoon to file for a divorce," and savored another bite of eggs.

"Wow! Divorce? Is that a good thing or a bad?" She closed her journal and took a sip of hot fennel tea.

"Well, it was inevitable, it's what my wife wants, and it will probably be good for me too. What about you? Are you getting divorced?"

"What? I am not ready to focus on anything other than becoming a member of Hope. I don't know who I will be when I am a Blue Band. I may see the world and even my ex in a different light; but for now, I have erased him from my mind. She waved her hand around encompassing everyone, her pen like a wand still in her hand. "I am totally working on being in the here and now."

James nodded knowingly, but as usual he could not understand where she was coming from. "I need to get my life settled before I can turn my attention to the things they do here. All I know is that I am staying here for now. I like the free rent and good food. I'll stay at least until I get the divorce and put my life in order. I've got kids to consider before I can think about housing. I'll talk to the lawyer about custody."

"I hope that goes well for you. I can't imagine having to deal with kids in my situation."

"Well, I'll see. I don't think I'll get custody. My kids don't seem to want to have anything to do with me."

"Why do you think that?"

James sighed. "They always have their nose up against a screen and treat me like a phantom, a background noise. They don't want to do anything with me anymore, and they answer me in one syllable, usually a grunt. I can't imagine they would part with their screens and engage in life the way people do here. No. I think I'm on my own."

"I am sorry, that sounds sad. I guess we are both going through major transitions. Would you like to keep in touch to compare notes?

"Okay. I'm in room S18 for now. I'll probably stay there until I figure out this custody thing with my kids."

"S18, got it. I'll get in touch with you after I settle into my new place." They exchanged Smartwatch numbers.

Making a friend seemed like a step closer to belonging here. The conversation became light and not as personal after that, which James found a relief. He liked Cathy, but she was intense sometimes.

"Come to my graduation if you can. It is at 3:00 today."

"3:00? Sorry, that is when I am meeting with the lawyer. Good Luck. I am sure you will do great."

She tried not to look disappointed. Graduating without anyone there to witness it felt a little lonely. "Think of me when you enter the lawyer's office. Then you will be with me in spirit. Now, I am off to meet my Guide, wish me luck. I just want a cozy little apartment walking distance from work. I am not sure what kind of work they will give me, but that will come soon enough." She took a last sip of tea, gathered her dishes and stood up. "Have a great day," she said as she turned to leave.

James took a breath and said, "We see you."

She laughed and said, "We see you. I'm glad you're staying."

James was just leaving the dining room when someone called his name. He turned to see Jordan. It took him a minute to remember where they had met. "Hi. You're from that Anger Management Group I visited, right?"

"Yes," said Jordan. "I am on my way to a meeting right now. Are you going?"

James was about to say no, when a voice in his head said, "Why not?"

Spontaneously, James said yes and fell into step beside Jordon. Katja was setting up the chairs in a circle when they arrived, so they pitched in and helped her. There were still a few minutes before the group was to begin, so Jordan and James sat down and waited.

Katja welcomed everyone and asked Jorden to begin the group with a brief check-in. He said, "I'm doing well with people these days. No one has pissed me off in weeks, but I can't say as much for my relationship with God. I try to walk the straight and narrow, but one can easily fall off a narrow path."

Katja made a mental note to ask Jordon why he believes his path must be that exacting. She assumed his beliefs came from growing up in a strict religious household. She planned to ask him questions that would lead him to discover this truth for himself. As a therapist, she knew realizations were far more powerful when the client discovers them for themselves.

"James, would you like to share next?" she asked. Last time James said, pass, but his time he felt ready to speak.

"I understand where Jordon is coming from. I also have a lot of anger at God. I used to love God, but when he stole my mother away from me, I never forgave him." Katja made a note to ask James later why he blames God for his mother's death.

Sergio went next. James felt so exhilarated after admitting this to the group that he could not pay attention to the next few people sharing. He was consumed by waves of anger, humiliation, release, and guilt. Each wave rose up after the last. Mostly he was aware of an intense pounding in his heart. Suddenly he had a migraine headache and felt dizzy. He had been getting these headaches for the past year ever since his father died last spring. They didn't usually come over him so quickly. He gripped his head and closed his eyes.

Katja saw the blood draining from James's face and wondered if he was going to faint. She kept an eye on him while the others shared. As soon as she could, she brought the focus back to him.

"James are you alright?" she asked. Jordan quietly put his hand on James's shoulder to help him stay in his body.

"Yeah, I'm fine," he lied. "It's just a little migraine. I'm sure it will pass soon, no need to fuss. I'll be fine in a minute." James was so embarrassed.

"There is no such thing as a 'little' migraine. Some intense energy must be causing it," she prodded. "What are you holding back? What is it that wants to be expressed but is difficult for you to say?"

He hadn't thought about it in years, but suddenly, the rage flooded back into him. "I am furious at God for taking my mother and my faith away." Tears threatened but he fought to hold them back.

"Your emotions are powerful things," said Katja "If you hold them back, eventually they can wreak havoc on your body. If you let it out, the pressure will subside.

"I just remembered something I had forgotten long ago." James could not believe he was going to tell this deep secret to a group of strangers, but he desperately wanted the pressure to subside.

"I was only six when my mother was first diagnosed with cancer. First it was breast cancer, then ovarian cancer, and finally bone cancer. I was fifteen when she died. I remember her being sick all the time."

His mind was suddenly filled with memories of his mothers' death. "She told me God would heal her, if he wanted to. She also said, if he decided to take her, she was okay with that too. She read the Bible and prayed every day, but no miracle came. I spent a lot of time when I was growing up, sitting by my mother's bedside, drawing fantasy cityscapes. I dreamed of drawing backgrounds for comic books back then.

"When she died, I was furious with God for taking her and for not giving her the miracle she needed to get well. When she was dying, she told me to be brave and make my father proud of me.

"Then the last thing she did before she died was hand me her Bible. What was I going to do with a stupid Bible? It didn't save her! I ran out into the backyard and told God to go to hell. Then I burned His Bible in my mother's precious rose garden."

The words poured out of James without his permission. They came through him like a tidal wave, and he could not stop them. Exhausted, he just sat staring at the floor, remembering that day, long ago, when he lost his mother.

The tears finally flowed, breaking through the barriers of his determination, washing away the terrible pressure in his head. He could not stop the flood. It had a will of its own. When it subsided, his headache was gone, and he felt utterly spent.

"Katja was silent for a minute. She let him ride the emotion until it released him. When the tears began to subside, she asked him if he still believes his mother's death was God's fault, or did he also believe it was the natural consequence of her disease?

"It was God's fault. He could have saved her. Somebody should have. My father used to stomp around the house, with a bottle in one hand and a fist in the other. He blamed God too."

"Tell us about your father. This must have been terrible for him too. He lost his wife and had to raise two boys by himself."

"He did the best he could!" James's tone was getting louder.

"Did he comfort you after she died?" she asked.

"Men don't cry. Crying is just for sissies. We had to buck up and get on with it," he barked at her.

She could hear in the rote way he recited these words that they were a quote from his father.

"You must have had strong emotions when she died, what outlet did you find for them?"

"We carried on as best we could. We were men and we had to be strong." This sounded like more quotes from his father.

"That must have put a lot of pressure on you. You were still so young." Katja sounded understanding, but she knew the statement would infuriate him. She also understood that James needed to blow up. He needed an intense emotion to get past his defenses and excuses, to see the truth of the matter. She understood that he, like many people, is protecting his father from blame for the traumas that he experienced as a child.

"Are you saying I'm mad at my father? NO!" he screamed. "My father was a good man. He worked very hard to put my brother and me through college, while paying off my mother's medical bills. He did his best. If anything, I look up to him and wish I could live up to his standards. He was a good man. Aloof and strict, but a good man. Everything he did was for my own good."

Katja knew his last few words were another quote. She needed to push him just a little further to get past his resistance and face the truth.

"I am sorry, you're right," she said softly, "I know nothing about your father and what your life was like growing up. Katja paused. "I was just wondering if your anger with God and your anger at your father are related."

"I AM NOT ANGRY AT MY FATHER!" he roared. "Everything he did was to make me a man. He had to do it. I was soft, too much of a mama's boy. It is a brutal world out there!" James felt a lump in his throat. His voice was still loud. Flames of anger were gripping him. "That's Love. My father was just looking out for me! He was right! I needed to be better and stronger to face the future. He knew I was too weak to make it in this dog-eat-dog world. He knew I would be a failure, and he was trying to save me from my fate."

Anger and grief had James in their grip. He could no longer sit still, so he jumped up and started pacing around the room. No one tried to stop him. They just looked sad, commiserating with his pain. He lengthened his strides around the room.

James pursed his lips and was fighting back his anger. He told himself that Katja was just trying to help. He wasn't sure he believed that.

After a few minutes, his pace slowed down. He found his voice and said, "You don't know anything about my father or me! I will control myself because I need all the help I can get right now, but in my heart, I really want to punch someone." His hands bunched into fists as he fought the rising urge to smash them into her all-knowing face.

Katja let him blow off the steam for a minute and then asked, "Are you saying that you think his anger was a show of love?"

"Yes, why? Do you think he was too mean? You think he was too hard on me, don't you? I thought so when I was young, but I understand him now that I'm older. I was too soft. He was right. I am a hopeless failure just like he said. Look at how badly I failed him." James stopped and leaned against the wall. The anger drained away and the tears returned.

"I am so embarrassed! Look at what you did to me! In front of everybody!" he accused.

"Don't worry about what we think," soothed Katja. "We are not judging you. We all have similar issues. What matters is the hurt you are feeling. We all carry similar pain. The source of our pain may be different, but we all carry it. This is what sparks anger and self-judgement.

"It is important for you to see that the pain comes from the beliefs implanted in you when you were young. You do not have to believe them anymore. You can let them go. You have the power to free yourself from now on." She spoke softly.

"This is why I ran away from home. I felt like a failure. I always do." The tears kept coming. Then he sank to the floor. "I always feel like a failure. He was right. He was right. I have always failed." James was talking about his wife and kids, his time in college, about not being an architectural designer, and about all the miserable jobs he was fired from.

He suddenly realized he was living out his father's prophecy that he would be a failure.

James stopped his frantic pacing and returned to his seat. He took a deep breath, and all the intense emotions subsided. He looked at Katja and said in utter defeat, "My father always said I would be a failure, and he was right."

"Remember, beliefs create reality. What were the beliefs that were creating your reality? Keep breathing. Deepen your breath. Make each one deeper than the last and see if you can find the underlying beliefs that created your reality."

"My father loved me. He knew I was not good enough at anything. I did everything I could to please him, but I failed. I always fail. He was right, I would always fail." His words rang in his head. There it was the core belief that drove him and made him screw up whenever things were going well.

Jordan quietly placed a hand on James's shoulder again as he sat there beside him. He did not say a word.

Katja said, "Keep breathing. You are doing great. You found the core belief behind the things you think of as your failures. You have had this core belief at least since your mother died, maybe longer. You believe you are a failure, so you set up the events in your life to fail to prove your father was right. Since you believed that you would fail, you did. You proved what you believed to be true. You did not fail because you were not good enough. You failed because you believed you would."

"Why would I do that? I've tried hard not to fail. This world didn't make it easy. It wasn't my fault the economy sucks, and my company had to lay people off. I am a victim of this unfair world!" James was shouting again, as he wiped his tears away.

"You're right. It is true that this world does not make it easy for someone to succeed. It is also true that you can create goals that are too lofty. You can also wind up creating debts if you let people push you into things you didn't really want. Not choosing to act is an unconscious invitation for trouble later. Since you believed you would fail. You consciously or unconsciously, actively or passively, attracted or created circumstances and people that led to failure."

To give James a chance to rest, Katja turned to the group and explained, "Our brains carve out pathways to beliefs, to emotions, and to all the information you ever learned. When we access those pathways often, they become like superhighways. That's why we repeat the same patterns over and over. When we get on one of those superhighways, it takes us to the same old place automatically. When you want to get to a new destination, you must consciously carve out a new road and travel it enough times to make it the primary pathway. Once you recognize your old patterns, and decide not to get sucked into them again, that carves out a new pathway. Habit sets your proverbial feet on the old path. It is up to you to assert your will and consciously decide to take the new road. Eventually, the old highway fades from disuse and the new road becomes your automatic response. You have rewired your brain, so to speak, to make good choices and access healthier more supportive beliefs with their accompanying emotions. It is a worthwhile endeavor, but it takes practice to make the new pathway become your normal choice.

"For you James, this old superhighway that your father carved out when you were young, led to failure. Now that you have uncovered the belief, you can consciously carve out another highway, one that leads to confidence and success. The important thing now is to change the belief that you are a failure, to a belief that you are a good man doing his best within challenging circumstances."

"James, you have made a great breakthrough, breaking ground for a new highway rather than automatically getting on that old superhighway to anger," Katja said encouragingly.

"Yeah really? I feel like punching someone right now!"

Katja spoke even softer, slower, and more gently than usual when she said, "Yes, but you told me what you are feeling, instead of automatically letting them control you, and make you do something you will regret later. You took a step back from letting them control you. That is the difference.

"With practice, it will become second nature to feel, observe, and choose your responses. You will become more and more aware of how it feels when a hot button is being triggered. Then, instead of blaming someone for pushing it, you can consciously step onto the new highway in your brain.

"The new road will lead you to the question, "Why are these words triggering me? Then the focus will shift from, 'that miserable person out there' to 'what is my next assignment, what issue in me is ready to be addressed?'"

It is always your choice. You choose whether to repeat old unhealthy patterns or choose a new one. The first rise of anger may be automatic, so you are not responsible for feeling that first spark, but what you choose at that moment is up to you. Are you going to let yourself be swept away on that old hurtful highway or choose to travel the new conscious healthy one?"

"So, you're saying all this intense feeling I went through today is not enough. I'm not cured of these compulsions. Then why did I go through all this?" He was just a hair's breadth away from having a fit of rage.

"Are you saying, my feelings are not real? They feel real to me." James was getting confused, and his anger was beginning to rise again.

Katja explained in a soft, kind voice, "From one perspective your emotions feel very real, but when your perspective changes, those emotions simply do not come up. These feelings are real only because of the beliefs that support them. When you change your belief, the feelings will change to match."

"Okay, so you are not saying my feelings aren't real, if I understand you, you are saying when my beliefs change, other feelings will arise and they won't be as angry or intense, right?"

"Yes, exactly. You might feel bad in reaction to something a person says because those words will trigger this belief that you will fail. When you no longer believe you are a failure, negative words just move right through you without triggering any emotion.

"The opposite is true also," she added. "When someone says something, and it may not even mean what you think it does, if you have a hot button connected to low self-esteem, and his words touch it, you will have an immediate angry reaction. Your reality is completely controlled by what you believe, and your beliefs create hot buttons which reinforce your negative beliefs.

"Are you saying that I'm driving myself crazy, trying to be good enough just because I want the approval of my father, mother, wife and kids? You mean, I'm not just trying to do the right thing, I'm trying to be good enough? I can't believe it!

"My whole life has been driven by this feeling that my father would love me only if I was successful; and he didn't love me, so I must be a failure. That is the belief you said we should look for - the one that hurts the most! He didn't love me, because I was a failure. I believed ever since that I was a failure, and I would always fail, so unconsciously I set myself up to prove it was true. Do people really work that way?!?" James looked up at Katja.

"Yes, the mind can work that way." Facing the group she said, "We were so young when these patterns were set in us that we forget how it all started. You have been thinking this way for a long time, ever since before you can remember. So, it's hard to think any other way. This is why we offer these groups. A new way of thinking can break your old behavioral loops."

James sat quietly, feeling spent; feeling lots of things and none of them felt good. This was too much to take in all at once.

Suddenly he realized Judy treated him just the way his father had. 'Yuk! I married my father! She is just like him, unforgiving, demanding, and emotionally manipulating. My God, I really did unconsciously set myself up to fail in this marriage! I'm still trying to please my father through her! Yuk."

When the session ended, James left the room feeling dazed and introspective. He was not ready to be around people, so he declined Jordan's invitation to get some coffee. He needed to be alone. He didn't want to go to his room. The space was not big enough to contain these thoughts. Then he remembered the labyrinth and how Tim said it was a place to think. What did he say? Oh yes. "Hold a question in your heart and the answer will come." So, James headed out to the garden. A few steps into the circle he heard a voice in his head.

"I am here," said the voice.

James froze, 'God, is that you?' he asked as a thought.

"Yes. Are you ready?" This time the voice did not sound like his own voice, but it was in his head. It sounded like an old actor, Sean Connery. James once watched him in an old movie and thought, 'If God had a voice, it would sound like that.'

James took a slow step forward. 'Uh, yeah, I guess. You're the All-Mighty, how could I stop you?'

"Quite the contrary. You have stopped me your whole life."

"You are God, how could little old me stop you?" James said out loud.

"All through your life, I have tried to help you and guide you. When you rejected and ridiculed my words, I sent messengers to deliver my messages. You have managed to ignore them all."

"Why would I do that?" James whispered out loud. He really did not know. There was a thought in the back of his mind that asking something he did not know would be a good test to find out if this voice was real.

"I respect your Free Will. I can give you hints, but it is up to you to navigate your way in this life. You must follow your inner calling and carve out your own path. It is up to you to do what you believe is right, decide for yourself what is true, and create the world in your own image."

'So, you are saying I created a world where God doesn't exist, and people are cruel to each other. I didn't know I was that powerful,' even in his mind the words had a snide and sarcastic tone.

"You are free to see it that way."

'What other way is there?'

"Are you challenging me or sincerely asking?" God patiently questioned him.

'You know I have always had trouble with the idea of Free Will. Why would you give us Free Will, if we do stupid things with it. It's a set up for sinning and failure and then you punish us for it!'

"Is that what you believe? Remember what you believe you will create. Be careful what you believe. I don't judge or punish. That is a belief you accepted whole. If you believe it, then you will experience it."

'How can I live differently? Really, I am not testing you. I want to know. I need to know!' He was obviously sincere, so God answered him sincerely.

"Listen to the voice of your Soul."

'Yuk. It always tells me I am screwing up.'

"That is not the voice of your Soul. When your Soul speaks, it inspires you and leaves you feeling transcendent. That critical voice is the Inner Critic. Your dad implanted it in you to make you behave. Many parents unknowingly do that because it was the way they were raised and they don't know better.

"If your beliefs are based on fear, your life will be filled with things and people to fear. If you choose to love people, you will find that love begets more love, you attract loving people and situations into your life.

"Know truly that I love you, that is why I gave you the freedom to choose your own path each moment of your life. You, however, have chosen to ignore what your Soul tells you. Instead, you listen to other people, because you are afraid to believe in Me, in your own Soul, and in yourself. I gave you the power to carve your own path, and you gave it away to your father, your wife, your bosses, and to all kinds of people in all kinds of situations."

"You love me?" This idea sounded so radically impossible that he said it out loud.

"If you really loved me, you would have arranged for my life to be easier. My father loved me too and I suffered. He was also trying to protect me from myself. He told me what I should do left and right. Do this, don't do that. I don't need that kind of love." James suddenly realized he was yelling in the labyrinth.

'So much for a meditative walk. I guess I am not in a meditative mood,' James scolded himself.

"You did not like it when your father told you what to do and here you want me to arrange your life for you? It would not be your own unique life, created in your own image, if I designed it."

'But you let me fail!' James accused.

"I respect your freedom. I believe in you. You refused to hear my voice in the past, but you are listening now. Now you can make different choices, conscious choices."

'You are just like my father. You say you love me and then you step back and wait for me to fail.'

"Is that what your father did?"

"Yes," he said out loud. "He convinced me that I am a failure and always will be. I was never loved by him. All he ever did was judge me. That is why I get so angry and feel like a failure. He programmed me to fail."

James suddenly realized what Katja said was true. His beliefs were creating his reality. He felt like a failure, so he took jobs he hated, and then did a half-assed job, because he resented having to do such grunt work.

He walked slowly, studying the ground beneath his feet to keep from listening to God, Katja (who now seemed to be in his head too) and his own thoughts.

He reached the center and stood there feeling quite tall. His feet felt strangely solid on the ground, and he felt quieter too.

On the return walk from the center, God spoke again. "Love is trusting, patient, and allows the object of your love the freedom to be who they are meant to be. It is respecting their Free Will, not judging them, and letting them walk their path even when it leads away from you."

'Why did you wait until I came here to talk to me? Why didn't you come sooner, before I lost everything?'

"Losing everything, as you put it, allowed you to let go of the reality that you were so invested in. It pried your fingers loose from all the 'have tos' and 'shoulds' that controlled your life.

"If I were to impose my will and judgement on you, like your father did, you would resent me, like you resent your father. I respect who you are and what you can accomplish too much to take your power away from you like that.

"Maybe it is time for you to accept that you are good enough and start loving yourself."

'Aren't you angry that I burned your book?'

"A book is only paper and ink. It has no value. It is the concepts and teachings that my Prince of Peace brought to this wounded world that have true and lasting value. If you can honor Him and His Teachings, if you can love yourself and love your neighbors, then the book is still alive in you."

James stared at the stones lining the path, thinking about that day, long ago, when his mother died. He missed his mother.

He was only six when she got sick and fifteen when she died. James only remembered her being sick. The sadness of never knowing her when she was well gripped his heart.

"You had the rare opportunity to spend so much time with your mother over the years. Very few children have that."

'My father taught me to be brave and show strength against hardship. I guess that is a virtue of some kind. But I needed something different. I needed him to love me and let me grieve.' A well of loneliness, miles deep, opened in his chest. It had been there ever since she died, but he always ran away from it, denied it, and accused himself of being weak because of it.

He wanted to run and be finished with all this nonsense. But instead, he forced his legs to keep a slow steady pace. He was not going to waste this opportunity like he wasted so many others.

"God, why didn't you save my mother? She was a wonderful woman. She loved you, believed in you, and trusted you. Why did you desert her?" he spoke aloud, oblivious to anyone else.

'Your mother was following her Soul's path and accomplished her Life Mission. She only came into this life for that specific length of time. To you, she left early. To her Soul, it was a whole life's worth. Her death changed you. Someday you will see how it was a turning point in your life. After going through a period of being bogged down, you will eventually learn the lessons you need and will become a more powerful Soul for having endured and transcended the experience.

"You are now on the path your Soul has chosen. If she had not died, you might have stayed on a stagnant path. It would have taken you much longer to complete your Soul's Mission. You were forced to develop courage, fortitude, self-reliance and several other virtues that will come to light when you need them."

'Right now, I do not feel brave.'

"You will, trust me."

James called Tim and asked him to meet him at the labyrinth. At first, they walked in silence for a couple of turns, then James shared his experience with Tim and told him all about his conversation with God. Tim was an excellent listener as usual.

Afterwards, Tim said, "It is time to give you your red band."

A feeling of pride moved through James as he put it on.

"Welcome to the community," said Tim. "Would you like to participate in a group ritual and take your vows, or would you prefer to do it in private just the two of us?"

"It would be more meaningful to me if we could do it here in the labyrinth with just the two of us." James answered.

Before Tim, God, and Mother Nature, James repeated the words after Tim and recited his vows, "The same gentleness and respect I pledge to show myself; I vow to show to everyone...ending with, "I vow to work on becoming the grandest version of myself in accord with the highest vision I have of who I am." As they parted company, a new sense of belonging filled James and left him feeling quiet and content.

CHAPTER 6

New Job

James woke up with a start and tried to crawl back into his dream. It felt so real and unresolved. As though it were a memory not a fantasy, he could see every detail of the drama he felt yanked out of and desperately wanted to go back there.

He was driving a tram with his whole family on board. His mother and father were sitting in the back with his brother, Donny, His wife and kids were in the middle, and he was at the wheel. Everyone was yelling at him, criticizing his driving. The tram was huge and hard to control. He was fighting to keep it on the road and a steep road it was. Suddenly the road led into a dark tunnel. He had to pay close attention because his headlights were dim. When the tram emerged from the tunnel, it was empty; huge, cavernous, and empty. He was all alone. He stopped the tram and ran back into the tunnel to find everyone. He was running breathlessly screaming their names, but the tunnel was silent. His own voice echoed back to him, mocking him. Suddenly he found himself in bed! He wanted to scream, no! and go back. He had to get back into the tunnel to find everyone.

Feeling incomplete and disoriented, he stumbled into the bathroom. Even after he showered, dressed, and left his room, a part of him was still stuck in the dream. He entered the dining room hoping Chatty Cathy would not be there. He liked her okay, he just wanted to be alone. He closed his eyes with every bite. To others, it might look like he was savoring his food, but in fact, he was imagining the tunnel. He was still looking for all the people he had lost there.

After breakfast, he thought of going to a group but promised himself he would do that later. He could not face a group, especially the Anger Group right now so he made his way back to his room. Maybe he could take a little nap before deciding how to spend this day. Without Tim waiting for him, he felt a little lost and unmotivated. Back in his room, he found the ComScreen flashing, 'you have 4 messages'.

"We see you. Kim Thorsten here. I am a psychotherapist, and I would like to arrange an initial interview with you. Please call me at your earliest convenience. I have openings at 10:00 on either day. Will that work for you?"

"We see you. My name is Taylor Compton, and I am with the Architectural Co-Op. Please come in for an interview this afternoon. We are in the new Architectural Cluster in L-Town," and he left an extension number.

"We see you. This is Dr. Fouche's office calling to schedule your Red Band physical." The message ended with a schedule button. He pushed it and three possible appointment times appeared. He picked one and hit SEND. Immediately an automatic response appeared reminding him to wear loose clothing and fast for four hours beforehand.

"We see you. James, Tim here. I hope you are doing well. I have set up a few meetings for you. They are all just part of taking on a Red Band. If it gets overwhelming or you just need someone to talk to, remember I am always here for you. Just give me a call."

'Wow, this day was off to a rapid start.'

James contacted Dr. Thorsten. He expected to get her receptionist or a voicemail. Out in the world, no one ever answers their own calls.

Dr. Thorsten answered on the second ring; she was a heavy-set woman in her late fifties in a loose flowing lavender blouse. Her eyes were cat-like, piercing but kind.

"We see you. James, is it? I am delighted to meet you."

"It's nice to meet you too Dr. Thorsten.

"Please call me Kim. I would like to be your new therapist. I would like to help you with your E-Training (Emergence Training) and PPS (Personal Process Support). Here in Hope, everyone has a support person. It is a very sacred and intimate experience they share based on a deep and mutual trust. My role would be to guide you into yourself and be a source of support for you, as you discover who you really are, beyond all the images of yourself you saw in the mirror of other people's eyes. Are there any questions that you would like to ask me?"

"We see you, Kim. I feel very comfortable with you. I have never had a therapist before. I don't know what to look for."

"You can only decide after you have had experience. Decision making is more accurate when you compare it to something similar. I recommend you interview another therapist. I would love to work with you. Before you choose me, interview a couple of other therapists, so you can make an informed choice. Perhaps you might enjoy working with a male therapist, at least set up an interview call with one.

"Is there someone you could recommend?"

"Yes, Alberto Fornelli. He is a good therapist. I wish you well. I hope you find everything you need in our community and remember my number."

They exchanged greetings and the screen went back to its Home Page.

James lay back on his bed and smiled to himself, 'That went well.'

Using the ComPad Find Friend function, James located Dr. Fornelli and called him.

James introduced himself and asked for an interview. Dr. Fornelli suggested the next day at 5:30 and offered him a choice of an On-Screen interview or an OA (office appointment). James chose the On-Screen because he might be working.

"Are you looking forward to working? asked Dr. Fornelli.

"Yes, but I have first day jitters. I am excited about getting my teeth into something meaningful, doing something I enjoy, and moving closer to my goal."

"What is that?

"Getting out of debt."

"Getting out of debt," repeated the therapist. "That's a good place to begin our session. 5:30 Tomorrow. See you then."

"Wait. I have never had a therapist before. Is it going to be like the Personal Process groups I went to? This is new ground for me. What will you do to me in a session? I'm going through a lot right now."

"My job is to be your support and help you get clarity on your decisions and your choices."

"Like my Guide, Tim?"

"Yes, Tim helped you get acquainted with our community. I will help you get better acquainted with yourself.

"Sounds good."

James hung up feeling more comfortable with the idea of therapy. Before talking to Kim and Dr. Fornelli, he was a little scared of the idea.

When the line was silent, James thought, 'He sounds efficient. Maybe he can whip me into shape."

The next call was to the doctor to make an appointment for a physical.

Now that the calls were handled, James collapsed on the bed for a moment. For an instant, he wished he still smoked, this would be the perfect moment for a puff.

"Now to go to Taylor Compton at the new Architectural Cluster in L-Town," he excitedly announced to the empty room.

He changed his clothes four times, the full extent of his wardrobe, wanting to make a good impression. Finally, he settled on a gray suit and called the number for directions. Then he realized he was trying to be perfect and understood that he was putting pressure on himself. He reminded himself that that path usually led him down a road of resentment and failure. He looked at that path and recognized it for what it was and decided not to go that way this time. He took off the suit and put on more casual clothes, a blue shirt and gray slacks. Shaking his head, he thought, 'Why do I keep doing this to myself? I guess I'm just scared that I'll make a mistake.'

Tim called again, "Having a busy day, are you?" he teased.

James laughed and rattled off all his accomplishments in the last hour.

He took a long look at himself in the mirror, and decided he looked as good as a middle-aged man with a paunch and thin graying hair can look. James took a tram to L-Town where he got a new journal. He wanted to write down his talks with God, Soul, therapist, and record his own thoughts to help him remember it all. He walked around glancing into shop windows as he slowly moseyed over to the new Architectural Cluster.

James was excited at the prospect of finally doing architectural design and was looking forward to working, nevertheless, his belly was tangled in knots with first-day jitters. 'Just focus on the goal,' he told himself. 'Feel the excitement. I am finally going to get my teeth into meaningful work. This is the moment I have dreamed of for years. Don't mess it up!'

He stood in front of heaven's gates, or rather, the front door of the architectural building high on the mesa. This aerodynamically designed building, with a cluster of lower buildings around it, was a serpentine shape, so the prevailing winds slid along its curved edge. Its four stories made it exceptionally tall for Hope. Crowning it was a spacious rooftop garden of colorful flowers and cool shade trees. On the far end of the roof, he saw the Wind Spinners and Solar Panels.

The exquisite surface of this serpentine structure was copper colored glass. The windows were framed with shiny copper reflectors to maximize their use as passive solar collectors. As he often saw here, it stood on thick solid stilts, so there was convenient space underneath for bicycles, electric scooters, segways, and all the other simple ways people got around. Leading up to the front doors there were stunning front steps in half circle concentric rings, inlaid with copper colored glass protected by a thick layer of resin. The glass panels on the front door had a beautiful shiny copper frame in an Art Deco design. All the other lines in the building were smooth and sleek, making this one decorative element stand out as ornamentally lavish.

Inside, a vast atrium was open to a series of mezzanines overlooking the central well. Standing on the faux marble floor stood several display cases containing prize-winning models of past projects. In the center, at a round desk, sat a lovely young woman with delicate golden braids laced over thick long flowing locks. She looked up from her ComScreen, smiled warmly, and said, "We see you. How may I serve you?"

"Hello. I mean, we see you. I'm James Dole and my Guide Tim arranged for me to meet with Taylor Compton." His excitement was increasing, and he was turning into a bundle of nerves.

"I will let Taylor know. Would you like to stroll around and look at our models while you wait? They are quite creative."

James studied the unique features of each model's design. They were brilliant and beautiful. He felt profound respect and admiration followed by the nagging question, Can I do as well? He welcomed the distraction because he was nervous. He strolled past a comfortable looking leather couch and chairs, facing a tall fireplace with a realistic natural gas insert. Despite the cavernous nature of the space, it felt cozy. Brightly painted ceramic pots filled with flowering plants arranged in clusters, defined separate areas. From a round copper colored skylight in the roof, golden amber light rained down, making the space bright and cheerful.

When James came to the elevators, he became mesmerized. There were three, one on each end and one in the middle. These small glass chambers revealed their shiny polished mechanical workings and the copper shaft. The walls between the glass elevators were decorated with a geometric mural of splashing random colors.

James completed his walk around the lobby and returned to the center desk. "This whole building seems to float in the light," he said to the receptionist. "Yes. If you can be here when the sun begins to set, you will have a marvelous treat. The setting sun reflecting off the glass will take your breath away."

"I hope to have many opportunities to see that. I want to work here."

"May the winds of luck fill your sails. Here comes Taylor."

A tall man wearing a lightweight sky-blue shirt, crisp grey slacks and expensive running shoes came jogging down a wide staircase that appeared to be floating in air. It was in fact, well braced by graceful powerful shining steel cables. It had a copper banister twisted in a geometric design. James looked up at the open stairs and was impressed with the vigor of the man. He had silver hair, a young-looking face, and a muscular body. It was hard to pin an age on him. He beamed vitality and youth. His hand, with its Blue Band, was extended even before he reached James. "We see you. I'm Taylor, welcome to the Art and Architectural Co-Op of Arizona, AACA as we like to call it," he smiled warmly.

James liked him instantly. His nervousness disappeared.

"I hear you want to design houses for our community."

James nodded.

"What are your qualifications?"

"I have a degree in Architectural Design, but I never got to practice in my field. The competition was too fierce. I have a wife, children, and debts so I needed to earn money. That's why I took whatever paid the bills. Taylor's eyes asked, where? so James squeaked out, 'Ford.' He felt embarrassed and quickly put in, "I may need some refresher classes to get up to par. I went to the Academy of Art University and did work on some designs, solar and passive, but then I ended up on the line at the Ford Motor company."

With a warm sincere smile, Taylor said, "We are glad to have another pair of hands and another creative mind. If you have the basics, we can teach you the rest. Don't worry."

"Let's place you in a group that is tackling design problems and see how you do. That will uncover where you need more studies."

Taylor gave him a quick tour. On the next floor was the Break Room, with a kitchen, dining room, and lounge. There was a reading area stocked with glossy inspirational picture books of amazing structures. Along the windows were vegetable beds and miniature trees bearing fruit. 'What fun,' thought James. We can read and nibble fruit right off the tree. In the opposite corner was the 3D video gaming area.

The next flight of stairs led them to the third floor, people were clustered in little groups, some around a table, others were stretched out on plush carpeting or sitting on Zen pillows, another group was sprawled on a circle of bean bags, others were sitting alone at a desk facing out a window looking out on the mesa.

James recognized Godfrey. He smiled, waved and went back to building a miniature variation of a mushroom building using a 3D printer, one of the four they had. It was in the printing alcove along with two blueprint printers.

Taylor led him to a small conference room. On the way, he asked, "What excites you about architecture?"

"Everything," said James, "I love the organic designs I saw in the market and restaurant districts, here in L-Town. I have never seen anything like them, and those domed houses are so out-there," he said, hoping he did not sound like a fool.

"Where should I put you?" He looked James over, like he was measuring him for a suit, or rather, what would suit him? Then the concentrating look vanished and his face brightened. "I have just the place."

"I think I will put you in a working group, so you can learn as you go. These are a great group of people. They will guide you and make sure you have what you need. This will be an exciting challenge and a good place to start. Let's see how you do with this project and then we can reevaluate your position in a couple of weeks when the project is done."

"Taylor," James said and paused to work up his nerve. He was not sure how to broach the subject of money. Normally the money was a primary focus of an interview, but who knows how it works here.

Taylor sensed what James was about to ask. "You will receive a salary with monthly reviews. If your work yields results, your salary goes up. Just sign-in and check-out on your ComPad, so we know when you are here. We suggest you attend your process groups before or after work. You also have the option of doing them during lunch or during Afternoon Breakout. We will continue to pay you until you tell us that you no longer need it.

"We prefer that you work seven or eight hours a day. However, you can choose your own working hours. Some members of our staff are night owls; others are bright and bushy-tailed in the mornings. You choose. Since you will be working on a team, your hours will have to interface well with the others."

"Sure, I will. Thank you for this opportunity."

"I hope you enjoy working with your team and like being a member of our cluster. Ready to meet them?"

James nodded enthusiastically.

Taylor introduced him to two men and two women, Pierre, Satyendra, Carla, and Yael all Red Bands or Orange Bands. For a minute James felt intimidated but then realized the color had nothing to do with the work and relaxed a little. 'Damn those first day jitters,' he thought.

"We see you James," said Carla, a cute, petite, twenty-four-year-old with honey colored skin from Buenos Aires. "Welcome to our brainstorming session. They were sitting in a circle of comfortable leather chairs around a table. Pierre pulled one over for him. Each person took a turn welcoming him and then Pierre summarized the problems they were facing.

Pierre, a tall, robust, good-looking man with large round eyes and long brown hair, clubbed at the back, from Algeria, age forty, said, "We are working on RBHs (Rapid Built Housing) for DRPs (Disaster Relief Projects). He gave James a brief history on quick *hempcrete* dome housing. They wanted to use it in Africa but ran into logistical problems.

Taylor left and the group continued. "Listen and feel free to join in whenever you are ready," invited Carla. "We are trying to create a series of designs appropriate for varying places and conditions," she explained. We have already looked at traditional tribal styles of building, and new resource ideas." He glanced at the pile of pictures on a table in front of them.

The day went by quickly. James enjoyed getting to know the members of his group and the project was a fascinating challenge. Their goal was to be able to erect a solid sustainable shelter in three days under dire circumstances. It had to be cost efficient and light enough to be carried in by hand or on a pack animal. Ideally, they wanted to use renewable resources that could be acquired in large quantities. James was beginning to doubt if there was a solution that met all the criteria.

The group took their Afternoon Breakout at 3:00. James was on his way to the coffeepot for his sixth cup of yerba matte coffee. Pierre laughed and said, "That stuff will kill you man."

James's eyes flared with fire. What business is it of his? He reminded himself to let it go. It would be bad form to get into a fight with a member of his team on the first day. Pierre was taken back by James's strong reaction to his playful banter. "There's an Anger Management group happening down the hall in Number 9, if you need it," offered Pierre.

"I have something even better," Carla chimed in. "Come with me. This will be fun."

"Anything is more fun than an Anger Group," quipped James.

Carla led him to a spacious room with a thick carpet and no furniture, just a pile of pillows in the corner.

"Welcome to Dynamic Meditation," she said as she took off her shoes and loosened the drawstring on her pants. Soft music was playing as the people filed in. A gong rang and the music stopped. Everyone stood still for a few minutes, then a new song came on. It was wild and raucous.

"Let go James. Go Wild!"

He looked around and everyone was dancing wild and crazy, flailing about, letting loose hardly described it. For the next ten minutes this chaotic dancing continued. James got into it. Some people had their eyes closed, some did not. No one was watching anyone else, and no one was judging. It was just a wild free for all! After a while, the music slowed down, and a gong rang. Everyone stopped and stood frozen. Then the lights were dimmed, and soft music began to play. Everyone grabbed a pillow from a pile in the corner and sat down. For the next ten minutes, he enjoyed the empty feeling of his body and the quiet of his mind. No one told him he was meditating, so he did not realize he was doing it. He was still for a long while, then this morning's dream slipped over him and stirred up a sense of longing, for what or who he did not know.

When the lights came on and the gong rang again, James felt peaceful and refreshed. On the way back to work, Carla and James passed a room where an anger group was just wrapping up.

He peeked through the door as they walked past. Twelve men and women were pounding foam bats against the floor and shouting angry words out loud. Some of them were leaving and others were in full swing. Godfrey was among those leaving.

He met them at the door. "That was great! Hi Carla. Good to see you man. What's your name again?"

"James. What group was that?"

"Anger Outlet. We start thinking about something that we are pissed about," Godfrey explained. "Then we scream louder and louder until we have expressed all the fire in our bellies. After that, we smash those bats on the floor imagining it is some stupid person's thick head. It is a good release. You should try it sometime."

"I will," said James. Then he and Carla turned the corner and went back to their room to attack the same problems that had had the group stumped for days.

On the way home after a satisfying day, he reviewed his performance and was satisfied that he did not embarrass himself. He wished he had all the answers they were looking for. Sitting on the tram on the way back to the hotel, he imagined himself as a superhero, walking into work on the first day and solving all their problems.

His eyes wandered aimlessly over the interior of the tram and came to fix on the seats. They were old-fashioned woven cane seats like trains had in the 1800s. 'How charming,' he thought.

James got back to his room right in time to call the other therapist for the interview.

"Hello. Dr. Fornelli? James here. How do we start? I am new to this thing."

"We see you, James. We can do a half hour session this first time," answered the therapist, "just to get acquainted. Tell me what you are dealing with, and I will help you work on it. That way you will get a feeling for my approach to therapy, and I will get a sense of whether I want to work with you."

"Right down to business, I like that. I lost my job and ran away. I didn't want to face my wife. She can be vicious sometimes. I like it here and hope it will help me to save money so I can pay off my debts, from all HER spending. That's about it."

"What bothers you most about this situation?"

"I felt controlled by my wife and my old job, which kept me on a hamster wheel running very fast but getting nowhere, while the debts were mounting. Now I have depleted the kid's college fund to keep us afloat and my wife is going to kill me when she finds out, even though it was to pay her debts."

"Have you ever had this feeling of being on a hamster wheel before?" Dr. Fornelli asked.

"Sure, all the years I was growing up. My father was just as demanding and controlling as my wife."

"Why do you think you married someone like your father?"

"What!"

"I asked you, 'Why do you think you married your father?'"

"I heard you the first time, but that's ridiculous!"

"How so? Many people marry someone who can help them resolve old issues with a family member. It happens all the time."

"Judy is nothing like my father!" James insisted.

"James, this is a good beginning. If you choose to work with me, we can go deeper into this dynamic and uncover your core beliefs, to see why you feel compelled to get into situations where you feel controlled and victimized."

James said goodbye and asked the therapist how he wanted to be addressed.

"Dr. Fornelli will do nicely. It is best that we keep our relationship formal."

Kim made him feel comfortable and safe while Dr. Fornelli really got down to business. He liked one and respected the other. This was going to be a difficult decision.

The ComScreen went blank, and he went to the bathroom for a minute. When he returned, a message was flashing. It was from Dr. Fouche's office confirming his medical exam for Monday at 5:30.

James ordered dinner in his room. He had a brief talk with Tim and spent the rest of the evening curled up in a comfortable recliner with his new books and went to bed early.

The next morning, he returned from another vivid dream. Back in his old life, he never remembered dreaming so much, and surely not in such detail. This time, he was in a vast desert all alone. A caravan went by and he wanted to join them, but they went over a sand dune and disappeared before he could catch up with them. He was thirsty, so he went looking for water. He was wandering through this wilderness when he saw a hill. Quickly he climbed it. From the top, he could see an oasis off in the distance. He ran to the oasis as fast as he could, desperate for water. It was covered in a dense thicket of bamboo. Huge shoots grew up from the moist ground. In the middle, he found a precious pond of fresh water. He was so relieved and so thirsty. He quickly kneeled down to draw up a handful of fresh cool water. Abruptly, he woke up. He didn't get to drink! The desire lingered for a long time, but he could not go back to sleep, and he had to get ready for work.

James showered, dressed, and went to the dining room for breakfast where he met Cathy. They had a pleasant chat, nothing he had to pay attention to. His body had started the day, but his mind was still in the desert trying to get that drink of fresh water.

He was at the door of his workroom before his mind and body settled into this realm. He grabbed a cup of that herbal make-believe coffee. It was beginning to grow on him. It had yerba matte and that gave him the caffeine kick he needed.

Pierre, Carla, Satyendra, and Yael were there already. The energy in the room seemed a bit dull. Pierre suggested they go over what they had established so far and a sluggish conversation ensued. Satyendra, a tall, thin man with stylishly cut hair, impeccably dressed, almond eyes, quite handsome, age twenty-two, from the Auroville Ashram in India, suggested they move their brainstorming to the gym. Everyone quickly agreed, jumped up, and headed out. James followed like a puppy trailing behind. A few minutes later, they were in a circle of treadmills with their legs running and their mouths talking just as fast.

"Sustainable Emergency Housing has unique requirements," said Yael, a six-foot-tall statuesque Amazon, from Jerusalem, a former army captain who stood very straight, had cropped dusty blond hair, and looked quite powerful, "that means we must keep thinking further and further outside the box."

Several ideas, which were successfully used in other projects, were tossed around but they did not meet all the requirements. James doubted that this was even possible. Yael suggested an African hut but it was made of straw and would not have sustainability in more northern lands. Carla said the Iroquois Longhouse would shelter many people at once. That was a virtue, but the weight of materials disqualified it. They would need trucks and reasonable roads to haul materials. Satyendra hesitantly suggested inflatable domes to be used as forms for hempcrete. That idea went round for a while until they came to the need to transport the mixing drums and bags of hempcrete. That threw the idea off the drawing board.

James was impressed with the way the group received a new idea and tossed it around trying to make it work before discarding it. Back at the architectural office where he once worked, new ideas were always shot down or torn apart. The group seemed to find satisfaction in tearing new ideas to shreds. James was afraid to suggest anything new because he was sure the vultures would tear him to shreds.

After an hour on the treadmill, everyone felt accomplished. The project had not advanced much but they felt better as though they were getting closer.

Carla asked him if he wanted to have lunch with her in the dining room. He accepted and Yael joined them. The food here was just as wonderful as the hotel. He thought, 'A man can grow fat on good food like this.' Carla had a salad with salmon and Yael ordered falafel, tahini, and hummus on a salad with pita.

James told the women this was his dream job.

Yael said, "Speaking of dreams" and went on to share the dream she had last night. "It was fantastic! I climbed up a high hill. I remembered in the dream having tried to climb that hill before, but I had a lot more trouble. This time it was a cinch. Pretty soon I was on top. I raised my arms and discovered I had wings, so I flew off into a blue sky and soared around in circles. It was exhilarating. I felt utterly free!"

Carla analyzed the dream. They all agreed that Yael was thriving in Hope and the dream was confirming it. Then Carla shared her dream of finding a secret door in her old house and inside was a treasure trove of plants. Carla went on to talk about her beautiful rooftop garden and all the exotic succulents she grew there. Then they asked James if he remembered his dream from last night.

James froze like a deer in headlights, took a few deep breaths, and decided to trust these women. They were so accepting in the brainstorming group, maybe he could trust them to hear his dream and not laugh or think badly of him. Taking a chance, he described the wilderness, the caravan, and the oasis. When he got to the bamboo thicket, Carla nearly choked on a sip of tea. It spurted out of her mouth all over the table, and she apologized. Alarmed, they both looked at her and asked if she was all right.

"All right. I am soooo all right! The God of Dreams has done it again! That's it! That's it!"

James and Yael were getting a little concerned about her. "What are you talking about?" They both asked at the same time. Had they been kids, they would have called, "Jinx."

With a cat-who-ate-the-mouse expression, Carla smiled, and laughed to herself, obviously enjoying a private joke. "You'll see soon enough," she sang in a tuneless way.

They ate the rest of their meal quickly to get back to the others. They were excited to hear Carla's secret.

CHAPTER 7

Virtual Reality

James was on the tram, going back to the hotel, after his third day at his new job. He was still feeling high from Carla's revelation. Her idea fit the bill perfectly. Now Satyendra, as their technical advisor, was running the numbers.

The nature of the team changed radically. Whereas they had spent the last few days always sitting together discussing ideas, now everyone was in their own world exploring different aspects of construction and feasibility. The excitement level in the room was high. They had moved to the plush, carpeted room James and Carla had attended Dynamic Meditation in. Everyone was draped around the room in an assortment of different positions. Different minds function best in different ways.

Pierre, their unofficial leader, was sitting at a desk in an ergonomic chair designed especially for him in their own shop. He was wearing amplifier earring buds and was seated in front of a ComScreen on a huge desk. He was deeply engrossed in talking to resource companies all over the world.

Carla was hard to see, buried deep in a pile of velvet pillows. On one side of her was a strong two-inch-thick metal arm made of braided copper. It was holding a flat surface upon which sat a pad of paper and various colored pens. Hanging on her right was a similar convenient table with a ComPad and various small information gathering devices on it. For a while, it looked like she was daydreaming, then she popped up and started drawing different models of the new RBH structure.

Satyendra was sitting on a Zen pillow in a beam of sunlight under a south facing window. His eyes were closed, and he was softly chanting to himself. After a while, he opened his eyes and began poking away at his ComPad, playing with various numbers.

Yael was on a treadmill. She was running to get her juices flowing. When she was high on a sense of prowess, she turned to her ComScreen and inspiration just poured out of her. For her the workout flipped a switch and all the power in her body went into her mind and sent her into hyper gear. She was working on transportation. She was untangling issues around the transport of supplies through danger zones.

James realized he did not know what made him feel creative. He just always sat in the chair his company gave him. No one ever asked him what kind of chair he wanted or whether he even wanted a chair at all. Suddenly he was aware of a disturbing fact, he did not really know himself all that well.

James needed to decide quickly, so he chose to get a chair like Pierre's. He reached for his ComPad to call the shop and order the furniture. They informed him that it will take three days and said, "Sergio will be up in a few minutes to scan a 3D of your body and take your measurements."

While the scan was in progress, a call came in on his ComPad. He noticed the blinking light and the one musical note. As soon as he was free, he glanced down at his ComPad and was surprised to see the call was from Sandra, his daughter. She also sent a text.

"Yo Dad," he read, "I downloaded your letter to mom off her computer. I tried to get her to talk, but she clammed up. Apparently, you are now a taboo subject in our house. All she said was that you were a "'_ _ _ _'coward who ran away."

"I did some cool detective work," she wrote "and discovered your whereabouts. I am thrilled that you are there! I know all about Trinitus Cities. Coincidently, we studied them in *Alternative Ways of Living*. It was part of my Social Studies Class. I was so blown away by this place that I plan to move there when I graduate. I didn't think I could get there sooner, but if you are living there I can! Dad, I want to live with you! I told Sammy about it, but he wants to stay with Mom, cause of soccer and his friends.

"Now I can join sooner! Let me know when I can come. Don't worry about school. I can finish my last year in Trinitus. I read great things about their schools. Please let me come now! Don't tell mom about this. She will blow a blood vessel and sabotage the custody hearing. She can make my life a living hell! She is royally angry at you! I don't want her taking it out on me. What is your side of the story, anyway?"

James reread the text. It was hard to believe his eyes. He poured a cup of Yerba Mate coffee and dropped down on a leather couch.

The thought, 'She had been planning this for a year,' went round and round in his mind. 'I lived in the same house as her and had no idea! I thought I knew her. How could I miss this big fact?

'I will have to keep her secret. Judy has a temper. She could give Sandra a hard time. She would probably do that badgering thing she does, until Sandra gives in. I remember how she used to badger me between jobs. I got off my sweet ass just to get her to stop. I was so desperate to go back to work that I took those miserable jobs that weren't even in my field. It was easier than listening to her drone on.

James touched his Smartwatch. "Text" he said. It immediately opened to a blank page. "I'm glad to hear that you want to stay with me, that would be great, but it is not my choice. We need to go through the courts and your mother. As you said, she is not too happy with me right now. I don't know how hard the fight in court will be. We may not get to choose so no promises.

"As far as coming here now, it is a nice dream, but I cannot imagine your mom letting you go. If you sneak away, it could jeopardize my chances of getting custody and bringing you here sooner. In one year, you will be eighteen and you can do as you please.

Know that you will always have a home with me."

"Send to Sandra." The little earring buds in his earlobes chimed, confirming the message was sent.

"I hope the court gives me a choice," she wrote and added six emojis. "I can't wait now that I know where you are. I want to finish high school there. Mom is going to fight us. In her mind, she already has me enrolled in college. She talks about it all the time. She is acting like my going to college will release her from prison. I don't know what to say to her. I don't want to go to college. I want to work in your community. It makes more sense to me. They have so many cool programs. I can join one of the teams that save animals from extinction or build robots that clean the oceans. They offer hands-on training. Who needs traditional college? So, what happened between you and Mom?"

"I like your passion, Sandra. What happened recently was just 'the straw that broke the camel's back.' It was just one small hurt on top of a lot of big hurts. What happened doesn't matter. Your mother and I fell out of love a long time ago. Our love died and we never buried the corpse. She has told me time and again that she wants a divorce. I can't fight her anymore. I have had enough.

"Be gentle on your mother. This is hard on her too. Maybe, if you help her calm down and cope with my leaving, she might be more amenable to agreeing to what you want. Please be patient. I know how hard it is for you to wait. If you meet her head on and tell her you are moving in with me, she will feel betrayed. She will be furious and might try to stop you from ever coming here."

"Send." He waited for the chime confirming that it was received.

"Okay Dad, I will take off the boxing gloves with Mom. I will try to be supportive. Do you like it there? What is it like? Do they control you by getting into your head and force you to expose your true feelings about everything? That's what my teacher said?"

"Yes and no. It's not quite like the way you make it sound. It's a good thing. If we are going to talk further, it should be On Screen, not in a text. I'm glad you wrote. We can talk more about Trinitus tonight, okay? Send."

"CUT"

"CUT?"

"Cool Until then."

A temporary desk and chair arrived with a huge new ComScreen. James was working on sources for growing bamboo. The RBH was going to be a Mongolian Yurt constructed from thick bamboo stalks sliced in half, lengthwise, and placed inside each other spooning fashion, then fastened together with strips of reinforced cane. The walls will be double insulated canvas containing Thinsulate.

James's assignment was to look for bamboo. He discovered that there are 1400 different species of bamboo, and it grows all over the world. In Asia: China, Japan, India, Indonesia, Korea, and Thailand, it is the most common. However, it has also played a significant role in the culture and economy of South America: Brazil and Peru; Africa: Nigeria, Ghana, Madagascar, and sub-Saharan Africa, where it is found in tropical areas; North America: Mexico, Guatemala, Honduras, and the southern United States; Oceania: Australia and New Zealand; the Caribbean islands and other islands.

Bamboo can grow in warm temperate climates, cool mountainous regions, and highland cloud forests. It is found in the Mediterranean climate of southern Italy, Portugal and in the south of France, where the climate is warm and sunny.

Bamboo was the lightweight renewable resource they were looking for. It can be grown in most places around the world, so it can be on hand everywhere for emergency housing.

He went on to study the attributes of the different kinds of bamboo. He had mostly decided that the wide species with thick shoots is the best suited for their purpose.

Each member of the team was ensconced in their own little nest; nevertheless, they were all carrying on constant dialogues with each other on their ComPads making a soft humming around the room. They were sharing each new discovery with everyone else. Despite being in their own little world, they remained on the same page together.

James took a break to get more coffee. As he sipped the soothing warm liquid, he mused about the call from his daughter. He had asked her to do something he could never figure out how to do. He never knew how to reach Judy and calm her when she was angry.

He hadn't realized it before, but it was true. As soon as Judy's face grew dark and scary, he felt like he was standing in front of his father and automatically shrank into silence. He could not stand up to her and be what she wanted. He honestly hoped that Sandra could reach her. Maybe his daughter wasn't as wounded as he was.

Sandra often looked like a stubborn teen, and he thought that was normal, but now, being here, he reconsidered. Maybe she acted like that because she thought she was supposed to, because everyone else did that. She wanted to be like everyone else, so she rejected everything her mom said and did. Then she turned it around and blamed her mother for the alienated way she felt. It was just the way they described it in the first Anger Management lecture.

Maybe all these lectures were affecting the way he saw the world around him. Understanding his own cowardice and what caused it did not make the idea of facing her any easier.

If he tried to stand up to Judy right now, he would catch all hell for it. He cringed. He was afraid this situation was going to explode in his face, but there was nothing else he could do about it right now.

It had been three days since he emailed Judy and sent the divorce papers. He was holding his breath waiting for her to respond.

James refilled his cup and plopped down on a sofa. He leaned back, his head hanging backwards and his legs outstretched. This had been a satisfying day. He accomplished a lot and pretty much filled his assignment for today. He still had half an hour before the final sharing circle where they were going to wrap up and review everyone's findings, so he relaxed.

He closed his eyes and imagined what it would be like to have Sandra live with him. At first, he was flattered and pleased that she was reaching out to him for the first time in years. Another thought rushed in on top of that one; what does he know about raising a teenage girl, a young woman, on his own! She wasn't old enough to take care of herself and who knows what special things a young woman needs to know. How was he going to talk to her about difficult, feminine kinds of stuff?

He still didn't know if he was going to stay in this community. He hadn't been here that long and still did not have the full lay of the land. Who's to say that coming here wasn't a mistake? It was just beginning to look like it would work for him. But how would her being here change things? He finally decided it is too soon to be sure.

The closing circle was very exciting. Everyone made progress in their different areas. James was especially proud of what he reported. When he was closing his ComPad, he noticed a message from Taylor that mentioned it was Friday, and therefore, his agreed upon salary, plus a bonus, had been deposited in his account. That brought a final glow on a wonderful day.

On his way home on the tram, in his mind, he organized his bills and made a mental note to send emails to each of his creditors to work out payment plans.

Tim met him in the lobby and this time James willingly walked the labyrinth in silence with him. Afterwards, they sat in front of the fountain and caught up on everything that had been happening.

"How is work? Are you settling in yet?" Tim asked.

"Yeah, it's great! I had this weird dream and when I told it to Carla, she and Yael were interpreting dreams, she decided mine was telling us to build Mongolian Yurts. So far, it looks like these yurts are the design we have been looking for. I am on a team designing RHB housing."

"Does that mean you are feeling comfortable there?" Tim coaxed him to share more.

"Absolutely. I am grateful to you for getting me this position. Thanks."

"I am glad it is working for you. Are you doing okay with everyone?"

"Everyone at work, yes, but a strange thing happened. My daughter called. She wants to live with me."

"I thought you said she was estranged from you."

"Yeah, well, it turns out that she has been planning on coming here when she graduates and she sees my being here as an in for her, so she is playing up to me right now."

"James, her motives may be suspect, but she is reaching out at this time. It could be the opening you have been waiting for to create a new relationship with your daughter."

"I am not in her mother's good graces. I doubt that Judy will let her come. So, it's just a pipe dream."

Tim softly commented, "It may be true that she cannot come here just yet, but the opening is still there."

"What can I do? She wants to live here. I can't guarantee that will happen. When it doesn't, she's going to write me off as a deadbeat dad and go back to ignoring me."

"James, it's too bad that you have it all figured out. It is a rather dead-end perspective. Do you think there could possibly be another way to play it?

"I'm open to suggestions," James said, but there was still a little resistance in his voice.

"If you cannot bring her into your world, maybe you can enter hers."

"What?" James scoffed. "Go back to the city and hang out with her high school friends???"

"Is that her real world?" his Guide said softly, hoping to calm his temperamental charge.

"No, she really lives in the ComPad all the time." When Tim raised an eyebrow and nodded, James scornfully responded, "Are you suggesting, I become a ComPad geek and run around in a make-believe world as an imaginary creature, like they do?"

"It was just an idea. If you really care about having an intimate relationship with your daughter, then it will entail meeting her wherever she is at."

"Doesn't the community forbid using the Outer Net?" James was relieved to find a roadblock to Tim's scary ideas.

"Very little is forbidden here, though some things are discouraged. We want people to have very little contact with the toxic outer world, because we are trying to establish a healthier way of life here. Using the Outer Net to create a rapport with your daughter sounds like a healthy use of technology. I can sign off on it and my Purple Band can open that door.

"I'll think about it. The idea seems a little daunting. These young kids are not going to like an old fart like me butting in."

"They won't know how old you are because everything is done through characters and yours can be any age you choose." Tim sounded reasonable.

"How would I start? I am familiar with a ComPad and ComScreen, but their stuff is a whole different software?"

"That's where the relationship work begins. Contact your daughter and ask her to teach you how. If you forge a teacher/student relationship with her, and she is the teacher, it takes you both out of the old roles and allows new ones to form."

"It sounds scary," James was being honest.

"Scary and exciting are the same emotion, filtered through different beliefs. Change your attitude and it might open a lot of new doors."

"Okay," James felt like a first-time skater venturing out onto thin ice, with cracks in it.

Later that evening, James decided to try it. Then he procrastinated. For over an hour he flipped through channels on the ComScreen while arguing with himself. Finally, he mustered his courage plus some false bravado and sent Sandra a text.

"Darling, I need a teacher to help me make one of those online characters. I want to experience the otherworld, but I don't know how to begin." He read this brief note over three times before he was ready to hit, SEND.

"Yo Dad, that is weird. I thought old people hate this stuff."

"I'm only forty-seven. That is not old, just older. Anyway, I am looking for a teacher. Do you want to teach me? Switch roles for a while?"

"Sure. Whatever," he could imagine her shrugging her shoulders and rolling her eyes.

"Do I have to make one of those things from scratch? Do I have to download an AI Vector Generator?" He tried to sound informed.

"No, just download a SIMS platform. Do you know what a platform is?" she asked like he was dumb.

He chose to ignore the slight and downloaded the program.

"Fill out the profile. Then pick and choose from the options being presented and build your Avatar. It is as easy as that. Give it a name, then you are off and running."

"Whoa. Could you slow that down and take it step by step?"

"Okay, go to the Character Builder dashboard. It has templates of people of all shapes and sizes representing different genders, races, and ethnicities. You can choose from various faces, bodies, and expressions. You can select one of the Avatars on the screen, or touch Shuffle until you find one you like.

"Can't I just be me?"

"Sure Dad, you can design an Avatar that matches you from your hairstyle to your everyday wear, but why do that when you can be anyone? You can take the form of an image of your real-life self, but a virtual character would be more fun. People create a character online to transfer their consciousness into the Avatar. This psionic link helps them make friends with people who might not give you a second glance in the RW (Real World) and it makes it easier to talk to people."

"Okay. The program is open, what do I do first?" asked James.

"Select, *Settings* and then, *Create New Avatar.* Choose *Customize* to change your Avatar's body and features. Then choose *Style* to change its clothes and accessories. Now select, *Save* and name it."

He chose a simple character, dressed him in plain clothes, and named him James Dole. He took a Screen Shot and sent it to Sandra.

"Dad, is that the best you can do? This Avatar is sooo boring. Let your creativity shine. Let your freak flag fly. You're not supposed to use your real name. Change it. I'm Taliya 456."

James went back to his profile page and changed the name to Big Dole 13.

This bonding thing was not working. He was so out of his comfort zone. He wanted to scream, not at her, just scream. She must have felt that because she softened the tone of the next text.

"Dad, take a picture of yourself and then play with it a little."

He chose the Photo option on the dashboard, stood straight and smiled. It came out pretty good, the picture that is, not his big paunch. He opened a submenu and began changing the numbers. It made the Avatar shorter and fatter, but it gave him the idea. He trimmed off sixty pounds of unnecessary pies and added half a foot to his height. While he was at it, he softened the lines in his face, which dropped thirty years from his age. Then he put on something he thought Sammy would wear and sat back to admire his new self. 'Not bad, not bad at all!' he mused.

"I have an Avatar I think you will like. His name is Big Dole 13," and he sent her another Screen Shot."

"The Avatar looks great. Now give him a cool name."

"Can I be Taliya's Dad?"

"No. Have you ever dreamt of being anyone else, or you had a special name when you were a kid?"

"Yeah, Buck. Can your character, I mean Avatar, interact with mine?"

"Of course," she replied.

"Great. How do we do that? How do I find you?"

"You need to put your Avatar in a Virtual World. Go to 'Download Virtual World.' Go down the list of worlds until you come to Trinitus. They offer a SIMS Platform.

He found 3D World Illustrated Backgrounds from the Trinitus Media Library; and was soon strutting down a street in New World town.

Chimes were coming from the screen and a light was blinking. He tapped on the lit button and a text appeared on the Avatar's watch. It said, "Dad, you can talk to me."

He touched the lit button again and mumbled to himself, "How do I get this damn thing to talk back?" To his amazement, those same words came out of the Avatar's mouth.

"Dad, look at your Avatar's watch." A cool-looking James, Buck 639, glanced down at his watch and saw a text from Taliya 456.

James was stunned at how real this Virtual World looked.

"Go to the Sanctuary Café," said the next text. "I will meet you there. I will be wearing a long red scarf with cats on it."

"Will do, CUT."

'Cool, you remembered. :) SML means smiles.

James' AVATAR strutted through the almost familiar town. It looked a lot like the real community he was in.

When he got to the café, he acted like he belonged. His AVATAR looked confident. Even though he felt like a phony, an intruder who did not belong, no one could see that.

The café had lots of tall round tables outside. He saw his daughter's Avatar standing at a table with three other characters. As his Avatar approached, they all said, "We see you!"

Their mouths were moving and it really looked like they were saying that. He made a mental note to ask her later how they were able to mimic facial expressions.

Taliya excused herself from her online friends and walked into the Sanctuary with Buck 639. They took a table near the wall.

"You're looking good, Buck. Well done. So now we have some time together. Tell me what is going on in your life. One day you went off to work like it was a regular day, and then poof, you were gone. Then Sammy and I didn't hear a word from you and Mom won't allow us to mention anything about you."

"Yeah, well, I got laid off from work because of automation so I wandered out to the desert and found myself in the City of Hope. I stayed because I did not want to face your mother's wrath. We have not been getting along with each other for years now."

He thought of saying, "You know how she can be when she wants something to go the way she wants it," but decided not to. Being Buck, he did not feel bitter. He would not bad-mouth his wife to her daughter.

"Losing this job was going to cause a fight. I just did not want to fight anymore. He thought of saying, 'I have had enough of my old life, enough of her yelling at me for something that was not my fault. I was so depressed and at my wits end.' Buck didn't want to say that either.

"I just couldn't go home so I drove aimlessly until I found this place. I just ended up here by coincidence. It was pure luck."

"What do you want to do about us? Are we ever going to be a family again? I saw the divorce papers. Is this the end of our family?"

"I don't know," he honestly admitted. This new, younger, taller version of him didn't feel a need to blame Judy for all his problems. Buck was not quick to offer false reassurances. He just wanted to connect with this stranger who reminded him of a little girl he used to feel very close to, a little girl who disappeared one day and a belligerent stranger took her place.

"When I came to Hope, I had no clue what Trinitus Cities were about. Then I stayed for the free food and lodging. Now I have a great job that I really like, so I am staying for lots of reasons.

"What's it like there?"

"It is very different than the RW, much calmer and friendlier. Life has no pressure, no need to give up the things that you care about, and no need to scramble to survive. People work together in ways that work best for them. Each person wants to contribute because so many people have given so much to them. They really care about each other. I have a guide named Tim. He chooses to be there for me. He listens to me, advises and helps me get whatever I need. He is patient with me and does not force me to do anything. He really helps me sort out my feelings and see the truth of things without telling me what to think. I never feel out on a limb all by myself. He's a good man."

"Do they try to brainwash you?"

"Not at all, they listen and support me in discovering who I am and what I really want. I get to talk about my feelings, but it is a good thing. There are too many hurts and fears locked inside me, and they make me act in ways that are not good for me or my family. When I get them out in the open and look at them, they lose their hold over me."

"It looked cool from everything I read about it. My teacher was a little skeptical. She compared it to Communism, Socialism, and a weirdo cult.

"Sandra, I hope you are not being brainwashed. School can indoctrinate you to believe a lot of prejudicial things. Sharing resources and taking care of each other within a community can be a very good thing."

"The teacher did not say it was bad; she just compared it to them because we were studying different styles of organizing society. She said that Communism only existed for about ten years during the 1930s. After that, it quickly morphed into Totalitarianism. They kept the name and ideology, but the government did not follow Marx's ideal of empowering women and children. The USSR and China promoted what they call, Communism. But Marx's 1875 slogan "from each according to his ability, to each according to his need" is not how their society operates. Their governments are Totalitarian Oligarchies."

"I can go along with that and Trinitus is also not a cult, because there is no one person or ideology that everyone must adhere to. In cults everyone drinks the same Kool Aid. In Trinitus, people are free to choose their own religion and beliefs, so it is not a cult. As for Socialism, if the community allows people to have more and succeed on their own; there is nothing wrong with making sure that everyone in the community has enough food, and access to collective resources. In Trinitus, they don't take away what people have, but rather, they make sure everyone has what they need."

"My teacher said something similar. I better get back to my friends. It's been nice talking with you. I don't know why we never do it in the RW. You are different here."

"Thank you, so are you. I'm glad we had this visit. If your friends are still there, I would like to meet them, not as your dad, just as Buck."

"This cute girl in the red scarf flung it over her shoulder, laughed, and said, "Sure, I have nothing to lose.""

The two Avatars walked back to the outdoor table. Taliya introduced Buck as a friend. Everyone said, "We see you," and they all hung out for a while. Buck was a little quiet at first but managed to say enough for everyone to feel he was part of the group.

After a while, the group broke up and Buck said goodbye. He wanted to ask Sandra to meet him again, but he did not want to scare her off by asking too much. So, he waved and said, "We see you. Catch you later, Taliya."

"We see you. I'm usually here after I do my homework. Stop by after work any time," Taliya said as she waved goodbye.

When he left the Virtual World, where he was young, and comfortable inside himself, he realized why his kids liked hanging out in a Virtual World so much. As an Avatar with a fictional nature, it is easier to be honest, open, and more truly yourself. It feels anonymous and therefore safer to reveal your true self.

CHAPTER 8

Escape

Judy Cordileone-Dole got off work a little early. She stopped and picked up some groceries. At home, she turned on her ComPad to check emails and began to put the groceries away in the refrigerator and cupboards. She was anxious to see if James would write again. When she found the email, she felt elated and angry. She bit her lip, reached into the bag for a box of cereal and dropped it on the floor. Her mind was elsewhere.

She loved this man and hated him too. He was always pulling something to disappoint her. He was a little boy in a man's body. He always promised to do things but rarely followed through. Time and again, he sabotaged his job and spent several months lying on the sofa watching videos, while she carried the whole family.

She worked, shopped, drove the kids around, came home to a messy house and a lump of a husband on the sofa. When she could not handle it anymore and exploded, he would act all wounded and say he was going back to work just to escape her wicked tongue. Again and again, every year or so, he would lose his job, and it would be the same.

He never even cleaned up his own mess. She would come home from a long day of work and chores, to make dinner; but first, she had to wash the dishes in the sink before she could even start.

That man could get her so mad. All she wanted was a real partner, someone who held up his end, a man who worked hard like her and was willing to carry half the household responsibilities.

He drove her to despair until she threatened to get a divorce. She hoped the threat would wake him up and get him to fly right. The first few times she said it, there was a temporary burst of improvement, but after a while, even that threat didn't work. She was so desperate, the desperation fermented into hopelessness, and now she was utterly miserable.

She had two ungrateful teenagers, who needed a taskmaster to make sure they did their chores. She looked in the mirror and saw their mother, a fire-breathing dragon; his wife, a nagging shrew; and the worker, a beast of burden towing its load. Where was Judy, bright, smart, hopeful young Judy? Nowhere in the mirror was even a trace of her. She wanted to break the mirror, instead, she poured a glass of wine. It would take her into a fuzzy place, maybe even a peaceful one, where she did not have her face pushed up against her miseries.

He had disappointed her so many times that she was at a point where she expected him to fail and blame his failures on her. He blamed everything on her, just as he had been doing from the very beginning.

Sandra came in and started helping her put the groceries away. From the look on her mother's face, she was sure mom had received an email from Dad. She said nothing, just went about putting things away.

Judy opened a bottle of wine and gulped down half a glass before she opened the email. She read the last one but did not respond. When she first read it, she assumed he would come to his senses, change his mind, and come home all contrite and apologetic.

When the divorce papers came yesterday, she was shocked. They had been fighting for so long; she assumed it would go on like this. She never imagined it would end. She opened the email and read it, reread it, and reached for the bottle of wine. She finished her glass, then finished the bottle, and then checked the cupboard to make sure there were more bottles. She was going to need quite a few before this night was over.

Sandra watched her mother without making it obvious. She was in the room when the divorce papers arrived. Her mom started cursing him out and then began throwing things. She broke an old vase, a full glass of wine, and an old trophy James had won in a bowling league.

The other day, after James called, Judy began shouting obscenities. In disgust, she tore her Smartwatch off her wrist and threw it with its evil message on the couch. Sandra was now ready for another outburst from her mom. Her mother looked just as mad as before, but now she just stood there looking off into space. Then she began some serious drinking.

Sandra decided to wade into dangerous waters. "What's wrong Mom, is it Dad again?"

Sammy came into the kitchen. He was oblivious to the tension in the room. Being fourteen, his mind was in his stomach. It always was these days. He was looking for something to snack on until dinner.

"You are both on your own tonight. Scrounge up your own dinner. I am going to my room and don't even think of bothering me," she slurred.

Sammy grabbed a fresh bag of cookies lying on the counter, decided they would make a perfect supper, and withdrew with his treasure to his bedroom.

Sandra cooked spaghetti in one pot. Then she poured a bottle of marinara sauce, and a handful of frozen meatballs, into another. Within half an hour she and her brother were eating dinner. Devouring a full bag of cookies beforehand did nothing to dampen his appetite.

Sandra cleaned the kitchen and put everything away. She did not want to do anything to set her mother off. The woman never used to drink, but lately she was packing it away.

Later that night, Sandra was getting ready for bed when she heard thumping around and the garage door opening. She looked out her window and saw her mom putting out the trash a night too early. She went to her mother's room and saw three empty bottles lying on her end table. The room was torn apart.

She heard her mother coming and dashed back to her room. When all was quiet again, she slipped out the back and looked at the garbage. It was just as she suspected, packed full of dad's clothes and music hard drives.

She returned to her room and threw herself on the bed. Her mind was racing. Then she calmed down and dictated a text which she sent to her best friend.

"Tammy, my mom has gone ballistic. Can you drive me to Arizona tonight?"

"Arizona? Are you running away to Trinitus?"

"Yeah, can you drive me? It is important. My dad is in the City of Hope. I need to see him!"

"Really? I thought you said he'd freak out if he knew you were planning to go there."

"Yeah, that's what I thought. Who would have guessed?"

"Is it as cool as we imagined?"

"Yeah, cool green. He likes it there!"

"He said he arrived by luck, but there are no coincidences, right? It had to be fate! I knew we were supposed to live there and this is the sign we've been waiting for. Are you with me?"

"Wow! OMG! You mean we are really going to do this? We've been talking about this for about a year now. I can't believe we are really going to just walk out of the Virtual World into RW Trinitus."

"Does that mean you are on board with this?"

"My dad said it is a great place. He likes it and wants to stay. He is all for my living with him."

"Okay, let's go. I'm in. I'll pack some stuff, charge up the car, and pick you up in an hour. Is that enough time?"

"Make it a little longer. My mom threw everything my dad owns in the trash. We can't leave yet. I need to wait for my mom to fall asleep before I can pack his stuff in your car. I will text you. Keep alert to your Smartwatch."

"Green. I am not going to tell Jack I'm leaving."

"I thought you and your boyfriend were getting on well."

"I like living with him, but I'm not sure he would be supportive of my moving to Arizona."

"Ok, CUT."

Sandra peeked out the window and watched her mom pack more stuff in boxes and put them out on the curb. She turned on her ComPad, went to the NEW WORLD SIMS where she hung out with some online friends, until her mom's room was quiet for a while.

The ComScreen was still on, so Sandra could not be sure her mom was asleep, but the room seemed still so she tiptoed over, cracked the door a bit, and peeked in. Mom was sprawled across the bed, still fully dressed, with four empty bottles lying on the floor beside her.

Sandra packed whatever she thought she might need and a few of her favorite things, wrote her mom a note saying she was with a friend and she was safe, then texted Tammy. She looked around her dad's office and then the garage to check if there was anything her mom had left behind. Mom was thorough.

Sandra tiptoed back to her room to grab her bag and slipped out the back door. She waited outside beside her dad's things for Tammy to pull up.

Once the girls were on the freeway, Tammy put the car in Auto-Drive, and they relaxed. They talked about the City of Hope for hours. By the time they reached the desert, they were tired and talked out. They both curled up and fell asleep while the Auto Drive drove on a nearly empty road, deep into the night. When their exit was on the horizon, and the sun was just rising, the Heads-up Display started to beep loudly and said, "Approaching exit, two miles ahead." It woke them up. Tammy turned off the Heads-up Display and the Auto-Drive.

The young man at the gate asked their ages, so they playfully flirted with him as a distraction. Then Tammy flashed her license proving she was eighteen, and he let them through. The tram operator helped them get everything onboard and took them to the Emergence Hotel. Inside, a sleepy busboy put all the boxes on a huge luggage cart.

James was awoken by the ComPad chiming. He looked at the time, thinking it was the alarm, but it said, 5:45 am, so he turned over and burrowed deeper into the covers. It chimed again. More awake this time, James realized it was an incoming call from Tim. Feeling confused, he answered without turning on the screen.

Tim's voice was clear and soft. "Your daughter is here with a friend and a mountain of boxes. Please come to the lobby."

"Sandra, she's here?"

"Yes, she is. She says she is here to stay with you, permanently."

"Oh! Give me a minute. I'll be right down."

James put his clothes on in a hurry. His head was spinning and a part of him thought he was still in the dream.

As he rode down in the elevator, he kept muttering to himself, "What the hell is she thinking? Judy is going to be so pissed!"

He met his Guide in the lobby. Tim studied James's appearance, disheveled and frantic. He could see that the man's blood was boiling. Calming down was probably the last thing on his mind, so he asked his charge to stop for a minute and suggested they breathe together.

While James was begrudgingly taking deep breaths, Tim envisioned James relaxing and beamed compassionate energy to him.

In a calm slow voice and a deep tone, Tim said, "Your daughter and her friend are in a comfortable room down the hall. Just relax and get your wits together first. You are going to need them. Take another deep breath. You can handle this without getting angry. Just feel yourself standing solid, know you are supported, and weigh your words before you speak. Ready?"

James nodded and they walked down the hall. It was on the left side of the building, an area he had not seen before. When they reached the room, Sandra jumped up and threw her arms around her father. The tension in his shoulders melted away.

When she let go, all the words came racing out, "Dad, I had to come. Mom was drunk. She was throwing all your stuff out! When she saw your email, she wouldn't talk about it. She got stinking drunk and threw out everything you own. I couldn't let her do that to you, so I brought everything here. This is my best friend, Tammy. She and I have been dreaming of coming to Trinitus together for a while, so I asked her to drive me."

The tension was mounting again in James. Through a rigid jaw he growled, "Your mother is going to be so pissed! You shouldn't have come here in the middle of the night. Does she know where you are?"

Sandra was not going to give up hope so fast. She set out to melt her daddy's heart.

"It's okay, Dad. I left her a note. She knows I am with a friend."

"It is so not okay. At sixteen, you can't just get up and leave. She'll report you to the police as a runaway!" With each word, his volume got louder.

Tim jumped in to calm things down. "Come. Let's sit down and quietly talk things out." He pointed to a circle of chairs with an outstretched hand and waited while they sat down.

Tim beamed warm accepting energy at James, and said to him, "We see you." Then he asked James, "Please look your daughter in the eyes and greet her. James had no recent memory of looking in Sandra's eyes. It took a couple of uncomfortable tries before he could do it. With a deep belabored breath, he tried to see the little girl he loved in this complex creature. He found a line near her brow and a dimple in her cheek that reminded him of his little girl, and he said with sincerity, "We see you." Sandra looked deeply into her father's eyes and thought about sweet easygoing Buck. With a very private smile, she said, "We see you." Then Sandra and Tammy exchanged the same greeting and the atmosphere in the room felt a lot calmer.

In a softly sincere voice Tim said, "Now everyone, before we talk, please take a deep breath, straighten your spine, and feel your feet on the floor. This will ground you. I invite you to hold an image in your heart. See yourself floating in the hand of God, safe and protected. I will be right here if you need me."

James, please take one more breath and then calmly explain to Sandra why you think this is not a good idea."

"Darling, I appreciate that you did not want to be with your mother when she is so out of control. Did she try to hurt you or your brother?

"No. Of course not," she was taken back by the question. Her mom was only hurting herself.

"I know it is hard on you when she drinks," James pressed the point.

His head finally felt clear, and he gathered his thoughts, "Sandra, I want to gain custody of you, and I want you to live here with me. To do that, I need to go through a custody hearing. Coming here has just jeopardized my chances. You must go back immediately."

Sandra realized that she really screwed up and responded defensively, "Yeah, well, I had to do something! Or would you prefer the garbage men take everything you own? What else could I do, just stand there and watch? What Mom did was wrong!"

James looked at his daughter and had to fight his way through the fear and anger that was gripping him.

He remembered being Buck and the easy rapport they shared in the Virtual World. He wished they could go back to that now. This memory helped his anger drain away and he said softly, "Darling, I know you were just trying to help. I should not have gotten so angry at you. I was just afraid that a rash move now could keep us from being together later."

"I'm sorry Dad. I had to do something. And you don't know what it is like being around her when she is drinking like that. She has been doing it a lot lately, even before you left. Can't I stay with you, Dad? I'll go to school every day, get good grades, and do my chores. You'll see, I won't be a burden."

"Darling, we are in the middle of a divorce, that means I am living under a microscope. One wrong move and we lose our right to be together. We need your mother to agree to mutual custody. She has not been feeling very generous lately. We need to get on the good side of her, if we want her to agree to our terms. Running away will not put you on her good side."

Sandra looked down in her lap. "Sorry, but I had to do something, I guess I wasn't thinking."

Tim said soothingly, "Sandra, you acted impulsively, but your heart was in the right place. James is lucky to have such a resourceful daughter."

James felt he should say something, so he said, "Well, I suppose. I am glad that my stuff is not in the trash. But coming all the way out here in the middle of the night was dangerous and without your mother's permission was stirring up a real can of worms."

He took a deep breath and said, "You can't run away from your problems," then he heard what he just said and felt compelled to add, "I don't have a right to say much about that. I haven't exactly been a good example for facing your problems," feeling a wave of exhaustion, he rubbed his face with both hands.

"It will only be a little over a year at most. I'll try to gain custody of both of you, if I can," James tried to reassure her. Seeing her sad face, he added, "I am so sorry. I wish you could stay, but it won't work."

A thought ran across Sandra's face lighting it up. "Maybe I can get emancipation. I can claim that, can't I?" It was something her online friends had talked about.

"If your mother continues to drink, maybe you can. It might be a costly legal battle. Let's not make it our first approach. It can cause a terrible rift between you and your mother, and between her and me, plus, Sammy will be left behind. We don't want to do that to him."

"I just don't want to be around her when she is drinking like that. She won't talk to me about anything."

James smiled weakly and said with a shudder, "I'll try to talk to Judy. I will call her in a couple of minutes. Maybe we can resolve this before the cops get involved. Tim, please get the girls a room, so they can rest. Thank you."

Tim smiled and said, "Follow me. Get some sleep. You must be exhausted after your long trip from San Bernardino. When you wake up, text me, and I will take you for something to eat before you leave."

Tammy, who had been silent until then, spoke up. "Thank you for your hospitality. I am over eighteen and I do not live at home. I would like to stay."

Tim accompanied them to the front desk, left them in Nicole's care, and returned to James. Tim offered to mediate the call and James agreed.

Tim showed him to a private room across the hall. "Let me talk first that will disrupt the dynamics you have with her. Okay?"

James nodded and accessed her number. It took several rings before Judy answered the ComPad.

"Do you know what time it is? Who is this?" she demanded to know. The pounding in her head echoed in her tone.

"My name is Tim Carriage and I'm with your husband James. He needs to talk to you about something very important."

"It is 6:00 in the morning! What the hell is this about!?"

Tim had them both on a conference call and signaled James to talk. "Judy, you apparently got stinking drunk and through all my stuff out!"

"So, what, you left!" she accused. "I can do what I please with the stuff in my house!"

Tim was signaling to him to soften his tone before he spoke.

James imagined what Tim would say and tried to imitate his tone. "Well," he said with an artificial calm, "the trouble is, Sandra got mad at you and she brought my stuff to me in Arizona. I didn't know anything about this until she showed up on my doorstep. Now she wants to stay, but I told her that it wasn't a nice way to treat you, so I am going to let her catch a few winks, and then I'll send her home to you." He did a rather good imitation of Tim. It took so much concentration that he forgot to feel angry.

"What! Sandra is gone!" she shouted. Then he heard Judy yelling down the hall for her daughter.

In a sleepy voice, Sammy asked, "What is wrong?"

Judy barked at him to go back into his room.

Then she growled, "What the hell are you playing at James! What the hell are you doing with my daughter?!"

Her tone ignited him, like a match to a flame. He was boiling now, "Sandra is my daughter too, and she has a right to see me! She ran to me because her mother was stinking drunk!"

"I am going to sue your ass off! It will be a cold day in hell before you get custody of my children. I'm their mother. I will win!" Judy spewed in rage.

Tim's soft voice entered the call and said slowly, "Now that you have both stated your positions, let's calm down and talk this through. Mrs. Dole, your daughter and her friend are safe here. We will make sure she gets home after she sleeps and eats some food. We will not keep her here without your permission. We called simply to put your mind at ease, before you found out she is gone, and began to worry."

James rolled his eyes. "You see what I have to put up with now!" James said to Tim, throwing up his hands in frustration. "I can't say anything!"

Judy heard this and it made her fume. "Who the hell is this guy? You've got no business interfering. This is between me and James."

"I'm a mediator. Breathe Mrs. Dole. A few deep breaths will make you feel calmer."

"It's Cordileone-Dole to you Mister, and don't tell me to calm down!"

In a soothing voice Tim said, "You have every reason to be upset. I am here to help you. I know you are hurting, and you had to drink yourself into oblivion just to cope with the rocky situation you're in right now. This is a very difficult time for you. I want to help you and your family. Please let's breathe and all calm down, so we can make some reasonable plans about what to do next."

"Talk to my lawyer. I don't want to talk to either of you! My daughter better be back home before I return from work tonight!" The line went dead.

"You see, she is impossible!" James threw up his hands.

"James, you succeeded in stopping her from calling the police. You overcame the first obstacle. Now how do we get her home?"

"Well, I was thinking of giving her my car. I don't need it here. Then she can drive herself home."

"At sixteen, she only has a Learner's Permit, so she needs an adult driver in the car.

The girls were too excited to sleep, so they hung out. They chatted until their bellies began to rumble, so they texted Tim.

Meanwhile, James sent Taylor a text asking to have half the day off. He explained that his daughter had arrived unexpectedly, and he wanted to show her around. Taylor responded quickly and wrote, "That's fine. We only look at what you produce, and you have been doing good work so far. Your hours are not important since you're doing a good job."

Tim and James met the girls for a late breakfast at 10:00. Tim suggested giving them a brief tour of L-Town and the Wildlife Park. James agreed on the condition that he could be at work by noon.

They boarded the tram. James and Sandra sat together so Tim and Tammy sat behind them.

"Dad, do you really want a divorce? Isn't that a little drastic and extreme? You always told Sammy and me to work things out, so why can't you? And don't play the 'you-will-understand-when-you-grow-up card'," Sandra said as she squared her shoulders to look taller and more grown up. "I am old enough to know."

"Your mother has been threatening to divorce me for years, just to control and belittle me. But don't get me wrong, I don't want to talk smack about her, I'm just being honest."

Sandra huffed and rolled her eyes. "Why do you let her make all the decisions? Are you afraid to stand up to her?"

"She can be pretty ferocious!" James said with a defeated look in his eyes.

"I agree. I love her, but she can be a real pain when she wants something. I've seen how she cuts you down. Sometimes she does that to me and Sammy when she is drunk. She thinks you're lazy and irresponsible. She always tells us so. My friends call this 'mental abuse.' I get why you left. I understand why you ran off. I wish I could too. Boy, after your call, she got plastered and called you every name in the book."

"Her drinking is totally not cool, especially in front of you kids. I didn't know about it before I left. I was so confused. I don't think I even knew what I was running from at first. But I do now. I was never running away from you and Sammy."

"I understand, Dad. She is impossible to live with. I tried to explain it to Sammy, but he is taking Mom's side. I don't know why."

"I don't want either of you to take sides. I'm not perfect. Just remember, this is not your fault. I love both of you and wish I could be with you, but right now, I need this place. It is helping me."

"Mom calls it a cult."

"Your mother hasn't responded to my email. We have not talked, but I am sure she will want you to finish school where you are, so I wouldn't count on her letting you live with me for a while."

"Stand up to her, Dad. Let her know this is a good place for us to grow up in. Tell her the schools are great, and the community is a healthy environment. She will like those words."

James smiled and sighed, "I will stand up to her and you should too. When she starts drinking, go to a friend's house and when she bad-mouths Trinitus, stand up to her. Just because she has grievances with me, doesn't mean she should judge this community harshly."

Tim had one ear listening to Tammy, and the other eavesdropping on James's conversation. Despite his training in non-interference, and letting people clean up their own mistakes, he could not resist sharing one small insight.

"James, it is not fair to pit Sandra against her mother. Just because you find it hard to stand up to Judy, don't program your daughter to do it for you. She only knows your side of the story, I am sure your wife has a different perspective, and that deserves to be heard too. It is unhealthy for you to triangulate like that."

When Sandra and her dad looked at Tim perplexed, he said, "Triangulation is where one person in a triad turns the second person against the third. The two are bullying up on the one."

"I wasn't doing that!" objected James. "I was just encouraging my daughter to protect herself."

"Rationalize it anyway you want," said Tim in a soft gentle voice, "but the result will be the same. She will get in trouble with her mom. You don't want her to carry the split between her parents as a division within herself. That lays seeds for problems later in life. Your problems with Judy belong between the two of you. You and Judy should keep the children out of it as much as possible; otherwise, they become pawns in your conflict and that can be very damaging to them."

"Sandra, I need to clear it with your mother first, but I don't need my car here and I was thinking of giving it to you as a birthday present."

"Oh my God, yes! That would be so green! Thank you so much."

"That way, if you stay another year, at least you'd have a car of your own until you move here. Then you can sell it."

"That would be super! I would love to have a car! But then I still want to come live here."

"I wouldn't put too much hope in that happening before you are finished with college."

"Isn't that the truth?" She sighed heavily. "Mom will probably blame you when I tell her I don't want to go to college."

"That's not new. She blames me for everything anyway."

"Don't worry about her forcing you to go to college. She already spent all your tuition. I had to use it to pay debts that were mostly hers. Don't tell her that. She doesn't know the money is gone. I need to tell her first. That might stop her from pressuring you to go to college."

"Okay, my lips are sealed."

Breakfast was wonderful. The conversation was mostly Tim describing all the interesting and unique aspects of the community. They took a tram around the city and then went around the Wildlife Park. The girls were charmed and both wanted to stay.

Tim agreed to help Tammy make the transition and spoke to Nicole about arranging a room in the Emergence Hotel.

When the topic of Sandra leaving came up, James offered to give her his car, but who would drive it? If Sandra got busted driving alone with a Learner's Permit, her mom might not allow him to have any visitation rights, ever. Plus, Tim discouraged them from breaking the law.

The time went by in a flash. Tim convinced Tammy to take Sandra home and settle things with Jack. It wasn't right to disappear and only leave a note. She also left a lot of stuff at his place. She agreed to go home with Sandra and return in a couple of days.

"Now Sandra," James said in his calm Tim voice, "Don't give your mother a hard time, promise? She is having a rougher time with this divorce than I imagined. I thought she would be glad."

"I'll try," she said with a pout, "but I don't think she is treating you right and that makes me really mad!"

"I understand, but if you go off on her, it will not help you get here before you're eighteen."

When they were ready to leave, Sandra hugged her dad and whispered in his ear, "Meet me at the Sanctuary Café in VR tonight. I will be there around seven."

"Yep, see you there," he smiled to himself.

"Drive safely. Use the Heads-Up Display. Set the alarm before you get to Highway 15 and stay wake on that freeway because it can get tricky, okay?" James picked up his ComPad and transferred E-Money from his account to hers, so the girls would have enough for the trip home.

He waved until he could not see her and then wiped tears from his eyes. He walked down to the tram and went to work.

The girls were quiet for the first hour. Each was lost in her own thoughts. But once they started talking, the seven-hour drive, with a few small stops, went by quickly enough. Her mom was home when she got there, and she was sober.

James went to work a little distracted. He finished the last of his research on growing and acquiring bamboo and shared it with his team. In the final sharing circle of the day, they all agreed that they had done enough research to submit a preliminary draft of their bamboo yurts. They ceremoniously push the SEND button to Tomas, the Program Coordinator, for approval. The proposal looked good. Pierre pulled out a small flask of something herbal with a sharp kick and they all took a sip to christen their accomplishment. They had good reason to believe their proposal would be accepted. They had dotted all the 'i's and crossed all the 't's. James went home tired and satisfied.

CHAPTER 9

Health and Well-Being

James dashed home from work excited to meet Buck again. It was fun to be young and looking good. When he was younger, it was easy for him to have a solid sensuous body, but the years stomp all over that self-image and he was left with a paunch and a slouch that were too hard to get rid of. After all, pastries are heaven's way of showing love.

With a swipe of his finger, he could be anyone. So, James turned on the ComPad and went to discover his true self. Surely, he was more than just a fat slouch. So, he gave a few verbal commands and there was Buck, looking dashing as he was about to explore the world.

Buck knew the way to the café, which made him feel a little less like a stranger in a strange new land. At the café, he met Taliya's friends. The first time Taliya introduced them, he was too scared to hear their names.

As he drew close, a tall, long-legged beauty with the purest white hair smiled and waved him over. "We see you," she said, "I'm Kitara 422," and she giggled. Then Ryan stood up from the table and said, "It's real green to see you again Buck. We met yesterday. I recognize you."

Kitara giggled again and Buck wondered why but had no idea what to say next.

"Has anyone seen Taliya?" he asked.

This drew another giggle from Kitara.

Ryan answered. "She's been frozen. Frozen is when someone takes away your ComScreen and you are stranded in the Dulls."

Buck was disappointed, but the feeling was fleeting. He was interested in testing out his wings, so he decided to stay and follow their lead. He was getting the hang of moving and posturing, everything was going well.

"Kitara, I'm new to this town, what should I know?"

"We see you. We see each other. Out there in the Dulls you need to be one person all the time. Here, you can have different personalities and different desires. New World is a safe, welcoming space. As the creators of our own world, we have all agreed to make it that way," she said and leaned closer to him, gazing seductively up into his eyes. It made James squirm, but Buck just sat there and smiled. James gave a command for that smile just at the right moment. It felt like a noteworthy accomplishment.

Ryan jumped in to add, "We don't have to clean up that overwhelming old mess they call a world out there in the Dulls. We have this clean slate. Here we can relax because we do not judge each other. We are free to be our natural selves. In the Dulls people need make-up, costumes, and props to make them believe they fit in. In truth, there is no room for your mind and Soul to really fly free in the Dulls.

"Lots of Avatars have different ideas on how to create this new world. So, many different worlds have emerged. Here in Trinitus, we are learning to pool our ideas and are co-creating an amazing environment that feels wonderful. In this virtual world, we have gathered like-minded people and envision together. It is exhilarating to have all these possibilities flying through your mind. Everyone can choose or create his own world. So, we have a lot of freedom."

James wanted Buck to nod but couldn't find the right setting for the tilt of his head, so nothing happened. He made a mental note to practice, so next time he would have more control over his Avatar's body.

Buck listened but failed to nod. Ryan took his lack of response to mean Buck was cool green, and assumed the new Avatar already knew all this.

Kitara asked Buck how he knew Taliya. He answered honestly, "I met her yesterday in this café." This made her laugh.

Her response surprised him, so he asked, "Why was that funny?"

"Okay, I will break protocol and tell you my name in the *Dulls*. It's Tammy. When we returned last night, I walked Sandra into the house for moral support. Her mom went totally ballistic. After a lot of yelling, she grounded and froze Sandra. We met online. Now Taliya is my best friend, in here and out there.

That really put him at ease. It took a minute for him to wrap his head around the fact that this long-legged white-haired vixen is in truth, the petite, bouncy, black-haired young woman, he met this morning.

For the next hour, Kitara flirted with him, and he responded playfully, while Ryan entertained them with interesting scenarios. He was a great storyteller. Feeling truly seen, Buck bid his new friends farewell, with the now comfortable greeting, "We see you."

Between all the events on Friday and beginning the new project on Monday, the weekend was just filler. He sorted through boxes, went to another Anger Management meeting, and attended a Process Group. One seemed like a continuation of the other because all he could think about, or talk about, was his boiling anger at his wife and his concerns about raising two children alone.

On Saturday, Cathy called and invited him to dinner. She emphasized that it was not a date, just a visit, so he did not panic. They both kept it light. He talked about Sandra's visit. She shared a spiritual revelation she had, full of other worldly energies. It was entertaining. A comfortable friendship was budding between them.

During a walk in the garden with Tim on Sunday, James said he hoped Judy's drinking would help him gain custody of the kids. Tim just listened and said nothing. He could see that James was coming from a place of anger and revenge, but he had to be patient. Those were realizations that James would have to come to on his own.

Monday morning finally arrived. At work, everyone was antsy. They were on pins and needles waiting for their proposal to go through proper channels. Occasionally, James got motivated enough to putter around with his designs, but like the others, he did not feel engaged in what he was doing. Time moved at a snail's pace. James had several bouts of anxiety throughout the day as he pictured his contribution bogging down the works.

James thought about seeing his therapist, Dr. Fornelli, but still wasn't sure that he was the right choice, so he called Kim. She was receptive to having a session with him and had an opening that evening.

The day dragged on until almost four o'clock, when the project approval came through. Then everyone was too excited to work, so they called it an early day. Tomorrow promised to be a busy one.

James was glad to leave the building and be outdoors. He took a tram to the Medical Cluster where he found Dr. Fouche in a small building, much like the others in the cluster. It was the usual mushroom on stilts, but the design had an unusual feature. Two staircases were tucked against the building, both leading to the front door. Above the door was a large, rounded glass canopy. Flowing over the canopy, was a stream of water falling into a small pool of water shaped like a heart, with the words, Wellness and Health Center written in aquamarine mosaic tiles inlaid among sparkling white stones in the pool.

James stood at the top of the stairs under the waterfalls feeling invigorated. The interior was more spacious than he expected. A sweet, kind-looking woman sat behind the desk. James assumed she was around his age, late forties. They exchanged greetings.

"We see you, James Dole. Welcome. You are here for your Red Band physical with Dr. Fouche, right? We received your questionnaire online. Is there anything you wish to add or change?" He nodded, no. "Please have a seat and the doctor will be with you in a minute."

James leaned back in a very comfortable seat. In his mind, he contrasted this office with the crowded medical waiting rooms he was familiar with. They usually had uncomfortable hard chairs as though they did not want you to stay long. Idly, he looked around and noticed a picture of the receptionist as a teenager at a diving match, wearing a first prize metal on a ribbon. It had a date on it. He automatically calculated her age. She was probably seventeen, so that means she is now... He was shocked to realize she is in her late seventies!

Just then, the door opened and Dr. Fouche entered. She invited him to follow her. He had waited less than two minutes. That was unheard of in the RW. That's how he was beginning to think of the world he had left behind.

"We see you, James. You are here for your Red Band physical. She placed a little cube on his finger and a thick wide bracelet on his wrist. She positioned the display over a main vein and touched a few words on the display. First, he felt mounting pressure on his wrist, then it subsided, and he felt a tiny pin prick. It hummed, chimed, and the display lit up with a lot of numbers on it. Some were written in blue, but several were in red. He figured the red ones were problems.

"Mr. Dole, you appear to have good core strength. Your stomach meridian is a bit weak. It is acting over-taxed. Your liver is strong but stressed. You are probably making it work very hard. That comes from eating a toxic diet. Your heart, liver, and lungs have good core strength, but they are also stressed right now. When the heart is stressed, it indicates that you are undergoing a period of emotional duress and instability. Be careful not to act with haste. The lungs are where you store grief. It indicates this is a time of loss. Life is demanding that you give up things that you may find hard to let go of.

"Your diastolic is strong and stable which is another sign of good core strength, but your systolic is higher than we like to see. It is another indication of agitation and stress.

"Your blood work looks good, though the cholesterol could be lower. I can see that you are new to the community, because you have been eating too much meat. The diet we have here will suit your body much better."

"Do you have any specific questions? Is there anything you want to talk about related to your body?"

"I want to get rid of this paunch. Is there a way without all these yoyo diets where I gain and lose, gain and lose?"

"Yes, I can recommend a program, but it will take determination and motivation. What would be your goal?

"To lose forty pounds and have a solid body."

"Envision what you will look like and when you can see it in your mind, nod your head." James nodded.

"I recommend that you download a picture of someone with this body and put your face on it. Put the picture on a mirror in your room and say a blessing over it every day. Never make comparisons.

"Think of this program as a train coming into a station. It may have to stop at a few other places first, but each one brings you that much closer to the station where your ideal body awaits you. If you make detours, it will take longer, but if you respect yourself and set your determination, you will reach this station eventually. I can also assign a Body Trainer to you. He will help you design a graduating food and exercise program.

"Will this program help me with my energy? I usually have low energy around mid-morning, but now that I think of it, that hasn't been happening lately."

"You mean, since you arrived here? That's because we do not have real coffee. Coffee is like sugar, it lifts you up and plunges you down, which is not just an energetic problem, it is an underlying factor in fluctuating moods. You will find that without coffee your moods are not as radical."

He was surprised to realize that this was true. What about the migraines?"

"I prescribe an Anger Management group to discharge the energy and Qigong to learn how to move energy through your body, so it does not get stuck in your head. I also recommend that you learn to be true to your own needs and desires. When you do what you think you should do, rather than what you feel is right for you, it creates a tension, which can mount into a migraine, an emotional explosion, or both.

"In summary, physically, you need a trainer to help you set up and maintain a diet that supports healthy functioning, and an exercise program to maintain the balance between how many calories go in and how many you expend. If you can keep your outlay slightly more than your intake, you will lose part of a pound every day until you reach a plateau. Then you will need to reevaluate your program. That is why we call it a 'graduating food and exercise' program.

"Your trainer will recommend a series of nutritional supplements, essential oils, herbal remedies, and Bach Flower remedies. The nutritional supplements add wind to your sails, they support organ functioning. The essential oils will help with various issues, like peppermint oil can relieve bloating and some forms of pain, clove oil can help with gum sensitivities, and Bach Flower essences can help stabilize your emotions. The trainer will tell you about Gut Connect 365, an herbal remedy for your leaky gut.

"I have addressed your physical, emotional, and mental issues. As for the spiritual underpinnings of good health, I recommend that you find a Spiritual Being, a Higher Self, a Spirit Guide, or a caring God, and foster that relationship. Having a strong spiritual relationship can iron out some of the bigger waves that life throws at us."

"That sounds good," he said, and surprisingly meant it. A picture of Buck flashed through his mind. Maybe he could be a little more like him in this world.

"I recommend that you meet with your trainer sooner rather than later. Here is the contact info to arrange a first meeting."

James walked out of her office thinking, "We see you," is an accurate statement. He felt like she saw him naked beyond the flesh, like she was seeing his cells.

James called the number and left a message. The call was returned within an hour. This was most assuredly a different world. People here are far more responsive and generally less busy. They do not put pressure on themselves to meet deadlines. Just the name 'deadline' tells you how unhealthy they are.

The trainer, Sven, proposed an On Screen visit first and then a meeting at the Permaculture Garden in his office cluster for the second one. He suggested the On Screen be tomorrow during Afternoon Break. James was feeling hopeful and a little scared. He had already tried lots of diets. They worked for a while. Then they always wore off. He gained back all the weight and then some, but he never had a trainer to support and oversee the process, so he hoped this would be more successful.

The next day unfolded in a flash. James, like everyone on the team, was totally involved in bringing their model to life. He had to set an alarm on his ComPad to remind him to stop for Afternoon Break. He was looking forward to talking to the new trainer.

James found a quiet corner and called Sven. After the usual greeting, Sven began discussing James's diet and gave him a list of healthy foods. Bread and pastries were on the list. That surprised him. He was sure they would be the first to go.

Sven explained, "Wheat, dairy, and sugar are not life-affirming foods, primarily because they have been genetically modified to increase profits, while being very hard on the digestive system. Therefore, they should be totally avoided. They are no longer food substances. However, here in Trinitus, we grow many healthy ancient varieties of wheat that have not been tampered with like faro and amaranth."

Sven recommended that James use discretion. He can choose one or two of these alternative grains a day, but no more than that, because even healthy forms of wheat are still carbohydrates. The body only needs small amounts of these grains for energy. The rest get stored as fats for later use.

He gave James a long list of foods that would support his health, most of which were fruits, vegetables, nuts, and plant-based meats.

"I usually get a list of foods to avoid when I go to the doctor," said James.

"That is a reflection on how some doctors think," Sven answered. "Here we are interested in encouraging good behaviors. We do not waste our time and energy avoiding bad things. The I Ching says, make so much progress in the good that evil has no room to exist. That is our philosophy here.

"We recommend that Red Bands attend a Body Care class to learn more about how the body works and how best to support healthy functioning. It covers nutrition, healing with food, homeopathy, herbology, and basic qigong. There is also a survey section that covers various physical support systems, like tai chi, Bach Flower remedies, yoga, breathwork, and several others. You will learn how to maintain your energy, nurture your stomach, balance your moods, and stabilize your weight."

"Thank you. I look forward to working with you. I've wanted to lose weight for a while."

James was so engrossed in his work that he lost track of the time. Luckily, Carla went to the snack area and called over her shoulder, "Does anyone want a power bar?" That dragged him out of his creative frenzy and back into this world.

"Sure, what time is it?" he answered.

"Just a little after five."

A brain cell fired and James remembered that he had a 5:30 in-person appointment with Kim. He jumped up in a flash and was out the door before the others could say goodbye.

James caught a tram to Kim's office. He was looking forward to meeting her in person. He found the unique shape of her building charming. It was a round structure like a wedding cake with tiers. Each of the four floors was a little smaller than the one below, which left marvelous balconies all the way around the outside. The top floor held a roof garden of fruit trees.

He entered through arched double doors and found himself in a huge open space with mezzanines overlooking the atrium, like the ones in his office building. The large round skylight in the center had hidden pipes around it, from which fell a fountain of water. Beneath it, a large round pool was lined in aquamarine glass mosaic tiles, which gave the water a soft blue hue. Colored lights embedded in the ceiling around the fountain beamed playful colors dancing off the falling water.

It was a very expansive and peaceful space that elicited a touch of the elated feeling one gets in a cathedral.

A circular staircase went around the walls leading from one tier to the next. Even though an elevator was tucked under the stairs, James decided to walk. It was partly because the staircase looked so inviting, and partly because he wanted to lose weight before he went for his physical tomorrow. He figured walking up three flights were worth at least half a pound and told himself, "Every little bit I lose helps."

Slightly out of breath, he huffed and puffed up the last flight. Muttering to himself that they were higher than they looked from below.

He caught his breath, found the right office, and opened the door. The first thing he noticed was sweet incense, something very soothing. Then he became aware of soft dreamy music quietly in the background, creating a relaxed atmosphere. He entered a small waiting room with light yellow walls. There were a couple of comfortable chairs and a small table with a tray of sand on it. A tiny rake was neatly arranged beside the sand and an open red silk covered box sat beside it. Inside were an assortment of little statues, animals, and temples. A printed note in lovely calligraphy said, "Please play with me."

While he waited, he made a squiggly design in the sand with the tiny rake. He carefully placed a little boy and a little puppy on one side and a tiny colorful red pagoda on the other. He stepped back. As he was admiring his creation, an inner door opened, and Kim came out. She smiled and led him into her room.

With a sweep of her hand, she indicated all the places where he could sit or lie down. He chose the leather sofa because it faced away from her. He felt safer talking without her eyes on him.

"James, it is good to see you in person. What is up for you today, and this past weekend? What are the story and the challenges underneath?"

"My wife threw my things in the trash and my daughter rescued everything. She called a friend with a car, and they came way out here. They asked if they could stay."

James felt a soft heat rising from the sofa. He melted into the invitingness of it and shared more. "I was amazed that Sandra would go so far out of her way to rescue my stuff and come see me. I was shocked that she wanted to live in Trinitus and spend time with me. At home, she was so into her internet games and friends that she hardly ever said a word to me. This is all a big surprise to me!"

Wanting him to feel safe, she playfully asked, "What are the cherries and the pits of this story, the highs and the lows, the concerns and the challenges? Why wouldn't your daughter be interested in you?"

He thought about that before he said, "I don't know. They grow up and their parents become a nuisance to them. The last few years, that is how I feel she sees me, just a nuisance. She and I used to talk, laugh, and play together. But then she got sucked into ComScreen games and Facebook and it became her whole life. She forgot all about her daddy!"

"Hmmm. What are the feelings, beliefs and challenges embedded in these events?" she gently probed.

"I don't know. Being ignored feels a lot like being unloved, I guess. Also, my relationship with my wife has been going downhill for a long time now. I guess, I just feel unloved in general."

"If I understand what you are saying, the cherry is that your daughter showed she cares about you and went out of her way to rescue your things. The pit is feeling unloved by your wife, daughter and employer, since you were laid off. Unloved on all sides? Please correct me if any of this is wrong. What are the beliefs underlying this feeling of being unloved?"

James thought she was reducing his pain to a mere belief, when it was real, so he felt insulted, "It's not just a belief! I am reacting to real things that are happening in my life!" Each word got louder.

He was getting frustrated, "They always ignore me and they don't care what I want, that's good reason to think they don't care about me anymore!"

In a soothing voice she explained, "In this unfolding process we call life, everyone holds beliefs inside them. Beliefs crave expression. They want attention so they introduce themselves to the rational mind by making something happen, an event that wakes up the mind and announces their presence.

"In other words, first comes the belief, and then the event that holds the belief inside it. Our job here is to look at your story, dig inside it a little, and try to uncover the core beliefs it holds. Beware, negative, self-negating beliefs can also peek out from time to time causing pain and mischief. So, what are the beliefs in this story?" she explained.

"When I was home, I believed that Sandra and Judy no longer loved me. But now, her coming here challenges that belief."

"Good. Tell me another?" Kim coaxed.

"Well, ignoring me all the time is proof that they don't love me, true? On the other hand, Sandra came way out here with my things, so that kind of looks like she cares. Her action challenged my belief.

"But how do I know she is not playing me? She really wants to live here, and I might just be an expedient path for her to get what she wants, a pawn in her game, and she doesn't really care about me at all?"

"Okay," Kim affirmed, "those are other possible beliefs, which one do you want to make real? Which one do you choose to believe? Which beliefs are you going to choose to direct your life?"

"I don't know," mumbled James. "I find it hard to believe she really did it for me. It could just as well be because she was looking for a way to stay here."

"I respect that," Kim said with sincerity. "Do you think those are healthy beliefs that will enhance your life or unhealthy beliefs that will cause you pain?"

James looked down into his lap and grunted. The feeling of being unloved and unlovable was up for him right now.

"What are you feeling?" she asked, and he felt she really wanted to know.

"I feel unloved and unlovable. I wonder if anyone ever really loved me. My father was a sergeant, whipping me into shape. Not much of a source of comfort, there. My brother deserted me, just like my mom did. Now Judy and Sandra are doing it again. One day, it feels like they care and the next day they make you feel invisible."

"Are you saying you feel unloved and invisible?" hearing the compassion in her voice almost made him cry. "James, this is an old feeling you have had before. Focus on it. Totally feel it. You can ride this feeling all the way back in time. Your feeling is like a magic carpet taking you back to an earlier time in your life."

James closed his eyes. For the first time in his life, he did not run away from what he was feeling. It was a relief not to have to cover his feelings with humor or anger. His shoulders slumped and he let out a big sigh.

"Breathe deeply and slowly," she whispered ever so softly. "Ride this feeling back, back, back to an earlier time, when you had this feeling."

In a small, tired, defeated voice, James quietly said, "I can see myself standing in the living room. People are filing through, and everyone is wearing black. I am fifteen and I am at my mother's funeral. The scene just flipped. I am at my brother's funeral. The two images get mixed up together sometimes. They deserted me. They left me alone with Father. I can't remember what he was like before Mother died, but I can assure you he was a stern taskmaster afterwards."

"After Mother died, my father was always hard and matter of fact with us. He did not grieve for my mother, and he did not let us grieve. I felt invisible, helpless, abandoned, and guilty that I could not do anything to save her. I used to bury my head in my pillow at night, so no one would hear me cry. I felt so guilty for crying. I knew I was supposed to be a man and buck up like my father always insisted, but I could not make the tears stop. I was utterly lonely. I desperately wanted someone to hold me and make me feel safe." It was like the words were speaking themselves. They just poured out. He suddenly realized how naked he felt and said in a strong voice, "I shouldn't have said that! How embarrassing!"

"You are safe here," she cooed. "Never feel embarrassed around me," she reassured him. "Your feelings are natural and deserve to be respected, not hidden away in dark places inside you. About being embarrassed, what is the belief behind that feeling?"

James wanted to believe she was a safe person to talk to, but no one else ever was, so he wasn't sure. In an angry voice he asserted, "Men don't cry!"

"Is crying the only thing you are forbidden to do?" she asked inquisitively.

"No, it is a lot bigger than that. Men must always have a stiff upper lip. You must handle anything and everything. You can't ever ask for help. You can't let anyone know that you are struggling. You must always have a stone face of strength and courage. That is what a man is and that is not me! I absolutely fail at being a man. No wonder no one loves me!"

"What beliefs do you think are hiding in this piece?" she guided.

His voice was a little unsteady when he answered. "Well, one belief might be that I have failed to be a man. Another might me that I hide who I am, so people don't find out." He glanced at her and felt reassured that she was there. Then he tried harder, "Maybe I feel like I cannot let people get too close to me because then they will find out what a fake I am."

"Thank you for sharing that with me. It helps me understand you a little better."

Inside his body, there was a little bird banging against the walls of his chest desperately trying to escape. How could he have said such naked things to her? The room was suddenly too hot, but he shuddered as though he had a chill. He was hot and cold all at the same time. If he wasn't already lying down, he was sure he would faint. Suddenly he wanted to hit someone.

Kim was silent and James listened to the soft peaceful music. After a bit, the urge to hit someone drained away. The room temperature evened out and the sofa he was lying on stopped spinning.

As he lay there staring at the ceiling, Kim touched a button and waves of warm water began to roll up and down under the leather covering on the sofa, blissfully massaging his back. Soon all his intense emotions disappeared.

A few minutes later he was drifting in bliss, when her soft quiet voice returned. "Let's step out of your beliefs for just a moment. You are welcome to pick them up in just a few minutes. For now, leave them on that table over there. Come with me. Let us look through another point of view.

"Let's look at your father. This man just lost his wife, and he was left with two teenage boys. Do you think it might be possible that he was talking to himself when he said, 'Buck up and be strong; you don't have time to grieve. You must provide for these boys.' If he came down hard on you for acting emotional, could it be that he could not allow himself to fall apart? He was fighting his own grief, and you got hurt in that battle he was having with himself."

"Wow! I never thought about that," he said with eyes wide.

"Now once again step outside your beliefs to see your children from their perspective. Your children were very involved with their own stuff. Important things were happening in their cyberworld, and it was totally consuming for them. So, their actions have nothing to do with you or how much they love you, they are lost in their own process. How does looking at it from this perspective feel in your body? Remember, there is no one absolute truth, just different perspectives."

"It could be true," he answered begrudgingly. He wasn't going to relinquish his version of reality that quickly.

"What if your father was projecting his process onto you and displaced his own guilt for not saving your mother, onto you. Is it possible that you were just a young boy full of love and caring, forced to live with a man who was in a lot of pain. He lost the love of his life and was unsure about how to raise two children on his own. Perhaps he was hiding his pain because he had to cope? Does any of this ring true for you? You have a few beliefs here that all came from this one intense traumatic experience."

"It feels true. It feels right," he reluctantly admitted.

"I am confused," she said, "how does this all tie together? We have the belief that you should be tough, a man as you call it; plus, your father's stern nature; and the belief that when someone is not paying attention to you, they do not love you; and that you are unlovable. How does this all tie together?"

"My father ignored me when my mother died. He never comforted me, and he kept me at arm's length. I felt like he hated me. I tried to figure out why and finally decided it was because he thought I was responsible for her death. He yelled at me all the time until I began to believe it was really my fault. His constant disappointments in me, for being 'soft,' made me feel like there was something wrong with me. He was always comparing me to my brother. Donny was better able to hold it all in, like we were supposed to."

"How well did you brother do with that?" she asked softly.

"He killed himself!"

"Oh," she said with a nod of her head, which he saw through the corner of his eye. So many things seemed conveyed in that one sound, "Oh".

"How are these beliefs playing out in your current life?"

"I get so mad at my wife because she never listens to me. All she ever talks and thinks about are her desires, her goals, her story, and her burdens. It is always all about her, never me. She could not care less about my needs! She is just like him. I am invisible around her just like I was with him. That is why I never stand up to her because she just cuts the legs out from under me. I feel like such a failure when I am around her."

"Thank you for explaining that to me. Are you willing to relinquish these beliefs? Do you want to continue to carry these beliefs onward? Do they serve you or do they set you up to be hurt?"

"How can I set myself free from these miserable whips I still hit myself with?"

"That will require doing a process. This is a good place to stop for today. You have done well. You now recognize that you have been a puppet, forced to act in certain ways, because of strings controlling you. Those strings are your beliefs. Now you are ready to reclaim the power you left behind, back then, when you took on beliefs that hurt and sabotage you.

"In our next session, I will take you on a little journey into yourself to rid yourself of these evil puppeteers. I will guide you to relinquish whatever negative beliefs are obstructing your happiness and undermining your self-esteem."

CHAPTER 10

Before the Beginning

Work was a busy beehive. ComPad chimes were ringing a symphony. They were always in use. Little details were being tweaked, supplies were arriving, and the general excitement was exhilarating. They were gearing up to build their first RBH structure, which they affectionately named Greenie.

The roof on a traditional yurt was generally made of canvas, leather, or a skin covering. James wanted to use hempcrete. The team had discussed it a few times, but it always came to the same dead end. It was a desirable medium because it was strong and durable, yet unfeasible because it had to be mixed in a heavy metal drum.

James tackled the weight problem. At first his thoughts followed the same options the others had examined. Then he thought outside the box. He narrowed the problem down to, what other substance is as strong, but has little weight? The answer seemed obvious, yet no one had thought of it before. It was just not the way it had always been done. No one questioned the accepted way of doing things until James did.

As part of all the therapy he was doing, he was questioning everything, every basic assumption he usually made. He was getting used to turning his thoughts around to see what they were based on and what was still true for him.

In the process of redefining his strengths, he wanted to be strong, but with a lightness of heart. His life had been too serious for too long. Then it came to him that the yurt needed similar things. He needed to redefine strength and unite it with weightlessness. Or try to come as close as he could.

He realized that to work and take care of two children, he would need flexibility. Balancing everyone's needs would require it. Being a good father in changing circumstances, where chaos seemed to be everywhere, would require him to be flexible, adaptable, and swift to respond to their needs.

He was thinking about how to handle all these complexities. His thoughts shifted to the project, and he realized Greenie seemed to be having a parallel process. The drum needed to be all these things. The answer was suddenly there in front of him.

Flexibility would also be an essential factor in building a structure in crisis situations, during turbulent climate shifts. Nature will buck no resistance. The building they create must work with the elements. If it is flexible, the crisis could pass through it, and it would survive. If the structure was rigid, as houses often were, the resistance it posed would be met by force head on. That could cause hurt and do damage.

That certainly applied to Judy. He planned to fight her for custody. That would be meeting the force straight on. Maybe he could exercise a little flexibility and try to work with her. That might avoid the full force of her anger.

Traditionally, divorce was an angry tug of war. That was the equivalent of following tradition and just putting a palapa roof on it. The most important thing to him was to have an ongoing relationship with his kids. Maybe he could let go of his attachment to the form it would take. He wanted sustainability, an ongoing relationship, and likewise Greenie needed sustainability too.

Greenie needs to bend with nature, ride her more turbulent moods without resistance. James tweaked the shape a little to give it slightly better aerodynamics until he felt it could live harmoniously with its environment.

When James presented these ideas in a more condensed form and ended by announcing that they could make the hempcrete in lightweight aluminum drums, you could hear a huge sigh ripple around the room. It was a brilliant idea.

Up until then, they could only come up with roofs out of palapa or straw, band aids not solutions. Wood was better, but it was not always available. Plus, all these coverings can burn. Hempcrete does not. It could provide longevity.

Everyone applauded and James felt embarrassed.

Pierre declared it a holiday and whipped out his wonderful herbal brew. It had the wakeup kick of coffee and the flowing ease of wine.

Awake and Content, Pierre thought he would name his brew, if he ever needed a backup business. It had a creamy texture with a nicely fermented kick.

Carla brought out a surprise. She baked pavlovas to celebrate the birth of Greenie. Yael swooned with each bite, and said, "These sweet little Meringue puffs with fruit and cream are absolutely heavenly. They are sort of like the way James describes his new drum, light in weight and strong in flavor.

"Are pavlovas a Russian pastry?" she asked.

"No," said Carla. "They come from Australia, but they were named after the Russian ballerina Anna Pavlova."

"Are they hard to make?" asked Yael.

Carla nodded, no, and said, "They are the easiest thing I ever made. I'll give you the recipe," and wrote it down for Yael.

After the party, everyone returned to their various tasks. Carla came over to congratulate James and stayed to chat. She happened to mention that she was struggling with the cane. She was planning to use cane to bind the spooning half-moons stalks of bamboo, that were going to be the primary support poles. Cane is flexible and strong, but not trustworthy for longevity.

James had been thinking about aluminum all day, so he said, "Cane is strong and flexible so is wire, they might make an even stronger duo."

"Of course!" she exclaimed, threw her hands up in the air, and ran off to see about reinforcing the cane with wire.

Pierre stopped by James's desk to share his excitement. He just found the perfect grower, Jose' Velasquez. "He is an expert in bamboo and is willing to join the team. He can show us how to teach the farmers how to grow this species of bamboo." James congratulated him and they both clapped each other on the back for a job well done.

Satyendra asked him if he thought they should order extra hempcrete and chicken wire, in case they needed to build a large structure. With all major obstacles resolved, they finalized their supply list for the trip. Wire, sheets of aluminum, hempcrete, and chicken wire were now at the top of the list.

Yael met James at the Drink Station, congratulated him, and let down her usual stiff shouldered posture. They took a table and shared a few minutes together during their break. Yael asked him how he liked being in the City of Hope. James said he was new here and he was still adapting. Then he launched into his usual story about Judy and the kids. Yael listened attentively. She glanced down at his wrist to confirm her suspicion. He was only a Red Band, so his victim consciousness was understandable.

Out of politeness, he asked Yael about herself.

"I was born the day I arrived here," she said. "This is the only true life that expresses who I am and allows me to live by what I believe. Out there, the world is full of madness. My country and that whole part of the world is tangled up in the idea, "it all started when *he hit me back.*' The victim is to blame, and the perpetrator is overlooked. I had to get away from all of it. Coming here was a breath of new life. I have found a sanctuary, a sane and functional place.

Are you an Israeli?

"Yes. I grew up in Jerusalem. Walking down the street, you would think it is the safest place in the world. Places like California sparkle like the sun off the ocean. In Jerusalem, I feel like I am living under a blanket of history. The air is thick with the echoes of great human beings who wrestled with life and battled each other.

"I was a soldier in an army trained to obey commands. One day, the clouds in my mind parted, and I saw the madness on all sides. Each country, even each person holds a piece of the truth, like puzzle pieces. They cannot make peace long enough to fit their pieces together. They are all missing the message because they won't work together long enough to see what their pieces can create.

"I am sure God is signaling us, giving us a map to guide us through these rocky waters into the future. We cannot read the map, because he gave it to everyone, and each person is hiding their secret inner truths.

"James, we see you. You have intuitive insight. It is a gift. We need your gifts. Thanks for being on our team."

James was walking on a cloud by the end of the day. On the way home on the tram, he mused about his day and felt warm all over.

Everyone went out of their way to be with him and acknowledge him. A deep satisfaction warmed his every limb.

The next day was hectic and harried for everyone, except Satyendra who was never ruffled. Each morning, when the sun streamed through the window, Satyendra always stopped whatever he was doing to pull out his pillow and meditate in the sunshine. Then he would stand up, draw the power of heaven down through his crown chakra, and the power up from the very core of Mother Earth. He imagined standing on a lotus filled with life force. After ten minutes of this each day, he was able to sail through every crisis and roll over every bump, with calm and grace.

Tomas, the Executive Project Coordinator, asked the team to write a summary about their personal experience of working on this project. They were asked to list each other's strengths. He wanted an insight into their interpersonal working dynamics. Trinitus needed a strong adhesive team that would successfully work together in a foreign environment, under challenging circumstances, facing unknown obstacles. In James's summary, he proposed Pierre for Foreign Project Coordinator.

Tomas invited James to join him at the Drink Station. "I was delighted with your last improvement. A small multi-powered crank for the drum, with a hand crank option, will be useful in more situations," he said.

"We are going to send your group to the Philippines for three weeks to test your new design in action. According to the questionnaires, the rest of your team unanimously voted for you to be Project Coordinator. They sighted your accessibility and your imagination.

'No one ever said things like that about me before. Maybe this really is a new life,' he mused.

"Do you accept the position?" asked Tomas

James was still waiting for the shoe to fall, to suddenly find that he had screwed up again. He was afraid to accept such a large responsibility.

"Isn't Satyendra more qualified? He is so calm and supportive," James suggested.

Tomas shook his head no.

"What about Pierre?" he pushed, "He has seniority. Or Carla? This was her idea in the first place. Her ability to interpret dreams started all this. What about Yael, she is stronger than all of us put together. Maybe she should lead. She was an army officer. She was trained to lead.

"In the questionnaire, your teammates wrote that they were individual elements working side by side until you arrived. You brought them together. They credit you for turning a group of co-workers into a cooperative interdependent team."

Tomas took another sip of herbal coffee and waited for James to think it over and respond.

James had mixed feelings about this opportunity. His head was spinning. 'On one hand, I am excited to go on a trip overseas. Also, I am happy that my ideas are successful, so far. On the other hand, overseeing the whole project sounds utterly daunting!

'My nerves are already stretched thin with this divorce and custody battle. I want the kids, but I am also terrified of having them. I hate my wife, and yet I still have flashbacks and remember how much I once loved her. My head is already spinning. On top of all that, I am just getting used to this place.'

His old daily routine flashed through his mind. 'I lived in that house with Judy for twenty years. Now suddenly, I find myself in a whole new world. I am just getting the hang of this place and they want to send me to the other side of the world.'

The color drained from James's face and Tomas was concerned that he was going to faint.

"Calm down," he said in a soothing voice and glanced down at James's wristband. That explained his reaction.

"These men and women know what they are doing. They like you and they will support you, just as it will be your responsibility to support them. Satyendra will offer his spiritual leadership. I have already asked him to facilitate qigong exercises to center the team each morning. I asked Pierre to host a morning and evening sharing circle review to keep everyone on the same page. I gave Yael the role of Timekeeper. She will keep the project moving according to the plan. Carla will be the Keeper of the Heart. I have charged her to oversee the team's physical emotional needs and act as the team's compassionate heart. These will be your roles beyond the logistical work you do."

James reluctantly accepted. He did not have a minute to reflect on what he had gotten himself into, because he needed to leave immediately to meet his lawyer. His wife signed the divorce papers and it was time to make a definite plan. She was going to fight for sole custody.

The lawyer asked why he left home so suddenly, and what he wanted from the custody suit. James went into his usual monologue about his wife's spending, drinking, and abuse.

The lawyer suggested that he acquire a house now, because it would make him look more stable to the court. He said Child Services would be coming to look at his home situation and informed him that the court date was set to be in three months.

James contacted the Housing Bureau. Lila answered in a friendly voice. She patiently listened as he explained that he was being sent on a community mission that would probably last three weeks, but the duration was not fixed in stone. Furthermore, he expected his two teenage children to arrive when he returned. However, there was a small chance that he might not gain custody, in which case, he would need a smaller place.

"We have two houses and a few units that could be reserved for that length of time," Lila assured him. He felt relieved and made an appointment to meet her in an hour.

He arrived at the Housing Bureau. It was in the Administrative Cluster. The buildings here were larger than most. Usually there was one large professional building in a cluster of smaller units, but this one was all large buildings. It still had Open Space for a stroll or activities, but it felt overshadowed by these lofty monoliths. They were all six stories tall, the tallest he had seen anywhere in Hope.

Lila greeted him and showed him to a seat. She handed him a special ComPad so he could answer a series of questions. He stared down at the screen and started feeling nervous at the idea of bringing the kids here. He was sure he wanted custody but was scared at what that would be like. He flashed on a vision of the future, when he would again be sent to a foreign place like the Philippines, and the kids would be here unsupervised. That made his skin crawl.

"How can I work and still raise my kids well?" he thought out loud and then felt embarrassed. Lila smiled reassuringly and suggested that he attend a Community Parenting group. She assured him that they would be able to answer all his questions and turn him onto whatever support he might need.

"That is what a cooperative community is all about," she said. "No one is left to struggle all alone, especially with home situations that everyone faces. Family responsibilities are shared among a cooperative group. Someone who is shopping for one child can easily do it for two. One parent taking a child to school can take three. Sharing the weight leaves no one overburdened.

Knowing about this option went a long way to helping James relax. He was beginning to believe he could do it. He wanted to be a good dad. He wanted to show his father what a good dad looks like. He craved family and always had. Being there for his children was very important to him.

One house was available in the Architectural Cluster. It had a labyrinth marked with stones in the Open Space, which he now was beginning to appreciate. He liked the house, but it was huge and he thought it might be a struggle to maintain such a large space.

Next, they visited a house in the Exercise Cluster. He liked it and was especially attracted to the well-appointed gym, and the obstacle course in the Open Space. He thought it would inspire him to work diligently on firming up his body and losing weight. An image of slim Buck flashed through his mind, and he decided he wanted to be in this cluster. The house itself was small and compact but well designed with multi-use spaces. She pointed out that he and his kids would be more likely to spend time together because the bedrooms were small and dark, conducive to sleep; and the shared space was open, spacious, airy, and bright.

Lila encouraged him to also choose an apartment in case the custody was postponed for a while. In times of change, having an alternative plan for each step is resourceful.

He asked if there was anything available in Cathy's building. Lila said, "No, but in three months there will be," so he reserved an apartment on the spot. He had been in her building and liked its open airiness. Like most structures in Hope, airiness, abundant light and solid sustainability were at the core of all architectural designs. It was shaped like a wedding cake with four tiers in descending size, like Kim's building, which gave each apartment lots of balcony space. It was lovely. He liked the idea of being neighbors with Cathy.

James's legs were hardly touching the ground on the way home. He was starving, but the idea of eating alone felt tiresome; so, he called Cathy and invited her to dinner. He needed to vent his excitement and fears. Her support made him feel good, and it also made him feel good about her as a friend. It was nice to have someone to talk to.

As he sat there with Cathy, enjoying dinner and laughing casually, he thought about how he and Judy were always at each other's throats. He could not remember a peaceful time when he and his wife just had dinner and laughed like he was doing now. They had fought for so long; they were now reduced to growling dogs always nipping at each other's heels.

Cathy was talking about how isolated she felt with her husband. James suddenly realized he too felt isolated being married. Over the years, family became his total focus, and friendships fell away. He had few friends and he did not keep in touch with them. He always thought it was her fault, but for the first time, he questioned that belief. Now that he dared to think outside the box, he had to admit that being a worker bee, and carrying all those responsibilities, was what isolated him.

So much was changing inside him.

Now that Greenie was finished and had approval on the drawing board, it was time to bring him to life. They gathered the supplies to build a prototype in their cluster's Open Space. This practice-run would hopefully iron out any kinks. Of course, they were working in ideal circumstances. Erecting the structure with violent winds blowing and torrential rains falling, would come with a hands-on experience. They had no way of replicating that beforehand.

Three half-moon bamboo shafts in spooning position, tied together with reinforced cane and wire worked well. The building held together and swayed in the wind. The finely calculated curve of the domes sent waves of wind or water around and over it with little or no damage.

The team continued to work well together. Every day they meshed better and better, as they became accustomed to doing the work like a dance. They each had their area of expertise, but it was up to each of them to see what needed to be done next and respond to it. Then each would check with the more experienced team member in charge of that aspect, to give their approval or suggestions. It became a dance where each one simply responded to what Greenie needed next and no one felt territorial. It was viewed as a dance with changing partners. James wondered if all Red and Orange Bands dance this well with each other.

When James arrived home after working on Greenie all day, his ComScreen was flashing. He had a message from Tammy.

"Hi, I mean, we see you, Mr. Dole. I am back in Trinitus. I have settled all my affairs at home and am ready to live here full-time. I was wondering if we could get together sometime. I only know you and Tim. We don't know each other well, but I would feel more comfortable if I had someone familiar to talk to sometimes."

"Yeah, that's okay, I guess." James flashed on the vixen, Kitara and had to remind himself he was not Buck, and likewise Tammy was not Kitara. Still, he was taken aback by the idea of being alone with her. He just didn't want to be alone with an 18-year-old. It wasn't that he distrusted himself; he just wanted someone to witness his good behavior. Anyway, he told himself that another woman would relate to her better. James sent Tammy a text inviting her to dinner and called Cathy and Tim to join them.

Tim smiled his soothing smile as he sat down next to Tammy. James was next to Cathy. The conversation was lively. They all seemed to get along well. James talked about his work, how well Greenie was coming along, and about how excited he was to go to the Philippines. Cathy and Tammy discovered they both love to bake and made a date to share organic alternative recipes for several traditional dishes. Tammy had a good one for lasagna that had no real meat, cheese, or wheat noodles, yet tasted wonderful.

Cathy offered to teach her how to make pavlovas. The night went well. James wondered how Sandra's night was going, especially after Tammy gave him the latest update. She said that Judy was holding a very tight rein on the girl and wasn't letting her go anywhere or do anything other than attend school.

Tammy apologized for driving her and said, "In retrospect, I am both excited and sorry for bringing her. I am sorry that Sandra got in so much trouble, but I am also elated, because I probably would not be here right now, if not for that night."

Cathy said it was very brave of Sandra to come, and everyone agreed.

Tammy thanked James for introducing her to Cathy, and said she really appreciated his kindness. He just smiled. He invited Cathy and Tim because he was afraid to be alone with her, but it was interpreted as an act of kindness. He decided not to correct her. He hoped Tammy would stay, so Sandra would have a friend when she arrived.

Tammy loved everything she was experiencing until later that night. When she was getting ready for her nightly excursion into New World, she found it hard to get online, so she texted James. He responded with "Trinitus does not have outside lines. All communications function on an in-house network."

"But Buck was there, how did that happen?"

"I petitioned and received permission from my Purple Band Guide. I had to convince him it was necessary to maintain my connection with my daughter."

Tammy was bummed.

James tried to explain that the real world of Trinitus would be a rich adventure. She would not need the other world anymore.

Tammy started rethinking her commitment.

James's thoughts turned to Sandra. He missed her and wondered how she was doing being grounded and frozen.

Sandra went straight home after school every day since she got grounded. She helped Sammy with his homework. They had gotten closer since she could not go anywhere or do anything. He enjoyed having her around, which surprised him. She was usually a pain in the neck to him and to Mother. He hated the way Sandra always sided with Dad, even when Dad was acting like a jerk. The first time her ComPad rang, and she could not answer it, he enjoyed watching her squirm. But the novelty of that wore off real soon, and he began to feel sorry for her. He volunteered to deliver messages from her to her friends. It made him feel like a co-conspirator on a dangerous mission.

One day, after she cleaned her room, she offered to clean his. She knew cleaning his room was on the top of his hate-to-do list. "What will it cost me?" he asked. He was young but not naïve, everything has a price.

"Let me use your ComPad to send a brief text and have some screen time."

"To whom?"

She knew if she said, Dad, he would turn her down, so she said in all honesty, "Buck, I want to meet him in New World this evening around 5:30. I'll be on and off before mom gets home. She never gets here before 6:30."

"Okay, if you clean my room and do my laundry." He enjoyed having the upper hand.

"Sure," she agreed. He handed over his ComPad and she sent a quick note to Dad's new number. He responded with a thumbs-up emoji.

James left work a little early and returned to his room. He quickly opened the ComScreen and within five minutes was strutting down the now familiar street on his way to the Sanctuary Café to meet Taliya.

Buck was so excited to see Taliya, he wanted to give her a hug but couldn't find the control button for that movement. He kicked himself for not making time to study Avatar movements.

"We see you Buck," she said, "I have missed you."

"Me too, what's it been like for you?"

"If you are asking Taliya, I have been very creative. My head is filled with ideas of returning to Trinitus. If you are asking about Sandra, she is making the best of a bad situation."

"What happened when you got home?" Buck asked and leaned forward to show he was interested. James was proud that he did that movement right.

"When I walked through the door, Mother was furious. She screamed right in my face, 'You are grounded until I'm not mad anymore. Give me your ComPad, Smartwatch, your car keys and your license. I don't think we need to discuss why you are grounded, do we?'"

"Boom! Just like that, right in my face!

"I was pretty pissed myself, so I screamed back just as loud. With her face point blank in mine, I let her know, I said, "Mother, you were wrong for throwing Dad's things out! You put me in a situation where I had no choice! Do what you will to me, but I would do it again!"

"Then Mom backed away, so I lowered my voice and softly repeated the same words.

"In a low dangerous voice, Mom hissed, "You can take that smart mouth of yours to your room and forget about dinner.

"I stood tall and told myself I am smarter than her. Without a fuss, I set my most personal things on the counter. With dignity and flare, I turned and righteously walked up to my room. I wasn't hungry anyway. We had a late lunch on the drive home, so missing dinner was no big deal.

"I picked up that beading project I used to work on. I always wanted to finish it but never had enough time. Once I got into the zone stringing beads, I didn't feel angry anymore. I felt calm and a little excited. I started planning how I was going to get back to Trinitus to live with you."

"Don't worry. Your mom never stays angry for long. It has only been a few days. She will probably lift the restrictions soon.

"Yeah, but this has already been the longest time that I can remember her being angry. You must really be on her shit-list."

Buck tried to put a hand on her shoulder to show support. The hand landed briefly on her head along the way, but safely reached its target spot and he said, "You know your mother. She will never admit she might be wrong. Please be nice to her. We do not want her on the warpath. P-l-e-a-s-e, he drew out the word, do whatever you can to defuse the situation if you ever want to move here."

"Okay Dad! Now that we have covered all that, can I hang out with Buck?"

That took him back. He took a deep breath and changed gears. 'Who is Buck?' he asked himself.

"We see you," said Buck. It is a relief to be here. I reserved a house for us in the Exercise Cluster. We can all get buff together."

"I was wondering, how did you wind up in Trinitus if you never heard of it before?"

"I saw the signs," he answered cryptically.

"Yes, you see lots of signs all the time, but what was it that made you take action?" she probed.

James wanted to pull back and make a joke about serendipity, but Buck answered with the truth, "I had a strange experience in the desert that made me realize I was being divinely guided. I followed the spiritual signs.

"Oh, do tell. I love stories about other worlds."

"When I lost my job, it was the straw that broke the camel's back. I felt launched out of my old life. I wasn't thinking. It was instinctual. I drove out into the desert. Maybe it was the only place big enough for me to think. My head was so cluttered with past, present, and future grievances. I just wanted to run away to a quiet place." He found it easy to talk to Taliya, and Buck seemed to listen so much better than James could.

A jarring alarm rang! It was time for Sandra to return the ComPad to Sammy before they got caught. She jumped up, said a quick hasty goodbye, and was gone. Buck stood there for a minute. He didn't recognize anyone and was not in the mood to make new friends, so he just signed off.

Sandra handed Sammy the ComPad. He curled up on the sofa and resumed playing his favorite game. She sat down at the dining room table and bent over her beading tray. When Judy walked in, not five minutes later, she was met by the sight of two quiet children entranced within their own worlds.

Sandra liked the calm repetition of the beading. While her mind and fingers were occupied, her deeper self was working out logistics and rehearsing what she would say in court.

She felt different now. Just last year, she probably would have found some way to defiantly get around her mother. Now she felt more mature, more able to handle things. She had proven herself to be brave and felt proud that she stood up for what she knew was right, no matter what the cost. She was sure she was now more adult than her mother.

CHAPTER 11

Philippines

James was covered in mosquito bites. He had just finished taking a shower and wondered why he wasted the time, he still felt just as sticky. Outside his tent, was a relentless beam of fire breathing down from the sky, the noonday sun. James was miserable. He finally allowed himself to rest. He flopped down on the straw mat covering his cot and gave a huge sigh. It was really a lot of sighs all wrapped up in one breath of utter exhaustion. This was already a long day, and it was only halfway done. He wished he was h-o-m-e. He pronounced it like one long moan.

As his body unkinked and released some of the built-up tension, he thought, 'Before we arrived, I assumed that by the end of the first week, we would have built a few Greenies. I imagined, we would be celebrating this accomplishment by today and now, we won't even begin until tomorrow.'

He looked through the little window in his tent and watched a flock of white birds flying away from him across an open sky. The whispering wind beneath their wings seemed to mock him with the words, "three weeks." He had told people in Hope that he would be home in three weeks. 'One week gone and we haven't even begun.'

The old James would have wallowed in the belief that, 'The clock wields a whip.' Normally, he would have blamed, raged, and moaned over the delay. But now he was learning to surrender what he could not change. Satyendra was teaching him to breathe in slowly, hold for a few seconds, and then let it go in a sharp release. All his tension rushed out of him in one hard breath!

Pierre had reassured him on the plane that whatever happens, they will ride it together. Pierre was always so focused on whatever caught his interest. He was intense or distracted most of the time. There seemed to be many channels running through his mind at once. He was a complex man with a simple heart. If someone as intense as Pierre can ride whatever fate throws at him, and still move forward towards manifesting his ideals, James told himself he can too.

After a few days in the jungle, this new idea of rolling with the punches had become his only sane choice. On the plane everything had looked so different.

When they first boarded, James was elated. He was excited to be embarking on a great adventure with his new friends, but the plane sat on the tarmac while last-minute repairs were underway. By the time it finally took off, James was in a panic. He spent this time worrying. It began with doubts about working with other teams. Three teams were coming from three different Trinitus Cities to cover all the different needs of the project. He knew his team could function well together but had no idea how they would interface with other groups. He also had fears about working with other Project Coordinators. They probably weren't just a Red Band like him. He wasn't used to being a leader. He knew he didn't like being a drone, but at least it felt safer. Would he be able to stand by his decisions, if the others disagreed?

By the time he finished worrying about his own performance and the challenge of dealing with other teams, his mind was in the full grip of negative thoughts, his emotions were boiling, and his stomach was screaming in pain. Fear was seeping through every vein. He imagined having to deal with a Filipino Chief and indigenous people, strangers he knew very little about. He knew the island had a history of exploitation and abuse and feared that they would be cautious and skeptical. After all, he was treading down a path strewn with a lot of old garbage.

In the books he read about the Philippines, he learned that in the past, developers, carpetbaggers, and vultures had come to gobble up this beautiful land and strip the lush forests of its precious trees. Kidnappers and slavers, thieves and smooth-talking industrialists had come before him promising improvements, but the improvements never benefitted the people, it just exploited them. How was he going to overcome their fears, when he could not even get a handle on his own?

In the new language he was learning, he looked for the beliefs beneath what he read. The driving belief was in the superiority of the White Race and their right to lord over indigenous people. He could see how these toxic beliefs had unleashed a tidal wave of poisons that polluted so many innocent lives.

How could he carve out a new path when so many had blown up the path before him? James could hardly breathe thinking of all this. The color was draining from his face, and his breath was labored. Satyendra, seated beside him, put a hand on his shoulder and asked James to meet his eyes. It took a few seconds to focus outside himself. There he found Satyendra's gentle eyes waiting for him. "Breathe with me," the young Indian said in his inviting and soothing voice. They breathed together for a while and James came back into the here and now.

Pierre asked James to tell him how the new multipowered crank works. He asked him to list each part and explain its function. That got James out of his emotions and into a safer part of his mind.

Once the wave of panic passed, Pierre assured him that they had come to give, not take and that would make the difference. James believed and disbelieved this. How was he going to get a village Chief to believe that they are dedicated to healing our planet and chose his little village as the place to begin?

With the help of his new friends, he was calm for a while. Then the plane ride ran into turbulence, and his stomach threatened to erupt. Again, he lost his composure, and his Inner Critic began to tear him apart with its threats, accusations, and Pirate Crew of negative emotions. Pretty soon, he was in a full-blown panic attack. Satyendra and Pierre patiently helped him move through it again. Pierre remembered when he was a Red Band, and his heart went out to the poor fellow. He was grateful to be an Orange Band with all the mental and emotional tools that come with it.

By the time the plane set down in Manila, James was hopeful and in full possession of himself once again.

The plane reached the airspace over the Philippines. From the sky they saw an archipelago encompassing 7,641 islands clustered in three major island groups. Pierre told James the names of the groups: Luzon, the Visayas, and Mindanao. He shared that only about 2,000 of these islands are inhabited; more than 5,000 are not even officially named.

From the airport in Manila, they drove for many miles until they found themselves at a sandy pier. Wherever they looked, the poverty was palpable. The roads were crowded with bikes, mopeds, buses, cars, oxen, and trash.

They boarded a large boat. Despite its ample size, their mountain of gear left space at a minimum. They set sail to Palawan, a small remote island.

After three slightly seasick hours, they reached the island. James helped unload the supplies onto a little caravan of wagons with tall, especially skinny wheels. They were strong but lightweight, designed to leave a very small footprint on the forest.

Within minutes of disembarking, they were approached by a private armed security squad patrolling the island to keep the people safe from kidnappers.

The wagons were connected by huge flexible coiled metal ropes and pulled by a Work Horse; a small powerful vehicle designed to pull a long line of wagons. James and his team rode in jeeps, which had arrived a week earlier. When everything was in place, they bumped along muddy roads for almost an hour.

From a distance, as they approached each town or village, it looked quaint, charming, inviting; but once they drew near, they saw more clearly, the streets were crowded and full of trash. Strewn around everywhere were the remains of damaged buildings in the aftermath of a wicked typhoon. Mosquito laden pools of water still stood all around.

The villages were smaller and cleaner as they became further apart. James felt a scary sense of isolation. The narrow road they followed led into the jungle. Satyendra sat close beside James and every few minutes reminded him in a whisper to breathe. At one point, when the jungle sounds were loud and threatening, he guided James into a meditation in which he accepted the jungle sounds as comforting. After a while, James calmed down and they reached the small remote village where they were expected.

The villagers and the other teams all came out to meet them.

Everyone wanted to get a look at the newcomers. It was late in the day and the sun was already splashing streaks of fuchsia across the heavens.

Johnnie, the Project Coordinator of the Energy Team, was a tall Norwegian man with long dirty blond hair and a long thick red beard. His real name was Johan, but everyone called him Johnnie.

James wanted them to be equal co-workers, but the truth is, he felt completely intimidated by this gentle giant who seemed to be so comfortable in his skin, and exuded self-assurance. James was sure that keeping this relationship equal was going to stretch him to the bone.

Johnnie welcomed them and then introduced him to the Project Coordinator of the Sustainable Living Team, "This is Suriya," he said. She is a refugee from the last terrible war."

"Poy!" She spit. "May such words never be uttered again."

James was intrigued by her eyes. He had never seen such deep dark wells before. She had been at Trinitus long enough to earn a Blue Band. He mimicked tipping his hat to her and then turned it into a salute.

She stepped forward and reached her hand out to shake his, "We see you. I hope we will work well together," she said, "My team and I are very resourceful. Whenever you run into problems, logistical or otherwise, let me know. I want us to have each other's back."

He felt he was off to a good beginning with her.

While James and his fellow Project Coordinators were getting acquainted, a member of the Sustainability Team showed the Building Team where to set up their tents. When James joined them, they gave him the place of honor, the cot and folding table nearest the door. The tent had a strong, musty old canvas smell to it. It had a long history of rushing into the elements, taking a beating, surviving and then moving on to help another community, in another part of the world. It was a well-traveled tent. Hanging on its central post were three solar lights.

The three teams met for an hour before dinner to meditate together. Then they walked into the feast, side by side.

The Chief gave a little speech of welcome at dinner. He was a thin older man who looked frail but was a lot stronger than he appeared. His wife, a large, heavy, jolly sort of woman, was always smiling. Flanking them were their four children, all young and fidgety. Seated around them were about eighty villagers. Johnnie introduced the other three leaders to the Chief and briefly explained their joint mission. It went well and James felt calmer.

Before turning in for the night, Johnnie proposed to James and Suriya that the three teams gather in the morning. The Building Team withdrew to their tents. Each person was soon submerged in their own activity. James needed this time alone to digest everything he had experienced since he had left his familiar little world. It was comforting, in this hot damp strange place, to feel the companionship of his teammates beside him.

Each one went to sleep at a different time. Pierre turned on a soft purring battery-operated sound absorber. It absorbed his snoring and the scary jungle sounds. Without the noises, the jungle was less scary. James lay down on the cot, wrapped his mosquito net around him, and prayed to the God of the Mosquitoes asking that He keep his creatures safely far away from James, for their good as well as his.

God laughed and said, "They were here first."

James reminded himself it was going to be an early morning. Between Satyendra's herbal remedy and Pierre's Rescue Remedy, they were gratefully not jet lagged. James fell right to sleep and slept deeply. He was utterly fatigued from the long journey.

The next morning, James stepped out into the light of day and saw his tent was one of six large Army tents set in two rows with two smaller ones further down the beach. They were just outside the village, near the edge of the trees, by the sea.

Johnnie greeted him and said, "Over there is our compost latrine." He pointed to a long narrow tent further down the beach. "The two small ones over there secluded in the trees, beside the river, are our showers. He pointed to two tents with pipes coming out from under them that ran down to the water. You can also bathe in the ocean, but I wouldn't recommend it, until we get the villagers to stop dumping their waste there."

First, they went to breakfast and then Johnnie took the other two teams on a tour of the village and its surrounding area.

James took a good look around for the first time. Mounds of freshly cut palm fronds perfumed the air. The once lush vegetation was now strewn about, and their precious bamboo was torn up by its roots. Scattered piles of supplies brought from Trinitus City added to the chaotic appearance of this once sleepy village. Stores of food, water, tools, piping, solar equipment, and building materials added more to the utter chaos.

"When we arrived," said Johnnie "the village was in shambles. It took a beating from a wild typhoon that hit two weeks ago. The garden area was wrecked; trees were upended by the wind, structures and animals were washed away by the rain and their food supply was trampled by loose pigs running wild in terror. The villagers have spent the last two weeks clearing away debris."

Even in the face of destruction, the people went gently about their daily lives seeming to be happy and content. You wouldn't know from their faces that their lives had been radically disrupted. Dealing with violent storms was familiar to them, it was part of the reoccurring pattern of their lives. They patiently handled one thing then the next, just as they always did. They rebuilt and recovered. James found this calm acceptance among the villagers to be reassuring.

They met up with the Energy Team and began the first joint meeting to launch their mutual project. Johnnie spoke first. He suggested that each team member introduce themselves, their area of expertise, their goals, and say something personal about themselves. Pretty soon these twelve strangers were beginning to feel like teammates and everyone relaxed.

Johnnie gave a brief history of the work done so far. "We have been here for a week," he said, "so far all we have accomplished is lending the villagers a hand in cleaning away the debris. We expected to have everything set up for you so you could start building as soon as you arrived, but we ran into a snafu in our plans. The Chief is not sold on the domes. I haven't even broached the idea of Trinitus buying the land, because I am still feeling him out. We are still dancing around each other. I cannot seem to pin him down. Everything he says one minute, he contradicts the next. He is going in two directions at once and we are getting nowhere. He is a stubborn clever man. Don't let the long beard fool you, there is a vigorous mind behind those tired, old eyes.

He talked about his team and the sustainable energy systems he had brought. They would maintain service even during unsavory weather conditions. Suriya and her team were here to work on sustainable living. They brought heritage seeds and enzymes that purify human waste and render it a healthy form of compost. Each team outlined their overall goals and a broad sweep of the steps they planned to take. Yael and the other Timekeepers coordinated their timetables for the project and its completion. Of course, they knew the schedule was mostly a fantasy, because nature makes mischief when men make plans.

Pierre gave an overview of the weather for the next few weeks. Wally, Satyendra, and Gloria, the Supply Coordinators from each team, confirmed that their inventories were all accounted for. Johnnie showed them where to erect a large building to protect their vulnerable supplies from the heat, humidity, water, and little creatures. It often rains this time of year. Gloria, from the Sustainability Team, reported that, aside from any unforeseen problems, they had enough food and supplies to stay for three months.

Johnnie thanked everyone for their reports, then explained, "Trinitus will be sending six teams in all. I was sent with the Energy Systems Team first to prepare the village for your arrival. The Agricultural Sustainability Team arrived only the day before the Building Team. Our goal is to prepare this village for a sustainable future. Once the building and energy systems are in place, our teams will leave. The Sustainability Team will stay longer to set up and oversee extensive agricultural projects. They will also be here to greet the other three teams when they arrive. The Medical Team is due to arrive a few days after we leave. The Water Team should arrive the week after that.

"The Water Team will have two missions. One is to pipe water up from the river and have it flow freely through the village. They will build a secure partially submerged holding tank with storage space for three weeks of water. Their second goal will be to launch a team of robots into the ocean and the river, which are designed to remove toxins.

The Education Team will be sent once the other teams feel the project is stabilized.

In closing he said, "Even though we are separate teams from different cities, we have overlapping and complimentary skills. I encourage everyone to follow our protocol, which is: If you see something needs doing, do it. But first, check with the team in charge of that function. That way no one will step on anyone's toes. Let everyone be a pair of helping hands for everyone else."

James turned to Johnnie and asked, "Why hasn't the Chief given his consent?"

"I couldn't get a foothold. This process has been much harder than I expected. These people have been raked over the coals so many times, they do not know who to trust."

Their first meeting ended, and the rest of the day was spent helping the villagers clean and salvage what they could.

That night, weary as he was, James's doubts and fears attacked him something fierce. The hour was late, and he was reluctant to wake anyone up, so he took deep breaths like Satyendra had taught him and he let them out slowly. He opened his heart, as they had done during the qigong exercises, and he called out for help.

"God, I am open to you. Please speak to me." After a few more deep breaths, he heard, "You are following your destiny. You are exactly where you are meant to be at this moment in time. Remain open and resourceful, flexible, and adaptable. You will be successful." God said. "I will help you succeed, but only if you banish worry and panic.

Johnnie said to the other Project Coordinators, "I have been negotiating with the Chief for a week and I haven't gotten his consent, who wants to try next?"

James and Suriya looked at each other. James thought she would probably be more qualified. After all, she was a Blue Band. But he wanted to try. If he also failed, he figured it was best to keep the big guns for last.

Suriya invited Francisco, a linguist on her team, to accompany them to translate. The Chief spoke English but talking in his own language might put him more at ease.

Johnnie, James, Suriya, and Francisco went to visit the Chief. He greeted them warmly, as he always did. Johnnie introduced James as their chief. He figured adding a little status to James's rank might make the Chief take him more seriously.

James stepped forward and reached out his hand in friendship. He smiled, relaxed his shoulders, and softened his body, as Satyendra had coached him to do on the way over. He took a deep breath and relaxed. Hoping his body was signaling that he was a friend. James and the Chief locked eyes and took the measure of each other. James felt tense inside but tried to hide it. So much was riding on this meeting. The Chief seemed friendly enough, but underneath James knew he was suspicious and cautious; not hostile, just resistant.

With their eyes locked on each other, the tension mounted. Each waited for the other to look away. Then to break the tension, James smiled and said, "We see you, Sir. I am impressed with all the fine work your people are doing to repair your village, homes, fishing boats, and nets. We came to help you and have lent a willing hand wherever we saw it was needed. Please tell me, what else would you like us to do?"

James hoped that deferring to him would put him at ease, but then he worried that he was conveying a position of weakness, so he added. "We are helping you now, and your villagers can return the favor when we need it."

Then James experienced firsthand what Johnnie had said about not getting a foothold. The Chief was warm, friendly, evasive, and avoided making any kind of a commitment.

Food and drink were brought, indicating that the business part of the meeting had ended. The Filipino Chief was interested in getting to know this foreign chief better.

James was invited to visit the Chief two days later. This time he only brought Francisco. After the formal greetings, the Chief said, "You want to build structures on my land; then you should build what we need."

For a moment James felt excited and thought success was at hand.

The Chief gave him a calculating look and said, "We need your architectural skills to build pens for our animals. I am told your medical team will be bringing the animals tomorrow. We need a strong pen for the pigs, another near it for the donkeys, and a long narrow chicken coop.

Although their animals traditionally ran free, they now needed pens to protect the new open gardens that the Sustainability Team was planting. A chicken house would make it easier to gather the eggs. His design mind automatically produced an image of the chicken house with an ample yard for exercise.

James heard the Chief's mocking emphasis on architectural skills and knew it was meant to be demeaning. His temper began to rise. Then he remembered Satyendra's warning on the way to this meeting, "This Chief will test you to see if you are really bringing peace or another variation on oppression."

Totally out of character, James laughed and turned it into a joke. "If my architectural skills can build good houses for your pigs, then maybe you will trust me to build good houses for your people. I will make them strong to last a long time even when Mother Nature has a blustery mood, even a typhoon."

The Chief laughed.

With his newfound awareness, James decided to address it as a test. "I will draw up the designs today and my team will begin building the enclosures tomorrow morning. We should have them done by the end of the day. Tomorrow, our Energy Team will see what is needed."

Even a few months ago, James would have been annoyed by the Chief. He would have left the meeting grumbling and muttering to himself. Now he felt differently. He knew he had these teams backing him up and so he could afford to be gracious. He set his team to build sustainable pens as a test to prove themselves and test out their skills in this not exactly conducive environment. The practice would do them good. By the end of the day, with all the teams working together, the pens were structurally solid and complete. By the end of the day, the little village also had a few Wind Spinners and limited Solar Power.

Despite himself, the Chief was impressed with the pens. This time, he made no snide innuendos. He just spoke plainly. James offered to build a safe place for the mother pigs to give birth. The Chief was pleased with the idea.

James planned to make the birthing house a miniature of Greenie. It would give them an opportunity to showcase their dome structure.

These proud people had their own way of doing things. He thought it was best to let the Chief lead.

James always addressed the Chief with great respect and looked him straight in the eye; another tip from Satyendra. It was hard. He was so tempted to look away from the man's piercing gaze, but he knew he was being tested, so he kept looking him in the eyes and spoke with absolute honesty.

He told the Chief, "Trinitus wants to preserve your traditional way of life. My people want only to trade with you. We will set up everything you need to produce healthy abundant crops. We can give you State-of-the-Art equipment, and share our knowledge about agriculture, but we are also willing to negotiate and adapt because we respect your time-honored traditions. Where we can concede, we will. We want a long-term relationship of trade with you. We will buy all the crops you produce beyond what your village needs. In exchange, we will provide you with excellent healthcare and educate your people in whatever subjects you choose, as Chief. We will not interfere with your traditions. We do not want to inflict our beliefs on you."

They only talked about the first steps. James mentioned nothing about long-range sustainable improvements. That would be a topic for a later date. Right now, he only wanted to get started. The only thing he was building was rapport and trust.

James understood that they were walking on a path strewn with broken dreams, broken lives, and broken promises. Satyendra counseled him to move very slowly and very respectfully.

James said to the Chief, "If you and I were sitting here in one year, and we were taking stock of all that we had accomplished from working together, what would your image look like? The Chief shared honestly, and so did James. They both came away feeling good about the vision they shared.

Two days later, James was invited to meet with the Chief again. Johnnie gave James a set of beautiful fish lores of the best quality, to give to the Chief as a token of friendship. In appreciation, James and all the foreigners were invited to share in a feast later that night.

"Tell me Chief James, why don't you want to rebuild our traditional bamboo huts?" the old man asked.

"The homes we want to build for you will also be of bamboo." James carefully explained. "We will use a special thick strong bamboo and give it a roof that will not burn or fight the wind. It will look a lot like your traditional homes with just a few adjustments to keep it from being blown away by a typhoon, or crumble when the earth rumbles.

"We plan to stay only for as long as it takes to build the new houses you need. Then we will move on to another place, to help them. We will take what we learn from your village to the next village, where we will continue to spread fellowship, goodwill, and open hearts. I have come to you with an open heart and an open hand. What better symbol is there for Loving Peace?"

The Chief wanted to believe this seemingly earnest stranger. He was excited when he first received the proposal months ago. He accepted their generous offer, but when the excitement wore off, doubts marched in. He did not want to lead his little tribe into a trap. Poison can come in a sweet package.

"Chief James, I have heard false promises before. There was a village not far away, where smooth talking men made promises to their chief. Sly, lying, silver-tongued men promised the stupid chief that they would give his village everything they needed, and the stupid chief believed them. Because he trusted these lying thieves, his village became enslaved, forced to convert to a foreign religion, their children were taken from them and sent away; their culture was destroyed. All those terrible things happened because their naive chief put his trust in the wrong people."

"After dinner, while an international array of musicians was making music together, James asked the Chief to walk with him. "Sir, please show me your land. I want to love it and care for it. I may never know it as you do, for I am only a guest in your gentle land. I want to be gentle too. How can we work together? We are extending our hands in friendship. Please do not be suspicious of our motives. I will make everything very clear.

"I understand that your greatest fear is that we will take your land and enslave your people. Please believe me when I say, we have not come to take, but to protect you from those who would. If we do not buy your land, others will. Now hear me out before you jump to any hard and fast conclusions. Please put aside your beliefs and your wounds. Just bring us your truth and we will match it.

"Trinitus wants to buy your land; but we will form a partnership with you. We will split our profits 50/50 with you. It will be a win/win experience. We have no interest in having Power Over you. What we want is Power With you. Together, we will have the Power To improve your lives and help your people thrive."

"Your religious beliefs will be held in high respect, and we will always be reverent of your soulful connection to this land.

"Trinitus will own this land, but we will immediately register documents transferring 50% of the ownership to the Palawan Cooperative, which will consist of every man, woman, and child in your village and their descendants. Your people and my people will work together, and we will all thrive.

"We will build a more comfortable life for your people, so they will prosper as a community and as a culture. We want to begin by building new homes that can ride the weather more gracefully and survive the storms. We will give you excellent tools to work the land. Your people will be educated. We can teach you what we know, and we invite you to teach us about your world. Your people and mine can create an equitable and harmonious relationship. Our accounting books will always be transparent and available to you, and as our partners, your people will be in on all decisions.

"I can honestly promise you that our underlying motivation is to reclaim and rebalance the world we share."

The Chief listened, nodded, and occasionally said, "Hmmm," but nothing more.

When they arrived back at the feast, the Chief thanked everyone for coming and announced, "Tomorrow the work begins."

James's last thought before he drifted off into sleep that night was, 'Okay Greenie, it showtime!'

The next morning, the teams converged shortly after dawn, Satyendra led qigong exercises and a meditation in the center of the village. A few fascinated locals joined them. It left James feeling grounded and centered. He felt ready to tackle the day.

Then everyone formed a circle where each person took a turn sharing what they were experiencing in their body, emotions, mind, and spirit. They also acknowledged the challenges they were facing. This sharing circle went a long way to put everyone on the same page. It made them aware of each other in more sensitive ways, which greased the way for them to have more patience with each other, when they faced the rocky forces that would undoubtedly assail them. After the check-in, they all went off to Suriya's breakfast feast where they relaxed and designed the day.

The next day was a busy one for this little village. Everyone over the age of three was engaged in some activity. James counted this as the first day and looked ahead at doing three weeks of work in two weeks. Or he would have to stay longer, which might not interface well with preparing for the divorce. He tried to reach his lawyer and gave up. The Internet was so slow, and the connection dropped so often, that it evoked a very high level of frustration. It was not worth it. He put the whole legal thing out of his mind for now.

Once he overcame his fear, he discovered that the isolation of this village had its virtues. He felt safer here than in San Bernardino. No one had to hover over their children. Kids ran freely, with every adult eye looking out for them. The landscape always took his breath away. The beauty of the rolling waves, the silver stardust on the dancing sea, the swaying palm trees silhouetted at dust against a passionate sky splashed with streaks of fuchsia and rose. He may not have come to love it in quite the same way as the natives, but its natural beauty took his breath away.

The morning after the Chief gave his consent, there was a typhoon of human energy. The Building Team and the Energy Team merged, and everyone worked together on the next few steps. Theirs was a synchronized dance. Solar Engineers milled thick stalks of bamboo beside the villagers and architects. Builders carried spools of wire for the Engineers.

For the Sustainability Team, 'Sus' as they called themselves now, it was just another day, no different than the last. Every morning, Suriya held an open feast to celebrate the dawn of a new day. She said they were celebrating living in paradise. Her feasts were a dignified way to feed the poor.

Then Suriya and her team strolled out into the fields. They were each carrying a large sack of seeds on their shoulders. Francisco drove the tractor with its raking fingers, in front of the team. While the team slowly strolled along planting seeds, they took turns telling lame jokes and funny stories. The natives came over when they heard the laughter. No one wanted to miss a good joke. Soon the villagers were walking beside the team, with a bag on their shoulders and seeds in their hands.

After a long morning of sowing, it was time for another feast. At the end of each midday feast, the team gave each guest a gift. Today it was warm waterproof woolen blankets. They were going to be well appreciated when the wind whipped through the village. Yesterday, it was wonderful colorful bolts of fabric; just perfect to thrill a creative imagination.

Since the afternoons were more freeform, Sus strolled over to lend the other teams a hand. The builders were responsible for every aspect of erecting structures, but it was a dance with the energy systems. The construction required energy for the tools, and the structure needed to be built before it could be wired. Two hands weaving one tapestry.

Wherever they could be useful, Sus and the villagers naturally gravitated towards each other and worked together. The people knew and trusted these loving hands that fed them and planted seeds for the village's future prosperity. Sus was growing foods they would not be here to enjoy. The villagers looked at these strange, wonderful people and remembered a story about a man who planted a tree for a generation he would never see.

The houses went up quickly. That night they twinkled with a warm orange glow through naked window openings. For winter, they were equipped with heavy, well-fitted shutters to keep the weather out and the warmth in. In summer, like now, the open space of the window welcomed in sea breezes to refresh sweaty brows.

Sometimes the land yielded to their will, and sometimes it acted like an unbroken mare shying away from the bit.

James felt the mission was unfolding as well as such things can, given he was working in a jungle with mischievous monkeys who regarded their supplies as delightful new playthings; dangerous snakes that demanded he have eyes everywhere; not to mention those omnipresent vicious vampire mosquitos ever vigilant, watching and waiting to devour him.

Keeping his emotions at an even keel was James's biggest challenge. Each day, (which felt like a week) gave him ample opportunity to give way to frustration and anger. But to his credit, he took everything Satyendra taught him to heart. He breathed deeply and slowly, he felt his feet standing firmly on the earth, he remembered to value the person over the issue, and he softened his total body so tension and stress could not get a foothold. Thus, he sailed through every obstacle, faced it, looked beneath appearances to its truer purpose, and assumed every blockage he encountered carried a message.

When he needed to circumvent an issue, a problem, a clash of beliefs, he called upon his three tenants: flexibility, adaptability, and resourcefulness. It worked most of the time. In the end, what was created carried the handprints of everyone involved. It was a true collage of beliefs, strategies, and a model for cooperation across cultural lines. People did not always understand what the other was saying, but their hearts always caught the gist of it.

The animals arrived a few days late, four donkeys, ten pigs and twenty chickens, along with a harried, harassed, exhausted medical team. Weather and Fate's whims controlled the schedule more than the people did.

The village threw a feast, and everyone gave them a warm welcome. Despite their exhaustion, they started vaccinating against Dengue Fever the very next day.

The little hamlet of Trinitus tents was growing. More showers and latrines were added. It got a little crowded when the Water Team got there ahead of schedule. Their surprise arrival was the product of missed messages and general communication snafues involving the nonexistent internet. The day the engineers erected a functioning cell tower, everyone celebrated. It was designed to look like a palm tree and was almost realistic.

Suriya elected to broach the subject of self-composting toilets with the Chief. He and his Council were confused by her suggestion. They didn't see a need to change something that had always worked. They figured the mighty sea could handle their waste and composting seemed too complicated to deal with. They argued that doing their business in the ocean was the way it had always been done, and it was cleaner.

Surya asserted that it may be cleaner for the people, but not for the sea. The fishing will be better when the water is cleaner. She explained that when you put human waste in the ground, it provides compost to grow bigger crops. Putting waste in the water just pollutes it. She offered to teach them composting step by step to show how simple it can be.

She laid out all the facts and benefits of composting human and pig waste plus she threw in a few statistics to impress the Chief and Council. Her bottom line was that their crops would grow faster and bigger.

The Chief insisted that pig waste was compost enough for their crops and human waste breeds disease. Suriya countered by telling him about enzymes that render human waste nontoxic and germ free. The stubborn Chief was taken aback and felt his dignity and authority was being challenged. An observer would have bet this was going to be an uphill battle for her. They would have lost that bet. Suriya used techniques she had learned in Process Group to alter her approach.

First, she summed up the facts, then she listed the current benefits their progress is currently yielding and ended with an honest assessment of the Chief and his nature. She did not attempt to falsely flatter him but rather, put a light veneer of gloss over his nature and process. She put in enough insightful evaluations to gain his respect, and enough reframes to make him see himself as a progressive and wise leader. She left him feeling in charge of her and his world. As an old man, it had been a while since he felt so virile.

Then she left the Chief and the Council to decide.

From this more centered place, he did not have to defend his views to her. She had helped him feel secure enough to step back and see that she had the well-being of the village at heart. He no longer felt threatened by what she was proposing and could think clearly about its pros and cons. Within an hour, they sent for Suriya and agreed to her requests, with added stipulations and terms. She graciously consented and the work began.

James was not as persuasive when he introduced the idea of building a large domed building for a school. Even though he emphasized that it would provide a strong shelter in times of turbulent storms, the Chief felt he needed to exercise his power somewhere. Suriya was so accommodating and open that flexing his muscles with her, held no satisfaction, but Janes was another story. The Chief looked at this big doughy white chief with thinning hair, who arrived with a gluttonous paunch. He enjoyed watching him squirm. After almost three weeks on the island, the paunch was greatly diminished, but the Chief still saw him that way.

The Chief listened to James, and argued unimportant little points, just to frustrate him. The Chief was fascinated by the way the white man so easily became angry. James felt like he was climbing a rocky road, facing a barrage of obstacles, which was shaving his patience down to the bone.

James felt his anger rise, closed his eyes, took a breath, and the red color drain away. After only a minute, he had a calm and accepting demeanor. The Chief found him fascinating. He was frustrating James just for the entertainment value it afforded him. Then he dismissed James and said he needed to think about it for a while.

He made the foreign chief wait a full day before consenting to building the school. He planned to agree from the beginning; he just wanted to see their chief squirm first.

The villagers were hard-working and even the older kids pitched in. The smaller children helped by picking up debris, bringing water to the workers, and chasing the loose animals and tying them up. The village women wove palm fronds for floormats and sleeping mats.

It rained that night, so the villagers crowded into the completed buildings and the teams retired to their tents. Everyone in the village was exhausted. James glanced at the book lying on his little table unopened. It made him laugh to realize he once thought he would have time to read. Every day required jumping out of bed on the run and falling into bed at the end of a long day, utterly exhausted. The work was satisfying. He had no time for himself, but he was experiencing moments of sheer contentment. That was a new and different feeling. He wanted to bottle it up and take it back with him. At home, he usually had a hard time falling asleep or staying asleep. Here, it was night, one minute and morning, the next. He forgot that he had ever had panic attacks. Now when something challenged him, he heard Satyendra's voice in his head directing him to maximize his power and minimize his stress. He enjoyed the comradery of the teams and the villagers. He felt good and solid in this peaceful little corner of the world.

Each sustainable hut had its own energy system. Running water and trustworthy electricity brought the village to unknown levels of comfort. New crafts were now possible for supplemental income.

Their traditional Nipa huts on stilts, were made primarily from bamboo and palm fronds with some hard wood framing. It was easily blown apart in the storms. The new building tried to echo as many similar design elements as possible, while being far more flexible, stronger, and more sustainable. The worst damage to the huts was done to the palm thatch on the roof, so James had his team make new roof tiles of hempcrete. In fact, James freely used hempcrete wherever he could.

Likewise, all the new buildings were elevated because of the omnipresent mud. The school would have a similar design, but it needed stronger support posts. Instead of using four cradled bamboo halves to frame the structure, they used six. This meant that an expedition of builders and locals had to venture further and further into the jungle to find the thick species they were using for the stilts and frames.

This village was specifically chosen because a large forest of thick bamboo grew not far from it and on other nearby islands. The land also hosted species of thinner bamboo, which could be made into strips, to be woven into lattice work for the walls and ceiling.

While the frames and supports were made of cradled bamboo tied with reinforced cane, the builders chose to make the floors and joists out of strong hardwood. The villagers also needed wood for boats, so a second expedition of locals and Sus set off into the jungle hunting for trees. It turned out to be a long week of logging. They were equipped with a couple of chainsaws and several machetes. The new donkeys were a blessing because they pulled the larger logs.

Poisonwood was strong and the wood had a beautiful grain. It would work well, but harvesting these trees needed to be done with cautious respect. Its sap acted on human flesh like poison oak and the symptoms tended to return after the blisters healed.

Deep in the jungle the humidity was brutal. They missed the sea breeze that was such a relief in the village.

The builders quickly erected a schoolhouse, forty feet round. Every member of the village and the Trinitus Teams participated. With so many hands, the labor easily progressed to completion.

Johnnie secured the water rights, and the builders designed a series of interlacing irrigation pipes to expand the farming area.

Each day the villagers and *Sus* prepared the land and planted new crops. Peanuts, pineapple and groves of bamboo would soon be growing in this jungle. They planted an orchard of rubber, mango, banana, guava, coconut, and papaya trees.

The villagers would now be well fed and have clean water. They were moving towards being independent and self-sufficient.

Trinitus finalized the purchase of the land, in and around the village, which preserved the jungle and protected the inhabitance. The partnership documents were signed the same day. The village was now protected from predatory companies and a corrupt government.

Suriya and Francisco held classes at night. Every adult, teenager, and older child in the village attended. She taught them how to manage the village as a Co-Op. She did not have to explain that they needed to treat every member as an equal employee/owner, it was already ingrained in their village. Suriya carefully showed parallels between their traditional values and the new concepts she was introducing. She was aware that a shift in consciousness takes patience, and she was aiming for nothing less.

James finally understood what Trinitus's Outreach Program was all about. They were creating a good quality of life for the people, while preserving the land, and their ancient traditions, which was a far cry from the way most companies, foreign and domestic, operated in the Philippines. Most companies were greed-based and paid barely survivable wages. Poverty forced young people to leave their villages and go to the city, where they lived in unsafe and crowded conditions. They had to endure contaminated water, trash filled streets, and no medical care. With no access to education, they had no way to better the quality of their meagre lives.

More supplies arrived from Trinitus, rice seeds, wheat seeds, clothes, fishing equipment, educational supplies, and medicines. They were all given to the village in trade for future harvests.

The Building Team and the Energy Team had completed their mission. The time had come to prepare for the long trip home. James felt divided. On one hand, he yearned for a world without mosquitos, on the other, he was reluctant to leave this beautiful island paradise and the wonderful friendships he had made here. This was an amazing experience; one he would never forget.

The whole village gathered to give them a worthy send-off. There was a pig feast, and the Chief gave a little speech. It was sincere and complimentary, which surprised James. He didn't think the old cantankerous fellow had it in him.

Six villagers accompanied them back to Manilla where they would be catching a flight to the States. Bayani, a young villager, was among them. He was on his way to a school in Manilla to learn financial accounting for the village. Bayani sat next to James and talked most of the way. He was nervous about leaving the village for the first time and excited about the new opportunities that lay ahead of him. Like all villagers, he was intrigued and afraid of the city. To avoid thinking about what lay before him, he chose to describe to James how life had been before they came.

"Survival in our village was difficult, yet we led happy lives. We took pleasure in the vast beauty of our land; the lush green mountain sides; the breathtaking beaches; our slow, relaxing, tranquil lifestyle; and our tight relationships with friends, family and neighbors. We were happy because of the great friendships we shared. I have the most wonderful and dearest friends. I know we will be able to count on each other for the rest of our lives.

"In the evenings, the whole village would gather in the streets to socialize and take advantage of the cooler weather after the sun had set. We had a sense of belonging and acceptance. We all shared the same religion, and the Church played a central role in our village life. We knew we were safe, and our children were safe. Our little ones ran about and played all around the village without parents having to worry about someone taking them or harming them. All the parents kept an eye on each other's children as they ran about from house to house.

"Daily life was very hard for us. Our money dries up in between rice seasons and the fishing is not always good. We often find it a challenge just to keep basic food and rice on our tables.

"In the summertime, there was no electricity for at least one day a week, and it would go out for few hours several times during the rest of the week. The internet was almost non-existent or at best, very slow.

"With our declining income from fishing, and the projects we started that failed, it was hard to produce a livelihood. Our village had little tax money to spend on improving the quality of our lives, and of course, we had to cope with devastating weather, which often destroyed our animals and crops.

"Young men, like my brother, Crisanto, were often forced to leave the village and move to the cities. He was desperate to make some money to feed our family. He was lucky enough to find a job. He had to work six days a week, for $3 to $6 a day and counted himself fortunate to have a job paying that much.

"Crisanto hated the city and wrote home often about how bad living conditions were. To survive, he had to live in a small apartment with a few other men, so he had no privacy. He wrote that the air was thick with smoke, smog, and pollution. It was especially hard for him to adjust to all the strange noises, having lights shining all through the night. People exploited him, and after a while he seemed to see himself as invisible. He missed the natural landscape, the mountains, hills, rivers, and lakes that fed his soul.

"Now you have given us a chance to keep our families together. No one will have to go away, except maybe to college to earn a degree, but then they can come home and enjoy a better social status, more opportunities for advancement, and a good life."

When they reached Manila, James and Bayani both felt a little overwhelmed by the crowded streets, the bottlenecked traffic, and the high level of pollution. James accompanied his young companion to the Financial School and helped him enroll. "Mabuhay! We see you," they said to each other as they parted ways.

James rejoined his team and flew home. Sitting back in his chair, looking out the window, James watched this precious emerald and aquamarine world recede. He had so many memories to savor on the long ride home.

James thought back to the day when he was in the jungle with Johnnie on an expedition to cut bamboo. Since Johnny was a Green Band, he asked him what he thought Trinitus's underlying motives were.

"Beside trade and helping the people?" he asked.

James nodded to encourage him to go on.

"We are transforming the world through our example. We are a responsible organization exemplifying how to do business without hurting the environment or the lifestyle of its people. We try to live in harmony with nature. We buy land to protect it from illegal logging, poaching, and human slavery.

"We go to places where there is still something to save; animals, water, biospheres, cultures, and national parks that are being sold off. We set an example that hopefully others will follow. We are creating a social movement based on Loving Peace. We are saving the environment. Hopefully our example is teaching the next generation how to live in Loving Peace.

Eventually, we hope to further the influence of our principles by becoming involved in local politics, so we can preserve even more land, and promote healthy methods for rebuilding cities and towns. We would also like to branch out into social justice to make rulings more humane.

"Another important goal is to improve the lives of the underclass. These people have nothing or close to it. Hamas, Hizballah and other terrorist groups gained their foothold by serving the underclass. They traded food, clothes and medical supplies for access to the basements of hospitals and schools, where they placed bombs. These groups do not care who gets killed. Since we began helping the underclass, and have asked nothing in return, there have been fewer places where terrorist gangs were able to get a foothold.

"The example we set offers children healthier models to live by. Rather than the dog-eat-dog competitive world that most kids are familiar with, we teach them the difference between *Power Over*, and *Power With*, or *Power To*. These are healthier models for children to follow while they are growing up. We show them that it is up to everyone on the planet today to preserve life in peaceful ways."

James thought for a moment, and asked, "Don't corrupt governments try to stop you?"

"No, they haven't yet," Johnnie replied. "We work quietly. One day we will have the political power to affect the laws of the land and have a direct influence on improving the quality of life for the citizens on a larger scale. Then we can expect to encounter opposition and sabotage. Hopefully by then, our grass root communities will be able to provide us with strong backing."

"Johnnie, do you really believe that Loving Peace will take root in a significant number of people? Won't there always be those who are competitive and greedy?" asked James.

"Loving Peace is not a passive force. We are fostering a peaceful evolution, rather than a violent revolution. We will never go to war to create peace. To do so is to lose before you have begun.

"We make change by guiding those we care for in the right direction. Our work unites people. It is a natural biproduct of their new healthy, more prosperous life. By lovingly supporting life-affirming rights and improving the quality of the community, we show our caring concern and build strong friendships.

"We never force anyone to do anything. We respect their right to have their own beliefs. We help people to free themselves from entrapping beliefs that cripple them, keep them small, and make them feel helpless. These beliefs have been imposed upon them to keep them obedient. We model healthy beliefs and help others create their own.

"People believe in us and trust us because they know we walk our talk. We practice the same loving acceptance that we ask of them. When we accept and respect people, they naturally feel loved."

James found this overview fascinating and felt honored to be part of such an idealistic endeavor. He asked, "Johnnie, in your Trinitus City, does everyone have to go through therapy and participate in ongoing Personal Process groups?"

"Yes. It is at the core of all our cities and projects. We are working to free people from the narrow destructive beliefs that have been inflicted upon us for the last 5,000 years, under patriarchal domination. Those beliefs have run their course and do not serve humanity anymore. Now they are a cancer eating away at the human soul."

"Why is Trinitus sending teams to foreign places on the other side of the world, when there is so much need in our own country?" asked James.

"Trinitus has many communities and many programs throughout the United States," replied Johnnie. "Those outreach programs are quite similar to what we have here. We rescue farms in small towns and trade locally for the products our communities need."

"The economy in many small towns and farming areas in the States is failing, so farmers are forced to sell to big agriculture companies. We provide a healthy alternative. Our Sustainability Team enters first, to teach economic development and host Personal Process groups in the schools. This is how we first establish ourselves in a town. The classes are free to townies and farmers alike. We offer them our outreach programs and those who are wise accept our terms. We help them return to healthy farming practices, offer economic alternatives to cattle-raising, and help them regain their water rights. We also teach them how to create Co-Ops, which help them flourish.

"The point is we are an example to the world of what conscious; cooperative, caring people can accomplish. We are guiding people to make self-reflection a daily practice and helping them grow their consciousness as well as their crops. Together we are exemplifying an advanced culture with social responsibility and maintains a harmonious relationship with the environment."

The plane landed in Arizona and James disembarked only one week later than planned. His face was slimmer and his waistline too. He felt his feet standing solidly on the ground and stood straighter. The buildings he designed were strong and flexible in the face of gale winds, and so was he. Whatever destiny was brewing to throw at him, James now had the skills to handle. This man was very different than the one who left a month ago. That scared, panicking, self-doubting, small-minded man never came back. This self-aware and confident man returned in his stead.

CHAPTER 12

Reentry

James stepped off the plane just after noon in Arizona. The humid jungle still clung to him. As soon as his feet touched the pavement, all the moisture was sucked out of his body. He could feel his skin fry and his lips crack. It was only 88° but there was no shade and no humidity. He dashed into the waiting air-conditioned van sent by Trinitus and gave a sigh of relief. An old rhyme went through his head, "Only mad dogs and Englishmen go out in the noonday sun." They must have meant Arizona in the summertime. Before air-conditioning, only snakes, scorpions, and lizards lived in this baking wilderness.

James had been gone for years, lifetimes, a little over four weeks. Throughout the day, he stopped to gaze off and remember. He remembered the smell of pigs baking underground, the sweet breeze off the sea, the strange and wonderful music coming from the improv sessions after dinner.

Most of his time in the village was spent working desperately hard and worrying equally hard. Only now did he have time and inclination to savor the beauty of the land and its playful people, the mysteries of the jungle, the comradery of his tentmates and the wonderful way all the teams worked together. He laughed to himself, remembering how intimidated he felt when he first met Johnnie, and what a great support the man turned out to be. James knew he would never have succeeded if it was not for Satyendra. This gentle man quietly in the background, taught him how to manage his energy and everyone else's.

He was proud of his accomplishments. It was a rare and wonderful feeling. He knew it was completely a team effort. Each person showed up one hundred percent and did their part. Qigong meditation with Satyendra grounded him each morning. Pierre's sharing circles, morning and evening, kept everyone on the same page with each other. Together, the level of unity and cooperation remained high, equal to the frustration, irritation, and annoyance levels they had to cope with from the project. He had a fantastic experience because of all the teams, without them, it would have been impossible.

James was looking forward to his Anger Management group. He had so many successes to report. He considered himself now cured of all his anger issues. All he had to do was ground, breathe, and relax. He entered the room, sat next to Shareen and offered to share first. It was quite a contrast to his usual reluctancy to share, his monosyllabic answers, and all the justifications and blame that were usually a big part of his sharing. His description of the Chief had everyone in stitches. They laughed so hard, a few had tears in their eyes. At the end, everyone applauded or cheered. Shareen was amazed at the transformation.

Tim, Cathy, and Tammy invited James to dinner to celebrate. He regaled them with his stories of the Chief, the teams, the jungle, and all the wonderful things he learned from Satyendra.

When the others left, James walked Cathy home. On the way, she asked him if he had any talks with God on the trip. He told her how God had said that he was in the right place, and this was his destiny. James said that it was very comforting.

Cathy agreed, and said that having the backing of God, made navigating through hard times, reassuring. This was her opening to share some private things that she did not want to share with the whole group at dinner.

"I've had a lot of occasion to talk with God while you were gone. I also missed talking with you. I filed for divorce. We don't have any children, so I don't think he will contest it. During the day, I feel relieved, but at night, I still have nightmares about the horrible things he did to me. Is it okay if I tell you about what I went through? You are my best friend here."

James liked her and wanted to be a good friend, so he nodded yes.

"I was pregnant once, but I lost the baby, after my husband used me as a punching bag. He was afraid of being a father. It freaked him out so badly that he started picking on me. When I said, "Leave me alone!" He went into a rage because I talked back to him. That's when he started swinging.

"He didn't usually hit me. Mostly, he liked to manipulate my mind. He always told me that I was crazy, and said if people knew, they would lock me up. He kept me afraid of being locked up and convinced me that I wasn't seeing things right. If he broke something, He would tell me that I did it, but I blocked out the memory. Even when my friend Clair saw something the same way I did, Bruce said that I convinced her to see it my way because she was my friend. He had me doubting myself and thinking I was crazy.

"After I lost the baby, I stayed in bed for two weeks. He wanted to get me up and going because his dirty laundry and dirty dishes were piling up.

"He suggested that I take some evening classes. I could not believe he was going to let me do something. I took a political science class. The teacher was inspirational. He gave me fascinating things to think about. One night, while I was washing the dishes, I had a vision of how we can all live together in peace. It wasn't very different than Trinitus. I stupidly mentioned it to Bruce. He immediately called the looney bin and had me incarcerated. They released me after a few days and said I had irritated boundaries. I think that means I let Bruce walk all over me. I did not have the strength to stop him.

"When I was pregnant and he hit me in the stomach, I stood up to him for the first time. I grabbed a shoe with a wooden heel and hit him. It left a cut on his eyebrow. His wound showed and mine did not. He called the police and told them that I was dangerous and said that I attacked him! The police arrived to take me back to the mental hospital. I just could not go back there again. They tried to push me into the squad car, I resisted, and they used a cattle prong to force me into the car.

"We were married for seven long years. I dreamed of leaving him every one of those days; but he kept me as his slave. I cooked, cleaned, and obeyed. He maintained his power over me by making me think I was crazy. He convinced me that without him, I could not survive. I believed that I could not take care of myself, and I needed him. He threatened to tell the doctors that I heard the voice of God and had since I was a child. If I didn't do just as he said, he would threaten me by saying, "I will tell the doctors, and they will lock you up and throw away the key."

James felt awkward and did not know what to do. She obviously needed something. Crying women were not his forte. So, he grounded his feet, took a breath, relaxed, put his arms around her, and held her to his chest. They stood like that for a long moment with her head on his chest. She felt like a wounded little bird, so he petted her head. She looked up at him through her tears with an expression of gratitude. He gave her a compassionate smile that somehow turned into a kiss. It was not a passionate, I desire you, but rather, a 'I am here for you,' kind of kiss. At least, that is what he told himself. He immediately wondered what kind of a kiss it was for her.

"I better get you home," he said. They started walking again and neither said a word the rest of the way to her house. In his head, there were lots of words, mostly around the question, 'what have I gotten myself into now?'

The next morning, James called Kim and let her know he was back. They made an appointment for later that afternoon. He went for a long walk to think about Cathy. He decided that the bottom line was that he liked her as a friend, but he wasn't sexually attracted to her. She seemed a bit clingy, and he certainly did not need more complications in his life.

When James checked in with Taylor, his supervisor told him to take three days off and enjoy his free time. James found a comfortable spot and finally began reading that book he dragged to the other side of the world and never opened.

Early that evening, James was still cozy in his comfortable chair, lost in the world of his novel. Suddenly the jarring ring of the ComPad broke his concentration. He was so startled that he answered it without even looking to see who was calling as he usually did.

"We see you," he said warmly assuming the caller was someone in Trinitus.

"What the hell are you seeing? My Facetime is not on," came the hostile, obviously drunk voice of Judy. That quickly brought him to full attention!

"Hello Judy," he said cautiously. "Why are you calling? I did not expect to hear from you."

"Stay away from my children, or I will arrange it so you never see them again. Sammy hates you. He will never go to that Communist Cult where you are hiding. Sandra is going to college. I am not going to let you ruin her life like you ruined mine."

James was gasping for air. He did not know which hook to grab first. Communist Cult? My son hates me! I ruined Judy's life! I am ruining Sandra's life! She's going to try to stop me from ever seeing my kids! He had the fleeting thought that he wished Satyendra was here to whisper in his ear. It was only a fleeting thought, a last remnant of his masterful enlightenment.

"You are going to pay for this, you bastard! I am suing for sole custody and supervised visits, unless I can arrange for no visits at all, ever!" She viciously spewed.

He was reeling and his blood was boiling. More hooks! Pay for what? What does she think I did? Sole custody! Supervised visits! No visits! There were a million horrible things he wanted to scream at her. He wanted to smash her in her smug drunken face! A flood of angry words rushed to his lips all at once, so luckily, none of them could get through. He just stared at the ComPad and gasped. There was a gurgling sound in his throat. Some words reached his lips, but before he could give voice to them, she screamed, "Go to hell," and pushed the end button.

The poor book became the victim of his wrath, so was the innocent mirror he threw it at. As the book left his hand and went sailing across the room, he felt a sense of release. The sound of tinkling glass hitting the floor brought waves of guilt, blame, regret, and fear.

James knew he should call Tim or Satyendra and do something to calm down and move the emotion through. He knew what he should do, but he did not want to let go of his rage just yet. He wanted to milk it to justify his pain. He kept repeating to himself how he was just sitting there minding his own business when this crazy hellion attacked him. He kept going over everything she said and everything he wanted to say, and should have said, and all the terrible things she had always done. His anger was boiling. He fanned the flames with thoughts of her drinking, of how unreasonable she was, and how she always got under his skin. These thoughts heated his anger into a bubbling explosive mix.

Minutes later, he was wallowing in self-pity. He listed all the many ways in which he was a poor helpless victim. Over and over, he regurgitated distorted views of reality. He walked around his room, around and around wearing a groove in the carpet. His mind went around and around poor me, poor me, and every variation on this theme.

When James made the appointment with Kim, earlier in the morning, he imagined telling her how well he had managed his anger in the Philippines, and how well the trip had gone. He was excited to tell her how he was now in control of his life.

On the way to Kim's office, he realized how fleeting his success had been. He felt like he was back at square one and it was all Judy's fault.

An hour before Judy flipped out at James, she came home from work with her arms filled with groceries. Sandra quickly went into the kitchen to help her put everything away. Mom cooked dinner and they all sat around the table eating in silence. Sandra was afraid to say anything for fear it would set her mom off and Sammy was preoccupied with thoughts about tonight's game. He wasn't going to bother asking Mom for permission to play. He watched her refill her wineglass again and again and knew she would pass out before it was time to go. He'd been doing it for a while and she never caught on.

Judy went to the kitchen for another bottle. She was drowning, not just in wine, in lots of things. They kept stomping through her mind. It was going to take a lot more wine to forget everything that was pulling her down. She was really frustrated by having a teenage daughter who blamed her for everything, a habit she picked up from her dad. Judy felt overwhelmed being the sole provider for two kids who knew how to spend money. The league that Sammy was on cost $5000 a year! She felt like she was pedaling as fast as she could and was falling behind.

Judy deserved a promotion at work, she had for a while, but men younger than her, newer to the company than she, moved up faster. One man, whom she trained, was now one of her bosses. That was utterly galling. She did excellent work but was always passed over because the bosses were men, and they wanted to keep it that way.

Her husband was no help. He was a dreamer. If he had made more money, it would have taken some of the pressure off her shoulders, but he was just a screw-up. Between the work, the kids, and her non-existent marriage, she was perpetually exhausted.

"I need a vacation," she mumbled to the stove, because no one else was listening. "James ran off to have a vacation. Don't I deserve one. Well," she sighed, "there is no time." She refilled her drink and raised her glass in a toast. "This is my vacation. I need a few more glasses and all my problems will drift away into oblivion. My sweet friend here will erase away all my miseries."

Judy went back to the dining room. She dropped into her chair and turned to Sandra. In the hopes of connecting with her brooding distant daughter, she probed her foggy brain for something they could talk about. They used to talk about things. They even used to laugh together, but that was a million years ago, when she was cute and sweet and they used to go on fun shopping trips together.

"Now that you are going to enter your senior year, it is time to think about the college you want to go to. You can go to a local one and live at home, or to an out-of-town school and live in a dorm. Which do you prefer, local or out of town?"

"Neither" said Sandra wrinkling her nose in disdain.

Judy laughed thinking her response was a joke, "We can begin looking now. I think a road trip would be great fun. We can begin ordering catalogues."

"Mom."

"If you live in the dorm, it would be cheaper. Your dad did not leave you any money for college, so you will need to apply for financial aid and get a job to cover your living costs. I can give you a small allowance to help you meet expenses.

"Mom."

"Maybe I can ask if they need anyone in my mailroom. It would be nice to have you work in my company, so you can save a little before you leave. You can work part time after school."

"Mom."

"Why do you keep interrupting me like that? It is very rude, you know."

Sandra took a deep breath and plunged ahead, "I'm not going to college, I'm going to work."

"Don't worry, it will be great fun. College was a great experience for me. You'll love it."

"Mom, you are not listening to me. I'm not going to college. I'm getting an internship." She said flatly. "I have looked at my options and I know where I'm going."

"Oh, really? You have, have you?" She sounded sarcastic, "What great plans do you have?"

"I don't want to fight with you. You don't need to worry about me; I have it all handled." She got up and put her plate in the sink. She was trying not to challenge her mother; she was just standing her ground.

"You have it handled? How about telling me and let me be the judge of that." Judy stood up. She was a little wobbly. She reached for a chair to steady herself. Her hand automatically reached out to pour another glass. Alas, the bottle was empty. She went over to the cupboard and took down another bottle.

To calm her mom down, Sandra said, "Let's table this for now, I don't want to argue with you."

Sammy disappeared fast. He could see where this was going.

"As long as you live in my house young lady, you're going to do what I say! Now tell me about this make-believe job of yours!"

"I'm going to my room. You're just going to try to talk me out of it, but I'm going to do it anyway! So, what's the point?"

"Your father put you up to this, didn't he? What's your plan, running away to that Communist Cult where your father is hiding out?"

"Yes, I am, they have a good school and guaranteed work...."

"This is bullshit!" Judy interrupted, her mood turning dark. "That place won't prepare you for the real world. You can't make anything of yourself without an education. Do you want to be a waitress all your life? You will never get a decent job!" Judy came around the island and put her face inches from Sandra's face.

"Listen to me Miss...."

"I can't go to college, Sandra jumped in and said, even if I wanted, which I don't! You made sure of that!" Sandra was trying not to shout but her volume was increasing a little.

"What the hell do you mean by that!" Judy had no qualms about screaming right in her daughter's face.

"You know what I mean!" Sandra hissed back. "There is no money for college! What kind of job am I going to get to pay for it? I can't get a student loan because you make too much money, and you already spent everything we have!"

Judy glared at her daughter. She had no comeback for that. "Go to your room! I'm done talking to you! Keep mouthing off and you are going to be grounded for a long, long time," she hissed vindictively.

"With pleasure!" Sandra walked off to her room.

'How dare she blame Dad for the missing money.' She seethed. 'I will live with my father when the divorce is final and never see her again!'

Judy poured another glass. She was furious. She went to change into her nightgown and remembered it was in the dryer. The laundry had been in the dryer for over a week. The dirty laundry was overflowing the hampers. She made a mental note to start another load in the morning. The note disappeared from her foggy brain. She reached for the hamper to take it downstairs. She got as far as the head of the stairs and put it down, was distracted by her thoughts, walked away, and forgot about it. As she put on a different nightgown, she mumbled to herself; "He has poisoned my daughter with that Commie Cult bullshit, and he is turning her against me! This is all his doing!" Absolutely furious, flames were shooting out of her nostrils when she told her Smartwatch to ring James.

James plopped down on Kim's sofa feeling utterly defeated. He talked about kissing Cathy out of compassion and said, "Maybe I should not have done that. I am not interested in having a relationship with her." Then he talked about Judy and how she exploded on the phone, accusing him of lots of things that weren't true. He told Kim that Sandra must have mentioned moving to Trinitus instead of going to college. He was annoyed with his daughter for riling Judy up, especially after he specifically told her not to talk about college with her mother. There were three women in his life, and he was not doing very well with any of them.

"It sounds like you are saying you are miserable because these women did various things to upset you. Is that correct?"

"Yeah," he said irritated with Kim for stating the obvious, "that's pretty clear."

"Do you think you might have a problem with blame? In our last session, you blamed your father and your wife for your troubles."

"Well, someone is to blame for the money being gone, and for all the insecurities in me!"

"Why does anyone have to be to blame?" she asked.

"What?" He was shocked by the question. He wanted to protest that this is something everyone knows but then figured she would not like him if he challenged her.

"Someone must be to blame, is a belief. One that may not work for you. Why do you need or want to believe someone is to blame?" Kim asked.

"Otherwise, I feel guilty." The truth slipped out unedited.

She seemed to have this power over him that made him confess his truth.

"Why do you feel guilty?" she asked in a soft compassionate voice.

"Well, when I am to blame, I feel guilty. It is important to find out who really is at fault." He wondered why she asked such strange and silly questions.

"That is another belief. Things go wrong from time to time for lots of reasons, many of which are beyond human control. Blame and guilt are a programed response to toxic beliefs.

"People change their beliefs all the time. Are you willing to change these or do you think they enhance the quality of your life?"

"No, of course not," he scoffed. "It's awful to feel guilty and blame creates a wedge between people. But how do I get rid of a belief, it is part of me."

"'It is part of you.' That is another belief. When you were three, you probably believed Santa rode on a magic sleigh and brought presents to children all around the world all in one night. Do you still believe that?"

James nodded no.

Kim asked, "Why?"

"Because I learned the truth," he answered, wondering where she was going with this.

"Good. Are you willing to learn the truth regarding these beliefs?"

'Oh boy, here comes the brainwashing, after all,' was the thought running through his head; but he answered what she expected him to say, "Yes, I want to know the truth."

"These beliefs were embedded in your consciousness to control you. The authorities in your life made arbitrary rules for you. When you broke one, you were punished. These punishments made you feel bad about yourself. They unleashed horrible emotions. That is how you learned to do whatever you could to not break the rules. You became afraid of those terrible feelings. To avoid punishment, you blame others. If you are willing to surrender these negative beliefs, that were implanted in you as a child to control you; you can be free to be your full beautiful self."

"But how?" he asked. Despite all his skepticism, this was beginning to make sense.

"I can teach you, but it will take dedication. These beliefs have been reinforced for a great many years. They may not let go easily. They might toss up resistance. If you think this will not work, or you need to shield yourself from people, or these people are brainwashing you, it is the Inner Critic fighting back. To do this work, you must learn to recognize beliefs embedded in thoughts. Then ask yourself, does this belief enhance your life? If it doesn't you can release it. The very first step is to realize that anything that makes you feel bad about yourself is a lie. It may be a lie based on events in the past. Nevertheless, it is still a lie.

"It works like this: You have a belief. That belief leads you to have expectations. Your expectations motivate your actions. Your actions prove the belief is true. It is a closed loop. If you were acting under another belief, you would get a different result and experience a different truth.

"This is an ingenious strategy to control people. Stories, the media, the news, it is all slanted to reaffirm collective beliefs, which were never true to begin with. If a belief makes you feel good about yourself, what you have done, and who you are, keep it. If it makes you feel bad, it is an embedded belief designed to control you.

"If you want to feel good about yourself and your decisions, this is how you start. See the lies. Are you willing to do homework?"

James nodded.

"Okay, make a list of one hundred beliefs that pull the strings of your emotions. Beliefs that control your perception of reality and of yourself in relation to others. Start every sentence with, "It is a lie that...." Such as, it is a lie that someone is always to blame. It is a lie that it was your fault that Judy is angry. Now it's your turn. Identify a few lies in your life."

"It is a lie that I cannot be a good leader. I did just fine in the Philippines."

"Good, say another."

"It is a lie that I am responsible for losing my job. Economics are tight and they had to lay people off."

"Good, say another."

"It is a lie that Judy is totally responsible for all the financial problems we are having. I made a bad investment, and we had some big bills. Sammy's obsession with soccer is expensive. There are steep dues, plus expensive uniforms and equipment. Last year, when he broke his arm in a game, it cost a pretty penny. Judy does spend too much, but there are reasons for that too."

"Good, a little compassion seeped in along with your honesty. When I see you next week, we can go over your list of one hundred beliefs that no longer serve you."

For the rest of the session, he talked about his beliefs around relationships, especially the ones that keep tripping him up.

James left her office feeling naked. He wanted to blame Kim for making him say things he never told anyone before. But then he realized it would be blaming her for his feelings.

Instead, he looked for a deeper truth and he found it. He saw the underlying beliefs controlling his feelings. He believed, 'it is dangerous to show your true feelings,' and a second belief popped out, "say what people want to hear instead of telling your truth."

He was amazed! He wanted to be free of these voices in his head, free of the guilt. He could see how these beliefs were not necessarily true, but they acted like puppet strings that made him dance. Then a warm feeling filled his heart as he realized he was setting himself free.

James received a call from Dr. Fouche's office informing him that he has a reentry examination this afternoon. None of his teammates returned with any tropical diseases, so he was likely to pass as well.

He had so many mosquito bites. The little vampires seemed to feast on him more than anyone else. He was worried that he had malaria, or dengue fever. On the plane coming home, Pierre and Carla assured him that if he was going to be sick, the symptoms would have appeared by now. James was relieved to go to the doctor. Once she gave him the all-clear, only then could he relax. Not that he could ever relax with Judy on the warpath.

Dr. Fouche greeted him and said, "You are looking good. Your paunch is virtually gone, and your skin texture looks firmer, good work."

"Hard physical labor and extreme heat cut my appetite in half."

She put the little box on his finger and the band around his wrist. It took his blood pressure, oxygen levels and drew blood. Within a few minutes it produced a readout. All his vital signs were in the acceptable range, except his cholesterol, which was still high.

"Did your Trainer give you a cholesterol lowering diet?" she asked.

James said, "Yes," and rattled off the rhyme just as he memorized it:

"Oats, whole grains, lentils, and beans,
Carrots, colorful veggies, and dark leafy greens.
Apples, pears, citrus fruits, just a light dish,
Berries, salmon, and fatty fish.
Nuts, flax seeds, chia seeds,
Avocado, and dark unsweetened chocolate, please."

"In the Philippines, they didn't have chia seeds or most of the other stuff; but a person can starve on this weird diet."

"What is weird about it?" she asked with a smile.

"Well, most of my staples are not on it. I usually have a normal breakfast," he said.

"What constitutes normal?" she asked, amused.

"Bacon, eggs, and toast or a croissant, with butter and jam, coffee with cream and sugar. I usually have your basic normal lunch, a club sandwich with ham, turkey, and cheese on white bread, with a coke. For my mid-morning and mid-afternoon breaks, I usually have a coke or coffee with sugar, cream, and a pastry, like everyone else at work. Dinners vary a lot, but often it is a typical dinner, burger on a bun with fried onions, French fries and a coke, or spaghetti and meatballs with parmesan cheese and garlic bread with a coffee afterwards, or spareribs dripping with barbecue sauce, mashed potatoes with gravy, dinner rolls and corn on the cob. Pasta with seafood in an Alfredo sauce, dinner rolls, breaded and fried onion rings, and canned green beans. Just basic food.

She had to hold herself back from laughing.

"Everything, every single food you mentioned may be part of the collective diet, but be sure, it is highly toxic, pure poison. If you continue to eat that way, you are well on your way to a heart attack or a stroke."

"But I'm only forty-seven," he protested. "I still have a lot of good years left. You told me before I left that I have good core strength."

"That is like having a hefty bank account, but you keep withdrawing five hundred dollars at a go," she explained. "It is going to deplete your account quite soon. Eating like this, even if you were thirty, could kill you. If you want to live long enough to see your son graduate from college, take the trainer's diet seriously. Your life is at stake.

"If I did have a heart attack, what kind of healthcare do you have here?"

"We have a hospital. It has State of the Art equipment and an excellent staff of doctors, nurses, healers, aids, and few patients. We have an excellent preventative Care program. We can handle most cases in a Trinitus City. We can set broken bones and cure most illnesses, but our medical system is very different here.

Out in the *RW*, people are bombarded with pharmaceutical commercials and most people think it is normal to take a handful of pills every day. They take a pill to cure a malady, which may or may not cure it. However, this pill produces a side effect, so the patient takes another pill to address the side effect, which could produce a side effect, on and on. There are even pills that help other pills work.

"If you have high blood pressure you take a pill for the rest of your life. If you have diabetes you take a pill to get your numbers down and swallow the pill with a swig of coke. It is all a form of addictive madness.

"Collective beliefs keep the pharmaceutical companies wallowing in gold, especially when they are legally allowed to mark up their prices 3000% above the cost of production.

"We supply you with everything you need including a support person to help you stay motivated. With healthy food and ample exercise, living in alignment with your body, mind, and emotions should keep you healthy most of the time.

"If you follow our protocol, all your medical expenses are free, no deductible, no copay, no premiums. The protocol is simple, live a healthy life. Your trainer will teach you how. It is a pleasurable way to live.

Here are the points of the protocol:

*Eat a well-balanced array of healthy foods, in moderation, with an equal amount of exercise.
*Drink upwards of eight cups of fresh clean water every day.
*Meditate when you go to bed before sleep, to ease your way into dreams.
*Drink all your water and eat all your food before nightfall.
*The largest meal is eaten at midday and a light meal in the evening.
*After your midday meal, lie on your left side for fifteen minutes. Then walk for fifteen minutes, alternating one minute of speed walking with one minute of your regular gait.
*Attend a process session, either in a group or privately, every day to monitor your emotional cycles. Learn to ride your emotional waves.
*When anger arises, go to the gym and work it out physically, then attend an Anger Management group and work it out emotionally.
*Rest when you are tired and eat when you are hungry.
*Eat food only when you are hungry, not as a strategy for dealing with agitation or boredom. Never use food to compensate.
*Have your pulses checked every month, to monitor the state of your organs.
*Learn to dialogue with your body and respect its needs.
*Be aware of your own cycles. Just because you were low on something last month does not mean you still need it now. Your body knows what it needs, ask it.
*When your body is feeling taxed, alter your diet and do qigong to give additional support to the specific organ that needs it.
*Practice qigong every day ideally, but minimally once a week, to keep your energy flowing strong through every organ.
*Have an acupuncture session once a month when you are well, and more often when your body needs more support.
*Develop a daily practice of fifteen minutes of yoga to keep your muscles limber and flexible.
*If you do break a bone, have it set, and take massive quantities of kelp to heal the break in a flash.
*For any impact, bruise, or overextended muscle, take homeopathic arnica, to speed recovery. Arnica gel or cream is also good topically.
*Make use of Homeopathy, Herbology, Bach Flowers Remedies and Essential Oils for everyday issues."

When you live this way, you stay healthy. When you need more help than usual, we have excellent medical equipment and staff to support you through a healing crisis. Only in very rare cases do we prescribe pills.

"Wow, that sounds like a lot. Do I have to spend all my time taking care of my body?" James asked, feeling overwhelmed.

"Your body spends all its time taking care of you," she quipped. Seriously, it is not much time when you add it up. Every day, there is a half hour added to your lunch hour. At night, once you are in bed anyway, instead of waiting for sleep to come to you, go out to meet it. Yoga and qigong require a half hour in the morning. It is a refreshing way to start your day, better than jump-starting it with coffee. Lastly, for the Afternoon Break, attend a process group. It is a way to refresh your mind and emotions. Otherwise, the rest are just strategies for dealing with things you would need to deal with anyway."

James left feeling like he was being renovated from the inside out.

Lila called from the Housing Bureau to schedule a date for James and his family to move into the new house in the Exercise Cluster. James was having doubts that he would get even partial custody. This was going to be a battle, and he never did well at fighting. He decided to be optimistic yet cover his bets. When they met to sign a contract, he mentioned that the divorce was not looking too good and asked if she could keep the apartment on hold.

Lila smiled and told him not to worry. "It will remain on hold until your divorce is decided. We are here to support you."

"Who owns the building, if I fall in love with it and want to buy it?" James asked.

Lila was startled by the question. "Mr. Dole, no one owns any property in Trinitus Cities," A quick glance at his wrist, and she understood why he was asking.

"Let me explain a little about how Trinitus functions. Your question shows you are looking at housing as one would in the RW. We approach housing a little differently. Are you familiar with our policies or should I explain them?"

Intrigued, James said, "Sure, I want to know everything about Trinitus and Hope."

"We prefer to look at the Earth as a living being far greater than a mere human. It seems like the height of hubris to say, "I own this piece of Earth." You can't own Her. However, we must interface with other cultures and other belief systems. According to state records, the Trinitus Foundation owns all the land. Of course, the Trinitus Foundation is comprised of everyone who permanently lives here.

"So, the answer to your question is, you can have your house for as long as you want it, but you cannot own it."

"Every member of the community is given a beautiful home. We all contribute our time and energy to the community and in exchange all our needs are graciously and respectfully met. Your guide, your doctor, your therapist, your physical trainer, we are all here to keep you healthy and contributory. This means we provide you with a high quality of life and you contribute to the wellbeing of the community. This is our formula for living in Loving Peace."

"Sounds great," James answered. His shoulders relaxed and a big weight fell off. Never again will he have to hustle to make the house payments or worry about falling behind on the mortgage. Wow!

"Go online to our VS Virtual Store and order the furniture and household items you want. It is usually delivered within one day. The *VS* will have everything you need. If not, let me know and I will see if we can get it. Once everything is delivered, you are welcome to move in. If the divorce goes awry and you need to move into the apartment, the *VS* will move everything for you and adjust the number of items."

"Thank you so much for making my life so much easier," he was overwhelmed by their generosity and compassion.

"Just doing my part, as we all do. Thank you for helping our friends in the Philippines. Good Luck with your custody suit. It will work out right eventually."

James bid her farewell and left. He almost let himself skip down the street, he was feeling so good. Of course, he didn't. 'Grown men don't skip.' A belief! He decided to keep this one.

CHAPTER 13

Back to Work

Tomas, the Executive Project Manager, gave James's team a choice. They could stay together or join new teams. Those who stayed together would go abroad to build more Greenies. The others would work in the office on designs for structures in other Trinitus Cities. He handed out two folders, one describing the positions abroad and the other listing new positions available here. Tomas gave a brief overview of each one. There were three in-house jobs and two different countries, Haiti and the Dominican Republic.

The others all picked Haiti because it was so needful of help. James wanted to go, but with the custody case coming up and the possibility of having his kids, Haiti was out of the question. He chose to stay. There were tearful farewells. He was going to miss working with these wonderful people and the close comradery they shared. It surprised him that he felt so abandoned when they left the room together and he stayed behind.

James wanted to learn more about Structural Design, so he asked Tomas where he could go to do that. Tomas walked him upstairs and introduced him to Pamela who oversaw blueprints and design. He thanked Tomas and wished him well. Pamela introduced him to her team Ibrahim, Sari, and Ryan, who were working on designs for a new city.

"Hello James, I heard you just returned from abroad," said Ibrahim, a young Palestinian, reaching out to shake his hand.

"Yes, I just got back from leading a team in the Philippines." James responded, noting what a strong handshake Ibrahim had.

"That sounds exciting!" said Sari with a bright smile. She was in her mid-thirties sporting a long black braid down past her waist.

"I am especially interested in designs like the ones built in this community," said James.

"Welcome to our team," said Ryan, a very handsome Italian TG (transgender) with large soulful brown eyes and wavy black hair who also reached out to shake his hand.

"Good luck James," said Pamela with a warm smile. "I hope you are happy working here. We are designing a food pavilion with a space age theme using organic art, lots of curves and oval openings. We plan to use smooth elements, futuristic technology, and fantastical plants and trees as sculptures and parts of work buildings. We want to integrate technology and plants, so they flow into each other." This was just the kind of thing James wanted to get into. He was excited to start.

Pamela showed him to a desk and helped him pull up related

blueprints from other pavilions in the city to study on his ComScreen. "These should get your creative juices flowing," she said. "Then you can doodle up a few ideas to submit to me. I'll get you copies of what we have so far."

"Thank you. I'm excited to work with this group," James said genuinely enthused."

"The more minds the better. I'll let you get to it then." She gave James a light pat on his back.

He watched her walk away. She was just his type, pretty, long legs, with an ample butt that showed well in soft flowing pants. He wondered if she was single. She was a Blue Band but wore no ring. James realized he was staring and quickly looked down at a blueprint.

James picked out his favorite elements from these blueprints and played with some ideas on the ComScreen Drafting Board. He focused on fractals using modular plant cells.

Towards the end of the day, Pamela stopped by James's desk to see what he had come up with. She handed him some hard copies of the blueprints he had asked for. She looked over his sketches. "Interesting, where did you get this idea from?"

"From an old movie set, I used it for inspiration."

"I like it. It is nicely organic and structurally interesting." She looked at the present drawing he was working on. "I like how you incorporated fractals, how green! Our next meeting is tomorrow. You can present these ideas then. I think yours will expand our ideas well. That's good, very good." She patted him on the back and left.

Encouraged, he worked out one more idea before he left for the day. James noticed how happy he was feeling. He was doing what he loved and getting recognized for it. It was a relief to no longer have the pressure of getting paid enough to pay bills and he was not filled with dread going home at the end of the day. Life was good, finally life was good. It almost brought him to tears.

At home, he wrote in his journal and read some more of the *Utopia of the Heart* book. This chapter described how a community could do socially beneficial outreach while acquiring needed supplies for the community without using money. This principle was the backbone of Trinitus trade. He had seen it in action in the Philippines. He decided to have dinner out before stocking his new house with groceries.

Shopping here was a novel experience. In San Bernardino, he used to go to big box stores where everything was in one place, and they sold lots of processed foods. No processed foods were sold here. There was a beautiful open market surrounded by gardens offering fruits, veggies, spices, and grains. Breads, cakes, and snacks were found in wonderfully fragrant bakeries. Meat was sold in butcher shops and everything else was found in niche shops. Each kind of store was located near each other. You need to go to many different shops for everything on your list. The whole market area had everything he could want. James enjoyed the walk, and the charming decor of the pavilion made it a pleasant place to stroll around.

James was in a goat's milk shop buying soap when he ran into Cathy. "Hello James, you like their soap too?"

"Oh, hi Cathy, I don't know, I was thinking of trying it. Do you like it?"

"Oh yes, goat's milk is great for the skin and this shop offers a lot of different natural fragrances," she answered.

They shopped together and then stopped in at a teahouse for a tea tasting. They each sat down on a large rattan winged chair beside a coffee table in the plaza out front. They discussed the taste of different sample teas. When there was a pause in the conversation, James thought this might be a good time to address his concerns about their relationship.

"Um, I, ah, wanted to talk to you…about us, just for a minute. We are both going through a divorce and I just want to be by myself for a while, until I get my head together. I like you as a friend. I have not had women friends before, so I just want to make my intentions clear."

"Oh, sure, no problem. I like you as a friend too. I guess I just got emotional after talking about my husband. Thank you for being such a good listener. I never had someone to listen to my problems before, you know?"

"Yeah, I understand. I don't have anyone also, but I didn't want you to misunderstand, that's all."

"No, that's fine, I just got excited that's all. No problem really." She drank some more tea out of the tiny tasting cups. They looked like a child's fancy tea set. "I love the cinnamon spice. I'm going to buy some for home. Which one do you like?" She changed the subject.

James was not sure she was okay with what he said. Something about her demeanor felt off. "Well, I'm not a connoisseur of tea, but I like the orange pekoe."

"Well let's get a half pound each then." She smiled and got up.

After leaving the tea shop, James checked in with her. "Are you sure you're okay? You seem a little off."

"Yeah, I'm fine, just a little embarrassed, I guess. I overstepped and I should not have kissed you." She said, her color slightly darkened.

"Don't be embarrassed, it just happened. It was fine, though unexpected," he reassured her.

She turned to him, her hands laden with shopping bags, and said, "No, it was too far, I'm not sure what I was up to there. I'm not used to being alone, that is the problem, but I'll talk to my therapist about it. You're right, we should just be friends. Don't worry about me I am fine."

"I'm sorry if I made you feel bad. I just didn't want you to get the wrong idea. I don't know how to navigate this." He made a waving gesture and added jokingly to put her at ease, "I have been married since the beginning of time."

"No, really, we are fine. It is good that you mentioned it," She smiled at him to show she was okay. "We are good."

"Good."

"Well, I should be getting home." She smiled again and left.

James was relieved it went as well as it did but was still worried that he had hurt her feelings. It was over anyway. He went home on the tram. He wondered if he was avoiding intimate relationships out of fear or maybe she was just not his type, and it was too soon anyway. He thought he would have to wait and see. Then he wondered how his kids would react when he found someone.

The following morning, he had a surprise visit from Child Services. Ms. Hydaburg, a heavyset woman in her fifties with large black glasses and sensible shoes, marched in saying that she was appointed by the San Bernadino court.

"Please come in. I just moved in and I'm still getting settled." James glanced at the mess on the dining room table from yesterday's shopping.

"That's fine. Where are the kid's rooms?" She gave off a business air about her that was not very friendly.

"This room here, and this one. I just have the basics in there until they come. I thought they would want to get their own stuff to decorate. I plan to take them shopping when they get here," he said as she quickly glanced into the rooms.

"I see," she said as she wrote something in her ComPad. "Let's sit down and talk about this community. What do you think about raising your kids here? I understand that Sandra already has an interest in this city and Sammy does not want to come."

"I think Sammy has no resistance to living here, he just does not want to leave where he is, friends, soccer, and all. That is a little different." She did not respond so he went on. "Sandra wants to finish school here, so she can acclimate and make new friends, before looking for work. I have been told the schools are excellent, better than those in San Bernadino, but I haven't had a chance to check it out yet. She wants to be involved in saving animals from extinction, a program they offer here." James was unnerved by this woman's cold stare.

"Yes, she told me as much." She wrote something else on her ComPad. "What do you think of the on-the-job training, verses going to college?"

"Well considering that my wife has used up the college fund we had for the kids, I think it is Sandra's primary option at this point. I wish she could go to college. I went. I think it is important, but the fact remains that it is not possible right now. Here at least, she will get the training she needs for an area she is deeply interested in."

"Yes, I have conducted other interviews here in the past and it has worked out well for them." Looking down at him as though he was a slug crawling beneath her, she said, "I'm surprised you haven't done the research yourself yet."

"Well, um, I was working abroad for the last four weeks. I was just given this house and immediately started preparing it for their arrival. I started a new job today and checking on the schools is high on my list. I just haven't gotten to it yet."

She scribbled down another note. "Mr. Dole, what is your opinion about this city?"

"Well, so far so good, I have been reading about its history and goals. I think they have strong healthy values. There is no coercion, indoctrination, or brainwashing here. The only unusual thing is their emphasis on self-reflection and being aware of your own beliefs. I've found it very helpful. I was noticing just yesterday how much happier I am now. This place is a little different than the outside world, but it is a better place for raising children. It certainly is safer." James wondered if he sounded a bit defensive.

"Yes, it is different. That is for sure," and wrote on her pad again.

James felt unprepared for this interview. He didn't want to sound desperate, so he opted for silence.

"Do you drink Mr. Dole?"

"I have a bit in the past but not now. This is a dry city. There is no alcohol here and I don't miss it. I don't need it. I am concerned about my wife's drinking though. It is stressful for my kids. It has been getting worse over the years."

"Yes, your daughter told me about her trip here and her mother's drinking. She is very upset about it. Your son on the other hand, primarily seems mad at you for leaving."

"Well, of course he is, but if he can visit me, or contact me, he will see. I want to explain to him that I left his mother, not him. I need a chance to talk to him, but right now I don't have his email or phone number and I can't get it from the only person talking to me in that house. Sandra is restricted and frozen. Judy will not let me talk to them, even if I try. She can be vindictive that way. These restrictions do not just affect Sandra; they also affect me."

"I see. How do you feel about this divorce and her role in it?"

"Well, I think now that it was inevitable. She can be unforgiving, demanding, and spiteful. I'm sure I had my part in it. Maybe I was too aloof and did not show my true feelings, but I was unaware of them back then. She is never satisfied and that drove me away. I'm getting therapy for that now, which will help me navigate being a single parent. I don't think my wife is open to it. I don't think she is aware that she even needs therapy. She suggested getting some at one time, but it was for me, not for her."

"Do you talk to Sandra about her?"

"Sandra is good at talking about her feelings. Yes, I did, a little, but we are not bad mouthing her mother. We just talked about some traits that make it hard to live with her. Unlike Judy has done, I'm not here to poison their brains against their mother. No good will come of that. Sandra told me that she understands why I left. She saw what Judy did to me and said Judy does it to them too."

"Yes, she mentioned that to me," she said, and scribbled down another note in her ComPad. So, do you want sole custody or joint?"

"Joint is fine with me. I don't think it is necessary to take them away from their mother. I would like her to stop drinking though. I think they're old enough to make up their own minds as to where they want to live, but I don't want to force Sammy, if he does not want to be with me.

"This place is different than the outside world. It wants people to come here willingly, not by force. Sandra wants to be here and has known about this community longer than I have. As much as I'd like them both to have the opportunities and safety of this place, I can't in good conscience force Sammy to come. I hope that he will come visit and check it out, but I am willing to wait and see."

She made another note on her ComPad. "I guess that is all I need. I'll see you in court then?"

"Yes, I'll be there."

"Good, thank you for your time." She got up and headed for the door.

James followed. "If Sandra wants to appeal to the court, is she going to have a chance to do that?"

"That depends on the Judge. I will mention her desire to him." She said without looking back and left.

James was unnerved by this encounter and paced a bit when she was gone. He felt that he had done the best he could, except for looking at the schools. He made up his mind to do it immediately.

James went off to work. He was looking forward to the meeting with his new group, and to sharing his designs with them. One of James's ideas was chosen to be incorporated in the plan. He was pleased.

The following day, he took a half day off to look at the neighborhood high school. There was also a smaller building for grade schoolers. The high school was huge. It sprawled over a four-block area and hosted six grades, not the usual four. The curriculum was the equivalent of high school, a two-year college, and an internship.

James met with Ms. Swenson, the principal of the High School. She was a friendly, outgoing woman who liked to talk, especially about her favorite subject, innovative education. She offered him a cup of tea, which he accepted and settled back in a comfortable burgundy velvet chair. He could feel this was not going to be a quick visit.

"Mr. Dole, we have a unique program here at Hope High. Do you also have a child in Middle School?" James nodded yes. "Well, our Middle School is structured on the same principles. We like youngsters to start at the beginning of the term, especially new ones who may be going through a period of adjustment.

"We will assign them each a partner to guide them in their process, not because they are new, but because it is our policy to assign a partner to every child. Your youngsters are free to choose a new partner whenever they wish.

"I sincerely hope they can begin on the first day of class. It is crucial to their success here. The first week is spent on bonding exercises. Missing out on all that fun would put them at a distinctive social disadvantage. It would be harder for them to feel like they are part of the group. During the first week, the students attend the Ropes Course. It is a series of daring physical challenges. Everyone cheers each other on and there is a wonderful feeling of support. Mind you, they always wear a safety harness, so there is no real danger. Even though they know they cannot get hurt, it is still just as scary. After they have endured these challenges together, they have learned to respect and care for everyone in the group. This provides an excellent foundation for working and playing together. As a result, we have had no problems in the playground, no bullying, and no negative behavior.

"The curriculum is well paced throughout the day. We provide ample opportunities for students to drink water and move around. We think it is unhealthy for youngsters to sit still all day. It causes all kinds of problems.

"Most classes are structured as group projects to teach them social skills, negotiating, and cooperation. We try to keep a balance between academic and experiential learning. Each group presents its findings to the whole class. Generally, a weaker speaker and a stronger one do the presentation as a team. When the weaker speaker presents, the stronger one stands close beside him or her with their shoulders touching to provide physical support.

"We do not have a competitive grading system. We offer a feedback system instead. In addition to students receiving feedback, the students also evaluate the teachers and give them feedback on their skills.

"There is no stigma in making mistakes. Everything is approached as a team exploration. By teaming up stronger and weaker students, the stronger students learn how to teach, and the mentoring helps the weaker ones to learn quicker.

"Our classes are small, intimate, and generally held sitting in a circle. This way the focus is not primarily on the teacher, but rather on the group. The teacher is not a disciplinarian, but rather a facilitator. Each day begins and ends with a Sharing Circle. The morning sharing is personal and the afternoon one is about their studies.

"In History Class, we spend one or two days summing up all the wars and their causes, plus another two days on the ramifications of these conflicts. The rest of the semester is spent covering humanity's accomplishments in all creative, explorative, and scientific areas of life. We offer a full spectrum of math, science, music, and art. We feed both sides of the brain, the intellectual and the creative.

"On Fridays, we spend the day developing physical skills, skiing, swimming, horseback riding, and any other requested skill. At the end of the day, students spend an hour doing a community Service.

"Most tests are given to assess where a student needs help, not as a measure of their worth or to judge them. Many tests are held in an open format. No one cheats because they would only be cheating themselves.

"Lunch is cooked, served, and cleaned afterwards by the students. We also have a full government body exploring alternative forms of governing. In addition to academic classes, we also offer classes in financial management, vocational training, and life skills, to give our students a well-rounded skill set. Every student is given everything they need and for those who need to feed their ambition, we offer incentive programs. Competition is not encouraged, cooperation is. However, for those who need competition, we find ways to provide it.

"Students are encouraged to explore innovative areas like Future Lifestyles and Future Technology. They begin by researching the people who pioneered these areas and the challenges they faced. We encourage our students to venture into new areas of study equipped and prepared.

"Our school is not about grades, status, and success. It is about developing successful strategies for living a balanced, healthy, individualistic, and creative life within a supportive and accepting community. We also validate following the dictates of your own soul. Thank you for your patience. This is only a brief overview. I did not want to tire you. Do you have any questions?"

James was amazed by this approach to education. His first thought was wishing he was a child and could attend. Then he felt grateful that hopefully his children were going to have this experience.

"Ms. Swenson, could you please give me a formal statement that I can present to the custody court hearing, describing why my children need to start school on the first day. The judge probably won't take my word for it."

"Certainly, Mr. Dole. As a member of our community, please call me Doris, the students do. We always want to remember each other's individuality, and I have no need to be an authoritarian. I guide my students with respect. I respect each student, and they respect me in return. I look forward to meeting your daughter. What is her name?

"Sandra. Sammy is in the 8th grade."

"Would you like me to introduce you to Butler Johnson, the principal of Hope Middle School. I am sure he would like to meet you," she offered with a warm smile.

James nodded yes, and they strolled over to another building. As they walked along, James briefly mentioned that he was new here, but of course, once she saw his Red Band that was redundant. He also told her about the divorce and the custody suit.

Butler was an outgoing middle-aged man with dark chocolate skin and plump round cheeks that made him appear much younger and always a little amused. His temperament was very sweet and easy-going.

Doris introduced them and told him that Sammy was going to attend if James got custody.

"We see you. I am pleased to meet you, James. I am so glad you are thinking of bringing us a new student. Tell me about Sammy. What are his favorite things?"

"Like most boys, it's soccer and ComScreens," James told him.

"Excellent. We have lots of both." Then he turned to Doris, gave her a warm smile and said, "Thank you Doris for introducing me to James. I hope you have a peaceful day."

Turning back to James, Butler said, "I am sure Doris gave you an in-depth description of our teaching style, curriculum, and philosophy. Is there anything else I can add to that?"

"Not really. But I should warn you Sammy does not want to leave his soccer team and friends, so when he arrives, he may have an attitude. His mother and I are splitting up. He is very attached to her and resents me. He is a sweet natured boy and not usually a troublemaker, but under the circumstances, I do not know what to expect," James wanted him to be prepared.

"Thank you for sharing all that. I will take it all into account. We will do everything we can to make him comfortable, and we have an excellent soccer team."

They shook hands and James left feeling excited to share this marvelous adventure with his children.

CHAPTER 14

Choice

With the new house set up, the schools looking exceptionally good, and settling into his new job, James was feeling very good about himself. He was impatient to tell Sandra and Sammy all about the schools in Hope. This inability to contact his children was getting harder every day. He could call Judy and simply ask to talk to Sandra, but stirring his wife up just before the court date would be the height of stupidity. He would just have to bite his lip and wait.

Back in San Bernardino, Sandra was going through a similar process. She was anxious to get back to Trinitus and this waiting was like being in prison. She was bored out of her mind. Without constant contact with her friends, and her adventures with her Avatar in New World, she was stagnating in the doldrums.

Sammy, acting as her go-between, acquired a catalogue on Trinitus from Tammy's brother, and sold it to Sandra for the exorbitant price of one week of laundry, cleaning his room, plus loading and unloading the dishwasher each night that week. It was just a small catalogue, but he knew it was worth its weight in gold to her, so she accepted his terms without even haggling.

She also had a college catalogue about the same size, so she slipped her contraband treasure inside it and thought herself clever. Judy walked by and saw Sandra engrossed in reading a college catalogue and thought happily that her daughter was finally getting on board. She complimented herself on what a good idea it was to keep her grounded all this time. Judy was relieved that her conflict with Sandra was coming to an end. She was so happy that she called Sandra over and told her that she was no longer grounded or frozen, and handed back her Smartwatch.

Sandra was so excited that she put down the catalogue and flipped through the directory to see how many calls she had missed. She flopped down on the sofa and was totally engrossed in reading her old text messages and emails.

Meanwhile, Judy was curious to see which of the colleges seemed to be so interesting to Sandra. She reached for the catalogue and out fell the Trinitus material. Judy felt utterly duped and betrayed. Sandra had made a fool of her. She was about to grab the Smartwatch back, when the thought crossed her mind that Sandra had no way to get this contraband catalogue unless James had found a way to smuggle it to her. He put her up to this. Her sweet little Sandra would not do this to her, or so her drunken mind convinced her.

She went into the kitchen for privacy and told her Smartwatch to ring James.

When he heard the chimes and he saw the number, he assumed it was from Sandra, so he answered, "Hello Darling."

"Don't darling me, you bastard! You convinced Sandra that she does not have to go to college. You filled her head with fantasies of living with you in that Commie Cult! Thanks to you, she has a rather uppity attitude about it too," Judy snarled.

"I had nothing to do with it," he flatly answered.

"Bullshit, you talked her into it, I know you did!"

"No, honestly Judy, Sandra knew about Trinitus before I did," he said defensively.

"Bull, I don't believe you. You talked her into this crap. I know you did!" She fumed.

"You are so wrong! She got into it a year ago online! She knew about this community before I found it," James was getting red in the face and his blood was boiling. Being falsely accused drove him wild.

"Online? Where?"

"It is called New World. Look at her ComPad! I'm not lying to you." He whined.

Judy opened her own ComScreen and looked it up.

Taking advantage of the silence, James said, "Judy, no matter what happens between us, I would never bad-mouth you to our kids. That is not good for them. Don't you agree?" He sounded innocent, but he knew he was baiting her. Sandra told him all the terrible things she had said about him to them.

Judy ignored the comment, as she often did when confronted. She found the site and read the blurb describing it. "How long have you known about this? This is just the type of site I warned her about and forbade her to visit. You let her go there against my wishes and then hid it from me."

"That is ridiculous. I just found out about it that day when she drove over here. It is one of the reasons she came with her friend. They had been planning to come here for a long time."

"Do Tammy's parents know?"

"I don't think so, she didn't mention them to me. I think she was living with a boyfriend."

"So now you are having intimate conversations with a teenager." she said, insinuating something perverted.

"That does it! I have had enough of your accusations! Don't call me again unless you can be a decent human being and can have a sensible conversation. You have no right to treat me like this! I will not take this kind of abuse any longer." He declared and pressed the end call button. He wished he had one of those old-fashioned phones so he could slam the receiver down.

Judy stared in disbelief at her Smartwatch. She was surprised that he stood up to her. That was a first! She sat back on the sofa feeling even more alone, utterly alone in the world. She could not list one ally that she could call on right now for support, so she refilled her glass. 'What has gotten into this family anyway?' She thought. 'At least Sammy is still a good boy. He's on my side.'

She looked at the website some more and read the Mission Statement under the picture. It was a cute town, she begrudgingly admitted to herself.

"In Trinitus Cities, we believe that the world will be a safer and friendlier place when we all learn to treat each other with Loving Peace and respect. We are making the changes in our own lives that we want to see in the world. We talk openly about our feelings, our needs, and our desires in a safe environment. We believe that by coming to know, love, and trust ourselves, so too we learn to love and trust others. We are creating a future where people are happier, more content, and feel fulfilled. We are creating a stress-free lifestyle by openly and caringly sharing our collective resources with each member of our community. We have learned that we can grow without hurting each other or the environment. We are creating a healthy future based on love, not fear."

Beneath it were options for exploring Trinitus further: About us, Contact us, New World, Trinitus Cities, Services, and Economic Opportunities. She closed the ComScreen.

James was in a rage. 'I hate that crazy woman! How dare she accuse me of all these lies! Who does she think she is! Why does she always have to see me as a bad guy doing something wrong? Boy, I wish I could ring her neck!'

He stomped out the door. He had to walk to keep his frustrations from eating him up. He walked faster and faster, but the hurt feelings were still there under the anger.

"God! What is wrong with that woman?!" he cried out into the night.

"You know the answer," he heard in reply.

"You mean because her parents never showed her love or tenderness, so she is insecure and constantly needs my assurance or else she goes ballistic."

"Why does she blame you?" asked the Divine voice within him.

"Because she wants me to save her, but I can't. I will be lucky if living here saves me. Her parents did nurture her, that happened a long time ago. She should get over it."

"Like you have gotten over all the hurts of your childhood?" asked God.

"Okay, so I used to do that stuff too, but I am not doing it anymore."

"Then you are healing from the help you are getting. Who is helping her?" asked God.

"No one," he mumbled.

"Perhaps for self-preservation, you need to reach out to her and reassure her," said this wise voice.

"I suppose I could react better than I am; but she says such infuriating things to me."

'Could it be a measure of her pain?'

"Yeah, but it would be a lot easier if she was nice to me," James grumbled.

"Could you be nice to her right now?" asked this bemused voice.

"No! I'm too angry and too hurt," he huffed.

"So is she," came the calm reply.

"I understand she is hurting but she never talks about it. Instead, whenever she feels upset, she blames me and immediately attacks. There is no getting a word in until she runs out of steam. After one of her explosions, she seems to feel better, but after all the mean things she said about me along the way, there is no way I can be understanding and reach out to make her feel better. She doesn't even acknowledge her pain to herself. What can I do?"

"Don't take what she does to you personally." God advised. "She is projecting the cause of her anger onto everyone around her. She is angry at herself and her parents, not you. Protect your boundaries and don't take it personally."

"Great! Now you want me to hug a raging dragon!" James quipped.

God let him have the last word.

James felt slightly better after his talk with God. Only a little better. He still needed someone to talk to, so he thought about calling someone. First, he thought about Tim. He is a good listener. Then he thought of Kim who would show him how to go deeper and use this to heal something inside of himself. He told the Smartwatch to ring Kim.

Even though his next appointment was not for two days, Kim had an opening in an hour, so he headed over there. Just making the decision to face this conflict inside him had a calming effect.

On the way over to Kim's office, James was practicing what he was going to tell her. He went over the phone call and the injustice of everything Judy said. Then he realized he knew exactly how Kim would respond. She was going to ask him what beliefs were underlying his intense emotions.

The ride was going to take a few minutes, so he started the therapeutic session by reflecting upon himself.

'What am I feeling? Anger, of course.' He remembered that Kim had once told him that anger is a secondary emotion, so he asked himself, 'What is under it? What is my anger there to protect?

'Hurt, she hurt my feelings. Yes, but that does not feel like it is my core emotion.

'Sometimes it is fear, but that does not fit this time.'

Then he realized, it was helplessness.

'I feel helpless, and I always have when she gets angry. If I want to help her, like I did in the early years, it makes this feeling of helplessness worse. What a tangled knot this is. She feels I am not there for her, so she gets upset and her mean words hurt me. Even though I know she is doing it because she feels I do not show up for her. I feel helpless, so I do nothing, and she feels even more abandoned. OMG! No wonder our marriage went belly up!

In Kim's office, James was confused as to where to start. It seemed redundant to repeat everything to her, so he recapped his process instead. He described the call from Judy, then his talk with God, and finally his process on the tram.

"I'm trying to let go of her accusing lies. It is hard. I am not angry anymore, but this feeling of helplessness is not an improvement.

"I can't make Judy see what she doesn't want to see. I'm not the same person I used to be, but she still thinks I am. Maybe I never was the person she thought I was, both the good and the bad parts. It makes me question our whole relationship even back to before we got married. Did she ever love me or was she in love with her image of me?"

"She saw you through her beliefs and desires, you saw her through yours. Humans are like that. We can't do much about it, but what we can work on is how you want to navigate forward.

"She is not going to be very loving during this divorce. How are you going to deal with that without being triggered into this feeling of helplessness? You will have to face her unloving attitude towards you. Right now, she can't help it. On the other hand, you have tools to use that can effect change. You cannot change her mind, but you can change your own thinking and that can affect her thoughts.

"Let's begin with understanding her. She may not be capable of self-reflection, but you can understand her position. Are you willing to try on her shoes?"

"Yes."

"Let's say, you're too wrapped up in all these intense emotions and are too confused to know what you feel. Got that?"

James nodded yes.

"You are angry at your husband because you are afraid of being abandoned. Every time he loses his job, and his income disappears, you must carry the finances alone. That makes you feel frightened and abandoned."

James nodded yes.

"You're hurt that your husband left you with the kids and a big debt. Now you must handle all this on your own. Your daughter, who you were once close to, now blames you for everything. Your husband blames you for spending too much money, but what else can you do to fill the vacuum within you?"

James just nodded, he could not think of anything to say.

"To cope, you drink. The more afraid you get, the more you drink. After a while, you know you should stop, but you can't. The need to escape now controls you. Are you still with me?"

He shook his head, feeling how overwhelmed Judy must be.

"Everything your husband does that obstructs you, triggers a panic response in you. Such as, you want your daughter to go to college and he wants her to live with him, or when he suddenly drives off into the desert without a word of warning and never comes back, or when he loses another job so there is no one to help with all your responsibilities. These all cause you to feel even more abandoned, so you feel helpless and yell at him."

"Yes," he said in a very small voice.

It sure didn't look like this before he came in here. It just looked like she was being abusive. He used to think that she was always abusive, and he never did anything to deserve her nasty tirades in which she listed every fault he ever had.

"Okay, now let's begin working on changing your feelings, so you are free to deal with her differently. This can potentially change the way she deals with you. Are you ready to begin?"

James nodded, closed his eyes and leaned back on the sofa.

"Have you ever felt abandoned and overwhelmed?"

He nodded yes.

"Go into your body and find where you hold these feelings." she instructed. "Focus on this feeling, breathe into it, and amplify it."

James closed his eyes and felt a dull throbbing pain in his stomach. For a few minutes he breathed deeply and slowly, his mind focused on the feelings in his body. The outer world and its realities drifted away, and he floated into a light trance state.

"We are going to do an exercise to gain insight into how to deal with Judy and your feelings about her," Kim proposed. "Okay?"

"Yes," replied James and nodded.

"Good. We will work with a phrase, and it will take you into all kinds of places, just follow the energy. Say, "I could be happy living with Judy except for..." and finish the sentence.

"I could be happy living with Judy except for her constant criticism."

"Good, what object feels like constant criticism? What object resonates with that quality of energy?"

"I don't know, maybe a broken glass?"

"Good. Visualize a broken glass................Can you see it?"

"Yes, I see a broken wine glass."

"Please put the broken wine glass over there on the floor beneath my window. Can you see it there?"

"Yes," he said.

"Now repeat the phrase, I could be happy living with Judy except for..."

"I could be happy living with Judy except for her drinking."

"What object feels like her drinking?"

"A rattlesnake."

"Please put the rattlesnake over there on the floor beneath my window right next to the broken glass. Can you see them? Feel the broken glass...feel the rattlesnake...and repeat the phrase," she guided him.

One by one he listed all the obstacles that stood between them and having a peaceful relationship, and each time he visualized an object to hold that quality of energy. He placed it next to the last. Again and again, they visualized each object as he placed a new one beside them. It was a long process, but eventually he said the phrase, and nothing came to mind. In fact, the last few were not actually negative things, not obstacles at all, but rather, slightly irritating endearments.

"Now we have come to the second part of this process. How do you feel?" she asked.

"Amazingly light and free. It is as though I was carrying a great weight on my shoulders and now, I am carrying nothing. I feel like anything is possible."

"All those things by the window were once on your shoulders. Now let us go through the list one last time. You need to choose what to take back and in what form. Or you can just leave them over there. If ever you want them, you know where they are."

The broken wineglass of criticism was taken back as praise, in the form of a ladder. Thinking and talking about the ladder made him realize that he was as critical of her as she was of him. This projection was going both ways. He promised himself that the next time they spoke, he would find something to praise her for. He would think about the ladder and find a way to raise her up. In lieu of the rattlesnake, he thought of a cane. He realized that Judy needed something to lean on, and whenever she tried to lean on him, he stepped back away from her. He thought to change the cane into a crystal tear of compassion. Having the power to change things felt good. He willingly took the tear and when he imagined holding it in his hand, he realized that he had treated her like an enemy, and she became his enemy. He now knew what he had to do. With each object he reclaimed in a new form, it brought with it an insight into something positive and supportive he could do for her. He realized she was inflamed and that is why she wanted to keep him from his children. There were things he could do to cool the flames.

By the end of the session, he felt exhilarated and exhausted but no longer helpless, hopeless, or burdened.

He slept very deeply that night and woke up refreshed. It was a strangely novel feeling. Perhaps years had passed since he felt so good.

The next day unfolded, and he did everything that was needed, but most of him was somewhere else. His feelings were like blowing bubbles and watching them pop. One bubble was compassion for himself, and one was for Judy. They floated on by. It seemed strange that it took him so long to come to such a simple realization; you get what you give. When forgiveness floated by, it looked like the beautiful and deadly jellyfish he had envisioned in his session, which he had transformed into a seed full of life. All through the day he saw again the objects and the understanding they bestowed. He always hated and feared her insecurity, now he need only see a cripple child changed into a woman with wings. It made him want to see her fly, see her whole and healthy. He marveled at how much of his life he had spent fantasizing forms of revenge. What a waste. Now he fantasized about how to rebuild the energy between them. He suddenly felt in control of his life. His thoughts of revenge were like acid dripping on his soul. It just caused him to feel more alienation and pain. Loving her, being compassionate for her suffering and the suffering he had caused her, set him free in ways that hatred and revenge never could.

He called Kim later in the day to thank her for setting him free and asked what that exercise was called. She said it was Focusing by a therapist named Eugene Gendlin.

CHAPTER 15

Divorce

On the way home from work that night, a letter wrote itself in his head. James was amazed and inspired. As soon as he entered his new home, he started recording his ideas in his ComPad. First, he acknowledged everything she had contributed to their relationship and acknowledged how hard she worked and what a caring person she was. It poured out of him, and he was startled to see that beneath the hurt and the pain, some of the love still survived. He didn't say, "I love you," he simply acted with Loving Peace. His time in Trinitus had radically changed him. He wanted to be free of all the old grievances.

He forwarded the letter to Tim and asked him to read it. Tim called a few minutes later and told him how impressed he was. He even acknowledged that James might be coming to the end of his Red Band time.

James was hoping for a response when he sent it to Judy but did not expect it. Sending it was enough to set him free of something dark and ugly that had been eating him up.

Judy was shocked when she read the letter and immediately assumed it was a trick. He was just trying to get on her good side in preparation for the custody suit. Or maybe he was trying to disarm her so he could try something exceptionally diabolical, like going for sole custody or revealing the extent of her drinking.

The next day, James met with his lawyer and told her that he wanted Judy to have everything, he would pay off the debts, but in good conscience, he could not bring himself to pay her charge cards. He wanted to be fair to her, but not at the cost of betraying himself. As it stood, what he was proposing was quite generous and equitable.

When Judy received a letter from James's lawyer stating that these were his terms, she did not know what to believe. Tears came to her eyes and she called herself a fool and tried to reaffirm that it was all a trick, but it did not feel like it. He even apologized for all the ways he let her down and listed them specifically. No justification, no excuses, no blaming her, just a simple straightforward acknowledgement that brought her to tears.

Finally, the day he was anticipating and dreading arrived, the day of the custody hearing. James wore a crisp new blue suit. As he got behind the wheel of the car, he realized it had been a few months since he had last driven.

James picked up his lawyer in U-Town (Up Town), an attractive young woman with a professional demeanor. After working with her for the last few weeks, he had great confidence in her abilities. While the Auto-Drive navigated the highways, they went over the terms of the divorce. Everything had been agreed upon already, except the custody of the kids. Judy was to receive everything they owned, except his car, which was to go to Sandra; and his personal credit cards, which he would keep. As he said in the letter, he planned to pay all their past debts, except those incurred on her personal credit cards. He held firm to this last point and offered everything else.

It felt both familiar and odd to be back in the RW again. He had gotten used to breathing clean fresh air. The commercialization on every surface assaulted his brain. The steel and glass of downtown looked sterile and drab to him.

Driving in traffic was nerve racking. On the sidewalks, many people were wearing TeleCom glasses and were only half paying attention to where they were going. He parked the car at a plug-in station in a huge parking lot behind the courthouse. The bad smell and toxicity of the air around him burned his eyes and throat. He had forgotten how dirty the city was.

James felt intimidated walking into the small courtroom, its formal wood paneling and the Judge's raised dais seemed to be designed just to make him feel small. He watched as Judy walked in looking elegant in a new power suit. He could not help wondering, 'How much did she pay for that?' then caught himself and thought, 'Bad habit, I don't want that one.'

Judy's lawyer was a distinguished gentleman in his late fifties. He talked first and did exactly as James and his lawyer anticipated. He portrayed Trinitus City as a cult.

James's lawyer countered with the truth and a series of statistics. He concluded with, "The schools are accredited and have an excellent record for job placement within Trinitus Cities and out in the world."

Ms. Hydaburg from Child Services, concurred. Her investigation found that the City of Hope was a solid stable community with excellent schools. The Educational System was safer and offered a better education than the San Bernadino public schools.

Ms. Hydaburg also reported that Sandra had researched Trinitus Cities and preferred to live there. In closing, she commented on Judy's extensive drinking and that her long hours at work were having a negative effect on the children. Not only were they home alone for up to four hours on workdays, but when the mother got home from work, she usually drank.

Judy seemed to shrivel up in her seat when the social worker said this. Much to James's surprise, he felt sorry for her and the humiliation of having that mentioned in court in front of everyone.

The judge asked Sandra to plead her case, and she talked glowingly about Trinitus and lamented her mother's drinking, citing that she had to do all the laundry and house cleaning. Then the judge asked Sammy what he wanted. The boy was feeling very protective of his mother and even protested that Ms. Hydaburg was exaggerating.

The judge decided in favor of joint custody and that the children would remain in their present schools. He declared that Sandra and Sammy would finish high school in San Bernardino and when they each reached eighteen, they could decide where they want to live. He said it builds character to participate in household chores. Until they come of age, they will live with their mother during the week and visit their father on the weekends.

The judge ordered Judy to stop drinking or he would do as Child Services recommended and give sole custody to their father. He also charged Child Services to make random visits to monitor her drinking.

After the proceedings, Judy was furious. She had some choice words with her lawyer. Sandra was unhappy about the verdict and cried quietly. Sammy was nervous and wondered how this divorce would change his life.

James asked Judy for some time alone with the kids in the hallway. Her Lawyer urged her to agree.

He told Sandra it was only a year and consoled her. Then he talked to Sammy. "I never wanted to leave you. I love you. I left because I did not want to fight with your mother anymore. I wanted to call, but I did not have my phone. Please give me your number and your email so we can stay in touch, okay?"

Sammy looked confused but gave him his number and email address. "I still don't understand why you cannot come home."

"Your mom and I have been fighting a lot. That's all. That is why I left. You did nothing wrong; do you understand that?"

"I understand, I guess; but Mom said you live in a cult. I don't want to live in a cult."

"It is not a cult. You can see for yourself when you visit. There is a Native American village and Western Town in a park that you can play in when you get there."

"Cool green! Sandra told me that, but I didn't believe her. So, it's real?"

"Yep, more real than you can imagine."

"Can I shoot bows and arrows?"

"Yep, and when you're good at it, you can even hunt real game!"

"WOW! Green! I want to do that," the boy exclaimed.

James watched his ex-wife approach. She was obviously impatient and concerned that her ex was filling Sammy's head with propaganda about Trinitus.

"Well, I'll see you next weekend, okay?" James ruffled his hair.

"Okay." Sammy smiled.

Judy whisked them away. She was furious that she had gotten called out about her drinking by her own daughter and by Child Services. She resented that there would be random checks to monitor her drinking.

James smiled gently at Judy, and she gave him a dirty look. He felt a wave of compassion; but the hate in her eyes made it fade quickly.

When James got back to Hope, he was glad to be home, and out of the dirty city. He thanked his lawyer, dropped her off in U-Town, and returned the car. James was exhausted. He had dinner, read for a while, then went to bed around ten.

Judy got the kids home and told them to behave themselves because she was going out. "Sandra, you're in charge. Go to bed at ten. There are leftovers in the frig."

"Okay, where are you going?"

"It's none of your business!" Give me your Smartwatch. You are grounded and frozen again young lady." she barked and marched out. She went straight to the neighborhood bar and drank to subdue her rage. She did not come home until three in the morning.

A few days later, Sandra waited until Sammy was asleep, then she slipped into Sammy's room and used his Smartwatch to email her dad. She wrote to him that her mom was now going out until late and returned drunk every night. She carefully put the Smartwatch back on Sammy's dresser and snuck back into her room.

James saw the email on the tram, on his way to work. It pissed him off. He tried to feel compassion and did but it did not diminish the frustration. He felt several emotions all at once. He quickly moved through the anger but that only deposited him in a cesspool of helplessness. He tried to recapture all the good feelings he had after therapy, but he could not remember why he felt so good.

He could not get past the idea that he gave her everything. There was no reason why she should be in such an awful mood. The helplessness rushed in on him again. He wanted to protect his children. He was not going to allow her drinking to continue. The old James would have spent all day fuming, or he would have taken revenge and called the lawyer and Child Services. The new James did not want to stab her in the back like that. He was stumped. He could not think of a Loving Peace solution.

He called Kim, but she was all booked up and could not see him today. His next session was still three days away. He called Tim and he agreed to meet James for lunch. He only had to hold it together for three hours. He arrived at work, tripped on a step and went crashing down on his left knee. That did nothing to improve his fragile mood.

James was working with his new design partner, Ibrahim. The young Palestinian was generally easy going. Although James kept reminding himself to breathe deeply, he could not keep the boiling rage from seeping out in his voice. Poor Ibrahim had a hard time with James. He felt like he could do nothing right this morning. James had a critical tone and a short temper, which he kept in check through great effort. Nevertheless, it was scary to be the focus of his displeasure.

When James finally exploded at Ibrahim, it was over a minor difference in opinion, either strategy would have worked as well. James tried to explain his point and Ibrahim made the mistake of interrupting and James went ballistic throwing out harsh words like incompetent, inexperienced, and myopic. James was completely in the wrong and some part of him was watching and knew Ibrahim did not deserve any of this. James had just been holding all his pain, anger, helplessness, hopelessness and downright rage in for too long. Ibrahim pointing out a different way of approaching the structural integrity issue became the straw that broke the proverbial camel's back.

Pamila immediately took James aside and asked, "What is happening James? You have not been yourself today?"

"Your right Pamila, I need a break," and he marched off to the Drink Station to pour a cup of Chai, his new substitute for coffee, which he had grown to enjoy.

Pamila followed him, poured a cup for herself and asked in a caring voice, "What is hurting you today?"

In the old days, he would have resented her butting into his business and would have growled, "Nothing!" but he was becoming accustomed to telling the truth when asked.

"I got an upsetting email from my daughter. My ex-wife has been drinking a lot." He took another sip and enjoyed its smooth warmth. He felt safe enough to be honest and was even a little surprised to realize he did not feel embarrassed over sharing something so personal. Here in Hope people talked openly with each other so he was honest.

"How troubling. Can I help in any way?" She put her hand lightly on his shoulder.

"No, thank you. I should not have taken my mood out on Ibrahim."

"Relax for as long as you want. If you need to talk more, let me know. Remember to apologize to Ibrahim."

"Of course." He faced her and said, "Thanks for your support."

"We all naturally have bad moments sometimes. There is no shame in it," she reassured him and gave him a warm compassionate smile.

James tried to smile back, but it came out as a grimace. Then he turned his attention back to his tea. She understood that he needed to be alone for a while, so she went back to Ibrahim to see how he was feeling.

James sipped his Chai and told his Smartwatch to contact his lawyer. He asked her what options were open to him. He did not want to get Judy into trouble, but he could not stand by and do nothing. "Look at your true motives. Look at what would help Judy. Does allowing her to continue to drink to excess really help her?"

"Legally, the only recourse is to tell the judge the extent of her drinking and have him order her into rehab. Then he will take the children away from her. I recommend that you look for a different avenue to get her into rehab. The legal one is public, humiliating, and much too permanent."

He thought of calling Child Services, but that seemed too drastic. He decided to hold back on the big guns for now.

He told himself, 'Well there is nothing more you can do. Calling her won't help, it might even make matters worse. I am going to have to let it go. Thinking about it will not change the facts. Worrying about it won't change anything either.' Then he heard Satyendra whispering in his mind, "Breathe deeply and slowly. Let it go."

He did the deep breathing, and it helped him calm down. Then he decided to call Satyendra. He calculated the time in Haiti and decided it was early afternoon, so he asked his Smartwatch to place the call.

Satyendra was delighted to hear from him. After a formal greeting, James dived into the problem and explained his dilemma to him. Satyendra was quiet on the other end for a minute and then responded. "If you were drowning and afraid, what would you want? How would you want any help offered to be given. She is the inner feminine in your soul and this part of you is drowning. Heal it inside yourself and you will know how to heal it in her. She is Shakti the feminine goddess inside you, and she is in despair, so is the Earth and all Feminine forces what are they crying out for? Answer this and you will know.

"I must go now. We are about to raise the walls of a structure. You called just as I took my tea. You see, your timing is impeccable, and everything unfolds in its own order. Things that could not work before can work now because this is its appointed time."

James thanked Satyendra and wished him well in Haiti. He finished his tea and went back up to the drafting table. Ibrahim was involved in drawing on his ComPad. "Excuse me Ibrahim, I am sorry. I was wrong to scream at you. You did nothing to deserve it. I am facing a very challenging personal decision." James sincerely apologized.

"I understand. What do you think of this design, does it work better?" James glanced at the screen.

"Sure, its fine." He swiped the drawing over to the larger screen and could see that the difference was small, but structurally sound. "Yes, that will work."

There were no further flare-ups. Pamila checked on them, saw things were going well, and smiled. Ibrahim acknowledged that he was young and not as experienced as James and James acknowledged that being young brings new ideas and fresh perspectives. Ibrahim agreed to respect James's experienced point of view and James agreed to listen and fairly evaluate new ideas. Once all this was said, they found that they work well together.

Lunch finally arrived and James met Kim in the dining room. With a couple of short sentences, he was able to bring Kim up to date.

"What decision have you come to?" asked Kim.

James was about to say, "I don't know. I have been too busy working to think about it," when he realized he did know. He saw in his mind's eye the rattlesnake turned into a cane and the cane into a crystal tear of compassion.

"I am going to build rapport, apologize, acknowledge, and offer an olive branch of peace. I am not going to say, 'How can I help?' Words are cheap. I am going to offer an array of choices, specifically the ways I am ready to help.

"Broken or not, she is mine. I will not be whole until I have done what I can to help her be whole. I am going to embrace the dragon. First, I will put on a fireproof suit. I will acknowledge all the mean things she could rightfully say or do and brace myself, so I am not triggered by them. Then I will repeat a mantra I read in a book written by Dr. Bebeau, 'If it isn't love, its illusion.' It could be my illusion, hers or both feeding into each other's. I will do my best and trust Spirit to do the rest."

Kim listened respectfully and then pulled out an orange band. She told James that he had earned it. "It may not fit perfectly right away but I feel you are ready to grow into it."

That night, James had the strangest dream. It started with him walking into a neighborhood bar and Judy was there. He looked around for her and found her sitting at the end of the bar chatting with a young bartender. He slipped onto the stool next to her and quietly ordered a drink. Eventually, she glanced at the man beside her and nearly fell off her stool when she recognized James.

"What are you doing here, gathering evidence?" she slurred belligerently.

"I mean you no harm. I owe you respect. I am here to show up, something I have owed you for a long time. I was not the husband you deserved. You work very hard, and you needed me to be a better man. Unfortunately, I did not know how to do that back then."

She was stunned and did not respond. She just stared at him.

He tried to match Judy's breathing pattern, just the way he had practiced in his therapy sessions. It was not smooth, and it was not easy, he kept losing the rhythm, but he persevered. He hoped breathing with her would make her feel safer. Then he slowly slowed his breath a little and she followed suit. Her breath slowed down.

The dream commentator said, "Building rapport, check. Now for an apology." James looked down at his orange band. In the dream, it was huge, at least four times what it was in real life.

Then he said to Judy, "It must have been awful for you when I left for work in the morning and did not come back at night. You did not know what to think. I could have been dead in a ditch for all you knew. That was cruel and inconsiderate. You deserve better than that. I was a coward. From the bottom of my heart, I am sincerely sorry to put you through that."

The dream commentator said, "Apology check."

Judy looked at him like he had two heads and said, "Who are you? My husband would never say these things. What kind of trick is this? What is your angle? What do you want?" She looked scared.

In the dream James said, "I am here to acknowledge that I caused you pain and contributed to making your life difficult. What I am saying is true, a long overdue truth. I have wronged you and I want to make amends."

He cringed waiting for her to meter out the punishment he knew he deserved.

Nothing happened. They just sat there for a long while.

Then wanting to break the silence he said, "Do you still eat pastrami sandwiches on rye at Bernie's Deli Café? I really miss their food."

They talked about pastrami sandwiches. Then James said, "I want to be your friend. No more fighting." She said, "yes" and confetti started falling from the ceiling, suddenly trumpets started playing a celebratory tune. James clicked his heels and suddenly found himself dancing with Gene Kelly in the famous movie scene, dancing in the rain.'

James woke up confused but strangely peaceful. He didn't resolve anything with Judy, but he did seem to heal something inside himself.

CHAPTER 16

Kids

Sammy was furious with Sandra. He was still extremely upset about the custody hearing, where Sandra told the Child Services lady about Mom's drinking. If Mom got caught, he could be taken away at any time and put in a Foster Home or worse, be forced to live with Dad in a weirdo cult. There was no one he could trust anymore.

They were hanging out in his room after dinner. Mom was gone again and they had a pretty good idea where she went.

"Yuk! I don't want to go to ugly old Arizona! I want to stay right here with all my friends and my soccer team!"

"We may not have a choice, if Mom can't stop drinking!" Sandra said flatly.

"I'll talk to her. She's not angry at me. We must do something

She heard the desperation in his voice but had little faith that anything would work.

"Try if you want," Sandra said, feeling a little hopeless herself, "but Mom is addicted to drinking. It is like it has a spell over her. I think if you say anything, she will just lie about it."

"This royally sucks!" he grumbled and kicked his desk, rolling back in his chair.

"Sammy, do you really want to live with her for the next four years while she keeps drinking?"

"I don't know. She is not mad at me. We get along okay."

"That doesn't matter. The laundry doesn't get done unless we do it. The other day, you didn't have anything clean to wear. The dishes stay in the sink until we put them in the dishwasher. She doesn't remember to give us lunch money anymore. If we didn't take the money out of her purse, we would starve! If she keeps drinking, it is just going to get worse. She has such a quick temper these days before she passes out. She can be dangerous.

"What are you going to do about college? If you don't get a scholarship for soccer, you will have to earn your own tuition, or get student loans, and graduate in deep debt. She doesn't have the money to pay for school. At dad's place, college is free, and they help you get a job."

"Sandra, I am not going to college for four years, that is close to forever. I don't want to talk about it anymore. Get out of my room!" he barked at her.

"Ok, fine. Put your head in the sand, but our problems are not going to go away." She left his room.

Sammy threw himself on the bed and started to cry. His whole world was falling apart.

Sandra felt sorry for him. She knew that his friends and soccer were his whole life, but she thought the school in Hope would be good for him. She was also going to miss hanging out with her friends, but she promised herself that she would keep in touch with them online. After all, it was worth it. How was she going to get Sammy to see it too. He can still play soccer there and make new friends on a new team.

Friday morning dawned bright and warm, like most mornings. But this one was special. They were going to visit their dad. Sandra was excited and started packing at 6:00 am. She woke up early because she was too wound up to sleep. Sammy was still in bed at 8:30, claiming to be sick, so he could stay home. Dad was due around nine.

The night before, Judy gave Sandra her Smartwatch, ComPad, and Learner's Permit back. She reminded them that they are going to visit their dad this weekend. James was going to pick them up at noon and told Sandra she could be the one to drive. She was excited to be driving all that distance. It made her feel really grown up.

Sandra knew Sammy was faking it. She debated between pouring water on him and bribing him. The bribe won out. She had twenty dollars saved and offered it to him. He miraculously recovered and was dressed on time.

Judy said goodbye to the kids and went off to work. She was looking forward to a weekend alone so she would not have to hide her drinking. Having no one spying on her was a relief. As she walked out the door, she was filled with anxiety, thinking that Sammy would like Trinitus too much.

James was excited and nervous. He designed a power packed weekend to keep them busy and engaged. The drive to San Bernadino took forever. He kept going over his plans, afraid he had left something out. Then he started second guessing himself and worried that they would find his plans lame. 'What if they hate it there and never want to come back.' Finally, he had to tell the nasty critic in his mind to shut up. He cranked up the music exceedingly loud, so he could not hear the negative words rattling around in his mind. Pretty soon he was sailing along and his excitement returned.

Sandra made breakfast, pancakes for her and Sammy once he got up. She also made some sandwiches and packed some cookies for the trip. When Dad drove up, she ran out to meet him and Sammy began to pack. Sandra and James helped the kid decide what to bring and packed his bag for him, otherwise, they would still be there at supper time.

The drive was painful. Sammy kept threatening to throw up and went into a monologue about how it was parental abuse to drag a sick kid out of bed. He conveniently forgot that he was well paid for the effort. Sandra put her earphones on and went into her own world. Sammy finally withdrew into his ComPad and played his games. For two hours, not one word was spoken. James was not sure whether to be concerned or relieved.

When they arrived at the house, everyone was glad to be out of the car and stretch their legs. Sammy scowled and asked why the houses were all up on pillars.

"It is for storage, bikes, and things. It has a low impact on the land."

"Are you sure it's not because there are lots of poisonous snakes slithering around here?"

"I have never seen one." He helped Sammy carry his bag up to the front porch. Sandra flew up the stairs carrying her own bag.

Inside, they took stock of everything. They threw their bags on the floor and headed to the kitchen at the back of the first floor. Sammy hopped up on one of the stools beside the big island and wondered aloud about lunch. Cathy had made calzones for them. She told James that the kids would be starving when they arrived because kids are always starving. James just had to nuke them in the microwave.

James was planning to learn how to cook. That's how he got the calzones. A couple of days ago, he called Cathy to ask her to teach him to cook, and when he mentioned that the kids were coming, she volunteered to make the calzones.

After lunch, Sammy sank into the comfy sofa near the front door to check out the ComScreen. It was mounted on the opposite wall. "Wow! This is a great screen. Did you just buy it for us?" Sammy squealed.

"It came with the house, so did the recliner, the coffee table, and all the furniture. I just had to choose what I wanted, and it was delivered. I only bought the minimum for your rooms because I thought you would enjoy decorating them yourself.

"Did you pick out that dining room table and chairs, Dad? They are really green," Sandra gushed.

"I think they are lame. Can we go pick out new ones?" Sammy criticized with a raised brow.

'He will probably criticize the clean air next!' thought James. 'Pick your battles carefully,' rang in his head as he softened his voice and said, "In your rooms, you can have full say. In the public spaces like the kitchen and dining room, we all get an equal vote. I like this table and chairs and so does Sandra so those won't change. However, is there anything else you want to change?"

"Dad, just ignore him. He is trying to bug you," said Sandra shaking her head.

"I know. It's okay. I care more about you both being here and being happy, than I care about which table and chairs we have.

"Let me show you your rooms. I bought plain sheets and pillows for tonight, but if you see anything else you like, perhaps themed sheets and stuff to match. Would you like to shop for things to decorate with?" James took the remote and began flipping to the shopping channel.

"Cool green!" said Sammy as he plopped back down on the comfy sofa. He planned to make this his spot for the whole weekend.

"What games do you have? I bet this ComScreen even has the newest Virtual Soccer," said Sammy showing his first drop of enthusiasm.

James took a deep breath for courage and said as gently as he could, "None. This community has a closed system, and it does not have virtual games. We can order a one-hour game in the evening, but that is the extent of it."

"I knew I was going to hate it here. This place is so barbaric. One hour? You can't get to a decent level in an hour! Why did you drag me to this God-forsaken place anyway?"

James did not answer, but while his son was ranting, he found the shopping channel and turned to the greenest bedroom stuff he could find, then handed the remote to Sammy. The kid looked at it, like it was a rattlesnake, and then glanced up at the screen.

"Wow Dad! Can I have this stuff?"

"Sure, whatever you want if you can fit it in your room."

"Green. Wow! Green!"

Sammy ordered way too much stuff, but the order went through, so James let it ride. Sandra patiently waited for her brother to finish. She understood that if Sammy liked this place and wanted to stay here, it would work to her advantage.

Eventually, Sandra got a turn and decorated her room exotically with an African animal motif. She wanted to become a veterinarian who specialized in caring for endangered species. She only ordered the things she thought she would need. They were going to share a bathroom. James could see that being an area of contention, but Sammy was in a much better mood after his shopping spree. They both agreed on seascapes and sea animals for the bathroom.

"We also have boutique shops in U-Town. If you like, we can go there sometime and find special things to add to your room."

"Thanks Dad. This is enough for now. Maybe another day. When will this be delivered?" Sandra reassured him.

"Today is Friday, so it will probably arrive on Monday. It will be here when you return next week. It is something to look forward to. Sandra smiled and Sammy rolled his eyes. He was excited, but he was not going to let them know.

"There's a soccer game about to start in half an hour, if you want to go. It is at the school, boys just your age will be playing," said James. He looked over at Sandra to see how her patience was holding out. To her credit, she shrugged and said, "Sure."

Sammy said, "I guess, since there is nothing else to do," which they both knew was his way of saying he would love to.

James and Sandra sat through the game and tried to look enthused. They both needed Sammy to want to live there. It would make things a lot easier.

"The kids went to get some snacks and James called Cathy. "What do you think we should do for dinner? I can take them to the hotel restaurant. Do you think they would like that?

"Sure, or I can come over in the evening with Tammy and bring a garden salad and tuna noodle casserole. I think kids usually like that. I will also bring the recipe. It is an easy dish to make," he needed some moral support, so he agreed."

After the game, Sammy said that the boys were not bad players, and they looked like okay people. That was the best they could expect from him.

On the way home on the tram, Sammy said it was a nice field and good-looking uniforms. They could see the wheels turning in his head. James was pleased. Things were going well. He had lots of great activities planned for Saturday and Sunday. Then just before they left, he thought it would be a good time to bring up the subject of Judy's drinking. He wanted to feel them out to see how they were doing with it. For now, he was going to spend all his time building rapport.

Sandra did not have the same sense of finesse. "Nice game. I bet those kids would love to have you on their team. Since Mom keeps drinking and is putting us at risk, the court is going to find out. Then we can come live here fulltime."

"They won't find out, if you two don't tell on her!" Sammy protested.

"Look Sammy. Don't worry about Dad and me. Mom is going to blow it all by herself," Sandra said, and James winced. So much for building rapport.

Sammy crossed his arms, shriveled up in his seat, and pouted.

"All we can do is try to love her through the crisis she is in." James said softly. "I'm not sure what we can do to stop her. She is sabotaging herself. When she drinks this often and this much, it is not fair to you guys. Whether she gets caught or not, this must be hard on you."

"It is not fair. You guys screw up your lives, and I suffer," whined Sammy.

I understand. It is unfair. Sometimes life is challenging and the only thing you can do is learn how to handle injustices. They happen in your life to teach you how to be a powerful warrior who stands up for what's right. You can't grow up to be a powerful man, unless you learn how to handle the curve balls. It is facing difficult situations that make you strong and able to persevere so you can reach your goals. This is your warrior training."

"I don't want to be a warrior, just a kid with a family, a whole family, in one place," Sammy barked at his dad and crossed his arms in protest.

James shivered though he was not cold. He did not want to make a scene here on the tram in front of a dozen or so people quietly listening. The words: rapport, apologize, acknowledge, and offer an olive branch of peace, ran through his head, so, he gave it a shot.

"I am so sorry that you are going through this. You are right. You are a boy, and you deserve to have a whole family. I wish I could give you that, but things have progressed too far to go back. I will be here for you, son. I will help you navigate the road ahead to the best of my ability. I wish I could make this world a fairer place for you, but I can't."

"You did not have to leave!" Sammy accused him.

"Son, our marriage was over a long time before I left. You just didn't know it. When your mom started drinking and my job ended, life became a force that carried us away from each other. Your mother and I love you very much. Sometimes life can grab you and spin you about. There are times when things look awfully bad, but you stick with them, and they work out in the end. Sometimes it takes a while to see why things happen the way they do. When you get older and stronger, you can look back on this time, and the puzzle pieces will fall into place. Then it all seems to make sense."

"Dad! You just use a lot of words, but they boil down to 'when you are older you will understand.' That is quite lame!"

"Here's our stop. I invited some friends over for dinner. They will be here in half an hour," James informed them.

James was breathing deeply and maintaining his composure, but just barely. This parenting stuff was harder than he thought. A small part of him yearned for the old days, when a father just roared at the kid and slugged him. The kid didn't dare talk back. That is how he was raised, but it screwed him up. He was committed to using the principles he was learning. He wanted his kids to grow up feeling good about themselves and their world.

"Whatever!" Sammy grumbled.

Sandra had her earphones in and was listening to her music on her Smartwatch. She did not want to hear what the guys were saying. She had pretty much given up on this family. She knew she was strong and would survive as long as those two did not screw things up too badly. Her mom already had that base completely covered.

When Tammy walked in, Sandra squealed. They threw their arms around each other and did a little celebratory dance. Cathy entered holding a casserole that smelled delicious. James gave her a friendly neighborly hug. Tammy brought salted caramel cashew ice cream, and they all moaned in delight.

Everyone was on good behavior. As soon as dinner was over, the two girls ran off to hide in Sandra's room, and James ordered a video game for Sammy. James and Cathy tried to play, but it was too complex for them to follow. They bowed out, so he just competed with himself, and was happy not to have to deal with adults.

All in all, the evening was a success. Maybe everyone would not agree, but some people enjoyed it.

Saturday morning, they got up early because James said he had a big day planned. Sandra made Frogs in a Hole for breakfast. She made a hole in buttered bread, dropped an egg in it, and cooked it to perfection. She served it with guacamole and sour cream on top. It was something she had seen on her ComPad and thought this would be a green time to try it out. It tasted delicious even though she had a hard time turning the eggs over without breaking them. Some broke, but most came out okay.

When they finished breakfast, James announced that today they were going to visit the Native American Village and shared their different options. Sammy chose to learn how to shoot a bow first and then he wanted to go for a short horseback ride. Sandra chose to sign up for an all-day ride up into the canyons, which included a campfire barbeque. She called Tammy and invited her. Tammy was thrilled.

James was glad this would give him some one-on-one time with Sammy. He also liked the idea that it would show Sandra that he trusted her. He was willing to give her time and freedom to be on her own.

They reached the park at 8:30 am and headed over to the Frontier Town's stables and barn where they met up with a supply wagon. The ride had a real purpose. The girls were going to join a weekly supply team traveling to an encampment deep in the canyons.

After the wagon train left, James and Sammy strolled around Frontier Town watching the craftspeople ply their trades. The town was authentic. The people who lived here wanted a simpler life. There were no actors, fake fighting, or shoot-outs here, in fact, there were no guns at all. The only thing here that was fake was the whiskey.

The park made money for the community, and for the Native American tribes that live in the four corners area. The shops had beautifully handcrafted jewelry, drums, clothing, and ritual items at reasonable prices. There was an entrance fee to the park, plus charges for the excursions and classes. However, for community members wearing colored bands and their families, everything was free.

James and Sammy headed over to the Blacksmith Shop down the wooden street from the stables. The smithy was working on making a fine hunting knife for a customer. Sammy watched in fascination. The smithy was an excellent teacher and explained each step as his work progressed.

After that, they stopped in at the General Store. It was well stocked with everything the townsfolk could need. There was a hand cranked ice cream maker in the corner and a soda fountain off to one side. Sammy stepped up to the counter and asked for some candy. James flashed his band and the candy was free. There were prices for visitors, but for members and Native Americans everything was free.

The farmers in this valley, who supplied Trinitus city, and the Native Village received most of their goods from this store, if not in the modern towns. They passed the hay and feed barn next door on the way to the Tannery Shop.

Here too a craftsman showed them, and a few visitors, how to work the leather to make it very soft and supple. The tanner also had a shop just outside of town where the more pungent work was done. They briefly visited the cobbler who was completing a new pair of shoes, a spinner and weaver making cloth. James could have spent days watching each of these talented people make their fascinating creations, but Sammy had a limited attention span, and he was anxious to get his hands on a bow.

The Archery Class was due to begin soon, so they left Frontier Town and crossed a wooden bridge over a dry creek to reach the Native encampment. The village was a real functioning community. Native Americans, who wanted to live according to their traditional ways, lived side by side with a mix of races and ethnicities, people who wanted to live this lifestyle. Some wore pioneer clothing, and some dressed in traditional deer skins. Pioneers and Native Americans were living together, as if the wars and betrayals had never happened. This was the primary theme of the park, exploring what life could have been, if the settlers had been respectful, and learned the ways of the land from the Native People, and they went on to live together in harmony.

The Archery Class was just outside the village. Four Native People and one White Man were the instructors. They sat down on strawbales while an instructor began with a history of the bow and arrow going back to the most ancient times. Then they covered the care and handling of this sacred tool and weapon, stressing how it must always be handled with respect. A second instructor went over the positions of how to draw and fire. Each student was asked to state the principles of safety before they were given a bow. "I pledge to always be aware of the people and property around me, keep my bow facing down range, never leave it on the ground, and always treat it with respect." Only then were they given a quiver of arrows. These arrows had blunt points, but they were still dangerous.

When it came to archery, James and Sammy were rather well matched. They both did poorly to begin with and seemed to progress at a similar rate. Sammy had some difficulty handling the bow and lining up the arrow. He got frustrated quickly. James did not do much better, but he had more patience.

After snaping his wrist with the string, Sammy cursed and was about to throw it down when he remembered that he had taken an oath to respect the bow. He turned to his dad and grumbled, "I'm never going to get this!"

The Native instructor came over and said, "Everything takes practice. You will get it. Just breathe for a minute and I'll show you again."

"No, I can't. I suck at everything," Sammy pouted.

James rubbed the boy's shoulders and said softly, "New things take time to get the rhythm. Remember how long it took for you to get good at soccer. Be patient. Breathe and calm down. You'll get better."

The instructor smiled at James and when Sammy was calm again, he gave the boy individual instructions. James watched and benefited from the lesson. After a while, Sammy and James got their first arrows down the range. The instructor stayed with them until they both had a feel for it. By the end of an hour, they were shooting in the target area.

The first time Sammy hit the target he gave his father a high five. James soon followed suit. It wasn't long before they hit the target on almost every shot. Sammy was brimming with excitement. "Did you see that one? I almost got a bullseye!"

"Yes, you're getting good already, see you just needed to believe in yourself that's all," his dad encouraged.

"You're doing pretty good too, Dad," Sammy replied. This might have been the very first time Sammy ever complemented his dad on anything, and it did not go unnoticed. "Thanks for bringing me here, this was fun," Sammy gave him a quick hug.

"We can come here and practice every weekend, if you like," James offered.

By the last hour, they were getting rather competitive with each other. James was doing very well. He was about to win, but then he saw the disappointed look in Sammy's eyes and aimed high on the last few shots. At the last minute, Sammy won.

They went to a large shed where they were fitted with a set to take home. They got sized for the bow and the right size arrows. James picked up a hay bag target as well.

"Now remember this is a dangerous weapon and must always be handled like one. Never cock an arrow unless you have a safe range set up and only shoot at the target bag, right? We expect you to always honor your pledge," said the instructor who fitted him.

"Oh yes, I understand," the boy said excitedly.

Sammy wore his bow and a quiver of arrows proudly on his back. His dad also wore his and carried the target.

They had lunch at the center fire pit in the village where they ate venison on fry-bread with wild onions and peppers. Even the food was authentic. The chief gathered the people round and told old tribal tales. After lunch they attended a circle where everyone was dancing and drumming. They even learned a few of the steps and joined in. Sammy danced until he was tired.

It was late afternoon by the time they made their way back to the Frontier Town across the creek to meet Sandra and Tammy. They were sore and tired from a full day of riding. Sammy laughed at them for walking funny. Sandra laughed too. "I can't help it. I think I'll be permanently bow legged from now on."

James gave them a choice. If they were too tired for more, they could take the tram home or they could go visit some boutique shops in U-Town and buy some green accessories for their rooms.

The kids took a raincheck, and they headed home. Sammy was eager to show Sandra how to shoot. James set up an archery range behind the house facing the back porch, aimed away from the exercise yard in the middle of the cluster. If an arrow went awry, it would just hit the porch or go under it.

James trusted the kids, but he also kept a close eye on them through the kitchen window as he made dinner. He called Cathy, and she walked him through preparing a garden salad, packaged veggie burgers and fresh potato fries. Everything came out rather good and he was quite proud of himself.

Sandra eventually got the hang of it, but she was shooting with a bow that was a little too small for her. Long before Sammy was ready to quit, Sandra gave up from fatigue, so she came in to help dad with dinner. When everything was ready, Sandra called her brother in.

James had a warm feeling in his chest. There was something timeless and satisfying about calling the kids in for a homecooked dinner after they had been playing outside. It was different than the usual hassle with kids to put away their electronic gadgets and sit down to eat a microwaved dinner.

While they ate, Sandra talked about her ride and described the village up in the canyons. It was a mixed tribe, primarily Hopi and they did not interact with park guests, except for the supply wagon riders. They wanted to live exclusively according to their traditions and felt a need to be isolated and separate. Sammy told her how he and his dad danced with the Native people. He jumped up and demonstrated some of the moves he had learned. Sandra and James applauded.

After dinner, James ordered a video game for him while he and Sandra washed, dried, and put away the dishes, something they never did together back in the RW.

"Sammy is sure excited for someone who did not want to come here at all," Sandra laughed.

"I'm glad he had fun. I was worried after yesterday," James admitted.

"Yeah, me too. I love it here and Sammy seems to be having a great time, so, how do we make this arrangement more permanent? If I report Mom to Child Services. She will know it was me."

"I don't think you should do that. Let your mother decide on her own fate. Let's hope she can pull it together. If not, and she gets caught, it will be on her head alone. It would be very wrong for you to betray your mother and alienate Sammy."

"Yeah, I guess so."

"I know you want to come here, but you cannot start a new life with a deceptive beginning," James advised.

"I guess you're right," she said with downcast eyes.

When Sammy's video game ended, they all played cards. In Hearts, Sandra Shot the Moon twice and Sammy accused her of fixing the deck, but all in all they got along well. No one had any meltdowns, and for that, James went to bed a happy man.

On Sunday, they had blueberry pancakes for breakfast, and then the three of them immediately went outside to do more target practice. James had to remind them to pack, it was close to noon. Sammy begged his dad to let him bring his real bow and quiver of arrows back to the RW. He wanted to show his friends. They were going to be blown away. Hard as it was to disappoint Sammy, James had to say no. He promised that Sammy could practice shooting all next weekend if he wanted.

James checked out a car and drove them home. There was a lot of hugging and Sandra even shed a tear when they parted. As James drove away from their house, he waved and felt like he missed them already. He was relieved that they both had fun.

When he arrived back at the community, he called Cathy to tell her all about his adventures with his children. They talked on the Smartwatch for over an hour. He thanked her profusely for all her support and for being such a great friend.

CHAPTER 17

Caught

The kids arrived home at the expected time, but no one was there. They settled in and Sandra made burritos for dinner. She opened a can of refried beans, warmed them and dumped the mush on tortillas. She added a dollop of sour cream, some grated cheese, store made guacamole, picante sauce, and dinner was ready.

A few hours later, their mom stumbled in. She was surprised to see them there. She thought they had gone to their dad for the weekend.

"Hi Mom, welcome home," Sammy greeted her warmly. He was about to give her a kiss on the cheek, but one whiff of her discouraged that.

"Hi Mom," echoed Sandra less enthusiastically.

"I thought you went to your dad for the weekend. Why are you here?" She asked, confused.

"Mom, its Sunday night. We came home right on time. Where were you?" Sandra had a bit of a condescending tone in her voice, which Judy picked up on.

"Don't use that tone with me, Miss High and Mighty. I am still your mother. If you don't clean up your act, you will be grounded for the rest of your life."

Sandra could not help laughing. It just came out. Judy's eyes were shooting flames. "What are you laughing at Young Lady?"

"You, telling me to clean up my act! That is hysterical," Sandra replied and there was a taunting tone to it.

Judy had no intention of hitting Sandra, but she was furious at this girl's rudeness and disrespect. The hand just leaped out on its own and slapped her across her rude little mouth. Though Judy would not admit it even to herself, it felt good. This girl's anger and resentment had hurt her for a very long time.

Sandra refused to cry but Sammy wasn't as stoic. He began to cry loudly. "Mom, why are you doing this to us? We love you. We need you to stop drinking. You should have been home waiting for us, like a real mom would. We need you to take care of us. We miss you terribly. It is like you are a Zombie not a mother.

Judy was listening and feeling sad until that last statement and it infuriated her. "Go to your room! I am not even going to make either of you supper tonight. You don't deserve it."

"What we don't deserve is a mother like you! We already ate. We always take care of ourselves, since we don't have a mother anymore."

Judy took one step towards her and Sammy threw himself between them to stop her from grabbing Sandra. "Please Mom. We love you. Calm down. We need you."

Sandra escaped into her room and locked the door. Judy stood there staring at Sammy like she wasn't sure what was going on and then went into her room. Sammy just sat where he was and cried. His whole world was slipping away. He felt like he was falling through space and there was no one to catch him.

Tuesday evening, Sandra was making dinner. Mom usually makes dinner. It was the one thing she was able to consistently maintain, but after the big fight on Sunday night, that stopped too. On Monday night, they did not see her after work until around midnight.

Now it was Tuesday night and Sandra was wondering when her mom's pouting was going to end because she was running out of food and dinner ideas.

There was a knock at the door. At first, she thought it was her mom and felt relieved. Then she realized her mom wouldn't knock. She answered the door and Ms. Hydaburg was standing there.

Sandra welcomed her in and asked her if she would like to have some tea.

"Where is your mom?" the woman asked.

"I think she went to the store. Excuse me for a minute. I'll ask Sammy."

She ran into Sammy's room and told him the social worker was here to see Mom. "Do you know which bar she is in? He nodded. "Hurry, get her here as fast as you can. Go out the front door so it does not look suspicious. I will tell her you went to the store. Put this grocery bag and this peanut butter and cereal in your backpack.

Sammy nonchalantly strolled past Ms. Hydaburg and said, "Hello, I will just go to the store around the block and let Mom know you are waiting for her."

He ran as fast as he could into the bar. He had the willies as he opened the door. If it was a prison door into hell, it could not have felt worse. He fought back the tears. It took a moment for his eyes to adjust to the darkness inside. As he looked around, he both hoped and dreaded that he would find her there. A wave of anger rose over him at this place that was stealing his mother from him.

Then he spotted her sitting at the end of the bar flirting with a young bartender. "Mom!" he called. She instinctively looked his way.

"What are you doing here?"

"Hurry Mom, the Social Worker lady is at the house. Sandra told her you went shopping. Here, take these groceries and let's go."

She stared at him for a moment, trying to make sense of seeing him here and what he was saying.

"Hurry Mom. You don't want her to come here, right?" he desperately urged.

"Judy, you had better go," said the bartender, which seemed to break her befuddled spell. She ran into the bathroom, splashed some water on her face, dug an Altoids mint out of her purse, popped it in her mouth, and hurried out with Sammy.

Judy arrived, all smiles and apologized for not being home when Ms. Hydaburg arrived. She dramatically put the grocery bag down and tried to act normally. She smiled at Sandra and said, "Thank you dear for making our guest some tea." Then she turned to the Social Worker and asked, "Would you like some cookies to go with that. We have some Ginger Snaps.

Ms. Hydaburg was not fooled. The Altoids may have sweetened her breath, but the alcohol was reeking out of every pore of her skin.

The Social Worker said, "Yes. Thank you."

As soon as Judy left the room, she asked Sandra if her mother had been drinking at home.

Sandra was relieved that the woman phrased it that way, so she did not have to lie. "No, my mother never drinks at home anymore, not since the judge ordered her not to." She swallowed the rest of the sentence, 'but she is drinking every night in the bar." She promised her dad that she would not betray her mom, so she was going to try.

The woman was about to ask Sammy, and he did not want to lie or tell the truth, so he thought fast and started talking.

"We spent the weekend with our dad, just like the court ordered. You know I really didn't want to go at first, but it turned out to be a great place. I learned all about early American life and how to shoot a bow and arrows. There were real Indians living there just the way they used to in the early days when the pioneers first went West." He said all this in one long breath. He was running out of things to say in his superfast monologue when to his relief, Mom returned carrying a plate of cookies.

Ms. Hydaburg leaned close to Judy ostensively to take a cookie, but her motive was more investigative. "Mrs. Dole, have you been drinking?"

"No, of course not," she feigned being insulted.

"Mrs. Dole, you smell like a brewery. Thank you for the tea and cookies. I am ready to make my report. You have wonderful children. They tried to cover for you. They deserve a better mother."

She knew she should not have said that but seeing these two beautiful children trying to cover for their mother just broke her heart. "I am going to report to the court that you are still drinking."

Judy protested and said it was just rubbing the alcohol she was using on her sore back. Ms. Hydaburg ignored her and walked out the door. Judy was still standing in the doorway shouting protests as she drove off.

Judy slammed the door. "Sandra Marine Dole, what did you tell that bitch from the court?!" She glared at her daughter standing in the hallway.

"Nothing Mom, I just talked about my weekend at Dad's place," she said truthfully.

"I don't believe you. You set me up and told her I was at the bar.

My own daughter stabbed me in the back," Judy accused her, acting mortally wounded. Then she turned to Sammy and said, "What did you tell her?"

"Mom, we tried to save you." He could not understand why she was turning on him.

Sandra was in a rage, "I wanted to tell her what a drunk you are and how you totally neglect us, but I promised Dad that I would not betray you and this is the thanks I get. You are so not worth it."

There were flames in Judy's eyes.

"Go ahead and slap me again. I expect it from you. That's what shitty mothers do. They abuse their children."

Sammy was stunned, Judy was furious, and Sandra had a hard steely look in her eyes. He burst out crying, Sandra reached down to comfort him, and he pushed her away. Judy grabbed her purse and left.

Sammy did not know what was happening. "She is going to the bar again isn't she," he was worried.

"I assume so," Sandra sounded sad. "I think we are going to end up with Dad, whether we want to or not."

"NO!" he shouted, ran to his room, and slammed the door!

Sandra could hear him yelling and slamming things around but opted to leave him alone for a while.

She got online to talk to her friends in New World. They always gave her solace. Especially now that she was talking to Purple Bands who offered her wise counsel.

After a while, Sammy's room was quiet, so she went to check on him.

She knocked. "You okay in there?"

"I'm not talking to you! Go away!" Sammy shouted. "Was Mom right? Did you tell on Mom while I was out getting her?"

"Think about it. Would I send you to get her and then snitch? Now unlock the door."

"Okay," He unlocked the door and went back to his chair.

Sandra opened the door and looked at the maelstrom. The room looked like it was hit by a tornado. Schoolbooks, papers, the posters from his wall, soccer balls, shoes and clothes were all strewn around the floor. A broken model plane was wedged under the door, making it hard to open. She had to push harder to get through. At first, it was hard to see Sammy in all this mess. Then she found him curled up in a ball in his chair with his head in his hands and a blood-soaked tee shirt wrapped around his head like a turban. His shirt and hands were covered in blood.

"What happened?"

"I hit my head on the corner of the shelf above my desk." He pointed to it. "Don't worry. I'm fine, I just cut my head, but it keeps bleeding. I am sure it is not as bad as it looks."

"Let me see it," said Sandra as she carefully made her way through all the debris to reach him.

She removed the blood-soaked tee shirt and parted his hair. "Ow, that hurts!" He complained and waved her away.

"I am sure it does." She had to pry his hand away before he relented. The gash was deep and still bleeding. "This is going to need stitches. I'm sorry."

"Are you sure? I don't want to go to the hospital!" he protested.

"Okay! I'll call an Uber, and we can go to the Walk-In Clinic."

"I'm scared!" he said with big round eyes. "What about Mom?" He looked up at her with blood dripping down his face and his tee-shirt soaked in blood.

"We can handle this better by ourselves. Mom is too drunk to drive us, and we don't want to run around looking for her, while you keep gushing blood. I think we need to get you to the Clinic right away and call her when we get there.

That made sense, so he agreed.

The Uber was there in five minutes. They walked into the Clinic and the receptionist took one look at the bloody turban and put his name at the top of the list. They were seen almost immediately. Sandra did not have time or thought to call her mother. She was worried about Sammy who was a scary shade of gray. Sammy was too frightened and dizzy to think of anything other than how he was bleeding to death, even though Sandra reassured him a few times that it was not that serious.

Sandra held his hand in the examination room. It was a measure of how scared he was that he let her. A nurse entered and asked, "How did it happen?"

Sammy answered honestly, "I bumped my head on the corner of a shelf," he did not add, "while I was jumping around throwing everything I own on the floor in a fit of rage."

A few minutes later, the doctor walked in and greeted them warmly. He looked in the boy's eyes with a light and examined the cut. He told them it would need at least three or four stitches. "You will be fine, young man," he assured the frightened boy and asked the nurse to flush and prep for stitches, then he left.

"You're going to be okay," said the nurse. "I am going to clean the area, so the doctor can sew you back together. Please lie down and I'll numb your head, so it won't hurt. It was a very long needle, but it didn't hurt too much. He was very brave.

"Now rest for a few minutes. The doctor will return when you are numb." Turning to Sandra she said, "Could you please step outside?"

Once outside the room, the receptionist asked her to sign in and fill out the forms. She thought she could just give them the address and they would bill her mom later. The forms were more extensive than she expected. She filled them out as best she could but did not know anything about the name of the insurance company or their information. She had to leave a lot of it blank.

"Has your mother been called," the nurse asked Sandra.

"No. I was too busy getting Sammy here to think of it."

She raised an eyebrow at that. She found it odd that this child did not think to call her mother. When she asked where Judy is, Sandra said, 'I don't know, probably at the store.' She didn't want to get her mom in trouble.

The nurse looked at the number Sandra had written down and called their mother. Judy glanced down at the chiming phone, did not recognize the phone number, and assumed it was a robocall.

It went to voicemail. She spilled the next glass because her hand coordination was a little sloppy. When she was blotting the wine off her Smartwatch, she noticed a missed call from the Walk-In Clinic. She straightened out her fuzzy brain and returned the call.

When the receptionist answered and informed her that her son was there, she sobered up a bit. She went to the bathroom, splashed some water on her face, popped an Altoids, slapped some money on the bar, and dashed out to her car.

Judy rushed into the clinic all worried and concerned about her child. She was playing the part perfectly until she asked the receptionist which room her son was in. The woman got a whiff of Judy and knew this woman was drunk. For procedure she asked, "How did this accident happen?

"I don't know. I was at the store," she said, trying to sound nonchalant.

Sammy was resting. The procedure was over, and he was relieved. Just then his mom burst into the room.

"Sammy darling, Mommy's here. How are you feeling sweetheart?" When she reached for his hand, he waved her away.

"I'm not a baby any more Mom, stop it." He was still too mad at her to let her touch him.

He was confused. So many emotions were rising at once. He wanted his mother there to comfort him. He was furious with her for drinking. He loved her and wanted life to go back to the way it used to be when they were a family. He wanted to scream at her that she was ruining everything. In the end, he just sat there feeling limp and exhausted. All the fight seeped out of him and the smell of her sitting close to him was making him feel nauseous.

Judy was trying not to look hurt by her son's rejection.

The receptionist behind the counter was just following procedure when she called Child Services.

Back in the waiting room, Sandra jumped up as soon as she saw her mother. "How is he? Is he going to be okay?"

Judy was upset and hissed at Sandra, "What happened to him? Did you guys get in a fight?" Judy jumped to a negative conclusion.

"No, of course not!" Sandra was totally insulted. "Sammy was having a meltdown over your drinking. He wrecked his room and, in his frenzy, bumped his head."

"That is so like you, blaming me for everything. Why didn't you call me?" Judy demanded to know and answered her own question. "You just wanted to make me look bad. You should have called me and waited for me to come back. That way, we could have come here together."

"Sammy was gushing blood. All I could think about was getting the bleeding to stop. I was completely focused on getting him here as quickly as possible. I didn't even think of calling you. You aren't available when I need you for the day-to-day things. Why should I think of you in an emergency? I just wanted to get him here. I knew they would call you," Sandra tried to sound innocent, "you would find out eventually."

"Still, you should have called on your way here. You made me look bad," Judy huffed.

"Sorry," mumbled Sandra. To herself she thought, 'Sorry you are my mom. Sorry you are messing up our lives. Sorry you care more about your damn bottle than about us.' "I am very sorry, Mom."

Once Sammy was all bandaged, he returned to the waiting room and sat down next to Sandra. Judy was just finishing up the paperwork. She asked Sammy, "So how did you bump into the corner of the shelf anyway?"

Sammy looked at Sandra then looked back at his mom, not knowing what to say. The truth was all he had, so he blurted out. "I was mad at you for going to a bar and for being drunk when Ms. Hydaburg was here. You need to stop drinking, but you won't. I don't want to live with Dad, but you are forcing me to!" He was crying by the end.

His mother was shocked. She did not want to cause a scene, so she just smiled and said softly, "Darling, I wasn't drunk. I just stopped for one drink after a long hard day at work."

"It doesn't matter, Ms. Hydaburg saw you drunk and she will tell the court. You promised the judge you wouldn't drink anymore and now they will make us go to Dad!" His voice was getting too loud and the receptionist could hear.

"Shh, we need to talk about this later, not here, not now." Judy was shaken and desperate to quiet them down.

Sandra was not going to let her off so easily. "Sammy is right, now is as good a time as any. You need to address your problem. What are you going to do to stop drinking?"

"I'll stop," said Judy in a very soft voice. "I promise. Now can we stop talking about it? I don't want anyone to hear."

A man from Child Services arrived. The receptionist took him aside and told him what she had overheard. He thanked her for calling him and walked over to Judy.

"Mrs. Cordileone-Dole, hello, my name is Officer Fredrick, I am from Child Services.

"Can you come with me to talk for a minute?"

"Umm, sure what's this about?" She knew she was in trouble; she could see it on the receptionist's face.

"Just medical procedure when kids come in alone, that is all, just a few questions."

There was no graceful way to avoid this, so Judy sheepishly followed him. "What is the problem? I was at the store, and he did this by accident while I was gone."

They kept walking until they reached the back hallway. "That's fine, just a few questions." He finally faced her and asked, "Are you drunk Mrs. Cordileone-Dole?"

"What do you mean? Do I look drunk to you?"

"Yes, as a matter of fact you do," he flatly replied.

"Well, I'm not, I had a few drinks before I got home but I'm not drunk."

"Mam, it only takes a few drinks. I believe you are under court order to stop drinking, are you not?"

Dean Fredrick had seen this all too many times and was disgusted. She was not so drunk that she could be arrested for disorderly conduct, but too drunk to drive. It would be tricky to get her into custody, which was the only way to get the kids away from her. He already had the police on alert. They were around the corner in the hall in case things escalated.

"I'm not that drunk." Judy insisted.

"Did you drive here?"

"Yes, of course I did," she replied.

"You could have gotten a DUI. You are too drunk to be behind the wheel." He was purposely baiting her to get her upset.

"That is for a cop to decide, and you are not a cop!" she belligerently retorted.

"Are you supposed to be drinking?" he pressed on.

"Supposed to be? What do you mean, 'supposed to be'?'"

"Aren't you under court order to remain sober?" He was direct.

Judy saw where this was going and lied. "No, of course not!"

"Are you sure about that? That was not what was overheard by the staff here. Why don't you tell me the truth, Mrs. Cordileone-Dole?"

"I don't know what you're talking about," she was scared and defensive.

"I am ready to make my report. If I find out that you're under a court injunction to stay sober, the judge will be interested in this report." This was a bluff. There was no way to check this right away. There would be days of paperwork before it could be established. But she did not know that.

"Okay, there is an injunction, but I can't just stop cold turkey! I'm tapering off. I will stop, soon," and she started to cry.

Now he had her where he wanted her. He could not have her arrested until she was behind the wheel. He had no grounds for removing the kids until then, but he could tell her to get help. He pulled out a pamphlet on AA meetings. "This will help you. I suggest you go to a meeting as soon as you are sober, Mrs. Cordileone-Dole."

"Okay. I will. I promise." She was relieved that she was not going to lose her kids. That worried her the most. Her hands were in a prayer pose as she pleaded, "Please don't make that report."

"I have to do my job," he said stiffly. "I cannot hide the facts. I suggest you take and Uber and don't drive home."

"I won't, I promise."

"Then you can go back to your son."

"Thank you, Sir," she could not leave fast enough.

Dean went to the cops around the corner. "Keep an eye on her and see if she tries to drive out of here."

"I bet she does," quipped one of the officers.

Sammy and Sandra sat alone in the waiting room worrying about their mother. "What is going to happen to mom?" the boy asked.

"I don't know, but we'll find out soon. I'm sure it will be alright," Sandra tried to console her frightened brother.

"You should have called her right away. Then they wouldn't be asking her questions right now!" Sammy was scared.

"I think they called him because she was drunk, not because she didn't come in with us. It is not my fault she wasn't home."

"I heard him say," Sammy persisted, "because they came alone."

"Sammy, he wasn't going to say 'because your mother was drunk' in front of us. He was just being nice."

Sammy crossed his arms in front of his chest and pouted.

After a while Mom returned. "You're still here, oh good," she sighed.

The boy was clearly relieved, "I thought they were going to arrest you, Mom." He stood up and hugged her.

"No, they just needed to talk to me. Just procedure, that's all," she hugged Sammy and glared at Sandra.

The nurse came out and handed Sandra the After Care Instructions and told her to bring him back in ten days to remove the stitches. She also presented Judy with a tablet to sign for the insurance payment.

Outside the clinic, Judy stopped. "Next time you call me and wait until I get home, you hear me?" she growled at Sandra.

Sandra just stood there biting her lip to keep from saying something smart mouthed.

"I'll drive you kids home and then Sandra, you are grounded for another month," she snapped.

As they got in the car, Judy whispered to Sammy, "Your sister is trying to get me in trouble. You know that, right?"

"Sure." That was all he could say. He knew it was partly his fault too.

Sandra approached the car and offered to drive. With her mom present, it would be totally legal. She thought of saying, 'because you have been drinking' but decided not to because it would probably cause another fight.

Believing that Sandra was trying to erase her from this family, Judy responded with an angry tone, "You are not a grown-up yet, Young Lady, I can drive my own car. Judy started driving and did not come to a full stop at the exit. Then she peeled out onto the street.

Out of nowhere a cop car pulled out in front of her. The policeman got out to talk to Judy. The other officer stood by the passenger side. The policeman asked Judy to get out of the car and motioned her to walk a straight line on the sidewalk to test whether she was under the influence.

Judy started getting testy with the policeman. He was not going to put up with it. He slapped handcuffs on her and pushed her into his car. The other officer leaned into the car and said to Sandra, "Are you, her daughter?"

"Yes, what are you going to do with my mother?"

"She is getting a DUI. Is there another adult at home? Do you have family nearby?"

"No, our father is in Arizona. He has joint custody of us," Sandra informed him.

"Please wait in the car," said the officer.

Sammy started crying and Sandra tried to console him. She hugged him and said, "It's okay they will take us to Dad or he will come get us. We will be fine."

"I'm worried about Mom," whimpered Sammy. "Now I am going to lose my friends. My whole world is collapsing because you didn't call her. This is all your fault!"

"Sammy, that is not true. None of this would have happened if Mom hadn't been drinking. It is not my fault."

"You didn't call! You could have!" Sammy was screaming now and pushed her away.

"I was too busy making sure you did not bleed to death. If I called her, it wouldn't have made a difference. They called Child Services because she was drunk not because we were alone! You bumped your head because she was drunk. She got arrested because she was drunk. It is her fault! Not mine!"

Sammy pitched a fit and repeatedly punched the glove compartment in mom's car. Sandra just let him.

Dean arrived. He walked over to the car to explain to Sandra and Sammy what was going to happen next.

"Hi, my name is Dean. Your mom is going to go to jail for the night. She can be bailed out sometime tomorrow. I am going to drive you to a special boarding house for children until we can find a family member or a foster family. Do you have family who might take you in?"

"Yes, Dad is in Arizona. He has joint custody of us." Sandra told him. Sammy just scowled with his arms crossed and stared out the window.

"Good, then it shouldn't take more than a day or two to do the necessary paperwork. Your dad can pick you up then. Your mom may even be allowed to visit you before you leave. It depends on the Judge."

Sandra told her Smartwatch to call Dad.

"Hi Sweetheart, you look upset, is everything okay?"

"No! Mom just got arrested for drunk driving. Child Services is going to keep us for a few days until you can pick us up."

James was shocked. "I can come right over now."

"I wish. No, first they need to do paperwork. We can't go with you today."

"Are you guys, okay? Were you in the car with her?" he was very upset.

Sandra could see the concern on his face. "Yeah, but it was only a short distance. She went to a bar. We were home and Sammy got mad and bumped his head on his shelf, so I had to take him to the clinic to get some stitches. Mom got questioned by Child Services at the clinic. Then Mom was driving us home and the cops came out of nowhere. I think they were waiting for us."

"How awful! How are you two doing with this?" James asked with genuine concern.

"I'm nervous but fine....." Sammy jumped in and shouted, "I'm pissed off!" toward her Smartwatch.

"And yes, Sammy is not too happy," she turned her watch toward him for a second.

"Well, I'm proud of you for getting Sammy to the clinic and making sure he was okay, how bad was it?"

"Just four stitches, but he bled a lot."

"Sammy, I know you don't want to come here, but I'll try to make it as good for you as possible?" She held her arm in front of him so he could see his dad talking to him.

"I'm going to miss my friends and the soccer team. It will be different there," the boy complained.

"Yes, but different can be good. Sammy, it is different here for me also, but I'm making new friends and I'm happier at work here. You can be happy too."

The boy crossed his arms again and pouted. He was angry that all this was happening to him and there was nothing he could do about it.

"Let me talk to the Child Service guy for a moment Sandra. Hand him your watch."

Sandra handed the Social Worker the Smartwatch, and he walked away from the car to talk to their dad. James asked how soon he could come and get them. Dean told him they would call as soon as the arrangements were made. James asked him to go over what had happened.

The boarding house was a scary place. The staff was stern. The kids looked tough and dangerous. There were four kids in each room with two bunk beds. The doors to the outside were always locked. It felt like being in jail. Sammy refused to talk to Sandra and did not want to play in the fenced-in yard with the other kids. He told anyone who was friendly to get away from him, including his sister.

The following day, Judy made bail and came for a supervised visit. She cried a lot saying she was going to get her drinking under control and get them back as soon as she could. She kept saying sorry over and over. The court had decided to give sole custody to their dad until she finished a court-ordered two-month recovery program.

Late in the afternoon, James arrived to pick them up. Sammy was somber and did not say a word. Sandra was more upbeat. She was glad to get out of there. Her biggest complaint was the boring food.

James took the kids to a hotel for the night and planned to get their personal belongings from the house the next day, before moving them to the City of Hope.

The next morning at the house, James stayed in the car so Judy could have her space with the kids. After a while, she came out to see him, while Sandra came out carrying another load of her stuff.

"I bet you are loving this, aren't you?" Judy quietly hissed through the window that James rolled down for her.

"Judy, I don't wish you ill of any sort. I am glad that you are finally going to get the support you need to heal your issues."

It was difficult to argue with his kind gentle words, but Judy found a way. "Sure, going to jail is great support. You are taking my kids away! Sandra you can have, she is as much to blame as you are for this, but Sammy wants to stay with me, and this is making him miserable. This is all Sandra's fault, and you put her up to it!"

There were so many lies, distortions, little daggers that he wanted to refute, but he knew better. All the therapy and training he was getting at Hope came in handy now.

He took a deep breath and said softly, "Sammy will adjust, Sandra may not have been tolerant of your behavior, because your drinking is really making her life difficult. But know for sure, your drinking caused this, not us." James was doing all he could to stay calm and be honest. He was not going to let her get him angry, this time.

"This may cost me my job. I had to take a maternity leave to go to an in-house rehab program. It is going to cost me a bundle. These new stricter laws are a pain in the butt. They took my car too, not just my license," she complained.

"Negative behavior begets negative results," he said and then regretted sounding so pompous. He tried to soften his words and come more from his heart. He was angry that she had endangered his children but then he remembered that she was suffering too.

"Maybe, some good will come out of this bad situation. You need some time to rest and not have to cope with all the pressures. It has been hard for you since I left. Maybe now you will get the support you need to redesign your life in a way that suits you better." James smiled softly.

He edited out the rest of what he wanted to say. It would only make her angry if he said, 'now you will finally have to face your issues, all those things you have denied for so long and think you are hiding, when everyone can see them except you.'

"Thanks! How wise of you!" she said sarcastically "You think getting arrested is a good thing! There is nothing wrong with me. I don't have any problems!" Her voice was rising.

"If you don't, then why do you drink?" he quietly asked.

"Because of you! We were doing fine until you started losing jobs and put us in debt." She baited him in a loud angry voice.

"I'm sorry," he said softly. "It's always someone else's fault. Always my fault! I suppose you think I held a wine bottle to your lips and forced you to drink. According to you everything that ever goes wrong in your life is always my fault!" His voice was rising, and he could feel them slipping into one of their usual fights. He stopped. Told himself he had a choice and chose to make peace.

He softened his voice and said as sincerely as he could, "I wish you well. Whatever unfolds, I hope fate is gentle on you and you succeed. We are all rooting for you to get sober and find what makes you happy."

She just stared at him stunned and could not think of a witty comeback, so she turned away. He rolled the window up and let out a huge sigh. That was probably the hardest thing he ever did. He was aching to yell at her, aching to answer all her accusations, aching to tell her his side of everything. He marveled at his self-control. Who was this new man he was becoming? He did not recognize himself.

The kids went back and forth twice carrying a mountain of things and stuffed them all in the back of the car.

Judy was shocked by James's response, so she just stood there waiting for the packing to end. Sammy stuffed his electric scooter and soccer gear into the car and slumped down in the backseat exhausted. He was teary eyed and still did not have his full strength back after losing all that blood.

Judy leaned in the window and said, "Sammy, take care of yourself and text or call me every day. I want to know how things are going with you. No matter what, okay? You'll be back home again soon. This is just for two months. The time will go by quickly."

"Okay Mom, I will." He hugged her. "I wish I didn't have to go."

"I know, but I won't be home anyway, so it is best for now. I'll get you back as soon as I can."

Sandra put in her last few things and shut the hatch. She came around to the front passenger side and stood near her mom.

"Good luck with your program Mom, I hope you get a lot out of it."

Judy ignored her and waved at Sammy who was looking out the window. Sandra shrugged and got in the car.

"Do you think she will learn anything at her program?" Sandra asked her father since he was the only one who would talk to her.

"You can lead a horse to water," said James and Sandra finished, "but you can't make it drink!"

"Well, let us hope she succeeds," said James and he meant it.

Then he shifted his attention to his pouting son. "Sammy, I know you are mad about this, but your mother needs some help. She has a drinking problem, and this treatment will help her get better. I know it is a sacrifice on your part, but you are doing it for a noble cause, to help your mother stop drinking. He looked in the rear-view mirror at Sammy.

The boy did not respond. He still sat sulking in the back seat.

Sammy turned on his ComPad and texted his friends to say that he was kidnapped by pirates and imprisoned on a huge ship that is lost at sea. He hoped to be rescued soon but had no idea how long this misadventure would take. Then he played video games for the next two hours. It made the time fly by. Sandra also took out her ComPad and journeyed into her online fantasy world to visit her avatar friends. James let them decompress. He did not mind the silence. It gave him time to think.

He marveled at the synchronicity. The principal wanted the children to attend school on the first day of classes and school is going to start in just a week. 'Sammy will need to enroll in the middle school, and I will have to arrange for him to be on a soccer team. I will have to talk to the school about finding out how to do that. I need to enroll Sandra in high school and arrange for her to have an internship. That should not be hard since she has good grades.

Sammy might pose some problems. His grades are not very good, and his attitude is bad. I wonder if they will try to hold him back. The curriculum is probably more advanced here and that will make it even harder for him. They probably do not just pass you, like they tend to do in public schools. I will have to arrange a tutor for him until he gets better grades. I hope he doesn't act up now. I am getting used to single parenting, that is going to be hard enough without a belligerent attitude making it harder.'

The ride was long and the road ahead even longer. For a moment he felt like a man standing on thin ice. Then he took a deep breath and reassured himself that in Hope, he would get a lot of support and help. He wasn't alone in this. He had a whole community there for him.

CHAPTER 18

Denial

Her family left and Judy was all alone. The world looked barren and desolate. All her strength seeped out of her, and she collapsed in tears. Alone in the house, rattling around like a lost penny, she ordered her emotions to get a grip on reality and stopped this foolish bawling. She reminded herself of the million dollar accounts she handled. Anyone who could do that could surely survive a couple of months in rehab. She had 24 hours to report to a facility or the ax would fall, a mandatory six months in jail!

"Jail? How far the great have fallen! Get a grip girl and just do it," She screamed at her image as she passed a mirror.

After a couple of necessary breaths to escape her own self-induced panic, she turned on her ComPad and started surfing Addiction Facilities. The first two resembled elegant resorts. This was going to be better than she thought. They looked wonderful and she certainly deserved a vacation after all she had been through. Just as she was settling into the pleasant idea of swimming, relaxing in a hot tub, and having gourmet meals prepared for her, she stumbled over the price tag, and her eyeballs nearly popped out of her head. She could buy a beautiful new car for that price!

Judy opened her financial spreadsheet and checked the figures. She worked them left and right, but they always came to the same result - impossible! There was no way to afford a place like this. She would be paying it off for the next hundred years. With regret, she left their glossy website and asked the ComPad to show her a free Addiction Facility. Free was about all she could afford. A drab depressing picture appeared on the screen, and it went downhill from there.

There were no amenities. It was run by the County in downtown San Bernardino. The rooms were small, gloomy and two inmates had to share this crowded space. It was a drab, locked-down facility, with a population of parolees. Everyone had to wear ugly blue jumpsuits. No ComPads, electronics, or Smartwatches were allowed. How could she live without her Smartwatch? Residents were only allowed to make calls once a week.

It looked like a depressing jail! Just picturing herself there made her soul shrivel up.

Judy was trapped between eternal debt and two months in hell, then she asked the ComPad if there were any other facilities that were free or almost free. She did not expect to find anything, but this was her last gasp of hope.

A link emerged and she clicked on it. A beautiful website

appeared. Soft music began and pictures flashed across the screen: serene and lovely gardens, an inviting swimming pool inside a huge glass atrium, a rustic and comfortable looking Great Room with plush leather sofas beside a huge fireplace in a log lodge. In the first three seconds these pictures sold her on this place. She immediately looked at the price. Sure enough, it was free. She scrutinized every inch of the website looking for a catch but could find none.

It was more beautiful and offered a more exciting program than the expensive ones. It had everything she could want. There was a Healing Center with a spa, hot tub, sauna, and exercise room. They offered free massages, acupuncture, acupressure, and psychotherapy. This was going to be like a day at the spa but for two months. She could get used to that kind of pampering, and for entertaining activities there was Martial Arts, Tai Chi, Dance, Cooking, and Self Care. Maybe she would expand her horizons and take one of their interesting classes: Qigong, Nutrition, Creative Expression, The Art of Relationship, and Anger Management. WOW!

This beautiful little hideaway was tucked into the San Jacinto mountains. She was swooning by the time she reached pictures of the bedrooms, private, tastefully appointed, attractive, with comfy-looking beds.

Judy bounced back and forth between suspicion and excitement, waiting for the shoe to drop. She combed through the site again, reading the bios on all the doctors, therapists (all accredited Ph.Ds.), teachers, and staff. She watched videos on their amenities, philosophy, the many forms of support and therapy provided, and the overall structure of the program. It was surprisingly comprehensive and innovative. She even took a virtual tour of the facility.

Judy found their Mission Statement inspirational. "The New Hope Substance Abuse Home is dedicated to addressing the needs of the whole individual, physically, emotionally, mentally, and spiritually. Our staff has taken it as their individual responsibility to enhance the overall good of our global community. We are a grassroots movement, a nonaffiliated community of organizations, businesses, and individual volunteers working together to enhance the common good. We are united in heart and are committed to providing our community with a more evolved and compassionate understanding of human nature. We are dedicated to healing wounds from the injustices of the RW, through a deeper understanding of social interaction, of our place within nature, of a natural way of life, of God, (as each sees Him/Her/It). We are dedicated to enhancing every person's spiritual and personal evolution."

On the website, it said, "At the New Hope Substance Abuse Home, our guests are given an array of opportunities to explore themselves and look at their version of reality. Guests receive free personal and group therapy. We offer classes that teach how to relieve stress, as well as detox programs, healing support groups focused on food, diet, and living a healthy life. These classes and amenities help our guests get to know themselves better and can transform into a new more conscious and capable version of themselves.

"We are an open facility with no locked doors. Once a week, we take our guests on an outing to visit the beautiful mountains around us. On the grounds of New Hope, our guests wear soft comfortable pajamas and a plush robe as their usual attire. To leave the world and all its problems outside our gates, we restrict the use of electronics. However, since we know how important connection is to our guests, we allow contact with family and the use of a ComPad or Smartwatch an hour each day."

When she got to the part about the food being prepared by a renowned chef and nutritionist, she was sold. Then the shoe dropped.

Judy recognized the Mission Statement, checked the logo, and sure enough, the facility was built and staffed by Trinitus, James's community.

She couldn't believe it. This was like a conspiracy against her. She was not going to go there, on principle. Judy was determined to have nothing to do with those people. She jumped up and stomped around the room for a few minutes and then reason returned. The choice was simple, this lovely welcoming place or that jail-like facility!

As much as she resisted the idea, she felt a sense of excitement at the prospect of going to the New Hope Substance Abuse Home. She called them, they had an opening, so she filled out the forms online to register. The die was cast, and a new chapter was opening in her life. Judy looked at this opportunity, like a desert traveler looks at a watering hole. It didn't matter who created it, she felt relief that it was here. This was the only way she could survive the DUI.

The next morning, Judy was dressed and ready to tackle the daunting challenges before her. She called an Uber and slid in the back seat with only a little overnight bag beside her. It held a bathing suit, underwear, socks and her ComPad. On her wrist was her Smartwatch. It felt strange to travel this light for a two-month stay, but they assured her that everything else would be provided.

Judy watched her old life flashing past the windows of the car and shuddered. She decided to focus her mind elsewhere. 'I wonder what they meant by saying, 'The length of stay is not predetermined, but rather, based on the guest's progress.' Did it mean they could keep her longer? That was a scary thought. Then she decided it meant that smart people could get through the program faster. In that case, she would be out in no time.

The car wound its way along a series of switchbacks on an unpaved dirt road. As her world sank out of sight, Judy began to feel nervous. 'After all, it is a rehabilitation facility where other people will have control over her!' That was also a scary thought. This time she had no witty little reframe. She did not like being in a situation that she could not control.

They arrived at a set of huge log gates where a warm, friendly gatekeeper welcomed her. The Uber dropped her off in front of a magnificent lodge and she found herself standing in front of two beautiful carved doors, made by a former guest.

She was feeling a lot more relaxed than she expected to be. All the tension of the long drive melted away as she stepped into another, gentler world. The doors opened into a Great Room with a huge fireplace. Big leather sofas and recliners were placed around the room, comfortably seating about thirty guests.

Two staff members approached and warmly welcomed her, Angela Beckman and Lisa Alexzander. They were dressed in purple suits with black lapels and white shirts. Angela, the Healing Coordinator, a tall blond woman in her fifties, supervised everything. Lisa, a young woman in her thirties, was tall and elegant. She was introduced as Judy's psychotherapist who would oversee Judy's personal program.

They led Judy on a tour of the Lodge and the grounds. Everything was even more beautiful than the pictures on the website revealed. They walked at an unhurried pace and took time to answer all her questions. "Yes, they were members of Trinitus. No, they do not recruit people to move to a Trinitus City. No, they do not promote any spiritual discipline or religion." By the time the tour ended, she knew where everything was located and sensed that they were living by a high set of principles. They exuded a sense of calm and peacefulness. Judy marveled that the woman, who was in charge of this whole facility, cared enough to take the time to show her around and make her feel comfortable.

When they passed Angela's office in the right wing, she suggested Judy call the court and notify them that she is enrolled in the New Hope Substance Abuse Residential Program. Once that was handled, Angela smiled warmly and said with sincerity, "It is nice to meet you, Judy. I hope you will find your time with us to be rich and rewarding. Now I will leave you in Lisa's able hands. I am always in my office in the mornings, feel free to stop by."

Lisa led her to a spacious bedroom with a comfy bed covered with a lovely fluffy comforter with a large lace fringe. There was a dresser, nightstand, and small bookcase built into the wall beside a small closet. Beside it stood a full-length mirror. On its frame were carved the words, "You are loving, worthy of love, and loveable." Neatly folded on the bed were a robe and pajamas. On the floor was a pair of fuzzy slippers.

Judy was given a bag for her clothes, shoes, and personal items along with the assurance that her clothes would be returned clean and pressed when she was ready to leave.

"Why does everybody have to wear pajamas?" Judy asked.

Lisa smiled. Everyone always asks that question. "There are many reasons but the simplest is that these loose soft clothes are very comfortable. You will feel more casual and relaxed in them. You will find it a relief to be free of tight binding clothes."

"Oh, I see."

Lisa also pointed out that six more pairs of pajamas were in her dresser, so she could change daily. There was a specific drawer for her to put dirty clothes to be washed and returned.

Lisa led her to the right wing where her office was located. It was the first one on the right. The room was furnished with two loveseats facing each other, a desk, recliner, and extra-large pillows on the floor. Judy looked around and chose to sit on a love seat, so Lisa picked up a folder from her desk and sat down on the opposite one facing Judy.

Producing a pen from her breast pocket, she asked, "Judy, why do you think your here?" Her tone was warm and friendly.

"Because my daughter betrayed me to Child Services at the clinic," Judy said in a matter-of-fact tone.

"Do you think you had any part in what happened?" asked Lisa.

"Well, to tell you the truth, no, not really. I drank a glass or two of wine when I got home after a hard day's work, to relax. My daughter decided that I have a drinking problem. My husband left us a few months ago, and she wants to stay with him. She is using my drinking as an excuse. She got me in trouble with the courts, just so she could live with him. I was given custody of the children during the week and James was to have them for the weekends. This wasn't enough for her. She wanted to go to school in his community."

"I see, so you think this is all about your daughter wanting to go away, not about your drinking?"

"Yes, exactly, I am glad you understand," Judy naively responded. "Child Services believed Sandra's lies and assumed I had a real drinking problem. Between that girl and her father, they convinced the judge that I am an alcoholic."

"Do you think being here will be a waste of your time?" asked Lisa.

"No, not really. I have been under a lot of stress lately. I can use a vacation," Judy answered honestly.

"It is unusual for the court to send someone here just on one person's word. Did anything else happen that prompted the court to require you to go to a facility?"

"Well, there was a mix up at the clinic. The doctor called Child Services because my kids showed up alone. You see, I went to the store and my son bumped his head on a shelf. My daughter did not call me or let me know that there was a problem at home. I didn't know until the clinic called.

"I had a long hard day at work, then I had to go shopping, so on the way home, I stopped in for a drink. The children went to the clinic without me, which made the doctor suspicious, so they called Child Services.

"I went to pick them up, and boy did I get the evil eye from that doctor. Then suddenly a Social Worker appeared and started questioning me and told me not to drive home. What was I supposed to do with my car? It is new and in perfect condition, there is no way I was going to just walk away and leave it in the parking lot. It might not have any wheels on it by morning. You know how San Bernadino is. I only had one little drink, and my house was only a couple of miles away so I carefully drove home. I knew I was sober enough to drive, but the cops were lying in wait for me. It was a trap, a set up."

"Judy, frankly, our program will not be able to help you. First you must be willing to take responsibility for being intoxicated while driving. There was a reason the police arrested you and the court insisted that you go to a rehab center."

"The cops are just out to collect fines. The legal limit is set so ridiculously low that they think one drink makes you an alcoholic. I can't walk a line that straight even stone sober?" Judy was getting frustrated with this stupid line of thought. Lisa was just beating a dead horse.

"You were warned not to drive, and the alcohol content of your blood was over the limit."

"Yes, technically, but more importantly, my daughter set me up. She went to the clinic without calling me first. If she had called, I would not be sitting here talking to you right now. Child Services would not have gotten involved, and the cops would not have been waiting to catch me."

"Maybe your daughter brought it to light, but you were drinking. If you had not been drinking, none of this could have happened. Can you agree to that?"

"I suppose so, but that doesn't make me an alcoholic."

"How much do you drink?"

"Normally, just a couple of glasses of wine after work."

"Does that mean that lately you have been drinking more than normally?" asked the therapist.

"Look, you have to understand, I just came through a divorce. I've been under a lot of stress lately. Then my teenage daughter snitches on me to the court. Teenagers are impossible! Because of her, I can no longer have a little drink in my own house, so that left me no choice, but to stop in at the bar on way home from work."

"If I understand you correctly, you said that you are drinking on the sly after the judge warned you not to, and you usually have two or more glasses of wine on most worknights. Is that correct?

"Yes, but you make it sound bad," Judy objected as her voice grew louder and more frustrated.

"I am just repeating what you said," Lisa said softly. Do you ever drink more than two drinks?"

"I am not an alcoholic! I don't drink at work, and I don't drink in the morning! I only have a few at night to relax. I should be able to do whatever I want in the privacy of my own home. I am not hurting anyone. Anyway, I can quit whenever I want."

"That is a description of a Functioning Alcoholic.' When was your last drink?"

"The day I was arrested."

"So, you have now been sober for four days?"

"Five, counting today. I promised my kids that I wouldn't drink, so I haven't."

"I am glad to hear that, and I am here to help you reach that goal. We will meet once a day, and you will attend group meetings twice a day. They could be an AA meeting or a therapeutic process group. You will be accountable for a writing assignment every week and participation in art projects. Creative projects provide non-verbal expressions. You can watch a film at night, go for walks, work in the gardens, exercise in the gym or in the pool once a day. You are welcome to use the spa, sauna, or the swimming pool, and receive massages in your unstructured free time.

"Do you have any questions?"

"Not exactly. I would like some information on Trinitus, at some point before I leave."

"Okay, I'll give you the URL for our website and there are books on Trinitus in the library. The activities I listed are mandatory. You will need to have a buddy to go to the pool or spa and you must notify a staff member."

"Okay, got it."

Judy was feeling a little frustrated with this woman for trying to brainwash her into thinking she is an alcoholic. Then she realized that this place may look like a resort, but it is a rehab center. She figured that they are required to label her an alcoholic to justify keeping her here.

"Please write a hundred words on what you think you can learn here and what sober will look like when you get out. In other words, what will you gain from being sober? Please have it ready by our meeting tomorrow. Would you prefer writing in a notebook or emailing it to me?"

Judy chose an old-fashioned notebook, one of those black and white composition books. It seemed quaint and portable. She thought she might want to find a place in the meditation garden to write.

"Judy, I'm glad you are here. This is an opportunity to transform your life; and lay a strong foundation upon which to build an even more successful way of living. We will meet each day before the Morning Meeting in the Great Room, which is starting now. I will walk you there."

The two women entered the Great Room. Lisa made her way to the back where staff members were standing, and Judy looked around. She saw a couple of vacant places on the sofas, but did not feel like sitting next to anyone, and the chairs were all taken, so she grabbed a large pillow and sat on the floor.

Judy noticed there were four kitchen people, the director Angela, and eight staff members wearing purple suits and white shirts with their names embroidered in white on black lapels.

A short balding man, sitting on a recliner among the guests, introduced himself as Frankie and started the group. He passed out laminated excerpts of Life Affirmations. Then he went over the rules for this meeting and the steps to a successful recovery. Three people were asked to read these inspirational words and then the sharing would begin.

"I am Frankie. We see you. I will be your facilitator for today. Before we begin, let's say, "Hi," to Judy, our newcomer."

"Hi Judy," everyone said in unison.

"Would you like to tell everyone how you got here? You are welcome to start the sharing or pass and watch for a while," he offered.

"I'll pass," said Judy with an embarrassed blush.

One at a time, people talked about their day, yesterday, or something that they realized while journaling. Some talked about how much they missed their families. Others talked about their struggle to stay sober. A few guests could not resist telling wild tales about the things they did when they were drunk. Alcohol was not the only addiction for some.

Each person began their sharing by saying their name and addiction. Judy realized, if she wanted to talk, she would have to say she was an alcoholic. This did not sit well with her. She refused to label herself like this.

At the end of the sharing circle, Frankie turned back to Judy again and invited her to share. Again, she declined.

When the meeting ended, Judy was told to report to the art room in half an hour, so she wandered over to the library and perused the bookshelves. She thumbed through the Big Book on the Twelve Steps of *AA* and noted there were books on drugs and alcohol, self-help books, a large set of books by Neil Donald Welch, and books on the Trinitus Cities, but there was no Fiction for just reading pleasure. She looked over the schedule on her pad and thought about going to the spa after art class.

The art room was a little daunting. She wasn't the artsy type. Tania, a tall woman with curly black hair, welcomed her and asked what she would like to work on. When Judy gave her a blank look, she rattled off a list, "We have painting, chalk drawing, Lego's, beading, crochet, and scrapbooking. There are also coloring books and puzzles of all kinds."

"May I think about if for a minute?" she asked and Tania smiled, nodded, and walked away. Judy did not know what to choose. Doing a useless activity to fill her time was something she never did. She was a workaholic. She either worked, rested, or shopped. She did not know how to choose, so she just sat on a stool next to a table watching those around her work on their creations.

Tania returned a few minutes later and asked, "Have you decided on something for today, just to begin?"

"I don't know," replied Judy honestly bewildered. "I never had a hobby. I work or rest, I never took time for this kind of thing."

"What did you like to play with as a child?" Tania asked.

"I played house and made believe I was shopping with my dolls. I had a big, beautiful dollhouse and a plastic kitchen set my size. I never did an art thing of any kind."

"I would suggest you come over here to the Lego table. You can use the Legos to build a big, beautiful dollhouse and we have Lego people you can put in it." The table had various colored metal plates stuck along one side. Against the wall behind the table was a cabinet filled with drawers that had colored knobs. Inside the drawers were Lego pieces sorted by type and color that matched the drawer knobs.

"I'm not a kid anymore. I'm not going to pretend like a kid." She walked over to the Lego table behind Tania.

"The point of this class is to be creative and let your Inner Child come out to play. Relaxing is part of it and so giving expression to the hurt part of your child self," Tania patiently explained."

"I don't have a hurt child self," said Judy with strong conviction. "I had great parents."

"Craft time is a healing process, and it will help you unwind. Try the Legos for today. Tomorrow you can do something else if you want."

Tania opened a drawer in a small file cabinet and took out a folder of ideas with easy instructions for building various styles of houses and offered it to Judy.

"Look through this folder and find something you like," Tania smiled compassionately and walked away.

Tania was gone and Judy remained standing there looking at the file like it was written in Greek. A round jolly looking man with a bulbous nose was sitting at the table building a firehouse and firetrucks out of Legos. Judy watched him for a while. He looked totally engaged in what he was doing. Finally in resignation, she sighed and opened the file.

"It's easier than it looks and it's fun," said the man with the fire truck. "Hi, I'm Jake. Would you like me to help you get started?" he offered with a smile.

"This is a kid's toy. Why are they making us play like kids? I don't get it," she sighed again.

"It helps me get in touch with my feelings. It's also an outlet for things I felt when I was a kid. Sometimes talking is just not enough." He laughed just a little nervously. "At least, we don't have to play with puppets, they are the worst."

"Puppets?" She didn't catch his meaning.

"Yeah, my son, he is eleven. His therapist used puppets with us. I had to pretend my puppet was saying things to me from my son. You know, things I thought he would say to me, if he could. When it was his turn, his puppet told me things I never realized. It was really painful and revealing. I found out that my sweet little son was afraid of me when I drank. The whole thing was really hard. After that I decided to come here."

She looked at him, not knowing what to say. "Oh, my son yelled at me for drinking and my daughter reported me to Child Services."

"Out of the mouths of babes. It really pulls you out of your own bullshit, don't it?" Jake lamented shaking his head.

"Yeah," was all she could say. She was not willing to open up to a stranger. Anyway, what could she tell him? That she does not have a problem with drinking and coming here was just her husband's way of stealing her kids.

Judy wanted to end this awkward conversation, so she started flipping through the folder. She came across a design that reminded her of her old dollhouse. The instructions looked easy enough, so she decided she could do it. It looked like a puzzle in 3D where you knew where all the pieces went.

By the end of the two-hour session, she was not finished. She wanted to stay a little longer to make a few modifications to the model, so it would match her childhood dollhouse. Tania offered to stay behind and Jake stayed too. He was putting the final touches on his firehouse. There were a few others that stayed for an extra hour.

Instead of going to the spa during her open time, she stayed, because she could not leave her house unfinished. Her obsessive, compulsive, perfectionism was in full swing.

"Legos are fun, a little hard on the fingers and manicured fingernails, but definitely fun," she said to Jake. He sat back and scrutinized his project, trying to decide whether it was done or not.

"I used to play with Legos a lot with my son, when he was little. I guess my drinking got in the way after that, Jake shared with her."

"I never bought my kids Lego's because I thought they would wind up on the floor and I would step on them. It was hard to get my son Sammy to put his toys away when he was little. Maybe I should have gotten Sandra and Sammy some. I didn't because I like being bare foot in the house," Judy justified what she saw as a mistake at this moment.

"Yep, that can be a problem. Stepping on them can hurt," he agreed. "I'm going to meditate on the porch. I'll see you around," Jake said as he walked out.

She gave him a distracted wave as she pondered her next piece. She was almost done when Tania came over and told her it was time for lunch.

"Judy, this is lovely. You have done very well. It is Lunch Time, so you should stop now."

"Oh, can't I stay for just another minute?"

"Don't worry, it is not going anywhere, you can come back and finish it later," Tania reassured her.

"I didn't think I was going to enjoy this as much as I did. Please just another few minutes," Judy pleaded.

"It will be here for you. Now go to lunch."

Judy reluctantly gave in.

Lunch turned out to be quite good for a vegetarian meal. There was still a free half hour before she had to go on a scheduled walk, so she decided to go back to the art room. On the way, she ran into Lisa.

"Judy, how are you doing so far?" Lisa asked with sincere interest.

"Okay, I guess. I built a house with Lego's. I did not realize how much fun they could be."

"I think they're one of the best creative toys out there," Lisa said with a smile.

"Didn't you have them as a child, or play with your children's Legos?" Lisa asked.

"No, I only bought them educational Video Games that would teach them something. I didn't think Legos were educational.

"Sounds like you're really involved with your kids."

"Not as much as I should be. Now that they are older, they keep to themselves. They are so busy with their online friends and video games, plus things have gotten more hectic at work."

"Oh, how so?" Lisa asked, sincerely interested.

"I'm in charge of several million-dollar accounts. I have a lot more responsibility now than I had when they were little, and I was just starting out. Sometimes I also need to work at home on my ComPad."

"It sounds like there are a lot of demands on you. Did you ever think about taking a break?"

"I am on a break now. It is not easy. I'm worried that my assistant, Mandy, will mess something up while I'm gone, and I could lose my job over it. I told her not to call me. She has Butch, if she needs help. He is rather reliable. I told them I am on Maternity Leave for a high-risk pregnancy to cover my time here.

I'm under a lot of stress, that's why I have a drink after work. Now, with the divorce, it's even worse."

"Have you thought of telling your boss that it feels like you are carrying too many accounts?"

"Oh! Look at the time! Thanks for chatting with me. I need to go outside right now to meet a group of people to go on a hike," she hurried off, feeling relieved to escape.

Judy was enjoying the fresh air, the mulch smell of the forest, the brilliant colors, and the fluid grace of her body as she hiked. Jake sidled up to her. "Hi, me again, do you like swimming?" he asked.

Confused by the out of the blue question, she answered, "I guess so, why?"

"Because we need a buddy to go swimming, so I was thinking that you and I could go together. My swimming buddy just left, and I don't have anyone to swim with. Most of these people have no interest in the pool, aside from their exercise class. The walk back to the main house can be a bit chilly when you are wet, and the dressing rooms are too steamy from the hot tub to dress in them. I was hoping that we could go sometime," All those words left him a little winded. He caught his breath and wheezed.

"Oh, I see. Okay, if you are willing to do a trade-off. Come with me to go to the spa."

"Ok, it's a deal," Jake gave her a warm smile.

At first, the afternoon sun was comfortable, but then it grew hotter and a nasty wind picked up. A few of the guests complained about the wind, so Ade, the young Nigerian man leading the hike, cut it short. He took them back inside and went into a small room just inside the front doors beside the Great Room. He led them through a series of stretching exercises until the time was up. This gave Judy an opportunity to count the number of guests. There were twenty-two.

Judy still had an hour before dinner, so she decided to go to the spa. She told Jake, and Ade called Paul, a staff member, over to accompany them. Ade also announced it to the group, in case someone else wanted to join them. One lady wanted to go too.

Judy remembered her from the morning meeting. Her name was Sasha. Now that Judy had another partner, Jake bowed out and said, "Next time, you have no partner, I owe you one."

Sasha introduced herself to Judy and they happily followed Paul to the spa. He was a big man, but very light on his feet, like he had once been a dancer. On the way, he introduced himself and asked what kind of massage they wanted. He also explained that while he was giving one woman a massage, the other one could luxuriate in the steam room, relax with a facial mask on, sit in the hot tub or do a foot detoxing soak. He offered to show them a list of the other services they could choose from, but Judy stopped him. She asked Sasha if she was willing to go first so she could do a foot soak. Sasha was delighted and chose a hot rock massage.

Judy chose to go second because she wanted to see if Paul was a good masseur. She was nervous about him being a man. He directed Sasha to the dressing room where she found a two-piece bathing suit. It would cover her private parts while giving him access to the rest of her body.

While she was changing, he set up the detox foot soak for Judy and put the rocks up to cook. Sasha jumped up onto the massage table. He turned on some soothing music and they began to relax. Judy could see that he was very professional and respectful.

Judy closed her eyes, leaned back and let her mind drift. She could come to like this kind of pampering. Boy does this beat that other prison like facility. When she opened her eyes a few minutes later, she was surprised to see the black foam in the water that had come from her feet. Paul suggested that she come back and do another soak later on this week to get more toxins out.

Judy listened to Sasha softly moaning. Apparently, she loved the hot stone massage. Paul turned this woman into a limp noodle. When he was done, he wrapped Sasha in a warm-mud body mask and she laid there content to bask in a cocoon of pleasure, while Judy received her massage.

Judy was more relaxed now and more willing to trust him. He was very gentle with her, but it brought her to tears during the massage. It had been so very long since she last let go and just relaxed. A lot of stored tears rushed to the surface. She felt overwhelmed. He ignored her tears but periodically cooed, "Relax, relax, let it all go."

She was embarrassed. He could feel the emotions moving through her. As his hands worked on her sore body, he softly whispered, "This is a time of detox. Your body is releasing toxins, physically through your feet and emotionally through your tears. Relax into them. These tears are just what you need. Release the tension. Release the tears, Release the stress. Release and let go."

His soothing voice lulled her into letting go more and more. By the end of the session, rivers of tears were flowing down her cheeks. He caressed her softly on her cheeks with a light tender and caring touch. It quieted her down. Then he said he was leaving, but she should stay as long as she liked. He returned to help Sasha up and led her to the shower to rinse off the mask.

Judy's sobs slowly subsided and she returned to a more relaxed version of her usual composed self. He invited her to come again so he could work out more of the trauma in her body and led her to another shower.

The two women walked back in contemplative silence. Dinner was already being served. They were running a little late. Judy had a voracious appetite as though filling a big empty space within her. She loved the savory breaded tilapia with a creamy cashew sauce and a medley of vegetables on rice.

After dinner, Judy sat down to do her writing assignment. She wrote, "I am not a drunk. I am under a lot of stress. I agree that drinking from stress may not have been good for my body and my kids." What else was there to write? She just stared at the pad.

She knew that her therapist was going to call this journal entry excuses and denials, but it was her truth. She had to look like she was trying to heal herself, but she didn't know how to do it honestly. She looked at her drinking and tried to see it as too much, but she didn't think it was, at least before the divorce it wasn't. Lately, it has been getting a little out of hand. But didn't she stop right after the arrest? Doesn't that prove she is not addicted? It proved that she could stop at any time.

She asked herself if she missed it. "Sure, she did. The wine was the only true friend she could count on. That does not make it an addiction. She admitted, but only to herself, that she was experiencing some symptoms from quitting. Her boss noticed that she was not feeling well and made a comment, which gave her the idea of lying to him about having a difficult pregnancy.

She lay back on the big sofa and closed her eyes. Writing was exhausting. This was difficult for her. These people refused to see that she was not an alcoholic. If she ever wanted to get out of here, she would have to play along with them, but to identify herself as an alcoholic in a group was so demeaning and untrue. Should she just say what they want her to say to get through the program? She hated to lie. She was sure the words would get stuck in her throat. She crumpled up her journal entry and started again. She wrote about the questions and thoughts in her mind, at least that would be honest, without her having to admit anything. She wrote that life without drinking would make her feel healthier and give her more energy. She would cultivate creative outlets for her stress and go for weekly massages to keep the stress out of her body. She did not mention that she could not afford weekly massages, but it sounded good and filled the space.

It was time for the night meeting. People filtered into the Great Room in twos and threes. She was early enough to snag a seat on a sofa. Sasha slipped in beside her. 'Hi, Judy. She looked up and smiled' It was time to put her book away. 'Hi' Sasha.

"Are you feeling better?" Sasha asked her.

"I'm fine. It was just the stress pouring out of me, that's all." Judy replied with a quick smile. "How did you come to end up here?" she asked to move the conversation off her.

"I was arrested during a drug bust in my apartment," Sasha said in a matter-of-fact voice that surprised Judy. "My boyfriend is a small-time dealer, just pot, but it was not legally grown." She smiled like that was a fine thing to be involved in.

This did not match Judy's idea of her. She was so innocent looking, small framed and too cute for a drug dealer's girlfriend. Judy did not know what to say. She was shocked.

When Judy did not answer, Sasha said, "Sorry, I just thought we could just get to know each other."

Judy blurted out, "You don't seem the drug dealer's girlfriend type to me, that's all. I was surprised."

Sasha laughed. "I'm not really. I didn't know he was selling it. I just thought they were friends of his that came over to smoke with him. I was too drunk to catch on, I guess. I did not care enough to see what was going on."

"Oh well, to tell the truth, I'm not an alcoholic. I just drank a few wines at night to relax. I'm only here because my daughter saw getting me busted as an opportunity to live with her father instead of me. She ratted me out to the Child Services and the divorce court. She made my drinking sound much worse than it was."

"Oh, that is so unfair," Sasha said with a pouty face. "I don't think being drunk at a party in my own apartment is grounds for me to have to come here either. It was this or jail, so here I am."

"That does seem extreme. You should be able to party in your own home."

Jose, another guest, overheard their conversation and interjected. "I think you two are swimming in *DeNile*."

"What?" Judy snapped. She did not like him butting into her conversation.

"You know, the river of sob stories, in Egypt. You are both in denial about your addictions."

"I'm not in denial of anything. You can stick your nose up your own ass, mister!" Judy growled.

Frankie came into the room carrying his meeting binder and was on his way to his seat, when he heard what Judy said.

"Woe let's watch the language, Judy. Calm down. What is the fuss here?"

"This man is butting in on conversations that is none of his business." Judy pointed at Jose.

"I'm just trying to help," Jose held up his hands like he was under arrest.

"I see. It sounds like you need to keep your two cents to yourself again, Jose." Frankie said gently. "Can you let this go, Judy?"

"I guess." She tried to sound sincere and failed.

Judy sat and stewed for a few minutes. Sasha left her alone. After the readings, when the sharing began, Jose was eager to share.

"Jose, alcoholic." Everyone except Judy said "Hi, Jose," in unison.

"I've been thinking about how much I sometimes go into denial about my drinking. I had two years clean and sober. Then I thought I could drink again without having a problem. Sure enough, I got another drunken driving arrest. I thought I could just have a beer or two one night and stay home. I wouldn't be driving, so I couldn't get arrested. But within a week, I was drinking a six-pack and driving to get another one. It is amazing how an alcoholic can think it is okay to have one or two drinks at a party once in a while, and that it's not going to lead them to drink all the time again. We lie to ourselves, and we don't even know it. Thank you." He was looking at Judy the whole time he was telling his story.

She burst out yelling at him, "You don't know me. You don't know my story. You don't know anything about me!"

"Judy, no cross talking. I know you're upset with him, but he has the right to share his story. Jose, it was wrong of you to direct your words at her."

"This is bullshit!" Judy stood up and yelled at Jose.

"I don't have to take this from anyone. I'm a successful Advertising Executive and I am NOT an alcoholic!"

"Judy, please take a breath and calm down."

Frankie got up and stood in front of her so she could no longer glare at Jose who was smiling tauntingly at her.

"Breathe slowly, breathe. Please sit down and relax." Frankie tried to get her eyes on him. He leaned his head down toward hers until he caught her eyes. "Let's breathe together for a minute." He patiently matched her quick shallow breaths for a moment and then slowly slowed his own breath. Hers slowed down as well.

Judy was embarrassed now. She had let this worm get her goat. Normally, she ignored worms like him. She prided herself on how she did not let people get under her skin. Finally, she sat down, scowled at Jose and looked away. She planned to ignore him and told herself that such a miserable little man probably has a miserable little life. He is not worth her anger.

"Okay Judy," Frankie sat down too. "Do you want to share your story with the group?"

"No, not really. I'm not convinced that I'm an alcoholic. So, I'm not going to call myself one. It seems to be required before I can speak in this meeting."

"You can share without calling yourself an alcoholic, just state your name and begin," Frankie soothingly offered.

Then he took a breath and added, "Why do you think you're not an alcoholic?"

"I don't drink all day long. I stopped the day I decided to. I just have a few drinks after work, but I don't drink all the time."

"Do you drink every night after work?" Frankie gently asked.

"Yes, but I quit when I was arrested. I will not drink again either. I can control it."

"What were you arrested for?"

"Drunken driving, but that was because my kids went to the clinic without letting me know. I was just having one drink after work when the Clinic called, and I had to pick them up. My daughter set me up and got me in trouble."

"I see. How many here, with a show of hands, think drinking every night is alcoholism." Twenty out of the twenty-four residents raised their hands, and all the staff did as well.

Judy looked around. "Well, you're all wrong! You don't know me. I have control. I stopped on a dime, and I can stay sober for as long as I need to. I don't have to drink. I have excellent self-control," she said with conviction.

"How long have you been drinking every night?" Frankie asked gently.

"I don't know, awhile. My work is very stressful. My husband has been losing jobs for years and the bills have been piling up. I need to make more and more money just to keep up. I see nothing wrong with relaxing a little when I get home." Judy was getting frustrated with him.

"If I understand you correctly, you drink to deal with your stress, right?

"Yes."

"I am sorry to tell you, but that is classic alcoholism," Frankie stated.

"I just do it to relax, that's all," Judy shrugged.

"If you can't relax without a few drinks that is alcoholism. You will have to determine that for yourself, but many here know it is easy to fool yourself into thinking that daily drinking is nothing. It's not nothing. It can ruin your life and has for many of us." Frankie was trying to help her without pushing her too hard.

Judy was not convinced, but she didn't want to be the focus anymore either, so she sat down, and the meeting moved on. Many people shared about their own denial and what it took for them to be convinced that they were fooling themselves. Two women said they were successful professionals like her, and they too only drank at night until it got worse for them. They started to drink at work, or they drank too much at night and it eventually affected the quality of their work. Judy listened and was sure it could not happen to her. She remained firm in her resolve.

At the end of the meeting, Judy got up to go to her room. Everyone else stayed while ComPads were passed out. It was time to call home, play games, or surf the net. She turned around when Lisa called out her name. "Judy, do you want your pad?"

"Oh, yes!" Judy came back. She checked her email and found a lot of congratulations on her pregnancy from co-workers, but no email from Sammy. She wrote to him saying that she was fine and missed him. Tears came to her eyes, and she went to her room for the night.

The next day, she awoke exhausted. She spent most of her dreamtime arguing with Jose who kept morphing into James and sometimes into her dad or mom. She was driving on a country road that climbed a very steep hill. She had to drive over the hill, but the road was unpaved, and the ruts were deep enough to swallow her car. It was all very disturbing.

The next morning bright and early, Sandra begrudgingly went to her therapy meeting with Lisa right after breakfast.

Lisa was warm and friendly, but Judy was guarded.

Yesterday, you said that you felt like there were a lot of demands on you and you needed a break. You have been under a lot of stress, which is why you were drinking, correct?" Judy cautiously nodded. "You also said that since the divorce, your stress has gone up at work. I think we left off at the point where you were going to tell me about your boss.

"There is nothing really to tell. He trusts me to do my job well and I don't want him to think otherwise. It has taken me a long time to get where I am. I can't just say, 'I'm tired I need to cut back on hours and accounts.' I need the job, and I need the money. I have two teenagers to raise, and they cost a lot!"

What keeps you from being honest with your boss?" Lisa pressed her a little.

"Not wanting to get fired! Even if I don't lose my job, I will be given fewer opportunities. I can't ruin my standing at work, I just have to try harder, that's all."

"Why?"

"Because that is how it is done!"

"Does that mean, you are going to do everything he hands you until you crumble? You are just going to let him keep piling it on until you crack? You have no choice in this? You believe he has the right to keep expecting more and more from you and you will comply without any regard for your health and well-being?"

Judy just sat there confused for a bit.

"Ok I get what you're saying, but I can do this. It is just stressful. I need to keep my position strong at the company, especially now that I'm divorced. I am on my own, with no one to depend on and we are deep in debt."

"The reality is, you can choose to work less, and have less, if need be, if you are willing to safeguard your health. Isn't your health more important than your job or drinking to cope with your job?"

"Sure, I can go to City of Hope and sit on my ass like my husband does! Is that what you think I should do?" Judy said sarcastically.

"I am saying that you have choices. You are making choices. I am just questioning whether you are choosing the healthiest options. Perhaps you could choose otherwise. You are in charge of your life, not your boss, and not your bills. You are choosing to carry the stress and drink rather than face your boss and tell him you are carrying too heavy a load for a mother with two teenage children. You can change your life if you choose to."

"So, you are saying that I should sell the house and live in a small condo, tell my boss that my limit is four accounts and cross my fingers that I don't get fired."

"That is one viable option. The point is to make conscious choices, rather than feel bullied by the people and circumstances around you. What do you need to do to have a sustainable lifestyle? How can you work and still be respectful of your health?"

"Look lady, I have been taking care of myself since I was eleven. I know how to take care of myself! I don't need you to tell me how to do it!" She yelled.

"The question you need to ask yourself is whether your health is as important as your work?" Lisa spoke in a voice smooth as silk and stayed calm.

"Look I get what you are saying, but I was doing fine until my husband jumped ship. He kept losing jobs. He wasn't bringing in the money, so I had to take this promotion. We are up to our asses in debt. And he's got the nerve to blame me for it!"

"So, this is his fault?"

"Yes, it is!" She yelled.

"Did you talk to him about the bills and together try to work up a plan?"

"No. There is no talking to him. It just leads to an argument about what we can or can't afford. I pay the bills as best I can." She sounded defeated now.

Judy thought about those arguments and how he always accused her of overspending. He never understood that someone who works as hard as she does, deserves a few treats to compensate for all that she puts into this family. That is one subject she did not want to touch on.

"Are you having problems talking openly to the men in your life about your needs?"

Judy exhaled loudly. "Yeah, sure, I guess," she said distractedly. She was still recovering from the wave of guilt she felt about her spending.

"What was your relationship like with your dad? Were you able to talk openly with him?"

"He was a good dad and so was my mom. We got along well."

"Was there any time when he demanded too much from you, and you felt you could not talk to him about your needs?"

"No," she said with downcast eyes.

Lisa noticed a sudden shift in Judy's overall energy, her now sunken shoulders and sad face.

"I suggest you give this some thought, and we can come back to it another day."

"Fine."

They clearly touched a nerve, something that Judy did not want to talk about. Lisa decided to shift gears, so she said, "Let's go over your writing assignment."

"I am just getting used to this place, I really haven't had any time yet," Judy lied.

"Well, this might be a good place to stop for now. We can talk again this time tomorrow."

CHAPTER 19

Adjusting

Sandra was excited! Waking up in her father's house in the City of Hope, she smiled brightly as she dressed, combed her hair, and brushed her teeth. Her head filled with plans. First, she would get into school here and make some new friends. Then she was going to get an internship working with animals, which would launch her into a career where she would travel the world helping wildlife. Feeling proud of herself, she spun around and danced off to the kitchen.

Her dad was already up and making breakfast. She skipped across the floor and jumped up onto a high stool beside the island. "Good morning, Dad. What's for breakfast?"

"Pancakes, I thought they might cheer Sammy up a bit. I'm glad to see you're in a good mood."

"Why wouldn't I be, I'm finally here in Hope. I'm ecstatic! Would you like some help?"

"No thanks, I have it, but you can get the plates and wake your brother up."

She knocked, opened the door, and called out, "Wake up sleepy head, Dad is making pancakes for you."

Sammy groaned and threw his pillow at her. He was still mad at his sister. She picked it up and threw it back at his head, just as he ducked under the covers. Sammy pouted and cried most of the way to Hope yesterday. At dinner, Dad tried to make him feel better by talking about the park and saying that now he could practice the bow more often. That did not seem to work. Sammy refused to talk to either of them all day yesterday.

"Your pancakes are getting cold. If you don't get up, I'll eat them all," she called over her shoulder as she walked back to the kitchen.

"I think he is still grumpy," she told her dad.

"Maybe we should give him some time to come around," James said patiently. "Let's go over and enroll you in school. We can give him the weekend to himself."

"I'm not a parent, but I think you are spoiling him. He needs to see his school and realize he will have start over. Once he makes new friends, he'll be just fine."

"Well, you might be right, but let's give him a little time to get with the program. We can get you enrolled first, then we can deal with his school next week."

James put the pancakes on the table and went to Sammy's room. "Hey Sport, are you going to get up for pancakes?"

Sammy peeked out from under his cover and glared at his father. "I don't want to go to a new school."

"I know, but you will have to, sooner or later. I know things are tough on you right now, but it will pass. You'll make new friends, and you can call or text your old ones. We will see about getting you on a soccer team too. Things will get better, I promise," and he sat down on Sammy's bed.

"This is all Sandra's fault. She knew I did not want to come here. It's like Mom said, Sandra didn't call her before we went to the clinic, just to get her in trouble."

"Well, I'll tell you the truth, when I talked to the guy on the phone, it sounded like Child Services got involved because your mom showed up drunk. Whether Sandra called or not, was not going to make the difference. So, maybe you could give your sister a break."

"Why didn't Mom stop after the court told her to? Why did she have to go to the bar and drink?" Sammy started to cry. Why did this have to happen to me? Why did you have to leave us?"

"If I stayed, I would have been miserable, and your mom would have kept drinking. She has an addiction. We used to yell at each other. It was not good for any of us. It really was inevitable that this would happen. The schools here are better for you, safer too. The whole city is. You'll see, you can have a good life here and over time you will come to be happier. Just give yourself some time to adjust." He rubbed the boy's head affectionately.

"I'm mad at Mom for drinking. I don't want to be, but I am." He rubbed his wet eyes.

"That's okay. You can be mad at someone and still love them at the same time. It is normal, you have the right to be mad. It's okay."

"Do I have to go to the school today?"

"No, but you need to come with us, unless I ask someone to stay with you. I have a friend who might be able to come over. I'll call her, if you want."

"I want to stay here. I don't want to go anywhere with that girl!" He looked up at his dad to see if he was going to react to his sarcastic tone.

"I'll make the call. Are you going to get out of that bed and eat some of my fine pancakes?"

"Yeah, I guess."

"Ok then. Get dressed."

James grabbed his ComPad and adjusted his wireless headphones for privacy. He called his therapist, canceled his appointment for today, and called Cathy.

"Hi Cathy, I was wondering if you could do me a favor and stay with my son. Are you comfortable with kids? I don't want to leave him alone on his first day here and I need to enroll Sandra in the high school. He is not feeling very sociable today."

"How old is he?"

"Fourteen. He can take care of himself, but this is a strange new place for him and he is feeling sad about his mother. She got arrested, so now they are both going to be with me."

"Oh my, that is sad for her, but lucky for you. Now you have your kids. That is wonderful!"

"Can you stay with him? You can call me if anything comes up, but I think he will be fine with you."

"Sure, I'll give it a go. Do you want me to come over right away?"

"Yes, if you can. I made pancakes, if you want some?"

"Thanks, I already ate, but I can come right over to meet him. I'll grab an electric bike and see you in a few minutes.

Cathy bounced in smiling and bright. She said hello to Sandra and Sammy. They briefly went over the introductions and James left with Sandra.

"So, My New Friend, what would you like to do with this fine day?" Cathy asked Sammy.

"I'm want to go back to bed and maybe text some friends, I'll probably just play some games on my pad." He sounded downcast.

"Okay. The sun is shining, and the day is beautiful. When you feel up to going out, there's lots to explore. Until then, we can just veg." Her heart went out to him.

"Thanks."

James and Sandra entered the high school administration office. Sandra had a bounce to her step. She was struggling to contain all her excitement. After years of planning and dreaming, she was amazed to be here! The principal asked a senior to give them a tour. He was a handsome boy with deep black eyes and mile long eyelashes. He made her feel very welcome and said he looked forward to getting to know her. His words rang in her heart again and again. Every place he showed her peaked her imagination. They offered a great campus, like a small college campus with a lot of amenities.

When they returned to the office, Mr. Salizar, the Grade Advisor, gave her a placement test. Sandra aced the test and was able to stay in her grade, even though this school was more advanced than her last one. They designed a schedule of classes based on her areas of interest and basic requirements. There were seven classes a day instead of the six found in RW schools, one of which she never heard of before, Emotional Intelligence class. This class alternated with study hall. Here they taught essential living skills and how to work with emotions. Another interesting class she chose was called Communication Skills and Unique Forms of Intelligence. She also chose an advanced ComPad class. Once her class schedule was complete, Mr. Salizar gave them a map. Sandra now had a good idea of the layout after her tour, and it was easy to find the rooms she needed.

On the way home, James stopped at a drugstore to get some fresh bandages for Sammy. Sandra went off to spend the afternoon with Tammy in U-Town.

As he entered the house, James asked, "Hi Cathy, how did you two get along while we were gone?"

"Sammy just stayed in his room the whole time. He's still sad and needs to be alone."

James knocked on the door and peeked in. Sammy had his headphones on and was playing a game. James waved at him to let the kid know he was home. Then he shut the door and let him keep on playing.

"Thanks Cathy, for letting him just do his own thing. He needed that and thanks for coming over. I appreciate it."

"He was no trouble at all," she said with a warm smile. "Are you going to enroll him in school too?"

"Not yet. He needs some time to grieve first. He didn't want to come here. I'm going to give him time to decompress, at least for the weekend."

"It looks like a lot has happened. Catch me up. What happened to his head?" Cathy sat on the sofa ready for a long story.

"His mother was drinking. Even though the judge at the court hearing ordered her to stop, she continued to drink. Child Services caught her and was going to report her to the judge. She got mad and went out to drink. Sammy got pissed and started trashing his room. In his frenzy, he hit his head on a shelf. Sandra took him to the Clinic. When Judy got there, they called Child Services because she was drunk. They told her not to drive but she did it anyway. Then the cops grabbed her for drunken driving with minors in the car. So, now she is in an addiction facility for the next two months. If she gets better, the courts may give her partial custody."

"Wow! That is so sad for her. How do you feel about all this?" Cathy asked and placed a hand on his arm to show support.

"Well part of me is glad to have the kids here. This is a better world to grow up in. The other half is nervous. Part of me is mad at her for messing this up like this. Now I must get my life on an even keel and fix theirs too."

"Did you want some time alone for yourself?"

"Yes, I know that seems selfish, but I was looking forward to it."

"It's understandable."

"Anyway, it's just hard now, but kids grow up fast. Pretty soon they will be on their own and I'll have plenty of time alone then."

Sammy walked into the kitchen and asked, "Dad, can I play with my bow now?"

"Sure Buddy, be careful. Remember to set up the target facing away from the exercise field. When you come back in, we can change your bandage."

He grabbed his equipment and walked out onto the back porch

Now that they were alone, James asked Cathy about her divorce.

"He's refusing to sign the papers. My lawyer needs to get the judge to order it. It's typical of him. He thinks he owns me."

"Well, you will be free of him soon enough. Can I get you something to drink? Help yourself to some fresh-made green juice. I am going to keep an eye on Sammy from the window."

"Sure. Hmmm. This tastes better than mine. Text me the recipe, can you? Thanks. I must get on with my day. It has been good to catch up with you. You and your family need some time alone. I'll see you later." She got up to leave.

"Thanks again."

"No problem." She smiled as she left.

James was not sure if he should go out and play with his son or leave the boy alone. He watched Sammy through the window for a few minutes. The kid was taking his frustrations and rage out on the bow. He drew the poor string as hard as he could and shouted every time the arrow hit its' mark. He clearly wanted to kill something.

James decided to leave his son alone and have a cup of tea while he continued to watch.

Earlier, when he spoke to Kim on the ComPad, she suggested that he bring the kids in for counseling as soon as possible. She could arrange a different counselor for each child. When the cup was empty, James strolled out onto the porch and just watched Sammy take a few shots. It was a cool morning, but the sun was up and the day was rapidly growing hot.

After a while, Sammy turned to James and said, "I'm hitting the bullseye more often now. Maybe I can hunt soon. I'd like to get an animal target."

"Well, do you want to go to the park? I think that is the only store with targets available. The bow range is a good place to start practicing, if you want to improve your distance shooting."

"Yeah, that would be great. Can we also have lunch there and eat Indian tacos."

"Sure, no problem," he smiled at his son.

Sammy went into the kitchen and took a cool drink of pineapple juice out of the frig. He wasn't going to try that weird green stuff. When he returned to the porch, he asked, "That lady, is she your girlfriend?"

"No, we are just friends. I think I need to be single for a while."

"Oh." He swung his legs and gently kicked the table leg of the outdoor furniture.

"I probably won't be seeing anyone for a long while, but just for curiosity, would you be upset if I dated?"

"I don't know," he shrugged. "I'd like you and Mom to get back together, but I guess you hate her now."

"I don't hate her. She needs to learn how to be nicer to me and how to stop drinking before I can even think about going back to her. Plus, I like it here, so I would want her to come to Hope."

"Why do you like it here? Is it because they don't use money?"

"That is part of it, but there is little crime here and people here are nicer. You know how you go through those Active Shooter drills at school, well here there is no need to. Everybody goes to counseling and talks about their feelings, so people are happier. They don't get all bottled up and explode the way they do in the RW"

"Oh, I guess that's good." He didn't know what to say.

"My counselor is going to help us find good therapists for you and

Sandra. They will teach us how to communicate what we think and feel more clearly and be honest with each other. Does that sound good to you?"

"Aww, do I have to?" he whined.

"It can help you feel better about your mom and help you make more sense of what happened this week. You're angry and you have a right to be. The new counselor can help you move through these feelings and feel happy again, when you are ready to let go of the anger."

"I don't want to be happy here. I was happy at Mom's," his voice was getting harsher and louder.

James took a deep breath and tried to make his voice softer. As gently as he could he said, "I know you were happy before, and I'm sorry that you could not stay there. Now things have changed and we have to make the best of our new circumstances. Your mom is getting the help she needs and hopefully you will be able to stay with her again afterwards. That is all up to the courts, and how well she recovers. Unfortunately, it is not up to us."

Sammy sat there pouting and idly spun a glass bottle of sparkling fruit juice. James wanted to say more, but he did not want to push him, so they sat quietly together for a while. Then Sammy went to his room and played his games again.

James busied himself with chores around the house, putting away things he bought earlier that week and doing the laundry that the kids brought with them. At lunchtime, he tapped on his son's door and walked in carrying clean clothes. "Are you ready to get lunch?" He said loudly enough to compensate for Sammy's headphones.

"Yeah, I'm starved." He got up and tossed his headphones on the bed.

"When we get back, I can help you unpack and put your room together."

"Sure, okay," Sammy mumbled.

"First, let's put a fresh bandage on your head."

They ate lunch in the Native Village and joined in the dances afterwards. Then they went to the open archery range where they practiced shooting. James hoped that sharing this with the boy would bring them closer. Sammy was so withdrawn; it was hard to reach him.

They were both ready for a more advanced range, one for practiced archers. They found one that had animal targets as well as bullseye ones. Eagle Elk, a Native American instructor, walked around helping anyone who needed it. He gave them both some tips on their stance and pull. It was clear that all his practice was making Sammy the better shot, but James had the muscle strength to get a full pull on his string and was able to drive the arrow farther down range. Eagle Elk showed Sammy how to use the bow as an exercise tool to build up muscle and James how to sight the target better.

Sammy was open to receiving help. This showed he had an

interest in getting better. It gave James hope that the boy would respond well to counseling and be willing to overcome his anger. If he was receptive to counseling, he might eventually come around to loving it here.

They got home at 4:30, the same time as Sandra. Sandra looked happy and Sammy was in better spirits too.

"Do you like that school?" Sammy asked as he hung up his bow and quiver on wall hooks.

"It's great! They created my schedule of classes based on my interests. It is so green. I'm going to do a study on the coyotes in the desert, estimate their real numbers, and look at the effect of feral dogs on the population."

"That sounds exciting," Sammy said sarcastically rolling his eyes and drifted back to his room. James put Sammy's new targets in a closet.

Sandra asked her dad about the animal targets, "Are we teaching Sammy to kill animals now?"

"Well, this is his interest right now," James spoke cautiously knowing her strong feelings on the subject. I hope that Sammy will learn to respect animals too. He is young, it may take a while for him to come to respect all forms of life. Right now, he needs an outlet for his frustrations, disappointments, and having to leave the home he wants to be in."

"Yeah, I get that, but killing animals out of anger and frustrations can only go wrong," Sandra said with deep concern.

"I'm sure his Native American instructors will teach him respect for life. It is core to their philosophy. I'm not too concerned."

Sandra and her dad talked a little more about the school while they worked together making dinner. James enjoyed sharing the kitchen with her.

He was getting quite good at cooking and enjoyed experimenting with different spices. He was determined to cook healthy and delicious meals for his little family. Tonight, he was making a nut encrusted halibut with roasted veggies. It turned out to be quite delicious. To go with it, Sandra made a wonderful salad with a variety of leafy greens, seeds, nuts, and veggies. After dinner, he helped Sammy put his room in order, hoping it would make him feel more at home. Sandra arranged her room by herself.

James and Judy were always vigilant about what kinds of games they allowed their kids to play on the net. They never permitted them to do violent shooting games or kill fantasy monsters either. Sandra had a point, so just to be sure, once Sammy was asleep, James checked his son's gaming list. He was relieved to see that the games were all acceptable. He felt better, but he did begin to question himself whether it was a mistake to get Sammy so involved in the bow. He looked at his motivation and had to admit that he was desperate to make the boy happy being here, and perhaps it was also a way to get the kid to like him more.

James decided to write about his children and his feelings in his journal before bed.

The next day was Saturday, so James suggested going to the park again. Sandra was overjoyed to go on another horseback ride into the canyon. James and Sammy went to the advanced range to practice. On Sunday, they relaxed around the house in the morning. In the afternoon, they went to little boutique shops in U-Town where they found some decorative elements for their rooms and new clothes for school.

By Sunday night, it was time for a talk with Sammy about school. The next day was going to be the first day of the new term. It was important for him to be there. He showed Sammy a website that had amazing pictures of the Ropes Course and all the awesome challenges. Sammy tried to say blasé, but it was hard to not get excited about this totally green obstacle course. All his resistance evaporated in an instant. He was never going to get a chance like this in the RW. He was sure wanted to do it. Then, if the school turned out to be lame, he could go on strike later.

"I guess, if I have to go to this boring school, this is not a bad way to start," he begrudgingly admitted. I hope they have an opening on the soccer team. It is the only thing that would make this school bearable."

"That's the spirit! I will wake you in time tomorrow. Wear loose-fitting clothes and your best running shoes. I'll make you Huevos Rancheros for breakfast."

James accompanied Sammy on the tram. He carried his electric scooter for the return trip. They arrived early so there would be time to introduce Sammy to Butler Johnson, the principal of Hope Middle School. Butler acted super-green, and Sammy liked him immediately. James filled out a few necessary forms and Chase, a young Lakota boy, was asked to be Sammy's partner. Chase asked him what he liked to do and Sammy told him about his bow and how he was already on the advanced shooting range. They became fast friends. Butler assured James that Chase was an exceptional student and a gifted empath. He would be a good guide and companion for his son.

James asked if Sammy could go into the next grade and confided that his son had faced some academic challenges in his last school. He said the boy is slow at math and technical material, but he tries hard. He also told him that Sammy was currently undergoing a difficult separation from his soccer teammates, friends, mother, and home. He warned Butler that the boy might act out a bit but reassured the principal that his son was a good-hearted kid who was usually easy to get along with. He also asked what tests the boy would have to take to decide if he would be held back a grade because this school is more advanced.

Butler reassured the worried father that his son would not be held back. He explained to James, that if the boy has difficulty with certain subjects, he will receive extra tutoring in those areas; and assured him that Sammy would not be judged by his challenges, but rather by his efforts.

"James, your son will be given every opportunity to succeed. Here in HMS, we are dedicated to individual attention. Each student counts. We are aware that there are different forms of intelligence, some are more left brained. They do well in math and memorize facts easily, but that is not the only valuable form of intellect. Some people are slower because they have a broader or deeper approach to the storage and utilization of information. We, in Hope, respect all forms of intelligence. We frame our lessons to accommodate both approaches to learning. Whatever his style, we will discover it and frame his lessons to maximize his strengths and help him feel successful in all his studies."

Butler suggested that Sammy meet with Roger, a high school senior doing a teaching internship as a tutor. He personally called the intern and asked if he was available. Roger said he could be free every day after school. James protested that that would interfere with soccer practice. The young man apologized but insisted that this was the only opening in his schedule. Reluctantly, James agreed. It would only be for a few months until the boy was caught up to his class. He knew this would upset Sammy and dreaded telling him.

As a single father, James was nervous about everything but reassured himself that Sammy would be fine. He was glad the kid ran off with Chase, which saved him from an awkward goodbye.

He was relieved to go back to work, where he knew what he was doing. It was refreshing after a weekend being with the kids, where he was always second guessing himself. Here at work, back on familiar ground, he breathed freely again.

After school, Sammy went home on his eScooter. He mostly remembered the way from his ride on the tram, and he also used the GPS on his Smartwatch. The address of the house was already programed into it.

Back at New Hope, Judy moped around the whole weekend. She did not even receive one email from Sammy, not one! She slouched down in her chair and barely listened during the meetings. She refused to talk, mostly grunted in response to questions, and was generally unresponsive. She still refused to identify herself as an alcoholic or acknowledge that she had a drinking problem. She was adamant that she had a right to drink in her own home, a right she earned by working so hard. She was at a stalemate in therapy and in group process.

Her writings showed no progress. She was also firm in her belief that her mother and father were wonderful parents who provided all that she needed, but her body language never agreed with that statement. There was something else that was buried deep that made her squirm with agitation every time anyone touched on the topic of her childhood. She also had a strange twitch in her eye whenever she talked about how supportive her parents were.

Judy was bored and frustrated with Lisa. The frustration was mutual. Lisa was being patient and approached Judy from several different angles, she asked her a *Chain of Questions*, but whenever Lisa got too close to the truth, Judy would show all these odd behaviors and clam up. Each day she was becoming more withdrawn.

On Sunday evening, Judy saw an email from Sammy and brightened up. It cheered her up for a moment, and then she read what he wrote. Sammy was having so much fun with his new friend Chase and was enraptured with his new school. It was utterly depressing to read. Now she was quite worried that he would never want to come home. She plunged into despair, imagining that she had lost him forever, forever, forever.

In rehab, there was no escape from therapy, even the movies were all about people working through their addictions. Her only escape was the art room and the Lego dollhouse she was continuing to expand. She kept improving the decor and the furniture. She even started to build a bigger house so she could make larger furniture. She also enjoyed going to the spa, sitting in the sauna, swimming in the pool, and receiving massages.

Begrudgingly, she went to therapy and complained about not being home with her son and that he was having too much fun at his dad's place. "That man is spoiling my boy. He won't come home after I'm done here. That whole place is spoiling them! In Real Life there are no freebies. Everyone must work for a living. That's what I do, and I do it well. He is filling their heads with unreal expectations. They will not be able to survive in the Real World after being in that La-La Land. What he is doing to those kids is far worse than my sitting at home and comfortably having a couple of glasses of wine after work. I have a God-given right to do that, and it is nobody's business but my own!"

"Whether or not Sammy comes home will be based on a judge's verdict, not on whether he wants to stay with his father, or on how the man is spoiling him. Can't you be happy for your son? Isn't it better for the boy to be adjusting and getting along well rather than being depressed and moping? Isn't it good that he has a friend? Would you prefer that he was miserable?" Lisa tried to expand Judy's perspective.

Judy didn't respond, she just glared at her. "You come from a Trinitus City; how can I talk to you? You are just brainwashed. You think people can live without money and no one needs to work."

Lisa laughed, "I put in ten hours a day, six days a week. It is interesting to hear that I am not working. It sounds like you're a little jealous of your ex-husband's situation." Lisa stated, or baited, hoping for a response. Any response would be better than her moping.

"Jealous, I'm not jealous. James is just being lazy as usual. He could never hold down a job for very long and now he doesn't have to."

"Trinitus helps everyone find work, so I'm sure he's doing

something. Do you blame him because you are working so hard?"

"I would be doing what I'm doing now regardless, but I do blame him for the debt he put us in because of his inability to hold down a job, and I blame him for pilfering the children's college fund." She exaggerated. It was easier to blame him, especially since he was not here to defend himself.

Lisa watched Judy as she shifted and looked away to the left. She knew Judy was distorting something she said.

"Judy, I want to understand your perspective. Please help me get the facts straight. If you like what you're doing at work, why does it stress you out so much? When did you start drinking on a regular basis?"

"I have always had a glass of wine or two when I got home from work. It's my treat for a hard day's work. I'm entitled to it." Judy picked at her pajamas and smoothed them out instead of looking at Lisa. She had an air of entitlement. Her legs were crossed, so were her arms, and her chin was raised high.

"If I understand you right, twice you said that you deserve wine at the end of your day, correct?

Judy raised her head higher and said, "Yes," in a defiant tone.

"What creates this sense of being entitled to your wine? Why do you need to have a treat after working?" Lisa probed.

"I work hard. There's a lot of stress involved and the wine unstresses me. Why is that so hard for you to understand? I deserve to relax," Judy was getting testy.

"You're right, everyone deserves to relax after a hard day's work. What confuses me is why you think you must have wine to relax. Aren't there other ways you can relax, perhaps ways that don't involve wine?"

"We've gone over this so many times," Judy said impatiently. I'm not drinking anymore. I'm here. I am relaxing in different ways, aren't I?"

"Please answer my question. How can you relax without wine?"

"Look," Judy said curtly, "I'm not addicted to wine. I shouldn't have to go through this BS. This is just a huge misunderstanding," Judy avoided Lisa's gaze again.

Lisa said very softly, "I want to believe what you are saying. I am confused because you are communicating two different things at the same time. Your words say one thing and your body is saying another. Which one am I to believe?

Lisa could see that Judy was ready to protest, so she held up her hand to signal, stop. "All I ask is that you ponder these questions for one day. How can you relax without wine? Why would your words say one thing and your body says the opposite? Which one is true? Are you trying to deceive me? Or are you deceiving yourself?"

Judy was about to repeat her usual monologue, when Lisa jumped in and said, "Please don't answer now. I just ask that you spend today thinking about it. It would serve you just to be with the questions and find out what your truth is."

Judy glared at Lisa. The heat was rising to her cheeks. In anger, she spit out the words, "I don't know what you're talking about! I don't lie to people and I don't lie to myself. I don't have a problem!"

"You're raising your voice. Why would you get so upset if you were not stuck between two beliefs and feeling trapped?

"I'm raising my voice because you frustrate me!" Judy screamed at her therapist. "You are trying to brainwash me into believing I am an alcoholic. You refused to accept the truth! I don't need alcohol, and I don't have a problem!"

"I want to give you ample time to think about my questions and write about them, "Lisa quietly continued. "Just write your truth, then sit quietly, and feel the words in your body. Do they feel right and true? Do they give you a peaceful relaxed feeling? Or do they make you feel unrest, agitated, unresolved? This is between you and you. Don't waste your energy fighting, rebelling against, and resenting me. Just be honest with yourself. That's all I ask. We have been meeting early in the day, so tomorrow, let's meet in the evening, so you have plenty of time to do this assignment."

Lisa took a deep breath and relaxed her own body. She did not like having to be this confrontative, but felt it was necessary in this case. She sincerely wanted to help this woman who was being compelled by something she was having a hard time facing. With this much resistance, it must be very important and very painful.

She took a few more deep breaths hoping that Judy would follow suit, but she did not. Judy just sat there glaring while her foot shook in irritation. "We have a few more minutes, please tell me, how is your Legos dollhouse going? I hear that you have spent a lot of extra time working on it. It must be lovely. How many rooms does it have? Are you having fun working on it?"

"Four bedrooms, living room, kitchen, den, a playroom, and a laundry room, so far. Is it fun? I don't know. It passes the time. After all, there's not much else to do here." The foot was slowing down a bit, but Judy was still quite agitated.

"What other rooms would you like to add? Are you going to have a garage too?" Judy answered the questions with controlled excitement. Lisa could see that she enjoyed building and talking about it but also noted that she was reluctant to let her enthusiasm show. After discussing more details about the building, Judy calmed down and by the end of the session calmly walked out.

Lisa felt spent. She leaned back into her chair and wondered what to do next to support Judy. How was she going to reach the sad, hidden child, within this driven woman?

Judy worked out hard during exercise hour and then went to the afternoon meeting. As usual, it began with three readings and then Frankie asked Judy to share.

"Hello, I'm Judy and I am not an alcoholic."

"Okay, fine. Please tell us about your first weekend here," Frankie said with a warm smile.

"I guess I'm a bit depressed. There's nothing to do around here. I'm so bored. My son did not email me even though I asked him to email me every day. Then last night, he finally emailed me and he says he's having a great time at his dad's house. I'm afraid he won't want to come home. I'm feeling frustrated because I'm used to working hard all the time. If it wasn't for the Legos and activities, I'd go nuts. Other than that, I guess I'm fine. So, that's all I've got."

"Thank you for participating, Judy." Everyone shared and then they closed with the Serenity Prayer."

Judy hated this part. Everybody held hands and said the words at the same time, "Higher power, grant me the serenity to accept the things I cannot change, the courage to change the things I can, and the wisdom to know the difference." She didn't like the idea that she should accept things first. She thought it should be the other way around. First you should have the courage to change things and only if that does not work, then you should accept them. As for not knowing the difference, that made no sense.

She was relieved that the boring meeting had ended and now it was time for comps, that's what they called all communication devices.

She checked her emails. Nothing, again! She took her pad to her room and called Sammy on FaceTime. He did not answer. His pad was at home. They were not allowed at school and now he was being tutored. Getting no answer added to her frustration. She called his Smartwatch, but the school had a policy that all comps had to be in their lockers.

The last person she wanted to talk to was James, but she was desperate to know what was going on, so, she called her ex using voice only. She did not want to be seen in pajamas.

James was working on a design issue at work when the call came in. He was surprised that Judy was calling. 'Could the program be working already?' he thought as he answered.

"Hello Judy, I'm at work right now, what is going on?" He sounded more cautious than he wanted to.

"Why is Sammy not picking up? I've been calling him?" She sounded annoyed.

"When did you call? He is in school right now until 4:30, then he rides his electric scooter home. It takes at least twenty minutes, so he gets home around five."

"Why do they make him stay in school so late?" she demanded to know.

James was cautious. He could hear the volitivity in her voice. He talked slowly and softly as he answered, "He is being tutored to catch up to his class."

"I see!" she said sharply. She had no reason to be annoyed but still sounded that way. "Well, can you tell him to call me tomorrow before he rides home, so I can have some time with him? I only have my pad between four and five. Okay?"

"Sure, will do." James was curious, "How are things at your rehab?"

"Boring. This having nothing to do is driving me crazy!" She didn't really want to talk to him about her situation, but it felt good to vent to someone who seemed to care.

"Are you working with a counselor?" James was taking advantage of her being in a talkative mood.

"Oh yeah, therapy is great fun," she said sarcastically. "My counselor called me a liar today! What nerve! She doesn't know me! No one here knows me, but they all act like they do," Judy vented. "They are just trying to brainwash me."

"Let them help you, that's what you're there for," James gently reminded her.

Changing the subject Judy said, "Oh, guess what? This place is run by Trinitus. It was the only place I could afford. Everyone on the staff is a Trinitarian. Funny that, huh! There are books here about your city, so I might read about it sometime. But don't get any ideas that I'm going there anytime soon, I still think it is a Commie cult!"

"I hope you find the books illuminating. At least you will understand why I stayed. It is a lot safer here for the kids, than it was in San Bernardino. I'm finally working at the profession I went to college for, Architectural Design. I love it here. I'm happy here."

"Good for you. It sucks here! I'm miserable. The only thing I have to look forward to is talking to Sammy, so make sure he calls me. Okay?" Judy was sarcastic and curt. She was finished with being nice.

James knew this call was over. It was pleasant while it lasted. "Well, I need to get back to work. Thanks for calling," he was about to hang up but hesitated in case she was going to say goodbye.

Instead, she added an afterthought, "I can't believe you two ratted me out! Now I'm stuck in here trying to tell these people that I'm not an alcoholic..." she raged.

James cut her off. "I'm not going to argue with you Judy!" and hung up.

Judy stared at the blank blue screen of her pad surprised. This was the second time he hung up on her. She was furious! She tossed the pad across her bed, and it hit the wall beside her. It had a rubber frame around it, so it didn't break. She sat there pouting until 4:30 and then tried to reach Sammy again.

"Hi Mom, that was weird. I just grabbed my Smartwatch from my locker, and it rang! You scared me."

"Sorry Sweetie, you haven't been calling and I miss you, so I thought I'd reach out. I can only make or receive calls between four and five. I hope this is a good time for you. I know you are between school and going home, but it is the only time we can talk without your father in the background."

"Yeah, sure. I'm out of tutoring about this time every day of the week."

"Good, how is your new school?"

"We're doing this Ropes Course. It is so amazing! I climbed a twelve-foot pole with cross branches to hold onto and then I stood up on the top. The platform was only twelve-inches wide! Boy, getting up that last step, with nothing to hold onto, was terrifying! I was so scared, even though I was wearing a harness. Everyone was watching and cheering when I did it. Then I jumped off! It was such a rush. They just lowered me down to the ground and everyone ran over and congratulated me and slapped me on the back. They acted like I was an old friend. It was so green!

We also went to our classes for a short time. They just introduced the curriculum. It looks a lot harder than my old school. It is a good thing I have Roger, my tutor. The sports meets are scheduled at the same time as my tutoring so I can't play soccer until I get a handle on math; until then I can't play."

"Oh, that is too bad. You do need to improve your math. Your math grades have always been low."

"They don't use grades here. They only have proficiency tests. It is not like you pass or fail. They just tutor you if you have a problem. They said that grades can make you feel bad about yourself, so they don't use them."

"Oh, I see. Well, if it helps you. In your email, you said you were having fun with your dad and your bow and arrow set?"

"Yeah, I'm getting very good at it too. Now I hit the bullseye almost every time! We go to this authentic Native American camp and eat tacos there. Then we do Native dances and after that, we go to the range. This range is more advanced, and it has animal targets. When I get good enough, they are going to take me on a real hunt with them!"

"Oh, I see," she sounded disappointed. "I think I should talk to your father about this. You know we never allowed you to play violent games on your ComPad. This hunting idea concerns me. I don't like it. I can't believe he is tempting you with this. It is a bad idea."

"Please, don't take this away from me. It is the only thing I have that makes me happy here. I can't play soccer yet, so it's all I have!"

"I know how much you must miss your friends and your soccer teammates, but a weapon is not a toy! I'm going to talk to your dad about this!"

She was oblivious to what she was doing. She thought she had a valid point. She believed she was just being a responsible parent who was appalled at the idea of her innocent little son being taught to kill animals. Subconsciously, she was sowing seeds of discontent. She did not want him to be happy there. She wanted him to yearn for his friends, his home, and for her.

Sammy remembered how his dad always caved in when his mother disapproved of something. His heart sank.

He knew just what his mother was going to say next. "I'm just trying to protect you. You know that right? Violence is bad. I'm just trying to protect you from it."

Sammy's anger exploded! This was the last straw. "Sure, you want to protect me! Like you protected me from your drinking! That is bad for me, you know. I would not be here at all, if it wasn't for your drinking!"

He had learned to throw guilt around from his mother. Well, now it was his turn to use it.

Judy was shocked. Sammy had never challenged her before, except at the Clinic. This was becoming a habit for all of them. Her whole family was turning against her. She was quiet for a moment as her eyes filled with tears.

"You know Mom, it is your fault that I'm here. If you had stopped drinking after the judge told you to, I would not be here, and you would not be locked in rehab!" Sammy unplugged his scooter, slammed his locker shut, and headed out.

"I know. I know. I'm sorry. I'll make it up to you, I promise," she said through her tears.

"Then don't talk to Dad about the bow. I don't want to have to give it up. I like it and I'm good at it!" Sammy used his new tool of guilt to his advantage.

Judy realized that she had lost her dominant position as a parent, and her ploy to make him unhappy had backfired.

"Okay. I won't, but please be careful. I just don't want you to get hurt. Is that such a bad thing for me to do? I'm just concerned for my favorite child," She tried to get back on his good side.

Sammy was feeling his new power and reveled in it for the moment. He decided to quit while he was ahead. He knew how manipulative she could be. "Well, I need to go and get home in time for dinner."

"Okay, Sweetie. Call me tomorrow after you're done with your tutor, okay?" The tears were still flowing.

"Ok, bye." He hung up feeling vindicated. On the road home, he felt like an accomplished warrior.

Judy found it hard to stop crying. She felt as if she was losing everything. She was hurt by her angry son and overwhelmed by her situation. She had never been in trouble with the law before. No one had ever been angry with her like this, except James, and he always backed down. This was all new to her. What had gone wrong in her life to cause this? Her drinking was innocent. It could not have caused all this!

If it was the drinking, that would mean this was all her fault. She tried to tell herself it was Sandra and James, but that argument was too old, too stale, and it just seemed to turn to dust. She looked around for someone else to blame, but there was no one. Finally, having exhausted all options, she looked at the drinking. She asked herself the question Lisa had so rudely posed, "Was she lying to everyone or to herself? No answer came to mind, but the flow of tears increased. She was drowning in tears when her Smartwatch chimed five and there was a knock at the door. Without thinking she opened it. Lisa was there. She came for the ComPad.

Lisa walked in and put her arms around Judy. She did not say a word. Judy let herself be held and surrendered to another torrent of tears.

After a long while, the tears subsided. "What is wrong, Judy?"

She pushed Lisa away, threw herself on the bed and buried her face in a pillow.

"Nothing! Go away!" The words came out muffled with her face still pressed into the pillow.

Lisa picked up the ComPad and asked softly with genuine concern, "Did the call to your son go badly?"

"I don't want to talk about it!" was Judy's muffled reply.

"Well, it's free time. Are you going to come out?" Lisa asked.

"Later, I want to be alone now," Judy mumbled and sniffled.

"Alright, I'm going to leave, but I'll come back in a while to check on you. I just want to make sure you're okay. Whenever you feel like talking, I'll be here." Judy did not respond. Lisa walked out and left the door open a crack. She came back every half hour or so and peeked in to check on her.

Judy wanted a drink so badly, but that only made her more depressed. It meant these people were right. Thinking about how much she needed a drink, sent Judy into another round of wailing tears. She tried to remember the last time she cried this much.

It was a very long time ago. She was young. Afterwards, she vowed to herself that she would never cry again. She had strong willpower and kept that vow all the way up to today. She had to be tough. She would never depend on anyone again.

She remembered the feeling clearly, but recapturing the event was harder.

'Oh, yes, that was the day, I realized I had to grow up. I was on my own now. How old was I? Eleven.'

She felt devastated back then, just as she did now. That was when she realized, if she depended only on herself, she would be safe. No one could hurt her if she was in charge and took care of her own needs.

"I've failed!" she wailed and melted into a new torrent of tears.

Judy felt completely rejected right now, just like she did when she was eleven. What happened? She asked herself again and again, 'Why did I feel so rejected back then?' She could not remember. All she could do was cry. Her heart was breaking.

Slowly, like focusing a blurry camera, a picture formed in her mind. It was when her parents didn't give her the horse she wanted for her birthday.

They promised her a horse. The tears stopped.

Pictures came into focus. Questions a child could never answer came into her adult mind. She was just sucking in the last sniffles when Lisa peeked in again.

She came in and sat on the side of the bed and did not say a word. She just reached over for some tissues and handed them to Judy. When the sniffles stopped, she waited another minute and then very softly asked, "Would you like a willing ear?"

An old feeling gripped Judy, "What do you care? Just leave me alone."

"I do care, I really do. That is why I chose this work. Give me a chance to help you. I can see you are in pain. Please let me in." Lisa petted Judy's hand, which was just laying nearby limply holding tissues.

Judy rolled her eyes at Lisa and turned away. "No one really cares about other people. You get paid for this job. I'm just a new challenge to you."

"I'm not paid in the traditional sense. I'm a member of Trinitus. You are not just a challenge for me. I am offering you unconditional love and I care. Maybe you did not receive unconditional love as a child. Something made you believe that people don't care for others. What happened?"

"People don't care. That is a fact of life. Everybody is just out for themselves. No one is going to care for me. I can only count on myself. That is just the way the world is." Judy was now curled up in a fetal position with her arms wrapped around her crossed legs.

Lisa took note of Judy's body language and proceeded carefully. "That seems to be a rather negative way to look at life. It is a sad way to live, don't you think?"

"Well, it's true." Judy said flatly.

"Maybe it only seems to be true. Maybe it is something you believe because of what happened to you. Or it is just the way the little girl in you saw it. What do you think?" she proceeded cautiously.

Judy did not respond, so Lisa continued. "You are not the only person who believes life is that way. Many people do and it has caused a lot of suffering, but there are also other people in the world who want to live differently. They are working to change the way people treat each other. They practice unconditional love. In fact, I'm one of them."

"I know your cult talks about changing the world with love, but there's no such thing. People will always be selfish. No one really cares about other people. They may care about their kids, at least until they grow up and turn on you; then they become selfish too. Just ask my kids."

"So, you don't believe in love, even though you love your children? Do you believe they have turned on you? Do you think they don't love you anymore?"

A new wave of tears grabbed Judy again. She was sobbing in despair. Lisa backed off.

"I see that you need some time alone. I am going to leave. Maybe when you feel a little better, you can think about what made you lose faith in love, and what effect it has had on your life."

Lisa quietly walked out and left the door slightly ajar.

Judy was consumed by the rejection she felt from her son. She was sure he no longer loved her. He was now just like Sandra, only looking out for himself. The close bond she shared with Sammy was gone. The mother part of her heart was dying without the love of her child. More tears of grief poured out of her. Everything was gone, lost, stolen from her. The only thing she had left was her job, her demanding, ever-running-to-keep-up, exhausting job. Her family finally defeated her after a lifetime of struggling to stay strong. Judy never came out for dinner, or the movie, she just cried until sleep swallowed up the tears.

In her dream, a pony was galloping towards her. She was clapping her hands in delight, but suddenly the horse started growing transparent. It disappeared just before he reached her, along with her happiness. She turned around, and in the distance, she saw her mother and father. She started running towards them, but as she got closer, they too grew transparent and disappeared just as she was about to reach them. She thought, 'Oh, they must be at home, but she could not remember where her home was. She started walking, hoping she would find a path. Along the way, she found a bottle of bubbles and started blowing them. She skipped along singing, "Bubbles and promises all go pop!" She never found her home, instead she woke up.

When James came home that night, Sandra warned him that Sammy was in a bad mood. At dinner, Sammy stuck to one-word answers when he was asked about school and his day. He returned to his room as soon as he finished eating. While Sandra was doing the dishes, James visited Sammy in his room.

"What has got you down, Buddy? Did you have a rough time at school?" James sat with his son on the bed.

"Not really, school was great." He didn't want to talk about his mom's call, just in case Dad sided with her about the bow.

"Did your mom get ahold of you? She complained to me that you haven't called her. She called me today to find out why. I told her that you were busy being tutored."

Sammy collapsed into his pillow. "Yeah, we talked," he said with a long sigh.

"Is that why you're in a funk? Did she say something that got you down?"

Sammy did not want to tell his father about what his mom said about the bow. He also did not want to talk about his feelings. He felt both good and bad about telling her off.

James just sat there patiently waiting for an answer. As time stretched on, Sammy felt he had to say something, or his dad would never leave.

"I yelled at her again for drinking."

"Oh, I see. Well, I think that's okay. She needs to realize that her drinking was a bad thing. You have a right to feel angry about it. You didn't curse her out though, did you? There is no need to go overboard."

"No, nothing like that! It was just that she was telling me what I should do, like she cares! She didn't care enough about me to stop drinking. Why does she get to tell me what I can, or cannot do?"

"I see your point, but we also need to remember that she is still your mother and still has a say in your life. Besides that, drinking can be very hard to quit. She is struggling. She loves you. Remember when you first picked up the bow, you really, really wanted to hit the bullseye, and you tried very hard, but you missed. Even though you wanted to hit the mark, you just couldn't. It is a little like that. You kept trying and eventually you got very good at it. She is having a hard time. Let's hope she keeps trying and she succeeds like you did. Do you understand?"

"I guess, but it doesn't seem right. If I can't hit the bullseye, I shouldn't be telling other people how to."

"Okay, you have me there. She hasn't set a good example, that is for sure. What did she tell you to do or not do?"

"Nothing, just my math stuff," he avoided the truth.

"Well, she loves you and cares about you. Just because she has made mistakes doesn't mean you don't have to listen to her anymore. Understand?

"Yeah, sure."

"Good. Do you want to play a game together? It might cheer you up a little," he patted his son on the shoulder.

"Okay."

Sammy was glad he didn't have to tell his dad about the bow argument. He felt relieved.

They played a game called Resources. You have a choice. You can play in one of two ways. One is to set prices on your goods and then convince people to buy them. Then you proceed along a route to see the effect your sales have on the economy of your town. Or you can participate in a system of mutual sharing and follow the effects of a freely distributed economy on your town. The game shows how sharing helps people, and how money creates divisions within a community. Some become rich and others poor, some are winners and others are losers. Sammy could see how sharing really works better.

The following Monday evening, Sammy and Sandra had their first counseling appointments. Sammy talked about his mother's drinking and how much he wanted to go back to California. His counselor, Antonio, was a young man in his late 20's, with brown hair and large soulful brown eyes.

"Do you think you would be happier back in California living with your mother, even if she is drinking?"

"No, but she is trying to get better now. She is in rehab, so maybe she won't drink anymore."

"It is really hard for people to stop you know."

"If she does it again, I'll make her stop. I can tell when she is drunk, and I'm not afraid of her anymore. I can stand up to her to tell her to stop."

"You cannot blame yourself for her drinking or think that you have the power to stop her, only she can do that. Do you understand that?" Antonio said gently. "No matter how much she loves you, it has nothing to do with her ability to stop. There is no equation here."

Sammy just sat there pouting so Antonio continued, "Not drinking is all up to her. You can't stop her. All you can do is be a loving son and be honest about your feelings. You can gently let her know that what she is doing to herself is affecting you. Do it gently because this is a difficult and sensitive subject that she is struggling with."

Sammy stared at his feet as he kicked the coffee table gently. "How does this make you feel?" Antonio asked.

"Mad at her for drinking," the boy quietly answered.

"That is perfectly normal. So, what do you do when your mad?"

"Throw things and hit things, I guess."

"How well is that working for you?"

"Well, it feels good, but I broke one of my favorite planes and I got this big cut on my head when I bumped into the corner of a shelf." He pointed to his stitches.

"What can you do to get the anger out in another way?"

"I don't know." Sammy was still somber. With downcast eyes, he mumbled, "I can punch my stuffed animals."

"That would work. How about exercising, could you run, or ride your scooter, or go to the gym, or go swimming, or throw some hoops, something like that?"

"Well, I just learned to shoot a bow and arrow. I can take my anger out on that." Sammy perked up and looked at his counselor.

"It may not be wise to put your anger into a weapon. That can be dangerous to you and to other people. However, you could use the bow to calm your emotions. Like approaching it as a meditation. Do you know what I mean?"

"Yeah, I guess," Sammy went somber again.

Between exercising, running, going to the gym, swimming, or throwing some hoops, which of these could you do the next time you feel angry at someone?"

"I can run," Sammy agreed.

"Where?" asked Antonio.

"I have a running track in my backyard. I live in the Exercise Cluster. We have all kinds of obstacle courses."

"Good. Now that you have a strategy for dealing with your anger, can we talk about what lies behind it?"

"I guess."

"When people get angry, it is usually to cover up hurt feelings like sadness, grief, or fear. Which one is it for you?"

"I guess I was scared. I didn't want to come here and live with my dad. I loved my life back home. I had everything I wanted. I had great friends, a winning team, and we did everything together. Life was perfect and then the grownups ruined it all. Now I need to go to my tutoring instead of soccer practice. I'm scared that I will be trapped here and never get back to California."

"That's clear. Let's go over what we covered. You now know what you can do when you get angry. You can go running until you feel better. You understand why you feel angry. It is to cover your fears, especially the one about being trapped here and never getting home. Remember, your mother is going to be released in two months, and if all goes well, you can go home then."

"You also said that you are no longer afraid of telling your mother how you feel, so you can express how you are feeling and ask for what you need. Now, you do not have to feel helpless or hopeless anymore.

"You see, there are parts of your life you can control, but there are others you can't. You can control how you express your emotions. You can understand why you are having these feelings. You can express how you feel and ask for what you want. You just cannot control what other people do. You cannot make your mother stop drinking. That is something she needs to do all by herself.

"Yeah, I guess. I just wish I had the power to make her stop," Sammy said sadly.

"I understand, but only she can make that choice for herself. The truth is you can't make anyone change unless they are willing to. Sometimes they really want to, but they still can't change. You are her son; it is not your job to teach her these things."

"But maybe if I tell her how mad I am, it can help her do it."

"You can tell her how you feel. It might help her, or it might not. You need to be honest with her, but if she fails, it's not your fault. This is her process not yours. Do you understand?"

"Yes, I hope she stops though."

After that, they talked about soccer and archery until his time was up.

James was waiting for his children in the open atrium in the middle of the building. It was the same building Kim was in. In fact, their twice-a-week appointments were timed with his Monday and Friday ones to be more convenient.

CHAPTER 20

Selfish

Judy was depressed all week. Sammy took her calls, but they were short. They didn't have much to talk about. She just complained about the staff and residents. She did not share in the meetings, hardly touched her food and did not even play with her Lego house. Instead, she just sat there, finger-flicking her Lego family figures into the rooms of the house. When Lisa called her to her office for their daily session, she moaned and slumped down in her seat.

Lisa asked her about her present family and her childhood but didn't get much of a response from her. As the week went on, Judy became more depressed, and Sammy stopped answering her calls. When Lisa asked her how her Comp times were going, Judy just sat staring at the wall.

"Okay, we can just sit here and not talk if you want, or we can talk about something else, like your parents or your upbringing. Would that be alright?"

"What's the point?" Judy sighed loudly, "I've lost everything that I tried to do in my life except maybe my job, and if they find out I'm in rehab, that might be gone too."

"Why do you think you have failed at everything?" Lisa gently asked, knowing how fragile Judy was right now.

"I tried to have the perfect family and marriage, but it failed. My kids hate me now. I'm divorced. It is all over. Everything I tried to do is gone."

"I don't think anyone has a perfect family. There is no such thing. We all have some troubles. You are in a bad spot right now, but that doesn't mean you can't get your family back. I doubt that your children hate you, even if they are acting distant right now."

"They think I'm a drunk and they are against me! Both of them!"

"I don't think they are against you, but they may be against your drinking."

"I've stopped now, I'm here and I won't drink again that's for sure!" Judy insisted.

"There may be more to it than just quitting cold turkey. You may have some underlining issues that caused you to drink and still give you the desire to." Then almost as an afterthought she asked, "When did your drinking to relax begin?"

"I don't know, college maybe. Everyone drank back then, so what?" She threw up her hands. "That doesn't mean I had problems. I had great parents, and I did well in school. I was a valedictorian, and I never got smashed drunk like others did. I always stopped after a few drinks. I never had a problem with it."

"Did you keep drinking wine at night throughout your marriage?"

"Yeah sure, why not? It wasn't hurting anyone. It never has."

"You mean, until now?"

"Well, until my daughter made a big deal out of it to get what she wanted. She got selfish. That's what happened. Now, Sammy is getting selfish too."

"Interesting, what do you mean by selfish?" Lisa delved.

"You know, wanting something and doing anything to get it, no matter who it hurts. It's not caring about anybody else's needs."

"What do you need right now?" Lisa prodded.

"Respect as a mother and a wife, and not have selfish kids, I guess."

"Do you think that maybe you have been selfish with your drinking?"

"I wasn't hurting anyone!" Judy retorted.

"You may need to think about that a little more," Lisa suggested. "It looks like you have hurt yourself and your family."

Judy just crossed her arms and stared at the wall again.

"You may have caught your addiction early, but it looks like you were well on your way to serious alcoholism."

"Maybe I wasn't. We will never know because I won't drink again."

"That's good. I'm just concerned that not addressing your deeper issues can set you up for failure. Just stopping may not be enough."

"Look, if I drink again, then all of you are right, I have lost control and therefore am an alcoholic, but if I don't, then that proves you are all wrong!" Judy felt she won that point.

"Is it important for you to feel you are in control?"

"Sure. Everybody needs to have control of their lives, that is how we get things done."

"That may be true, but having to always be in control can cause a lot of stress and stress is the reason you gave for drinking. We Trinitarians believe that the need to control creates negative behaviors. Needing to have control stems from fear and anger, which probably came from when you were very young. What do you think of that?"

"I think you're fishing, I had a great childhood," Judy said flatly.

"You said that you have been taking care of yourself since you were eleven. Isn't that a bit early for a kid? Why did you have to do that so young?"

"I just grew up early. My parents worked a lot and had Benefits to go to, so I had to take care of myself. That's all." Judy foot, the one crossed over her knee, started to shake.

Lisa could see she was getting close to something Judy did not want to admit and gently pressed on. "Did you feel bad because they did not pay attention to you?"

"I don't know. They were busy, that's all. I had to grow up and do my own things."

"Like what?"

"When I was younger, I played with dolls and a dollhouse and talked to my friends online. I had a lot of sleepovers with them. I got into fashion and as I got older, I did a lot of shopping with my friends," a hint of a smile touched the edge of her mouth.

"Did you ever shop with your mother?" the smile disappeared.

"Once in a while for Christmas to get something for Dad, but she usually had her own friends who she went shopping with."

"Sounds like she could have spent more time with you than she did. Did you ever get into trouble?"

"No, not really. I was a good kid. I stayed out of trouble, so my parents did not need to check up on me. We had a butler and at first, a nanny too. They would tell my parents if I did anything wrong, so I always behaved. If I did something bad, they locked me in my room."

"Tell me about a time when you got in trouble."

"Well, the biggest one had to be the time I did a sleepover, and the butler found out that we were drinking. I got three weeks restriction for that one," she smiled mischievously.

"How old were you then?"

"Eleven or twelve, I don't recall."

"What did you parents say? Did they yell at you?" Lisa asked.

"Nothing, they just told the butler to lock me in my room. He said that I had to grow up and I had three weeks to think about it, so I did. I got rid of my doll house and dolls, and I grew up. My parents were not hard on me. They did not beat me or anything like that. Like I said, I had good parents."

"Did they ever talk to you about the dangers of alcohol or about the choices you make?"

"They did not have to. They got their point across. I did not drink again, not until college."

"Did they ever sit down with you and just talk about life, puberty, school, or ask how you were doing?"

"No, it was not necessary. School and my nanny taught me all I needed to know. My parents were too busy. We sometimes went out for dinner and talked, but it was for major changes like college or retiring my nanny. I really didn't have the right to say anything about the matter. They were just informing me."

"Do you resent them for not considering your needs and desires?"

"I don't resent them. They did what was best for me. When I went off to college, I was on my own, and I made my own decisions." Judy's leg was shaking again.

"Did they hug you and spend time with you when you were young?" The shaking became even more pronounced, but Judy did not seem to notice.

"No, I don't think so. I was raised by the nanny, Ms. Tailor, but she did not play with me or hold me either, not that I remember." Judy stated all this matter-of-factly, as if this was natural.

Lisa was saddened by Judy's obvious neglect and her obliviousness to it. She decided not to challenge her today. It was too soon. Judy wasn't ready to hear it. She continued to question her about college and the drinking she did there. Judy saw no fault in that either. She believed that it was just normal young adult fun. However, it became obvious to Lisa that this was where Judy's nightly drinking habit started. She had worked hard to get good grades and afterwards, it was party time.

"Let's get back to this idea of selfishness, as you define it. What happened today during your call that made you so upset?"

Avoiding the real problem, Judy said, "That selfish ex-husband of mine gave my son a real bow and arrows to play with and I think it is a terrible idea. Sammy is mad about this divorce and his dad having left them. The last thing he needs is a weapon!"

"You mentioned that they are living in the City of Hope, right? Then he is probably seeing a therapist who will help him with his anger and direct him away from violence using a weapon. The counselor will teach him how to express his anger properly. I wouldn't worry too much about that."

"Still, I should have had a say in it. That worthless bastard didn't even tell me about it!" She stewed and looked at her therapist to confirm her belief.

"Now let's refrain from name calling, he is the father of your children. Can you contact him and talk about how you feel about the bow in a cordial way?"

"I don't know about cordial. We have not been cordial for years!" she snapped.

"Does he yell at you a lot?" Lisa was probing why Judy resisted confronting James with a legitimate complaint.

Judy did not want to answer, knowing that she was the one who yelled most of the time. She also did not want to talk about how Sammy was trying to guilt her out of mentioning it, so she deflected.

"I have lost all persuasion over them. Now I'm just a drunk to them. James hung up on me twice! There is no point in trying to talk to him. I'm all alone now, without a family. I have lost everything, even my house," with downcast eyes she sighed and said, "I'm going to have to sell it once I'm out of here."

Lisa noted the deflection and the body language that told her Judy was avoiding or distorting the truth. Trying another tactic, Lisa focused on the obvious depression instead.

"You sound depressed and defeated. What is going on for you?"

Judy needed to get back in control. She was unwilling to be labeled by anyone or admit defeat.

"I'll get through this rehab, sell the house, get a condo, and start over. I'll be fine! I will not be defined as a drunk by these selfish people! I will work hard and get back on my feet. That will show all of you that I'm not a failure." Mustering up false bravado, she held her head high for the first time in this session.

Lisa was concerned now. Judy was unwilling to sit with her depressed feelings or admit to them. She was avoiding her feelings.

"It may be good that you are letting yourself feel depressed and feel the hurt over losing your family. You are learning about yourself by feeling your pain. It is better than hiding them in a glass of wine. At least, you are not avoiding them."

"I am in control. I won't drink ever again. I'll just find a healthier way to relax. I don't need my family or alcohol to succeed. I'll be fine." Judy announced confidently.

Lisa could see that this sudden show of bravado was another distraction from facing the truth.

"When people stop drinking, but they do not address the cause of the drinking, it can lead to hurting yourself and others, or to bad behaviors, even when you no longer actively drink. These feelings do not go away just because you want them to. You need to face them and disarm their power over you. We call that processing."

"I'm just accepting what is and moving on. What is wrong with that? I'm a strong person. I can do that. There is no point in crying over forgotten promises. I need to take care of myself. That is that!"

"That was an interesting sequence, it led to an interesting belief, 'there is no point in crying over forgotten promises.' Who forgot their promises to you? Your parents? Did they promise things and forget them?"

Suddenly, Judy felt trapped by her own words. She had to escape.

"I don't know what you're talking about. I had great parents. I was given everything I needed," she insisted.

Lisa knew she had hit a nerve. Judy's body language was strongly responding. As a therapist, Lisa knew that Judy could not go any further at this time, so she gave her the writing assignment and ended the session.

"Let's stop here for today. For this week, write about 'forgotten promises.'"

Judy jumped up and could not leave fast enough.

Since the therapy ended a little early, she had some free time before the daily exercise session at 2:00. She marched over to the art room. She was on a mission.

Just as she did when she was a child with her dolls and dollhouse, she tore down her Lego house.

A feeling of abandonment was trying to rise into consciousness, and she had to bury it, just as she did long ago. She buried her feelings of abandonment and put her mind to the task of working hard to take care of herself. She vowed to start fresh and look for a better husband.

Tania noted the viciousness with which Judy was taking the Lego house apart and walked over to her. "What are you doing?" Tania asked softly.

Judy jumped a little. She did not expect anyone to take notice. "Putting away kid toys. I'm not a kid anymore, so I don't need toys!" She answered sharply.

"I see, the adult in you is taking away your toys, so your child self can't play. Why?"

"My child self needs to grow up and get on with the business of adulthood."

"What does it mean to you to be an adult?" she cautiously asked.

"It means not pretending and dreaming of things that will never be given to you. It means getting things yourself," Judy continued to tear the walls down.

"What have you been pretending?"

"That I had a perfect life! Perfect kids! A perfect marriage!" Judy started banging pieces of walls against the house. When this became painful and her hands hurt, she broke down in tears and threw chunks of the wall at the table.

Tania had taken the *Chain of Questions* as far as she could with Judy.

"Please come away from here and calm down, okay?" Tania reached for this angry woman's hands, but Judy pulled away. She pushed pass Tania and the other staff women who were coming toward her and fled to her bedroom.

She was not alone for long. Frankie and Lisa came in with Tania. Judy was on her bed with her face pressed into her pillow. She was embarrassed by her crying. She did not want anyone to see her like this or know that they got to her, but she couldn't stop either. Her walls were crumbling, crumbling like her Lego dollhouse.

Tania repeated Judy's responses to Lisa and then returned to the art room. Judy was embarrassed that they were talking about her.

"Just go away and leave me alone!" she shouted.

Lisa nodded to Frankie and signaled to him to leave. He nodded and left. Lisa sat down on the corner of the bed. "I'll stay until you feel ready to talk."

"You'll be waiting a long time!" Judy shouted and put her face back into her pillow.

Lisa waited.

Judy cried a bit longer until embarrassment took over. "Why won't you let me be?"

"Honestly, because leaving you alone is what your parents did, and I don't think that's what you need. You can have all the time you want, but I am going to wait here by your side, so you are not alone with these feelings. I will be here for you when you are ready to share your pain with me," Lisa spoke softly. "You need to share your feelings, and you need someone to listen, someone to care about you and I do. I really do care."

"No, you don't! No one really cares. You're just doing your job that's all." Judy spun around and sat against the headboard with her pillow between her chest and her drawn up knees. She looked as if she was trying to stay away from Lisa.

"I picked this job precisely because I care about people. I want to help you get through these painful feelings," Lisa said with a soft and caring tone.

Judy looked away and sulked. Lisa continued. "Maybe this belief that people don't care comes from your parents. You wanted them to talk to you and ask you about your feelings." She waited for a response but received none. "Does some part of you feel that your parents didn't take the time to listen to you?" No response.

Lisa tried another tactic. "It is interesting that you told me you got rid of your dollhouse and now you went after your Lego house right after we spoke. You looked quite angry. Was the child self in you angry? When you were getting rid of the toys, was that a way of getting rid of her? Were you avoiding your feelings by getting rid of your hurt inner child?"

No response, so Lisa went on. "You see, when we are traumatized as children, we carry that child part with us even when we are older. The inner child never grows up, it stays the same age forever. Their beliefs about life live on in the adult, like your belief that no one cares. That belief lives in your inner child and was learned from your parents. Your core beliefs come from the things you learned as a child."

"I was not traumatized. I had good parents." Judy said flatly.

"I know you believe that. I agree, your parents did the best they could. They didn't mean to hurt you, but you felt abandoned, and you hide those feelings by drinking. It is like your family situation now. You are very upset because again you feel abandoned."

"Of course, I feel abandoned! James left me and took my children! That has nothing to do with my past."

"I understand, it hurts regardless of your past, but if you look, you'll see a connection across time. For right now, can we focus on the belief that no one cares. That is a painful belief that leads to more pain. If you keep believing that no one wants to help you, then you cannot accept our help when we are here for you. This belief makes your life hard and having to carry everything alone is very stressful. This program is here to help you put your burdens down, rest, and continue with support, so you do not have to be alone with your struggles. We really do care, and we want to help you, but first you need to let down your guard and let us in. Expressing your feelings will keep you from burying them in the wine."

"I told you! I will not drink again! You can't help me because there is nothing wrong with me," Judy shouted defiantly.

"Why do you need to believe that, when your body is crying out for acknowledgement?"

"Oh, really, so what's wrong with me?" Judy asked, bracing herself for the answer.

"Since you ask, I'll tell you what I have seen. You are hiding your hurt child self and covering the pain with anger, which you express at anyone who will listen, and you hide by drinking. You are denying that you have painful feelings of abandonment, which seep out in lots of ways. You believe that no one cares about you and you are shutting out anyone who tries to help you. I'm not saying that there is anything mentally wrong with you, just that you have some unresolved issues from your past that are messing up your life right now. If you let us in, we can help you. Be open and honest with us without all the protective coverings."

"I don't have protective coverings. I just don't think I'm as messed up as you think I am. Why wouldn't I feel abandoned by my family right now, they abandoned me. Of course, I'm angry about it! Why wouldn't I?"

"That is a sincere and honest statement. Let's talk about that. Besides anger, how do you feel about it?"

Lisa began the *Chain of Questions*.

"Sad, I guess," Judy shrugged her shoulders.

"Good, why does it make you sad?"

"Because, I don't have a family anymore!"

"Why is that important to you?"

"I don't know, I guess because that's what I thought about when I was a kid. I thought that is what a woman did." Judy shrugged again.

"Is that what you did when you were playing with your dolls and dollhouse?"

"Yes." Judy looked away embarrassed.

Lisa noticed the body language. "Why does admitting that embarrass you?"

"I'm not embarrassed. That's just what kids do!"

"You're covering your feelings again. Kids play house with their dolls, adults can too. That's all fine, but your body language says you were embarrassed by this. Why did you think that you had to get rid of your dolls when you were eleven?" Lisa guided her toward a deeper realization to help her face herself.

"I'm not covering anything up! I just needed to grow up. My parents said, "Grow up," so I did!"

"What was it about pretending that was not grown up? How did pretending relate to broken promises?"

"I don't know. Pretending is a child's way to play, so growing up means no more pretending. I don't know how it relates to broken promises."

"You said, 'There is no point in crying over forgotten promises, I have to take care of myself.' You related 'forgotten promises' with 'take care of myself' and with growing up. For you, there was a relationship between them that you may have forgotten.

"Think back to when you were eleven and you got rid of your dollhouse, what did you feel at the time?"

"I don't know, that was a long time ago. I haven't a clue!" Judy deflected again.

"Breathe deeply and slowly. Close your eyes. Look deep down inside you. Let your mind drift back to the past. This feeling you had was very important. It was painful, so painful you had to hide it. It had something to do with feeling abandoned. These feelings are here now in the present, but they echo with the same qualities as that day long ago when you were eleven. Take another deep breath and let it out slowly. Look at your current situation and let your feelings move through you, just feel them and let them move through. You can do this."

The tears returned. They silently filled her eyes and overflowed, rolling down her cheeks. "Good, just keep breathing and stay with these feelings. There is nothing to say. Nothing to do. Just let these feelings move through."

Lisa was quiet as she patiently watched Judy sitting staring off into the pain as the tears kept rolling down her cheeks.

When the tears stopped, Lisa took her hand and patted it.

"Good work. Rest for a few minutes and then write about your feelings while they are still fresh. Try to answer these questions; What made you think that you had to take apart your Lego house, how did that relate to your dollhouse as a child, how does this relate to your belief that you shouldn't cry over broken promises, and lastly, how does it relate to growing up? The keys we are looking for are hidden in this event. They will unlock a mystery and explain many things about your life, including what underlies your need to drink. When you find that key, it will set you free."

"Ok, I'll try, but I don't see the feelings you think I'm having. I don't know how these are all related."

"Just try. Skip the exercise period for today and spend this time writing. Just start and see where it takes you."

Lisa knew how they were related, but Judy had to make the connections for herself. Otherwise, she would just see it as Lisa's idea and fight it, just as she was fighting the idea of being an alcoholic. She had to make the discovery on her own. She had to feel the feelings she was repressing.

"Take your time but try to come to the afternoon meeting at 3:00."

Lisa left her to work on her own.

The *Chain of Questions* led Judy to a door. If she can open it, she will find the traumatic event that left her feeling abandoned all these years.

'Why did Judy feel abandoned when her butler locked her up that day. Her parents didn't confront her or chastise her for drinking at the slumber party. If that was all that happened, it would not have had such a lasting effect. There must be another piece to the story,' thought Lisa

Lisa mused about how being a therapist was a lot like being a detective. They both had to piece together clues to find the truth. 'Judy's parents had a dinner party to go to. They were busy. Too busy to pay attention to this little girl, even when she drank to get them to notice her, and how did the horse fit in?'

Judy started to write. At first, she was digging for ideas. Then they started to flow, and soon it was bringing up all these insights. She began to write, "It was a sleepover on my birthday. My parents made all kinds of promises about what a special day it was going to be, and how they were going to give me my very own pony.

"Then another of their dinners came up and they sent me to a sleep over at my friend's house instead. I told the kids it was my birthday, and they said we should celebrate, so we sneaked into the liquor cabinet, drank some vile stuff, and got caught. The butler was called, and he took me home. He called my parents, and they just said, 'Lock her in her room.' He locked me in, and I had to stay for three long weeks! He told me to grow up, so I got rid of my toys and tried to grow up. I thought that would make them love me but instead, they sent me away to a boarding school. They got rid of me.

"They promised me a horse, but they didn't give me one. Instead, they said I was growing up and did not need toys anymore. At least at boarding school, they had horses, and I learned dressage and jumping. I tried to grow up, like they said. I tried to get in their good graces again.

"That's why I felt abandoned. They sent me away because I was bad. At least, that is what I believed back then. I always believed that they were just doing what they thought was good for me. That is what they told me, and I believed it."

The tears were flowing so hard it was difficult to keep writing, but it was also hard to stop.

Judy was coming to grips with the feeling of being abandoned, even though she thought that was not their intention. She still did not fully see the general neglect, not yet. She thought about 'forgotten promises,' and began to write again.

"I remember there were lots of times when they promised to give me a special gift, if I did what they wanted. I did what they said, but I never got the toys and books they promised me. Never."

She winced. This thought made her feel really spoiled. 'Didn't my parents always say something about that? What was it? Give too much and spoil the child. Something like that.' She picked up her pen and then remembered, it was 'coddled too much'. What does coddle mean anyway?'

She began to write again, "Every time I pouted, my parents used to say, 'Coddle too much and spoil the child.' I certainly did not feel coddled as a child, but rather, ignored. Whenever they did not give me something they promised, they would also say, 'Sometimes you don't get what you think you deserve in life. That is just the way it is.' They never admitted that they had forgotten what they promised me.

"That is why I worked so hard at school, and went into advertising, I wanted to make my own money, so I could buy whatever I wanted by myself. I married James for the same reason. I thought he would make good money like me, but then he couldn't find a job in his field, so he started getting odd jobs and losing them. Now I am broke and will have to work even harder." Her thoughts trailed off into thinking about what she had to do to get back on her feet.

The afternoon meeting came up fast and Lisa knocked on her door to remind her. "Did you get any writing done?" she asked.

"A little." Judy shrugged, feeling she didn't do enough.

"Can I read it while you're in the meeting?" asked Lisa.

"Sure, but I'm not even close to being done yet."

Judy went to the meeting, but she did not share when Frankie asked her to. After that, it was time for comps, so Lisa handed her a pad and her notebook.

"Try to expand on what you wrote. It's very good so far. Also, if you have bad feelings after your Comp time, let's talk. Come see me if you need someone to talk too."

Judy nodded and went back to her room. She worked on her writing some more until she could FaceTime her son.

"Hey Sammy, how are you doing?"

He answered, slightly guarded, "Fine. I'm getting better at understanding the math more. I'm hoping that I can get out of tutoring, so I can do soccer sooner rather than later."

"That's good to hear. How's everything at home?"

"Good, Dad comes home the same time we do, so we can play a game or watch TV before dinner. They don't have many channels on TV, so we mostly play games. They don't have soda here and Dad doesn't buy any cookies or sweets either, so we snack on veggies and dips, or peanut butter. Sometimes we eat nuts. Dad is on a health kick. He's been cooking good dinners, but they're healthy ones, I miss mac and cheese. Things are so different here."

"Well, I suppose healthy is good, but when you get back home with me, you can have all the cookies and mac & cheese you want." Judy secretly liked hearing that he was not happy with everything there. "So, how's your bow practice going?"

"Fine, I practice most days after school, if I'm not playing a game with Dad and Sandra. I go to the range on weekends. I'm getting very good at it."

"You're being careful?"

"Yes Mom, I'm careful," he sighed. She was trying to manipulate and control him, and he knew it.

"Well, I guess you're as happy as you can be there, so that is good. I miss you so much. I'm bored out of my mind here. They only have Hallmark movies here and no TV time at all; so, count yourself lucky to have some TV there. I was playing with Legos for a while to pass the time. They have a swimming pool and a spa. so that's nice for me."

"I thought you did not like Legos."

"I do now, they are fun. I just did not like the idea of finding them the hard way on the floor. They hurt when you step on them. I'm sorry that I didn't get you any. They have cupboards here to keep them neat and off the floor. I wish I had thought of that when you were little."

"I can't imagine you playing with Lego's. Why do they have Lego's? Are there kids there?"

"No. They're trying to get us to play like kids, to help us remember what it was like when we were little. They think people drink because of something that happened to them in their childhood."

"Oh," Sammy mumbled. "Dad has me and Sandra seeing a

therapist too. Mine is Antonio. He's nice. He's helping me with my anger."

"Oh, well that's good." She changed the subject because this one was causing her to feel a wave of guilt. "Maybe they can help Sandra learn to respect her mother."

"Well, Sandra is happy here. The only thing she does not like is that she needs to go to high school for two extra years, but she said it will help her find new friends. She is already working with animals."

"Well, she got what she wanted, that's for sure." Judy said spitefully.

Not wanting to hear his mother complain as she tended to do, he took this as a good time to sign off. "Well, I have to get home, I'll talk to you tomorrow," he said in closing.

"Okay sure, tomorrow," Love you, Sweetie!"

Judy felt better after having a nice conversation with him and sighed as she hung up. She considered calling James to complain about the bow but decided against it. She was in a good mood and wanted to stay that way. She hadn't lost Sammy and therefore everything.

Judy sought out Sasha and Paul so she could have a massage at the spa. She cried again under his touch. At dinner, Sasha sat with her. "Are you okay today, do you want to talk about it?"

"Thanks, no, I feel better now but I don't want to talk."

After dinner and a movie, she sat on a sofa in the Great Room to work on her writing assignment. Since it was a way to get out of here, she had to at least look like she was doing the required work. As the words began to flow, she came to see that her parents were not as attentive as she thought they should be. Then she realized that she was mad at them for never spending time with her.

'Is that neglect?' she asked herself. A wave of embarrassment came over her and she stopped writing.

'This can't be true! Did they love me at all? Was I just in their way? One reason I tried to be an adult was so they would see me as an adult and be willing to take me to dinners and events with them, but they never did. They sent me away to private boarding school instead.'

Judy wrote this all down and her eyes grew moist, so she left the sofa and went to her room. There she let herself cry. She realized that she had been neglected and maybe even unloved by her parents, or at least, they seemed unloving at the time. Whether they loved her in their own way didn't matter, she had to admit now that she felt unloved by them and still does. She realized how selfish they had been.

Whenever she talked to her parents on the phone, they only talked about her work and how successful her marriage was, which, in later years, she felt compelled to lie about. She realized that she lied so they would not judge her and think she was a failure. She was still concerned that they would not see her as an adult and successful.

She realized her life had been all about showing them that she was a worthy adult, so they would want to spend time with her, and to prove to herself that she could take care of herself. Suddenly, she felt angry. She dropped the notebook on the bed and began to punch her pillow. She was surprised by the intensity of her anger. She hadn't realized it was there. Then she broke down in a torrent of tears. Afterwards, she just lay there until the lights went out.

CHAPTER 21

Grieving

James waited in the atrium after his appointment with Kim for his children to finish their sessions. Sandra walked out first. She was smiling from ear to ear. She waved her right arm in the air. She was wearing a new orange band. Samantha, her therapist, said she had a good grasp on processing, so she graduated to the next band. "All that time on New World really paid off. Now I only need to go to therapy once a week."

"That's great honey! "Congratulations," James hugged his daughter.

Sammy walked out of the other elevator. He was solemn again. For the past two weeks, he had been struggling with depression, feeling angry toward his mother and upset about the divorce. He wasn't taking her calls either. He just did not like acting as if nothing was wrong when it was. His mother did not ask how he was feeling, she just complained about people at rehab. He didn't want to talk to her. His dad had been more understanding about his feelings. He always asked him to talk, any time he felt up to it. He was now doing well with his tutoring and with other classes but had withdrawn from other kids. He just didn't feel like talking to anyone, not even Chase, his school partner. He preferred to work on his homework at lunch, so he could have more time for bow practice at home. He often practiced until dark or until dinner time, whichever came first.

"Look I received my orange band today!" Sandra flashed it at her brother as he walked over.

"Great," Sammy said sarcastically and rolled his eyes.

"Let's go home, so you can get ready for school," James said to break the tension between them.

They took the tram and walked the three blocks to their house. James went in to get their lunchboxes and backpacks while they got their borrowed E-Bikes from under the house. James gave them their packs and wished them a good day at school. Sammy stopped just beyond the corner, watched his dad walk to the bus stop, and waited until his dad boarded the tram. Then he returned to the house, dropped off his backpack, picked up his bow and arrows, and took the tram going the other way, to the shooting range in the park.

Just as James was settling into his project, he received a call from Sammy's school. "This is the Attendance Monitor at Hope Middle School; my name is Jaffa. I see that the schedule has Sammy out this morning until third period. He is still not in school. Did he have to stay out later today?"

"No, I sent him to school for third period. He's not there?"

"No, third period has him listed as absent. We called his comps but there was no answer. Would you like us to send a Truancy Officer to your home?"

"No, I'll find him. He has been struggling emotionally. I'll talk to him and bring him to school if he's up to it."

"Okay, I hope you find him. Have a good day."

James told Pamila and Taylor that he was going to take the day off to help his son. They wished him good luck on finding him and said, "Family comes first." James went to the share lot and picked up a small E car and went home to see if he was there. He found Sammy's bike under the porch and his backpack on the sofa. In his pack was his Smartwatch, so there was no way to call him. He drove the route to the school to make sure he wasn't in an accident. Then he checked the nearby clusters that had parks in them. Nothing. Now he was getting worried, so he went home again to see if Sammy had returned. He looked in his room, and then in the kitchen where he noticed the bow and quiver were not hanging on the wall. It dawned on him where Sammy was, the only place that made him happy, the shooting range. James drove over to the park.

Sure enough, Sammy was at his favorite lane, shooting the bow. He walked over to him, "Don't forget to breathe." James said as if he'd been there all day. Sammy jumped and turned around. His shot went wild.

"How did you know I was here?" Sammy's heart was pounding.

"The school called, so I went searching to make sure you didn't get hit by a car. Then I returned to the house and saw that the bow was missing. Why don't you have your Smartwatch on?"

"I'm sorry, I just didn't feel like going to school today. I just wanted to get my frustrations out. I guess I left my watch in my bag."

"Sure. I understand, but all you had to do was say so, and I would have taken the day off with you. You are my first priority, you know. You scared me when I could not find you or call you." He came up to his son and gave him a hug. "You need to at least have your Smartwatch with you at all times, okay?"

"Sorry, I didn't know they would call you. I was going to skip today, and I just forgot my watch."

"Well, I found you, and you're safe, that's all that matters. So, where were you planning to go for lunch, the village?" He looked at his son at arm's length, hands on his shoulders.

"Yeah, Cool green!" Sammy chirped up.

"Well let's go then, I'm hungry!" They quietly walked to the village.

At their favorite place, they ate Native tacos and listened to the storyteller's stories. He was telling the tale of a Native man who turned into a jackal because he did not respect the animals that he hunted. James remarked on the story, "Do you hear how important it is to have respect for the animals that you may hunt? You can't just go out and kill them for no reason. That's not right. The Native people use every part of the animal and waste nothing."

Sammy nodded his head as the storyteller went into another tale. After the stories and lunch were over, the dancing began. Sammy joined the circle and danced the steps well. Afterward, an older Native man gave Sammy a feather tied to a leather strap for his head, as a sign of his dancing prowess. He mentioned that there were dancing lessons during the weekends, if he wanted to learn more. Sammy was excited by the offer.

When James came up to them, the Native man said, "My name is Abornazine, and I was just telling this young man about our dance classes on the weekends."

James smiled as he placed a hand on Sammy's shoulder. "Well, first I'd need a promise that he will never cut school again," James feigned a scowl at his son.

"Oh, I promise, never again. If I really feel bad, I'll tell you first, I promise!" Sammy was jumping up and down like a pogo stick.

James smiled, "Okay, what time do they start?"

"It is early Sunday morning at 7:00. I noticed his bow, if he is interested in hunting too, we have a weekend program for those who want to immerse themselves in our culture. I, or one of the other Native people would adopt him for the weekend as one of our own and teach him everything about our Native culture; how to hunt, dance, be a good man, respect for life and spirit. We have hunting practice all day Saturday. You could bring him Saturday morning at 7:00 and we would take care of him until Sunday evening at 7:00."

"I don't know about that," James was taken aback by the offer.

"Please Dad, I'll be good, and I want to learn to hunt too!" Sammy begged with his hands in a prayer pose.

"Thank you for the offer, but I need time to think about this."

Sammy was dejected and pouted. James pulled him close, "I'm not saying, no. I just need time to think about it."

"Let me give you a pamphlet on the program, so you have some more information on it," said Abornazine. This was when James noticed that he was a Purple Band.

Abornazine went to his teepee and returned with the pamphlet. It was more like a four-page booklet. James thanked him and they headed back home for the day. Sammy asked for the booklet in the car and read it on their way home. He excitedly told his dad about everything he read in the booklet. Once home, James got out some fizzy fruit drinks and asked Sammy to sit with him on the sofa. "So, tell me what caused you to skip school today?"

"I just didn't feel like it. I was depressed." Sammy looked down at his pop bottle and spun it around in his lap.

"What happened with Antonio? Did something upset you?" James prodded.

"He keeps telling me that I have to accept that Mom may not get well from her drinking, and I might have to stay here. He wants me to get the angry feelings out that I got from Mom's drinking and about how that made me end up here. It just depresses me that I can't do anything about it."

"Is being here that bad for you?"

"Well, I miss soccer, but I'm catching up in math, so that may change soon. Mostly, I miss my old friends, but I talk to them on weekends, so it's not that bad, just different."

"Well, life is sometimes full of changes. We learn how to adapt to them. At least, many of the changes here are good ones. I miss that old life too, but I've found many new things that are very good. So, I don't mind giving some things up to get all the good things that I have now."

"Yeah," Sammy shrugged.

"What about your new friends? I remember you mentioning several after the Ropes Course."

"I just don't have anything to say to them, because I feel so sad. I just do my homework at lunch and avoid people. Antonio said I should try to connect and spend time with some kids, but I just don't feel up to it yet."

"Hmm, well, maybe this weekend, the Native American thing might be good for you. You might make some new friends, and it could give you something to talk about to the kids at school. What do you think?" James smiled at his son.

Sammy jumped up and nearly spilled his bubbly fruit drink. "Yes! Thank you, Dad. I think it will be so green," he hugged his father. "I'm going tell my friends in California." He rushed off to his room. Then he realized that his pack, which had his ComPad in it, was on the lounge chair so he spun around to get it.

"First you need to call the school and get your homework for today. It is almost 4:00, so do that first."

Sammy groaned but then asked the big screen in the living room to ring the number. The TV, phone, and ComPad came to life at his voice command. His homework came through the printer under the ComScreen and went to his room.

James looked over the pamphlet. It described the weekend immersion in Native American culture. There were classes and time to explore other interests. Adults were given a teepee to themselves. Children could stay with their parents, or with their adoptive Native family. They offered weeklong immersions and month-long ones too. They even had resident placement for those who wanted to stay a year or two, or permanently. Basic survival techniques were taught; hunting, leatherworking, clothes making, camp cooking, basket weaving, horse husbandry, adobe building, and desert gardening. Everything would be taught from a Native American mind set, which was basically a spiritual way of looking at all life. James decided that this would be a good distraction for his son and a way to ensure good hunting practices.

Sandra came in with Tammy. They had been spending a lot of time together and she often stayed for dinner. She did not know how to cook, so James was teaching her. It gave James a good reason to break out some cookbooks, try new recipes, and show Sandra how to make some new dishes. There was still an hour before it was time to begin, so Sandra settled down at the island to do homework while James focused on household chores like sweeping, sand was always a problem in the desert.

James checked on Sammy in his room to see if he was doing his homework. He was hard at work, so James returned to the kitchen to start cooking with the girls. Once the homework was done and Sammy emerged from his room, his dad tried to get him involved too, but the boy didn't take to cooking much. James suspected it was because it involved working with his sister.

After dinner, Tammy went home to her apartment. Sandra picked up the pamphlet on the Native American immersion courses. "What's this?"

Sammy perked up and told her about the dancing and hunting courses. "Wait, you cut school today?"

James interjected, "Yeah, I had to leave work to look for him and I found him at the shooting range, so, we spent the day there."

"You let him stay out of school?" she sounded critical and accusing.

"Yes, he's been having a hard time adjusting, you know. So, he needed some time to just have fun. I think it was good for him. But he is not going to skip school again, are you." He directed the last part to his son, who adamantly shook his head.

"If Mom was here, she would've had a conniption fit! Are you going to ground him?" Sandra demanded to know.

"No, not this time, but if it happens again, I will. Right Sammy?"

"Yes, but Mom is not here, so stay out of it, Sandra. You're not Mom!" Sammy's anger flashed at his sister.

"Sammy's right. You've been taking a parent role with both of us. I can handle Sammy on my own. He needs to know we care about his feelings first, not just punish him for his mistakes."

"You're right, I'm not the mom, but this is big. I wonder if we are spoiling him just because he is mad at the situation."

"Sandra, this is no bigger than driving all the way out here with my stuff! I'm not your mother and I don't have to react like her. She never asked how you feel. I take your feelings into consideration," James did not like having to explain himself to his daughter, but it needed to be done.

"I guess you're right. I've been acting like Mom, and she is not the best example. I guess, I felt Mom's absence and tried to fill the space. It was not my responsibility. I'm sorry for not respecting your boundaries and Sammy's. I'll work on that behavior, and I'll talk to Samantha about it."

"Good, I should not have to explain my parenting to you."

"No, you're right. You shouldn't. I'm sorry. So, are you going to let him go to this weekend thing?"

"Yes, I think it'll be good for him. I was thinking we could all go this weekend. It would be like a camping trip. Does that sound good to you?"

"I was going to go clothes shopping with Tammy. She didn't bring much with her."

"That shouldn't take all weekend, maybe you could leave to do the shopping for a while, then come back to the park?"

"Yeah, I could do that."

"Good, then it is settled. We'll get up at 6:00 in the morning on Saturday to go to the park."

Sandra went to her session on Friday and told Samatha about how she was trying to fill the vacuum Judy left in the family. She shared with her therapist how disrespectful that was to her father. She also told Samantha that after talking with her dad, she went to her room and did the *Chain of Questions*. It uncovered some feelings she was not aware of, and she talked about them for much of the session.

James and his children arrived at the park on time, which was a measure of how excited they were. James was looking forward to meeting the Native couple who would take Sammy for the weekend. He wanted to talk to them about the boy's problems. He instantly liked them and appreciated that they were Purple Bands. They put him at ease and he felt comfortable with the idea of leaving his son with them for this weekend, and perhaps future ones. They were a mixed couple; the father Alo, was Hopi and the mother Chenoa, was White. They had two older children of their own.

During the weekend, Sammy went on a hike, hunted with his foster family, and practiced his bow. Alo killed a rabbit. He taught Sammy how to prepare it for dinner and Chenoa taught him how to cook it.

Early in the day, Sandra joined the women of the tribe and learned how to weave. She was enjoying her time until the men returned from hunting. The sight of the dead rabbits upset her, so she took off to go shopping before the butchering began. She did not want to see it. Sandra returned after dinner to participate in the dancing. Sammy was engrossed in everything. He loved living and dressing like a native, hunting, and learning to tend the fire. He was beaming.

The next day, Sammy and James went out early to hunt with Alo again. Then they attended the dancing classes. They had no luck hunting, but for dinner they ate deer meat that Chenoa had roasted all day in a pit. Sammy was disappointed that he didn't shoot anything when he hunted. James was relieved; he liked being on a hunt but had no desire to hurt an animal. Alo patiently explained to Sammy that Great Spirit would let him succeed only when he was ready.

Sandra helped Chenoa gather herbs in the wild and vegetables from the cold storage, where they kept everything that they had harvested from the gardens. The family was content. They all enjoyed the weekend and returned home exhausted.

Judy was disappointed. Sammy did not take her calls or email her. She was feeling isolated and abandoned. Other than complaining about Jose and the other residents, she had nothing to say. She was still not comfortable talking about her feelings to anyone, especially a group. Instead, she felt consumed by her feelings of being a failure as a child and as an adult. It is the only way she saw it.

Lisa was trying to help Judy see that they were not failures, but rather, she simply did not know how to deal with her feelings because her parents never taught her. Perhaps they could not, because they did not know themselves. These past two weeks seemed like a month to her.

Lisa worked with Judy's anger towards her parents, but she could not get her to move past a feeling of being a failure. She failed to be adult enough for her parents. Changing gears for the moment, Lisa addressed Judy's intense guilt.

"No one at eleven is an adult, nor should they be. There is no failure in this. You were a child. You could not expect yourself to know how to be an adult at eleven years old. Parents usually teach a child how to mature while they are growing up, but yours didn't know how to do that. They should have been more attentive to you, but they weren't."

"They never gave me a chance. They just sent me to that boarding school. I had to grow up there and I did, but they still treated me like a child. They did not want to hang out with me," Judy lamented through her tears.

"Does that make you angry at them?"

"At the time, I was ashamed, now I'm just sad. I still can't get them to see me as an adult. At least, that is how I feel. I'm still trying to prove myself to them. If I told them the truth about my life, I'm afraid they would see me as the failed child I was, when they put me away in that school," Judy said through a torrent of tears.

"There is nothing for you to be ashamed of. You tried so hard. It isn't that you failed, only that they failed to see you, and all the effort you were making to gain their respect. You were not given opportunities to express your emotions, so you did not learn how to properly deal with them as a kid or even now as an adult. There is no fault in that. It is just something you need to learn. It was wrong of them to push you into being an adult long before the appropriate time. They demanded too much from you." Lisa patiently explained.

"You keep saying that, but I can't help the way I feel. As you've said before, I need to grieve in my own way until I'm done. I understand what you are saying, but I can't shake these feelings yet. I have had them for so long. I can see what you're saying but it still hurts."

"You're right, you need time to grieve; time to realize you did everything in your power to fulfill their expectations, but they were not capable of seeing your successes. They never gave you the recognition you deserved. It was always an open issue in the past because you believed that if you tried harder, it would work. Now you are coming to the realization that there was nothing more you could have done. They led you to believe that if you were an adult, they would want to do things with you. Now you are an adult, and they are still not seeking out your company. The fault lies with them not you. You can be healthy and whole, without their recognition. You can be everything they could not be. You can be an attentive parent, to yourself and to your children. You are on your way to healing now."

"How long do I have to grieve?"

"Everyone is different. Each person grieves differently. It takes as much time as it needs. When you are done, your feelings will shift. Once you are free from these old false beliefs, which trapped you, made you feel bad, and gave you a need to hide who you are and what you feel, the grief will end. Then you will feel a new vitality and be ready to begin a new phase of your life. You can't force the shift before its time. However, you can aid the process by being more open about it. It would help you move through the grief quicker, if you could share your feelings in the meetings."

"I'm too embarrassed to do that. No one needs to see my pain. Look how long it took me to share it with you, even though I knew I had to do it to get out of here."

"Everyone in that room, carries a similar pain. They won't judge you because they do not want to be judged either. Pain is a tenderizing process; a part of our humanity and it seeds compassion. If you can listen to their pain and share your own, you help each other heal. It is a tool to help you heal, I promise. It has power just like your writing does."

Judy sighed heavily and blew her nose, still recovering from her sobs. "I'll try, I guess."

"Good, let's wrap it up for today."

"Okay."

Her free time was not over yet, so Judy hid her swollen eyes in her room. When it was time to exercise, she went into the bathroom and washed her face first. After rigorous exercises, she felt better. She went to the afternoon meeting and Frankie called on her. She wanted to decline, but then she looked at her therapist, who was prompting her to talk.

She took a deep breath, stood up, and said, "Judy."

Everyone said "Hi, Judy," simultaneously.

"I haven't shared for two reasons; one is that I don't think I'm an alcoholic, so I didn't want to start with that, and two, I'm not one to vent my feelings before other people. I want to get out of here in a month and my therapist said talking in this group will help. So, here goes. In the past two weeks, I figured out that my parents ignored my feelings and didn't want me to be a kid. I didn't realize that until now. I thought my childhood was normal, until Lisa pointed out to me that they didn't spend any time with me or ever asked how I felt about anything. I realize now that 'grow up' was the only message I got from them. So, I grew up fast, but not fast enough, so they sent me away to a boarding school. It felt like they were just trying to get rid of me." Judy started to tear up, so she stopped. "That's it for today."

Sasha, who always sat next to her, handed her some tissues. She begrudgingly accepted. Her therapist gave her a thumbs up.

After the meeting, while they waited for their ComPads, Sasha said, "Congratulations on your first real sharing! That must have been hard. I know mine was."

"Thanks Sasha, it was totally embarrassing. I don't know if it will help me as much as Lisa thinks it will. I feel so dumb for not knowing that my upbringing was not normal."

"I don't think anyone knows that until someone points it out to them. I didn't know either." Sasha got her Smartwatch; Judy got her pad, and they went their separate ways.

Judy went to her room. She wanted to call but hesitated because she felt she could not take the heartbreak of not being answered again. She thought about calling James, while she paid some bills online. He had sent a text with his number, but she didn't want to FaceTime him with pajamas on. The truth was, she was embarrassed to talk about what was going on with her. Admitting that she was wrong or broken in some way did not sit well with her. She decided to wait until ten minutes to five to call James on his Smartwatch.

James made it a point to be home when the kids returned from school. He did not want them to be alone, so he was taking off early from work until Sammy felt better and could be trusted to be home alone with the bow. He was just walking in when Judy called. Sammy was not home yet, and Sandra was staying at Tammy's tonight after school.

"Hello, Judy, how are you doing?" he said in a friendly voice.

"Fine, I guess, but I haven't been able to talk to Sammy in over a week. He is not answering my calls," she complained.

"Well, he has been very upset this week, upset with your drinking and with having to come here. He has been talking to a therapist about it, but still, he is mopey and depressed. He can't play soccer yet and that is bumming him out. He has had a hard time connecting with his friends at school. We will just have to give him time."

"My calls to him are the only thing I look forward to. Have I said something to upset him?"

"I don't know, he didn't tell me. I didn't ask him about your calls. I felt that was a private thing between you and him. I thought you'd want it that way."

"Yes, that's true. I do but can you talk to him and find out why he won't answer my calls?" she said in a pleading voice.

"Sure. He may be here in a minute, if you want to talk with him," James offered.

"I don't want to force him to talk to me, but I would like to know why."

"Ok, I'll ask him. So, how are you doing anyway, are you making progress?"

"Yeah, I guess so. My therapist is digging into my past. She thinks it's what's making me drink. I'm not so sure about that, but I'm finding that my past is not as rosy as I always thought it was, and it's depressing. I feel abandoned by you, my kids, and by my parents too. So, I'm not having a lot of fun," she said with a mixture of blame and sarcasm.

"Well, I can see that. I'm dealing with the same problem. I felt abandoned by my mother and brother."

"Didn't they die? That is different."

"Yes, it's different but it feels the same to a kid. You may need to grieve about it either way," James replied.

"I'm sure doing a lot of that. Well, I don't want to get into a conversation about it right now, I just wanted to find out what is going on with Sammy," her tone became a little curt.

"I think Sammy is grieving too," he replied.

"Well, I have to return the ComPad, so shoot me an email with what you find out."

"Sure, will do. Glad you're making progress. We're all three going through the same thing. If you want to talk to someone you know who'll understand, feel free to call me."

"Sounds good, talk to the very person who abandoned me, that makes sense," she said with acid dripping off her tongue.

"Just remember, you pushed me away. I gave you what you said you wanted for years, a divorce. I don't want to argue about the past. I think it would be good for us to talk," James kept his cool.

"Not likely to happen, but I'm glad you are just as miserable as I am," she spit out.

"Ok, that's not nice, so I'm going to hang up on you now," and he did.

Judy tossed the pad on her bed. She was tired of getting hung up on. She lay on her back and crossed her arms and thought to herself. 'The nerve of that man thinking I'm going to open my soul to him! I wouldn't do that if he was the last man on Earth!'

Lisa knocked and opened the door. "Are you done with the pad? It's time."

"Yeah, quite done," Judy answered with the caustic tone still in her voice.

Normally, Judy was sad at the end of her Comp time, so Lisa took notice that she was angry now. "What is wrong? You sound upset."

"I just talked to my ex. Would you believe he had the nerve to suggest that we could talk about our feelings with each other," Judy looked at Lisa in disbelief.

"It actually sounds like a good idea to me, that is, if you can do it nicely."

"He abandoned me, why should I talk my heart out to him?" Judy accused.

"You were married, so he is the closest person to you other than your parents. It could be good for your relationship with him. You will need to patch things up with him eventually because you want to have shared custody of your kids. The better the relationship between you, the better it is for the kids."

"I can't believe you're on his side!" Judy felt betrayed.

"It is not about sides. It is the most loving and possibly healing thing to do. It could be good for both of you. If he is willing to talk to you, it's a good thing!"

"He just wants to check up on me. Just wants to know if the drunk is safe to be around the kids, that's all." Judy spit out.

"He may have some concerns, but what better way of showing your progress then to talk to him?" Lisa said in a loving voice.

"He doesn't need to know what is in my heart of hearts. That is private."

"You seem to think that about everyone. You are afraid of people knowing your pain and thoughts. That is why you don't share at the meetings. What are you afraid will happen if someone finds out how you feel? This is your next writing assignment." Judy groaned.

When Sammy got home, James asked him to sit on the sofa for a talk. "Your mother called. She was wondering why you weren't answering her calls lately."

"Because all she does is complain about the people there and ask me the same questions about school over and over again," he sounded exasperated.

"I see. Do you want to talk to her? It is ok if you don't."

"No, not really. She goes on about the past fun we had and that makes it worse about being here. It feels like she is trying to upset me, and I'm still mad at her too. She acts like nothing happened."

"Sammy, you don't have to talk to your mother until you are ready. She's really upset because she doesn't know why you won't take her calls. I can talk to her for you, if you like?"

"I don't want to hurt her feelings. I just don't want her to call," he whined.

"I understand. What do you want me to do? I can tell her to call less often, like every few days, and not complain or bring up the past, would that work for you?"

"Yeah, I guess," he mumbled weakly.

"Sammy, please tell me if you want me to handle this. You don't have to talk to her if you don't want to. You can wait until you feel ready. No one is going to force you, but to be fair, someone needs to tell her."

"I don't want to. You can call her and tell her I'm still mad at her right now. That is the truth."

"Okay, I'll send her an email right now."

"Tell her not to send anymore emails also. She keeps asking why I won't answer her calls and saying sorry a lot."

"Okay, I'll handle it," James said softly and patted his son on the shoulder.

"Thanks Dad, for understanding. I thought you were going to make me talk to her. I've been worried about it this whole time."

"I believe you have a right to say no. I won't force you."

Sammy was clearly relieved.

James immediately sent Judy an email telling her that Sammy needed more time before he would be ready to talk to her. She will receive it tomorrow. His heart went out to Sammy, and Judy. They were so close and shared such a warm bond, now they can't even talk to each other.

CHAPTER 22

The Process

Judy had a rough week. First, she received an email from her ex saying Sammy did not want to talk to her, then Jose got in her face again about denying her alcoholism. On top of that, she had to open up to the group about her feelings and her past. It was humiliating. She often broke down and cried or felt embarrassed. She had plenty of fodder for her writing assignments about her need to hide her vulnerability and feelings from others. Her parents' judgement made Judy feel that any perceived failure on her part was unacceptable.

Lisa explained the Eleven Affirmations for Life to Judy, and she had a problem with the first three steps. The idea of a conscious loving Self that is somehow separate from her perceived self was hard for her to grasp. She also had a problem with seeing abandonment as a type of fear, because she could not admit that she had fears.

"I just don't get it!" Judy said in one of her sessions. "I am, who I am. There's no other me."

"Treat it as an exercise. Imagine you have a Higher Self. Pretend there is this other version of you, a calm, loving, non-judgmental you. See her in your mind as a part of you that was able to express emotions her whole life and was never hurt like you were. You could see her like a guardian angel who always speaks and acts in a loving way."

"I don't believe in angels or gods," Judy affirmed.

"You don't have to. This is who you would be, if your parents had been loving, kind, and respectful to you. She would have no anger, grief, or sadness. She just has love. This is your Essential Core Self. To find her, imagine this ideal version of you that is not controlling or judgmental. Do you understand now?"

"I get the idea, but it is hard to picture someone truly loving, when I don't know what that looks like. I thought my parents were loving, until I got here; and now, I see that they weren't. What does real love look like? What does it act like?"

"That's a fair question. Love is being honest, caring about how the one you love feels, as well as being gentle and kind. Being loving is caring more about the person and how they feel, than about any issue that arises. It is being willing to share yourself, your deepest self, and your possessions, because when you love someone, they become an extension of who you are. When you love someone, you want what is best for them even when it requires sacrifice on your part. Loving brings out the best in you and in the one you love.

"When you love yourself, it is similar, you honestly look at yourself and accept your virtues and your faults, without judgment, criticism, or embarrassment. They are just part of the wonderful package that is you. You assume that everyone has different parts that work or don't work to some extent, and these are yours. They just are, with no bad feelings attached.

"It means being gentle, kind, and patient with yourself. It is caring about how you feel more than about any issue that arises. It is being willing to share yourself with others and finding at least one person with whom you can share your deepest self, your deepest thoughts and feelings. It is valuing and respecting your own nature and your things. It is knowing that you are an individual of value. You want what is best for you, so you avoid anything that will harm you and your body. Sometimes that requires sacrificing something pleasurable, because you know it is not good for you. When you love yourself, you express the best in you.

"In contrast, when a child grows up without feeling loved, whether they are or not doesn't matter, it is feeling unloved that carves out the child's view of the world and of themselves.

"The first thing the child does is try to explain why they aren't loved. They generally decide that there is something wrong with them, that they are unlovable, they do not deserve to be loved, or that there is something bad inside them. This explains why.

"In order to get the love, they need, they try to do or be whatever they think will find favor in the eyes of the adults, they want to be loved by. For some, it is trying to be prettier, or smarter, more helpful, or more grown up. Often when a child is not loved, the problem does not lie in this adorable little person, but rather in the parent who has been too wounded by life to give love. This adult probably does not love themselves or the inner child within them, so they do not have the love to give that this adorable little person deserves.

"In any case, being prettier, smarter, helpful, or more grown up, does not fully get them what they want. It may bring many kudos from other people. They may become very successful in their lives, but not in their heart of hearts. They never received the love they wanted from their parents. They never received the respect and acknowledgement for all their efforts from their parents, so they keep trying harder.

"They are doomed to fail, because they want something their parents are not, and never were, capable of giving. That is why they didn't get it when they were young.

"To cope with the disappointment, and to hide the thing that they still believe makes them unlovable, they construct what Carl Jung called, a Persona, a social mask. They put on this pretty, smart, helpful, mature mask, and people respond favorably towards them. They get the attention, appreciation, and success they want, but it never satisfies them. It never heals the wounds inside them, because they think people only love the mask, and not who they really are inside.

"Over time, the difference between the outer world, which is often successful; and the inner world, which is hurting, lonely, angry, and filled with disappointment; grows wider apart. Eventually the distance causes a crisis and necessitates a major healing. It could be an illness, accident, heart attack, mental breakdown, divorce, addiction, or some other calamity that forces the person to reevaluate their life.”

“So, the me I have always been as far back as I can remember, is a fake front that I put on just to keep me safe from the bad feelings I have inside and from being rejected again the way my parents did? And there is another me that has been hiding inside me the whole time that is loving, kind and good?” Judy said with great skepticism.

“Yes, you got it! Your rational self, your ego, thinks it must protect this tender loving Self, so it leads you to lie, hide who you really are, and does not let anyone get close; but your Wise Loving Self, your Higher Self, your True Essential Self, can take care of itself.

“Once you learn to process your feelings openly and honestly, you will easily be able to distinguish between the negative thoughts and behaviors of this overprotective ego and the loving supportive thoughts that come from your Loving Self. See it as the wise part of you.”

“Okay. I think I get it. The conscious wise part of me is the loving Higher Self. Every day until now, my thoughts and actions have been controlled by an overprotective, fearful, rational ego. Have I got that right?” Judy had an edge to her voice.

“Yes,” Lisa said cautiously, hearing her tone.

“I don’t have a clue how I’m supposed to be this loving conscious Self. I’ve been plain old me for a long time, bad or good. I’ve thought I needed to protect myself all this time. Let’s be realistic. The world is not a nice loving place. This Loving Self is not going to pay my bills or protect me from a bad marriage.”

“Maybe it could have, but you have not tried it yet. First let’s just let it love you and forgive yourself for your imagined failures. Then we will show you how it can do other things. Right now, we just need you to process your feelings honestly and begin to love yourself, despite any beliefs you have about the past.”

“I didn’t fail in my marriage! It was a bad choice to marry James. He looked like the kind of man who would make a lot of money, but he didn’t. That’s what led to the marriage failing. I could not have seen that ahead of time.”

“No, of course you couldn’t, neither could he. That’s just it, why be angry at him or at yourself, for something that neither of you could have foreseen? Life sometimes throws unpredictable things at us, and no one is to blame. We cope as best we can, but sometimes through no fault of our own, nothing can be done to prevent it.

“Let’s try to understand your situation and his. Obviously, you were living beyond your means, otherwise you would not be in debt. Due to whatever circumstances, he had bad luck in the job market. He didn’t bring in enough and too much was going out. There does not need to be any blame here. The two of you could have handled your combined income better, but emotional and other needs got in the way. You brought in more and perhaps you spent more. Alcohol can lead to a bad habit of shopping too much. Shopping can be an addiction too. The point is, you can try to stop blaming and start understanding your part and his in a loving and compassionate way."

Judy said nothing. She just sat there staring, deep in thought. She still had not admitted that she had a part in the financial problems, and now she felt trapped by Lisa's words. She did not want to admit that she was at fault for any of this. She needed to change the subject, but to what?

Lisa noticed that Judy had shut down. 'There is that secret again,' she mused. 'It seems to come up every time finances are mentioned.'

"What are you holding back on? What is it about money that makes you shut down completely? You always blame him for the debt, but you are the one that gets embarrassed by the mention of money. Tell me what is on your mind."

Judy squirmed in her seat. How was she going to avoid this?

"James could not keep a job. That was the major problem in our relationship. That is why we argued so much. It is why we were in credit debt; and when he did get a job it was a low paying one. He had a degree in architecture; he should have done better."

"You're in blaming mode. This process will only work if you are honest. Blaming is a way to redirect our focus away from the real problem. Let's use the *Chain of Questions* to get around this.

"What are the feelings that make you deflect to blaming him?"

Judy sighed heavily. She knew she was not going to avoid this subject. "He thinks I spend too much money. We argued over it a lot. He did the bills and would point out how I was spending too much. I know what the problem is, I just don't want to admit it."

"There, that was honest. Thank you for telling me the truth. Telling yourself the truth is a very important part of this process. Now that we have that out of the way, we can get to the real problem underneath. Using the *Chain of Questions* will bring us to the core of the problem. What feelings do you have that makes you avoid the truth?"

"Embarrassment. I don't handle money well, and I should be able too. I handle million-dollar accounts at work, and I can't keep my credit reasonable. It's ridiculous!"

"Let's find out why. Remember how I taught you to use the *Chain of Questions*?" Judy nodded.

"What is the next obvious question about your feelings, not about the situation?"

Judy thought for a while. "Why do I spend money, I don't have?"

"That question is situational. Remember to ask for a feeling. Okay, reword it."

"Why do I feel I need to spend money that I don't have?"

Lisa eased her onward. "Good, and the answer is?"

"I think I need stuff for work to fit in, and to feel better about myself. I want to look the part of a top Account Holder and look professional."

"Good, now what is the next obvious question about your feelings? Focus on the part where you said, 'to make me feel better about myself and fit in' the rest of your answer was situational."

"I do need to look professional though!" Judy objected.

"Yes, that is true. However, for this process, it doesn't address your feelings. We want to stay with the feelings."

"The feeling I get is pride when people comment on my new clothes or car." Judy said, with a smile playing at the corners of her mouth.

"Yes, that is your objective. The question is, why do you need it? To continue this Chain, tell me why you feel you need to fit in and feel better about yourself?"

"Because I don't feel like I do," the words jumped out.

"There it is. Why don't you feel like you belong? Why do you feel less than everyone else?"

Judy sighed, "This is tedious. These Chains of Questions always lead to the same answer, because my parents did not make me feel valued and loved."

"There you go. If that is the true motive, then you are dealing with an addiction not a fault. The cause of your shopping addiction is this feeling of being unloved and not valued. Right?"

"Yeah, I know. I'm a loving person inside and I need to love myself and forgive myself. Yeah, but that is a lot harder to do then just saying it?" Judy was now utterly exasperated.

"Yes, it is. I know it is hard, but you must do what your parents could not do. You need to retrain your brain to love yourself, despite these negative beliefs they implanted in you. That is why we have mirrors in every room that say, 'You are loving, worthy of love, and loveable.' Every day as you get up and go to bed, you can read these words and remember who you really are."

"I didn't realize how much I didn't love myself. I thought I did. But my persona covered it up with false pride. I have been lying to myself and everyone else for a long time. The truth is, I don't feel worthy of love at all." There was sincerity in Judy's voice. The sarcasm was gone and honest tears were flowing.

"You'll need to grieve over this for a time. But eventually, you will come to really love yourself and feel better about everything.

"There is a theme throughout many of your behaviors. You were embarrassed to let people see the real you, you were reluctant to talk about your feelings, and you were unwilling to admit even to yourself that you have an addiction to alcohol. All of that was about maintaining appearances. You were unwilling to admit your true feelings and believed weaknesses, even down to insisting you had good parents. You want to appear normal and balanced. It is part of the persona's job to look normal. It naturally strives to hide any believed weakness. As a child, you did it to survive in the boarding school. There is no reason to blame yourself. It was a basic survival mechanism.

"So, we all lie to ourselves, even you?" Judy said with spite.

"Most people lie to themselves to some extent. It is a measure of how much they love or don't love themselves. They do it as a coping mechanism."

Lisa felt that Judy was ready to go deeper. Even though she was still acting defensive, it was much less than usual.

Lisa ventured into deeper waters. "This need to look normal and be accepted is why you drank in college. You were not only trying to fit in but covering up your feelings of unworthiness. College had a competitive atmosphere. You had to do well to prove yourself worthy to your parents, to yourself, and to others; that generated a lot of stress in you. You needed something to help you relax, that would also keep you from feeling your feelings, because they were too painful. Alcohol became your answer."

Judy just sat there with nothing to say. She felt furious and sad at the same time, and her tears flowed freely.

Lisa knew it would take time for Judy to absorb all this, so she called an end to the session and gave her the next writing assignment. "Write about how you feel in regard to all the things we talked about today."

James was struggling to feel his grief because he was happier now than he had ever been in his life. The only thing he was worried about was Sammy. Kim helped him get in touch with his feelings of abandonment through a visualization. They were working on feelings of worthlessness in connection with his past jobs and his relationship with his wife. James understood that the past affects the present, nevertheless, he was so happy with his life now that delving into the past did not seem worth the trouble.

In Friday's session, Kim was saying, "Getting in touch with your feelings of grief can help you better understand what your son is feeling."

"Yeah, I guess that's true, but I'm having a hard time connecting to this feeling outside of your office. If we were doing this therapy back when I was still with my wife or still in a job I hated, I think it would be easier to feel the rawness of it."

"It might have been easier, but this is when your destiny brought you to this point. If this is when it is coming up, then this is the right time. Feelings don't go away. They just become buried, lying under the surface waiting for the right time to rise again. There is a big difference between suppressing an issue and resolving it. One buries it and the other disperses the energy locked in the memory. Life is cyclical. When issues are not resolved, they rise again.

"After the honeymoon phase of this new life wears off, and the kids spend more time on their own, you will enter another cycle and these old issues can rise again, bringing up painful unresolved feelings. Right now, while we are working together, I can give you the tools, so when the time comes, you will be equipped to deal with these feelings and have less pain. On the other hand, I think we can see each other less often. How about once a week on Mondays, so it is still coordinated with your children's appointments?"

"That sounds good. Do I get an Orange Band yet?"

"Have you been going to Eleven Affirmations meetings?"

"No, not since I moved out of the hotel."

"I will give you a list of the ones in your area or near work. I think it would help you to go at least once a week. They will give you more tools to work with. Then we can talk about the band. Being able to use these tools when you're stressed is the key to getting the next color band. You are using the tools well, but you still have a few more to learn."

"I know that I've been avoiding my more negative feelings to just be happy, but I thought I had this down."

"You do, in a lot of ways, you know the *Chain of Questions*, which is a big part of it, and you can get in touch with your feelings when pressed to do so. Now you need to work on your knowledge of the Affirmations and learn how to use them when you are under pressure. This is still new to you."

"Okay, if I'm not there yet, I'm not there yet," James said in resignation.

After work, James got home at the same time as Sandra and Tammy. Tammy offered to do the dishes as she often did when she came for dinner. Sandra helped. James took care of the laundry. Sammy came in shortly afterwards and immediately went out to practice his bow as he usually did after school. He generally did his homework at lunch or in tutoring, so he could practice before he lost the light. Sandra and Tammy did their homework together at the island before cooking with James. After dinner, Tammy thanked them again and went home. Sammy went to his room to talk with his friends in California.

James asked Sandra to sit and talk with him. "I noticed that Tammy still has a Red Band, but you two visited the same website, so how did you get your Orange Band so fast and she didn't?"

"I went to the Affirmations meetings in New World and learned to do personal processing there. Tammy just hung out with her friends and talked. She found the meetings boring. I did them, because I saw the value of them. They helped me deal with Mom."

"Oh, I see. Well, that's good. Good for you doing that."

"Are you jealous?" Sandra asked, with an amused smile.

"Just a little. I haven't gone to those meetings since I moved into the new house. I talked to Kim about it and she thinks I should start going again. I'd like to do that after dinner on a weekday, so I don't lose more work hours. There's a meeting tonight in half an hour, but I don't want to leave Sammy alone. Would you be willing to stay with him tonight and on Fridays?"

"Sure. Is there another night in the middle of the week? I want to go to Tammy's for the weekend, and I'd like to go on Friday nights."

"Sure, there's one on Wednesdays at the same time."

"That would be better for me, and you can go tonight if you like. I've got a paper to write on the dog-yotes, they're half-bred coyotes."

"Great, I'll tell Sammy and be on my way. Call me if there are any problems. I'm going to take one of the E bikes.

James went to the nearest community center that hosted a meeting and arrived just in time. They passed out three reading sheets: on Co-Dependance, the Eleven Affirmations, and Meeting Rules and Traditions. Most of the people wore red, orange, or yellow bands, but a couple had green bands or blue ones. That made James feel, better for some reason. The leader of the group was a Purple Band. He introduced himself as Bryant.

When it was James's turn to share, he identified himself as an Ex-Spouse of an Alcoholic. After everyone said, "Hi James" he continued, "I'm trying to grieve over my mother's death from cancer and my brother's suicide, which is hard for me to do right now because I'm the happiest I've been my whole life. I can work in my preferred field for the first time, I got a divorce from my abusive wife, and I even have custody of my kids. This has all happened since I arrived in Hope. It is hard for me to grieve the loss of my childhood family when things are going so well, besides it was a long time ago.

"My daughter got her Orange Band last week and I feel like my own daughter has a better handle on life than I do. I'm a little jealous. I'd like to get my grieving out of the way, so it doesn't mess up my good life, but it is hard to bring up old feelings from the depths.

"I'm worried about my son. He resents coming here, so he mopes around sad and depressed. He's angry at his mom for drinking and for getting caught by Child Services. That is how I got custody of them. He misses his friends and playing soccer. He gets down on himself too easily, but I have him doing archery and spending time at the Wise World Park. It's helping his mood. I hope it doesn't distract him from processing his feelings toward his mother. Well, that's all I have right now."

In their sharing, a few people mentioned they related to what James said. It felt good to know he wasn't alone. He picked up a book on the Eleven Affirmations that he didn't read at the hotel. He didn't finish the last book he was working on, so he felt he'd better get a new one. He realized he needed to make time to read, maybe before bed.

On the eBike riding home, James thought about asking God for guidance with his son. He opened to the voice of God and heard, 'Sammy is on a good path for him, don't worry. Sometimes it takes a village to raise a child.' James immediately began to relax.

At home, James said goodnight to Sammy. Sandra was still working on her paper, so he sat down on the sofa and began to read his new book and refresh his memory on the Affirmations. A little while later, Sandra came over. "I know a secret about you that you haven't told me." She said in a coy tone.

"Oh, what's that?" James echoed her coy tone.

"You talk to God."

"Oh that. Yes, I do. I was not sure how you would react to that, but I was going to tell you when the time was right."

"I thought you didn't believe in God?" Sandra asked with sincere curiosity.

"I didn't for a while, but I was raised to believe in God. Your grandmother used to pray a lot. When she died, I felt angry at God and shut Him out. Since I have been here, I have learned to dialogue with God, rather than just pray to Him. Tim and Cathy encouraged me to do it and I find it very comforting at times. It feels good to know there is someone who can always give me guidance and reassurance when I need it."

"Cathy told Tammy and me something about a cactus. Please tell me the story," Sandra coaxed.

"Well, on the way here, I got very frustrated with myself. I didn't know whether to leave, or go back home, and I had a little rageful fit on the side of the highway. It caused me to fall on a cactus and a half dozen needles were stuck in my leg. There were pieces of paper on the needles from a tattered child's book that had gotten stuck on the cactus. While I was ranting at God, I asked him, 'What do you want from me?' Why are you torturing me? and What do you want me to do? On these little shards of paper, were the words, "Nothing," "I'm not," and "Listen to me." They were perfect answers to my questions. I was too mad at the time to be amazed, but I am now. I have a piece of paper with those words on it taped on my bathroom mirror. It was given to me by the Founder's Proxy on my first day here. She channeled the words. There was no way she could have known. Do you know what channeling is?"

"Yes, I've read the Founder's books, I know what it is. Can you teach me how to do it?"

"I haven't the foggiest Idea how I do it, let alone how to teach it. Cathy once explained to me that everyone has intuition. Most people can learn to enhance it, but not everyone is open to it. The right-brain is the part of the mind that channels information. Cathy explained to me that the left-brain functions rationally, and the right-brain connects ideas by associations, how things are related to each other. The left-brain separates the whole of reality into details, and the right-brain weaves details into a whole picture. Most people have access to both functions. Those who have a highly developed right-brain naturally receive intuitive information.

"Unless the right-brain is impaired, or the left-brain is overly dominant, anyone can learn to channel. It is a matter of understanding the language of the right-brain and not subjecting the information to the critical eye of the rational mind. Skepticism blocks the flow of the channel.

"Tim mentioned once that most children under the age of five naturally channel information. As they get older, indoctrinated beliefs and other people's expectations cause children to doubt themselves and reject the information they receive. For many people, this makes them become closed, until such time as the trust is rebuilt and the person is willing to be open again.

"In my case, the trauma of losing my job and everything that went with that, made me desperate. My desperation pushed me past the editing-out part of my rational mind, so the intuition could reopen.

"I want to take a class on it. They are held on Fridays in town, can I go?" asked Sandra.

"Oh, that's why you need Friday nights. Sure, I don't see a problem with that. Good luck, I hope it works for you."

"Since you are going to send Sammy to the park on weekends, I was wondering if I can spend weekends at Tammy's. We can do our homework together and just hang out." Sandra held her breath waiting for her dad's reply.

"I'll make a deal with you. You can spend the weekends there as long as you follow a few basic rules: No boys involved, unless I meet them first. No parties or going to a dance club, without me or Cathy there to watch over you. No leaving the city without me coming along. No alcohol or drugs, legal or not, and if you think I wouldn't like you getting into something, don't do it until you run it by me first. Do these game rules sound fair to you, and do you promise to follow them?"

"Yes, very fair. I'll follow all of them. Thank you, Dad. Thank you! Thank you!" She jumped up and hugged her father, with the same level of joy she had as a child.

"I want to go with you to the park and do the canyon ride again, then I'd like to go to Tammy's. I'm going to call Tammy, then I'll go to bed."

James read for a while. Then, listened at Sandra's door, but there was no sound. She was probably asleep, so he went to bed.

The next morning, they all went to the park as planned. Sandra was looking forward to visiting the canyon village again to talk to the Native people about dog-yotes. James dropped Sammy off at his foster parents, Alo and Chenoa. They told him what they wanted to teach his son. James approved and gave them permission. Then he went home to catch up on cleaning and reading. It was nice to have the house to himself, but it also felt a little empty. He realized that he had rarely been alone. Even in college there were roommates and friends around and then he got married.

"Well, I did want some time alone, so this should be good for me," he said out loud to the empty room. He read a little but soon he was feeling a rising anxiety. He thought of taking a drug to bury the feeling. There was some Hydroxyzine in the medicine cabinet, but he remembered all the things he was learning and decided to do the dynamic meditation on his own. He put on loud music and danced wildly while shouting odd sounds. He let himself be completely crazy until all the panicky feelings subsided. Then he sat down and surrendered to a deep meditation. After forty-five minutes, he felt utterly spent, so he ran a bath, added some calming bath salts Sandra had in the bathroom and called Cathy to chat. He wished he had more friends, so he didn't have to depend solely on her all the time. He invited her over for lunch, but she already had other plans.

He asked the ComScreen in the living room to tell him what entertainments are available in town tonight. The list was long. There was a music event at the shell concert hall, but it didn't start until 7:00 that evening. He thought about having lunch and playing a few games at the bowling alley. That would keep him occupied until the concert. Then he got the idea to join a league. It would be a way to meet new people. He had a plan.

He brushed up on his bowling, ate an early lunch, and found a list of leagues. Calling one to see if they had an opening, was a little intimidating. Could he be consistent enough in his scores to be worthy of a league?

Under each league's name was a brief description. Some sounded rather laid back about getting high scores. They appeared to be more about socializing. One was for divorcees. They were coming in at noon. 'Perfect!' thought James.

When the group arrived, James introduced himself and they seemed genuinely glad to have him join them. There were five men and three women. Everyone ate pizza and drank non-alcoholic beer, which tasted good enough.

They were bowling in pairs. James was paired up with Maxine, a good-looking woman around his age. She had lovely curves, a little extra weight, curly brown hair, and sweet dimples in her cheeks.

James scored a one hundred ten and was happy with it, considering he had not had much practice. After three more games, the group took a break in the lounge. Maxine had an outgoing nature, so, she started the conversation. "What brought you to Hope?"

"Well, the signs on the highway did, more or less. I needed a place to stay for a while and I took advantage of the free hotel," James said somewhat sheepishly.

"Oh, you didn't know about this community before you came?" that piqued Maxine's interest.

"No. I once saw a 20/20 program on communities like this but never thought to visit one. I was looking for a hotel when a sign for Hope appeared. It was the right place at the right time, far more than I could imagine."

"Then you just stayed? What brought you out to the desert in the first place?" she probed.

"Well, I lost another job, my wife at the time was intolerable, and I just had enough, I couldn't take any more of her yelling and screaming, so I left work and just kept driving until I ended up here. It was a synchronicity, as a friend of mine calls it. I had no idea how much I needed this place, until now."

"What made you stay?"

"Well, honestly, at first, it was that everything was free, then it was finding work in my field, and then it became the way the counseling was changing my life." James omitted the part about God guiding him.

"Well, I'm glad you found what you needed. How long have you been here?"

"Only about four months."

"Oh, so you haven't been divorced very long?"

"No, just about three months or so."

"I'm surprised that you joined a group like this so soon. Are you ready to move on?"

"Oh no. I'm just looking for friends who can relate to my situation. I'm not looking to hook up with anyone. I'm not used to being alone. My kids are doing other things this weekend and I was rattling around in a big house alone, so I came here."

"Oh, I see. Well, there are good people in this group." She leaned into his ear. "Make your intentions known to Katrina, she gets attached too easily."

"Oh, okay."

"She is always hitting on new guys and wants to get married. She hates being divorced." Maxine proceeded to tell him everyone's story, like it was her job to inform him. It was interesting, but hearing all this gossip made him feel uncomfortable. As soon as he could slip away, he joined the men's conversation about sports.

They bowled another set of games. This time he was paired up with Katrina. She did not seem clingy, like Maxine claimed. At the end of the evening, James was not sure about staying in this group. Other than divorce, which no one talked about, he did not have much in common with them. He decided to try again before he made up his mind. It felt good to meet new people, even though his insecurities made him feel shy and the whole experience felt forced.

Afterwards, he went straight home and did some reading, then he called the kids to check on them. Sammy was having fun, but again he was disappointed that he didn't shoot an animal in the hunt. Sandra and Tammy were at a poetry reading in the conversation house.

The next day, he did some chores around the house and then called Cathy. They went shopping together, talked about the loneliness they both felt, and the things they were trying to do about it. Cathy was very easy to talk to.

"My therapist said that I don't trust myself," said Cathy. "That's because I've been down on myself for so long. Now I need to learn to trust myself again. It is so hard to stop those old tapes in my head. I haven't been out much with others except for the Affirmation meetings. It is hard for me to talk to new people, because I keep second guessing my motives. I've been spending time with only women because I want to avoid getting into another relationship. I'm glad we already clarified where we stand with each other. It makes me feel safe with you. If a man was pursuing me, I don't know if I could say no." Cathy shared with him.

"I can relate," James responded. "My loneliness is a lot stronger than I thought it would be. I'm questioning my motives too. I don't want to start a relationship just because I'm not used to being alone and I know what you mean about trust issues. The tape loops in my mind are hard to stop. They make me feel out of place in social situations. I am pretty good at talking to people, but I still feel out of place, like I don't belong there.

"At least you're getting out," said Cathy. "I need to find things I like to do, otherwise, I just stay in the apartment all the time. I haven't done much in my life. What is bowling like? Would you be willing to teach me? Then maybe we could go there together and support each other?"

"They could use more women on the team," he offered. "So yeah, that might be a good idea. If we feel uncomfortable, we can at least talk to each other. If you're not doing anything now, I can teach you. It is a simple game to learn."

They went home to put their groceries away and met back at the bowling alley. Everything was going well. She picked up the basics quickly and was good at aiming the ball. But then, Cathy got her first strike and was so excited that she threw her arms around James and hugged him in her delight. James automatically hugged her back. Then they both froze and backed away. Cathy got red in the face and tried to cover her embarrassment. "I'm sorry, I should not have done that."

"It's okay, you were just excited. That's all."

She sat down on the bench. "I don't know what I'm doing. I don't trust myself. I don't know whether I have ulterior motives or not," she said with a heavy sigh.

"Do you really think you had an ulterior motive for hugging me, or was it just that I happen to be a man whom you feel you can trust with your emotions? I mean we have talked about a lot of deep things, and it has created a level of trust. You may not have any motive other than the sheer joy at making that strike." James sat beside her to console her.

"Maybe you're right, but I did a *Chain of Questions* with Angi, my therapist, and it led me to realize I want to be in a relationship where I feel safe, and I am attracted to you. I don't know if it is just that you are someone, I feel safe talking to, and you happen to be a man, or if I want to be with you because you're a man I am attracted to. Do you know what I mean?"

"Yeah, I get it," James sympathized. "I don't know if I'm interest in having a relationship with a woman or just attracted by her beauty. I never had a friendship with a woman before, so this is all new territory to me. I'm learning through you how to just be a friend."

"So, you feel no physical attraction to me?" she asked, slightly hurt.

"Don't get me wrong, you're pretty and you're a good person too, but you're not the type of woman I go to for just sex, and I have no idea what kind of woman I need for a relationship. To tell you the truth, I wouldn't know what to look for. My wife was convenient. I married her because my father wanted me to, not because I loved her. I don't know what falling in love feels like!"

"I don't either. My ex-husband and I got married right out of high school. I don't think it was for love either. It was more for safety. We just didn't want to be alone."

"Boy, we are pretty messed up about relationships, aren't we?" James observed.

"Isn't commonality a part of attraction?" she quipped.

"Perhaps, but it doesn't mean we are destined for each other." They both smiled. "So, you want to play a game or two with the scoreboard?" he asked.

She agreed, and they played a few games together. From then on, when they got good scores, they did high fives. James felt good being so honest and open about his feelings with Cathy. 'The openness here at City of Hope is a very healthy practice. It puts interactions on a whole other level of clarity, no games, no second guessing. It is refreshing.' thought James.

CHAPTER 23

Awakening

Judy was crying her heart out. "I can't believe how I made such a mess of my life!"

Lisa had just read Judy's writing assignment out loud. "There is no fault here. You were doing the best you could with the tools you had. Blaming distorts the truth. Don't blame yourself. Your conscious loving Self can help you reach forgiveness."

"I don't want to forgive myself. I messed up everything with my drinking and my shopping. I should have done better! I knew the truth, even when I was lying to myself! But no, I felt entitled to get what I wanted. I was selfish! I hate the fact, but it's true. There's nothing I hate more than selfish people and I was selfish the whole time! I hate myself!"

"It is okay. This is a genuine feeling. Feel it and then move on. You need to recognize that you were simply protecting yourself from painful feelings, and that is a normal behavior. When you face a feeling, it can be very strong at first, but then it subsides, and you can forgive fate for not being kinder, and forgive yourself for doing whatever you had to do to survive. Once you forgive, you can put your life back on track. It is unfair to punish yourself for this or hate yourself. What you did as a child and as a young adult could not be helped. Anyone in your situation would probably have done the same."

Judy just sat there drowning in tears. At her morning massage, which she had every other day, she became overwhelmed by intense emotions. Afterwards, instead of going to art class, she sought out Lisa.

Judy was using the *Chain of Questions* to find out why she had failed in her marriage and why drinking and shopping were the only answers she came up with. When she asked why she did these things, the answer was a feeling of entitlement. Her parents promised her presents and those promises made her feel loved. Then they often forget. Not only did they not give her those things, but they belittled her desire for them. She wanted to fulfill their promises, so she bought herself beautiful clothes. It was one of her motives for being successful. She was compensating, trying to fill the emptiness caused by all those unfulfilled promises. As her parents would say, she was coddling herself. She hated how spoiled she sounded.

"My parents tried to keep me from being spoiled, but it made me more so. I indulged myself. I have no one to blame but me! I was angry when they broke their promises, and I vowed to make up for it when I became an adult. I vowed to get what I wanted, no matter who it hurt," Judy admitted between wrenching sobs.

"You reacted to your neglect and the broken promises as any child would. You had to satisfy yourself. You needed love, but you created a persona that approved of you only when you felt successful. It pressured you to fit in, so you drank. You needed to dress the part you were playing to succeed, so you bought clothes and accessories. You were desperate to cover up your feelings of abandonment and being unlovable, so you pretended that your life was, and always had been, perfectly normal. These are all common reactions for a young person. You had no other tools and didn't know how to do otherwise. You had no other recourse, but now you do. You can learn to love yourself and learn to be less selfish. You can deal with your feelings better now and consciously change your behavior. This is not the end, it is the beginning of your new life," Lisa sounded hopeful.

"I feel like a spoiled child who needs to be locked up for being a brat. I'm exactly what my parents were trying to avoid."

"Perhaps they just went about raising you the wrong way. They didn't know better, but you do. Blame is just a dead end. It prevents healing. I suggest you don't stay there too long. Feel the anger and then release it. Holding onto it will not serve you. Let it go as soon as you can. Avoid making any decisions about your life until you have let go of the anger. Don't bargain with yourself either. Just be mad until you see how it is keeping you stuck and let it go. You had no choice. There is no blame.

"This is your next assignment. Write about what your life will be like when you have stopped blaming yourself and others for what happened in the past. When the anger has subsided, how will you go about healing yourself? Anger does not heal, only love does. What will your life look like when you are loving yourself and no longer need to be selfish?"

Judy begrudgingly agreed. She picked up her notebook and left. She didn't bother washing away the tears like she usually did. Now, she felt she had nothing to hide. The secrets of her life were out. There was time before the afternoon meeting, so she sat down on a sofa in the Great Room to think and write.

She could not help feeling angry about her failures and ashamed about how spoiled she thought she was. She could not blame her parents either, they told her not to care about material things and to be selfless. She blamed herself despite everything Lisa said. She felt depressed. She understood what Lisa said but putting it into practice was very hard. Only this loving, conscious Self could help her, if it existed. It was her only hope. This idea of unconditional love and being loved no matter what, was the only help she could think of to get out of the hole she was in. She had no idea what such love would look like or feel like.

As she languished on the sofa in the living room, she imagined her child self at the age of eleven, before she decided to grow up. She thought of her child-self, playing with her dolls and dollhouse, pretending to raise a family. She was the wife, and she had this perfect husband, and a little baby boy. Everything was peaceful in the house. The husband came home and played with their child and the mom cooked dinner in the kitchen. They always ate together and talked about their day. There was no butler or nanny in her fantasy. It struck Judy that her idea of family was a lot more loving than her real one. She knew something was not right about her upbringing even then. She bolted upright and started writing this down. She did know what love looked like. People talked and spent time with each other. Her child self knew that something was wrong with her parents. She saw things on TV. There was a difference between other families and hers.

She raised her kids the way she wished she was raised. She talked to them and played with them. They were close, until they got older and disappeared into their video games and FaceTime. Then she started feeling rejected by them, especially Sandra. That's when her drinking started to increase. She knew what love was, how it felt, and what it felt like when it was no longer there. James played with the kids too and felt rejected when they became so self-absorbed. He drank more then, too.

'James was not the perfect husband, but it was good in the beginning,' she remembered. 'What went wrong?' She asked herself. 'Was it losing those jobs? No. It was my spending. James mentioned it all the time and I ignored him. That's when we began to draw apart emotionally. I can't blame him for that. It didn't help that he kept losing jobs, but in truth, he always found another one rather quickly. I never realized how much that probably upset him. He couldn't have been happy. He never found a job doing what he really wanted. This is the first time I ever really thought about what he was going through.

Judy pulled out her notebook and wrote this all down. She made a tisk tisk sound with her tongue to herself. 'I was so selfish that I didn't even care about how he might feel that his dream work was never available to him.'

Lisa saw that Judy was writing, so she didn't bother her. She could see that her client was rounding a corner in her treatment and smiled to herself. She knew the gates of honesty were open now and there was no going back.

People began strolling in for the 3:00 Meeting, but everyone left her alone on the sofa. She listened to the things they shared and told herself that she would tell the truth and deserved whatever comments came her way, even from Jose.

When she was asked to share, she said, "Judy. I'm a selfish alcoholic and shopaholic. There I said it!" She looked at Jose and at her therapist who was leaning against the kitchen door while everyone said, 'Hi Judy.' She willingly shared, "I hope you are all happy now! I admit I have been fooling myself for a long time about a lot of things, but I'm not going to drink and I'm not going to lie to myself anymore. I'm going to do whatever it takes to get my addictions under control. I don't know if I can forgive myself for being so stupid, but I'm definitely not going to waste money on frivolous things, and I don't need to drink anymore."

Frankie looked at Lisa and then back at Judy. "Do you really think you can just control everything with your will?"

"Yes. I can control myself, if I don't lie to myself," Judy replied with a matter-of-fact tone.

"Thinking you can control emotions, is itself a lie, Judy. Without facing your feelings and working through the painful emotions, there is no healing, no resolution. Controlling and burying feelings because you do not approve of them causes problems in the future. Controlling and conquering negative behaviors, just buries them for a while. You have to learn to love yourself. When you do, then, and only then, can you overcome bad habits. It is not a matter of willpower but rather, the power of love," Frankie explained in a smooth gentle tone.

"Yeah, okay. I will do that too," Judy mocked defiantly.

Jose raised his hand to share next and Frankie called on him. "Jose, alcoholic."

"Hi Jose," everyone said in unison.

"What Frankie said is right. I thought that I could control my drinking with the sheer power of my will. I thought I could have one drink and stop. But over time, one became two, and that led to a six-pack. I still haven't delt with my anger issues and it is driving my drinking. I didn't know how to love myself or other people, really. I'm a control freak. I was always trying to control others, maybe I still am. Controlling others was easier than controlling myself. It felt like the solution to my imagined problems. I'm learning now that my problems with other people are mostly in my head. I'm judgmental of others, just as I judge myself harshly. I butt my nose into other people's problems that are none of my business. I'm the only one to blame, or fix, for that matter. I can't and shouldn't try to fix others. That is the Fifth Affirmation and I'm working on it."

Judy felt that he was directing his comments to her again, but this time there was a tone of apology in it for getting in her face before. Other people commented on their Fifth Step process also. After the meeting, the comps were handed out. Lisa offered one to Judy, but she declined, "I don't need it. I have no one to talk to."

"Isn't there anybody you want to do your Fourth Step with? You're working on that one right now, aren't you?"

"Yeah, but I don't think I'm ready to do that yet. To admit I'm wrong in here is one thing, to admit it to my ex is quite another."

"Take the pad anyway and think about it. It could be good for you to admit your shortcomings to someone you know, especially someone you've hurt."

Judy took the pad and sat there thinking about it. Then she went to her room. She thought of writing an email instead of calling. This way she could compose the perfect words and not disturb James at work. She thought it would be better to do that with the kids also. She wished she did not have to do it at all, but if she was going to prove she was serious about healing, it had to be done. It was her homework, and she was aiming for a good grade. The Third Step of the Affirmations was about taking responsibility, so she knew she had to do that too.

Judy composed a draft. "I'm working on my Fourth Affirmation step. I'm assuming you know what that is, since you are in the City of Hope. It has come to my attention of late that I was drinking too much and that was one of the reasons for the split between us. Another factor was the finances and my compulsive shopping. I have recently realized that these are my addictions, which I used to cover my feelings of abandonment that I felt from my parents. I had no idea that these feelings were even there in me, so I didn't realize I was addicted. That of course is no excuse for my behavior. I take full responsibility for my actions. I'm sorry for the hurt I have caused you in the last few years. Part of my pain was the kids growing apart from us. It made me drink even more, but some was from the stress from my work and the finances."

"The finances were my fault. I used shopping to feel better about myself. I realize now that I didn't consider that you may have been unhappy with your jobs. I am sorry I didn't support you emotionally back then. I blamed everything on you and gave you a hard time with it too. I am so sorry. I'm going to email the kids and make amends with them too. Please, if you could make sure they read it, I would appreciate it. Thank you for taking care of the kids and putting up with me for so long. I am on the mend and I'm taking this healing process very seriously. I will not drink or excessively shop ever again, I promise.'

Judy wrote shorter versions for the kids. She admitted to Sandra that she was wrong for being angry at her and blaming her for getting in trouble with the court and Child Services. She said she was sorry they had grown apart. She wrote to Sammy that she was sorry that he had to move and give up his soccer practice. She asked him not to be mad anymore and repeated something Lisa had told her. 'Anger hurts you more than it hurts anyone else.' She said she understood if he was still mad. With a deep breath, she raised her finger, and it stayed in the air for a second before she hit the SEND button.

When Lisa came to pick up the pad, Judy showed her the drafts.

"This is good! You did well. How does it feel to get this off your chest?"

"Well, good now, but it was hard to get started. Talk about feeling weak and remorseful. I hate admitting my faults."

"You did a good job. There was no blaming or excuses, well done. This will go a long way towards helping you to stay clean and could improve your relationships with your family. There is no guarantee though."

"I know. I realize I can't have any expectations. I don't know what will happen. They need to go through their own process, and it may take time if those bridges are not already burnt. I want my family back, but not the way it was these past few years. Even if I can get them back, it still won't be the same as it used to be. Sandra is grown up now. She is going to leave the nest soon. Sammy has, or will have, his friends and soccer. I have no illusions about trying to get back with James for the kid's sake. I don't even know if he would want me anymore."

"Things are going to be different." Lisa agreed.

James read the email on the tram ride home. He was glad the program was getting through to her. He was surprised that she was writing so soon and was worried about how authentic Judy was being. She could fool herself into whatever lie she wanted to believe, but the recognition of his struggles felt satisfying, and made him feel vindicated.

When he got home, he wrote Judy a response. "I'm glad to hear that you are letting the program work for you, and that you found the source of your pain. I'm thankful for your apology and the recognition of my distress. I'm not faultless either. I didn't realize how bad your distress was, or mine at the time. We didn't know that back then. Now we have therapists to point it out to us. I'm sorry for my emotional distance and for leaving you without a warning. I didn't know how to talk to you. I'm sorry about that and about the drinking I did. Thank you for your apology and I hope you will accept mine as well.' He felt a little lighter once this was sent.

Sandra came in with Tammy. "I received a text from mom. She apologized for her behavior and drinking." Sandra sounded astonished. "Did you get one too?"

"Yes, in fact I just sent her a response. I think the Trinitus rehab is having a good influence on her from the sound of it."

"Do you think it's real? I mean she was all apologetic and crying at the Child Services dorm, but I did not believe for one minute that it was real," said Sandra as she took a seat next to Tammy at the island.

"I think it might be real this time, at least I'm hopeful. You are going to have to decide for yourself how or if, you are going to respond." James advised.

Just then Sammy came in. They all looked at him.

"What? Did I do something wrong?" he was startled.

"No. Your mom just texted all of us and we were wondering if you saw yours yet?" his dad informed him.

"No, I haven't looked at it yet. She hasn't been bugging me since you told her I need time."

"Well, this is different. She is doing her Fourth Affirmation step, apologizing for her past. It is kind of like an official apology. You can choose whether you want to read it and respond or not. She would probably like to know that you saw it, and whether you accept her apology or not. It is up to you. We all got one, even your sister. I already responded to her and accepted her apology. You can do what you want to. It is up to you Buddy," His dad reassured him.

"Can I do my bow practice first, before the light fades?"

"Sure, go ahead. There is no rush on this. Your mom won't see it until tomorrow anyway."

Sammy grabbed his bow and went out onto the porch. James looked at Sandra. "Are you going to respond?"

"Yeah. I guess I should. I also have things to apologize to her for." Sandra pulled out her ComPad.

James asked, "Am I cooking for two or four tonight?"

"Two. Tammy and I are going out to dinner on the way to her place."

"Okay." He pulled out some food to cook, while he watched his son through the kitchen windows.

Sandra took the moment to answer her mother's email. "Thank you for your apology. I accept it. I have some apologies to make too. I'm sorry I got you in trouble with the law, I thought your drinking was very harmful, and I did what I thought was right. As it turned out, this process is good for you. Now you have the support to heal. It looks like you are starting to see that. Good for you. I'm glad this is working out. You may not think it is true, but I do love you and I miss you. I hope we can talk like a normal mother and daughter someday soon. Love Sandra."

Sammy felt agitated so his shots missed the mark. He became frustrated after a while and took off to run on the track behind the house. His dad noticed his absence and went to the porch to look for him. He saw him running. Sandra came up to him. "We're ready to go. Where is Sammy?"

"He's over there running," James pointed to him. "I think the email made him frazzled."

"We'll see you Sunday night, okay?"

"Okay, Sunday." He turned around and gave her a hug. He nodded to Tammy, then looked back at Sammy.

James let him run until it was getting too dark to see him. Then he went out to bring the boy in. "Let's go in, Buddy. It's getting late."

"I'm still mad at her," Sammy grumbled as he came in.

"I get it. I do. It takes time for the anger to go away. You don't have to respond to her if you don't want to. Take all the time you need."

"If she gets better, will you let me go back to California?" Sammy asked.

"If you want to and you are not mad anymore. I think it would be good for the two of you to repair your relationship. But then again, it is not up to me anymore. It will be the judge's decision. Do you want to go back?"

"Not right now. I like my weekends with Alo and Chenoa," Sammy asserted.

"Do you have friends at school?"

"Yeah, some," Sammy shrugged.

He patted his son on the back and smiled. "Do you want to go out for dinner?"

"Did I hear pizza?" Sammy said excitedly.

"Pizza? I don't know if they make pizza here," His dad teased. "I know you like the one we went to, but I know another place that makes good pizza too, I'll take you there." They went to the bowling alley and bowled a few games. They also played some video games and an old pinball machine.

The next morning, James took Sammy to his Native foster parents for the weekend. He thought of telling Judy about this development but then decided against it. She tended to be overprotective about Sammy. She was once banned from the soccer games for yelling at the coach too many times. He knew she would have a fit over this whole Native thing.

He and Cathy did their weekly shopping together and then they met to go bowling with the divorcee league. Sunday, he spent time cleaning the house, reading, and exercising. James was glad to have some time for himself now and felt better about it.

Sammy shot a rabbit when they went hunting and felt very proud. He prepared it himself that Saturday night and everyone said it tasted particularly good. During Sunday dinner at home, Sammy talked about how the Spirit of the animal chooses to give its life, when you are one with nature. Sandra announced suddenly that she was going to be a Vegan and stopped eating her dinner of buffalo stew.

"What is this all about?" James asked, surprised.

"I've been thinking about it for a while now. I just can't eat animals anymore," she left the table and went into the kitchen.

"Okay, do you want me to make a salad for you?" James got up.

"No. Enjoy your buffalo stew. I spung this on you, I'll make something for myself."

"There are some strawberries in the frig, if you like." James sat down, looked at Sammy, and quietly said, "I think your story of Animal Spirits got to her."

Sammy nodded. He had an amused smile on his face.

The next morning was therapy day. James told his therapist about the emails. "I'm just surprised by the speed with which she came around to an apology. She avoids apologies and hates admitting she is wrong."

"Well, we Trinitarians are good at what we do when it comes to personal healing. She is in the right place."

"Like me, she went there because it was no cost, but she is getting more help than she may have bargained for."

"What if Judy turns over a new leaf and wants to come back to the family?" Kim asked.

"Judy come here to live, I doubt it, and I'm not leaving Hope, no matter how much she has recovered," James insisted.

"Let's say she wants to come here, what then? How would you handle that?" she asked.

"Well, I don't know. I can't keep her from her children. That would be wrong, but right now Sammy wants nothing to do with her. I would not let her come if he was not ready. I can't stop her from living in the city, but she cannot live in our house."

"What will you do, if she asks to live here?"

James repositioned himself in his chair. "I don't know. We have a lot of water under the bridge. If she is willing to work on her behavior, I suppose we could try to be friends. It all depends on how she treats me. I'm not going to let her belittle me ever again."

"Good, we can work on your boundaries before that issue comes up as a possibility. I'm going to give you a book on Co-dependance. It will help you with your boundaries." She went to the bookshelf and pulled out a book for him entitled, Co-dependance No More.

"Great, another book. Well, I carved out time to read on the weekends. I'll make this one a priority," he said as he took the book.

"How is it going? Are you still taking your son to the park for the weekends," She asked as she sat down again.

"It's going well. He's learning to respect animals, while having fun hunting them. My daughter doesn't approve, but I think it's good for him. She became Vegan all-of-sudden. I could also use a book on Vegan recipes, so I can make something for her to eat, but I digress. Sammy really seems to enjoy his weekends. I'm thinking of talking to his foster parents the next time I see them. I want to know how he is doing. I just hear his hunting stories."

"That sounds good. How are you coping with your time alone, now?"

"Better. I have a way to make friends, I spend time with Cathy, I have time to read, and I do things around the house. I'm not getting panic attacks anymore. I have settled into a new normal. Reading books and watching videos about this community has helped a lot, as far as any reservations I might have had about this city."

"Are you going to Affirmation meetings?"

"Yes, on Wednesdays, when my daughter can stay home with Sammy. She's been spending the weekends at a friend's apartment nearer to town and goes out on Fridays."

"Good. How are you doing in your grief process for your brother and mother?"

"If we are not doing something in here, I just don't think about it, but I think what we have done has helped. Mostly, I think about and process my feelings of unworthiness. I feel shy at my bowling league. I also feel like I don't know the difference between liking a woman, verses sexually desiring her. I didn't do a lot of dating in high school or college, so I didn't learn the difference."

"That is not uncommon for men, and women too. Men particularly tend to appraise most women as sexual objects. Women often assess most men as potential mates, rather than as friends. It is a problem that most people have, especially if they had bad examples as parents."

"What can I do about it?"

"Just what you have been doing with Cathy. Working on your

boundaries will help. Think about what you really want in a relationship and don't just listen to the little man downstairs. You are working on being comfortable in your own company. Not being comfortable alone is a major motivation for getting into unhealthy relationships. The book I gave you will help you with this. Being aware of your neediness is the key. You are on the right track, James."

"That's good to hear."

"What do you think is making you feel shy at the bowling alley?"

"I don't know. I guess I'm worried that I'll be judged about my past, that my old inability to succeed in life will be judged."

"Do you still think you failed?"

"I know we talked about this, and you said I could not help how things went before, because of my lack of support from my father; but yes, I guess I still feel like a failure."

I'm doing better now. I like my job, and I think I am doing well at it. It is just that I wonder how I appear to others."

"You have no control over what other people think. Most of the time, a person's opinion of you is no more than a projection of their own process onto you. They see what they want to see. Those who are critical of you, are not true friends."

"Yeah, you're right. This group is all divorcees so they should understand."

"What do you think held you back from making friends before?"

"I don't know. I guess I felt I was just going to be a nuisance to them. Like I was trying to unnaturally force something."

"Is that how you felt at the bowling alley? What was the feeling there?"

"Oh yeah, that was totally how I felt. I was inserting myself into a group of friends that didn't need me there, but no one treated me that way. I just felt like it."

"You brought that feeling to the group. Okay, focus on that feeling. Where is it in your body. Good. Put your hand there. Breathe into your hand and ask your body, where does this feeling come from?"

James closed his eyes and brought his awareness into his body. He noticed a sensation of heat around his head and ears, so he mentioned it.

"What is it that you don't want to hear?"

"That I'm not worth their time." His eyes popped open as he realized, "That was my dad's primary message to me! That's what I learned from this work we are doing around my dad."

"That is right, and you extended your dad's negative attitude to the rest of the world."

"Yeah, but the truth is, I'm worth being a friend. I can be a good friend."

"Yes, you can."

"So, I guess I have to put another note on my bathroom mirror."

"In regard to your boundaries, what would you need to feel more comfortable putting yourself out to others. What would help you talk to people and honestly say what you feel without holding back?"

"I've been honest and open with you, Tim, and Cathy. I need to practice doing that with other people too. This is what makes this city unique. It is the intimacy people can have here with each other."

"Have you gotten involved with your neighborhood Cluster Association?"

"No, I haven't made the time yet. I'm just getting my feet under me, but it might be a good place to meet new people."

"Take your time. Go at your own pace so you don't feel overwhelmed."

James spent the rest of the session doing a visualization about making friends and focused on feelings of self-respect and feeling worthwhile. James did not realize he held such a negative opinion of himself when it came to making friends.

After his appointment, he waited for his kids in the atrium in the center of the building. Sandra walked out wearing a happy smile, but Sammy looked like he had been crying. "Are you okay, Buddy?"

"Yeah. I just did an exercise to get my mad feelings out about Mom."

"Oh, I see," James gave him a warm hug.

He took the kids home to get their bikes and then hopped the tram to work.

CHAPTER 24

Communication

Judy looked at her emails at Comp time. One was from James, and one was from Sandra, but Sammy did not write back. This made her cry. The next morning, she went to get another massage from Paul and cried some more.

Later that day, in her daily therapy session, Judy talked about grieving. "I can't seem to stop myself from crying all the time. I miss my family. The family that I should have had before I messed everything up. You know what I mean?"

"Yes, I do, but as hurt as you feel, it is good that you are allowing yourself to grieve. Just let it out, you are safe here to grieve as much as you need to."

"I don't have a choice, I can't stop. All I ever wanted was a perfect family who would love each other, instead of ignoring each other. I see that now. I was aware of the lack of love and caring from my parents all along, so, I tried to build my perfect family with James. Then my shopping and drinking destroyed it," she dissolved in another wave of tears.

"Now that you can see this, maybe you will be able to repair your family in time. Regardless of whatever happens, you have learned something valuable. Learning to love yourself and forgive yourself is the key now. Self-love is the key to stop your addictions and to help create harmony within yourself and maybe with your family too," Lisa explained.

Judy threw up her hands. "I don't know how to do that! I know you keep reminding me that I could not have known that my child self was going to protect itself this way, but I still feel at fault. My persona is still part of who I am. I was the one who did these things!"

"Not forgiving yourself is not going to help you put the pieces back together again. Being angry at yourself is not a loving behavior. It is destructive and will only make things worse. Love is the only way to gain peace of mind. The only way through these feelings, is through forgiveness."

"I'm not there yet," Judy protested.

"That is okay. Grieve for as long as you need. When you're tired of blaming and being angry at yourself, you will get to a point where you will have to make a choice. Maybe then you can stop giving yourself such a hard time. Eventually, you will see that this anger is not helping you and love is the only way out."

Judy sighed loudly.

"Did you get any response to your Fourth Step letters?" Lisa asked.

"Yes, James and Sandra wrote to me, but Sammy didn't. They said they are sorry too for their parts in all this. They accepted my apologies and are open to talking. So, I guess that's good."

"Since they are in therapy, I'm not surprised. I'm sure Sammy will come around in time. You should talk to them about how you feel and what you're learning. It can help you re-bond with them."

"I hate talking about how I feel. I don't want to complain to them," she complained.

"Then don't. Just tell them how you are doing and what you are working on, just like you do in the meetings. You need the support of your family to get you through this. You are lucky to have them. Many people here only have the meetings and us."

Judy sighed again.

They did a visualization for the rest of the session, in which her conscious loving Self forgave her. This made Judy cry even more.

Lisa let her sit out during exercise time to calm down and absorb the visualization. Judy opted to not share in the meeting. Then came comps. She did not call anyone. Instead, she cried in her room over messing everything up. She did her own visualization of forgiving herself and then fell asleep early. Lisa did not wake her up for dinner. She let her sleep through the night.

The next morning, Judy felt a little better. Forgiving herself was the only thing she could do, and she felt relieved when she did it. How could she know how to process her feelings as a child or a young adult? Until she came here, she had no idea how to do it. She protected herself the best way she could. Hiding faults and pretending that everything was okay was all she knew how to do. She didn't have the tools she has now. Today, she can deal with her feelings directly instead of hiding them.

In the morning meeting and in her therapy session, Judy expressed forgiveness for herself and said she was going to choose to love herself and forgive herself in the future. Lisa was happy for her and reminded her that she may have to forgive herself repeatedly when other issues come up.

When Comp time arrived, Judy went to her room to call James on his Smartwatch. He was surprised to hear from her at work and excused himself from a meeting with Pamila. "Sorry, I should take this."

"I'm at work Judy, what do you need?" He walked downstairs to the Break Room and put his earpiece in.

"I know. I'm sorry, but this is the only time I can call you. I was hoping you could take the rest of the day off so we could talk. It is just an hour, right? You go home at five, don't you?"

"Half an hour. At 4:30 I usually take the tram, but you just interrupted a meeting I was having with my group leader. I can wrap that up and call you back on my ride home."

"Okay, please call me back," Judy requested with sincerity.

"Is something wrong?" James asked, concerned.

"No, I'm fine. I just want to talk to you about my progress here."

"Okay, I'll call back soon. Bye for now."

James went back to Pamila and apologized for the interruption. They concluded their business. James left and called Judy.

"So, how are you doing?" He asked as he walked slowly to the tram stop.

"I realize that I gave you a tough time about the money and the jobs you lost. I want to apologize again. I yearned for a perfect family, so I tried to hold you up to an imaginary standard. I was trying to live out a fantasy I had as a child. It came from not being loved by my parents the way they should have. I'm so sorry about that. I realize now that my shopping was a way to get what I thought I deserved, because they often did not give me what they promised or what I wanted. I realized that in their attempt to not spoil me, they made me feel deprived, which led me to feel this need to indulge myself.

"My addictions were an attempt to fill the hole left in me, by the lack of love and attention I needed. I'm sorry, I also expected you to fill that hole. When you didn't, I aimed my anger at you, when it was really meant for them. I hope you understand what I'm talking about. I transferred my anger from my parents to you. Does that make sense to you?"

"Yes, it does. I understand you perfectly. Sounds like you are learning a lot there. I'm glad for you."

"Oh good. I thought you might think I've lost my mind. About my drinking, it was not only a luxury I gave myself, but also a way of covering up my feelings of worthlessness from my parents' neglect. That realization is going to take a while to heal, of course, but I'm not ever going to drink again. I'm sorry I was acting like a spoiled brat. I had no idea that I was. Well, maybe I did, but not consciously. Anyway, I needed you to know this. This is important, if you are ever going to trust me again."

"I needed this too," said James. "Thank you for being so honest. I had my own fault in this also. I realize now that my way of dealing with anger is to hold it in until I explode, or I just shut down and say or do nothing. That's why I left without a word. I was afraid that you would be furious. I just didn't want to fight anymore. I didn't know how to properly communicate my anger to you. I had no real plan or idea of where I was going. I just couldn't go home that night and face you. I couldn't get you to stop spending money that we didn't have, so instead, I used the college fund. I did it to avoid arguing over money, and I did not tell you which was wrong. I felt like I was backed into a corner."

"I get it. I was impossible to communicate with. I didn't listen to you when you told me to stop spending so much. I argued my points and then shut you down. I was awful to you. I wanted what I wanted, and no one was going to get in the way of my getting it. I felt so entitled, which was my parents' fault. Well kind of, they tried to not spoil me, but it had the opposite effect," Judy honestly admitted.

"Yeah, I get it, my dad tried to make my brother and me emotionally strong by not showing any feelings. All it did was teach us to shut down, which led to my troubles with you and to my brother committing suicide. I'm now learning to open up about my feelings and be honest," James shared.

"It is not fair that we spend half our lives messed up, and after we screw things up, we find out that there was another way. They sure don't teach us that in school. I'll never have my fantasy of a perfect family now, not that perfection is possible anyway. Do you know what I mean?" she sadly lamented."

"I agree, it's not fair at all." James did not want to get into his new spiritual beliefs about learning to love.

"Well, that's what I wanted to tell you." Judy wanted to bring this part of the call to an end.

"There is also the matter of the house and the kids. I've been thinking that I need to sell the house to get out from under the mortgage. I don't know if I can afford an apartment after that or what. I need to have the roof done before I can sell the house. It is old, as you know. Then there's my job. I don't know if I want to keep living with this much stress if I can't lighten my load there. Anyway, I don't know what to do after I'm done here. How would you feel about me staying with you and the kids, until I get back on my feet and I decide what to do next?"

"Well, I've been giving that some thought. You can stay here in Hope for free, if you go through the emergence process and see a therapist. It might be good for you, but I don't think I want you to live with us right now. I'm still working on my boundaries and being honest about my feelings. I'd hate for us to fall back into old habits."

That stung more than she thought it would. "Oh, I see. Well, at least I know where I stand with you. I do want a chance to reestablish my relationship with the kids though."

"That's fine. If you have an apartment in San Bernardino or in Hope, we can make it work. I think it would be good for the kids if they're ready for it. Sammy may need some more time to deal with his anger, but after that, I think it would be helpful."

"So, I need to get a place in San Bernardino then? Does Sammy still want to come back to California?"

"Not as much as before. He's found some things he likes here, and after he finishes the tutoring, he can play soccer again. I know he still misses his old friends, but the schools are better in Hope, so I think they should both stay here during the week. Their weekends are quite full too, so you may want to come here if you want to have any time with them. We have a better quality of life here. I don't know what you would do for work in Hope. You wouldn't have to work unless you still have bills to pay, but there's not much call for advertising here."

"Oh. Well, I haven't decided about my present job, or worked out how to pay the bills, but it sounds like you think it would be better for me to come there?"

"Definitely. Plus, you would be in a place where you can continue to get therapy and there is no alcohol, or money to shop with. You'd be safe from temptation."

"Well, I haven't decided on those things yet. I just wanted to see where I stood. We are divorced and all, so it makes sense I guess," she sounded sad.

"You sound like you want to try again. Do you?" he tentatively asked.

"I don't really know. I don't know if we ever really loved each other. Did you love me?" she bravely asked.

"I don't know either. I've realized that I'm not sure I know what love is, but I'm still working on it, James was vulnerable and honest.

"I feel the same way. I just wanted a child's dream of a perfect family, and I thought you were my way to get it," she sincerely shared.

"I discovered that I married my father in you, someone who makes demands of me that I cannot satisfy. No offence intended. This is just my truth," James said without malice.

"You may be right. I can't say I didn't fit the bill there, but that is awful. So, now what? Is there anything between us that is salvageable?" Judy sadly asked.

"I don't know. Maybe if you come here, we can just start out as friends. First, we will need to build trust, that's for sure." James proposed."

"Fair enough, friends then," Judy brightened a little.

"I need to get home for the kids." James saw the tram coming up the road.

"Sure, okay. I said what I needed to, sorry for calling while you were still at work, but I thought we needed to talk about all this."

"It was good that we did. I'm glad we can finally have this kind of honest conversation. This is a healthy step for us both." James meant it and that surprised him.

"I agree. Well, I better let you go then. I'll shoot you an email next time before I call, if I need to talk to you." Judy said, as a way of apologizing for intruding on his work time.

"Or call at 4:30. I'm walking out the door by then," James said as a peace offering.

"Okay. Bye then," she said in an upbeat voice.

"Bye," he replied, sounding friendly.

James stood there dumbfounded. He never thought this kind of conversation was possible with Judy. Even when they first got married, there was a distance between them that kept them from talking like this.

The tram arrived and James went home.

Judy put down the pad and cried some more. She punished herself by thinking, 'there isn't any love to save,' and whipped herself with another distorted view of what just happened. 'I'm as bad as his father! How terrible is that?!' She was filled with remorse over her lost fantasies.

When Lisa came in to get the pad, she saw Judy crying. "Did your call go badly?"

"No, it went well, but there is no love to save. Neither of us married for love. I was fooling myself about that too. I did it for money and he did it because I was like his father, and I mean that in a bad way. He wants us to try to be just friends now. I guess I was hoping that if he loved me, I could try again to love him better, but there is no love to rekindle. Now that I'm being honest, I may never have another chance to love. I don't want to start over with someone new. James is a good man and I royally screwed up this one."

"Starting over as friends might give love the space it needs to grow. You might rebuild the love and trust now that you're being honest. You don't know. There may be love hiding under his need to be emotionally safe. You have to reexamine your boundaries first though."

"Do you really think so? I don't know. I've messed things up pretty bad, Judy lamented."

"You never know. If you learn to love yourself, things can change."

"I guess, I don't want to give myself false hope either."

"Honesty can lead to love, is all I'm saying," Lisa reiterated.

"That would be nice." She got up to go wash her face.

Judy used her free time to work on her writing assignment. "What will my life look like?" Judy asked herself, feeling like she was holding pieces of a puzzle that did not seem to fit together. She wrote, "Will I live in San Bernardino or in Arizona? Will Sammy forgive me? Can I ever get my whole family back together? What will life look like with no drinking or shopping?"

"The idea that there are no vices in the City of Hope is tempting. Then again, I want to prove to myself and others that I can quit my vices. I can't prove that, if they don't exist. Do I really have to prove something? If I go there, wouldn't that be proof enough?" Judy tried to think of other contingency plans.

James was still amazed by the call from Judy. After Sandra got home and Sammy went outside to practice his bow, he talked to Sandra about it. "I mean I was shocked by her email, and this was so not like her!"

"I'm having a hard time believing it too." Sandra said, shaking her head. "Could Trinitus rehab make this much difference?"

"Processing here is more direct and faster than normal. But some of it needs to be that losing this family has hurt her deeply. She told me that we are the most important thing in her life. This fantasy of a perfect family was what drove her. She never talked about her family much, but when she did, it was always positive. I had no idea that she was neglected. She didn't go into details, but she said that they did not give her any attention."

"Well, if she didn't feel loved, that shines a light on her drinking too," Sandra added.

"She always seemed so confident and independent. I never imagined she felt worthless! But if she did, she maintained her façade the whole time. She had to blame me because she couldn't blame herself for anything, that would have revealed it was only a facade," this was all such a revelation to him. It shocked him how little he knew about his own wife after all these years.

"Could she be replacing one deception with another, making us believe she is healed now?" Sandra wondered aloud.

"I suppose that's possible, but if she comes here it wouldn't matter. She has no access to alcohol or expensive shopping. She might hoard clothes and things, but someone would notice, and she would have to get help. Best of all, she would have a therapist to help her along."

"Do you really think she would come here to Hope?"

"She sounded open to it, so it is possible. She wants her family back."

"What would she do for work?" Sandra asked, being practical.

"I don't know. Maybe nothing, but I think that would drive her nuts after a while. She likes to stay busy, but that may be part of her ignoring her feelings too. She can't process all the time, it is too grueling," said James, shaking his head.

"Did she want to stay here at the house?" Sandra asked, feeling a little alarmed.

"I think so, but I told her she would have to get an apartment. I don't want to live with her yet, if ever. I think she was hurt by that, but I need my space right now."

"Good, I'm glad to hear that. You have only been divorced for a few months and I can't believe she is totally healed already. It's good that you are holding to your boundaries. She's going to try to muscle in I'm sure, so I'll help remind you why you got a divorce in the first place," Sandra offered.

"Hmmm, well I might need that, but I should be able to do it myself. She wants her fantasy family back so bad I can feel it. She has a lot of trust to rebuild before that can happen."

"I hope so, because it's not just the drinking and spending, it's also the way she abused all of us. Whenever things were not perfect, like Sammy's grades, or you having lost a job, or me not going to college, she would be nasty. That's why Sammy feels like he needs to do things right or he is not good enough. Mom did that to him trying to help him with his math," Sandra had a little bitterness in her voice.

"I see that now, but I think you need to give her a chance too. Don't be so hard on her. You need to work on your forgiveness. She really is trying, I think," James defended Judy.

"Maybe. I'll talk to Samantha about it," Sandra said.

"She really sounded committed to this healing. Give your mother a chance, okay?"

"Yeah, I'll try," Sandra said with a weak smile.

The next day, Judy talked to Lisa about what she will do when she leaves rehab. "I don't really want to lose my job, but I think my family is more important to me. If I'm where I can't drink or spend money, then I can't fall off the proverbial wagon either."

"What happens if you can't get your family back the way you envision it?"

"Well, like you say there are no guarantees of anything, but I have to try. It is important to me."

"Why?" Lisa asked, sensing there was something underneath what Judy was saying.

"It's my family! I don't need any other reason!"

"True, but are you sure you're not also trying to prove something to yourself, to us here at rehab, to your family, and to your parents?"

"I don't need to prove anything to anyone!" Judy asserted.

"That's right. You don't. This is what I've been trying to help you see. It is important that you stop trying to prove to your parents that you are worth loving. It could mess up everything you are trying to do. Your happiness and well-being cannot depend on anyone else, not even your family. If you cannot rebuild your family, you don't want the disappointment to send you into a deep hole and lead you to drink again.

"Accept that you are a worthwhile individual. You are lovable. There is nothing bad in you and there never was. Your parents were preoccupied with their own lives and had no space in their reality for incorporating a child. Granted it hurt you a lot, but you cannot change those circumstances now. All you can do is forgive them, forgive fate, and above all, forgive yourself for coping in whatever way you were able to." Lisa gave this overview in the hope that Judy understood it now and was ready to move on.

"I think I understand. It is time to stop trying so hard to win an old argument with my parents about how I was raised."

"That's right. This is why you had to have a perfect family, and why when your fantasies and your reality didn't match, you drank to hide your feelings. Drinking and hiding feelings are connected. This is why it feels so important right now to fix your family, so you can stop drinking. Repairing the damage is a good thing to do, but do it for the right reasons, not so you can have another chance to create a new version of the perfect family. Make sure your intentions are not tainted by old nagging needs."

"I get your drift, but how do I know what my true intentions are? I think I am doing this for the right reasons, but then I always thought that."

"When some people grieve, they go through a step called Bargaining. That's when you say to yourself, 'if I quit my vices, I will get my family back.' There is no guarantee. What if you don't? Does that mean the bargain is off and you drink again? At this point, since the trust is broken, there will be more to getting your family back than just stop your drinking and shopping. You will need to work on reestablishing that trust. You also need to change behaviors, like blaming and demanding. These can trip you up and stand in the way of getting your family back. Remember, these are real people who want to be loved and understood for who they are, not for the role they play in your fantasy of a perfect family."

"That sounds overwhelming. How do I even begin?"

"First, you release the need for a perfect family and close the past. It was what it was, and now it is gone. You don't fit into the little dress you wore at the age of five, so you gave it away, and never tried to wear it again. Same here. Close the past.

"Once you have done that, have some honest conversations with your family about your behaviors. You don't need to prove yourself to them, you just need to be present and responsive to whatever they say. Be open to accept their truth, their pain, and hear their grievances. Accept and acknowledge what they say, then forgive yourself, and forgive them. No bargaining, just honest dialogue and remain present. When their words hurt you. Stand in the fire, feel the pain, and let it move on through. It was what it was, but it is no more. Practice feeling the pain and let it move on through. I recommend, when you try to rebuild the trust, start with one person, and choose the one who is the least challenging.

"Remember, there are no guarantees that any of this will work. An odd thing about life is that when you fight something, it persists, but when you forgive and release, it creates a space where things can change. First, you must sincerely accept the way things are right now and even face the possibility that they may always stay that way. This provides an honest platform from which to begin."

This idea was totally daunting to Judy. "Stand in the fire and let it move through. Wow! When they accuse me of the things I did and I feel guilty and ashamed, you are saying that I need to stand there and do nothing, really?"

"No blaming, no deflecting, no excuses, no bargaining, just open receptivity." Lisa replied calmly.

"Do you think I'm a saint?" Judy sounded flippant, but it really seemed to her that only a saint could have that much strength.

"Blame and shame only hurt you when you feel you deserve it. Once you have forgiven yourself and forgiven the past, those emotions will no longer take hold of you. Sadness, regret, and compassion for yourself and your family can arise. They too will move on through, if you let them."

"So, if I understand right, what I must do is listen to their complaints and feel their pain. Acknowledge that what I did was wrong and say I'm sorry. Nothing more." Judy felt a little scared at the prospect.

"It's a good place to begin. Let's do the *Chain of Questions* to uncover your deeper feelings, so you can be totally honest with them."

"Sure," Judy said, settling back in her chair.

Lisa took a deep breath before diving in. She reminded herself that delving into the soul like this was a sacred process.

"Drinking and shopping are symptoms of a much deeper problem. Are you ready to be honest?

"Yes, as best I can." Judy said cautiously, a little afraid of where these questions would take her, and how she would feel afterwards. Sometimes this process left her feeling free and unburdened, and sometimes it felt like the roof was caving in on her.

"When a person wants something to be perfect, they try to control circumstances to move things and people in the direction they want. Do you think you have control issues?"

Judy was about to automatically say no, but before she could, several instances flashed across her mind. Remembering her commitment to be honest, she said yes. I do try to control my family," Judy reluctantly admitted.

"In what ways?" Lisa guided.

"Well, I guess, I shut people down if I disagree with them, like when James would talk about the finances, I argued until he walked away frustrated. I ignored things I didn't want to hear. That's all I can think of right now."

"This is a good start. Thank you for being honest. Do you know what triggers you to do this?"

"Well, the financial thing is obvious. I didn't want to hear that I had a problem with money or that I needed stuff to make me feel better about myself."

"What was the deeper problem?"

"My parents neglected my emotional needs."

"What feeling is at the core of neglect?"

"That I wasn't worth loving?"

"That is a thought. What was the feeling? Take your time, let the feeling rise, and feel it.

"Empty. Deep loneliness. Falling through space with no one to catch me. Abandoned and alone," tears enveloped her, and she sobbed uncontrollably. She felt the terrible deep pain of that little girl, alone in the world with no one who cared about her.

Lisa sat back in her chair and waited for this wave to subside. After a couple of minutes, she leaned forward, put her hand on Judy's and said in a soft and tender voice, "Just let me know when you are ready to continue," Judy gave a last sniffle and nodded.

"The *Chain of Questions* brought you to these core emotions. From these emotions, you formed core beliefs that motivated your behavior. We need to uncover these beliefs. The ones that lead to negative consequences need to be reframed into healthy ones. What is the belief here?

"I guess, I believed that I deserve to get what I want and that includes a perfect family. But this belief hurt all of us. I guess, I could reframe it into, I deserve to be part of a family. That might be more attainable."

"Judy, you also must face the possibility that you might not get your family back. Even if you must grieve that loss, and come to accept it, it is better than hiding from the pain, which would just put you back where you started."

"I want my family back. I will do whatever I have to do to succeed," Judy asserted.

"You cannot push your way through this, you m love must yourself and out of that feeling, love them. Only gently loving them has the possibility of earning back their respect.

"I am sure I can make them love me! I'm their mother."

"Judy, to be loving towards yourself or someone else, requires gentleness. If you are controlling, manipulating, angry, ignoring, or complaining, those express a closed, unreceptive state of mind. When you are loving, you feel open, and accept the others' views, even when they disagree with yours. When you are loving, you allow people to have a choice, you respect their perspective. You don't try to stop them from doing what they want, but rather, lovingly support them. You can tell them about your experience and how you faced a similar choice, and how it affected your life. However, in the end, you need to respect that the decision is theirs and trust that the consequences will teach them what they need to learn. Sometimes, you have to let the one you love fall on their face, if that is the consequence of what they have chosen. Trust that it was a lesson their soul needed to learn.

"Every time you find yourself starting to control, stop and ask yourself the *Chain of Questions*. Find out what you are feeling. Why do you feel threatened at that moment? What need is driving you to want to control the world and people around you?"

"Why do I need all these questions when the answer is always the same, my parents neglected me," Judy whined.

"These questions reveal the pattern of your thoughts and uncover important beliefs. It makes you aware of why you do these controlling behaviors and explains what is driving you. This is how you discover the beliefs that control you and get you into trouble."

Lisa continued, "Let's use your spending, and arguing with your husband about it as an example. He says to you, 'You are spending too much on clothes. We cannot afford $50 for pants every month,' and you say?"

"I must look professional. It is not like your jobs, where you walk around all day in overalls!"

"Judy, you countered him with an insult about his work and underlined that it wasn't as important as yours. Why do you think you did that? You could have said something true like, 'my upbringing made me feel I deserve it.' Knowing this is the core of your problems doesn't help you understand your beliefs. That is why we follow the *Chain of Questions*.

"Why did you feel the need to put him down?"

"Because I made all the money, so I had the right to spend it any way I wanted," she stuck out her chin defiantly.

"There. That is the belief we were looking for. Is it actually true?"

Lisa challenged her.

"No. He made money too. Even if I made more, I shouldn't spend it however I desire. I just wanted to believe that, so I didn't have to face my problem with spending money," she admitted.

"Continuing with the *Chain of Questions*, what feelings are associated with spending money?"

"Guilt and pleasure. The guilt I bury, and the pleasure makes me feel good about myself."

"And the next obvious question about your feelings, is...?"

"Why do I need to feel good about myself? As always, the answer is my parents."

"You are jumping the gun. The answer is that you don't feel good about yourself. The question is why," Lisa asked.

"Because my parents didn't pay attention to me or give me the things I wanted and needed," she recited her now pat answer.

"No. Why did you need to shop to feel good about yourself, and why did you need to cut your husband down and make him feel bad?"

"I didn't want to feel bad about myself. I needed the lack of money to be all his fault," Judy admitted.

"These questions led you to uncover this belief, which was actually not true. This is how you uncover negative beliefs that harm you and others. Once you see the truth, you can develop new positive beliefs that enhance your life. Following your emotions to discover the negative beliefs that control your behavior is why we don't just jump to your core problem."

"I understand," said Judy. She was really beginning to see what Lisa was talking about.

"For your next assignment, write about how doing the *Chain of Questions* on your own can work in your life. Then pick a negative behavior that you know you do and ask the *Chain of Questions* to uncover the core emotion, the accompanying belief, and the behaviors that result."

"Ok, but I don't know what my negative behaviors were. I thought I was trying and succeeding at being my perfect self."

"If you don't know what you did, ask your family to tell you."

Judy thought about her assignment and realized she needed some help, so she waited until 4:30 and called James.

"Are you leaving work?" asked Judy. "Can we talk?"

"Yeah, just a second." James shut his office ComScreen and put the Bluetooth earbud in his ear. "Okay, I'm ready now, go ahead."

"Well, I was wondering what I did that was bad or mean to you? How did I resemble your father? I am trying to make sure I don't do those things again, but I'm not sure that I remember all of them. I need to process them, so I won't do them again. Please, be honest with me. I'll try not to get mad."

"Ok," James said cautiously. "Well, you bullied me. Whether it was about money, the kids, or my work, you would bully me about it until you got your way, or thought you won the argument. By win, I mean; I would shut up, give in, and walk away. When you wanted something to go the way you thought it should, you would argue endlessly until the person was exhausted and just gave in. Remember when you argued with the referee at Sammy's game, and they threw you off the field?"

"I remember that night. They didn't call a foul when they should have, and they did not let Sammy play center."

"It didn't matter what you thought was right. It is up to the referee and the coaches. Not you. You can't control other people."

"So, you are saying that I tried to control you?" she wanted to rebuttal but caught herself and didn't.

"You try to control everyone. Every decision must be your way. You even bullied Sammy with his math homework. You called him stupid for not understanding a complex principle. Now he has confidence issues because of it."

"I was trying to help him!"

"I know you were, but you did it in a way that was mean and demeaning."

"Why didn't you say something at the time?"

"Because I was afraid that you would turn everything into an argument, especially if I told you something you did was wrong. You either ignored what I said or turned it into an argument," James said.

"You feel you have to be right all the time."

"Not all the time, it can't be all the time," she objected.

"That's another thing you do. You make arguments out of things that don't really matter, just to change the subject. Who cares if it is 90% or a 100%? It is just how it feels. It is just a phrase." James's voice was starting to sound agitated, and he noticed. "Look, I don't want to argue with you. You wanted to know, so I'm telling you how I felt."

"Ok. Ok. I don't want to argue either. I get it, I bullied you. Did I do it to the kids too?" Judy asked, trying to calm him down.

"Yes," he regained his composure and was ready to continue. This truce felt very fragile.

"I guess, I needed to be perfect, and everyone around me had to be too. My therapist keeps hounding me that there is no such thing as perfect. Being a control freak is about trying to control everything to avoid the guilt and shame I feel when I think I've done something wrong, because it proves I am bad. My parents made me believe that there is something wrong with me so everything I do is to get their approval in the never-ending hope that they will love me."

"I can identify with that. I also did that when I went to college to please my father. I only went because he pushed me into it."

"I had a little fun with it once. After I received my degree, I called him and said I got a degree in 'drawing pretty pictures of buildings,' he did not laugh."

"I don't get the joke either."

"He pushed me into going to college by telling me over and over that I couldn't make a living drawing pretty pictures of buildings for comic books. Never mind, you had to be there."

"Well, I got what I called for. I guess everything I did that hurt you and the kids was because I had to control everyone and everything. I felt so guilty and ashamed when I was wrong, that I did everything to avoid facing my mistakes."

"You always pretended that there was nothing wrong with you."

"Yeah, I know I've been lying to myself about all of this. I'm not going to do that anymore."

"One more question James. I understand that I yelled a lot, but even so, why didn't you ever stand up to me? What was your process around that?"

James was comfortable talking honestly to Judy when the focus was on her process, but now, he had to reflect on his deeper motivations and confess his truth, not just to her, but to himself. Telling the naked truth to Judy was something he never imagined doing, but she deserved it. She went out on a limb calling him and initiating this conversation, now she was inviting him to join her.

"Well, um, I try to avoid any conflict. Most of the time, I like to think I am above petty issues. I want to see myself as tolerant, accepting, and easy-going, so mentioning little things feels like it is beneath me. I always want to be liked. I don't want anyone to think badly about me, so I avoid conflict with everyone, not just you. I usually need some kind of reassurance that the person will still like me, before I can admit something is upsetting me. I don't want to be a problem, so instead of admitting a little annoyance, I stuff it. I keep stuffing these little things until I can't take it anymore and then I explode. Maybe that was a factor in losing some of those jobs.

"When I reach my limit, I start to argue with myself. I build up a case to justify making a fuss. I don't want to be a nuisance. My father was so critical of me, I don't want to do that to anyone else," his voice broke as he fought back tears.

"I know now that I was setting you up by not telling you about the little things that bothered me. So, it must have looked like when I got angry, it came out of nowhere, like when I suddenly drove away into the desert without a word of warning."

"In your therapy, do you practice the *Chain of Questions*?"

"Yes," James dreaded where she was going with this.

"Everything you said were behaviors and thoughts, what were you feeling?" She asked in the kind of voice Lisa used.

"When I am forced to confront anyone and tell them how hurt I really feel, I feel guilty, worthless, and petty. Admitting my pain makes it hurt more. My father could be very cruel to me and my brother, when we showed any emotions," he choked up and fought back the tears.

Judy waited. Several different emotions were swirling around in her. She was tempted to block them, but instead, she breathed deeply and slowly. While he regained his composure, she felt a deep sadness, regret, and compassion.

To distract herself from this wave of emotion, she began to argue with herself that she wasn't a tyrant like his father. How dare he make that comparison. This wave of indignation passed quickly, and she saw the truth of it. When she found her voice, she said, "Thank you for sharing your truth with me."

"Judy, thank you for calling. This has meant a lot to me. I'm glad that this place has led you to think about these things. I'm proud of you."

"Don't patronize me," she objected.

"I'm not. I really mean it. You have turned a major corner, maybe so have I. I'm amazed and grateful that we can have a meaningful conversation. This is more than I hoped for. I'm glad that we can talk honestly like this. It feels really good."

"I was really awful to you. I'm having a hard time believing that you've really forgiven me for all the things I did," she confessed.

"Like you, I'm just learning, but being angry will not help either one of us, so I really have forgiven you. Like me, you probably didn't know what you were doing at the time," James said sincerely.

"You're right, I had no clue, and the clues I did have, I hid from myself. Do you have a problem connecting with your conscious Self? I do," she sincerely asked.

"I see it as the me I was meant to be. My soul Self is the real me that I'm trying to be now," he shared.

"I'm having a hard time getting it. I'm trying to see the soul Self as my unspoiled child, the kid who played with dolls and knew things were wrong with my parents. The me I was, before I started to lie to myself. That is all I can think of," she explained to herself as much as to him.

"Fine. The important thing is, it works for you," he confirmed.

"All I can think of is a child who is somehow smarter than me. It is at least humbling."

"Humble is good," James acknowledged.

"I bet you're glad that I'm eating a lot of humble pie right now," she said only half sarcastically.

"I'm sure it's not easy for you to find out all this stuff and have to deal with it. I know it was not easy for me either. As humbling as it is, I don't wish it on anybody. I don't hate you; you know."

"You don't love me either," she said, feeling hurt.

"I'm learning that no one can love another, until they love themselves. Neither one of us knew how to really love given our issues, but we didn't know that at the time."

"You are probably right. I did love the kids though."

"I am sure you loved them in your way, but it was not enough to stop you from drinking when they pleaded with you," he pointed out.

"I did stop! I've been sober this whole time," she defended herself.

"Yes, but not when the judge ordered you to stop, before you got arrested," he reminded her.

"You're right," she paused and then said, "Well, I better let you get home."

"Yep, the next tram is coming."

"Bye, have a nice evening," Judy said, and meant it.

"Bye. Keep up the good work." James was left with a feeling that there was hope for her yet.

CHAPTER 25

The Move

Judy took another look at her finances. It looked like the only thing to do was sell the house to pay off her credit cards and her car. Moving was going to eat up the rest of her money. There was only a buffer of savings for emergencies, but that was it. The only options looked like getting a small place at an affordable price and staying with her job or moving to the City of Hope. She was worried about living above her means. She didn't trust herself. Leaving rehab sounded great, but it meant she would have to face being alone on her own and that scared her.

Judy began to read *Utopia of the Heart*. It gave her a better idea about the city her ex-husband and children were living in. During her last month in rehab, she made it a point to talk to James weekly and share her progress with him. She also talked to Sandra every week. Sammy finally wrote an email accepting her apology and even started answering her weekly calls. Neither Sammy, Sandra, nor James mentioned his weekends in the Native Village for fear of her overreacting.

Judy worked hard on her process, so she could go back to her family without the need to be perfect messing her up again. She wanted her family back, but hopefully without all the old baggage. She felt ready to live a new life for herself and her family.

Lisa was teaching her the steps in the Affirmations for life program and worked on her fears. Judy was afraid of living alone because she didn't trust herself with money. That was why she always depended on James to handle the finances. She began to realize how much she was afraid to be by herself. She needed people around her. She needed the attention to feel good about herself. She could not shake the fear that she would never be loved again, and she would be abandoned by everyone she cared about.

Lisa taught her that there are two primary states of mind, love and fear. Love comes from the conscious loving Self and fear comes from the Inner Critic, based on old beliefs that came from never knowing unconditional love. Fears learned in childhood generated a fearful belief system. Turning to the conscious loving Self was the only true security she could have. It was taking a while for her to learn to love herself. She found it hard to forgive herself for the automatic defense mechanisms that caused her bad behavior.

"I'm afraid to live alone in San Bernardino," she told Lisa. "As much as I'd like to keep my job, I just don't trust myself to handle my bills and not go shopping. I've promised not to spend beyond my means ever again, but I've never had to handle my own money before.

The bottom line is that I just want to be with my family. One of the reasons I drank so much when James left, was because I was afraid of the financial responsibilities and the debt we were in. When I left boarding school and went to college, my parents paid for everything. If I wanted money beyond my college requirements, I worked for it, but I overdrew my accounts right away and got into debt. I was never good at handling money," Judy lamented.

"If you do go to the City of Hope, you won't have that problem. Of course, avoiding a problem does not teach you how to overcome it. The problem with living in Hope is that it takes the pressure off you, so you may never learn to deal with your problems. It does make life easier." Lisa was careful to remain neutral about the City of Hope or any Trinitus City.

"Yeah, I would not have to deal with my fears or my addictions, but I will have to face my biggest one, that of having a real relationship with my family."

"That is true. Your fear of intimacy is one of your biggest challenges. Trying not to control your relationships will take constant vigilance."

"I've been giving it a lot of thought since James mentioned it. He is right, I do try to control everyone, if I can. That is going to be my hardest challenge. I think, it is attached to my need for perfection, which is still such a struggle for me."

"Whether you go to Hope or stay in San Bernardino, you will need to continue going to therapy and meetings. They can be AA or Affirmation meetings. It will help you to have someone to talk about your progress and personal process."

"I just hope it keeps me from lying to myself and covering up the emotions I don't want to face. I have way too much experience with that."

"Next week, I'm going to give the court a good report. "I think you have come far enough to go home," announced Lisa.

"Really?" Judy was excited, then she suddenly felt overwhelmed, followed by a wave of fear. "I'll need to get busy on arrangements then. I must sell the house and decide where to live. I think I'll go to Arizona. I don't want to disrupt the kid's schooling again."

"I think you are on the mend and ready to work on rebuilding the love. You're in contact with your conscious loving Self and you know the steps to help you navigate your emotions better. Now it is a matter of dedication and practice."

"And no more perfection!" Judy interjected.

"That's right," Lisa said, with a smile.

That evening Judy called James at 4:30. "Hi, I just got the news that they are going to recommend my release next week."

"Oh good, have you decided where you want to live?" James was just heading out.

"Well, I'm pretty sure I will go to Hope, so I can be with the kids and continue to have access to therapy. There is no sense in tempting fate by staying out here. The job doesn't hold me anymore. I am far more interested in being with my family, so I think it is settled. I know we have only been talking for a few weeks, but I was wondering if you still think I should get my own place. I know we still have a lot of healing to do, but I was hoping to avoid having to move a second time if we do get back together. Do you think it's possible?"

"Well, I'm not sure about that. I need more time. First, you and I need to prove that we can get along well. I still think you should have your own place for now. I'm sorry."

"That's okay. I can be patient. I'm just afraid of living alone, that's all. Maybe facing my fears would be good for me. At least, I wouldn't have financial problems there. So, um, I was hoping to ask for your help with the moving and putting the house up for sale. I don't have the foggiest idea how to do that. I guess I can call some movers and a realtor, but packing, deciding what to keep, and how to get the best price, I just don't know how to do all that stuff."

"I see. Yes, well, I guess, I could come over this weekend and help you out. Maybe I can even take a few days off and make it a short week. I'll bring the kids to help too."

"That would be wonderful. I'd appreciate it so much. I'd be a mess without you!"

"No problem. I get it. I think they even have panel vans here that we would not have to pay for."

"Oh good, one less expense for my dismal finances. I plan to pay off my credit cards and keep a savings account for emergencies. Can you borrow a van, so, I can sell my car?"

"Yeah, sell it after all the packing is done."

"It is an economical environmentally friendly electric car. I'm sure they would approve of it in Hope, but I probably wouldn't need it. You don't have a car and you seem to be getting around fine."

"Yeah, the trams here are great, so you don't need a car."

"Good, I'll sell it and pay off some bills. I'm looking forward to being out of debt," Judy said, enthusiastically.

"It will be a relief to have those all paid off," James agreed.

"I'll have to find something to do with my time that makes me happy. I have a few ideas. I've always liked clothes and fashion, so I might open an art studio and make clothes. They have stores and galleries there, don't they?"

"I'm sure you will find support here. There might be some sort of art guild or co-op you can join."

"That sounds like fun. Please give the kids a heads up on all this," she made her voice extra light and happy.

"Sure, no problem," he responded in a similar tone. "Call me when you're free, so we can make plans,"

"Will do, good night then," she said in parting.

"Bye," James sounded friendly, but inside, he felt fluttering butterflies.

Judy was hopeful after the call as she sat down to write about the Seventh Affirmation, the one where she showed how she is redefining herself and finding her true self-esteem through her personal process work and how it was changing her perspectives.

The week breezed by quickly. Judy focused on her Affirmation Steps and visited her therapist to talk about her growing anxiety. Thinking of being alone in her house for even a day filled her with fear. Living alone in the City of Hope was weighing on her. Though she looked confident to others, the truth is, inside she was quivering. She had rarely been alone and was afraid that loneliness would drive her to drink.

Angelica, the Healing Coordinator, gave her the URLs for several meditation sites and a list of things she could do to calm herself down. She also did a hypnotherapy session with Judy on the day before she left to help her feel calm and grounded. She did a process called Changing Personal History. In a hypnotic trance Angelica took the adult Judy back to accompany and protect the eleven-year-old child, while the child confronted her parents and told them about the neglect. When Angelica instructed Judy, while still in trance, to bring this experience to its healthiest conclusion, Judy imagined her parents throwing their arms around her, apologizing, telling her they loved her, and saying, what a wonderful daughter she is.

The next morning, before Judy was scheduled to leave, Angelica put her in a trance and embedded the suggestion that with each step out into the world, she would feel more confident and relaxed.

Judy stood near the gate of the rehab center and took a dozen full deep breaths. She spoke to her conscious loving Self and felt a little better. Standing out in the world, feeling naked and new, was exciting and daunting. The old wound of neglect may no longer be motivating her, but a history of poor financial judgments, and the reality that her family did not trust her, hung over her head. Without her family, she felt alone in the world. It made her feel very lonely.

She composed herself and called James. "Hi, I know you are at work and that we planned for you to come up tomorrow, but I don't want to be alone on this first night. Could you please come over. I feel so raw. I'd rather not be alone. Could you please come today?"

"I should be able to, but I'd have to pull the kids out of school and get their homework, it would still be at least 5:00 before I get there."

"Okay, I can go to a mall and watch a movie, maybe buy a pair of running shoes just to kill some time. I probably won't be wearing heels in Hope. I'm feeling okay right now but when it gets dark out, I'm afraid I'll freak out. If you and the kids are here, I'll feel so much better. If I get too lonely, I'm afraid I'll drink. I feel so raw. I don't want to have to fight temptation on my first night out."

"Well, I understand. I'm glad you called me. I'll talk to Pamila, my supervisor, and get the kids ready. Do you want me to call when I'm on my way?"

"I'll call you after the movie. You should be well on your way by then."

"Yep, okay. I know what it feels like and I'm glad you're going to the movies. That's a good plan. Remember to breathe deeply and slowly as often as you can remember. It really works for me. Call me if you need to and we can visit on the Smartwatch while I'm driving, okay?"

"Yeah, will do. I'm glad you understand, I feel so stupid, but I had a lot of hidden fears that I'm only now starting to deal with," she was being honest and sincere.

"I completely understand. Call me if you need to," James offered, but a little voice in his head said, 'what have I gotten myself into?'

"Okay, I'll let you go. The sooner you get here, the better. Thanks again, bye."

"I'll see you as fast as I can, bye."

Judy took an Uber to the nearest mall. She found a movie that looked interesting and shopped around for shoes while waiting for the theater to open. She had time for a quick bite in the food court. It felt good to have all these people around her, like they were all part of something. That was the hard part about leaving rehab, she wasn't a part of anything anymore, not even her job, since she was about to quit and go to Hope.

The shopping was relaxing and the afternoon unfolded well enough. She found just the kind of shoes she wanted, but then automatically started looking for more things to buy. She caught herself, recognized the addiction creeping back in, and reminded herself that she is in the middle of downscaling. The last thing she needs is more stuff to pack.

The movie was good. She cried when the actress walked out on her husband and stood at a crossroads, all alone, facing an empty road, and needed to decide where to go. After the movie she called James. It had been four hours, so he should be relatively close.

"I'm an hour past Kingsman in your direction. It's a little more than two hours still, depending on the traffic in Barstow and Highway 15."

"Okay, I'm going to find a place that sells sewing machines for my clothes idea, then I'll go home."

"Good, see you soon."

James arrived at the house first and parked the panel van in the driveway. He still had a key. The house was stuffy after being empty for so long and needed some fresh air, so he went around opening the windows. The kids ran up to their rooms to gather the rest of their things, and the neighbor next door came over with the mail.

"Hello, Judy asked me to collect the mail. Is she back from her vacation yet? I bet she loved Italy. I always dreamed of going there."

"She is on her way now. Thank you for keeping the mail," he took the box from her.

The kids came down with armloads of their things and piled them in a corner.

"Are you moving?" the nice neighbor lady asked.

"Yes, to Arizona."

"That sounds nice. Good luck to you." He could see that she wanted to be nosier, but he walked her to the door, and she went back to her house.

James instructed the kids to put their stuff in the garage, because he wanted to load it last. He looked around for anything that he wanted to have. There was not much, but he wanted to discuss who would keep the things that belonged to them both, like family pictures.

Judy's Uber got there a half hour after they arrived. "Sorry the traffic was awful in town."

"That's okay, the kids were just gathering their stuff. There are few things that belong to both of us that I'd like to have, but you may want some of them."

She turned to the Uber driver who came up with a new sewing machine in his hands. "Where do you want this?"

"Oh, just anywhere in here. Thanks," Judy said, feeling disoriented. She almost reached into her purse to pay him before she remembered that the payment was deducted when the Uber was called.

"Can we just talk before we get to packing, say hello first?" Judy asked, sounding upset.

"Yeah, sure. How was your time at the mall? Are you okay?"

The kids gave her timid hugs and said a quick obligatory hello.

"I was fine, yes. The traffic was brutal, but I'm fine. Let's close this door and sit for a while, shall we? We haven't seen each other for months now."

"Sure, no problem." James noticed she was out of sorts. He closed the garage door, and they all sat down in the living room. The kids didn't know what to say and James wanted her to start, so they were quiet for an awkwardly long time.

Judy felt she needed to say something. Just sitting here like strangers was uncomfortable. "I'm sorry, I'm not ready to pack just yet. I was hoping for a warm hello, but I guess that was too much to ask," she looked exasperated.

"I think we just need to start over. We all have had a lot going on during these past few months and things have changed a lot," James explained.

"I guess, I was expecting too much, but I'm still your mother," she accused, and gave the children a look meant to make them feel guilty. "I just thought I'd get more than a quick forced hug from my own children."

"Mom, it's not going to be like nothing happened. We must start over and learn to trust each other again," Sandra spoke up.

"Yeah, I get that, but we had conversations on the phone and talked about our feelings in texts," she threw up her hands in dismay.

"I thought we would be better than this."

"Maybe the kids are not as far along as you would have hoped, but that's okay. We have time. Give them space and things will develop naturally," James advised her.

Judy sighed loudly. "You're right. I expected too much. Expectations are another form of control." She remembered Lisa's words. "Sorry, I didn't mean to put you on the spot. We do need to start over. I don't know why I expected a warmer welcome." She fought back the tears.

She changed the subject to regain her composure. "So, how was the trip here?"

"Long, but I played games on my pad." Sammy was relieved to finally have something he felt comfortable saying. "The truck was really bouncy, and Dad's seat bounced up and down. It was funny."

"In fact, I think we should rent a car. Then the kids can ride back with you. There really isn't enough room for four of us in there."

"Oh good. That will give us some time to just talk," Judy said, looking happier now.

"I'm going to shut the windows. The stuffiness is gone, and it is starting to get too hot in here." James got up and walked into the other room.

Judy saw this as an opening and said to the kids, "It's almost Christmas, we should think about shopping for gifts. Do we want to do that here, before we go to Hope? They may not have a Virtual Reality Deluxe VR Lab 4.1."

"Wow! That's green!" Sammy exclaimed. "Can we get a Virtual Reality Deluxe VR Lab 4.1, Dad?"

"Sure, I don't see why not," James said, as he closed the kitchen window. "We are going to have some money to play with after we sell the house. But you two will have to share that together, because we are still going to be broke after that."

James did not want to disappoint Sammy, but he was mad at Judy for doing this again. She would make promises in front of them like this, so he couldn't object. He was going to talk to her later about it. He finished closing windows as Sammy and his mom discussed the games they could get. Sandra got up to help James and followed him into her old bedroom.

"Mom is being manipulative again. First, she tries to make us feel guilty and now with Sammy and this game."

"Yes, I see it too. I'll talk to her about it but first let's get her packed without an episode."

After James and Sandra closed the rest of the windows, they sat down with a pad of paper and a pen.

James took charge and addressed the family, while Sandra took notes. "Now let's make some plans. We need to go through the house. I brought different colored ribbons to mark everything we're taking. Judy, we cannot bring cleaners and toiletries, because they use only environmentally friendly ones in Hope. Anything that is not recyclable or all natural, just leave here. Tomorrow, we need to make some calls." He listed them and Sandra wrote down who would do what. "Judy, tonight we can talk about the things we both own, who gets what and what will be left behind. We can call Goodwill and have them pick up everything we don't want. We can also do a quick sale with a realtor tomorrow. Does that sound good?" He sounded so efficient.

Still needing to feel a connection with them, Judy asked, "Can we go out to dinner tonight, just to get reacquainted?"

"Yes, that sounds good. First let's finish discussing what we need to accomplish." James kept his cool, though he could see that she was stalling.

"Pizza!" shouted Sammy.

"Mommy needs a steak and I'm sure your dad does too," Judy firmly suggested. "How about it?"

"That sounds okay," James continued, "but first, we have to walk around and tag a few things, just so we get a start on this."

Judy relented, "Okay what did you want to discuss."

"The first things are in the garage. I pulled them out already. Kids, if you are finished with your stuff, you can play your games until we go to dinner." They ran out to get their pads that were still in the van.

Judy and James went to the garage. He showed her some family photos and some decor that were wedding gifts or things they bought together, things he thought one of them should keep. Judy was gracious and cooperative. This was good, but he wondered if she was trying to butter him up because she knew she spoke out of turn earlier. He did not want to argue, so he didn't mention it.

They went through the house and cordially decided on things. He marked them with ribbons. Blue ones were going to his house and red ones to hers.

Within an hour they were in an Uber on their way to their favorite steak house for dinner. James was looking forward to his steak. Sandra got an all-you-can-eat-salad-buffet.

"What's with all the salad, Sandra? You're not fat," Judy probed.

"I've decided to be a Vegetarian, Mom. I don't want to eat animals anymore," Sandra answered flatly.

"Since when?" Judy's tone was mocking.

"Since I DECIDED TO a month ago." Her emphasis clearly conveyed that she was not going to put up with her mom's mocking tone.

James stepped in as an arbitrator. "Now Judy, I think it's her prerogative to decide what she needs to do to stay healthy. The choice is up to her."

"But James, she's as skinny as a rail!" Judy protested.

"It's her decision to make, not yours!" James was firm.

Judy was shocked by his assertiveness. He reminded her that she is not in control here anymore.

"No, no. You are right. I'm not in control. Sorry dear, I have to practice not saying things like that. Old habits take time to overcome.

I'm still learning." She paused, took a bite of food, regained her composure and asked, "So, what brought this on?"

"I love animals, as you know, and I've been thinking about it for a long time. I knew you'd be upset by it, so I didn't try it until I was with Dad."

"She sprung it on me in the middle of dinner one night," James added, "after Sammy told a story about animal spirits."

"Animal spirits?" She directed her question to Sammy.

Sammy knew his mother had not heard about his weekends at the Native village, so he looked to his dad for help.

James swallowed his food, took a deep breath, and bravely proceeded, "Sammy has been spending weekends at a Native American village in the park where he learns dancing and hunting skills. They teach him to respect nature and the spirits of animals. It has helped him with his self-esteem and anger issues."

"Oh, that sounds good. What do you mean by 'spending the weekends?'"

"They have a foster parent program. He is supervised by a family, while he is camping with them. They teach him the ways of their culture and help him with personal growth."

"I see. Why can't we teach him those things in our own culture?" Judy spit out the words, feeling angry that she was not consulted on this. She was trying not to show her anger, but the words just jumped out.

"He is interested in Native American culture, and I see no harm in that." James retorted knowing full well that Judy was pissed. James knew this was the best place to tell her, because Judy would never show her emotions in a restaurant.

Judy wanted to know why he didn't consult her first but knew it would lead to an argument, so she opted to get more information instead. "Well, tell me Sammy, what are you learning?"

Now that the hard part was over, and his mom did not freak out, Sammy talked about the dancing, the hunting, and how there is Spirit everywhere.

Then Judy turned her attention to Sandra, "So, how do you spend your time on the weekends?"

Sandra was guarded, but felt she had nothing to hide, so she shared, "I spend most weekends with my friends at Tammy's apartment. We do our homework and play games. On Saturday nights, we go to the Conversation House and listen to poetry. I also do a lot of research on coyotes and the desert." She purposely did not mention her channeling classes.

"I see, are any of those friends, boys?"

"No. Dad said, 'No boys, no drugs, no alcohol, and no leaving town,' and I've kept all the rules."

"She's been really responsible," James quickly interjected, "so, I have been giving her a long leash. I think it is good for her to have more freedom now that she is getting older." James knew Judy was going to give him an argument on this too, so he tried to head her off beforehand, "Hope is very safe, so I feel good about it."

"Speaking of older," Judy said, to change the subject, "what do you want for your birthday, Sandra? We may need to buy it before we leave because they may not have it in the desert." She was trying to sound calm.

"I'd like to go to a bead shop to get some beads and supplies. I'm going to take an Indian beading class with Tammy and Susan, my new friend."

They talked about the way the schools were different in Hope and how much they liked them. Then the conversation turned to what they wanted to keep from the house. After dinner, they all went home and tagged some more things for the van.

James slept on the sofa despite Judy's urging him to come into the bedroom. James knew it was a trap. She wanted to get him alone, so she could argue with him. He was not falling for it. He hoped that time would give her perspective. The next morning, she seemed better. She woke him with coffee and sat with him on the sofa.

"I'm sorry I got testy at dinner. I'm not as sure as you are about these new developments with the kids, and honestly, I'm angry at you for not consulting me first."

"I understand your anger, but I had to do what I thought best for them, and I had to do it without you. I needed to discover my own boundaries as a parent. Also, we were under the impression that you would never move to Hope. In the past, I was not able to discuss things with you and have any real say in a decision. I needed to find my own path in parenting. I hope you understand."

"I don't know if I do understand. In my opinion, Sandra is not ready to be turned lose on the town, and I don't like the idea of someone else influencing my boy either."

"Sandra is just weeks from her seventeenth birthday, and she will be an adult in just a year. She needs the practice of venturing out while she still respects my guidance. As for Sammy, after taking an interest in the bow, I wanted him to be responsible with it, and I didn't know how to teach him that, so this was the best way for him to learn."

"You should never have given him a weapon in the first place," she asserted.

"Granted, but he came up with the idea at the courthouse. He needed something to look forward to when he came, so that's how it happened. I did the best I could under the circumstances. It would have happened anyway. Besides, it has been good for him to have something to focus on, since he can't do soccer yet. He needed it for his confidence. You didn't have to deal with his anger about you, or his feeling that he was at fault for the divorce, I did, and the bow helped him get through it all."

"There it is! Everything is my fault!" Judy fumed. Her mounting anger suddenly burst out.

"No, I didn't say that. I'm not blaming you. I was just stating the facts. Let's not argue and wake up the kids," James tried to calm her.

"You should have consulted me first," she scolded him.

"Like you did with the Virtual Reality Deluxe Lab. We are both in the habit of not consulting others. Besides, you were in rehab, and I didn't want to upset you."

"Yeah, because you knew it would!" Judy was still angry.

"You are being over controlling and overprotective of them. They are fine and they're learning good things, including how to be more independent."

"I don't like all this spiritual stuff that Sammy is learning." She threw this out as bait for another argument.

"I know we agreed on no religion a long time ago, but I think it's time for them to make up their own minds. Besides, it is just a good way to look at life, and it's not a religion."

"I don't know, but there is nothing I can do about it now, is there?"

"No, the wheels are in motion. You would just come off as controlling. They are doing well considering, so I'm happy about it."

"Well, I'm not! But I guess this is something I have to learn to accept now. Can we agree to consult each other in the future, on things like this before a decision is made?"

"Yes, of course, but that goes both ways after this, like the Virtual Reality thing."

"Yes, your right. I'm sorry."

"I'm trying to ween them away from video gaming. I'm sorry too, but it was good for me to make some decisions on my own. Now that you're here, that changes things. We can work together and not make decisions without talking it out first. Okay?"

"Yeah."

They woke the kids and made some calls. After a breakfast of toast and eggs, the kids packed up the kitchen and started on the movies, games, and music in the living room. Meanwhile, Judy and James showed a new realtor around the house. She promised that in this market, it would sell quickly, even with the old roof. She took pictures and left.

Then Judy went through her clothes with Sandra's help. She tried to get Sandra to take some of her expensive suits, but Sandra insisted that she did not need them. Finally, Judy gave up. She did not need them either, so she put them in the box for Goodwill. She saved a couple of her favorites, just in case.

Around mid-morning, she called her office and told them she was leaving. She said her reason was that her husband got a new job in Arizona, and they have to move. It was partly true, and now she could get a Letter of Recommendation, if she needed it down the line. She hoped that they would beg her to stay and offer her a raise, but instead they accepted her resignation and said, "Sorry to see you go," but it sounded a bit perfunctory. 'I guess I was a control freak there too,' she admitted to herself.

The panel van was coming along nicely, so they took a break for lunch. James suggested that Sandra take Judy to the bead store and have lunch together, while he and Sammy ordered a pizza at home.

Judy was well behaved in the bead store where she bought a hundred dollars' worth of beads and supplies. At lunch, Judy asked a bunch of questions about Tammy and her other friends. Sandra answered them, understanding that her mom had the right to field them for her safety.

"I'm being good and I'm safe, Mom. You don't have to worry," Sandra patiently reassured her.

"I'm not ready to let my little girl go just yet, that's all. Especially after what happened between us. You were right, I was not being fair to you two and I needed to get the help I got. Now I'd like to make amends with you, but you're gone all weekend and in school all week. That leaves no time for us," Judy complained.

"Maybe we can have a weekend just to ourselves once a month, or something like that. How's that sound, Mom?"

"Once a month? How about twice a month but for only one day of the weekend?" Judy countered.

"That sounds fair," Sandra accepted the offer. "Are Sundays alright?"

"Sure. Every other Sunday."

By the end of the day, everything was loaded except the beds and the sofa. The rest was going to Goodwill. The van was only half full. They had done a good job, trimming down to just the necessary things for the smaller place she would likely get.

The next morning, Goodwill came by and took everything else. They spent the day cleaning and throwing away the stuff that was not needed. The realtor came by with the E-Forms they needed to sign and told them that there was already a bidding war for their place. It was likely that the sale would be finalized by morning. They stayed another day to sign the final forms. They canceled the power, water, and garbage for the following day.

The next morning, they loaded the beds and sofa into the van and waited for the realtor. She arrived early. They signed the papers and James was soon on the road driving the van. Judy paid off her bills, picked up her car from the police in-pound lot, and sold it to a used car dealership. She rented a car and allowed Sandra to drive. They bought a Virtual Reality Deluxe VR Lab 4.1 and were on their way.

That night, Judy settled in at the Emergence Hotel. James picked up the kids and drove the van to the house, where they unloaded their stuff, leaving Judy's things in the van for later.

Monday morning, James and the kids went to their sessions and told their therapists about the weekend.

"I'm so proud of myself for holding to my boundaries and voicing my opinions to her," James said with his chin held high.

"I'm glad for you. Kim complemented him. "Now that you know you can, you can keep that up."

"Well, I think the therapy she underwent at the rehab center helped, because she's not immediately shutting me down like she used to, and that's making a big difference. Without this attitude change, I don't think I could deal with her at all. At least, it feels good to be more empowered."

"I am sure it does. To help you stay empowered, I suggest you both go to co-dependance meetings; separate ones, so you can talk about each other freely. It will help you continue your work on boundaries. I am sure her new therapist will suggest this also. Judy may want to get started with a meeting in the hotel until she finds a therapist."

"Thanks, I'll suggest it to her."

"Is she still going to have her own place here?"

"Oh yes. I'm not willing to live with her. She's still manipulative. I don't trust her yet. It may be a while before she gets over those old behaviors of hers. I'm not sure I'm interested in getting back together with her, ever. Friends maybe, but not lovers. Now that I have learned to process my feelings, I can see more clearly how badly she treated me. Nope, I'm not putting myself in that trap again."

"It's good that you see that clearly. What does she want to do for work? I remember you said you didn't know what she could do here."

"She talked about making clothes, she has always liked fashion, many of her advertising accounts were clothing lines. She even bought a fancy sewing machine."

"That sounds nice for her. That will keep her busy, and not in your hair too much."

"Yeah, I'm hopeful about that. She is having some trouble with being alone right now, so I'm worried that she'll want to be around a lot, mealtimes especially. She always used to make a point of having the whole family eat dinner together. I'm not sure how to handle that. I don't want to keep her from the kids, but I don't want her around all the time either. I'd like her to see them just on weekends, but the kids do their own things on the weekends, so that just leaves weeknights, but I don't want her over every weeknight."

"How about every other night; Monday, Wednesday, and Friday?"

"Even that's a lot," James said honestly, "but yeah, I guess, we must do something like that. I need my alone time with the kids too."

"That is fair, but how do you think she will take it?"

"I don't know," he shook his head, "she's different now, more unpredictable. It might go badly, and then she might relent, or not."

"Just be clear about your feelings, so she can empathize with you."

"Thanks Kim, that helps."

In her session with Samantha, her therapist, Sandra said, "My mom asked me to spend one day every other weekend with her. She is still being manipulative, but I can understand where she's coming from. She wants a relationship with me. I sort of do too."

Samantha was a young woman about twenty-five. She had a

pretty face, long lashes, blond hair, and penetrating blue eyes.

"Having a scheduled time will help you maintain your boundaries around Judy. It is also a good exercise in setting boundaries that you both agree to."

"Yeah, I'll see her beyond that too. I'm sure she is going to insist on some family time also. I just hope it is not every night for dinner. She makes a big deal over family dinners. I like my time with just Dad and Sammy. I guess, that's up to Dad but he used to cave in to her much too easily. Though he did surprisingly well this last weekend. He stood up to her about our extracurricular activities, which she did not approve of. You should have seen it, he practically hit the table, when he said it was my choice to be a Vegetarian. I was so proud of him. I was sure he'd cave in and my weekends with Tammy were over, but he didn't. He stood his ground and acknowledged that I was a young adult and had the right to more freedom. It was really green!"

"Good. Now all you must do is keep to the rules to show them that their trust in you is not misplaced. I'm glad things worked out for you this weekend."

"Me too," Sandra said shaking her head. "I thought that it would be a disaster. She started manipulating right off the bat, but Dad nipped it in the bud. She was startled and stopped. In fact, Mom was the one who apologized and backed down. It was refreshing to see."

"Did that make you feel safer?"

"Yeah, but I still don't trust her. I will have to constantly guard my boundaries with her. She is still trying to use emotional manipulation and bribery to cajole me into things."

"Have you told her as such?"

"No. I'm giving her some time to settle in. I hope she'll realize it on her own, once she has her new life established here, and is working with a counselor. But if she tries it again when we are alone, I will. I just hope it does not come to that."

"It might be good for you to go to co-dependance meetings to acquire some more tools for dealing with her."

"Yeah, I'll look for one."

Later that afternoon, James and Sandra were sitting in the living room. She was working on her homework, and he was reading a book on co-dependance, when he received a call from the court about a new custody arrangement. They were giving him control over Judy's visitation rights.

James and Sandra started looking for co-dependance meetings. There were two in their area on Mondays and Fridays, located in the same community center that hosted the affirmations meetings.

"Well, I know you don't want to do Fridays, so that leaves Mondays," said James. "I don't want to go out on the nights that your mother visits, so that makes her nights, Tuesdays and Thursdays, plus, you have her every other Sunday. When she gets here later, I'll tell her our schedule."

"She may put up a fight. I'm sure she is expecting to stay every night," Sandra warned.

"I'm sure she will, but this is what we're comfortable with, and this is what the courts ordered too, supervised visits at my convenience, at least twice a week, so that's that. Later I may consider all dinners and when I'm at meetings, but not yet."

"I promised to visit your mom at the hotel tonight and tell her what the court ordered. Can you hang out with your brother?"

"Sure."

Sammy arrived just as he was leaving. "I must see your mom. I'll be back in a little while," James tussled his son's hair as he walked past.

James met her in the lobby, and they went to her room. In a calm matter of fact voice he said, "Well, I got the court order today. It stipulates your time with the kids. The days after work and school are Tuesdays and Thursdays. You already set up unsupervised visits every other Sunday with Sandra. That is more than the court agreed to, but I'm fine with that. They do not have to know."

"That's all! Just two nights a week and I don't get any full days with Sammy!" Judy objected.

"That's all we have. It's based on our schedule and your visits must be supervised. The courts will reconsider this again in four months."

"Sammy's foster parents get more time with him than I do! If he didn't go there, I could be with him for a whole day on the weekends."

"I'm sorry Judy. That is the way it is. I'm not going to take his weekends away from him. Besides I can't be there to supervise on Saturdays. That's the day I shop for the week, and I go bowling. When you no longer have supervised visits, maybe then we can do more nights. Eventually, if he gets tired of camping, or he doesn't play soccer on the weekends, there may be more openings. It could get better over time."

"They're my kids too! I shouldn't have to be supervised!" Judy objected.

"I had nothing to do with this. The court set it up. Those are the nights I can be home to supervise. That's the best we can do now."

"It's not fair!" She fumed.

"Try to look at it this way, you get some time to yourself. You can work on your own process, learn to overcome your fear of being alone, and get settled in your new life. This could be good for you."

"It is still not fair," Judy started to sob.

James sat down next to her on the bed and rubbed her shoulder. "It's only temporary, Judy. You just must bear with it for now."

Judy wrapped her arms around him and hugged him tight. "Why did I have to mess everything up. I'm a terrible person. I'm so selfish. I didn't mean for any of this to happen," she sobbed.

James did not want to look like he was rejecting her, but he did not want her to push this further. He didn't know what to do or say, so he decided to just be comforting. It was the kindest thing he could do. He could afford to be gracious.

"I know you didn't, neither did I. It'll be over soon. Things are going in the right direction. Soon you'll have a counselor, and she will help you. Things'll get better."

"What about us? Are we going to get better?" She lifted her head and looked up into his eyes, with feigned innocence and vulnerability.

"Yes, but I don't know if we are destined to love each other. I need more time before I can even think about that, and so do you." He took her by her upper arms, pulled away from her, and stood up.

Judy flung herself on the bed face down and cried. Some of it was sincere disappointment and some was a plea for help. "I don't want to be alone, James. Please stay with me, please!" her eyes were begging.

"I need to go home, Judy. I'm sorry. This is not what I want to do right now," and he quickly left.

He couldn't get on the tram fast enough. Her reaction surprised him. He wondered how much was genuine and how much was contrived to get his attention. Next time, he planned to talk to her downstairs and stay out of her room.

Once he reached home, he busied himself with making dinner. Sandra helped him as they tackled a new recipe for a Vegetarian meal that they could all enjoy.

"You look out of sorts Dad, what happened?" Sandra gently asked.

"Your mother tried to get frisky with me." He looked over his shoulder to make sure Sammy was still practicing his bow. "She claimed she was lonely, but I think she just wanted to get her way about the child custody issue. Granted, she's lonely, but she was trying to manipulate me."

"Sounds like she has changed her tactics, but not her goals. She sure is working the 'feel sorry for me' angle," Sandra observed.

"Yeah, I'm afraid so. I'm glad the court ordered supervised visits only, because I'd hate for her to manipulate Sammy without us around to prevent it. This is new for all of us. Let's give her time to surrender her expectations and adapt."

"Your Mom is trying. She doesn't shut me down anymore or make-believe she's perfect. She sincerely wants to rebuild the relationship with us and there's been a lot of progress. Old habits can be hard to overcome. Sometimes they just jump out automatically as her default strategies.

"We need to keep our boundaries strong and be honest with each other, as well as with her. It is important that we stick together and support each other in upholding our own truths. You have your interests, which you should not have to give up for her. Sammy has his and I have mine. We are not going to make her the center of our world. She must learn to be a contributing member of this family, equal to everyone else, and not try to be the pivotal center."

CHAPTER 26

No Control

Chalondra met Judy in the Great Room of the Emergence Hotel.

She introduced herself and welcomed Judy to the City of Hope. As Judy's Guide, she explained that her role is to help Judy adapt to her new home. Chalondra, a tall athletically built African American woman, was about the same age as Judy.

While they were getting acquainted, Judy shared the story of how she came to move here. Then she launched into complaints about the lack of visiting time she had with her kids.

"Two nights a week, James could've given me more time than that! He wouldn't listen to me. I think he's power hungry now that he has the kids."

With a no-nonsense attitude, Chalondra responded with, "Maybe that really is all the nights he has. They must be supervised visits, right, but he must have meetings to go to on other nights. Many newcomers go to affirmation, co-dependency, and cluster groups. He is probably just busy on the other nights."

"He can leave the kids with me, if that's the case. I don't need supervision," Judy protested.

"The courts disagree and apparently so does James, or he wants to stick to the letter of the ruling for now. The point is, you can't change his decision, and you must accept that. You are not in control. James and the judge are."

"I can fight it in court. That's what I'll do. You have lawyers here, don't you?"

"Yes. I can help you find one, if that is what you want to do. But think about it first. Do you really want to start your new life being adversarial and start a whole legal thing soon after coming here?"

"I don't know. I want to see my kids more than twice a week!" Judy repeated.

"It sounds like you came with expectations, and you are having a difficult time adapting to the real situation you have found here.

Judy became visibly agitated and started pacing around.

Let's calm down. Please, breathe with me. Take a deep breath and slowly let it out.....Good.....Now take another one very slowly. Make each breath slower than the last.....Good.....Let it all out. Take another deep breath.... slowly let it out. Let's do three more....Good. How do you feel?

"A little calmer," Judy admitted.

Then tears welled up in her eyes and she whined, "I just want to see my kids."

Take another slow deep breath. Let's do this until the tears subside.

Once Judy seemed to regain her composure, Chalondra said softly, "You are going to see your kids. That is not the problem. Your expectations are. It may not be as often as you had hoped for, but this is only temporary. It won't last long. You said there will be a review in four months. If you work with a therapist daily, while you build the trust between you and James, adapt to the situation you are stepping into, soon you may be able to have unsupervised visits and arrange to see your children more. Keep breathing slowly and relax your shoulders.... Good. James is already showing a willingness to work with you in that he agreed to more than the court ordered two days a week. He is giving you a full day unsupervised with your daughter."

"Yeah, I guess so, but it's just not fair," Judy protested.

"Life is not fair. It perpetually poses problems and challenges that you have to overcome. Meeting fate with openness, conscious awareness, and a willingness to embrace rather than reject love rather than hate, is generally more effective. That is what is required to reach your goals. If you can love James and the children, if you can adapt to their needs, in the end they will want you around more and willingly give you unsupervised visits with your children. That is what will work. The question is, are you willing to do this? Are you willing to adapt and be loving?"

"I just don't get why he is so afraid to let me see the kids every day?"

"You said he is rebuilding his relationship with the kids. Maybe he is still working on getting his footing as a parent. Being newly divorced, he may also need some space from you. Can you think of any reason why he might need some space? Put yourself in his shoes."

"Yeah, I guess he would."

"Here sit in this chair, close your eyes and for just a minute make believe you are James. Can you just be James for a minute."

"Okay.

"For what reasons would you need space from Judy."

"I don't know. We need to build trust again. That's what he said, or it was Sandra, but I think he would agree. I don't know what they mean by that, other than my drinking.

"Any other reason?"

"Maybe it could be my need to control things, and my need to have things perfect. He did say I bullied him."

"Well done. Control and bullying sound like manipulation. Do you try to manipulate him?"

"That's what Lisa, my old therapist said. I guess I did that, but I'm not going to do that anymore!"

"Are you sure? It can be a hard habit to break. Haven't you already tried to manipulate him about this court order?"

"I don't know, maybe," the words came out without conviction. She knew the truth.

"Your body and tone do not match your words. They say you did and you know it."

"But I was so lonely, I just wanted him to stay with me for a while and he didn't want to."

"What are you afraid of, Judy? You have to face it, or it will control you and manipulate you."

"I am afraid that no matter what I do, they will never trust me, and I will never have my family back again."

"The terrible thing about fear is that it makes the very thing you are afraid of more likely to happen. Fear and control are just as much addictions as drinking and compulsive spending. Your fear leads to behaviors that make your family not trust you. This kind of behavior can end up sabotaging everything you want."

"How do I stop?"

"That is a good question. You know the answer. Tell me," Chalondra pushed her to reach for the answers she had within her.

"Well, I guess, it comes back to loving myself and trusting myself. If I can't trust myself, how can they. If I don't forgive me, how can they? Maybe it's like you said before, I must be willing to adapt to the way things are, instead of always trying to make the outer world conform to my inner pictures," Judy stretched to find the answers within her and was totally amazed that she could do it.

"Lisa said that I must accept that I may never get my family back, at least not in the form I imagine. It doesn't make sense to me. She said accepting that they may not come back was the first step to getting them back. Do you understand this paradox?" Judy was lost.

"Yes. Trying to get them to conform to your expectations pushes them away. Accepting that they may not come back makes you surrender. When you surrender and stop pushing, it leaves space for them to come to you," Chalondra explained.

"Accept them, surrender to what is happening, give up manipulating, don't try to control them, and don't let fear control me. This is all too strange, too weird. I'm their mother! They should love me!" Judy had to stop herself from shouting in this big open room.

"Judy, this is all very simple. It all boils down to one thing. If you can understand it, it will heal you, your family and your life. You broke the trust and now you must rebuild it. You pushed them away with your addictions, now you must earn their love back. Every time you do any of the old behaviors, it pushes them further away. Do you understand?"

"Yeah, but how do you do this?" Judy threw up her hands in despair.

"You know the answer. What is it?" Chalondra persisted.

"Accept that they are not going to do things the way I want. Start working on my own life. Follow their lead. Accept the visiting hours and work on building up the trust level. Listen to their needs and not try to change them. Make my primary focus working on loving myself and learning to have boundaries," Judy repeated everything Lisa and Frankie had tried to teach her. She knew the concepts but remembering them when life was happening was another matter.

"There were times when I told myself not to drink, and the next thing I knew there was a glass of wine in my hand. Or I promised myself that I would not go shopping that day, and sure enough the next thing I knew, I was holding an arm load of bags and boxes. This addiction to control and manipulation is no different." Judy said and moaned like she was really in pain. somewhere inside her she was.

"Relax Judy. Let the reconciliation happen naturally. Do not try to force your will upon circumstances, that will just backfire. You can't make them change their minds. You can only wait until they do it themselves. You are never going to control other people's minds. It's trespassing into their private space. Trying to control and manipulate them will just drive them away. Love yourself, it will make you very attractive and then you have a better chance of winning them over. You can't change them; you can only change yourself."

"Like the affirmation steps say," Judy remembered.

"Yes, the affirmations are there to guide you."

"Ok, I get what you're saying, but it sounds exhausting," Judy whined.

"If you don't do this, you could lose them all together. You must let go and trust that they will come back. Focus on loving yourself and beam the same unconditional love on them. No conditions, just appreciation. Period.

"I've tried to be a good mother. I made them dinner every night. They always had beautiful clothes and lots of toys. I was a good mother."

"Sure, you were. Now it is time to focus on building your own life, and practice appreciating yourself. Go to your visits with a loving attitude and avoid any form of manipulation. Expect nothing. Give everything. Be loving, gentle, and kind. And don't give them a lot of stuff either, that is another form of manipulation. Give them your time and attention, listen to them and try to really hear what they are saying. Be truthful about your process to yourself and to them, and please don't complain. When you complain, it is like being an energy vampire."

Judy just sighed and wiped her eyes, "I don't complain!

Chalondra chuckled and gave Judy a bemused look.

"Okay, maybe I complained a little." The humor made Judy feel a little less defensive and she added, "I guess I can try to do all this. I'll get cleaned up," Judy headed for the bathroom.

Then they went to the breakfast lecture. It was already 9:00. They ate together and listened to the '*What is* Trinitus' lecture. Afterwards, they had a half hour before the '*Introduction to Personal Process*' lecture, so they sat in comfortable armchairs in the Great Room and talked about processing, Trinitus, and the community's goals.

This conversation with her guide gave Judy an opportunity to voice some of her concerns. "So, wait a minute, I've been reading '*Utopia of the Heart*' and it says that if everyone did daily personal processing, the world could be at peace and people would love each other. Do you really believe this?"

"Yes, that is it in a nutshell. The only reason life is so hard is because most people are traumatized by their unloving upbringing, and they perpetuate those traumas generation after generation. The collective belief system in the outer world, which governs most everything people think and do, is cruel and harsh. It is divisionary and pits people against each other. Miserable people make other people miserable. That's why so many people turn to drugs and alcohol to numb the pain. Basically, our culture uses fear as a driving force. Fear is behind many actions. It is perpetuated by harsh, negative, prejudicial beliefs that are accepted as cultural norms."

"Do you really believe that just complaining that your parents didn't love you will change the world?" Judy scoffed.

"Processing creates opportunities to look at what you believe and look at what is driving your behavior. Processing gives you an opportunity to reflect on your life and gives you a chance to make conscious choices, rather than continuing to be like a lemming walking off a cliff, following behind another lemming walking off a cliff, in a perpetually destructive reality.

"Processing helps you relinquish negative beliefs and consciously choose a healthier view of reality, which allows you to be free from fear. Once the fear is gone, the love, which was your natural state, can freely be expressed. When you honestly love yourself, it brings you joy. You want to share this joy with others. Processing also leads to self-acceptance. Once you are happy with yourself, it is easy to be happy with others. Once you can accept your diverse nature You can accept it in others.

"This ability to love and act in loving ways, becomes your normal way of dealing with the world. Life has its natural cycles of abundance and scarcity, ease and difficulty. However, when difficulties arise in a loving environment, people naturally bond together and help each other. That's how we all grow together and share a more comfortable humane world," Chalondra explained all this in detail in the hopes of overcoming Judy's resistance. She could feel how fear-driven this poor woman was and how it was making her miserable.

Judy still had doubt written on her face, so Chalondra decided to talk from a more personal perspective. "Dr. Bebeau once said, "What you visualize, you can create." I have lived in Hope for almost twenty years. I come from Inner City LA. When I arrived here, I was filled with rage, ancestral rage, and personal rage. Now I am living a wonderful quality of life and so are all the people I know. I enjoy helping people and am grateful to all the people who help me. You are welcome to be a sceptic. I see and feel the truth of Trinitus in everyone around me and inside myself. I hope one day you can embrace this pleasurable state of being. We live in love, not fear."

"Wouldn't that be nice, but you will never get everyone to do this," Judy liked the story but regarded it as a 'make-believe, wish upon a star and all your dreams will come true,' kind of story.

"I'm sorry you feel that way. I think processing is like a daily bath for the mind. It cleans and clears the way for a healthy day. By continually processing whatever arises, we clear away the old beliefs and heal old wounds to remain honest with ourselves and each other."

"You are a cult! A good cult maybe, but a cult nevertheless." Judy said it too loud. A few people turned and looked at her.

"We are not a cult. Cults manipulate and control what people believe. We simply teach love and self-reliance. Here people are encouraged to think for themselves and not to kowtow to controlling beliefs. Furthermore, we do not make people stay."

"Sure, but if I wanted to leave, I couldn't because I would have no money." Judy said in a soft, but challenging voice.

"The community leaders would give you the money to get started in a new life and help you move for free. We do not want anyone in Hope who does not want to be here. Do you want to be here?"

"Well, my family is here so, yes, I do, but if I had a choice, I don't know. I like that there are no temptations here to deal with. Plus, I'm broke, so I don't have much of a choice."

"Many newcomers arrive at their wits end, but if they want to leave after they get their heads together, we don't mind at all. In fact, we hope that they take what they learned here and use it to influence people out there in a loving way."

"Well, maybe you're not like other cults, but you do believe in spirituality," Judy scoffed at the word, 'spirituality', like it was a form of voodoo.

"Everyone has their individual beliefs, and no one pushes theirs on anyone else." Chalondra would have liked to say more about that, but the speaker walked in.

Kauffman entered with four people who sat down on the chairs placed on the stage and began his presentation. Judy got a lot out of the skits they did and saw processing a little more clearly.

As soon as the lecture ended, Judy asked Chalondra how one acquires an apartment. "You will need a red band. To earn it, you must attend all the introductory lectures. Then you can visit the Housing Bureau, and they will tell you what is available."

"Can we just go there now to see what they have, even though I still have a black band?"

"Sure, you can reserve something," Chalondra assured her.

Between lectures, they went to the Housing Bureau. Judy wanted to live close to the kids, so she took a two-bedroom apartment in a cluster near theirs. To get all the requirements out of the way, she attended all the meal lectures in one day and earned her red band.

The next day, she called James to tell him she was ready to move into her new apartment and asked if he could come over. James saw the kids off to school and headed for her hotel.

As soon as they met up, she apologized for the other night. "I'm sorry for trying to manipulate you that night. I was scared. I didn't know how to respond when I found out that I have no control over seeing my kids. I talked to my guide, and she helped me see that I was manipulating you and that it was not going to help me gain your trust. I am willing to accept that you're leading now. Again, I'm sorry."

"Thank you for the apology. I was going to talk to you about that. I guess it'll take some time for you to overcome all your manipulating habits. I think it would be helpful if I point them out to you when you do them. I plan to stand my ground, and I'll give you feedback without any anger." That was a relief, he was dreading having to address this issue.

James emptied the van and helped her set up the bed and sofa.

"That should get you started," he said as he stood up and stretched his back. "You can do the rest. I must go to work," he said wiping his brow with a hanky.

"Can't you please stay longer?" Then she held up her hands in surrender and said, "I'm sorry, no manipulation. Go to work. I'm going to face my fear myself and meditate. If I need more support than that, I'll call Chalondra."

"I know how you feel Judy, I rattled around in my empty house when I first moved in. I had a list of ways to work with my emotions. I did some of those, plus I had a lot of talks with my guide, and I spent a lot of time doing things to get ready, mostly as distractions and time-fillers. I would stay. Honestly, I'm helping you as much as I can, but I do have to go to work. Call Chalondra."

"We are having dinner together tonight. Right? It's Tuesday," she brightened a little.

"Yes, come over at 5:00."

Judy watched him leave and plopped down on the sofa. She said to the empty room, "I love you little apartment. I love that I am out of rehab. I love you, Judy. Thank you for this new life." That actually felt good.

Then Judy looked around at all the boxes cluttering the floor and sank into the sofa, closed her eyes, set her will, and tried again. The room was cluttered with boxes and stuff everywhere. The panic set in. Remembering to breathe deeply and slowly, she breathed consciously for several minutes and that calmed her enough to pull herself off the sofa and grab a box of kitchenware. At least, where it goes was obvious.

Judy opened the box and there was her coffeemaker and a bag of ground coffee inside. She hunted around for a cup, and with a sense of great relief made a fresh brewed cappuccino. She returned to the sofa and savored the warm liquid. After that, she got herself to pick up one box and empty it, which made her feel very accomplished. She glanced around trying to decide which box to tackle next, but nothing stood out, so she figured she had done enough for one day. She moved a few boxes around but did not have the heart to do more.

She looked at her list of coping skills and the words, "Go for a walk," jumped out at her, so she decided to explore her new neighborhood. By the time she returned, she was in much better spirits. She found the towels and a bar of handmade soap she had once bought at a Farmers Market, so now she could take a hot bath. That relaxed her. She was feeling proud of herself for surviving this day. She carefully dressed, put on make-up and wrote on the mirror with a red lipliner, "I love you, Judy." She smiled at the silliness of that and walked over to James's house for dinner.

On the way, her Inner Critic whispered in her ear, 'I am going to James's house, his house, where his family lives. I have an apartment with no family. How did this happen when he was the one that ran away?'

She remembered Lisa telling her that she had a choice. She does not have to listen to the lies that the Inner Critic spews.

"I am healing from a very old and deep wound. I am bravely overcoming my addictions. I have pulled myself out of a dark place," she whispered as she walked along, but the tears still welled up.

She tried to focus on the houses she was passing, but the Inner Critic persisted, trying to get its claws into her again. "You fucked up, that's what happened! You should have let Sandra drive you that day." This evil voice in her head accused, "but no, you could not admit you were drunk!"

"Shut up! It all happened to get me to rehab, so I could get the healing I needed. It happened the way it needed to," she stood up to the liar in her head and it stopped.

'I can't go in there with streaked make-up. No more tears,' she ordered herself and underlined her resolve with a few sniffles. 'I'll get this straight without using manipulation. I really love my kids. I just have to beam that love towards them. I am not going to run away from my life anymore. I can do this!' she told herself.

'They will never love you," the evil voice rose up again to threaten her.

Terrible feelings were rising in Judy. She began feeling desperate and yearned for a glass of sweet soothing wine. Then she remembered all those hours with Lisa practicing how to handle this very moment. She began to sing an old Irish song, she didn't even know what it was called, but it went, "Hay, look me over, lend me an ear, all decked in clover, mortgaged up to here. Don't pass the plates boys. Don't pass the cup. Whenever I feel I'm down and out, the only way is up......"

After several rounds of singing this lively little tune, she was up. By the time she reached the house, she was ready to face them with love and honesty.

She asked Sandra and Sammy about their schools and their hobbies, and she was able to do it without judgments or feeling concerned. Sammy offered to show her some of his Native American dances and Sandra talked about dog-yotes and coyotes. James set up the Virtual Reality game and they virtually bowled until bedtime.

James walked her home. At her door he smiled and said, "You did very well tonight. There was not one ounce of manipulating concern.

Thank you."

Judy took a deep breath or maybe it was a sigh of surrender and answered, "Well, I realize I don't have the power anymore. I never did and I was pushing you all away. I can't keep trying to make this family perfect. There's no such thing as perfection anyway. I'm trying to go with the flow. I still don't like that Sammy is hunting and killing poor little animals, but what can we do? It's too late now."

"Yeah, well, maybe when he gets back into soccer, he'll forget about the bow. You know kids, they get bored with things and move on."

"I hope so. Well, I'll see you Thursday. Good night."

"Good night. I hope you sleep well."

"Well, if I can't sleep, I can always unpack. There's lots to do," she smiled and went inside without inviting him in.

James was grateful that she did not invite him in and was surprised that the night went so well. 'She is either really turning over a new leaf or faking it by doing what she thinks she has too, to get what she wants. I wish I knew which. Maybe she doesn't know either.'

Judy spent Wednesday unpacking and getting the place organized. Her craving for a glass of wine was strong, but she kept herself busy and was able to fight it off. She decorated her bedroom and arranged the second one as the sewing room. She looked at the sewing machine on the floor and planned to get a table with wheels and a comfortable chair. She still did not feel up to facing people, so she put off shopping for tomorrow. She looked through her clothes, which weren't very many, now that she gave away all her suits. The thought came to her that workaholics don't have many casual clothes. 'Anyway, I need to see what people are wearing to get an idea of what to create as my signature style.'

Toward the end of the day, she picked up her ComPad and went to the emergence website. She sat on the sofa and read through the articles, one by one. Having attended the lectures, her time in New Hope, and her talks with her guide, Chalondra, most of the material was familiar and by now acceptable to her. She still had doubts that the world could make this transformation that the book, *Utopia of the Heart* hoped for. Nevertheless, these were good ideas and couldn't hurt.

The last article was called *New Spirituality*. First, she bristled, then she sat back and looked up at the ceiling. She closed her eyes, shook her head, and decided to read it with an open mind. She never believed in God, or in any religion. She grew up with no religion and always found people who did to be illogical. To her, it was all fantasy that people pretended was real. After she gave up her childhood fantasies, she had always judged others harshly for theirs. That was one thing she liked about James; he did not believe in God or religion either. She acknowledged her own beliefs and with an inquisitive mind read on.

'We Trinitarians, in the United States and abroad, respect other people's religious beliefs and do not push any religion or idea of God on anyone. We respect that everyone deserves to believe as they wish, as long as they do not force their beliefs onto others.

"We do, however, invite people who are struggling with their beliefs and with self-love, to consider a more positive view of God and Spirit, to aid in forgiving and loving themselves. We encourage those who believe in a deity to see Him or Her as a loving and forgiving Presence. Those who have no belief in a deity may still believe in the oneness of all things, with or without spirit. We promote a belief in oneness and in forgiveness to help the individual feel a part of a larger community and experience the wholeness within themselves.

"The Affirmations for Life steps accept the New Spirituality ideal of a Higher Self. This aspect of one's natural state looks after your wellbeing and helps you pay attention to the motivation underlying your behavior. It also helps you evaluate your beliefs. This awareness of your Conscious Self is helpful in cultivating self-love and forgiveness.

"The Affirmations is a New Spirituality version of the more Christian Twelve Steps of Alcoholics Anonymous. We hope that you find a Higher Power that works for you, whether it is spirit or just your wise conscious Self.

"The core beliefs of New Spirituality are in line with the goals of the Trinitus organization. We believe in the oneness of humanity and nature and uphold that unconditional love is the central generating force towards global peace. Kindness and sharing resources are the key to creating and maintaining that peace. These ideas differ from the core beliefs operating in the world, which is rooted in fear, loss, separateness, and unworthiness.

"We believe that these three destructive beliefs underlie all the misery in the world today. It is through a sense of worthiness and self-love that the world can heal current feelings of separateness and fears of loss. We propose that we all work together to face the trials of our future and thus grow as a species.

"The next great frontier is becoming emotionally intelligent and consciously aware to get along better as a cooperative planetary community. We believe that unconditional love is the answer to life's dilemmas.

"These are the basic principles of the Trinitarian way of thinking, which we offer to all who come to our communities, schools, and self-help programs. We are not a Church, nor do we teach the New Spirituality in our communities. We are not a new religion. We have a new way of thinking of ourselves. We are a conscious community, a world community, members of one collective human race."

The rest of the article discussed how Trinitarian differs from religions, and other ideologies. How Trinitarians are independent from the old monetary system of capitalism. They do not condone a belief in a punishing God, in sin, or in the need for salvation. People who are healthy in mind and spirit carry no guilt of Original Sin and therefore have no need for redemption. Trinitus does not escribe to a hierarchy of rich and poor or adhere to a governing system of professional politicians.

Like the introduction to the city, and the New World website that Sandra found, Judy could see there was no indoctrination, no adherence to any set of ideas being pushed on anyone. Judy was satisfied with that. Hopefully that was really the case. She did however have concerns about the talk of spirits that Sammy seemed to be getting from the Indians.

Judy noticed a text that had come in earlier. It was from Chalondra, saying that she made an appointment for Judy with a therapist named David Shoemaker for 10:00 the next morning. Judy responded with a thumb up emoji.

Judy went to bed, but falling asleep was a problem. She had another night of insomnia and used the time to finish reading, *Utopia of the Heart*. Having insomnia was new for her. It started after her depression lifted in the New Hope Substance Abuse Home. She usually went to bed drunk, so she wondered if that was the problem. As she tossed and turned for hours, she blamed the court for keeping her up. Her mind kept grumbling over the idea of supervised visits.

Judy had only four hours of sleep, so she had to drag herself out of bed to arrive at her appointment on time.

She made her way to the tram stop and asked the driver where to get off for her appointment. The address turned out to be a tall round building in U-Town. She followed Chalondra's instructions and arrived on time.

"How have your first couple of nights in your new apartment gone?" David asked.

"Not well. I can't sleep and the space between actions is scary." Judy chose a chair tucked in the corner of the room. There were other chairs in the middle of the floor, but she did not feel that safe with him yet.

He brought his chair close, facing hers. Judy felt cornered.

"I'm sorry to hear that," David said. "What is keeping you awake?"

"Old grievances and new ones," Judy felt guarded and wondered if a male therapist was a good idea. She missed Lisa.

With a small ComPad in hand, he took notes. David was about forty with thick brown hair just starting to grey at the temples.

"In five minutes, tell me everything I need to know about you to help you." He glanced at his Smartwatch.

Boy was he different from Lisa. She was so informal and nurturing.

Judy just stared at him and finally got out one word, "What?"

"You have already gone through several months in a rehab center and talked extensively with a guide. It does not serve you to keep rehashing all the details and belaboring your past. I am here to help you move on. I want to know who you are now, not who you were then.

These five minute are just a formality to help you close the past and open to the present,"

Judy understood but was still taken back. She took a breath and began, as David glanced at his Smartwatch again.

"I was an add...addict." It was still hard for her to get the word out. "I was sent to rehab for being an alcoholic. My well-to-do parents were very busy, so I was raised by a nanny and a butler. The nanny was dismissed when I was eleven, and I was shipped off to boarding school until I went away to college. Basically, after the age of eleven, I was on my own and had only myself to rely upon. I married James and we have two children, Sammy, fourteen, and Sandra, seventeen. They live here in Hope. I was living in San Bernardino until I got arrested and sent to rehab. James has custody of the kids. He and the courts decided that I can only have supervised visits twice a week. I also have an unsupervised visit with my daughter for one day twice a month. It is ludicrous! I don't need supervised visits. They say the trust is broken because I drank and was perfectionistic and maybe manipulative, but I'm not anymore."

"Thank you. That is clear and concise," said David and he smiled. It was amazing how that smile lit up his face and he didn't look intimidating anymore.

"Were you an alcoholic?" He jotted down a note.

"I didn't think so for a long time, but the craving to drink is overwhelming, so I guess it's true. It's hard to really fight the urge to drink. I thought it would be simple to control, but it's not!" She brushed some imaginary lint from her pants.

"Alcohol, like other drugs, creates a chemical dependency in your body and in your brain, so they yearn for their usual fix. Behavioral and emotional addictions carve deep pathways that you habitually follow. Overcoming the cravings and consciously choosing not to follow the old pathways, takes a lot of vigilance and determination. It also takes compassion, gentleness, and kindness. Remember, the part of you that is addicted was stymied at a very young age. It does not have all the skills you have. The yearning and the habits urge you to drink. You are going to have to be firm and gentle all at the same time," David patiently explained. "If I understand you correctly, you are only in Hope to be with your children, is that correct?" he asked.

Judy nodded.

"Do you not want to be here?"

"I don't know," Judy answered honestly. "The premises seem good, and I read 'Utopia of the Heart.' I like the ideals well enough, but I question how realistic they are. They sound like a fantasy that will not work in the real world."

"The city helps people change their lives for the better." David tried to expand her view. "The growth rate of Trinitus communities is continually rising. Communities such as this one are part of a huge movement all over the world. The important question is, why do you think it is a fantasy?"

"I don't know. It is just so different from normal life in the outside world. It goes against the grain of how things have been for centuries. I agree that people have become greedy and lost in their fears, but I am not sure unconditional love has the power to change basic human nature."

"Briefly, the way the world is and has been, is the product of social conditioning, not a commentary on human nature. Secondly, if love can't heal the pain in people, nothing can. These are topics for discussion with your guide, in lectures, and at meetings. For our purposes here, the important element is, why are you concerned that the Trinitus way is a fantasy? Fantasies become reality. How do you think any invention came into being? The inventor fantasized and then created it."

"Lisa, my therapist in rehab, told me my fear of fantasies is connected to a fear of making a fool of myself. I had to give up my childhood fantasies to be an adult, so I could be treated like a person of worth. My parents' neglect left me with the fantasy of a perfect family. The driving urge to have a perfect family was a core factor in my losing them. All the things I thought were important in my life, now look like fantasies. I went from one fantasy to another. I don't know what's real. I'm afraid that coming here to be with my family was a fantasy, and so I'm doing it again," she put her head in her hands to hide the waves of tears she could hold back no longer.

"Am I fooling myself that I'll get well, no longer need alcohol, and have a perfect family again in a utopian city?" She grabbed a few tissues from a box on the table next to her.

"You cannot have a perfect family, but it can be a loving one, and if this city doesn't satisfy your needs, you are free to leave."

"I don't feel safe on the outside anymore. I don't want to be alone and the urge to drink is too strong," she said between sniffles and tears. "If this place can't save me, I'm lost. My ex-husband will not leave; he loves it here."

"I just want to be with my family, but the court ordered visits only twice a week, and my ex is letting me have an extra day with my daughter every other Sunday, but that is not enough. I miss my career. At least, I knew who I was there, and it filled my days. Now my life is empty. I only came because my family is here, it is a dry city, it's free, and I'm broke. Without my family, I'm lost. I have no purpose!" she dissolved into tears.

Judy was in a catharsis. David let her cry uncontrollably for a few minutes then began to gently guide her through it. "You want to know what fantasy is, and what is real. You still have your family. This is real. You are working to regain their trust. You are not alone. You have me and Chalondra to help you get through this hard part at the beginning. And you have already come to know yourself so much better than you used to. You are working on loving yourself. There are moments when you do. You are not lost. You are finding your true self for the first time. You are discovering that you are worthy of love and learning how to forgive your past. You're struggling not to drink, and so far, you have succeeded. These are all real, solid truths. You can count on them and build a future on them.

"I don't know, I don't love myself right now and my parents never loved me," she sobbed some more.

"You are working on it. It is just taking longer than the time you allotted for completing the process. Give it an extension. This process takes longer than anyone expects. As for your parents, they probably loved you but couldn't show it in the way you needed. You can love your children better, and that will redeem the past. You just need a little more patience with the process. It is unfolding perfectly at its own natural pace."

When the tears subsided, David asked, "Do you feel better?"

Judy sniffled and nodded.

"You have just come through a catharsis. Whenever this happens and these intense emotions come over you, just list what is real. When you tell yourself the truth and recognize that you are hearing lies, it stops the Inner Critic. This evil tongued liar exaggerates and phrases words just to make you feel guilty, ashamed, rejected, and whips you into despair. It was implanted in your mind when you were a child to control you. It is a compulsive liar. You can tell it by the terrible way it makes you feel. Nothing hurts like this evil tongued beast. Wean yourself off believing its lies." David said with a warm smile and a look of great sincerity.

"Lisa used to say that too," Judy confirmed between sniffles.

"How do you feel? Take a moment, really feel the emotion first, then tell me."

"I feel really angry that this evil voice has controlled me and made me suffer for so long."

"It is natural to feel anger, but it is not healthy to hold onto it. Be grateful that you know now what it says is not true, and you don't have to believe it. As for all the other grievances you carry, it is time to put them down. Forgiveness is the key to letting go of anger. When you are willing to forgive everyone who has wronged you and forgive yourself for whatever part you think you played, you have taken the first step towards being free of your addictions."

"Are you willing to do homework?" asked David.

Judy nodded.

"Write a very detailed letter to your parents that you will never send them. Express every grievance, everything you're angry about that they did or didn't do. When your emotions reach a crescendo, put the letter aside and go for a very speedy walk or beat up your pillow. Let your tears flow freely. Do not stop them. Let them continue until they stop on their own. When the letter is finished and the emotions subside, write a second letter. In this one forgive them for each and every grievance. Bring them to tomorrow's session."

"I'm going to have dinner with my family tonight. I don't know if I can finish it by tomorrow.

"You have all day today. If you don't sleep, you have all night. Once the letters are done, sleep is more likely to come," he offered her a little ray of hope.

They made another appointment for the next day.

Judy walked out feeling exhausted but also freer. She went to the car share lot by the main tram station and got an SUV to go shopping. She needed materials to make some new clothes for herself. The heads-up display sent her straight to the shopping district in the L-Town.

She found three kinds of clothes. In the stores there were new and resale clothes from outside, and cottage industry natural fiber clothes from Trinitus Co-Ops. In stalls under the shops, she discovered handmade clothes created by people like her. They were also made from all natural fibers like hemp, bamboo, fleece, silk, and wool. There was a shop of weavers making fabrics and a cloth store displaying an assortment of wonderful bolts of cloth.

She browsed around, taking in all the different styles of local clothes. Most were simply made. Judy concluded that simplicity in style was valued here, but there was also a wide array of bright and natural colors.

The loose flowing drape of this style mimicked desert people, Middle Eastern and Tribal clothes. Some were old Roman style, and still others were like Kimonos. She found sewing patterns for all these styles. This was a great place to begin to polish up her skills on these simpler designs. All the patterns said, *low waste*, on the front, Apparently, low amounts of scrap material seemed to be important to this community, Judy observed.

She chose several interesting fabrics and an adjustable mannikin. After she put them in the car, she got some clothes as examples of finished products. She wanted to wear them, so she could get ideas on how to make them more stylish. It delighted her to carry them out and not have to pay. As she headed for the car, she thought about how she had expected it to be expensive. What freedom this gave her to experiment, and she did not have to worry about wasting money if it did not work out.

She walked through the furniture stores and found some great tables, which they would deliver to her apartment. One table was for her sewing machine, and one was for cutting patterns. She also found a few things for the apartment; a kitchen table and chairs, end tables, a dresser, and a nightstand. The old ones went to Goodwill. She picked natural light wood to brighten up her new abode.

At home, she put all the stuff on the sofa until the tables arrived. She tried on the new clothes, then hung them in the spare bedroom closet. Most came with sashes to create a waistline. But some did not. Most could be worn by a woman or a man. She thought that making more feminine styles would be a nice idea.

While Judy waited for the furniture to be delivered, she looked for something to do, afraid that if she wasn't busy, the craving to drink would grab her, or a panic attack would start. She reminded herself that she was not going to listen to any lies her mind threw at her and looked for something constructive to do.

She used her ComScreen to order groceries to be delivered and found a Sewing Circle near her, which met every other Saturday. She took note of the community center's address and looked it up on Map Quest. It was walking distance. She wondered if she could just drop by and see the kids after the Sewing Circle, in the future, of course. That is, when the kids are home. This thought led her to the idea of asking to visit the Indian camp this coming weekend, so she could see it for herself. She had some questions she wanted to ask those foster parents. At dinner tonight, she would ask to see the park on the weekend.

Judy curled up in the corner of the sofa, the rest was covered in bolts of cloth. Her desire for a drink was very strong right now, so she took out her coping list and saw 'do homework'. That reminded her that she needed to write the letters. Getting started was hard, but within a few minutes the first letter was writing itself.

She was interrupted by the arrival of the furniture movers. When they left, it was time to go to dinner at James's house. She put on a white kimono-like robe with blue flying cranes on it. Underneath she wore a tee shirt and tights. She drove the borrowed car to his house.

James made game birds and potato salad. Sandra had the potato salad and a nut pate'. The kids told stories about school and Judy described her new therapist. The dinner was going very well and everyone seemed at ease, so Judy asked about going to the park with them this weekend.

"I know I don't have weekends right now, but I'd like to meet Sammy's foster family."

"Well, how do you feel about that Sammy?" James asked with caution in his voice.

"I'm okay with it. She can see how good it is for me," Sammy said confidently.

"Okay then, Sandra, do you want to come?"

"Yeah, I would not miss it!" Sandra said, with caution in her tone too.

"Okay, we can all do a camp out. I'll call and reserve two teepees."

"Judy, we need to be there by 6:00 am, so Sammy can be on time for his hunting trip," James pointed out.

"How long are you going to be gone hunting?" Judy asked her son.

"Most of the morning, and if we are not lucky, part of the afternoon too, but we'll be together most of Sunday."

"Oh, good," Judy said, trying to sound enthusiastic.

When the evening was over, James walked her out to the car and asked, "I can't help thinking you are up to something. No offence, but I am curious if you have an agenda?"

"I have no agenda," she lied. "I just want to meet the Weekend Parents of my son. I am his mom, and I did not get a chance to meet them before all this was decided, that's all. I still have a right to be involved in decisions like this, don't I?"

"Yes, of course, you do. But I don't want you to make trouble for him, he's happy there."

"No trouble, I promise."

"All, right then, I hope you'll keep that promise."

Judy smiled and got in the car.

James quickly went back in. Sammy already retired to his room to call his friends and tell them about his weekend plans. Sandra was clearing the table. "Do you trust her?"

"Not one bit," said James.

CHAPTER 27

Finding Faith

Just before dawn, as the sky slowly brightened, Judy's Smartwatch chimed to wake her up. It was Saturday morning, and she needed to catch a tram to the park. She was both excited and nervous about this day. 'What if these foster parents turned out to be great, how will that make me feel?' Judy asked herself. She also did not want the people training her son to be bigoted and selfish. This was a no-win situation. Judy was prepared to dislike them if they were good and if they were bad. She quickly dressed in jeans and a soft sweater, grabbed what she thought she would need for camping, and ran out to catch a tram.

James and the kids met her at the park entrance. They were in line waiting to go in and waved her over to them. She hugged them with her pillow and bag in hand.

"I see you. You won't need all that, just a change of clothes. Sorry, I should have told you that at dinner," James apologized.

"That's okay. I'll just have more to choose from." She said with a smile.

"I reserved two teepees. How did you want to divide us? We can put you in with Sandra or with me. Sammy is staying with Alo and Chenoa."

"Can't Sammy be with me, and you stay with Sandra?" Judy was trying to keep her disappointment from showing, but it peeked out.

"No, he has to get up really early tomorrow to go with Alo." James made an excuse he thought she would believe. He did not want her to be alone with Sammy. The boy understood what his father was doing and agreed, nodding his head. He did not want to be with her solo either.

"Oh well, then I'll bunk with Sandra," Judy was avoiding staying with James. Sleeping in the tent alone with him would bring up too many feelings and confusion.

They walked over to the Native Village. It wasn't far. There were at least fifty tanned teepees around a large central fire pit. A large adobe building stood to one side and thirty more canvas teepees stood near another pueblo building behind them. The canvas ones had numbers on them for guests.

"We're in eleven and twelve," James reported. "We can put our things in the teepees, and then Sammy can take us to Chenoa and Alo. I don't know if I remember which one it is. Sh, walk quietly, people may still be sleeping."

As they approached his foster parents' teepee, the smell of herbal coffee and biscuits announced that they were already up. Speaking in

Hopi, Sammy asked if they could come in. He was picking up the language little by little.

Inside, the space was warm. On top of a little cast iron stove, in a Dutch oven biscuits were cooking. A pipe vented it through the top of the teepee. Guide wires, about five feet off the ground, held the pipe centered. Clothes and herb bunches hung from the wires. Chenoa bent under them to check the biscuits.

The bare dirt floor had a few animal skins strategically placed in front of each of four wooden cots covered in skins. They stood a few inches from the walls to avoid condensation. The beds also served as seats. They were only six inches off the ground, so it did not feel much different than sitting on the floor.

Sammy's foster parents greeted their guests with "I see you" and everyone sat down. They talked in quiet voices, because it was still quite early and the teepees were close together. Chenoa handed out hot biscuits and wooden cups of herbal coffee. They needed the warm liquid to get down the dense, but delicious, biscuits.

After breakfast and pleasantries, Alo announced that they needed to leave. He invited James to join them. James was taken back and considered it for a minute but knew that if he was confronted with an animal, he doubted that he could take its life.

"Thank you, but no. I'd just slow you down, besides I have things I must do later," his smile was warm and genuine, even if his words weren't.

Everyone wished them luck, except Sandra. She was rooting for the animals.

Chenoa handed Alo a cloth sack containing deer jerky, coffee, and biscuits for later. Alo kissed his wife, then he and his charge set off on their hunt.

The sun was now beginning to rise.

Chenoa looked at James, Judy, and Sandra, "Is anyone still hungry, I can whip us up some eggs and bacon. The boys like to eat light before hunting, but I like a little more."

"Thank you, that sounds good," James said. Judy agreed. Sandra smiled and said she just wanted another biscuit.

Chenoa was adept at navigating the small space. She took the eggs from a box wedged between the cots. The bacon was wrapped in wax paper hanging in a bag above it. She squatted in front of the stove and put the bacon in the deep cast iron skillet, in which she had baked the biscuits. From another space between the cots, she pulled out three wooden plates. She poured more herbal coffee in everyone's cup, then checked the fire in the stove, and poked the bacon in the pan with a two-tine fork.

"Judy, we are glad you are here. We wanted to meet you too. Do you have any questions for me?" Chenoa graciously asked.

"Sure, do you live like this year-round?"

"Yes, Alo and I do. We enjoy living a traditional lifestyle. Not all Native people do it all year-round."

"Why do you like it?" Judy asked making sure her voice sounded friendly even if she still felt nervous and uncomfortable. She would have preferred a proper chair and table, so she didn't have to hold the food on her lap.

"Many Native People want to get in touch with their roots. They want to feel their natural spirit and the spirit of Mother Earth," Chenoa explained with simplicity and grace.

"But you are white. Why do YOU do it?" Judy blurted out.

At this, James almost spit out his sip of coffee.

"Yes, that is one of my identities. I believe as Native People do, that we need to get in touch with our land and its spirit. I like the simplicity of an old-fashioned life. With the General Store in the Old West town, I'm not roughing it too much."

"What do you mean by spirit?" Judy asked, trying to filter out any hint of the prejudice she was feeling.

James stiffened, for fear that she was about to be rude or challenging.

Chenoa took a breath and reflected for a few seconds, then answered, "We believe that spirit is everywhere, in everything. When AI and comps define your view of life, you can become detached from spirit and from life. City life can be too busy and distracting to allow the mind to be conscious and aware. Here we live in a relationship with the land and its resources. We feel connected to the land and to nature. This is how we stay in harmony with our spirit and to the spirit of our world."

"Oh, I see. Are you happy living like this?" Judy probed more.

James relaxed a bit, relieved that she did not challenge Chenoa.

"Yes, very much," Chenoa said as she flipped the bacon. "I understand that you are divorced, but I see you're wearing a red band, are you living here in Hope now?"

"Yeah, I could not very well do supervised visits, if I lived in a different state. Plus, I have no money to start over."

"Oh, I'm sorry to hear that. Life out there can be extra hard for no good reason, that's for sure," Chenoa sympathized.

"Yes, well, the therapy here is helping me."

"Good, I'm glad to hear you are doing well," she gave Judy a sweet compassionate smile.

"As well as I could be anyway," Judy grumbled.

It got quiet for a while as Chenoa stirred the eggs in a bowl and added a drop of water.

To break the silence, James asked, "So, Sandra, I thought your mother and I could go shopping today and walk around the town. Do you want to come with us, or do you want to ride up the canyon?"

"I think a ride sounds good to me. There are always more people I can interview about the dog-yotes."

"Okay, well, we still have some time before that starts." James said.

"Can I interest you in a craft?" Chenoa asked. "I would be

delighted to teach you how to make baskets, dream weavers, weave cloth, or sew leather. At the big pueblo, they offer classes on throwing clay bowls and vases, if you prefer," Chenoa wanted to help her guest enjoy the park and the gifts of the village.

"Is that a loom hanging on a peg over there?" Judy asked as she pointed to a teepee pole.

"Yes, it is. Would you like me to show you how to use it after breakfast?" The bacon was almost done, so Chenoa turned down the heat by adjusting the flue. Chenoa asked Sandra and James, "Can I get you started on something, which you can finish later?"

"Oh, I would love to learn how to make a dream weaver," Sandra volunteered.

"I think I'll just watch." James copped out. "I'm not crafty with my hands,"

"Then we will get started right after we eat," Chenoa filled the plates and served them.

The food filled their bellies nicely and soon the women were busy with their projects. Chenoa showed them how to start and attentively went back and forth between them offering words of guidance. James sat and watched for a few minutes. Then Chenoa asked if he would help her by cleaning some rabbit skins outside the door. As he set to this task, he watched the dawn break, and the camp come alive.

An older woman started the central fire and women gathered around it to cook. They placed big iron kettles and pans on a large iron grate. Meat was brought over and laid upon any space that remained on the grate. A smoker nearby was fired up and a group of women prepared fresh fish to put in it. James wondered where the fish came from, the creeks were still dry.

James was about to ask Chenoa, when he glanced at his Smartwatch, and realized Sandra needed to leave for her ride.

He stepped inside and said, "Sandra, it's time for us to get going. Judy, do you want to come shopping with me?"

Judy was sitting just inside the doorway where it was cooler and had the best light. "You can go and I'll meet you later. I'm just getting the hang of this. I would rather not stop yet." She was trying to be alone with Chenoa but did not want it to look obvious.

"You're not going to miss seeing Sandra on a horse, are you? I think it makes more sense for us to all go together. It is a big town. It might be harder to reconnect later," James was not falling for it.

Judy relented, "Ok I'm coming," and she tried to look innocent.

They said their farewell and James told Chenoa they planned to have lunch in town.

The temperature was comfortable, but the sun would soon take command of the day. Sandra reached her ride on time and James showed Judy around the town. They visited the General Store and bought some smoked salmon. It came from another tribe living on a Trinitus land. It had a Rare Tax, so James had to use his Smartwatch to pay for it with E-Money. He also found some real coffee there and was thrilled. It also had a Rare Tax and was from a Trinitus community in South America. They were expensive, but worth it.

Judy was delighted to acquire a beautiful Native dress with beads on it, made from hemp cloth, a pair of soft comfy moccasins to go with it, and a warm pair of moccasin boots. "I will need them for warmth in the winter." Judy explained to relieve the guilt she felt for taking so much.

They walked around the shops and restaurants until noon, then chose to have lunch at an outdoor barbecue. As they chowed down on buffalo and boiled potatoes, Judy said, "We've been getting along well. Today is fun, don't you think?"

"Yes, it is going well," he acknowledged cautiously, suspicious of where this statement would lead.

"You know, my threats of divorce were just that, threats. I think I was deflecting to avoid the real problems I created."

"Really?" James stopped walking, turned, and looked her in the eyes. "I took them seriously. How do you think that made me feel?"

"I'm sorry. I had to make you feel bad in to protect myself from seeing my problems. Lisa at New Hope taught me that."

"I'm glad you went there and received some good help. I honestly did not expect this much change in such a short time. You can be stubborn in the best of times," he said in a good-natured way.

"Well losing everything, including our marriage, woke me up."

"Then it was a good thing for both of us." James concurred.

"How did it help you, James?"

"When I first left, I assumed you would file for divorce immediately. I totally believed that you wanted one since you mentioned it so many times. But when you didn't, my guide, Tim, helped me see that what I really wanted was a fresh start. I looked at how you had treated me, and I didn't want your threats hanging over my head anymore, so I did what I thought you wanted, I filed."

"Well, I know I gave you that idea, but no, I did not want it at all. I probably would never have filed."

James was stunned, "That's interesting. Why not?"

"It would have been like admitting we failed. I was still running after my grandiose ideal of a perfect family. I could not face the failure of it all. I guess my being here is spoiling your fresh start, huh?"

"Well, maybe, but I'm glad I can give the kids a better life here and they still have you in their lives, so it's a good thing."

They quietly walked along for a bit, then James broke the silence. "I'm glad you are here for the kids, and I'm glad we can talk like this, openly and honestly about our feelings."

"I'm glad too," she looked at him and sincerely smiled.

"Well, we should head back. It's time to meet Sandra. She should be back from her ride soon and Sammy might be back too."

They picked up Sandra who was all bubbly after a successful day of interviews. She shared her stories all the way back to Chenoa's teepee.

No one was inside.

A neighbor told them that the men took down a deer and she pointed to an area behind the adobe style Community Building, a little way up the hill. Sandra volunteered to stay behind and put their purchases in their teepee. She wanted to avoid the blood and gore of the butchering.

Up the hill, behind the building, they found the prepping station for meat with hanging racks, stainless-steel tables, and a watering hose. Alo was showing Sammy where to cut to get the hide off. They were so engrossed in their work, neither saw them until they were upon them. Chenoa was cutting the heart and liver into smaller pieces on a steel table next to the rack where they were working.

"Always keep your other hand away from the stroke of your knife and be aware of where your legs are when you dress an animal in the field.

"That's it. Short accurate stokes, you got this," Alo was telling Sammy.

Sammy looked up to see Alo's pride in him, and he saw his parents over his mentor's shoulder. "Look Mom and Dad, I took down a deer!"

"That is wonderful, son. Good job!" James said looking closer.

"Good for you, Sammy," said his mother as she stepped back away from them. She did not want to get too close to the blood, even though there was not much there.

Sammy had some blood on his shirt and pants, and Alo had some on the side of his buckskin pants, but it had long dried. Sammy turned back to his work.

"Your son is a man now, according to our traditions. I know you may not feel that way yet." Alo told them. He watched Sammy take the skin off with only a glance at his parents.

"You're right." Judy said, with a touch of venom to her tone. "I think it will be some time before I see him as a man yet. But you are right he is growing up, too fast for my taste," she tried to lighten up her tone.

James and Chenoa caught her inflection and exchanged knowing glances.

"Maybe your values and the legal age see people differently than we do, but we see this as a milestone for your son. He has become one with the land. He has provided for the tribe and the family. This is an important event in a young man's life." Chenoa explained.

"Well, it may be a big deal, but to tell you the truth, I'm not sure it is a good thing to kill poor little animals. I just don't like it. I'm sorry Sammy. I know you're feeling proud, and you should be, but I just don't like it, that's all. I'm just being honest."

"Judy!" James whispered to her.

Sammy turned to face his mother, "Well, I'm proud of what I've done, and I feel more grown up." He was pointing with the knife as he spoke, "I like hunting, and I'm going to keep on hunting. You're not going to stop me either!" then he turned back to his work.

Everyone was quiet. Chenoa and Alo would not interfere with a family matter. James and Judy were in shock. A smile slipped across James's face, and he covered it with his hand. Judy just stood there in shock waiting for her son to apologize. He did not relent one bit.

Chenoa looked at Judy and said softly, "We all have different opinions, that is okay. We don't need to push our opinions on others." Chenoa gently reminded Judy.

Judy did not want a lecture right now, so, she left. She went around the building and stood against the wall pouting. What infuriated her the most, what seeped through her mind like acid was, 'I have no influence over my own son and these Indians do.'

Alo cautioned Sammy not to take his anger out on the hide. "We need to make sure we don't put holes in it, so we can make you some clothes with it."

James let his smile show now and nodded to Chenoa knowingly.

Then James put his hand on his son's shoulder and asked, "Are you okay?"

"The work is a good distraction for my anger," Sammy sighed, but this is a big day for me, and she just had to ruin it."

Sammy's excitement, all those wonderful feelings of being successful, of attaining a goal he had worked so long to accomplish, now evaporated, reduced to 'killing a poor little animal.' It left him agitated and irritable.

He mumbled something venomous about his mother. He didn't know Chenoa was near enough to hear. She smiled compassionately at the lad and reminded him, "She is the mother who gave you life. Without her, you would not exist, so she deserves your respect."

Sammy bowed his head to Chenoa in acknowledgement but remained moody for the rest of the weekend.

Chenoa walked over to James and asked, "Should I talk to Judy, or should we give her a moment?"

"Give her some time first, then you can try. Judy can be very stubborn," he warned.

Chenoa turned back to her work. She put pieces of meat into muslin bags, cleaned up at the hose and washed off the table, then told James, "I'm going to see if I can find her now."

"Good luck," James said with a skeptical half smile.

Sammy walked over to his dad and said, "I am worried about Sandra's feelings. Do you think she feels like Mom, that I am just a murderer?"

"I don't know how she feels, but we can deal with that later."

Alo stood quietly listening to all of this and now felt it was the proper moment to speak. "Everyone has their own beliefs. That is their business. Your job is to respect your own. You stood up for yourself and stood by your truth. That is a good sign of growing up."

"I must define my boundaries around her. She can be very manipulative," Sammy said as he continued to work on the skin.

James wondered if Sandra or his therapist told him that. Now he did not have to hide and protect him from the truth.

Judy was crying when Chenoa found her. She wiped the tears away and faced the woman whom she felt was replacing her.

Chenoa said in the most compassionate tone, "I know you love your son, and you want the best for him, but children don't always take the path we want them to."

"And your path is better?" Judy spit out.

"I don't think our ways are better, they are just different. The important thing is that this is the path Sammy has chosen for himself."

"Yeah, because you brainwashed him into this fantasy world of yours." Judy waved her hands around to include the whole park.

"I'm sorry you feel that way," Chenoa said gently. "Before we accepted your son, we spoke with your husband, and he gave us permission to teach Sammy our traditional ways. We were very clear with him about what we teach. We are very respectful of the parent's wishes and only share what has been approved by them."

"Yeah, James allowed this to happen. I'm not happy about that, but I know he didn't say you could teach him about spirit. We don't believe in that stuff. He would have never allowed that!" Judy insisted.

"On the contrary," Chenoa continued in a soft respectful voice, "we were specific about that, and he did agree to it. We were very careful to cover this."

"Bullshit, he hates religion as much as I do. He would not allow that!"

Patiently Chenoa stood her ground, "I assure you he did. I'm sorry if it offends you. What can we do to..." Judy walked away in the middle of Chenoa's words. She went to the corner of the building, in view of the prep station, and barked out the order, "James come here!"

James felt a little guilty for letting Chenoa take on Judy alone, so he responded immediately. As he came towards her, Judy demanded, "Tell this woman that you did not say she could teach our son about spirit."

"No. I said she could," James concurred with Chenoa.

"What! Why?" Judy was shocked.

"I've changed my beliefs about that since coming here. I think it is good for Sammy to see animals as having a soul. He is learning to respect that soul and the life he takes."

"What do you mean you have changed your beliefs?"

"I have grown to understand God and spirit in new ways. I think it's a good thing to teach Sammy, considering his desire to hunt."

"You believe in God and spirit now? Why, just because this place believes in a made up unconditional loving God?"

"I have my own reasons for my beliefs. I once lost my faith, but now I have it back. That's all," James crossed his arms and leaned against the building. He still did not want to tell her about his experiences with channeling God.

Judy threw up her hands, "Well great, I thought we agreed on that. Now I don't know what we agree on." She paced around for a bit mumbling to herself. "Now he beliefs in God. What am I supposed to do with that? Sammy is being indoctrinated into a fantasyland and I cannot do anything to stop it!" she grumbled to the open desert.

Chenoa approached Judy cautiously and softly asked, "Please tell us what you are afraid of. What fear lies behind your reaction?"

"That my son is being brainwashed to believe in this fantasyland, this..." she gestured to the park and the city. "This is all make-believe!"

Chenoa chose her words carefully, "This is the City of Hope. We are pioneers with the hope that this experiment will work. We see it as a light of hope in the darkness of the world. We are working for the only future mankind may ever have. This is not a fantasy! We are changing the way people treat each other. The world outside is filled with threats and danger, but here we are an incubator cultivating a new form of society, one that satisfies human needs. We work diligently to heal old traumas and remove old fears. What we are accomplishing is real and it is having a real effect on the lives of all the people we touch. Isn't it helping you too?"

"I don't know, maybe," Judy just walked off down the hill.

"Let her be, Chenoa. I think you got through to her as best you could. She has a thing about God and religion that only her own spirit can rectify."

"I agree. She is still holding onto something old and painful, so she needs to maintain control. She will let go when she is ready."

Judy wandered aimlessly for a while, then ended up at her teepee. She pulled back the flap and saw Sandra dosing on a buffalo hide covered cot. She quietly stepped inside.

"How was the butchering going? Is he proud of himself?" Sandra asked.

"Oh, I didn't mean to wake you. Yes, he is proud as punch, so are your father and his foster parents," Judy's anger showed in her tone.

Sandra perked up and put her head on her crossed arms, "Oh, you sound mad. What happened?" Sandra expected her to brush the question aside, but she answered.

"I am so miffed! Suddenly your father believes in God and is okay with these Indians teaching Sammy that everything has a spirit. I don't think believing in spirit is going to change his desire to kill animals, which I don't approve of anyway. I can't believe your father is letting this happen!"

"Well Mom, there is nothing we can do about this. Sammy likes hunting. I'm glad they are teaching him about spirit, so he thinks twice about the value of life."

"I would have thought, with you being Vegetarian, you would be on my side."

"Oh, I disagree with killing animals alright, but you can't force people to be like you want them to be. You can't try to manipulate them to do what you think is right or best. They control their decisions and choices, not you. You can only change how you feel about something."

"I don't want to change how I feel about it. Killing is wrong! This whole place is wrong!" Judy was getting more upset. She wrapped her arms around her knees and sat on the side of the cot.

"Mom, what are you really afraid of?" Since her mom seemed open to talking, she thought maybe she could help by doing the *Chain of Questions* with her.

"That this whole place is a fantasy, and it will not work."

"What is so scary about a fantasy?"

"I don't want Sammy to fall for a dumb way of thinking."

Sandra had to get her mother back to how she feels to make the *Chain of Questions* work, so she asked, "Do you feel dumb about coming here?"

"Maybe. Are you processing me right now?"

"Yeah. I think this thing with Sammy is more about you. You're projecting your issues onto him. He's not having a problem with it, you are." Sandra explained in her best therapist voice.

"It's cold in here. Let's get a fire going," Judy was trying to change the focus.

Sandra was not going to give up that easily, "We don't need a fire, we're going to Chenoa's teepee as soon as they're done up there. You are dodging my question. Can you see that thinking this is a fantasy is not going to help you heal?"

"I'm not dodging. I need to think. I honestly don't know how I feel about this place." She got some wood and paper from the neatly stacked pile between the beds. She was going to at least build the fire for later. She needed a distraction.

"Maybe you're afraid that you are falling for a dumb way of thinking?" Sandra pressed on.

"Sure, okay, I am worried that I might be fooling myself," She was kneeling in front of the stove waving small pieces of wood around in her hand.

"Where does this belief about fooling yourself come from?" Sandra sat up and wrapped the warm buffalo hide around her.

"I don't know," Judy lied. "I don't want to talk about this with you. You're not my therapist. I'll talk with David and process with him." Sharing all this with a professional was fine but feeling that her daughter was wiser than her was just embarrassing. Judy finished filling the stove with wood.

"I can't force you to process with me, but I think you are more worried about yourself then Sammy. You're discounting this place as a fantasy to self-sabotage your healing process. That's my two cents worth."

"What do you mean by self-sabotaging?" Judy sat down in the sand and dirt near the unlit stove.

"You're afraid that Trinitus is a fantasy world. This is where your healing comes from, so you're afraid that the possibility of healing is a fantasy. You're afraid to trust this place, afraid to trust that you can heal," Sandra was insightful in her analysis.

Judy looked at her daughter in astonishment and said nothing. To herself she thought, 'Is Sandra right? Am I afraid to believe I can heal?' She wanted to stop thinking, so she picked up the matches and lit the stove anyway.

Sandra saw that the conversation was over and realized that she had struck a chord in her mom, so she curled up in her sleeping position and left her mom alone. The only sound in the teepee was the crackling of the fire. Judy sat on her cot staring at the stove, needing its warmth.

Alo showed Sammy how to cut up the deer. Chenoa put the pieces into muslin bags, salted the hide, and rolled it up. Then Alo instructed Sammy to take some of the meat to give to the elders of the tribe. In this way, he was teaching the boy about respect for the elders which included his mom.

James, Alo, and Sammy were on their way to the other end of camp to find a smoker not in use. "Your mother is in a bad state of mind right now," instructed Alo, "but you still need to respect her. Maybe you can help her if she listens to you. You are a man now. After we finish smoking the meat, we are all going to celebrate you and your success."

James helped by holding the heavy bag of cut meat while Alo showed Sammy how to drape it over the sticks. Once the meat was handled, they went to Chenoa's teepee for coffee and freshly cooked heart and liver with wild onions and rosemary. While Chenoa was cooking, James went to find Sandra and Judy. He saw smoke coming from their teepee, so he headed over there.

James tapped on the teepee flap. "Hello in there, we are going to eat soon and celebrate Sammy's success. Chenoa made a veggie stew for you, Sandra."

"We'll be right there," she answered.

The men ate most of the meat that Chenoa cooked and some of the veggies. With Alo's encouragement and urging, Sammy told the story of his hunt. "The deer looked right at me, but did not move, so I took the shot. It gave itself to me."

Judy was quiet for a long while, then she went over to Sammy and said, "Congratulations, you accomplished what you set out to do. You killed that poor deer. Now I hope you are finished with this nonsense. I know that lots of kids like to play Cowboys and Indians, but it is time for you to grow up. You are almost fifteen. It is time you started acting your age." The boy said nothing. He just looked down at the ground until she returned to her seat.

After the meal, Sandra helped Chenoa carry the dishes to the pueblo area where there was a large kitchen sink. While they were washing them, Sandra asked what had happened at the prep area with her mom. Chenoa was not keen on gossiping but did say that Judy thought the park was a fantasy.

"That's what she told me too. I told her she was projecting her doubts about Trinitus and the healing process onto Sammy. I think at the core she does not believe in herself. She thinks her healing process is a fantasy."

"She will believe when she is ready, until then all we can do is support her, as best we can." Chenoa was putting a stop to talking about Judy without her being there.

Sandra got the message and worked quietly.

Later, the women came together in a circle to work on their weaving. Judy went back to the loom and Sandra finished her dream catcher. The men stood around the big central fire with other village men talking about hunting strategies. Sammy was included, which made him feel even more like a man. By the time he went to bed, he was glowing with pride.

Alo and Chenoa had a hard time falling asleep. They were worried about their foster son. Alo said, "Sammy wants to be a man, but his mother steals his power. The lad cannot get a footing. If she wasn't there today, he would have made a leap forward. He tried, but she kept pulling him back into childhood. At fifteen, he certainly is old enough to act like a man.

Chenoa returned from the land of dreams with guidance on how to help Sammy. She dreamed of greeting the lad upon his return from a Vision Quest.

Early the next morning, while Sammy was alone with his foster parents, before the others arrived for breakfast, Alo spoke of a Vision Quest. He explained to the boy that it was an ancient coming of age ritual. A young man would spend three days without food, alone up in the canyon. He would go to seek a vision of his future, to find his totem animal, and to prove his manhood. Alo asked Sammy if he wanted to go on a Vision Quest.

Sammy was excited about the idea, so Alo talked to James about it. They agreed it would take place next weekend. Since this was a sacred ritual among men, women were not necessarily consulted or informed. Thus, Alo and James felt no need to tell Judy. James wished he had had an opportunity like this when he was young.

Judy woke up very early and stoked the dwindling fire in the stove. She cried quietly, not wanting to wake her daughter. She thought about what Sandra said about her fear of fantasy. 'Is it just in my head, an echo of throwing out my dolls as a kid? Lisa told me that there is nothing wrong with fantasy if you know that is what something is. Not knowing the difference is where the problem lies. Are these people all deluding themselves, or am I? What is real? What is not?'

She wrapped the buffalo skin around her. 'Life is real, this place is real. It's here. It exists. What is just in my head is not necessarily real. Lisa taught me that. So, is my fear real or just something I tell myself. I'm afraid of deluding myself, but the therapy is real. The city is real, so, I can believe in that. So, what about the rest, Sammy and the hunting? It is real to him, and he is not going to give it up. These Indians believe in this lifestyle, so it is real to them too, but what about spirit? It's not real to me, but it might be to others. Hard to debate that, it's a matter of faith. I can't tell people what to believe. My healing counts, and I can do that here or elsewhere, but I need to stay with my family, so here I am. This is a place of hope and change. Can it work? Well, I hope so. I guess I need to have faith in it?'

Judy crawled back into bed. Having faith in something was hard for her, but she needed it to stay sober and get over her fears. She had to pick something to have faith in. The therapy and the city were all she had. Her mind went back to her parents, her disappointments, and how she lost faith in life in the first place. In a moment of utter clarity, she saw how she stopped trusting people, their faiths and beliefs and came to believe that she could only trust herself. She was alone because she didn't trust someone. She had to have faith in life again and faith in herself. As she surrendered into faith, she drifted off to sleep.

It was raining the next morning. They went to Chenoa's for breakfast and the women stayed inside weaving. The men, including Sammy, had to leave the teepee to check and package the meat from the smoker. Alo had gone out several times in the night to stoke the fire. In the collective kitchen, they used an airless sealer to keep the meat safe from spoilage.

When the men were gone, Chenoa asked Judy how she was feeling today.

"Okay I guess," Judy replied. "I thought about what you both said yesterday, and you are right. I am projecting my fears onto Sammy. I need more faith in myself, in this community, and in my therapist, or I will fail. This place is real, and my fears are fantasies. Thinking no one can help me is sabotage. I must have faith in something, and this is what I have."

Chenoa was sewing the rabbit skins James cleaned yesterday. As she worked, she offered a word of advice, "I'm glad to hear you feel better, and glad we could help. We all need a Higher Power to get through our healing."

Sandra finished her first dream weaver and began working on a second. When the rain let up, they went to the cold storage to get food for dinner. After dinner, there were warm farewells. Chenoa and Alo gave the lean and tender backstrap venison to Sammy and his family. The weekend had come to an end and the visitors left.

CHAPTER 28

Vision Quest

On Monday morning, in her therapy session, Judy related everything that happened that weekend and ended with, "It is hard to have faith in my Higher Self or even myself. When I look in the mirror, I see a fearful, unworthy failure. I don't feel love, I feel shame. I'm scared, plain and simple, I have no control over my life."

David responded with, "You cannot heal by will alone, it takes a shift in perspective. It is realizing you never had control in the first place. That is the fantasy you are still living in. Life cannot be controlled. It requires acceptance, allowing, and forgiveness. You need to let go and let life be what it is. The same is true for people. You have to let them be as they are. When you bargain control for protection, it backfires.

"When you give up control and stop bargaining, you come face to face with your fear. When you surrender and give up, you feel completely lost. That is catharsis, a turning point. It happens when you hit bottom. Then there is nowhere else to go but up. That path begins with forgiveness. You forgive life for not being easier or kinder and you forgive yourself for the part you were compelled to play.

After that, as your value system resets itself, you come to the point of loving and forgiving yourself, if for no other reason than it is the only path out of the pain. You learn to love with no conditions and for no reason. You do it because nothing else has worked.

"When you feel threatened and have an urge to control the world around you, stop. Take a deep breath and let it out slowly. Then do the *Chain of Questions* to reach a catharsis, which will come when you are face to face with your true fears. Eventually this process will become second nature."

"What if I disagree with someone and I know I am right?" Judy asked.

"People can disagree and still be warm and loving with each other. It is only fear that causes problems. Fear feeds insecurities and makes you think things are a threat to you. When you do not trust yourself, you see threats everywhere. Your son's choices are not a threat to you, nor are your husband's beliefs. They are just different. Confidence comes with a true love of yourself."

Judy was finally ready to hear this. "So, if I love myself unconditionally, I'll be able to love other people unconditionally." Now that she had the principle, she still needed to do the work.

Alo and Sammy set out early in the morning and climbed a hill, then they walked past cactus and tumbleweeds for almost half an hour until they came to a large flat mesa. There they entered a clearing where the ground was hard and barren. In the center of the clearing was a huge boulder, almost a rectangular shape, like an altar stone. Beside it stood a spindly tree. Sammy thought the tree looked like it had been there since the beginning of time, because it was so weathered and gnarly.

Alo held three rocks in his hand and said a blessing over them. Then he dropped them on the hard packed ground beside the altar stone and handed the boy a large water bottle and a sack of supplies.

"Every day when the sun is highest in the sky, come here and place a rock on this boulder. On the third day, place your stone at midday as always. Later, when the sun descends in golden light, before twilight surrenders into darkness, meet me here. We will return to the village together."

"Walk now until you find a special place to make camp. You will know it when you get there. It will feel right. You must trust your feelings in all things. It is what will keep you safe. I will come every day in the afternoon to check that you have left a rock and know that you are well and safe.

"Everything that happens has a deeper meaning. Keep your mind open. Keep your heart pure. Spirit will find you. I leave you now a boy and will return to accompany you back to the village as a man."

Sammy watched Alo walking away. He felt excited and a little scared. He turned and started to follow a small path, probably made by a little animal. It soon petered out, but an unseen path drew him forward. About twenty minutes later, he came upon a huge cactus in full bloom, covered in brilliant red flowers. In autumn, it is very rare to see a saguaro in full bloom. This was clearly a sign welcoming him to this spot. He took a sip of water and opened the sack. Inside he found a blanket, a knife, a lighter, a notebook, and a pen.

He decided the first thing he should do is build a shelter. He wore his bow and a full quiver of arrows, as much for confidence as for use. He gathered a lot of dry tumbleweeds and made a good size dome, large enough to sleep in. It would not keep out rain or wind, but it might keep a large animal at bay. He thought of Sandra's research into dog-yotes and coyotes. By mid-morning, his shelter was complete, and he was getting hungry. Alo had told him he must fast, so hunting for food was forbidden.

Sammy set his will, ignored his demanding stomach, and went exploring. He was walking along when a small iguana ran out from under a creosote bush, right across his path with a huge Lizard chasing behind him. Sammy stopped to watch the drama. The big fellow caught the little one and wrapped his whole mouth around its middle. Suddenly Sammy's shadow fell across them. The big iguana looked up at the huge terrifying creature looming above him. He froze and dropped the little lizard. The little fellow quickly scurried off, while the large lizard slowly backed away, retreating to the safety of the creosote bush.

Sammy pondered the meaning of this strange little scenario. He was sure his presence saved the little lizard's life. He wondered what the message was in it for him. He decided that one of his missions in this life would be to always advocate for those in need of help. He would follow the path of the hero. When these thoughts walked across his mind, they were accompanied by a solid sense of certainty.

He came across a tall cactus that cast a big shadow and sat down in its meager shade to write in his journal. Then he returned to his campsite. He threw his blanket over the dome and crawled inside. He took off his shirt and carefully spilled a few drops of water on it, then laid it over his face. Now that he was safely out of the sun, he took a nap. Mostly he lay there with his eyes closed thinking about his life, the move to Hope, the Native teachings, and asked the Great Spirit, "Who am I really?"

At one point, he drifted off to sleep and dreamed that a large bird was feeding its young in a nest. One of the baby birds fluttered its wings and rose a few inches into the air. It did this several times, then waddled over to the edge of the nest and was about to try its first flight, when the big mama bird grabbed the little fellow by the neck, threw it back into the nest, and sat on it.

Sammy woke up sweating, as much from the dream as the heat. He was thirsty, so he carefully metered out his water knowing it had to last for three days.

When he first came to Hope, on the drive from California to Arizona, he watched the desert zoom by his window and thought it was a barren empty place. Now as he slowly walked alone, he was amazed to see that the desert was filled with all kinds of life. He just had to be patient and quiet. He made a point of walking with Native feet, heel first, then he slowly lowered the rest of his foot. It was a careful way of walking that made him very aware of his steps. Good thing too, because a scorpion zipped out of a hole and passed right where his foot would have fallen if he were not could see with his feet.

The entire day unfolded with little creatures living their ordinary lives while Sammy found them to be fascinating and extraordinary. He began to notice that all cactuses were not alike and began to identify the distinct species. There was so much diversity here in what he had once thought was empty space.

Late in the afternoon, he gathered several armloads of brush to make a fire. He felt safe enough in the daytime, but he held a city boy's fear of the desert at night. He thought about coyotes and dog-yotes and quivered. Sammy gathered enough kindling and branches to keep a small fire going all night. He would have liked to make a big one to keep monsters away, but the Arizona heat was hardly bearable without the added flames of a fire. The day did not lose its heat until a little before dawn. At first light, Sammy was up and moving.

After a ritual drink of water, he sat down on a small stone just large enough to hold his body and initiated a talk with the Great Spirit.

"Are you real? My father says that we have a Higher Self, and an Essential Self, people talk of Jesus as a God, there's also the Old Testament God, the Native People talk of The Great Spirit, and my mother says you are just a make-believe fantasy. What is true? How does this world all fit together?" He breathed deeply and slowly the way his therapist had taught him and patiently waited. His mind wandered around in aimless thoughts for a while, then one thought stayed and grew stronger, "A room can have many windows."

He repeated these words and realized it meant that all these deities were one life force that was being seen from different perspectives. He recited these words and sang them making up different tunes. After a while he returned to being silent. He listened to the tiny sounds of the world around him. Soon another phrase got stuck in his thoughts, "Different men climb a mountain on different paths." Sammy wanted to remember these exact words, so he repeated them again and again until more words attached themselves to this phrase.

Now he recited, "Different men climb a mountain on different paths, so they see different vistas." He repeated this phrase until another idea revealed itself. Again, he repeated the two phrases together and a third appeared. Soon he had the whole idea. "Different men climb a mountain on different paths, so they see different vistas, but as they come together at the top, they see it is all one mountain and one path is not better than another, though some are easier."

Sammy pondered the meaning of these words for a long time as he wandered around watching, observing, and growing more comfortable with the world around him. At high noon, he returned to the altar stone and placed a rock on top, to mark that he had survived the heat, the desert, and its creatures for an entire day. He felt proud of himself.

He walked and explored until the light began to change, then made his way back to camp well before nightfall. He watched a gorgeous golden sun surrender this precious first day and felt a passionate finality that deeply touched him. When the sun disappeared off the end of the world, a lavish display of colors splashed across the sky. It went on forever and ever. It was glorious, transcendent, a written message from the Great Spirit just for him.

Then the darkness began to descend, and Sammy got very nervous. He started talking out loud. First, he wanted his loud voice to scare off any would-be predators, then he wanted to make sure that if a spirit or deity was listening, that he would hear him, and lastly because the loud voice kept him company.

"I'm afraid to be alone. I have never been alone at night by myself, let alone out here where animals can eat me!" His heart reached out as strongly as he could, inviting a protective deity to watch over him.

He imagined himself wrapped in a buffalo skin in Chenoa's teepee and remembered the wonderful smell of her venison stew. This image made him feel safe. It eventually faded and he was alone with the night again. He watched the crackling fire for a while. In the flames, he saw images.

At first, the fingers of flame were reaching for something they never attained and fell back down. He thought of how hard he had tried to get his mother to stop drinking and how he had to give it up and let it go.

A branch popped and a burst of little golden sparks fluttered upward into the sky. He thought they looked like a troupe of fairies flying up to the stars, and remembered Antonio, his therapist, saying, "You have to rise above the limitations of your past and embrace all that you can be."

This led him to ponder how we are all little sparks of light, and how some people hoard that light and keep it just for themselves, while others hold their light aloft like a lamp to guide those who come up behind them.

Then he asked himself what he wanted to do with his light. He thought of the iguanas and remembered that his mission in this life was going to be helping people in their struggles with destiny's challenges.

He fell asleep imagining himself as he wanted to be when he was grown up. He had many dreams that night. At home he was lucky to remember the last dream he had before waking, but here under the vastness of the night sky, he walked through the land of dreams with his eyes wide open. He woke up often and each time he remembered the dream. Sometimes when he woke up, he forgot that he was alone in the desert and just fell back to sleep, but other times things happened that made him sharply alert, and he definitely knew where he was. He heard an animal cry, a breaking twig, a sudden unknown sound, or worse, a recognizable howl.

Morning came and rescued him from the night. He had his ritual sip of water and decided that he could have a little more than yesterday when he was being too cautious.

Sammy walked most of the morning, nourishing himself on the stark beauty of the desert. He was feeling many things. His heart was filled with all this power shooting through him. He felt love for the desert, and for his two families. Having two suited the two sides of his nature. He never thought about that before, but there were two sides of him.

He used to live in a noisy crowded city where so much was demanded of him, that he had to peddle very fast to keep up with it all. By the time his school day ended, he was hungering for solitude, so he sought the diversions of the ComPad and the Virtual World. There the parameters of life were clear, good and bad, right and wrong. The real world was far more complex. There were lots of variations of what was right and wrong; and far too many people telling him what to believe. Sammy felt very young and very timid. The world seemed too big and too threatening. There was no place carved out just for him. Competition was everywhere. The ComPad ironed all that out.

This scared and harried person was someone he had once been, and it was still part of him, but since he came to Hope, another side of him has emerged and it is really him too.

The new him likes to feel the dirt under his feet in the teepee of his Native family. When he is with them, he is a part of a family that focuses inward not on the world. Our family here is part of a small tribe of caring and nurturing people who work together and give each other space. Here, he feels both connected and free. The words came to him, "Free as the wind and fastened forever." Repeating these words warmed his heart and filled him with a solid sense of belonging.

Sammy was excited as he explored this new man he was becoming. Standing on the brink of a great adventure, those little fire sparks he had seen in his fire were now crackling in him. The day unfolded with a wide array of miracles, and he savored each teeny tiny one. As his bare feet touched the earth, roots of pure life force surged through his body. He felt young, powerful, and utterly free. He was an extension of the earth, a marvelous unique life form. This led to a million other thoughts.

The sun celebrated the glory of this day and when it touched the roof of the sky, Sammy returned to the altar stone to place his rock and mark another passing day. Time moved too slowly and too quickly here in this vast strange world.

Sammy was feeling quite full and content by the time heaven put on another great show for him. He put down his bow and removed his quiver of arrows, leaned back and watched as the sun celebrated the ending of this precious day with a glorious golden sunset and then as great splashes of vermillion washed over the vast sky. Sammy's spirit was soaring. As the lavender light of twilight turned the visible world into silhouettes, the boy made a good size fire and followed his thoughts into magical views on his life. When the darkness swallowed up the light, Sammy walked over to the beautiful saguaro, as red as the sky had been, and begged the Great Spirit to delay the darkness. He was not ready. Again, he cried out to the night repeating his plea, "I'm afraid to be alone. I have never been alone at night by myself, let alone out here where animals can eat me!"

The short hairs on the back of his neck quivered. There was a rustling behind him. Very slowly he turned, feeling cautious and apprehensive, aware of his footing, in case he needed to run for his life. He was prepared to quickly assess his visitor and swiftly act, as he fought back a feeling of terror. Suddenly he realized! He left his bow and quiver by the fire when he stepped away to talk to the Darkness. A sense of being naked with no way to defend himself came over him. All these thoughts and feelings flashed through his mind at lightning speed as he completed the turn. There standing only six feet away, staring right into his eyes, was a white-tailed deer just like the one he shot.

The deer was not afraid of him, so he did not feel scared. They just stood there staring at each other for a long while. Sammy was ready to sit down by his fire, but the deer stood between him and his destination. Sammy moved one leg closer, stood stock still and very slowly shifted his weight onto the extended leg. He repeated this again and again. He slowly moved one leg, stopped, and stood absolutely still, then slowly shifted his weight and froze. In this way, he was able to move within one foot of the deer. The animal did not feel threatened, aware, and alert, but not threatened. Eventually, Sammy sat down. He assumed the deer would now run away, but it did not. The deer walked over to the tumbleweed dome with its black blanket on top and sat down on the ground right beside it.

After his ritual sip of water, Sammy banked his fire and crawled into his nest. He lay down so that his head was near the deer's face. He whispered good night to his companion and felt very, very safe. The deer had come to forgive him for taking its life. Its presence made him feel that his spirit now belonged to Sammy. The lad knew in his heart that there would always be a sacred connection between them. Life and death, the parameters of existence are totally sacred. This was his rebirth as a man, so it was sacred too.

For the first time, he made peace with the earth upon which he lived and regretted that he had always taken the ground plane of his existence for granted. The land is sacred.

He fell asleep feeling wrapped in sacredness and gratitude. Sleeping with a wild free animal was a remarkable honor and gift. He felt that there was a sacred trust between them that they would protect each other. Sammy felt the deer spirit covering him as he fell into a very deep sleep, cradled in the arms of the Great Mother desert land.

In the morning of the third day, Sammy awakened, truly awakened, feeling filled with life force, filled with passion, and filled with a sense of destiny. When he opened his eyes, the deer was gone. He questioned whether the deer was ever there or was it just an illusion. By the time he processed all the thoughts that followed, it was time to leave his little nest. He looked at the spot where the deer had slept, but the ground was too hard to have a print.

Sammy placed his last stone on the desert altar and sat there just feeling what it was like to be in this moment, open in all his senses, experiencing the extent of being alive right here, right now, with destiny calling him forward.

His heart yearned to answer destiny's call. He wished he could see himself in twenty years and know what would emerge from the profound gift he was experiencing. No one had to say, "Now, you are a man." The desert christened him as one of its own. He looked at the third rock on the altar stone and went off to savor his remaining few hours.

His stomach reminded him that it was quite empty, and his mind wondered how long it would be until he ate. As much as he had felt elated over the spirit stuff, he was now more aware of his stomach and its "feed me" mantra that never stopped.

He was walking down a new path and instead of using his Native feet, he was moseying along. His mind was not guiding his feet. He was too busy listening to his stomach and drifting in a fantasy of all the wonderful foods he would eat when he arrived back at the village. Without an alert mind, all kinds of chaos can ensue.

A small snake slithered out and Sammy jumped back. He did not look to see what was behind him. All he could think of was getting away from the snake! It was a harmless little fellow who was just passing by, but the sharp stone he fell on inflicted a pain that did not pass by as quickly.

He washed the wound with some of his remaining water. Knowing his quest would end today made him a little more generous. Then he tore a piece off his shirt and wrapped the bleeding wound. The bleeding soon stopped. He returned to the altar stone and stayed there until Alo returned. He found a small flat stone to sit on and felt he only needed a small patch of earth to feel he was home.

When Alo arrived, Sam was both glad to see him and sad to leave. What other miracles was he going to miss? He did not initiate conversation, so his mentor respected his need for introspection, and they walked back in silence.

Sam expected them to go to Alo's teepee for dinner. He was starving. When they arrived at the little village, Alo led Sam to a large teepee set away from the others. This special teepee, one of the largest in the village, was the men's teepee. They entered and were welcomed by a group of men sitting in a circle. In the key position was the village Chief. On his left, sat the young leader of the village. On his right was an empty place. Sam was asked to sit in this place of honor beside the Elder Chief.

The village leader brought forth a clay pipe with a long wooden stem. He explained that the bowl represented all the feminine receptive aspects of life. The wooden stem represents all that is masculine and active. Together working in unison, life is in balance. Both need each other. Thus, it is a symbol of cooperation, and the balance of all things. It came to be called a peace pipe because when all opposing forces work together it produces peace.

The pipe was ceremoniously filled and sent around. The Chief drew on the pipe first and blew a small puff of smoke to each of the four directions, then turned it around and passed it to Sam. Alo whispered to his charge, "Slow and gentle." Sam did just that and never even coughed, though he had never smoked anything before.

Like the Chief, he offered a small puff to the four directions and turned the pipe in a circle before he passed it on. Now, a young boy, not yet a man, entered the teepee with a bowl of fruit and set it before

Sam. The Chief encouraged him to eat. When the boy returned, he was carrying water and set it before Sam. After that a group of boys brought Sam and all the men steaming bowls of delicious venison stew. While Sam was enjoying his feast, he looked around the circle and recognized several of the men. One by one these men recounted a praiseful story about Sam, what they experienced or observed about him, and made favorable comments on his character. Sam became visibly taller as the circle of commentaries continued. Alo went last and he was the most detailed and favorable of all.

The Venerable Chief turned to the young man and addressed him with respect and called him, 'Sam.' It was the first time he heard his name spoken in its short form and felt how well it fit. The Chief told him that he must always remember this experience and live with the honor he possesses today. Then he removed a beautiful little green suede pouch, covered with colorful beads, from around his neck and called it a medicine pouch. He said, "This pouch contains symbols of all that you will become," and passed it to the man on his left, who dropped a small shell into the pouch and said, "The shell is curved, so you cannot know what is in its innermost heart. Remember always that no one can know this about another, so with patience, caution, and trust approach each new experience." One by one each man put some object into the pouch, a bit of flax, a seed of truth, a pebble to hold unchanging truths, and a fragile petal for the precious fleeting things of life that must be savored and surrendered.

When the pouch returned to the Chief, he hung it around Sam's neck and welcomed him into the world of men. After that, Sam was asked to share whatever part of his story he wished.

Sam shared the events but not his thoughts or the meanings his experiences held. These were too private, and a man knows how to keep private things to himself, for his own pleasure and awareness.

When James and Sandra arrived to take Sam home, he greeted his father and sister warmly and said, "Now I prefer to be called Sam." They smiled at him and agreed. The next day he went to school as usual. After school, while his dad was making dinner, Sam marched up to him with newfound confidence and said, "Dad I know that you and Sandra have been trying to protect me from Mom's manipulating behaviors. Thank you for your good intentions. I appreciate it. I don't think that'll be necessary anymore. I need to deal with her on my own. She's always going to be my mother, so I need to set my own boundaries with her."

"Okay Sam. I understand," James replied feeling very impressed with his son's tone and confidence. It was very different from the little boy he always seemed to be, sheltered under his mother's wing as he had always been.

"I am going to invite Mom over tomorrow and talk to her by myself. What would be a good time, when we can be alone?"

"You could do it around 4:00 or do you need to be at tutoring?"

"Thanks Dad. I am just about caught up. I am sure I can take a day off. I'll tell Sandra."

Judy was excited when she received the invitation to spend time with her son. He greeted her at the door and said, "Thank you for coming. I wanted us to have some time alone to get reacquainted. We haven't spent much time together over the last few months and this has been an important time for both of us. We are both changing and growing. I am no longer a little boy who needs mothering. I am a young man now and I want to establish a more mutually respectful relationship between us." His newfound maturity was clearly apparent, which sent her into panic. She was losing her baby! She felt threatened, so she attacked him.

In a harsh voice she spit out the words, "These people have turned you into a killer. Don't you realize it's wrong to hunt and kill animals? Haven't I taught you better than that? Your father and these Indians are poisoning your mind. I love you and I only want what is best for you, so I forbid you to ever use a bow again. Furthermore, I cannot as a responsible parent continue to allow you to make believe you are an Indian. It is not your heritage, and it is not preparing you for a productive life. It's just escapism into a fantasy. It's no better than living in a computer and playing video games all the time."

Sam stood before her and politely listened. Whatever he felt was not visible in his face or body. For the first time in his life, he did not whither under her harangue. He simply said in a gentle respectful voice, "I am grateful that you gave me life, but now that life belongs to me."

A lot of mean things ran through Judy's mind, but the training she was getting in therapy made her stop talking. She was not going to give in to the anger. Instead, she said, "Sammy, you know how I feel about the awful things you are doing. I am going to leave now. Don't contact me until you learn how to be more respectful."

Judy mustered up her dignity and walked away. As she was walking down the road, she started doing the *Chain of Questions* with herself and discovered that she was feeling threatened. She realized that she strikes out when she feels this way. By the end of the *Chain of Questions*, she was ready to apologize to Sammy.

Sam was totally calm through the entire encounter, but once she left, agitation seeped in. He had hoped to establish a new relationship with his mother and clarify their boundaries. He thought that by showing her respect, she would do the same.

To release her negative energy, he paced around the living room; then decided he could regain his center with target practice. Shooting always calmed him down, so he grabbed his bow and a full quiver of arrows. He was excited to set up his new moving target on the porch for the first time.

His shots kept missing the target, because he could not

concentrate. He still felt an agitated undercurrent. He focused and tried harder. Hitting a moving target was still new to him, so missing the target was not entirely caused by his annoyance.

He checked his posture and how he was holding the bow. In his mind, he reviewed Alo's teachings. He took another shot and hit the edge of the target. So close! He was thrilled and determined to hit the outer ring, if not one closer to the center.

The light was fading, but he was determined. The next shot also hit the rim. It was so close to the outermost circle. He was almost there, but the light was fading. He totally concentrated on his posture, his aim, on relaxing his shoulders and narrowed his eyes, so only his target existed in his field of vision.

He let the arrow fly.

Just then, Judy stepped onto the porch. In the fading light, she saw Sammy, but not the flying arrow. Before it could reach the target, the arrow pierced her shoulder.

Sam ran to her, and stood there horrified for a few seconds, then called an ambulance and his dad. James called Sam's therapist, Antonio, and rushed home. They all arrived at the same time. Judy was taken to the hospital. Antonio asked James what had happened, and he repeated what Sam had told him on the phone.

Then Sam's father and therapist went to his room to comfort him. He was gone! They searched everywhere around and inside the house. He was definitely gone. They called Alo and Chenoa to ask them to keep an eye out for the boy. James called Sandra at Tammy's house, and they also joined in the search.

The whole community was now aware that Sam was missing. Sandra knew she should feel sympathy for her mother, but all she felt was anger. Her mother always messed things up.

"Tammy, this is all my mother's fault. I am sure it was an accident, but now Sammy is so upset, he has run away. He is such a gentle soul and she can be so cruel. Poor Sammy, he must feel really guilty. If anything happens to him, it will be because she came here and ruined our lives."

"Don't you think you are being a little harsh towards your mother? After all, she is the one in the hospital," said Tammy.

"She is always the victim. She turns everything around to be about her. We would have been so much better if she never showed up."

"Sandra, don't you think your anger is a little out of proportion here? What are you truly angry about?" Tammy tried to calm her down

"She is a terrible mother. She is so selfish; she would destroy all of us just to get what she wants."

"Wow, that was harsh. What is behind all this? Maybe we should do a *Chain of Questions* and find out where all this venom is coming from," Tammy offered.

"Okay. There is this sinking feeling inside me when I think of her."

"Where is this feeling located?"

"In my stomach. I feel that people like me, and I am successful at the things I do, but when she is around, I feel like I can't do anything right."

"When you think about not being able to do anything right, what comes up for you?"

"I see myself as a guttersnipe, a dirty, worthless, discarded child."

"When you see yourself as this child, what memory comes to mind?"

"I remember a time when I was around six. She dressed me up like a little doll in a lacy pinafore with black patent leather shoes and ribbons in my hair. I felt so silly. Nobody dresses like that. Anyway, my friend next door and I were playing hide and go seek, then we just ran around chasing each other and I tripped in a puddle. I got mud all over the dress. Mom called me terrible names. She said I looked like a worthless guttersnipe, and I did not deserve pretty clothes because I could not take care of them. I guess I have always secretly felt like I am dirty and worthless, just like she said."

Tammy asked, "That was a long time ago, do you still feel that way?"

"When I'm around my mother, I try to show her how I've grown and improved, but she never seems to notice. She still blames me for being a perpetual disappointment to her. I guess I have been carrying this grievance and a list of others for a long time."

Once Sandra admitted how she felt, the anger dissipated and was followed by a sense of relief. Getting that memory off her chest cleared the way for Sandra to let go of her anger. Then she thought of her mother in the hospital and finally was able to feel some compassion and sympathy for her.

James sat beside Judy's bed for hours. She was sleeping and he was beating himself up. He blamed himself for what happened. 'I should not have given Sam the bow and let him shoot it on the porch. I should not have left Sam alone with her. God only knows what she said to him! Mostly I should not have let Judy come to Hope in the first place. I didn't think she would be a good influence on the kids, but then I convinced myself that the children had a right to see their mother. I had hoped that spending time with her, now that she was healing, would repair the damage of the past. Judy is so much better than she was before, but she still has a lot of those old negative behaviors.' Round and round these thoughts chewed up his serenity and left him feeling guilty and filled with regret.

James went out into the hall for a breath of fresh air. He needed to escape the evil voice in his head that was browbeating him for everything he had done.

In the hall, he ran into Antonio who had just arrived. "You look really upset James. What is bothering you? The doctors reassured us that Judy would fully recover."

"I am feeling guilty for all the ways I have contributed to making this accident happen."

"James, you weren't even there, and it was an unpredictable accident."

"I know all that with my mind, but in my gut, I feel to blame."

"Would you like to process this feeling? I would be glad to guide you," Antonio offered.

They went into a small private waiting room. Antonio took James through the Chain of Questions. It led him to admit that his relationship with his father left him feeling powerless, unsure of how to guide his life. That is why he depended on Judy to lead in so many ways throughout their relationship; but then he resented her for dominating him. He now realized that if he could have accessed his personal power, she would never have been able to bully him like she did. His own fear of power laid the groundwork for the whole situation. Once he understood what lay under his actions, he felt better. Now that he was working with Kim, his therapist, to develop a stronger sense of his personal power, he realized that he would never give his power away like that again.

Tammy and Sandra sat beside Judy in the hospital until she woke up. Then they took a break, and a stream of neighbors arrived to give the girls a rest and make sure Judy was never left alone. Someone from the community was always by her side. Antonio accompanied James home to wait in case Sam returned. He was there for support, while everyone was out searching.

That evening, when Sandra returned home tired and worried, she began to rub her dad the wrong way. It almost developed into an argument, but then they both acknowledged what they were feeling and the pressure they were under. With the skills they had learned, they did not have to give in to the tension, guilt, and helplessness that was trying to create a distance between them.

Cathy showed up around 6:00 with a hearty dinner and brought a delicious fresh warm pie.

Everyone was invited to a prayer vigil for Judy and Sam. The community was on the alert, and everyone helped in whatever ways were needed.

The next morning Chenoa awoke from a dream and knew exactly where Sam had gone. She told Alo and they went up into the canyon to the place where Sam had left the rocks on the stone. Sure enough, there was a new rock sitting there. That meant he was somewhere within walking distance. Alo followed Sam's tracks and found his camp.

Judy stayed in the hospital for a few days. It was a turning point in her life. These people were all so kind to her even though they did not know her. She realized how cruel she had been. A steady stream of people showed up at the hospital to keep her company and cheer her up. She thrived on all the attention. It filled a very old need in her.

Kim, James's therapist, organized the volunteers who took turns visiting Judy in the hospital. They brought her sweet treats and read to her. When she could sit up, they played cards and games to entertain her.

When Judy was released, she went to stay with James and the children for a few days. His bowling team brought over a week's worth of delicious warm food. David, Judy's therapist, stayed with her for a couple of hours helping her process all the new insights and feelings that were running through her. Everyone was gentle and kind to her. She began to appreciate all the special moments she shared with each visitor.

This was a turning point for James too. He worked through all his resentments against his father; by realizing how difficult it must have been for the man to raise two boys on his own. He felt sympathy and compassion for this man whom he had resented for so long. He even realized that he had become the father he always wanted. He was supportive and affirmative.

Judy was sincerely grateful to James for letting her stay with them while she recovered. One evening, when Sandra checked on her before going to bed, Judy invited her to sit down beside her.

"Sandra, I owe you a huge apology. I had some unresolved issues from my childhood that made it hard for me to be a good mother. I never acknowledged what a kind and wonderful daughter and sister you have been. I picked on you because I was not really seeing who you are. Now that the veil is removed from my eyes, I am so proud of who you are and what you are accomplishing. You are a great young lady, and I am proud to be your mother. I hope someday you can forgive me for all the mistakes I made, all the darkness I carried, and how I mistreated you. You did not deserve it. I am so lucky to have you as my daughter and grateful that I can finally see that clearly.

These were words she always wished she could hear from her mother. It cleared the air between them and healed something deep inside them.

Sam returned home reluctantly. He wanted to stay with Alo and Chenoa. It was decided that he could stay for a couple of days. First, he faced the guilt he felt over the accident, then he worked through old grievances he was carrying towards his mom.

He worked them through with Alo's help and came to feel that he really knew himself now. His newfound maturity had been tested and demanded a lot of self-reflection. It was a good price to pay to become the man he wanted to be. He returned home feeling secure and responsive to his family. He felt great love for each of them and for his caring and supportive community.

Sam had been distancing himself from his classmates for months because he thought no one could understand what he was going through. Now, they all rallied around him as though that separation had never occurred. His friends from school visited him often and showed him that they did understand and were compassionate. Each one went out of his way to tell Sam how much they liked and respected him.

Alo and Chenoa came to visit Judy. They told her about themselves, their beliefs, and their experiences with Sam's maturing process. Respectfully, they asked Judy not to take their foster son away from them, because he brought them great comfort. Judy thanked them and this time she meant it. She agreed that they could be one extended family.

James, Judy, Sandra and Sam had traveled a long hard road, pitted with struggles and disappointments. They arrived in Hope with their own list of wounds from an unjust and insensitive world. In this loving community, they received the support they needed to venture into their past and into their deep intimate psyches. Thus, they were able to heal the wounds that drove them to behave as they did. Now they keep their minds and emotions healthy and clear, through their on-going personal process work.

They continued to live in Hope, secure in the love of their community. They forgave the past and the pain that lay back there. Life still had its ups and downs. There were always new challenges, but now they each had the tools to deal with them. They were no longer crippled by hidden agendas caused by the residue of old grievances. Each in their own way came to know peace.

Our story has ended, but for the destiny of conscious communities, life is just beginning.

Acknowledgements

Nicholette Pavlevsky

I wish to thank my wife for the time and safe place to do my writing. She has changed my life for the better. I'd like to thank Nin for her helpful collaboration with me. And I thank spirit for the courage to speak my heart.

N•I•N Sharyn Bebeau

I wish to thank Nikk (Nicholette) for inviting me to join her on this wonderful journey into the future. Her brilliant and insightful story became the perfect platform for me to embroider my visions and understandings of how to live more consciously. I would like to thank Marie and Rich Ruster who have lived in a conscious community since the 1980s. From them, I learned about the many highs and lows of this challenging and rewarding way of life. I want to thank Dr. Charles Bebeau for teaching me about human nature and about how the therapeutic process transforms lives. I thank my dear ritual sisters in Boulder Colorado for my knowledge of the Vision Quest. My gratitude goes to Vanessa Bebeau and her red pen. She has always been my final editor removing all the extra words, leaving a fresh sharp copy that smoothly moves the reader along. Many thanks to my large wonderful extended family and my many sisters who have expanded my heart and taught me how to live in unconditional love.

About the Authors

Nicholette Pavlevsky

Nicholette was born into a military family. They moved around a lot, and she had a hard time adjusting to new schools. Her parents were abusive, and she was neglected. She suffered from PTSD and spent her young adult life getting therapy for her traumas. She felt a need to create a better and safer world. Nicholette wants to help people heal and have a happier loving life, not just as individuals but as communities. She believes there are just two paths - fear and love. It is her dream and hope that you will resonate with the ideas in this book, that it changes how you see and live life, and has a healing effect on collective hearts. It is her dream and hope that you will resonate with the ideas in this book. Nicholette is not a therapist, but she knows we are all looking for the same things. Peace of mind and a safe environment to live in. Peace comes from within.

N·I·N Sharyn Bebeau

N*I*N has a wide background in psychology and spiritualty. She founded four graduate schools in Archetypal Psychotherapy and Jungian Psychology with her husband, Dr. Charles Bebeau, in Boulder, Colorado. She created the Qadisha, a priestesshood worshipping life itself and honoring our Divine Mother Earth. She traveled around the world giving talks on how we can all work together as a global family based on unconditional love and cooperation.

In Florence, Oregon, Nin was the founder of FOR, Florence Organizes; an organization dedicated to enriching the community by protecting human rights and the environment

She has written several books. See her website, NinSharynBebeau.com for a list of all of them. One especially, *The Wise Woman and The Goddess* offers another version of how people can develop and live in creatively conscious communities.

N*I*N currently resides in Illinois, where she is developing a series of short videos entitled, *Why the World Appears to be Falling Apart: A Deeper Look at What is Really Going on.* These videos present a spiritual, psychological, historical and emotional look at the underlying currents defining the events unfolding in our world today.

Other Books by the N*I*N Sharyn Bebeau

Meshka, the Wise Woman
The Wise Woman and the Goddess
The Eternal Goddess
The Saga of The Sages
Tarot: Looking Beneath Reality
Weavers of Life
Haggadah: A Celebration of Freedom

Please support authors. If you are interested in purchasing any of these books, please order them directly from N*I*N or Nicholette. When you buy from online distributors, authors only get aproximately a dollar, the rest goes to the publisher and the distributor.